I0762266

INTO THE DARKWOOD

ANTHEA SHARP

Into the Darkwood omnibus copyright 2020 by Anthea Sharp. All rights reserved.
Characters are purely fictional figments of the author's imagination. Please do not copy, upload, or distribute in any fashion.

Cover by Mulan Jiang. Map by Sarah Kellington Professional editing by LHTemple and Editing720.
Visit www.antheasharp.com

QUALITY CONTROL
We care about producing error-free books. If you discover a typo or formatting issue, please contact antheasharp@hotmail.com so that it may be corrected.

A complete epic fantasy trilogy brimming with intrigue, royalty, and fairytale enchantment from USA Today bestselling author Anthea Sharp. Includes Elfhame, Hawthorne, and Raine

Subjects: Fairy Tale & Folklore Adaptations - Young Adult Fiction/Coming of Age Fantasy - Fiction/Romance-Fantasy-Young Adult Fiction

ISBN 9781680131512 (hardcover)

ISBN 9781680131505 (ebook)

Don't miss the DARKWOOD TRILOGY: *White as Frost*, *Black as Nigh*t, and *Red as Flame*

ELFHAME

ACKNOWLEDGMENTS

Thank you to my fabulous editor, Laurie, for catching chapters as I flung them at you, and keeping pace with me in a mad dash to the finish line. You are a treasure.

Another big tip of the hat to Arran for the fine copy editing work and quick turn-around, not to mention cleaning up my semi-colon abuse.

Special thanks to Mulan Jiang, cover designer extraordinaire, for the gorgeous work. And to Sarah Kellington for the beautiful hand-drawn map.

I'd like to acknowledge the work of Leonard and the wonderful folks who compiled Parf Edhellen, a free online dictionary of Tolkien's languages. The Dark Elf language is deeply inspired by Sindarin, with many thanks to this excellent resource. https://www.elfdict.com/about.page

And finally, this series wouldn't exist without Scarlett Dawn and her extraordinary vision for the Skeleton Key book world. Thank you, Scarlett, for being an indie pioneer!

DEDICATION

For love, in all its forms.

This book is dedicated to the memory of those slain at the Pulse shooting in Orlando 6/12/16

CHAPTER 1

There was no music at Castle Raine, little light, and the fresh-quarried stones still bore the clammy chill of the earth.

A chill that Mara Geary was supposed to banish as part of her duties as one of the new maids. Not that she thought Castle Raine would ever be warm, not even in midsummer. It certainly was frigid now, in spring, with no hint of the softening air outside penetrating the tall stone walls or creeping in through the narrow windows.

Mara's tallow candle sent flickering shadows dancing over the grey walls, lighting the way as she and Fenna, who had only been hired two days ago, hurried to the Great Room to light the fires. Mara's wooden bucket of kindling bumped against her leg and the whisk broom at her waist rasped over her wool skirts with every step she took.

"It's not what I imagined," Fenna said as they knelt to clean the ashes out of one of the great hearths. "Somehow I thought it would be more exciting, serving at the castle."

"Well, Castle Raine has only been finished for a month," Mara said. "Perhaps once the weather turns warm and more lords and ladies come to visit, it will be more interesting."

Fenna frowned and cast a look over her shoulder at the dark recesses of the Great Hall. "Dunno why anyone would want to come visit *here*. The castle's grim enough, and then there's the Darkwood just outside."

Mara refrained from pointing out that the King of Raine lived at the castle now, and soon enough it would become a hub of activity. Fenna was a sweet girl, but not quick to put all the pieces together.

Still, it was true that life as a maid in Castle Raine had been dreary so far. If she were honest with herself, Mara had to admit that she, too, had thought working at the castle would be less full of drudgery and more... She tried to find the right word for it. More lively.

"You don't have to worry about the Darkwood," she said to Fenna. "I know you're from the coastlands, but the forest isn't anything to fear."

"But the stories..." Fenna trailed off, the sibilant echo of her words hanging in the shadowed air.

"Just old tales." Mara finished sweeping up the last of the ashes and deposited them in Fenna's bucket. "Nothing interesting has happened in the Darkwood for centuries. Not since the Dark Elves disappeared."

"Were they real, then?" Fenna paused in laying the kindling and stared at Mara with wide eyes. "What if they decide to come out and murder us all in our sleep?"

Mara laughed. "Believe me, that won't happen. There's no magical doorway in the forest anymore. People have searched for generations."

She didn't mention that strange things still happened sometimes in the Darkwood. No point in frightening Fenna any further. And strange didn't necessarily mean dangerous.

She brushed off her skirt and rose to her feet. "That's this fire done. One more in here, and then we move to the smaller rooms."

Only one peculiar thing had ever happened to Mara in the forest, and even now she wasn't entirely sure it had been real. It had been on her thirteenth birthday, nearly four years ago. Mara had gone out with her siblings to fetch wood for their dwindling stores. Birthday or not, there was always work to be done.

As the middle child of five, she was used to being left on her own. Her older brother and sister were twins, and always paired up, even when they were fighting. Sometimes it seemed that they lived in a different world from the rest of the family, a world full of the secret language of shared birth that no one else could penetrate.

Mara had tried for years, and when she'd finally given up and resigned herself to being nothing more than the tagalong, she'd found that her two younger sisters had made an alliance of their own, with no room left for annoying older siblings.

So there she was, the odd one out, quite literally.

The air had been cool that day in the Darkwood, and moist enough that dew still clung to the new leaves of the underbrush. Mara practiced walking silently and smoothly through the trees, letting the moss cushion her steps. She'd become used to her solitude, though she didn't necessarily embrace it.

A few black-capped birds chirped and fluttered from bush to tree, their wings flashing whitely as they flew. She tried not to feel jealous that even the chickadees had companions when she did not.

Perhaps it was because of her birthday, or that the yearning inside her to belong *somewhere* was beginning to blossom into true misery, but she paused, tilted her head up to the feathery needles of the hemlock trees, and spoke.

"I wish that my life were different," she said. "I wish something exciting would happen."

There was no answer but the rush of the wind in the high branches. Sighing, Mara dropped her gaze back to the forest floor, searching for deadwood to stick in her burlap bag.

Then the breeze changed, murmuring down to pull at her brown hair and push against her skirts. The air felt thicker, as though filled with invisible mist, and she could no longer hear her siblings calling to each other through the trees.

Small, twinkling lights darted and danced in the shadows ahead, bright as candle flames. Mara's breath hitched in fear, and in wonder.

Something was happening.

The dark evergreens shivered, like animals sensing danger. Mara didn't know whether to run toward the glimmering motes, or dash away in panic. Her heart thudded beneath her simple woolen dress.

Not yet.

It was a whisper of regret, rolling through the Darkwood. The breeze quieted and let go of her dress. The air grew lighter. The glowing lights abruptly winked out. Loss ached through her, but for what, she did not know.

"Mara, aren't you done?" her older sister called, her tone sharp. "We're ready to go."

Mara wanted to shout back that they should leave without her. Maybe if she stayed, she would rediscover whatever little bit of magic she'd just seen.

But it was the cardinal rule of living beside the Darkwood: no one ventured there alone until they were well of age. The forest might not hold uncanny dangers any longer—though after what she'd just experienced, Mara wasn't so sure—but there were plenty of other threats lurking in the wild depths of the woods.

Bear, boar, and even wolves who howled in the winter at the far-distant moon. Not to mention poisonous mushrooms and spiders, sinkholes where a body could disappear forever, treacherous snags, and deep ravines.

Heaving a sigh, she turned and lugged her sack of branches back toward her family. She sent a single glance over her shoulder, but there was nothing to be seen but empty underbrush and ancient trees.

Later, she'd tried to tell her next-youngest sister what she'd experienced, but Pansy only looked at her.

"There's nothing special about the Darkwood," Pansy said. "I can hardly wait until I'm grown up and can marry a rich merchant and move away from here. Do you want to rot in Little Hazel forever?"

Mara didn't know *what* she wanted, beyond a future that felt important and real. And though the idea of seeing the wider world was quite appealing, she was fairly certain her life wouldn't feature a rich merchant.

"Where do we take the ashes?" Fenna's question jolted Mara back to her work.

She blew out a breath and turned her mind back to tending the cold hearths of the castle. Back to a life that was small and exceedingly unimportant.

"The compost heap is behind the kitchen gardens," she said. "I'll show you."

She led the other maid through the chilly stone corridors and into a grey morning filled with mist. The fog would burn off later, but for now everything was seen through a filmy veil. The tall trees of the Darkwood rising beyond Castle Raine's walls were soft blurs, and the newly risen sun a flat coin barely rolling into the sky.

"The heap is here." She dumped the bucket and powdery ash drifted down, covering the onion skins and withered greens on the top of the pile.

Something else slid out, too, with a soft clatter.

"What's that?" Fenna leaned forward.

"Careful—sometimes there are still live coals buried in the ashes. Let me poke at it."

Mara cast about and found a discarded stake at the edge of the heap. She prodded gently at the item. It glowed faintly, as an ember would, but the light was much cooler, a pale blue instead of the orangey-red of coals.

A puff of wind made the ashes swirl, and when it cleared, Mara could see what lay there.

It was a key—but the strangest one she'd ever seen. Cautiously, she poked at it again. The stick clicked lightly against the surface, which seemed to be made of glass. The key was as long as the measure of her fingertip to her palm. Eerily, the bow was formed to look like a grinning skull, the shank formed like a bone, and two teeth protruded at the end.

"A key?" Fenna asked.

"Seems to be."

Mara gave it a wary glance. She didn't remember sweeping it up, but somehow it had ended up in the ash bucket. It shone from the middle of the compost heap, and almost seemed to be laughing at them.

"Whatever do you think it opens?"

"I've no idea." There was something very unsettling about the key.

"Suppose we'd better take it in to the housekeeper," Fenna said doubtfully.

"Yes."

They both stood there, unmoving. Clammy mist curled around them, and a bird called mournfully from the hazy trees beyond.

"Pick it up," Mara said.

"What, me?" Fenna tucked her hands in her apron and backed up a step. "I'm the new girl, remember? It's your job to do such things."

Unfortunately, she was right. Mara pulled her handkerchief from her pocket and plucked the key from the compost, careful to keep the glass from touching her skin.

"Is it hot?" Fenna asked.

"No."

It wasn't cold, either, but the warm temperature of something alive. Mara slid the key into her pocket. As soon as she and Fenna finished with the hearths, she'd have to turn the uncanny thing over to the housekeeper.

It might be adventure, a voice in her mind whispered. *It might be important.*

This was true—but Fenna had seen the key, too. It would mean instant dismissal if a maid kept any trinket she found lying about the castle, and this glass key was no exception. Mara couldn't keep it, even if she wanted to.

She and Fenna completed their early morning chores, and then Mara went to find Mrs. Glendel, the housekeeper.

"I'm sorry, I have to return you," she whispered to the key, patting her pocket as she went down the narrow servant's hallway to the housekeeper's office. However it had come to be in the ash bucket, surely it belonged somewhere far grander.

Mrs. Glendel was going over her household lists by the light of an oil lamp, and looked up sharply when Mara came in.

"My apologies for bothering you," Mara said, "but Fenna and I found something while cleaning out the hearths."

"Very good." Mrs. Glendel stood and held out her hand. "Give it over."

Mara reached into her pocket, then paused. A knot of discomfort formed in her belly as her fingers met her handkerchief—and nothing else. There was no warm, heavy weight in her pocket.

"Well?" The housekeeper waggled her fingers. The starched cuff of her brown dress drew a sharp line across her wrist.

"It's here," Mara said, her breath tightening. "I know it is."

She felt about in her pocket, jamming her fingers into the corners. Was there a stray hole the key had slipped out of?

All the seams were tightly sewn, however. In desperation, she turned out both pockets of her heavy woolen skirt. Her empty kerchief fluttered to the slate floor. Mrs. Glendel's thin eyebrows rose higher in her seamed forehead.

"It seems you've misplaced the item, Miss Geary. What was it, pray tell?"

"A key. A strange glass key with a skeleton head."

"Hm." The housekeeper gave her a disapproving look. "No one's reported such a loss. But you know that the place of every maid here depends on complete honesty. You have until tomorrow to find that key and bring it to me."

"Of course." Mara swallowed the sour taste of her own saliva.

"Then you are dismissed for now." Mrs. Glendel sat back down and turned her attention to her papers.

"Yes, ma'am." Mara bobbed a curtsey and let herself out the door.

She'd have to retrace every step and find that blasted key, wherever it had gotten itself to. Her job at the castle—little though she might love it—depended upon finding that key again.

CHAPTER 2

In the double-mooned realm of Elfhame, the halls of the Hawthorne Court were hushed, the dim corridors even more shadowed than usual. The Hawthorne Prince, Brannon Luthinor, strode in and out of patches of starlight thrown from the high windows onto the flagstones.

Although he was not pleased to be summoned to his father's court, Bran let no hint of his feelings show. For this audience, he had replaited his black hair into formal warrior's braids on either side of his face, and donned a court tunic of indigo silk embroidered with silver.

He'd even washed the mud off his boots. Court opinion was brutal, and though he was protected somewhat by his rank and power, it was always best to give the gossips nothing to fasten upon.

Just outside the ornately patterned silver doors of the throne room, Bran paused. He'd rather face the gyrewolves and twisted spiderkin threatening their border than set foot inside this room filled with courtiers speaking untruths and twisting their actions to suit their ambitions. But the robed servant standing outside the room was watching him expectantly, and there could be no escape.

Settling his jeweled sword more firmly at his hip, Bran took a deep breath, then nodded at the doorman. The servant waved his hand, summoning the small magic that would open the double doors.

"His Highness the Hawthorne Prince, Brannonilon Luthinor!"

The doorman's voice rang out, and Bran stared impassively at the far wall as all eyes turned to him. A few gazes held admiration, others envy, but the worst were the ladies who viewed him as a means to an end, either for themselves or their daughters. That end being the Hawthorne Throne.

Their court was not the most powerful in Elfhame, but it was one of the oldest, and well placed among the seven ruling families.

Luckily, the circumstances of his birth provided an easy answer for why he was not yet married. It did not, however, provide him with a reasonable excuse for not taking mistresses—a fact that many of the women of the court liked to remind him of.

He'd had his share of dalliances, of course, but had no interest in weakening himself or his mission with misplaced attachment. Need for love made one vulnerable. He'd grown up learning that lesson, and had no desire to repeat it.

At the far end of the hall stood a raised dais, and upon it sat the Hawthorne Throne, occupied by Bran's father, Calithilon Luthinor. The years lay lightly on his face, as was the way of their people, but silver threaded his once midnight hair, and his dark eyes held a weary cast.

Beside the ornately carved Hawthorne Throne stood a smaller, less elaborate chair where Bran's mother, Tinnueth, sat. There was no trace of warmth or greeting in her expression, but that was no different from the reception he'd received from her all his life.

According to the gossip, the moment the prophecy had been pronounced over his newborn head, his mother had distanced herself. Although even with his younger sister, Anneth, their mother had never displayed an excess of affection.

"A heart like ice," the nursery servants used to say after Tinnueth paid her obligatory visits to her young offspring.

Bran wasn't supposed to understand, but he did. He'd grown up thinking he was flawed, unworthy of his mother's care, and perhaps it had made him hard, but all good weapons must be made of stern stuff. Without that core of stone, he would not be half the warrior he was.

A warrior who held the fate of Elfhame on his shoulders—and that fate was growing more perilous every day.

From his dais, the Hawthorne Lord lifted his hand in a clear summons, his eyes meeting Bran's. Letting no hint of his reluctance show on his face, Bran made his way toward his parents. He murmured greetings to the courtiers as he slid past them like water. Most let him go with a nod or reply, but his passage was halted when a particularly cloying young woman named Mireleth gripped his sleeve.

"I'm so glad you're back at court, milord," she said, in a low voice that was meant to be seductive.

He nodded and disengaged himself from her hold. Despite their few dalliances, he was not interested in pursuing a connection with the woman. She, however, seemed unable to grasp that fact.

"I'll visit you later," she called as Bran strode away.

He did not respond. Even if he'd fancied Mireleth, the prophecy was very clear concerning his fate. He was destined to marry some ungainly mortal. There was no escaping it, but his life would be a little less miserable if he did not fall in love in the meantime.

Soon enough he reached the dais and dipped into a formal bow before his parents.

"Prince Brannon, you took your time in coming," his father said. "I sent that summons a quarter moon ago."

"Your pardon, my lord." Bran kept his tone level. "I could not leave the front until we'd closed the current breaches and reinforced the barrier."

Even then, it was risky for him to be gone. As one of the leaders, and the strongest magic user among the Dark Elf forces, they couldn't afford for him to be away from the battle for long. But ignoring his father's summons would have been worse.

His mother gave a delicate sniff, conveying her disapproval and disappointment. Bran ignored her.

"Is the fight going well?" his father asked.

"Well enough."

It was an outright lie, but Bran would say no more where the sharp ears of the courtiers might hear. Later, in the privacy of his father's chambers, he would confide the desperate position the Dark Elves were in.

And although he'd been dreading the fulfillment of the prophecy his entire life, if it didn't happen soon there would be nothing left to save. The Void creatures infiltrating their world would destroy Elfhame and all its courts. By now, Bran almost welcomed his fate. Almost.

"It's good to have you back in the Hawthorne Court," his father said. "Meet with me later in my library, and you can recount to me your glorious tales of battle."

The look in Lord Calithilon's eyes promised that Bran would know then why he'd been summoned. It was not something he looked forward to hearing—though if it had to do with the prophecy, then perhaps the news would not be so unwelcome. The fate of Elfhame was paramount to his own wishes.

"My lord." Bran bowed again, then stepped away.

He hated the dance of protocol, the layers of meaning hidden behind veiled words. And he hated to wait, especially when the barrier was not nearly as strong as everyone thought. As soon as he could escape the court for the haven of his rooms, he'd contact the front and see how they were holding.

Halfway across the throne room, he glimpsed his sister standing near the wall and altered his course to meet her. She was alone, a glass of nectar in her hand. As he approached he could see her struggling to keep her features composed in the cool expression required of court protocol.

"Lady Anneth." He bowed before her, and could not prevent the corner of his mouth from curling up into a brief smile. His sister was the one person at court he truly cared for, and missed.

"Bran." She held up the golden glass of nectar to hide her grin. "I'm so glad you're home. How long can you stay?"

He glanced about, checking to make sure no eavesdroppers hovered nearby. "Not long, I'm afraid. They need me back at the battle."

Anneth's blackberry-colored eyes lost their merry sparkle. "Truly?"

"Don't look so unhappy. I'll sup with you at eventide, and you can tell me all the gossip of the court. Have you any suitors?"

A faint blush stained her pale skin. "Not to speak of."

Bran arched a brow at her. "We'll see about that."

"You have your own future to think about, as well. Now that father..." She busied herself with her glass of nectar.

"What?" Cold foreboding swept through him.

"It's not for me to say—and besides, he's only dropped hints here and there." She gave him a wide-eyed look. "I don't know anything for certain. You'll have to ask him yourself."

"I will." The sooner the better.

Bran glanced at the dais, to see Lady Tinnueth watching them with a calculating expression. What scheme were his parents brewing?

"I'll see you at supper." Bran made his sister a bow of farewell, then strode from the hall.

He did not slow his steps until he'd reached the privacy of his rooms in the family wing. Although he was not much in residence lately, everything was kept clean and ready for his arrival.

He wanted to throw the bedroom shutters wide to the dusky air and fill his lungs with freshness instead of the stultifying formality of court. Instead, he made sure they were firmly latched. To counter the dimness in the room, he conjured a flickering ball of foxfire. The pale blue light bobbed at his shoulder as he checked the door, then went over to his saddlebags. On his orders the servants had left them undisturbed, though the head houseman had frowned mightily when Bran requested they leave the unpacking for him to do.

He drew out his silver scrying bowl, then poured a measure of water from the ewer on the nightstand until the bottom of the bowl was covered. Slowly, he sank down on the forest-green carpet in the center of his bedroom. It was not as soft as the mosses he was used to perching upon, but it did have the advantage of being dry.

With the ball of foxfire hovering above his head, Bran took several deep breaths to focus his magic. He held the bowl between his cupped hands. The surface was lit with pale blue, and the dark shadow of his silhouette.

He spoke the Rune of Scrying. The hiss of the word of power twisted round the bowl. Light flared up and Bran squinted against that brightness. When it faded, he bent over the surface.

"Show me Hestil," he said.

The image of the second-in-command of the Dark Elf forces appeared, shivering over the top of the water and then coming into focus: thin nose, narrow eyes the color of malachite, dark hair braided back from a battle-weary face.

"Well met in shadow," Hestil said.

"And in starlight," Bran answered, the code words assuring her that he was alone and not under duress. "How goes the fight?"

Her lips tightened. "We're holding, but your magic is sorely missed. How soon can you return?"

Bran gave a sigh that fluttered the surface of the water, making Hestil's reflection waver. The Dark Elves could not win. Every time they threw back the invaders, another breach opened and more twisted creatures flowed out of the crack between the worlds. Even if Bran revealed how dire the situation was and brought every magic-wielding elf to the front, it was only a matter of time before they were overwhelmed.

But he would not share such hopeless thoughts with his second.

"I meet with my father later," he said.

"Well, I hope your precious prophecy chooses to manifest soon. Doesn't it say that during Elfhame's greatest need, a doorway will open, bringing help?"

"That's one interpretation." Other than specifying that Bran must wed whatever mortal opened the door, the prophecy was annoyingly vague.

Hestil's eyes narrowed. "I'd say the moment of need is fast approaching—especially if you dawdle overlong in your father's court."

"I'll return as quickly as I can. I know how desperate our situation is." He made his voice cold. It was not for Hestil to question her commander.

She dipped her head in apology. "I must go."

"Of course. I'll come soon."

He waved his hand over the bowl and Hestil's image disappeared. His own reflection stared up at him, skin pale as moonlight, slitted eyes filled with violet shadows, dark slashes of eyebrows drawn down in a frown.

Though he knew it was useless—he'd tried it hundreds of times—

he spoke the Rune once more. The silver light flared about the circumference of the bowl, and he gave his command.

"Show me the woman of the prophecy."

As usual, the water remained a blank pool of light, revealing nothing. Bran stared into it, willing something, *anything*, to appear. The force of his need and frustration burned through him.

"Show her to me," he demanded again, pulling deeply on his wellspring of magic.

The surface of the water shuddered.

He leaned forward, barely breathing. As if through a mist, he made out the figure of a mortal woman running through a forest. Her long mud-colored hair was tangled, and he glimpsed her face for one moment—the smooth curve of her cheek, a stubborn tilt to her chin, desperation in her strange blue eyes.

Then she was gone.

Only empty water stared up at him. His power subsided and the tremble in his fingers sent a faint ripple across the surface. Bran passed his hand over the bowl, dismissing the magic, then gently set the silver bowl aside. Closing his eyes, he fixed the glimpse of the woman firmly in his mind.

She did not seem old or disfigured, she looked healthy, and even through the scrying bowl he sensed the determination of her spirit.

Thank the double moons.

Now if he could somehow drag her through the sealed doorway, there might be hope for Elfhame.

CHAPTER 3

A soft chime rang through the halls of the Hawthorne Court, signaling that the Lord and Lady's reception hours were now at an end.

Bran rerolled the scroll of border maps he'd been studying, and rose from the table. He knew the seven courts of Elfhame by heart, of course. Four of them, including Hawthorne, lay in a rough square along the magical barrier protecting their realm. The other three were enclosed by the outer courts.

He'd spent more than a turn concentrating on the courts flanking Hawthorne—Nightshade and Moonflower. So far, he'd found nothing that would give the Dark Elf warriors an overlooked advantage in their war against the Void. The barrier between the worlds that his forebears had erected still pulsed with magic, standing strong. Unfortunately, this time the Void was stronger.

A tap sounded at the door.

"Come," Bran called, dropping his hand to rest on the hilt of his bejeweled court sword. Despite its ornamentation, it was a sharp and serviceable blade.

"Your Highness." The door swung open to reveal a pageboy. "Your father will see you now in his library."

Bran nodded. He stepped out and reset the magical lock securing his room, then followed the boy through the patches of faint moonlight filling the halls. He had no need of an escort to his father's library, of course, but there was no arguing with the rigidity of court protocol.

The boy left him before the tall ebony door. Bran rapped once and went in, smothering the spurt of nervousness that tried to rise up in his belly. He was no longer a child, but commander of the Dark Elf forces and a powerful magic wielder. Whatever his father wanted, Bran had no need of fear.

"Brannon." The Hawthorne Lord turned from the window, where the landscape of dark trees was turning silver from the light of the newly risen palemoon.

"My lord." Bran bowed. "I must tell you of the battle."

"Of course—but we can sip wine and sit like civilized folk. Pour out two glasses, if you please."

Bran went to the sideboard, where his father kept a decanter of elderberry wine and several crystal goblets etched with twining vines. He deftly poured them each a glass. The scent of the wine tickled his nose—dark and pungent, the color a deep purple that was almost black.

Lord Calithilon had settled in one of the armchairs in his sitting area. His indigo eyes glowed softly as Bran approached and handed him a goblet.

"I believe this is one of the finest vintages we've yet produced," Lord Calithilon said. He brought the glass to his nose and sniffed appreciatively. "Now, sit and tell me of your exploits in battle."

Bran took the chair opposite his father and set his wine on the small side table.

"I'm afraid I've no heroic tales to recount. The fighting is brutish and difficult, and we're sustaining losses we can't afford."

Lord Calithilon raised one thin, dark eyebrow. "When the Void opened the first breach to our world, our warriors had no trouble containing the creatures. Like every other incursion in our history, the Void attacks, we repel its efforts, and it passes us by once more."

"This time is different," Bran said. "The first small breach opened nearly five doublemoons ago. For a time, the creatures issuing forth were easily dealt with. But now bigger creatures have begun to emerge

—things not so simple to kill or return to the Void. The barrier is weakening, with more breaches opening every brightmoon. Our forces are spread dangerously thin. Surely you and the other court rulers have read the reports?"

"It is difficult to believe that our forces cannot prevail, as they have in the past. Dark Elves are the most powerful magic users and warriors in the known worlds."

Bran's fingers itched, and with effort, he kept his claws from springing forth. It was that kind of complacent arrogance that would be the downfall of Elfhame.

"Not powerful enough for this," he said through gritted teeth.

Lord Calithilon looked taken aback for a moment, then leaned forward and smiled. There was something very uncomfortable in his smile, and Bran knew he was not going to like his father's next words.

"If things truly are getting so much worse," Lord Calithilon said, "then I'm sure you'll be eager to put a new plan in motion. You know, of course, that the whole realm, and certainly our court in particular, has been waiting to see the prophecy foretold at your birth come to pass."

"High time for it," Bran could not help but say.

A pleased expression crossed his father's face. "Exactly. Which is why we think the best course would be to announce your betrothal."

"My betrothal?" Bran rose to his feet, unable to contain his visceral reaction. "No. Out of the question. The prophecy is very clear on the fact that I am to wed a mortal woman."

"Which is why your mother and I are in complete agreement." Lord Calithilon stood as well, facing Bran. "For years we've been waiting for the prophecy to manifest. It's time to help it along—past time, judging from your accounts. By announcing your betrothal to a Dark Elf, surely fate will take note, and produce the mortal you are supposed to marry."

"You can't dictate to fate." Bran stared into his father's eyes, aware that the power and will he saw there was a match for his own. "The woman will appear when it is time."

Lord Calithilon waved an impatient hand. "You said yourself that time is running out. Before you leave the Hawthorne Court, we will celebrate your betrothal and set a date for the wedding. Say, in one double-moon? How will the battle be going at that point?"

"Badly." Bran pulled in a deep breath through his nose, trying to contain the temper simmering in his belly. "I don't believe this is the answer."

His father gave him an arch look, then paused to take up his goblet and have a sip of wine. "Has the prophecy showed any signs of stirring?"

"I glimpsed a mortal girl today, when I was scrying."

"See, then! Our plan is working already. Your mother will be most pleased to hear it."

"It's not because of this ridiculous scheme," Bran said.

"Can you prove otherwise? Now sit down and stop baring your claws at me. We can discuss this like sensible men, not animals."

Chagrined, Bran glanced down to see the sharp ebony tips of his claws protruding past his fingertips. It was very bad manners, and a sign of how quickly his father had upset him that he'd lost control of his reactions.

"Your pardon." He retracted his claws and sat. "If I were to agree to this plan—which I'm not saying I am—who would the lucky fiancée be?"

Even as he asked the question, he had the creeping suspicion he already knew.

"I understand you've always had a fancy for Mireleth Andion, and she has already agreed to undertake the role of your sham fiancée."

His father's words confirmed his guess, and sourness settled in Bran's belly. He took a sip of wine to try and clear the taste of defeat from his mouth.

"Mireleth and I were once companions," he admitted. "But that affair is long over."

"All the better—she won't distract you from your battles."

Bran's gaze went to the window, where the moon was now sailing above the trees. Silver light illuminated the pale blossoms in the nearby meadow and filtered through the forest, stitching patterns of leaf and shadow over the mossy ground.

"What if the mortal girl from the prophecy never materializes?" He spoke his greatest fear aloud.

What if, somehow, they had all misread the intent of the prophecy?

What if he'd spent his life in service to an empty promise? The thought made him cold.

"Then, according to the blasted thing, all Elfhame will be lost, and it won't matter *who* you marry. Come now, Brannon. Things can't continue as they are, you've made that clear. We must take charge, and this is the best way to do it. Will you agree to the betrothal?"

Eyes still fixed on the moonlit forest, Bran gave a slow nod. "Very well."

He could see no use in defying his parents. Perhaps they were right, and such a drastic action would wake the slumbering prophecy. He must take the chance, before everything he cared for slipped into oblivion.

CHAPTER 4

That night, as Mara hung up her serviceable woolen skirt in the small wardrobe she shared with Fenna, she felt a hard lump in the pocket.

Brow creasing, she reached into her skirt pocket. Warm glass met her fingers. Carefully she pulled it out to find the skeleton key had reappeared.

"Where were you hiding?" she asked it, not a little annoyed.

She'd scoured the Great Hall and the corridors in a fruitless search for the key—and it had been in her pocket all along. How could she have overlooked it? She held it up to the light, just to make sure it was really there. The skull grinned back at her.

"I thought you were giving that to Mrs. Glendel," Fenna said from where she sat cross-legged on her bed, brushing her hair.

"I tried," Mara said. "Truly, I did. I turned my pockets out and everything."

"You can't keep it." Fenna's tone clearly conveyed that she thought Mara was lying.

"I know." *Blast it!* "I don't want to lose my position here any more than you do."

She'd just started settling into the rhythm of life at the castle, for once making a place for herself that was not defined by her family.

Not that she imagined herself as a maid for the rest of her years. This was a stepping stone out of her predictable life in Little Hazel, the first rung on her journey toward something better. When the announcement had come from the castle that they were hiring new servants, she'd been one of the first applicants in line.

"Are you quite certain?" her mother had asked.

"Oh, yes." A year of hard work, maybe two, and Mara would have saved up enough to travel.

To the coast, at least, and perhaps she'd even book passage on a ship bound for foreign lands. Somewhere out there in the wider world her life was waiting for her—she just knew it.

All that waited for her back in the village was a boy besotted with her that she had no feelings for whatsoever, a family immersed in their own lives, and a hopelessly monotonous future.

The key rested, heavy in her hand. Mara pressed her lips together in thought as she stared down at it. She'd never seen any door in the castle that it might open; they all had large cast-iron locks that would require a much longer and wider key than this.

The glass shone as if lit faintly from within, full of promise. Full of magic.

"I'll keep the key for you," Fenna said, twisting a tie about her hair and standing. "Give it to me for safekeeping and tomorrow morning we can go together to give it to the housekeeper."

"Come with me if you like." Mara closed her hand around the key. "But I'll just put this back in my pocket for now."

The other girl gave her a hard look. "If you say so."

"I do." Mara slipped the key back into her skirt pocket. "Stay there," she told it sternly.

What if you find the door it opens? part of her whispered. *If you give the key back, it will stay locked forever.*

Mara glanced at her roommate. Fenna had her arms crossed, a suspicious look in her eyes.

"I don't want to get in trouble along with you," Fenna said.

"You won't." Mara shut the wardrobe door, closing the key safely inside.

She blew out the candle beside her bed and climbed under the covers. Fenna did the same, and the room was soon filled with the other girl's gentle snores.

Sleep did not come so easy for Mara, and when it finally arrived, it pulled her down into nightmares.

She ran through a dark forest, something immense chasing her, and she knew she'd never reach safety in time. Monsters shambled in the shadows, watching her with glowing eyes. A bell tolled midnight.

Gasping, Mara sat up in bed, the sheet wound tightly around her body. The castle was silent. Fenna still snored in the other bed.

It was just a dream, Mara told herself, though her hammering heart insisted otherwise. She needed to go back to sleep. A maid's work began at an ungodly hour, and she'd never been fond of waking before the dawn.

Instead, she ignored all common sense and silently slipped out of bed. The stone floor pulled the warmth from the soles of her bare feet as she padded over to the wardrobe and opened the door.

Silvery radiance lit the inside of the wardrobe, and Mara sucked in a breath. The key glowed from within the pocket of her skirt like a tiny, vibrant star. If she took it out, she feared it would blind her.

"Stop it," she whispered. "I can't keep you."

She couldn't go haring off in search of some mystery door when she had yet to receive her first month's pay.

The light dimmed somewhat, and she found herself wondering if the key had any value. But that was silly. If she ran away from the castle bearing a magical key, certainly the king would send riders after her. She wouldn't make it to Little Hazel, let alone the city of Meriton beyond.

Slowly, she closed the wardrobe door, then crept back into bed. As her feet warmed up again beneath the blankets, she turned the problem over and over in her mind, but could find no way she could possibly keep the key. Even if it was magic.

First thing in the morning she would have to give it to Mrs. Glendel, and that would be the end of it.

Mara and Fenna stood before Mrs. Glendel's desk. The whole chilly walk to the housekeeper's office, Mara had kept her hand closed tightly around the key, reassuring herself it hadn't disappeared. The narrow corridors were dark and unfriendly, and it had felt like miles, but at last they'd arrived. Good thing, too, as her hand was starting to cramp.

"Mara's here to give you the key we found," Fenna said.

"Good." Mrs. Glendel gave Mara a stern look. "Let's see it."

Mara pulled her hand out of her pocket and opened her fingers. A knobbled stick sat in her palm, and she stared at it, cold disbelief running through her.

"Very funny, Mara." Mrs. Glendel did not sound amused. "The key, if you please."

"I... But... I swear it was right here, in my hand."

Anger swept hotly through her. The key was playing terrible tricks on her, and was about to cost her everything.

"She has it," Fenna declared. "I saw her with it last night, clear as you please. And she refused to give it to me to look after."

Mara set the useless twig down on the housekeeper's desk. She stared at it, willing it to change back into the glass key, but nothing happened.

"Produce the key." Mrs. Glendel's voice was cold.

"I don't know where it is. Search me, if you like." Trembling with hot frustration, Mara turned out her pockets.

There was no explanation she could make. The key existed, and Fenna had seen her holding it the night before. Any talk of magic wouldn't be believed, and instead would be taken as Mara trying to make weak excuses for her behavior.

"Fenna," the housekeeper said, "run upstairs and make a thorough search of your room and all Mara's belongings. Mara, you will remain here."

Fenna made Mrs. Glendel a quick curtsey, then sent Mara a sour look as she left.

"I must say, I'm disappointed in you," Mrs. Glendel said. "You showed promise as a maid. I didn't pin you as the lying, stealing kind."

"I'm not!" But there was no way to prove it.

"You do realize your time here is at an end? Whether Fenna returns with the key or not, I'm going to have to dismiss you. And I'm going to have to ask you to strip to the skin now, so I can determine you're not hiding anything."

It was humiliating, but Mara did as the housekeeper asked, handing over each item of clothing and then turning about with her hands in the air. Of course, Mrs. Glendel found nothing.

"It's a good thing no one has reported any such key as missing," the housekeeper said. "If they ever do, you'll be hunted down and arrested by the king's men."

Mara didn't think it likely that would happen, as the blasted key seemed to have chosen her alone for its pranks. In fact, she had a nasty suspicion it would rematerialize in her pocket the moment she left the castle grounds.

She hastily re-donned her clothing, trying not to shiver from the cold castle air. Frustration scraped her lungs with every breath.

"Will I receive any of my pay?" she asked, trying to keep the temper from her voice.

The housekeeper regarded her for a moment, her expression softening slightly. "You were a hard worker, I must admit. I'll see that you get half of it. No references, of course."

Of course. The unfairness of it flared up inside Mara, and she clenched her hands. Half a month's pay was a trifling amount, and certainly not enough to travel on.

She'd have to return to Little Hazel in disgrace. Her parents would take her back, of course, but she could just see the look of reproach in her mother's eyes when Mara told them she'd been dismissed.

Her siblings would be unbearable, and Thom, the woodcutter's son, would no doubt renew his wooing of her with his usual single-mindedness.

Was that what her life was meant to be? A resigned marriage to an uninteresting fellow, and then picking up kindling in the Darkwood until her body was too bent with age to venture out?

"Sit." Mrs. Glendel nodded to the straight-backed chair in the corner. "I'll arrange for your pay while we wait for Fenna to return."

Trapped, Mara sat, mentally cursing the key. She'd wanted adventure in her life, but not like this. What good was magic if it only booted her back into the life she was trying to escape?

After a few more uncomfortable minutes marked only by the scratching of the housekeeper's pen, Fenna returned.

"I didn't find anything," she reported.

Mrs. Glendel nodded, as if she'd expected as much. "Very well. Mara, you are free to gather your things. Stop by my office when you're packed up. And Fenna, you'd best get one of the other maids to help you with the hearths."

"Yes, ma'am." Fenna bobbed a curtsey, then turned to Mara. She looked a little regretful, but perhaps that was because her workload had just doubled. "Goodbye, Mara."

"I wish you well," Mara said. She refrained from telling the other maid to steer well clear of strange keys shining in the compost heap.

Fenna hurried off, and Mara made her way more slowly to the servants' quarters. Although the room she shared with the other maid was in disarray from the girl's search, nothing was torn or destroyed. Fenna had a good heart, despite her suspicions.

It didn't take long for Mara to bundle up her extra set of clothing and her two books. She donned her cloak, relaced her boots, and soon enough was back in Mrs. Glendel's office.

"Here you are." The housekeeper handed her a small sack. "You'd best be off now."

The sack clinked when Mara took it, the weight dismayingly light. But what could she do?

"Thank you," she said, though she didn't mean it, then tucked her paltry pay into her pocket and heaved up her bundle.

It would not be a comfortable walk back to Little Hazel, but at least she'd be home before sundown.

Steps heavy, she traversed the cold corridors of Castle Raine one last time and let herself out the servants' door. The morning fog was burning off, showing glimpses of pale blue sky, though the air was still chilly.

Servants bustled about in the courtyard, and she heard the muffled whinny of a horse, but no one paid her any mind as she went to the small postern gate. The shadow of the tall grey walls fell over her as she stepped out, leaving the castle—and all of her hopes for the future—behind.

CHAPTER 5

Mara's seventeenth birthday dawned sunny and clear. She lay beneath her colorful quilt for a moment, staring at the familiar ceiling of the bedroom she shared with her sisters. The bumpy plaster had always seemed like a miniature landscape, and she'd spent hours imagining herself as a tiny being walking over the ceiling, armed with a needle for a sword, encountering strange creatures and having all sorts of adventures.

Too bad her attempt to leave home had ended in disaster, and she'd nothing to show for it but a thin bag of coins. The blasted key had not rematerialized after all. It seemed to have done its work in ousting her from the castle, then disappeared for good.

She blew out a long breath, pushing away the creeping sense of defeat that shadowed her thoughts. She refused to believe that she would wake to this view every morning for the rest of her life. Surely she must belong somewhere, beyond Little Hazel, or even the country of Raine itself. One day, she'd find that place.

Holding that determination close, she got up and donned her favorite dress. She'd used all her pin money to buy it off a traveling merchant last summer. Clearly some noble's castaway, there had been enough salvageable material for Mara to combine it with one of her other gowns and make a whole new garment. The sleeves and overbodice were light blue silk, with bands of gold-embroidered trim, flowing down to the full skirt. It was rather impractical for doing housework, but she didn't care. She'd put on an apron. Today was her birthday, after all.

When she came downstairs, her mother looked her up and down, then handed her the wooden spoon to stir the porridge.

"Good morning to you," she said. "Up bright and early, I see."

Mara snagged an apron from the cupboard, then took the spoon and replaced her mother in front of the cast-iron stove and began to stir the lumpy oats.

"This is sleeping late, compared to the hours at the castle. We'd be up before dawn to light the hearths."

"A pity your time there wasn't a success." Her mother's voice held questions.

Ones she'd never get the answers to, as far as Mara was concerned. She concentrated on stirring. "I'm sure something else will come along."

She hadn't explained why she'd been turned out of Castle Raine. It wasn't as though she'd *actually* stolen anything. She could try and tell them about the magical key, but her parents were the practical kind. Despite living at the edge of the Darkwood they gave little heed to the old tales, and always had a commonplace explanation for any odd occurrences.

The dancing lights she'd glimpsed that once in the forest? Nothing more than fireflies out of season. The enormous black boar with glowing eyes that roamed the deep ravines? A frightened hunter's exaggeration.

They did not approve of the book of fanciful stories she'd discovered in a used bookshop during their yearly visit to the city of Meriton, and they certainly did not understand why she wanted to leave Little Hazel.

"Thom the woodcutter's son is a perfectly nice boy," her mother had remarked on more than one occasion. "Give up your silly notions and settle down, Mara. I'll help you look after the children."

Heavens, no.

"Come with me to market today," her mother now said. "Perhaps we can find you something nice for your birthday."

"I wondered if you'd forget," Mara said, sliding the pot of cooked oatmeal off the stove.

"Forget the day you were born? Not likely. You were a noisy child coming into the world, Mara Geary, yelling to wake the dead. It was a morning much like this, in fact, clear and with a bit of warmth. Now, is our breakfast ready?"

Mara dished up wooden bowls of porridge while her mother called the rest of the family to breakfast. They all gathered around the long table, and Mara couldn't help smiling. Much as her family might annoy her at times, she still loved them.

In addition to the oatmeal, there were dried apples, honeycomb, and milk from the neighbor's cow. It tasted much better than the food the servants were given at the castle, and Mara gave a contented sigh as she took a bite of honeycomb.

"Mara and I are off to market after breakfast," her mother said. "I thought we could take some fresh nettles for barter. Lily and Pansy, cut me some before you go off to school. And Mara, we'll take eggs along, as well. Mrs. Weir is always happy to give us some good trout in exchange."

"Don't cut all the nettles," Mara's elder sister, Seanna, said. "We need some for our studies with the herbwife."

Their mother gave her a sharp look. "Plenty of nettle patches all over. Old Soraya doesn't need to raid ours."

Sean nudged his twin's shoulder. "We can gather some from beside the baker's."

The twins had been apprenticed to the herbwife since last fall, in an arrangement that seemed to suit everyone.

Mara's father, a man of little words, finished his breakfast, gave his wife a peck on the cheek, and departed for work at his small brewery located on the outskirts of the village. He and a good friend had started it up ten years ago, and everyone scoffed at the notion. Little Hazel was too tiny a village to support a brewery!

But their beers and mead had turned out to be excellent, and they now had a nice export business going, with vendors and even a few inns all over Raine carrying Geary's Meads and Ales.

Mara glanced around their cozy cottage, at her family who all seemed content with the fit of their daily lives. Well, except for Pansy, who had already mapped out her future away from Little Hazel and seemed to have no doubts about it.

Mara wondered, not for the first time, what was the matter with her. Why did she never quite belong? What was the restless itch she'd felt just under her skin ever since she'd been a child?

Swallowing the last of her tea, and with no answers, she rose and helped her mother clear the table.

"Look." Mara's mother prodded her in the ribs. "Thom is over there, by the potato seller. Go and say hello."

Mara glanced up from the tray of silver jewelry she'd been admiring. The necklaces were beautiful, like spun moonlight—and far above what they could afford. When her mother asked, she'd say she'd been looking at the braided copper rings instead.

"Oh look, he's seen us." Mara's mother waved and called a greeting.

Thom saw them and, smiling widely, started to make his way to where they stood.

Too late to escape. Mara dredged up a pleasant smile. It was always difficult, trying to be kind to Thom without giving him undue encouragement.

"Mara!" Thom fetched up before her, his brown eyes shining. He took off his cap and made her a clumsy bow. "You're back from the castle."

"She missed you too much to stay," Mara's mother said.

"Mother!" Mara glared at her mother, then turned to Thom. "She's teasing, of course. They found they'd hired too many maids, and I was let go."

"That's a pity," he said. "But I can't say I'm sad about it, since now you're home where you belong."

More than ever, Mara felt as though she did *not* belong—but it was hardly the time or place to try and explain.

"It's Mara's birthday," her mother said. "Seventeen—such a good age to think about starting a family of her own."

"I disagree," Mara said, but the damage was already done.

Thom gazed at her, the adoration shining in his eyes making her quite uncomfortable. For the first time that day, she regretted wearing her prettiest gown. While she'd always thought Thom a nice enough boy, if she thought of him at all, she'd never returned the force of emotion he so clearly directed at her every time they met.

"May I come and call upon you soon?" Thom asked, crumpling his cap between his hands.

His intent was plain: he meant to begin courting her in earnest.

"I really don't—"

"Mara will be delighted to see you," her mother said. "Come visit us tomorrow after supper, if you're free."

"I am. Yes. That would be marvelous." Thom grabbed Mara's hand and planted a moist kiss upon it. "I can hardly wait. Thank you, Mrs. Geary."

"We'll see you tomorrow then, Thom," Mara's mother said. "Have a good afternoon."

"Oh, I shall." Thom jammed his cap back on his head and walked away, glancing back at Mara every few steps.

"He's like a puppy." Mara wiped the back of her hand on her cloak. "Mother, did you have to be so encouraging?"

"Well, you weren't." Her mother shifted her market basket. "Come, we don't want to be late to Mrs. Weir's stall, or we'll miss the best fish."

"I don't want to marry Thom." She hurried after her mother. "I wish you'd understand that."

"Puppies grow up in time," her mother said. "And you need to do something with your life, since the castle didn't work out."

"I thought I'd travel."

"Alone? The world is full of troubles waiting to beset an innocent young woman. Besides, you haven't any money."

Mara felt she'd be able to handle most difficulties that might arise on her travels, but her mother's last words were depressingly true.

"Not much," she said.

"Perhaps you can convince Thom to spend a little time seeing the country, once you're married."

"He doesn't seem the adventurous sort," Mara said.

"Then he'll settle you down nicely." They halted in front of the fishmonger's. "What do you think of that fat trout there, on the end?"

Clearly their discussion about Mara's future was at an end. She swallowed back her words of protest and privately vowed that, no matter what happened, she would *never* settle for a life in Little Hazel, married to Thom the woodcutter's son.

CHAPTER 6

The only redeeming feature of the Hawthorne Court's formal dinner was that Bran was seated beside his sister. Although it was rude, he ignored the woman on his left and spent the meal conversing with Anneth.

During the soup course, she made him smile with tales of her escapades in the court, including raiding the library and making off with as many lurid tales of mortals as she could carry.

"One of us needs to know what you'll be getting into when your human woman finally appears," Anneth said, giving him a teasing look. "Did you know that mortals prefer strong light—even stronger than our brightmoon—and like to eat snails?"

"That sounds most unappetizing."

"What, the light or the slugs?"

"Both." But the prophecy demanded he bear with honor whatever challenges a mortal wife would bring.

"What is afoot with our parents?" Anneth glanced to the head of the table, where the Hawthorne Lord and Lady presided over the feast. "Mother looks as though she's swallowed something surprisingly pleasant, and Father is absolutely gloating."

Bran leaned back to let the servant take his bowl, and did not speak until the man had moved away down the table.

"They have a scheme that they hope will force the prophecy to manifest."

Anneth frowned. "I was afraid of that, from the tidbits Father let drop. But is it even possible to make a prophecy happen? Can you tell me more?"

Bran paused again as the fowl course was served, and took the opportunity to take a deep draught of elderberry wine. His father was correct: it was one of the finest vintages yet.

Anneth took a bite of pheasant, patiently waiting until Bran was ready to speak. It was one of the reasons he was so fond of her. She never pressed, never scolded, but simply accepted him as he was.

Which was more than their parents had ever done.

Bran made himself eat, though he'd lost his appetite. He needed all his strength for his return to the front, and it would be foolish to refuse the food set before him.

As soon as conversations rose about them, he leaned toward Anneth.

"They think that making a formal announcement of my betrothal will activate the prophecy," he said.

She stared at him a moment, her dark eyes flaring with sympathy. "So they *do* want you to marry someone. That's absurd. You didn't tell them yes, did you?"

"I did."

Her expression turned to dismay. "Bran, no. Was that wise? What if the prophecy abandons us altogether? I'm sure such things don't like to be dictated to."

"Something has to happen." He could not entirely suppress the note of urgency in his voice. "The battles are getting desperate."

He took another swallow of wine. By all the stars, he should be there now, not enduring a formal banquet while his parents gloated over forcing his hand. His mother, in particular, had always hinted that she did not quite believe in the foretelling that had accompanied his birth.

Anneth laid a sympathetic hand on his shoulder. "I trust we'll prevail. Surely the fates would not desert us altogether."

"I wish I shared that trust." He took another bite of tasteless meat, made himself chew and swallow.

"But who is the lucky—"

"I beg your pardon, Lady Anneth." The syrupy-sweet voice came from just behind him. "I need to borrow your brother for a moment."

Bran turned in his chair to see Mireleth standing there, a predatory look in her eyes. Anneth's gaze met his, and her eyes widened. She knew how he felt about Mireleth, and he read horrified sympathy in her expression.

"Lady Mireleth." He set his napkin aside and rose smoothly. "It would be my pleasure to attend upon you."

"Good." She twined her arm through his, and he felt the delicate prick of her claws through his shirt.

As soon as they stepped out of the dining hall, she turned to him. Her pale cheeks were flushed with emotion, and her eyes glowed dangerously.

"Do you think so little of me," she said in a tight voice, "that you force me to seek you out in the middle of dinner?"

"My most sincere apologies," he said. "I was busy in strategic meetings until the dinner bell rang. I had every intention of finding you after the feast, to discuss matters between us."

"Discuss matters?" The words came out in a hiss. "You have a duty to me now, Prince Brannonilon Luthinor. Our fathers signed the agreement."

Cold twisted in Bran's chest. "You *are* aware that we won't actually be married."

"Oh, Bran." She ran one hand possessively up and down his shoulder. "Who's to say what might happen? Now, I've brought the vow bracelets. You must say the words."

Bran closed his eyes briefly. Of course, he should have guessed that Mireleth and her politically grasping father would take every advantage to seal the betrothal as tightly as they could. He'd hoped it would be a mere formality—a tactical error on his part.

Now he had no choice but to ask Mireleth to become his fiancée, and even wear the cursed bracelet. But no way under the moons would he allow the full betrothal bond to be forged. Luckily, even Mireleth would not overstep protocol by dragging him away from the rest of the feast to put her permanent claim upon him.

"Here." She handed him the smaller of the silver-runed bracelets.

"Lady Mireleth Anion," he said, reluctantly taking it in his palm, "will you pledge your future to mine, under star and shadow, by pale moon and bright, through fire and storm?"

"Prince Brannonilon Luthinor, heir to the Hawthorne Throne." Her voice was exultant. "I will do so, under star and shadow, by pale moon and bright, through fire and storm. Until the day we are wed, let these bracelets seal the depth of our vow."

She held up the bracelet meant for him, kissed it, and then slid it over his hand. He was hard-pressed not to make a fist to keep it from encircling his wrist. The veins in his hands corded, and he forced himself to breathe evenly.

The cold metal closed over his skin, latching with a click that reverberated through him like a slammed door.

"My turn," she said, a hint of threat in her voice.

Dutifully, Bran raised her bracelet to his lips, then pushed it onto her hand. It slithered over her skin like a metal snake, eagerly snapping shut the moment it reached her wrist.

The bracelets flared in tandem, and Mireleth gave him a smug smile. "Now there will be no doubt when our betrothal is announced at the end of dinner."

"As you say." He felt numb.

If this betrothal did not call the woman of the prophecy, he would be shackled to Mireleth for life. Fortunately, that life would be very short as the creatures of the Void overran Elfhame and destroyed everything in their path. It was a bitter consolation.

"I'll come to your rooms tonight, after moonset," she said, lifting her hand to caress his cheek. "We'll seal the bracelet bonding then. Leave your door unlocked."

His heart was a stone, his mouth full of pebbles. He said nothing.

"You could show a little more emotion," Mireleth said, huffing out a breath. "After all, we've been companions already. This will only formalize things."

"We ought to return to dinner," he said, catching her arm and deftly steering her back inside the dining hall.

He could not bear another moment in her company, and he absolutely refused to bond their bracelets by welcoming her to his rooms later that night.

He escorted Mireleth to her seat, bowed and kissed her hand, then hastily retreated to his place.

"Oh dear," Anneth said, once he sat down. "She's determined to get her claws into you, isn't she?"

Bran glanced at the pinprick holes in the arm of his linen shirt. "I'm afraid she already has."

His sister grimaced. "And making you wear the vow bracelets, too. Does she really think she's more important than the prophecy that will save our realm? Oh, don't answer that. Clearly she does."

The fruit course was served, and Bran made his decision.

"I'll be leaving right after dinner," he told his sister in a low voice. "I must return to the front. I'll leave a note."

"She'll be furious." Anneth glanced down the table, to where Mireleth sat, showing off her bracelet to anyone whose attention she could catch.

"Stay well out of her way until she calms down," he said. "And send for me at any sign of trouble. So far we've been able to keep the border secure, but I fear some creature might slip through. Do you have the dagger I gave you?"

She nodded. "I wear it at my belt, always."

"And are you still practicing the moves? Go to Garon at the first hint of danger—he may be old and lame, but the man still knows how to fight."

"Yes—he complains constantly to anyone who'll listen that he ought to be out fighting with the rest of the warriors."

"He's needed here as captain of the guard. Remind him of that next time he grumbles. And that I've entrusted my sister's safety to his hands."

"Surely it won't come to that?" Anneth ate a slice of moon melon, but he could hear the fear in her voice.

Before he could reply—and really, he had nothing but empty reassurances to give her—Lord Calithilon stood from his place at the head of the table.

"Attention," he said, his voice enhanced with magic to fill the room. "We have a very important announcement to make."

The clink of cutlery and babble of conversation faded. Tinnueth rose to stand beside her husband, her expression austere and regal.

"It gives us great joy to announce the betrothal of our son, Prince Brannonilon Luthinor, heir to the Hawthorne Throne, to Lady Mireleth Anion. Let us toast to their happiness!"

A shocked murmur ran through the room, and Bran heard the questions rise: *What of the prophecy? Does he love her that much? Is the Hawthorne Lord mad?*

He ignored the buzz of speculation and concentrated on not openly scowling.

"You look very forbidding," his sister murmured.

"It's the best I can do," he replied.

In contrast, Lady Mireleth was smiling broadly. She lifted her arm so everyone could see the betrothal bracelet.

"I'm so delighted that Bran has asked me to marry him," she said in a voice pitched to carry. "I'm sure you all know we've been madly in love for years."

Anneth nearly choked on her wine, and Bran tried not to wince at the outright lie. If he hadn't already decided to leave immediately, Mireleth's words would have sent him running.

So much for the brave warrior, he thought cynically. He was fearless in battle, but in the face of Mireleth's court-sanctioned grasping, he felt like an untrained youth facing his first enemy in the field.

"Congratulations!" one well-wisher shouted, and the toast was taken up through the dining hall.

Bran raised his goblet and wet his lips with wine, acknowledging the cheers. He needed a clear head to travel on, despite the impulse to drain his cup.

He was gratified to note that several people sent him looks filled with commiseration, however, rather than congratulation. Not everyone believed Mireleth's fabrications, or thought the betrothal was wise.

The Hawthorne Lord and Lady resumed their seats, and the musicians in the gallery struck up a jaunty tune on flute and cittern. As people's attention returned to their food, Bran considered how quickly he could depart.

He'd make it through the last course, pen a note for Lady Mireleth saying he'd been unexpectedly called back to the battle, fetch his mount, and be well away from the Hawthorne Court before the pale-moon set.

CHAPTER 7

The rest of the market trip was uneventful, but despite the bright sun on her face, Mara's mood turned gloomy. As expected, her mother had bought her the braided copper ring, and she twisted it back and forth on her finger as they returned home.

"We'll have trout and spring greens for supper," her mother said. "And honeycakes to celebrate your birthday."

"That sounds lovely." Mara tried to sound enthusiastic. "I'll cut a bouquet for the table."

She helped her mother put away their supplies, then took a pair of shears and a basket and went outside again. The late afternoon sun warmed the front stoop of their cottage, and mint and wallflowers were already growing there in profusion.

Mara cut a few stems of each, then went down the lane toward the Darkwood, adding forget-me-not and sweet rocket to her basket. Near the forest, she took a few ferns for greenery.

Other flowers grew deeper in the shadows between the trees: delicate columbine and pale lady's mantle. She was tempted to venture in, even though she had plenty of flowers to make a pleasing arrangement. For a long moment she stood, staring into the forest and hoping to see golden sparks of light dancing toward her.

"Mara!" Her younger sisters waved to her from down the lane, carrying their slates and schoolbooks.

Nothing sparked or glimmered in the Darkwood. Well then. Mara took up her basket and went to join her sisters.

The rest of the afternoon and evening was pleasant enough, in a humdrum sort of way. All her siblings had remembered it was her birthday, and after supper they presented her with a book-shaped package.

"We put all our pocket money in," Pansy said. "Of course, that was when we thought you'd be away forever, working at the castle."

She sounded a little put out that they'd splurged for nothing, and that there would be no lavish reciprocal gifts bought with Mara's salary as a maid.

Seanna rolled her eyes. "I'm sure Mara will enjoy it, regardless of her surroundings. Go ahead, open it."

Mara carefully unwrapped the brown paper, pausing when the gilt-edged corner of the book was revealed. Had they found her another book of fabulous tales? Quickly, she pulled the rest of the paper free, and couldn't help a little yelp of joy.

"It's the sequel to my storybook! Oh, thank you all so much." She went around the sitting room, giving each of her siblings a hug and a kiss.

"You'll have to read us out the best ones," Lily said.

"Hmph," their father said. "An impractical waste of money."

Mara's mother did not agree, as she usually did. After all, she'd bought Mara a ring with the leftover market money. Despite her obvious disappointment that Mara had lost her position at the castle, it seemed she was happy to have her middle child home again.

If only to marry her off. Mara banished that thought and ran her fingers over the green cloth binding of the book. Tonight she'd stay up late, reading by candlelight, and let the tales take her away from the drab future awaiting her.

"Off to bed, the lot of you," Mara's mother said. "Morning comes early enough."

Pansy and Lily made noises of complaint and dragged their feet upstairs. Sean and Seanna followed them, displaying far less reluctance. Mara stayed in the faded armchair, her new book in her lap.

"Happy birthday, love." Mara's mother kissed her cheek, then took up the oil lamp. "Don't stay up too late, mind."

"Foolishness," her father said with a glance at her book, but he set a fond hand on her head. "Bank the fire when you go to bed."

"I will. Goodnight." A rush of warmth filled her as she watched her parents step down the hallway, a circle of lamplight surrounding them. They worked hard, and it couldn't be easy raising five children, especially with all of them still at home.

No wonder her mother was in favor of Mara taking up with Thom.

But she wouldn't let herself think of that—not now, not with the solitude of the night folding sweetly about her, and a new, tantalizing book of tales waiting for her to dive in.

Mara lit a fat beeswax candle from the flames still dancing on the hearth, then settled in to celebrate her birthday.

The cottage quieted as she devoured tales of dragons and magic and impossible quests. Although she wanted to read the entire book in one sitting, she made herself mark the halfway point and stop. She needed to have something to look forward to over the coming days.

Quietly, she rose and banked the fire, smiling at the thought that she wouldn't have to rise before dawn to stoke it up again. She picked up the candle, noting how the reflection of the flame danced in the night-darkened windows.

Then she froze, eyes fixed outside. Carefully, she lifted her hand and shielded the candle flame, blocking its reflection.

The bright spark flickering beyond the window did not disappear. Her breath trembling with excitement, Mara blew the candle out.

At the edge of the Darkwood, a golden mote bobbed and beckoned. All around her, in the darkened cottage, Mara's family slumbered.

Now.

She did not know if she breathed the word, or if the breeze rustled it through the distant trees. In the dimness, she set the extinguished candle down on the kitchen table. After a moment's hesitation, she laid the book beside it.

Moving quietly, she slipped on her boots and cloak, then grabbed a kitchen knife and slid it through her belt. It wouldn't do much to protect her from the wild beasts of the wood, but she felt a little better taking some kind of weapon, no matter how small.

The door creaked softly as she opened it. A cool breath of moist night air circled around her, carrying the scent of mint. Her heart thumped in her chest. Before she could question herself too closely, Mara stepped out and closed the door behind her.

Overhead, the stars winked brightly. The moon had already set. It felt very late; the still, deep hours of the night, when the fussiest of babies quieted and even the village cats slept. Mara moved like a shadow down the lane, past the few other cottages that stood between her family's home and the Darkwood.

The light at the edge of the trees bobbed up and down, as if aware she was coming. A breath of cedar and hemlock issued from the forest. She quickened her step, but as she came closer to the forest, the spark receded, dancing back into the shadows.

She stopped, and the light stopped, then bobbed again. Clearly it wanted her to follow.

Mara glanced up at the tall trees, the peaks of the evergreens feathery against the starlit sky. What if she got lost in the Darkwood, or fell into a sinkhole, or was attacked by a wild beast? Her family would never know what had become of her.

Ahead, a second light joined the first, darting and dancing around the hemlocks as if urging her to hurry.

Standing just outside the forest, she knew she was on the edge of something momentous. This choice would never come again—return to the cottage and the safety of her familiar life, or go forward to meet the dancing sparks beneath the trees.

Now, the forest breathed.

Taking a deep breath, she stepped into the Darkwood.

The two motes of light twirled up into a spiral, then parted and continued to float expectantly beneath the boughs.

"I'm coming," Mara said softly.

Gathering up her skirts, she strode through the sparse underbrush. The forest floor was soft beneath her boots, and faint starlight filtered through the trees, giving her barely enough light to avoid tripping over downed logs and getting tangled in briar thickets.

She glanced up from navigating around one such thicket to see that her guides had doubled in number. Now four sparks glimmered through the forest. They seemed a bit larger, too, as if she were closer to them.

What could they possibly be? Not fireflies, as her parents had suggested. They did not pulse and glow as insects did, and their movements were far more purposeful than the random flittings of bugs.

Increasing her stride, she made an effort to catch up to the motes of light as they wove in and out of the trees. The smell of moss and loam filled her nose. Around her, the wind stirred the trees and they sighed and whispered in the language of the forest. The sparks—now numbering five—glowed ahead, shedding a golden radiance through the Darkwood. But no matter how Mara quickened her pace, she couldn't draw any closer.

A sound came from behind her, a low, guttural growl filled with menace. Her heart leaped into her throat, and she cast a fearful glance over her shoulder. The forest revealed nothing; only tree trunks receding into shadow, with pure blackness behind.

A sudden flare of light made her look up to see one of her elusive guides hovering just above her head. She sucked in her breath when she saw it was a small creature made entirely of light, its slim body borne aloft on butterflylike wings.

Her temporary wonder was smothered by another growl, closer this time. The light-creature fluttered urgently. Mara grabbed up her skirts in her clenched fists and ran, as fast as she could.

The bright flyer kept pace, lighting her way while the other sparks flew ahead, marking the path she must follow.

A rank scent drifted in the air: matted fur and old meat. Lungs tight with panic, Mara leaped over branches and dodged around tangled underbrush. Whatever was following seemed to be gaining, the crash of its passage growing louder as she sped through the forest.

Please. Just the one word, keeping time with her gasps for breath. *Please.*

The lights winked out, and she lost her footing in the sudden dark. A roar sounded from behind her as she tumbled over the edge of a hidden precipice. Stones and roots scraped her hands as she tried to slow her fall. After a sickening eternity she landed, dazed and breathless, at the bottom. She scrambled into a crouch, heart pounding, and fumbled for her kitchen knife. At any moment the dreadful creature chasing her would leap down to devour her.

Nothing happened.

No wild beast crashed over the bank. No growls filled the air, not even the crackling rustle of the underbrush. Only the rasp of her own breathing. After a few moments where she was not, in fact, mauled to death, she forced herself to stand. The kitchen knife was still clenched in her right hand, though somehow she'd lost her cloak.

The Darkwood was quiet about her. Stars peeked between the branches overhead. She pushed her sweat-dampened hair back from her face and tucked her blade away, then took a careful step forward, glad to discover she was only a little bruised from her tumble.

But where was she? She'd never be able to find her way home now.

Her fall had deposited her at the edge of a clearing. Two standing stones rose from the mossy ground, positioned about a meter apart and taller than her head. Her glowing guides hovered above them. The stones emitted a soft silver light that mixed with the golden radiance of the winged sparks, until the clearing was illuminated with uncanny brightness.

Mara pulled in a reverent breath. Clearly this was one of the deep secrets of the Darkwood.

She stepped closer, to see mysterious runes carved into the stones. The sparks whirled into a flurry as she approached. One of them flew down, made a circle around her, and then darted into the space between the tall stones.

It winked out. There one moment, gone the next.

The hair on the back of her neck prickled. This was true magic.

The night wind kicked up at her back, pushing her forward. Clearly the forest wanted her to step through.

Mara set her hand to her knife, took a deep breath, and walked directly between the two standing stones.

The air flickered. For a moment she glimpsed a land steeped in indigo shadows, a sky full of strange and brilliant stars. The sweet scent of unfamiliar flowers wafted on the warm air.

And then it was gone, and she fetched up on the other side of the clearing, the stones behind her. The wind died to a quiet sigh. Slowly, Mara turned to look at the doorway she had *almost* stepped through.

An owl hooted from a distance, the mournful cry giving voice to her disappointment. Whatever that place had been, it was full of a wild magic that stirred her senses.

"It didn't work," she said.

Perhaps this wasn't to be her adventure after all. But why had she been led to these stones, if she was not meant to go through?

One of the other sparks spiraled down, flying close to the right-hand stone. Bits of mica glinted in the rock as it passed. Halfway down, it hesitated, then flew *into* the stone. No, not into the solid granite. It had gone into a small hole in the rock.

A keyhole.

"Oh," Mara said, more sigh than word.

Slowly, she slipped her hand into the inner pocket of her dress. Her fingers brushed against something warm and solid. Holding her breath, she pulled it out.

The skull-headed key grinned at her, shining whitely against the shadows.

"You trickster," she whispered. "You didn't abandon me."

She felt as though her heart would take flight like the bright-winged sparks now darting ecstatically above the stones. This was the moment she'd been waiting for her entire life. Her body was a bell, reverberating in a single, sure peal.

She took three steps forward, until she reached the stone. The golden light darted out of the keyhole, and slowly Mara inserted the glass key.

It slipped in smooth as water. She turned it carefully to the right. A soft chime filled the clearing, and the air between the stones shimmered. The key fell out into her hand.

She tucked it back into her pocket, lifted her head, and walked through the doorway between the worlds.

CHAPTER 8

A shower of sensation drenched Mara's skin, as if she'd stepped through a curtain of warm water. She took a gasping breath of flower-scented air while her body realized it was not, in fact, drowning.

She stood between two standing stones in a clearing, similar to the one she had just left. Similar, and yet the air held a wild tang, and an unseasonably warm breeze wafted against her cheek. The sky above her was violet-black and spangled with unfamiliar constellations, including a bright spiral of seven stars high overhead. Silver light illuminated the tall evergreen trees surrounding her, and beneath them grew strange flowers that glowed dark purple and scarlet.

The trees, at least, were still hemlock and cedar, though they whispered to her in a language she could not understand.

A flicker of light danced through the air, and Mara was glad to see that one of her guides had accompanied her. It flitted to the edge of the clearing, then bobbed impatiently up and down.

"Very well," Mara said. There was no reason to linger near the doorway when a magical new world awaited her.

She patted her pocket to make sure the key was still there—not that she trusted it to remain—then checked the knife at her waist. Before stepping under the trees, she turned and studied the clearing. The stones stood tall against the night sky. She could see no distinguishing landmarks—no twisted bushes or ragged stumps to signal the way back.

Well then. She'd just have to trust the winged sparks to guide her when it was time for her to return.

But first, she was truly embarked on an adventure.

The glowing creature lit a path into the evergreens, and Mara followed, her steps taking her through a deeper, richer version of the Darkwood. The scent of cedar and rich loam tickled her nose. The glowing flowers grew in clusters between the trunks, along with a soft moss that shed a faint emerald light. The trees were much taller than in her world, the trunks wider—some even as broad as a cottage. High overhead, the wind waved the branches in a hushing lullaby.

The light grew stronger, until she stepped out of the woods into a meadow filled with tall, silvery grasses. The little golden glow she'd been following swooped back to circle three times around her head, then flew straight up into the sky.

"Wait!" Mara cried.

She stared up at the night until her eyes watered, but the mote had settled itself in among the stars. Now she was alone, and the wind suddenly blew cooler, bringing with it a dank whiff of something rotten.

Where did she go, now that her guide had abandoned her? She turned a slow circle, wrinkling her nose at the stench. It seemed to be coming from her right. Moving quickly, she headed away from the smell and into the meadow. The grasses were almost as high as her chest, but parted easily as she passed.

No matter how fast she went, though, she could not get away from the nasty smell. In fact, it was growing stronger. There was a noise, too, a chittering sound that made the back of her neck prickle with fear.

She broke into a run, pushing through the grasses. The sound grew louder. Breath coming fast, Mara risked a glanced over shoulder, then wished she had not.

A hideous creature scuttled out of the forest. It looked like an enormous spider—if spiders had hard shells and pincer claws. It had at least six red eyes that swiveled to fix upon her. Quicker than she thought possible, it hurtled into the meadow, clicking and emitting a high-pitched screech.

Mara dug her feet into the earth, praying she could outrun the monster. A noxious shadow passed over her, and then the creature landed ahead of her, pincers raised.

A moan of fear curdled in her throat. Though it was hopeless, she drew the kitchen knife. It trembled in her hand. It seemed her adventure this night was going to be very short-lived, indeed.

The monster opened its mouth, and the stench that emitted nearly brought her to her knees. Then it jumped again, directly for her.

Mara dodged and went to her knees, slashing out blindly with her knife. Miraculously, it connected with one of the creature's legs, sending out a spatter of green ichor that burned her arm. She let out a cry of pain and dropped the blade. Her forearm felt seared to the bone.

The monster screeched and pivoted, raising its pincers, and despair washed over her. *Goodbye, my family,* she thought. *I wish I'd had the chance to tell you all I love you.*

Then, from out of the blackness of the night, a savior arrived. With a deep battle cry, he launched himself at the spider monster. Blinking away her tears of pain, Mara saw that he looked like a human man, Mostly. His eyes were slitted like a cat's and glowed with violet light, and his bone-white features were contorted in a fierce grimace.

He wielded a long, curved sword in one hand. As she watched, stunned, he cleaved through one of the monster's legs, nimbly dodging the acidic spray of green blood.

"Vende!" he shouted, pointing at her.

Get away, she heard, echoing in her mind.

Cradling her injured arm across her chest, she scrambled back, but could not take her eyes from the fight.

The spider monster hissed, swiping at the man with its claws. He dodged the attack and raised his free hand. A ball of purple fire flew from his palm, hitting the creature in the head. The smell of scorched flesh joined the rank odor of the monster, and Mara swallowed back bile.

With a shout, her rescuer leaped gracefully forward and plunged his sword into the creature's body. It let out a screech that rasped the air, then collapsed, legs and pincers twitching. One claw rose feebly and he set it ablaze with another gout of fire. After a few seconds, the monster stopped moving altogether.

"Rhanc na," her rescuer said. *It is dead.*

He pulled his blade from the carcass and wiped it clean on the silvery grasses. While he was thus occupied, Mara scanned the battle-trampled ground for her kitchen knife. It lay near the dead monster, nearly buried by the churned-up soil. She scrambled forward, gritting her teeth against the pain in her arm, and grabbed the blade. It was a poor weapon, but better than nothing.

Gasping, she rose to her feet, knife awkwardly raised in her left hand.

"Who are you?" she asked. "*What* are you?"

"Nahtadh!" he exclaimed. *You are hurt.*

With two quick strides he stood before her, ignoring the feeble waving of her knife. He was tall and lithe, and wore dark leather armor. Pointed ears poked up through the midnight-black hair framing his pale face. Even without the battle grimace his features were forbiddingly strange—the sharp planes of his cheeks too angular, the set of his mouth too harsh.

Worst of all were his eyes, the irises widening as he studied her. She glanced away from the sight, trying to calm her galloping heartbeat.

She was not sure if she was in any less danger from her erstwhile savior than she had been from the spider monster. Although he'd come to her rescue, he was nonetheless quite terrifying.

With a shaky breath, she steeled herself and looked up into his glowing eyes.

The unfamiliar stars spun above his head, and the world seemed to tilt.

He reached to steady her. She flinched, and was surprised to feel his hands were warm on her shoulders, not corpse cold. A strange sensation coursed through her, a buzzing that centered on her injured arm. He dropped one hand and gently took her arm, and she let him straighten it, though the movement made her hiss with agony.

Thin lips turned down in a frown, he passed his hand over her arm. The pain lessened somewhat, and she let out a relieved breath, though she could not help noticing that his fingertips ended in hard ebony claws. In some ways he seemed more monster than man.

"Naresta," he said. *Help is nearby.*

"I don't trust you," she said. "What kind of being are you? Do you even understand what I'm saying?"

He gave her a look she could not interpret. "Tolo." *Come.*

She wasn't sure she should go with him - but he was offering to help, and she didn't have any other options. Mara took a step, then nearly collapsed. The adrenaline that had carried her through pursuit and attack had gone, leaving her shaky and filled with pulsing pain.

With a muttered curse, he swept her up in his arms. She barely had the presence of mind to keep hold of her knife as he bore her through the silvery grasses.

His stride was smooth, and it seemed to take no effort to carry her. Some of his long, dark hair fell forward and brushed her face, and she smelled the dusty scent of hawthorn blossoms. She was too weary to struggle in his arms.

"Gartong," he said. *Hold tight.*

He was a man of few words—but at least she was able to understand them. Though it seemed their communication was only one-way.

He shifted her in his arms, then lunged up. It took a moment for her stomach to settle, and then she realized they were on a horse. A very large black horse that seemed to have neither saddle nor bridle. He resettled her across his lap, holding her securely yet carefully. Her head rested against his chest, where she heard the steady beating of his heart. Her legs draped over his, and had he been a human man it would have been embarrassingly intimate.

But this strange, stern warrior was certainly not a mortal man. If she were to guess, she would name him one of the fearsome Dark Elves out of legend. And she had fallen firmly into his clutches.

The horse moved into a walk, then a faster gait that was smooth as water. Mara listened to the Dark Elf's heartbeat beneath her ear and wondered what her fate was to be, and how she might escape it.

CHAPTER 9

By *the seven bright stars!* Bran could not believe he'd found the human woman he'd seen in his vision—and nearly lost her to a creature of the Void.

He didn't know how the abomination had penetrated the barrier undetected, but it was a very bad sign. As was the appearance of the girl, if the prophecy was to be believed. Elfhame's darkest hour must be nearly upon them.

She was a brave thing, he had to admit, even armed with that laughable blade. The fact she'd managed to cut the monster was impressive. But how strange she looked, with her soft, blunt features and small, clawless hands. She'd said she didn't trust him—as if she had any choice in the matter.

His first impulse had been to take her back to the Hawthorne Court, so they might be married immediately. But she was injured, and the camp at the border was much closer than his father's court. After they tended her wounded arm, and made sure she was well enough to travel, then the prophecy could be fulfilled.

Cautiously, he glanced down, to see that she was sleeping in his arms. The determination that had filled her face was smoothed away, and she looked vulnerable and young. His muscles tensed again at the thought of the Void creature attacking her, and a strange possessiveness welled up in him. He made a swift vow to the absent moon to do whatever he must to keep her safe.

In less than a half-turn, he crested a rise and saw the soft glow of the border camp ahead. The woman in his arms made a quiet moan of pain. Without thinking, he gently smoothed her mud-colored hair away from her face.

With his knee he nudged Fuin, his faithful steed, into a canter. The guards at the perimeter lifted their hands in silent greeting as he passed. On the horizon, the first light of the brightmoon washed out the stars.

When he reached the center of camp, he slid off his horse. Though he landed as lightly as he could, the girl's eyes flew open and she stiffened in his arms.

"Hush," he said to her. "All is well."

Whatever magic lay between them, she seemed to understand. Her body relaxed, though she raised her head, surveying the tents and warriors.

"Are you at war?" she asked.

He made no reply. There would be time enough, later, to explain the dire situation the Dark Elves were faced with, and her part in saving them.

The healer's tent was lit inside with golden everflame lanterns. Avantor, leader of the healing hands, hurried over when Bran strode in. He glanced at the human, and his eyes flared with questions.

"Void ichor burn," Bran said. "Her right arm."

"Lay her there," the healer said, gesturing to an unoccupied cot.

Bran gently deposited the woman, then stood back while Avantor peeled the sleeve of her gown away from her blistered skin. She let out a hiss of pain, then looked up at Bran.

"Will it leave a scar?" she asked.

He did not know, and only pressed his lips together in reply.

She let out a low breath. "I don't know why I bother asking. You don't understand me, and all you do is give me that hideous glare."

Bran opened his mouth to answer that he was not glaring at her, let alone considered hideous, but Avantor waved him back.

"Give me room to work," the healer said.

Bran nodded and took a step away. He had some rudimentary ability to heal, but Avantor was far more skilled, and had spent years honing his abilities.

Humming a song of soothing, the healer passed his hands over the mortal's burned flesh. She closed her eyes, a look of blessed relief crossing her face. It had been brave of her, to bear the pain so long without protest.

As Bran watched, Avantor made a second pass, golden light radiating from his palms. The reddened skin turned to pink, the blisters faded, but the ichor would leave its mark, a faint etching of lines on her skin. Thank the distant moon it had not burned her down to the bone.

"Her forearm will be weak and the skin tender for a quarter moon," Avantor said. "And it will leave a scar. I'm sorry. The injury was not serious enough to call forth my deepest healing songs."

"I understand." Though Bran wanted his bride whole and unscarred, Avantor must conserve his power to tend more grievous wounds. There were few enough Dark Elf warriors standing whole upon the field as it was.

"Rest now," Bran said to the woman, who seemed already half asleep.

She opened her eyes fully at the sound of his voice.

"Wait," she said. "What is your name?"

He hesitated a moment. His full, formal name might be too difficult for her. Should he introduce himself as the Hawthorne Prince, or would that make him even more intimidating in her eyes?

She clearly took his silence for incomprehension. With an exaggerated movement, she pointed to herself.

"I am Mara." She tapped her chest with her uninjured hand. "Mara. You?" She pointed back to him.

It was a simple name, and he decided to return it in kind.

"Bran," he said, putting his own hand on his chest.

Her gaze followed the motion, and he saw her shiver at the sight of his partially sheathed claws. Then her gaze darted back to his face. Her eyes held more gold than mud, illuminated by the everflame, and he stared, caught by that brightness.

"Bran," she said.

The sound of his name in her mouth sent a jolt through him, as though the prophecy had been waiting for a moment of weakness to pounce. He suppressed the feeling, and made her a slight bow.

"Mara," he said. It was not displeasing, as far as mortal names went.

Her lips bent into a slight smile and she closed her eyes.

Bran stared at her a long moment, studying the curves of her face—so different from the angular planes of his own people. Avantor cleared his throat.

"Are you in need of anything else, my lord?" the healer asked.

"No." Bran gave himself a mental shake. "I'll be consulting with Hestil. Summon me if there's any change."

"There should not be. She'll sleep for quite some time, and be a little unsteady on her feet when she wakes."

"Fetch me when she does," Bran said.

He hoped there would not be an attack while Mara was convalescing. The sooner he could get her away from the front and to the safety of court, the better.

Hestil was in the command tent, leaning over an array of maps spread out on the low table. She straightened when Bran walked in, and raised one eyebrow.

"My scouts tell me you arrived with a human woman. Could it be that the long-awaited prophecy is finally in motion?"

"Yes." He nodded at the maps. "Have there been any more incursions beyond the ones marked?"

She made an annoyed sound. "For just a moment, forget you are a commander, and answer as though you have a heart. What do you think of her?"

"It doesn't matter what I think." It never had, not when he'd grown up bound by prophecy, hemmed in at every turn.

"Nonsense. You have to marry the girl. It's better if you don't find her odious."

"She's human." He shrugged. "They are somewhat different than our kind."

"*Our kind.* You know as well as I that before the doorway was closed, Dark Elves and humans interbred. Just because the Hawthorne line never intermingled doesn't mean she's of completely alien blood."

"My mother would disagree."

Tinnueth had always found the idea of the Hawthorne Heir married to a lowly mortal quite distasteful. Which was why she'd probably concocted the scheme to betroth him to Mireleth.

"Just because part-blood mortals almost never showed Dark Elf characteristics doesn't mean they're not compatible mates," Hestil continued.

Mates. Bran frowned. His little mortal was strange of appearance, and it was clear she found him equally unnerving. "The prophecy says nothing of breeding. Only that we must wed."

His second-in-command regarded him a long moment, then gave a small shake of her head and turned back to the maps. "There's been a breach further south. We were able to contain it, but the forces are spread too thin."

"One creature got through," Bran said, his voice tight. "It attacked Mara, and that might have been the end of us all, right then. We must increase the patrols."

Hestil's eyes widened. "Muck and mire. Was she badly injured?"

"Burned, but not too badly. She's resting in the healer's tent. I killed the creature."

"Of course you did. Though you know we haven't enough warriors to add extra patrols."

Bran clenched his fist and tapped it against the sword at his waist. What Hestil said was true—they were desperately shorthanded.

"Up the ration of puffdust," he finally said. "We'll all be short on sleep, but the alternatives are worse."

Hestil frowned, but made no argument. They both knew prolonged use of the stimulant could cause debilitating headaches, sometimes lasting for moons. Still, they had no choice.

"I'll go out to the perimeter now," Bran said. "Who's in most need of a rest?"

"Lieth. She's been pulling double shifts since you left."

There was no censure in her voice, but Bran felt a stab of guilt anyway. Lieth was the strongest magic user the Dark Elves had, after himself. But she was not also heir to a court, and subject to the beck and call of an imperious father.

"I'll send her in right away," he said.

The brightmoon had just cleared the horizon, spilling milky light over the land, as Bran stepped out of the command tent. He blinked, letting his eyes adjust to the light, then went to fetch Fuin.

It took a turn of riding to find Lieth. The glow of her magic was a simple guide, though Bran noted the light wavered unsteadily as he approached. He dismounted at Lieth's rough camp and tethered Fuin, then hurried to the clearing where she held the Void at bay.

She stood, bathed in a halo of purple light, one hand upraised to try and maintain the barrier. With her other hand, she directed a stream of lightning at a huge, lumbering creature who had obviously issued from the Rift. Its five eyes glowed menacingly atop an elongated neck and it sported a maw of wickedly sharp teeth, but thankfully its stumpy legs did not propel it very quickly.

Bran summoned his magic, adding his own powerful blast to Lieth's attack. With a wet *whump*, the creature exploded. Lieth staggered back a step, but to her credit kept the flow of power going to the barrier. Quickly, Bran stepped up beside her, ready to lend a steadying shoulder.

"Prince Brannon. Good to see you," she said with a weak smile.

By the light of the risen moon she looked wretched, her pale skin tinged ashen, her eyes faded and barely glowing.

"I have the barrier," Bran said, opening his hand and letting magic flow from his palm. "You need a rest."

"I'll just lie down in my tent—" she began.

"No. I insist you return to the main camp and see Avantor. You're dangerously close to draining your magic dry."

She regarded him a moment, then slowly nodded.

"I won't argue with you, commander. The breach here is nearly sealed, but I couldn't close it and fend off the creatures at the same time. I'm sorry to say that I lost my mount to a gyrewolf." She dropped her gaze to the trampled grasses.

"The Void attacks are growing more aggressive. You did well to hold the border for this long."

And he was an idiot for letting Hestil send her out alone.

It was fortunate that one of the slower Riftlings had emerged, not another gyrewolf or spiderkin. Had he been much later, Elfhame might have seen an influx of creatures they could not contain.

Thank the prophecy the mortal woman had appeared at last.

"Take Fuin," he said. "I'll finish closing the breach, then come back on foot. That way I can check the border more closely."

He did not want to be unable to reach Mara quickly, but Lieth was nearly dead upon her feet. He could not make her march back to the main camp, and he did not want her to wait until he finished sealing the border—not with the way the light in her eyes was dimming.

As if to mock his thoughts, the breach in the barrier bulged, and two creatures emerged: a chittering spiderkin and a red-eyed wolf.

Lieth raised her hands, but Bran grabbed her arm. "No. I command you to go. *Now.*"

He knew she would obey. None dared go against the Hawthorne Prince when he used such a tone.

A poor leader he would be if he allowed the second-best magic user they had to drain her powers to the bone. As it was, it would take at least a brightmoon for her to regain her strength.

He was powerful enough to handle two foes and maintain the barrier by himself. Not with perfect ease, but he could not be distracted by worrying that Lieth was about to collapse from exhaustion.

As she turned and trudged over to where Fuin was tied, Bran sent a blast of magic at the spiderkin. It flew backward, temporarily disabled. He drew his sword and, still keeping some power flowing to the breach, ran forward to meet the gyrewolf.

It was overeager, and leaped straight at him. Bran ducked and thrust his sword up into the wolf's belly, then dodged the shower of ichor as the creature thudded to the ground. It twitched once, then was still.

Behind him, he heard the thud of hooves as Lieth left.

The spiderkin righted itself and began scuttling toward him. Bran sent an extra jolt of power into the breach to keep it closed, then turned his magic on his attacker. It would take more force than he wanted to use to dispatch it the way he and Lieth had killed the lumberer, especially since he must make sure the border was secure afterward.

With a grim smile, he raised his sword again. One of the reasons he was the strongest magic user among the warriors was that he knew when to conserve his power and use his blade instead. True, he had unusually deep reserves of magical energy, but his fighting prowess helped him maintain that power rather than constantly spending it in battle.

As the spiderkin circled, claws clacking, Bran pulled out his dagger with his left hand. Best to end this soon. He must seal the breach and return to Mara before she woke. He balanced the blade, then sent it hurtling toward one of the creature's glowing red eyes. It struck true and the spiderkin let out a screech of pain and anger.

In that moment of distraction, Bran leaped forward, sword swinging. It did not take long before the carcass of the spiderkin joined that of the gyrewolf. He retrieved his dagger, then carefully wiped the ichor from both blades before re-sheathing them.

Now to seal the border.

He studied the small tear in the barrier surrounding Elfhame. Behind it, he could feel the pulsing power of the Void, hungry and relentless.

As he had told his father, the Void had never before pressed so closely against their world. It was concentrating its attack on the portion of the barrier guarded by Hawthorne and Nightshade, and every time their warriors sealed a breach, the Void managed to open a new one. The other courts had sent reinforcements as well, keeping only enough warriors to patrol the boundaries of their own territories.

But there were not enough Dark Elves to contain the sustained assault from the Void. Not this time.

Bran drew in a long breath and glanced at the full orb of the moon. Planting his feet firmly in the soil, he lifted his hands and drew upon his wellspring of power.

Blue light streamed from his hands, splashing across the invisible barrier that encircled Elfhame. He found the edges of the tear, and pulled them back together, weaving his magic back and forth to create a strong seal. When it was mended, he raised his voice and spoke the word of binding.

White light flared across the clearing. The border was secure.

Just below hearing, he was aware of the Void's rage, a black hum of fury. If he had to guess, he would say the Void had exhausted the other worlds it preyed upon. In the past, Elfhame had been too much trouble, but now he could sense a desperation in its hunger.

He thought it no coincidence that the Void's efforts to break through were concentrated near the doorway to yet another land: the mortal world where humans dwelt. They would stand little chance against the creatures now attacking the Dark Elves.

Humans were weak, despite their iron swords and masses of soldiers. It was not because of their fighting prowess that the Dark Elves had closed the doorway and returned to Elfhame. Mortals, with very few exceptions, lacked the magic to repel the creatures of the Void. They would make a sweet feast for its devouring energy.

But he should not dwell on such dark thoughts. Now that Mara had arrived, an end to the battle was in sight. And it could not come soon enough.

Bran strode back to Lieth's small camp. He bundled up her sleeping roll and struck her tent, stowing it and most of her supplies in the waterproof saddlebags she'd brought. Without a horse to help transport everything back, he'd have to leave most of it for later retrieval.

He made up a smaller pack for himself with the food, water, and a blanket. It would take him a turn or two to return to the main camp, and it was always wise to be prepared.

As the brightmoon rose high in the star-etched sky, he set off. He paralleled the barrier, keeping a tendril of magic lightly touching the boundary that walled off the world. For a half-turn, all was quiet. Silver light filtered through the trees and cast radiance into the open glades where white-petaled flowers bloomed. Their faint perfume drifted on the air, along with the quiet coo of ashdoves.

Then Bran sensed a tremor in the barrier. He paused and extended his power more fully, then shuddered at what he felt. The coldness of the Void seeped into his soul.

A large breach had opened ahead—and if he was any judge, it was near the main camp. If Mara was in danger...

Quickly, he withdrew his magic and began to run, cursing his lack of a horse. His heart beat, fast and strong, as he dashed through the silver-lit forest that lay between him and the threat to Elfhame's entire future.

CHAPTER 10

Mara blinked, emerging from strange dreams of moonlight and poison-filled spider monsters. She felt cold; her bedroom fire must have died down and she'd kicked off her quilt.

But... something was not right with the ceiling. Unease curled through her as she blinked again, trying to clear the muzz of sleep from her head. Pale fabric rose above her, and she lay in a narrow cot. Shouts filtered from outside, voices raised in a language not her own.

A jolt of wrongness went through her.

She was not lying in the bedroom she shared with her sisters. She was not in Little Hazel. Not even in the world she called home.

She was in the Dark Elves' world, where they were fighting a battle against strange creatures—and now it seemed the fight was taking place right outside. Strange glows lit the tent walls, and she heard screeches and howls that raised the hairs on the back of her neck.

Carefully she sat up, relieved to find that beneath the tatters of her sleeve her burned arm was only tender and pink. The blisters and searing pain were gone, and she let out a low breath of gratitude.

There was one other patient in the tent, an older Dark Elf, judging by the pale silver of his braided-back hair and the lines at the corners of his strange dark eyes. As she watched, he stood and moved slowly to the door flap.

"What is happening?" she asked.

"Dagor," he said, giving her a curious look. "Na echil?"

"I don't understand." She shook her head. Whatever ability she had to know Bran's meaning was gone, along with him. "Bran? Do you know where Bran is?"

"Ernil Brannonilon?" His eyes widened as he stared at her, and then he gave a slow nod.

Outside, the sounds of fighting grew closer. The elf glanced about, snatching a sword set just inside the tent's door. He raised the blade, then stepped back as another Dark Elf entered.

It was Bran.

Mara's heart gave a huge thump, then settled. Despite the fierce look on his stark features and the ichor-stained sword in his hand, she was strangely relieved to see him.

Something flared in his dark eyes and his grim expression softened a bit. Without a word, he sheathed his sword and strode to her bed. A light green cloak was neatly folded at the foot, and he picked it up.

"Lenweta emme," he said. *We must go.*

Good thing she had healed so quickly. She swung her feet to the canvas-covered floor, glad to find her boots tucked beneath the bed. She put them on and stood, and Bran wrapped the cloak about her in one swift move. It was a little too long for her. Something in the inner pocket bumped her hip—her kitchen knife. She pulled it out and stuck it through her belt.

The barest hint of approval softened his mouth, gone so quickly she thought she might have imagined it.

"I'm ready," she told him.

He paused at the tent door to exchange a quick conversation with the older warrior. She caught a few words—*hold* and *magic* and something that sounded like court.

Wonderful. She glanced down at her gown, stained with mud at the hem, the skirt hopelessly wrinkled, one sleeve partially burned away, the other ravaged by brambles. Just the thing to wear to meet the Dark Elf king.

If they even had a king. She knew so little about this world. The thought of an entire castle filled with terrifying Dark Elves made her shudder.

Bran took her elbow and escorted her out of the tent. The acrid smell of scorched flesh and the reek of ichor hung in the air. On one side of the camp, two Dark Elves sent blasts of magic against a pack of red-eyed wolves. On the other side, a band of warriors held three of the spiderlike creatures at bay.

A huge golden moon hung in the sky, much brighter than the silver disc she was familiar with. Its light showed all too clearly the desperation in the faces of the fighters. Mara closed her fingers about the handle of her kitchen knife, her breath tightening.

The air in front of them shimmered, and a wolf sprang out of nowhere, directly at her. She yanked out her blade, but Bran was already between her and the creature, sword swinging. A gaunt woman ran up, pale fire sputtering from her hands. It did not take long for the wolf to die.

"Taur coth," the woman said, her voice ringing hollow with exhaustion.

"Savamarth," Bran replied. *Trust fate.*

"Manen?" The woman gestured at the besieged camp, frustration clear in her voice.

Slowly, Bran sheathed his sword. He raised his hands, blue light flickering from his fingertips. The light intensified, washing over the tents and trampled ground, the bands of fighters and their dreadful enemies.

Mara squinted, her attention focused on Bran. His dark hair flew back from his severe face, and his strange eyes were closed. Magic streamed from his hands, and the attacking creatures began to disappear with sickeningly wet pops.

Bran swayed, and, without thinking, she stepped to his side. She slipped her arm about his waist, bracing him. It was foolish to think that she could lend this tall, muscular warrior her small mortal strength, but somehow she knew she must try.

Heat streamed from his body. He gave a grunt of approval and leaned more heavily against her. Mara dug her booted feet into the ground and braced herself against his weight.

The Dark Elf woman came to lend her aid on his other side. Mara drew in a deep breath and held on. Her side and arm began to pulse where they were in contact with Bran, as though he were not simply made of flesh. Perhaps it was his magic she felt, and she prayed it would not harm her as it did the invading creatures.

As if summoned by that thought, a strange prickling swept over her, as though she'd rolled in a patch of stinging nettles. Despite the discomfort, she screwed her eyes shut and continued to hold Bran up. Then, as if she were an egg, something inside her cracked open.

Pain, and light, and a surge of sensation that made her gasp and nearly double over.

Bran let out a shout. Blue light flared against her closed eyelids, then faded. She was not sure if she still upported Bran, or if were now the other way around.

"Mara?" His arm around her shoulders, his hand gentle on her cheek.

She forced her eyes open. The camp was quiet, the invading creatures gone. The Dark Elves spoke quietly to one another, and the woman next to Bran did not look nearly as spent as she had mere moments ago.

"What happened?" Mara asked.

"We closed the breach," he answered, his voice stiff with surprise. He studied her, brows lowered.

"Wait—I can understand you. And you understand me?" Relief blossomed in her chest. Suddenly, she felt far less alone.

"I always did." His voice was dry.

"Oh." Her cheeks heated as she recalled some of the things she'd said to him. Fortunately, he didn't seem to be too upset with her, but she'd mind her words from now on.

Another Dark Elf strode up to where they stood, her hair in elaborate braids, a sword in either hand. She glanced at Mara's arm about Bran's waist, and his around her shoulders, and raised one thin brow.

Mara tried pulling away, but Bran's hold tightened. Very well—she still felt shaky after whatever had happened, and his support was not unwelcome.

"That was an impressive show of power," the warrior woman said.

Mara drew in a breath. She could understand everyone! Whatever magic had just touched her, it seemed to have brought her more fully into the Dark Elves' world.

"That effort nearly drained me," Bran said. "Until Mara's wellspring opened. It was her power blended with mine that you saw." He sounded bemused by the fact.

Not nearly as stunned as Mara, however. Was he truly saying that she possessed magic of her own? How could that be? Her mind scrambled, trying to make sense of it.

"Well." The Dark Elf warrior frowned in thought. "The prophecy appears to be functioning correctly. I suppose you'll take her to court now?"

"I must, as soon as possible."

"I'll stay here," the woman on Bran's other side said. "My powers are restored enough to be of use again."

"Are you certain, Lieth?" He gave her a stern look.

"One of us has to remain, and it can't be you. I'm sure Commander Hestil agrees."

The woman with the braids gave a short nod. "The camp appears to be safe for now, and the border secure. It's high time you fulfilled your destiny."

She shot Mara an unreadable glance, then looked back at Bran.

"We'll depart immediately," he said. "I assume Fuin is with the other horses?"

"Yes," the woman he'd called Lieth said. "I can make up a pack for you—"

"I have one. Both of you, contact me if the Void attacks again, beyond the usual small breaches."

"Of course," Commander Hestil said. "Good luck."

Bran inclined his head to her, then looked at Mara. "Can you walk?"

"I think so." Although she had to admit her legs felt like wilted stalks after a hard frost. "What's going on? What do you mean by my 'wellspring'? What—"

"I'll tell you as we travel."

His arm still about her, he turned them both. She took a step, and nearly fell. With an annoyed sound, Bran swept her up in his arms. It was becoming a habit of his, to cart her about like a sack of grain. Nevertheless, she didn't have the strength to protest. This time.

"Lieth, my pack is at the edge of camp, there," he said. "Be so kind as to fetch it."

The other woman nodded and went to get Bran's supplies.

He strode to where the horses were tied, and his tall black steed whickered at their arrival. Lieth stowed his pack in the saddlebags and bade them farewell.

Soon enough they were mounted and on their way, Mara seated in front of Bran as before, his strong arm holding her in place. She tried to ignore the sharp claws at the ends of his fingers.

"Where are we going?" she asked. "Is it far?"

He did not answer immediately. She was coming to understand that he was comfortable with silence. Long silence. Still, she tried to curb her impatience and wait for his reply.

"We are going to the Hawthorne Court," he finally said.

"By court do you mean something like a castle, where your rulers dwell?" She must discover more about this strange land, though she might dread the answer.

"Yes. Something like."

Why did he always reply so quickly when the answer was unpleasant? She grimaced, glad he couldn't see her face. It seemed she was to meet the Dark Elf nobility after all.

"Does the king live there?" she asked.

His chest vibrated with a short, mirthless laugh. "We have no king, not in the way of mortals. There are seven courts, each governed by a Lord or Lady. They meet in council when necessary, but mostly the courts are content to rule themselves without interference from their neighbors."

It did not sound like an arrangement that would work in her world. "Do you not fight among yourselves?"

"No." His arm around her tightened. "There are plenty of outside threats to occupy us."

"Like those creatures."

"The Void, yes. And other things."

"Your world doesn't seem particularly pleasant," she said, then glanced about at the shadowy landscape they were riding through. "Does the sun ever shine here?"

"We do not have a fiery orb in the sky as you do in your mortal world. But the brightmoon casts plenty of light. And, in its defense, Elfhame currently is not appearing at its best." His voice had turned grim. "But once the Void is defeated, you'll see how lovely your new homeland is."

"What?" Panic swept through her. She turned to look at him and nearly fell off the horse, staying on only by grabbing his linen shirt. "My new *homeland*? Are you saying I'm trapped here?"

He pulled the horse to a stop, and cocked his head at her. "It is not so bad."

"How would *you* like to be ripped away from your home and family, away from everything you've ever known?" She let go of the silky fabric of his shirt, and pushed hard against his chest. "Put me down this instant."

Still holding her, he slid off his mount, then set her gently on her feet. She took a step away from him and balled her hands into fists, wanting to strike him, wanting to strike the entire twilight world of Elfhame.

"I don't belong here," she said fiercely.

He folded his arms. "It is your fate."

"It is no such thing."

She wanted to go home, to a sunlit world filled with the scent of baking bread and the good-humored teasing of her siblings. The thought of being trapped in this shadowy place, menaced by horrible creatures for the rest of her life, was unbearable.

"Since the day I was born," he said, "I've known that a mortal woman would come through the doorway into Elfhame. It is the prophecy."

"That's all very well for you." She ground her boot heels into the soil. "I didn't grow up surrounded by some kind of magical destiny, and I don't believe in your so-called prophecy. Can't you send me home?"

"No." His expression was hard.

"Then what good are those powers you like to fling about?"

"I remind you they've saved your life twice. And you have newly awakened magic of your own—magic that does not belong in the human world. Magic that can help us fight the Void and save Elfhame."

"I don't care." She crossed her arms, mirroring his stance. "I won't use it, not if it means I can't ever go home."

The wind brushed the tall grasses around them and sent silver shadows dancing through a nearby grove of trees.

"You have no choice." He stepped forward and took her shoulders. "You cannot fight fate."

His hands were warm, and he smelled faintly of some exotic spice—cloves, or sandalwood. But those things didn't matter.

Mara narrowed her eyes. Her stubbornness was her most exasperating quality, according to her mother. Well, she had every intention of putting it to full use.

"If you can't send me home, I'll find someone at the Hawthorne Court who will."

His lips flattened in disapproval. "I very much doubt that. I'm the strongest magic user in the land."

"But you've never gone through the doorway between our worlds. I have." A wild hope ran through her. "Take me there, right now—the place where the door stands."

He shook his head, one of his thin, dark braids brushing his angular cheek. "It's too dangerous."

She twisted her shoulders, and he dropped his hands, freeing her from the warmth of his grasp.

"You said you need my magic to help save Elfhame?" she asked.

He did not answer. Secrets swirled in his dark eyes.

"Well?" she demanded. "Isn't that what your so-called prophecy says?"

"Something akin to it," he said. "Your presence is essential to saving our world from the Void."

"Then I'll help you. But once the Void is defeated, you must promise to help me return home. To the mortal world."

He turned the silver bracelet on his wrist back and forth, the harsh planes of his face unreadable. “I do not know what you are accustomed to among humans, but in Elfhame we do not give promises lightly.”

“I’ll keep my word.” She lifted her chin, determined that he believe her. “If I tell you I’ll help, then I will. I’ll even learn to use whatever this new power is, if I have to.”

His lips twisted slightly, as though he tasted something sour. “It is not your side of the bargain I am concerned about.”

It took a moment for her to catch his meaning.

“So you *won’t* try to help me get me back home?” It felt like a betrayal, though she had no real reason to think of this forbidding warrior as her ally.

“It is not a matter of what I can and cannot do,” he said. “There are other elements in play.”

She folded her arms. “Then why should I help you?”

His eyes flared. “If you do not, you will perish along with Elfhame.”

His words rang with truth. The Dark Elves were hard-pressed, from what she had seen.

And she was somehow bound up in their future, whether she wanted to be or not. There was no winning this argument—and she was no closer to finding a way home. Defeat wrapped around her like a clammy cloak.

“Come,” he said. “When we reach the Hawthorne Court, matters will be made clear.”

CHAPTER 11

Bran mounted Fuin and settled Mara in front of him. She sat stiffly, and he could read her anger and unhappiness in the set of her shoulders.

He let out a soundless sigh. If only they had more *time*, so that he might ease her into his world and better prepare her for what was to come. But the Void was relentless, and the prophecy must be fulfilled.

Still, he had a little sympathy. He'd grown up with the prophecy woven into the fabric of his life. For her, the revelation of her unexpected magic—and her destiny—must be quite unsettling.

Perhaps that was why he hadn't yet told her about the wedding...

Her magic had come as a surprise to him as well, but a welcome one. He had never tried to second-guess his fate, but he'd sometimes wondered how a mortal woman could possibly be so important to the Dark Elves' future. Now he knew.

And soon, Mara would too.

Once she accustomed herself to her role in Elfhame's future, he had no doubt she would do what needed to be done. After all, she was the woman of the prophecy.

Fuin bore them through glades washed with the radiance of the brightmoon and past a silvery lake where glimglows danced with their reflections. The moon was sinking low in the sky when she finally spoke.

"What is this wellspring of magic that I supposedly have?"

He considered for a moment how best to explain it to her, relieved that she'd softened enough to lean against him. Or maybe she was simply too tired to care.

"Every Dark Elf has magic within them, in differing amounts," he said. "Some can perform only basic tasks—creating light and illusions, moving small objects, and rudimentary forms of offensive and defensive magic."

She let out a short, weary laugh. "That sounds impressive enough to me. But I'm not a Dark Elf. Why would I have any of your powers?"

Because it is your fate, he almost said, then thought better of it.

"You know that our people intermingled freely, centuries ago?"

"So the legends say. I suppose it's true. After all, there *is* a door between our worlds. Why did you leave and lock it behind you?"

"Dark Elves were no longer welcome among your kind," he said. "It would have been foolish to stay and fight for a place in your world—not when we had no great stake in the doings of mortals, and no real benefit to remaining."

"So you just took your magic and left."

"Not all of it, clearly. Some humans carry the blood of my ancestors. Like yourself."

"I've never done anything the least bit out of the ordinary back home," she said. "And it's not for lack of wanting."

"Then you have a latent power that only awoke when you entered Elfhame."

He did not mention that it was shockingly strong. Not as powerful as his own, but impressive for someone with so much mortal blood.

Of course, fate had arranged it so. Clearly her newfound powers were part of the key to saving his land. They must marry as soon as possible, then return to the front and defeat the Void once and for all.

"How do I learn to use this new magic of mine?" she asked. "And how long does it take to master?"

"I will teach you," he said. "As to how long? Dark Elf children are tutored for at least three years as they develop their powers and hone their skills."

"Three *years*?" She sounded aghast at the prospect. "That's far too long."

"I agree." At best, they had only a handful of moons. Her appearance in Elfhame heralded the beginning of the end. "We will begin your training now."

"Now?" She twisted around and glanced up at him. "While riding?"

"I will not let you fall. Close your eyes and reach deep within yourself. Remember the feeling of your magic unlocking, and see if you can reach it again."

With her pressed against him, he could sense the warm glow of her wellspring—but could she?

"Now," he said, "lift your hand and imagine a small ball of light hovering above your palm."

She dutifully raised her hand, palm open. Nothing happened.

"Feel your power, waiting for you to call upon it," he said.

"I don't feel anything," she said, frustration clear in her voice.

"You must try." It was essential she be able to harness her power before they returned to the battle.

She blew out a sharp breath and splayed her hand wide. No ball of foxfire materialized to dance above her palm.

"It's not working," she said.

Bran pushed away his disappointment. It was a temporary setback —but fate had brought her to Elfhame. Surely she would be able to access her powers with a little more training.

"We will try again later," he said.

"I thought we didn't have any time to waste." She dropped her arm to her side.

"You are tired and still recovering from the injury and healing done to your arm. No doubt the journey through the doorway was taxing, as well."

"Are you making excuses for me?" There was a sharp edge in her voice. "I must say, I don't think much of your training."

He lifted his eyes to the setting moon and prayed for patience—for both of them. "I can't expect you to instantly grasp a power you didn't even know you possessed until very recently. You are not a Dark Elf, born with the knowledge of magic running through your blood."

"No, I'm not. I'm just a lowly mortal girl."

"You are far more than that. You are the answer to a prophecy."

She gave a snort. "It doesn't seem to be working out all that well."

"Once we reach the Hawthorne Court—"

She swiveled again and stared at him with her strange blue eyes. "You keep saying that. What, exactly, will happen, when we get to the court?"

"There is to be a ceremony."

She stiffened within his grasp, and he felt her pulse leap like a startled animal. "Dear gods, am I to be sacrificed? You need my lifeblood, don't you?"

"No! Nothing like that. I swear it. You will not be harmed."

She stared at him a long moment, meeting his gaze without flinching. She must have read the truth in his eyes, for she relaxed slightly, and her heartbeat steadied.

For a moment he considered Mireleth's reaction to his true bride appearing. She would not be pleased—but there was nothing she could do about it. Thank the seven stars he'd escaped court before bonding their bracelets. Extrication from a fully activated betrothal bond was quite painful, or so he'd heard.

"What will the court think of me?" Mara asked. "Are they all as terrifying as you?"

He did not know how to respond. Probably, in the case of his parents, the answer was yes.

"My sister will like you," he said, avoiding the question. "She has spent much time studying everything she could find about mortals. And as the woman of the prophecy, you shall be well received at the Hawthorne Palace." He hoped.

Mortals had not visited the Dark Elf courts for nearly a hundred years. She would be stared at, and her strange appearance and manners remarked upon. Probably even mocked. But once she helped save Elfhame, everyone would respect her role in their fate, and in his life, no matter how unappealing they might personally find her. Like him, they would have no choice.

He urged Fuin along the base of a low hill. The setting moon cast their shadow ahead of them over the silvergrass, and the woman in his arms swayed with weariness.

Were he alone, he'd press on to the Hawthorne Court, but it would do neither of them any good to drag Mara, exhausted, into the palace. Despite the impatience pulsing through him, he must give her time to rest.

"We will bed down in the grove, ahead," he said, pointing to the small copse of trees just beyond the hill.

She stiffened, and he let out a breath, wondering what it was he'd said wrong this time.

"I'm not..." she began, then cleared her throat. "I warn you, I'm sleeping with my knife at my side."

He blinked a moment, before catching her meaning, and then let out a short, humorless laugh.

"I have no intention of compromising your maidenly honor," he said dryly.

She swiveled to frown at him. "Are you saying you think I'm ugly?"

Lips pursed, he stared back at her. It felt like a trap, where nothing he said would land him in her good graces.

After a long moment, she let out a *hmph* and turned back around. "Well, I think you're fairly horrible looking, too."

That surprised the warmth of real laughter out of him. "You are not horrible to behold, Mara. Just—different than what I'm used to. But I promise you will come to no harm while under my care. From anyone, including myself."

CHAPTER 12

They reached the little grove of trees Bran had indicated, and Mara let out a weary breath. She was glad to be stopping, and though she'd teased her dour escort, she wasn't truly afraid that he'd take advantage.

Although they scarcely knew each other, she sensed that he valued his integrity and would keep his word. Not that he was telling her everything, of course. She had the suspicion there was far more going on, but didn't have the energy to try to puzzle it out.

Not at the moment, anyway. She was exhausted and off-kilter, thrust into a strange land in the middle of a frightening conflict—and apparently trapped there until she was able to harness her newfound magic to help the Dark Elves win their war.

Magic.

She shook her head, still finding it nearly impossible to believe that she, Mara Geary from Little Hazel, possessed the power to help save worlds.

Bran pulled his horse to a stop and gracefully dismounted. She slid off far more clumsily, grateful that he was there to catch her. Though she'd meant to step away from him immediately, she instead found herself clinging to his solid arms, leaning into the warmth of his broad chest.

For a moment he held very still, then gently wrapped one arm around her.

"I'll make up a pallet for you," he said. "Meanwhile, sit here."

He led her to a fallen log and helped her settle onto the cushioning moss.

"I could just sleep right here," she said, patting the thick emerald mat. "It's nearly as soft as my bed at home."

He gave her a long look. "That will not be necessary. I assure you I can fashion a better bed than a fallen tree."

She'd meant her words partly in jest, but simply nodded. Her Dark Elf protecter took things rather seriously. Which, given the circumstances, she supposed she could understand. His land was under siege by terrifying monsters, after all, and from what she'd gathered, they were losing the battle.

And needed her, and her shockingly unexpected magic.

She'd meant her earlier promise, too. She would help them, and then she would go back to her world. Indeed, she hoped that whatever the rulers of the Hawthorne Court required—whatever ceremony Bran had alluded to—it would be over quickly so that she could return home.

A lump of homesickness rose in her throat at the thought of their cozy cottage in the lane, the ruckus of her siblings, the smell of her mother's bread baking. She hadn't been gone terribly long, but everything was so *strange* in this new realm.

She let out a sigh and rested her elbows on her knees. Maybe she'd been a fool to go running off looking for adventure, after all.

While she'd been lost in her thoughts, Bran had unsaddled his horse and deftly made a rudimentary camp. He strode over, a water flask in one hand, a strange green sphere in the other.

"Eat," he said, holding the food out to her.

"What is it?" She plucked the round object from his hand and gave it a sniff. Some kind of fruit, she guessed. The skin was almost the color of a green apple, though slightly bumpier.

"Yava. It is sweet."

Well, that wasn't terribly helpful. "Do I peel it, or?"

"Simply take a bite. But watch for seeds."

She took a careful bite, her teeth going through the skin and encountering the pale flesh of the fruit, which had a creamy texture. It was delicious, and the large black seeds were easy enough to pick out.

"Very tasty," she said after a few more bites, when she realized Bran was still watching her, brow furrowed.

He gave a single nod. "Good. Save the seeds."

The ache of hunger in her belly eased as she ate the fruit and sipped clear, cool water from the flask. When she finished, there was a neat pile of seeds beside her on the log, and she felt a bit more herself.

"Let me help." She rose and joined Bran, who was gathering armfuls of dried bracken fern. "Will this be for our pallets?"

"Yours."

She shot him a look. "There seems to be enough material for two beds."

"It is not necessary. I'll be keeping watch."

She glanced at him. Despite the unfamiliar planes of his face, she could see the lines of weariness bracketing his mouth.

"You need to sleep, too," she said. "I can take first watch. Besides, I'm not very tired."

It was a blatant lie, but she summoned up a cheerful expression and smiled at him when he met her gaze.

"I could not let you—" he began.

"It won't be for long," she said briskly. "Just take a little rest. And if one of those Void creatures scuttles over the hill, I'll scream. I wager you'll be on your feet in an instant, ready for battle."

His hand brushed over the sword strapped at his back and he nodded. A small thrill of victory went through her, that she could win an argument against her stern protector. He was stubborn, no doubt, but not completely immune to reason.

Together, they finished piling up the bracken, and then Bran laid a thin sleeping roll atop it, made of two silky pieces of cloth sewn together.

"You have your blade?" he asked, giving her an intent look.

"Yes." She pushed her cloak aside so he could see the kitchen knife tucked into her belt. "Don't worry. I'll be fine."

Lips firm, he stared at her a moment longer. His eyes were flecked with violet sparks, and for a brief instant she felt as though she was falling into their mystical depths...

Then he blinked and looked away.

"See the edge of the hill?" He pointed to the silver-grassed slope. "When the palemoon begins to rise, wake me."

"I will. Now go lie down."

He took a deep breath, his leather-armored chest rising and falling. Mara realized she was staring at the breadth of him, noticing the clearly defined muscles beneath the pale skin of his arms, and she quickly averted her gaze.

When she looked back, he was sitting at the edge of the makeshift pallet. He unbuckled his sword and laid it on the ground within arm's reach, then pulled his cloak around him and stretched out on top of the bedroll. Still wearing his boots, of course—ready to leap up at a moment's notice.

With a shake of her head, Mara returned to her perch on the log. By the time she was settled, Bran seemed to be fast asleep.

She occupied herself for some time looking up at the strange stars and trying to find shapes in their patterns. There was no Plough, no Huntsman, but she thought one clump looked a bit like a rosebush, and another resembled a ship.

When she started to yawn, she turned to the pile of seeds, lining them up by the faint glow of starlight and trying to echo the shapes overhead.

Finally, even that failed to keep her attention. With a sigh, she tucked the seeds into her pocket and stood. What did guards do to keep awake, anyway? She thought back to her time at Castle Raine, which felt like a thousand years ago.

The men there had played dice, and told ribald stories. They'd tended the bonfire in the courtyard and the one near the gates. They'd walked back and forth—now *that* she could do.

Hoping her movements wouldn't wake the sleeping Dark Elf, she began to pace about their camp, every now and then glancing at the hillside. No sign yet of any moon.

Bran's horse had laid down in a small hollow filled with grasses, and seemed to be slumbering as deeply as his master, with only a faint snuffle of exhalation. The trees about them rustled softly in the night breeze, which was warm and held the faint scent of flowers. Truly, Elfhame wasn't so bad—except for the lack of sun.

"Stay awake," she muttered to herself as her footsteps slowed.

It was the least she could do. Besides, it was in her best interest to make sure her guardian wasn't dropping from exhaustion, himself.

When she realized she'd halted again, she took hold of the skin of her arm and pinched, hard.

Then a stick broke farther back in the grove, and she came wide awake. Breathing shallowly, she pulled out her kitchen blade and turned. Was something there? Heart beating rapidly in her chest, she peered into the darkness, making out only the dim trunks of the trees. Why was there no *light* in this dratted land?

For a long moment, she stood very still. Nothing moved. No glow of red eyes shone from the shadows, no chittering rush of an attacking spider-creature reached her ears.

Maybe...maybe it had been nothing.

Swallowing, she leaned back—and bumped into someone standing directly behind her.

She let out a panicked yelp and pivoted, knife held shakily before her.

"Hush," Bran said softly, seemingly unconcerned that she might've stabbed him.

Of course, he probably would have just batted her blade away with one hand. She exhaled as he gently drew her back behind him, careful to avoid the naked sword in his hand.

"Is something there?" she whispered, following his gaze into the trees.

He made no reply, but shifted forward on the balls of his feet.

Something flashed silver in the shadows, and then a sudden flurry of glowing balls appeared, shedding their golden light. By their soft radiance, Mara thought she could make out a shape between the trees: a pale, majestic stag crowned with antlers.

Bran exhaled and lowered his sword, and the creature turned, looking directly at them.

Then it gathered itself and made a powerful leap, up and away. The shining little creatures whirled like windblown sparks from a fire, a half-dozen golden specks gone as quickly as they'd come. When Mara looked back at the grove, the stag was gone.

"What..." She wet her lips and tried again. "What was that?"

Bran glanced down at her. "The White Hart. Have you no tales of it, in your mortal world?"

"We do...I think." She pursed her lips. "My grandmother told me an old legend about a prince who followed it into the forest in order to grant a wish. Do you think it's the same one?"

"Likely so. It is a creature possessing great magic."

"But what does it mean?"

"I know not." He sheathed his blade, glanced once more into the shadows beneath the trees, then led them back to the center of their camp.

"Surely it's some kind of omen?" she persisted. "Maybe good luck?"

He lifted one shoulder in a shrug, and she folded her arms, irritated by his lack of answers.

"Maybe someone in the Hawthorne Court knows," she said tartly. "Someone with a bit higher breeding, that is."

The corner of his stern mouth twitched, but whether with amusement or annoyance she couldn't say.

"Your turn to rest." He gestured at the makeshift bed.

"I'm fine, honestly." The encounter with the White Hart had cleared her mind of its exhausted fog. "You go back to sleep."

"Look." He nodded to the hill behind their camp. "The palemoon is about to rise. Your watch is over."

She turned and squinted. The sky looked just as dark as ever.

"I'll keep you company until it comes up," she said.

"Hm."

"Truly, I will." She swallowed back the yawn that threatened. The stubborn part of herself wanted to prove that she could keep her word—that she would help guard the camp until the little moon rose in the sky.

"If you insist." He strode over to the log and sat, then patted the moss beside him.

She joined him, making herself sit stiffly upright. *I will stay awake*, she promised herself.

"Tell me more about the court," she said. "Will we reach it tomorrow?"

"After another day of riding, yes. Which is why you should rest."

"I'm truly—" This time she couldn't hold back her yawn.

Bran exhaled, a short puff of amusement, then reached over and scooped her against his side. The warm smell of woody spice tickled her nose and she looked up at him in surprise.

"To keep you from tumbling off the log," he said, "since you so stubbornly insist on keeping me company. Now look—there's the palemoon."

She glanced over at the hillside, finally able to make out a very faint glow in the indigo-purple sky. As she watched, it grew stronger, sending a sheen of light into the sky before it, like courtiers clearing the way for the king.

Finally, the pale, curved edge peeked over the horizon, round as an egg. She let out a sigh, and Bran settled her more comfortably against him.

She wanted to protest, to move away, but she was so comfortable...

Her eyes closed. She opened them, watching as the moon crested the horizon, pulling free like a reverse drop of water floating up into the sky. They closed again.

She was sleepily aware of Bran gathering her up, carrying her to the bed and tucking her between the silken layers of the bedding. He brushed her hair from her forehead and murmured something in elvish.

Then a soft touch, like moth wings against her cheek—his fingertips, his lips, she didn't know, but it felt comforting. Safe.

Cradled in the bracken ferns, she slipped down into dreams of a stern-faced, violet-eyed warrior.

CHAPTER 13

Bran watched Mara sleep—his peculiar, stubborn wife-to-be. Despite her odd eyes and her mud-brown hair, he couldn't help admire her strength.

She'd promised to do whatever was necessary to help his people, in return for passage back to her own world. Still, he was reluctant to tell her exactly what that entailed.

Especially as she'd made it clear she found the Dark Elves unpleasant to look upon. Informing her that she must marry him would shatter the tentative trust forming between them.

No. Better to let their bond, slight as it might be, grow as strong as possible until the moment he must reveal the terms of the prophecy.

The White Hart had been an auspicious omen. He glanced at the grove of lindens surrounding them and let his magic spread out. There was no sense of the magical creature, and no threat, either. Which was to be expected. They were far enough from the rifts that it was nigh impossible they'd encounter a Voidspawn.

That was the only reason he'd let Mara take first watch. And he had to admit he felt the better for catching a bit of rest. His wellspring was recovering. As for the tiredness of his body, he could carry on for some time. Once the Void was defeated, then he could sleep for a half-dozen palemoons if he so wished.

With Mara by his side…

He banished the thought. She would *not* be by his side, and truly he had no wish for it. The terms of their bargain were sound. And on the morrow, if all went well, the first step would be completed.

Their betrothal.

~

He let Mara rest until the palemoon had nearly set behind the grove, then gently shook her awake.

"Oh." She sat up, pushing her sleep-tangled hair off her face. "It's so strange to wake up and have it still be night."

"Are you ready to eat?" He refrained from reminding her that Elfhame did not have night and day as she knew it, and instead handed her the water flask and a dried honeycake.

"Yes, thank you." She scooted out of the bedroll and sat cross-legged on the bracken ferns, making short work of her meal.

"Here." He handed her another cake.

She looked at it a moment, then up at him. "What about your breakfast? Or lunch, or whatever meal it is."

"I've already eaten." It was the truth—although it had been some time since the hurried rations he'd downed at the battlefront.

"Hmph." She took the cake, then broke it in half. "You say that, but you still look hungry. Take this."

She held a piece out to him. Frowning, he hesitated.

"Don't be foolish." She shoved the honeycake toward him. "Besides, you said we'd get to the Hawthorne Court today. There should be plenty to eat there, I'd imagine."

It was true. He took the food from her and inclined his head in thanks.

She finished her cake, brushed the crumbs from her hands, then turned and rolled up the blankets. While she'd slept he'd tidied the rest of their little camp and saddled Fuin, ensuring that they'd be able depart the moment she was ready.

"Let me just..." she nodded to the grove.

"Of course."

While she tended to her needs, he tucked the bedroll away. The moment she emerged from the trees, he beckoned her to his horse. "Ready?"

She nodded. "I'm a bit stiff, but I suppose it can't be helped. Let's go."

He lifted her to the saddle, sprang up behind her, and between one breath and the next they were over the hill and away. Bound for Hawthorne, and the fulfillment of his destiny.

The brightmoon rose, chasing after her little sister, and Mara glanced about, clearly happy for the illumination of the larger moon. She asked about the flowers—the glowing *quille* and others that he could not name, and about the stars, and coaxed him into conjuring a ball of foxfire to dance before them.

As they rode, they spoke. Well, mostly *she* spoke, like a bird chirping away in the branches. She told him of her life and her family, a wistful note in her voice.

"You'll return to them soon," he said.

"Yes." He could hear the smile in her voice. "But tell me about your family."

He stiffened. "There's little to say. My parents are distant."

There was no need to elaborate. She would encounter the Hawthorne Lord and Lady soon enough, and see for herself.

"Don't you have anyone?" She twisted, sending him a sympathetic look. "A favorite uncle, perhaps? Or any siblings?"

"My sister." He felt his expression ease. "I am fond of her."

"Well, good." Mara faced forward again. "I was beginning to worry you were all alone in the world."

He couldn't help his quick snort of amusement. The Hawthorne Prince was never alone.

They stopped for lunch beside a stream cutting through rolling hills, and, at her insistence, split the last honeycake. Afterward, she dozed in his arms as they rode through meadows and in and out of scattered groves.

Bran found himself strangely content, as though there world had stopped and there was nothing but him and Mara riding through the silver-lit landscape. Their breaths matched, and their heartbeats, and he let himself be at peace for that small amount of time when they were neither at one place nor the next.

The brightmoon had reached its zenith and begun to roll back down the star-spattered sky when his human finally stirred and sat upright.

She rubbed the sleep from her eyes. "Still riding, I see."

"Mm." He leaned forward, urging Fuin up the long, gentle rise of hill stretching before them.

The grasses waved gently, one side purple, the other silver, and he felt his heartbeat beginning to speed.

Mara glanced about. "How long was I asleep? Oh, never mind, it doesn't matter. Are we getting close to the Hawthorne Palace?" There was a plaintive note in her voice, and she shifted, clearly uncomfortable after the long hours of riding.

He nudged Fuin into a trot, then a canter, making sure to hold Mara securely against him.

At the top of the rise, they halted.

"There it is," he said. "The Hawthorne Court."

"Oh." The woman in his arms let out a low breath at the sight of the palace spread out below.

He tried to view it through her eyes—the spiraling towers and vine-covered arches leading up to the central dome, the entire court surrounded by a profusion of white blossoms sending their dusty scent into the air. Balls of foxfire illuminated the open corridors and floated in and out of doorways, while glimglows danced in the courtyards over beds of purple moonflowers.

"It's beautiful," Mara said in a low voice.

He was pleased that she would find it so, since his kind seemed so frightful to her.

"What are those shining things flying over the flowers?" she asked.

"Glimglows. They possess all the intelligence of a butterfly. Do you not have them in the mortal world?"

"We have butterflies. But the first time I ever saw one of those glowing things was when they led me to the doorway. They're smarter than you think."

"Perhaps." He had no intention of arguing with her. Fate used whatever tools were at hand—himself included.

She looked down and plucked at her travel-stained dress. "Will I be allowed to freshen up before I have to meet anyone of importance? I'd hate to come before a prince or something, looking like this."

"A prince would not mind."

"That's all very well for *you* to say, but I suspect your nobility takes themselves seriously here, just as they do in the human world."

"There is a certain formality expected at court," he admitted.

He'd not really considered her appearance, beyond the blessed fact that his mortal woman had arrived at last, and was not hideous to look upon. Now he glanced from her tangled mud-colored hair to the torn and dirty skirts of her gown, and allowed that perhaps she was right.

"We'll go in the back way," he said, "and try to remain unobserved. Once we arrive, my sister will know what to do."

"I hope so," she said in a soft voice, her gaze fixed on the glowing court below. "I truly hope so."

CHAPTER 14

Mara could not take her eyes from the fanciful towers and high, glowing dome of the Hawthorne Court. The sense of dread that had shadowed her adventures had been receding ever since she and Bran had seen the White Hart, and now her terror was firmly buried beneath a renewed sense of wonder.

Certainly she was beyond nervous about meeting the Dark Elves of the Hawthorne Palace, but she would have Bran to defend her if any trouble arose. She was strangely sure of his support. He'd rescued her from the Void creature, after all, and during their travels she felt as though they were beginning to understand each other—at least a small amount.

Besides, there were worse things than having a Dark Elf warrior mage as her champion.

She was aware of the heat of his body at her back, the shifting of his muscles as he guided his horse down the rise.

They skirted the tall, columned gates that she guessed marked the main entrance to the palace. Bran kept them in the shadow of the encircling wall. Hawthorn hedges bloomed there, the flowers white smudges in the dim light.

She was sorry the large moon was setting. It seemed to be the closest thing to daylight she would ever see in this land.

As if sensing her need for light, two of the bright motes Bran had called glimglows darted over the hedge of greenery. Her spirits lifted as they danced in the air above her head.

“They had better not reveal our position,” Bran said in a low voice.

“I think we’re safe. Surely they flit about all over the grounds.”

He made a noise in the back of his throat, but did not argue with her, or blast the sparks out of the air with his powers.

They came to a break in the hedge, and Bran guided them through. The glimglows followed, dipping and bobbing in the air. Ahead of them spread a velvety lawn edged with luminous blue flowers. On their right a wall of pale stone extended, broken by a few arched windows. As they passed beneath one, Mara heard a soft whinny and caught the scent of hay and manure. The stables.

When Bran rode into the building, a smaller Dark Elf hurried up to take his horse.

“Welcome home, milord,” she said. “How goes the battle?”

“Well enough,” Bran said shortly. Gathering Mara against him, he slid down and landed lightly on the straw-covered floor.

The stable girl stared at Mara, her dark eyes widening.

“Is that...the mortal woman?” she asked. “What a strange-looking creature! Where are her claws? What about—”

“I trust you to remain quiet on this matter,” Bran said, his tone hard. “Discretion is essential. Now, see to Fuin, and speak no more of what you have seen.”

The girl gulped back the questions Mara could see filling her eyes, and ducked her head in obedience. She clucked to the horse and led him deeper into the stables, sending one quick backward glance over her shoulder at Mara as she went.

Bran shook his head, his features set in a frown.

“Hurry,” he said, taking her arm and leading her back into the star-spangled night. “Word will spread quickly of your presence.”

“I thought she wouldn’t say anything.”

“She’ll hold her tongue, but not for long. It is in the nature of stable hands to gossip. And she will probably not be the only one to see you.”

He ushered her toward one of the graceful towers. Vines grew about its arched doorway, bearing starry blossoms that scented the air with exotic perfume. Mara drew in a deep breath as they passed under, trying to fix the smell in her mind. It would be a memory of her time in Elfhame, once she returned home.

"My sister's rooms are not far," Bran said, quickening his steps and bypassing the staircase spiraling up the inside of the tower.

Mara had to nearly run to keep pace. The corridor was dark, and she stumbled over a slight irregularity in the floor. Only Bran's grip on her arm kept her from falling.

With an impatient flick of his fingers, he conjured a ball of pale blue light to keep them company. The glimglows had abandoned them at the stable, and Mara was sorry for it.

The light revealed carved doors made of golden wood set on either side of the hallway, and a subtle mosaic of stars and flowers on the tiled floor.

"Here." Bran halted before a door that looked like all the others and tapped softly. "Anneth? Are you within?"

Further down the corridor another door opened, and Mara heard a gasp of surprise.

Frown deepening, Bran turned the crystalline knob and pushed open the door of his sister's room. His hand firm at Mara's back, he urged her inside and closed the door behind them.

"Anneth?" he called again, gesturing for the ball of light to rise into the room.

The blue glow illuminated a richly appointed sitting room, with two open archways leading off on either side. Bran snapped his fingers and warmer light sprang from filigreed lanterns hanging from the ceiling.

Eyes wide, Mara surveyed the room. Richly woven rugs covered the floor, and beside the silk-draped couch a carved shelf held delicate glass orbs in varying sizes and hues. The rooms were very rich. Too rich.

Suspicion curling in her stomach, she turned to him. "Is your sister married?"

"No," he answered.

The opulence of the room could not be denied, and it spoke clearly to his family's station within the court. He was not a mere soldier. Not that she'd ever really thought so. And the stable hand had called him *milord.*

"Then you are of noble blood," she said flatly.

He was silent a moment—one of those pauses she was becoming accustomed to.

"I never implied otherwise," he said, though he would not meet her eyes.

"You are impossible! Prying information out of you is like pulling thorns out of woolen cloth."

He looked back at her. "Then you may add it to my list of faults, along with being hideous and terrifying."

She stared at him, torn between irritation and amusement. Their gazes met, and once again she felt that strange, giddy sensation in her belly.

"Bran!" The door flew open.

He took a step away from Mara—somehow he had come near enough she could feel his breath against her hair—and turned to greet the black-haired young woman who stepped into the room.

"Anneth—close the door."

"Oh, my. Of course." She complied, then leaned her back against the door, her gaze going to Mara. "You found her! Oh, Bran, this is marvelous. We must let the court know as soon as possible."

"Wait." Bran lifted one claw-tipped hand. "Not before she is presentable. That is why we are here." He glanced at Mara. "Mara, meet my sister, Anneth. I leave you in her capable hands."

"Wait." Mara frowned as he turned to go. "You're just leaving me alone?"

Her throat tightened with anxiety. He was the one known thing in this entire strange world. Without him by her side, she felt lost.

"You will not be alone, for Annett is here. I will return for you in a half-turn."

"She can speak our language? Perfect." Anneth grinned at her—a slightly frightening baring of her teeth. "But Bran, I can't make her presentable in less than a turn's time. Come back then. Besides, you have plenty of other arrangements to tend to."

He nodded, then reached and laid a gentle hand, claws withdrawn, on Mara's shoulder. "Do not fear. You are safe with my sister."

She had no choice but to believe him. And she still had her kitchen knife, if it came to that.

He turned to Annett. "Do your best."

Mara's temper flared at the implied insult, and she felt her cheeks heat. Did he truly find her so ugly? The thought bothered her more than it should.

"Might I remind you that you're not so pleasant to look upon, yourself," she said tartly. Though she had to admit she was growing accustomed to his strange features.

Anneth laughed. "There's a blow to your vanity, brother."

"I am not vain," he said stiffly, which led Mara to believe he was considered quite handsome among the Dark Elves, hard as that might be to fathom.

She crossed her arms, uncertainty sweeping over her in the wake of her outburst. She was an outsider here, and felt it far more keenly inside the palace walls than when it had just been the two of them riding beneath the star-dappled sky.

The thought of her coming presentation to the Hawthorne Court made her stomach clench. Once again, she longed desperately to go home. Her life in Little Hazel might be boring, but at least there she trod upon sure ground. Elfhame was fraught with danger, and she was finished with this adventure.

Unfortunately, it was not yet finished with her. No t until she held up her end of the bargain and helped the Dark Elves would she be able to go home.

"One thing," Bran said, turning to her. "Do you go by any other name than Mara?"

"My full name is Mara Geary. Why?"

"The formal court presentation," he said. "Mara Geary will do."

She had a suspicion that Dark Elves had long, elaborate names, despite what Bran chose to call himself. It was another knot in her belly, another place she was judged and found wanting.

"Go." Anneth pushed her brother to the door.

"Set the lock behind me," he said.

"Of course. Now, shoo. We have work to do."

He slipped out. Anneth shut the door, then turned to Mara.

"Well," she said, her berry-colored eyes glowing, "this is going to be fun."

Mara studied the Dark Elf's expression, trying to read the intent in her eyes. She couldn't tell if Bran's sister was mocking her, or was actually pleased at the idea of helping her. Though Bran *had* said Anneth was interested in learning about mortals. Perhaps her interest was genuine.

And if not, there was nothing Mara could do about it, except hope she would not make herself an utter fool in front of the entire Hawthorne Court.

CHAPTER 15

"First, I think, a bath." Bran's sister looked Mara up and down. "That is, if you agree."

"A bath would be nice," Mara said, adding hastily, "I'm usually much cleaner than this."

She didn't want Anneth to assume that mortals were some kind of inferior creatures, happy to wallow about in their own dirt. In truth, Mara wanted nothing more than to wash off the sweat and grime left by running for her life, falling down a hillside, and battling a frightful spider creature. Not to mention being scarred by vicious ichor, using raw magic, sleeping in a bed of ferns, and being hauled about the countryside on horseback.

No doubt her hair was in an equally dreadful state.

"I'll help you draw and heat the water," she added.

There didn't seem to be many servants in the Hawthorne Palace, unlike her experience of Castle Raine, which held more maids than nobles.

"That won't be necessary," Anneth said. "Come this way."

She stepped through the arched opening to the right of the sitting room, and Mara followed.

The filigreed lanterns hanging from the ceiling winked on as they entered, shedding a dim golden glow over the room. Anneth raised her hand, and the light increased until the room was bright even by human standards. Mara's eyes widened at the sight of the round stone tub filled with water in the center of what was clearly an elaborate bathing room. One corner of the room had a drain set into the tiled floor.

A nearby shelf held colorful bottles and small metal containers filled with aromatic powders. The long counter along one wall boasted a sink shaped like a flower, and held a pile of fluffy rose-colored towels. The far end of the room was a screened-off area that Mara guessed must be the privy.

"I'll prepare the water for you," Anneth said. "Would you like me to stay and assist you in bathing? I'm unsure of your mortal customs."

"I don't need any help," Mara replied.

Although Anneth seemed kind, Mara would feel far too vulnerable standing naked before any Dark Elf, with their sharp claws and fierce eyes.

Bran's sister nodded. "The scrolls I've read tell of human women being aided in many aspects of their lives. Bathing, dressing, and the like. So I wasn't certain what you expected."

"That's for noblewomen," Mara said, feeling self-conscious. "I'm simply a commoner."

Anneth shook her head. "Here in Elfhame, you are ranked above the nobility. You are the woman of the prophecy, after all! Don't be shy about who you are. Now, let me tend to the bath."

She stepped to the tub and waved her hand over the water. A faint glow hung in the air, then drifted down, infusing the bath with subtle light.

"What's that?" Mara asked.

"I'm heating it for you. But before you get in, you must rinse yourself off."

Anneth flicked her fingers in a sharp gesture, and water began cascading out of the wall in the corner. The room was in no danger of flooding, however, as the stream curled easily down the drain. Seeming not to notice Mara's awed silence, Anneth went to the shelf and pulled out a bottle filled with creamy liquid, and one of the metal tins containing a pinkish powder.

“This one is for your hair,” she said, holding out the bottle. “And the other, your skin. I’ll just set them by the waterfall. Towels are on the counter. Come out when you’re ready. I’ll start laying out gowns.”

Before Mara could thank her, Anneth left the room in a flurry of skirts and optimism. Well. She certainly was a contrast to her silent, dour brother.

Quickly, Mara removed the long green cloak, laid her knife upon it, then stripped out of her once-favorite gown. She sadly regarded the tattered skirts and ruined sleeves. There would be no salvaging it, and she hoped Anneth could find her something suitable for her to wear. In general, the Dark Elves she’d seen had all been very tall, even Bran’s sister. Mara could just see herself tripping over her skirts as she was presented to the nobility of the Hawthorne Court.

But first, her bath awaited. She stepped into the waterfall, delighted to find it was warm. The water cascading over her head felt heavenly, and the soaps smelled like roses and starflowers. Though she could have spent hours under the waterfall, she made herself step out once she was clean. As if aware she was finished, the flow of water coming from the wall shut off.

She eyed the tub a bit doubtfully. But Anneth had gone to the trouble of heating it for her, and there was no reason not to trust her good intentions.

Mara sat on the wide rim and dipped her toes in. That was all she needed, and a moment later she was submerged to her neck in warm, silky water. She lay back and let out a contented sigh. The Dark Elf bathing customs were strange, but she could easily get used to such luxuries as waterfalls on demand and self-heating tubs.

She was just drying off with one of the absurdly fluffy towels when Anneth called out, “Are you almost finished?”

“Yes. I’m coming.”

Mara wrapped a towel around her body, then draped another over her shoulders to absorb the water dripping from her hair. She felt awkward going before Anneth barely dressed, but she couldn’t bear the thought of putting her soiled and ragged gown back on.

With a deep breath, she walked into the sitting room. Anneth wasn’t there, but in the room beyond, and waved at her to enter.

"Come see what I've selected." The glee in her voice was unmistakable.

Mara stepped into Anneth's bedroom. She was dimly aware of a desk, tall shelves along the wall, and a pair of windows looking out to the dark gardens, but her attention was focused on the glimmering fabrics spread across the wide bed. Peacock-blue silk and silver gauze like moonlight, scarlet velvet deeper than rose petals, satin studded with dewdrops. Tiny gemstones winked from the hems and edges, and the scent of sandalwood hung in the air, as though the garments breathed out opulence.

"I can't wear these," she said, reluctantly joining Anneth beside the bed. "They're far too grand."

Anneth made a tsking noise that was endearingly human. "Of course you can. All eyes will be on you when you're presented to the Lord and Lady. We must give the court something impressive to look upon."

Mara privately doubted she could ever be made to look impressive, but there was no point in arguing with Anneth. And she had to wear something, after all. Appearing before the court draped in a towel would make an impression, but certainly not a favorable one.

"You don't want to let Bran down, do you?" his sister asked. "Now, which one do you like the best?"

Mara stared at the rich fabrics. Most of them were cut in such a way she couldn't quite fathom how they would be worn. There were no sleeves, to speak of, no obvious bodices and barely any clearly-defined skirts. Just yards of beautiful, drapey cloth.

"The silver one is very pretty," she said at last.

"It is. I thought we'd save that one for later." Anneth gave her a conspiratorial smile. "For tonight, though..."

She tilted her head, studying Mara with her dark eyes. It was difficult not to feel inadequate, but Mara lifted her chin. No matter which gown she wore, she would find a way to attach the kitchen knife. It might be silly, the blade next to useless, but now that she'd lost her cloak and ruined her dress, it was the one token she had from home. She refused to leave it behind.

"How about this purple one?" Mara reached out and slid her fingers over a velvet-soft skirt the color of ripe plums. It seemed a little less complicated than some of the others.

"Let's try it on—and get you out of that towel. What was I thinking?" Anneth turned and hurried through yet another arched door, though this was smaller than the rest.

She returned with something that resembled a chemise, made of silky, cream-colored material.

"Put this on. I won't look." She handed the garment to Mara, then shut her eyes.

Hastily, Mara shed her towels and pulled the silky cloth over her, grateful to find it had armholes and a place for her head to come out.

"Done," she said, plucking at the length of fabric.

It seemed oddly twisted around her body, and she snuck a quick glance at Anneth. Dark Elf women did not seem to be made that much differently than humans. Other than her height, and claws, and strange eyes, Anneth's shape much resembled her own.

"Let me wrap you." Anneth took up the trailing piece of fabric and deftly draped it twice about Mara's torso, tucking here and folding there.

When she was done, the garment fit much better, and felt surprisingly comfortable. Mara shot the elaborate plum-colored gown a look.

"I don't suppose I can just wear this?" she asked, indicating the underdress.

Anneth let out a peal of laughter. "Ooh, I'm tempted. But no. You would create quite a sensation, but I don't think Bran would appreciate the joke."

"I don't think he finds many things humorous," Mara said. It felt generous to say even that much, but she could hardly tell Anneth that her brother was the most grim and taciturn individual she'd ever met.

"Once you get to know him better, you'll see his dry wit," Anneth said. "He carries the weight of Elfhame on his shoulders, and it has taken a toll."

"I'm sorry. I didn't meant to imply—"

"Oh, Bran can be a sour stone, we all know that. I only hope..." She gave Mara a look she could not interpret.

Discomfited, Mara turned back to the purple gown spread across the bed. "Shall I try this one on?"

"Yes." Anneth shook her head, as if dispelling some melancholy thought. "I have just the gems to go with it, too. And we'll have to spend some time considering what to do with your hair."

Mara tugged a strand in front of her face and studied it. "Does everyone here have black or silver hair?"

"Yours is a most unusual color," Anneth confirmed. "But I think the key is to play up the difference. Now, lift your arms. Bran will be back soon, and we want him to be stunned by your transformation."

Mara did not think he was the type to be easily stunned. But for the next little while, she would allow Anneth to do whatever she thought necessary to turn her poor mortal self into something worthy of the exacting standards of the Hawthorne Court. If such a thing were even possible.

CHAPTER 16

Bran hesitated before Anneth's door. He had alerted his parents that the woman of the prophecy had arrived, and now the entire court was waiting impatiently for him to produce the mortal.

What would they think of the bedraggled, mud-haired creature he'd rescued? For a moment he imagined the looks of shock and pity on their faces, and his stomach twisted. He'd spent his life making himself into someone that would never be pitied or looked down upon. Except by his mother, but there was no salvaging that relationship, ever.

Wedding Mara was his fate, and he would accept it gracefully. He'd do anything to save Elfhame, and there were worse sacrifices than a blow to his pride.

Bran squared his shoulders. No matter Mara's appearance, he resolved to be stoic in his reactions. It would shame them both if he were seen to be a reluctant bridegroom.

"Anneth?" He rapped on the door. "It's me."

"One moment," she called.

He could hear whispering and the rustle of cloth. Then the lock chimed and the door swung open.

Despite his resolution to remain unmoved, Bran froze, struck dumb at the sight of the mortal woman standing before him.

She was gowned in a purple dress that emphasized her mortal curves. A half cape flowed from her shoulders, and amethysts sparkled at her neck and wrists. Her hair was woven with strands of glowing gold, transforming it from mud-colored to the dark amber of winter honey. Her round-irised human eyes were accentuated with purple gems affixed at the corners. Instead of drawing attention to her strangeness, they made her look exotic and mysterious.

"Don't just stand there like a lump," Anneth exclaimed. She caught his arm and pulled him into the room.

He could not stop staring at Mara. His woman of the prophecy. His soon-to-be mate. For the first time, the prospect did not seem so terrible.

She gave him a shy smile, and something strange happened to his heart: a sudden squeeze, and then surge of blood, similar to the battle rush he felt upon the field, yet different. His gaze went to the ornate gold belt at her waist, and he let out a surprised laugh to see her homely human knife hanging there.

"By the bright moon, he laughed!" Anneth said. "Call the historians, quickly, so they might set it in the record scrolls."

"Mara." He found his voice again. "You look lovely."

She smiled again, color rushing into her cheeks. He did not find it unbecoming.

"You see." Anneth sounded very self-satisfied. "I told you he'd be stunned."

"I am not," he said. "Merely admiring your handiwork. Well done, sister."

Anneth raised a brow at him. "Afraid she's going to outshine you now, aren't you?"

He did not bother to reply, only held his arm out to Mara. "The court awaits. Are you ready?"

"I suppose." She pulled in a deep breath. "Is it all right if I wear my knife?"

"It is a blade that's seen honor in battle. Wear it with pride."

It was also a reminder that she was not entirely helpless. He'd already spread the story about her wounding the spiderkin, and the knife added to the mystique that Anneth had woven around her.

He had to admit his sister had worked wonders. And though he would never admit it to her, "stunned" was the perfect description of how he'd felt when he looked upon Mara's transformation. Wedding her would be an honor, despite all their differences.

It was not just the physical change that a formal court gown and well-dressed hair made. Her determination and bravery, her resilience, even the way she chattered on—all these facets were like a gemstone polished in a tumbler.

She had been Mara from the first, but now something had shifted inside him, and, somewhat to his consternation, he could truly see her shine.

Mara thought she saw a flash of approval in Bran's eyes when Anneth opened the door. His sister seemed to think he was impressed, and he *had* told Mara she looked lovely. She didn't think he was the type to give empty compliments. He'd also laughed at the knife tucked through her ornately woven belt, though it had been an approving sort of laugh.

Why was she so worried about what Bran thought of her? She should be far more concerned about the Hawthorne Lord and his lady. Anneth had not said much about them, her expression clouding when Mara asked, so she hadn't pressed the matter. She didn't want to alienate the only other person she knew at court by insisting on talking about what was a clearly a difficult subject.

As Bran led her down the corridor, thoughtfully providing a blue sphere of fire for illumination, Mara couldn't help but fret. Anneth had evaded her question about the rulers of the court. She could only assume that they were dreadful indeed.

"Do not be afraid," Bran said, as if sensing her thoughts. "No one will harm you, and if they try, they will have to deal with me."

It was a comforting thought, and she gave him a quick, grateful glance. She might be wearing her kitchen knife, but she noticed he had a bejeweled sword at his hip and a dagger hanging from his belt, as well as a second blade tucked into his boot. He'd changed his clothes, too, and now wore a midnight-black tunic with gold embroidery around the sleeves and neck. His hair hung in elaborate braids on either side of his severe face.

"You could go a little faster," Anneth said from behind them. "I'm sure the court is in a frenzy by now."

"Give Mara a few moments," Bran said. "This won't be easy for her."

"I've no doubt she'll carry herself well."

"I'm right here," Mara said dryly. "No need to speak as if I'm absent—or hang back on my account."

The sooner they arrived, the sooner she could dispel her looming apprehension. Surely the reality of the Hawthorne Court couldn't be worse than her fearful imaginings.

Their footsteps echoed over the mosaic floor. Mara wore her boots, though Anneth had flicked her fingers over them, and they'd not only gained a high polish, but turned the exact hue of the gown she wore.

"It's a temporary spell," Anneth had said. "A small glamour that will fade by tomorrow."

"That's a handy bit of magic. Are you as powerful as your brother?"

Anneth had let out a short laugh. "Not nearly. No one in all of Elfhame can match Bran—though don't tell him I said that. He's already too proud of himself as it is."

Bran did not seem overly prideful to Mara. Rigid and exacting, perhaps, but she'd wager he demanded more of himself than anyone around him.

"Nearly there," he said, laying his hand over hers where it rested on his arm.

"Ignore the gossips," Anneth said. "They're petty and spiteful. Pretend you don't hear a word they say."

Mara pressed her lips together. She hadn't grown up in a court, learning to harden herself against hurtful words—but she would do her best.

The hallway opened into a crescent-shaped foyer dominated by tall double doors made of some glowing silvery metal. They were decorated with a design featuring the blossoms and thorny spikes of hawthorn branches. Mara hoped the gossips of the Hawthorne Court would not be as sharp as their namesake thorns.

A Dark Elf dressed in a flowing robe stepped forward as they approached, and gestured at the doors. They swung open by themselves, and Mara swallowed back her impending panic. Bran pressed her hand, as if he understood her anxiety, but did not slow his steps.

Carried along by his momentum, she crossed the threshold of the Hawthorne Court.

"Prince Brannonilon Luthinor, heir to the Hawthorne Throne," the doorman announced. "Lady Anneth Ithilden Luthinor. And the mortal woman called Mara Geary."

Shock swept through Mara, clearing the fog of fear rising in her brain. *Prince* Brannonsomething? Heir to the throne?

"You're a prince?" she hissed at Bran. Curse him for being so close-mouthed! "What else haven't you told me?"

He gave her a look tinged with apology. "The court is watching."

To perdition with the Hawthorne Court, and its lying heir. Mara pulled her arm free of Bran's and held her head high. These Dark Elves were no better than humans, no matter how fearsome they looked, and she would not be cowed by them.

"Good girl," Anneth murmured from behind Mara. "Go straight forward, then stop a pace from the dais and curtsey. Ignore everyone to either side."

Fueled by her anger, Mara marched forward. She didn't care if Bran kept up with her. The crowd murmured as she passed, but she paid them no mind. Her attention was fixed on the two thrones set upon the dais, occupied by the Hawthorne Lord and Lady.

Bran's parents.

She could see the stern cast of Bran's features in his father's face. His mother assessed her coldly from eyes the same dark violet hue as her son's.

Mara gritted her teeth. She should have wondered *why* he had a prophecy surrounding him. Why he was given such deference at the camp, and why his magic was so strong. She'd been a fool, imagining him to be, at best, a member of the minor nobility.

No, she was keeping company with the Hawthorne Prince himself.

No wonder he'd been so possessive of his prize. The connection she'd felt building between them evaporated like mist under strong sunlight. Bran only wanted to use her to save his kingdom. She was nothing but a pawn on the board of Elfhame's future, and she resented it bitterly.

She halted in a swirl of purple skirts before the dais and made the rulers her most formal curtsey—the one she and her sisters had practiced in front of the mirror for hours, pretending they were going to visit the queen. Mara held the pose for a heartbeat to show her respect to the Hawthorne Lord and Lady. Their son might be full of deceit, but she was in their court now, and at their mercy.

She refused to be trapped in this wretched dark land for very much longer, though. Bran owed her answers. And there was still the mysterious ceremony to get through. Soon, however, she'd do what she must, escape Elfhame, and return home.

And never come back.

CHAPTER 17

Standing just behind Mara, Bran made a formal bow to his parents. Though he kept his gaze low, he was watching their reactions closely. His father seemed amused by Mara's fearless demeanor, and his mother taken aback. No doubt Tinnueth had expected a meek and cowering human, not this fierce girl with a bare blade at her belt.

By the seven bright stars, he was proud of his mortal woman for marching so boldly into the throne room. He supposed he should have told her he was the Hawthorne Heir—although the moment had never seemed right—but ultimately her anger at him had proved to be well timed.

A buzz of whispers rose as Bran's father welcomed Mara to Elfhame and extended the hospitality of the Hawthorne Court. Tinnueth looked like she'd bitten down on something sour, but she could hardly deny the prophecy any longer.

"A hideous creature," someone said, loudly enough for Bran to hear. The voice sounded suspiciously like Mireleth's.

Bran glanced down at the silver bracelet shackling his wrist. He'd seek her out immediately after court to dissolve their false betrothal.

The flush of color on Mara's cheeks was the only sign she'd heard the malicious words.

"Thank you," she said to his parents once the welcome speech ended. "I am honored."

This prompted another wave of murmuring when the Dark Elves realized Mara could speak their tongue, as well as understand what was said. A flash of satisfaction went through Bran, though he kept his expression impassive.

"We will hold a feast in your honor," Lord Calithilon said. "Until that time, we grant you the run of the palace. Prince Brannon will serve as your guide. So that we might all make ready for the festivities ahead, I now declare our court hours at an end."

He raised one finger, and the sound of the dismissal gong rang through the room.

Mara curtseyed again to the lord and lady, then took a step backward. Bran caught her elbow as she began to turn.

"Wait," he said. It was the height of rudeness to turn one's back on the rulers before they stood from their thrones.

He bowed to his parents, aware of the look of warning in his mother's eyes. Tinnueth would pounce upon any misstep Mara made, and they would both pay the price.

The Hawthorne Lord and Lady rose and regally paced to their private door behind the thrones. Sometimes they stepped off the dais to mingle with their court. Bran was relieved it was not one of those days.

The moment his parents were gone, he pulled Mara's arm through his, then turned them back toward the tall doors of the throne room. Beside him, he felt her take a quick breath. None of the assembled court had departed yet, and she and Bran were the center of attention. Everyone wanted a good look at the woman of the prophecy, after all.

Anneth came up to them and took her place on Mara's other side. Approval shone from her eyes. She would not praise Mara here, in front of the court, but Bran could tell she was pleased.

As was he. His future bride had a core of strength that would serve them both well in the coming days.

An awkward circle of space formed around them, with no one willing to step close enough to have to speak to Bran or Mara. Despite that, the pathway to the exit was blocked. It would be unpleasant to have to force their way forward.

Then his old master-at-arms, Garon, strode forward, his blackthorn cane knocking on the floor with every other step. He bowed stiffly, and Bran held out his hand.

"No need for such formality," he said.

"It's not you I'm honoring." Garon turned to face the mortal woman standing bravely beside Bran. "Lady Mara, it is a pleasure to meet you. I know I speak for everyone when I say I'm glad to see the prophecy fulfilled in such a satisfactory manner."

He sent a fierce look toward the bystanders, and most of them had the grace to nod and murmur their agreement. All except Mireleth, who glared at Bran, and a few other members of the nobility who clearly sided with her.

"Thank you, sir," Mara said.

"Not all of us are so easily satisfied." Mireleth stepped up beside Garon. Her claws were unsheathed, and malice glittered from her narrowed eyes.

Bran set his hand to his dagger, and called his magic to his fingertips. If Mireleth had the stupidity to physically attack Mara, he would not hesitate to defend her.

"Lady Mireleth," he warned, "consider your actions carefully."

"Is this so-called Mara Geary actually a mortal?" Ignoring him, Mireleth whirled to face the crowd. "How do we know this is truly the woman of the prophecy, and not some trick meant to deprive me of my intended? You all saw us pledged to one another! Now he arrives, dragging in some so-called human girl from who-knows-where?"

Her few supporters voiced their approval, and Bran could see questions arise in the eyes of some of the nobles. He clenched his jaw. Trust Mireleth to stir up trouble.

"Your accusations are ridiculous," he said. "And our betrothal nothing more than a sham, as you well know. Be careful whom you call a trickster."

Mireleth stared angrily at him a moment, then raised her voice. "Members of the court, consider this. How is it that this *mortal* newly come to Elfhame is fluent in our language? And would a real human be able to stand before the Hawthorne Lord and Lady without quivering in fear? I think not."

Garon tapped his cane on the floor. "Now see here—"

"Everyone knows Prince Brannon is the strongest magic user in the land," Mireleth continued. "He's quite capable of casting a glamour none could see through." She pointed at Mara. "How do we know this isn't simply some Dark Elf girl in disguise?"

Before Bran could speak in her defense, Mara set her hands on her hips and took a step forward.

"Truly?" she said. "If it's true that Bran was once betrothed to you, I don't blame him for changing his mind. I wouldn't want to marry you, either."

Her words caused a riffle of amusement among the courtiers.

Mireleth turned to her, teeth bared. "Can you prove that you are a mortal woman?"

"Who would willingly put herself through all this?" Mara waved at the assembled court. "Who would come here to be looked down upon by your lord and lady, insulted and sneered at, forced to submit to some prophecy she's never even heard of? I'd happily leave you all to your fate this very moment and return to my own world, if I could."

Her words rang with unmistakable truth, and Bran could see the effect they had on the crowd. No Dark Elf would ever speak so. And although he was dismayed at Mara's words, he was equally pleased to see Mireleth withdraw her claws and slink back into the crowd.

"Well said." Anneth linked her arm through Mara's. "Excuse us."

She strode forward, not waiting for the assembled nobles to clear a path. The courtiers between her and the door scrambled to get out of the way.

Bran considered following. He would like nothing better than to remove himself from the room. But first, he must officially end his betrothal to Mireleth. She had no claim on him, and her display of rudeness toward Mara could not be tolerated.

Mireleth had sequestered herself in a circle of her supporters. When they saw him approaching, however, they parted like water.

"Lady Andion," he said formally, paying no mind to the poisonous look she turned on him, "speaking of trickery, I remind you that you were well aware our so-called betrothal was nothing more than a ploy to activate the prophecy. I am pleased that it succeeded, and am here to officially break our bond."

Her nostrils flared, but she could not deny the truth.

"Then I repudiate our vows," she said bitterly. "By fire and storm, pale moon and bright, star and shadow, I want no part of you, Prince Brannonilon Luthinor."

She shook her arm, and her silver betrothal bracelet opened and fell to the floor with a clang.

Bran caught his as it slithered off his wrist, then held it awkwardly, for once at a loss. He would not offer Mireleth an empty apology.

"I wish you well with your horrid little creature," Mireleth said.

She tossed back her hair and stalked away, kicking her betrothal bracelet aside as she went. Her allies scurried after her.

"I'll take charge of the bracelets," Garon said, limping up to Bran. "Nasty business."

Bran didn't know if he meant Mireleth, the bracelets, or the entire sham betrothal. Likely all three. He held his discarded bracelet out.

"My thanks," he said.

"You'd best go see to Lady Mara," the old soldier said.

"Indeed." He clapped Garon on the shoulder, then strode out of the room.

What a tangle. He was only glad his mother hadn't been there to witness the entire thing—though no doubt Mireleth was already on her way to tell Tinnueth her own slanted version of events.

By the pale moon, at times like this he wished for the simplicity of battle.

Boot heels ringing over the patterned stone floor, he made for Anneth's rooms, and the mortal woman that was his destiny. It was time he told her truth—if she had not guessed it already.

CHAPTER 18

Mara's fury carried her all the way to Anneth's rooms before subsiding to a dull smolder.

"I made a mess of things," she said, perching on the silk-draped couch in the sitting room. "The court must hate me now for speaking so bluntly."

"Not in the least," Anneth said. "You were wonderful. I'd venture to say you even won the respect of the Hawthorne Lord, which is no mean feat."

"Your father." Mara crossed her arms. "I can't believe Bran didn't see fit to mention the fact that he was a prince."

Anneth let out a sigh. "Getting my brother to part with words is like prying gold coins from a dragon."

"You have dragons here?" Mara leaned forward, temporarily distracted by the thought.

"They are very rare, and possess cloaking magic that cannot be penetrated by Dark Elves. No one's seen them for nearly a century. But enough of that. I think we both could use some refreshment."

"That would be wonderful. It's been ages since I ate."

In fact, the knot of anxiety in her belly had been replaced by gnawing hunger. She recalled the meager breakfast she and Bran had shared before breaking camp and riding to the Hawthorne Court. It felt like eons ago.

Anneth closed her eyes and spoke a few words Mara didn't understand.

"There," she said after a moment. "I've ordered nectar and cakes from the kitchens. We must clear a space on the table. And afterwards, you may rest in my room."

"Thank you." Mara had been trying to hide her yawns, but Bran's sister had clearly noticed how tired she was.

She helped tidy the low table set in front of the couch, and as soon as it was clear, a tray materialized there. Mara blinked at it, understanding more clearly the lack of servants at the palace. Why employ people to transport such things as trays of refreshments when one could simply make them appear by magic?

Anneth sat in the chair next to the couch and kicked off her jeweled sandals.

"Fruit nectar and Amaranth cakes," she said, offering a goblet and plate to Mara. "I hope you like them."

Mara took a bite, and sighed. The cake tasted like sunlight on her tongue. The nectar was a perfect blend of tart and sweet.

When she'd finished the cake and drained half her goblet, she felt much better. She wiped her fingers on one of the linen napkins, then glanced at Anneth.

Ever since the scene in the throne room, where that nasty Dark Elf woman had stepped up and started throwing accusations about, a horrible suspicion had wormed through Mara. Although her mind shied away from the thought, she could not run from it any longer.

"Was Bran really planning to marry that dreadful woman?" she asked, hoping to discover her answer in a roundabout way. The stark, unvarnished truth was too awful to contemplate.

Anneth coughed and set down her goblet. "How much did my brother tell you about the prophecy?"

"Not much. He said my presence was essential to saving Elfhame, and that he'd known of the prophecy all his life."

"He didn't quote the exact words to you?" Anneth asked tightly.

"No." Foreboding prickled the back of Mara's neck and she feared she'd been right in her suspicions. "I take it he neglected to tell me something of extreme importance."

Please, no.

"One might say that." Anneth glanced down and busied herself with breaking one of the cakes into smaller pieces.

"So, what was all that about betrothals and marriages—and where do I fit in? He's not really going to marry that horrible woman, is he?"

At that moment, Bran opened the door and strode into the room. Clearly he'd heard Mara's question, for he fixed her with his violet-flecked gaze.

"No," he said clearly. "I am not going to marry Mireleth. The only woman I plan to wed is you."

She jumped up, overturning the tray. It was as terrible as she had feared.

Juice splattered on the floor, and cake crumbs scattered over the table and couch cushions. Bran's sister rose and hurried off to fetch a towel, but Mara simply stood there, staring at the Dark Elf prince.

"What did you just say?" Her voice came out a whisper.

"I am marrying you," Bran repeated. "As soon as the next bright-moon rises."

"No." She clutched her skirts in her fists, no doubt rumpling the fine fabric beyond repair, but she didn't care. "I'm not getting married to you."

Bran's gaze flicked away from her, then back. "I know you find my appearance distasteful, my manner overbearing, and my land full of shadows. Nonetheless, I'm afraid the prophecy is very clear. If Elfhame is to be saved, I must marry the mortal woman who opens the door between our worlds. That woman is you."

She shook her head so hard some of the golden lights tumbled from her hair. "I can't."

Marry Bran? It was unthinkable. When she'd promised to go through with the Dark Elf ceremony, she'd never imagined *this*.

Her adventurous dream had truly become a nightmare.

"I am sorry," he said in a low voice. "I'm to blame for not better preparing you for your fate."

"I feared you were going to kill me, but this is worse than I could've imagined."

She crossed her arms tightly in front of her, wishing she could wake up, wishing she had some place of refuge to flee to. Instead, she was trapped in the Hawthorne Palace, required to shackle herself to someone who wasn't even *human*.

"If you do not marry me," Bran said, his voice tight, "then we will all die. The Void will destroy us, Mara, and soon. Would you rather perish than make this sacrifice that will save not only yourself, but all of Elfhame?"

She almost said she preferred to die than be forced into such a union, but even through her bitter anger she could see how foolish that was.

"Please tell me that marriage is a passing thing in your world," she said, clinging to a shred of hope. "Something we can dissolve once the battle's won."

He slowly shook his head, his eyes filled with shadows. "I wish I could give you the answer you want. But in Elfhame, a wedding vow is a lifetime pledge. Is it not so with mortals?"

She almost lied—but he would not believe her, and Anneth surely knew the truth from her studies.

"Marriages are not often broken," Mara reluctantly admitted. "But surely there is recourse among the Dark Elves? What if the union is a miserable one?"

"Then the couple may choose to live apart. But the bond will not be broken."

Her throat constricted, and she could barely breathe. She would have to do it. She would have to marry the fearsome Dark Elf who stood before her.

She'd promised to aid his realm, and cursed herself for making that foolish vow without knowing what it entailed. The only consolation was that once she helped save his world, she would leave it—and him—forever.

Gathering all her strength, she made herself stand tall and meet his gaze. "By the terms of our bargain, if I marry you, you must promise me you'll do everything in your power to send me back home. Swear it."

He regarded her for a long moment, his dark eyes glowing with violet sparks. At last he gave her a slow nod.

"Mara Geary, I swear to you on the seven bright stars and the pale moon, on my own blood and breath, that after you marry me and we defeat the Void, I will find a way to return you to the mortal world. You have my oath."

She drew in a ragged breath. There was no mistaking the sincerity in his voice. And he *was* the strongest magic user among the Dark Elves. Surely he would be able to free her from Elfhame, and open the doorway back to her home.

But first, the final battle with the Void was looming—if his prophecy was to be believed.

The moment it was over, though, she would insist he honor his promise. Her time among the Dark Elves would be finished soon. Until then, she hoped she was strong enough to bear being his bride.

"Very well," she said, her throat dry. "On that condition, I will marry you."

He made her a low bow. "It will be my honor."

He almost sounded as though he meant it. Before she could respond, he turned and let himself out the door. It closed firmly behind him.

Anneth stepped into the room and tossed a towel over the spilled juice.

"He will do his best for you," she said. "I pray you give him as much in return."

"I will try." Mara had a promise to keep, too, much as she might dislike it. "Now, tell me everything about your Dark Elf weddings."

CHAPTER 19

The palemoon skimmed the horizon and cast soft shadows over the palace gardens. Bran walked the paths between the glowing flowers, paying no heed to the beauty of his surroundings.

It seemed Mara would never forgive him.

But despite everything, she would wed him. He was thankful for that, although the prospect was clearly odious to her. In return for her sacrifice, he must find a way to undo a hundred years of magic and open the door back into the mortal world.

There would be repercussions from that act he did not want to contemplate. But it was the price he had sworn to pay, and pay it he would. The pang he felt at the thought had nothing to do with Mara leaving forever. There was no point in her remaining in Elfhame to live out a life of misery married to a man she detested.

He let out a low breath. Not quite a sigh; princes didn't sigh.

They would wed soon, then return to the front and hope for a miracle.

Bran balled up one fist and tapped it against his leg. They needed more time! Time to teach Mara how to access her wellspring of power and harness it to her will. Time for her to learn more of Elfhame and his people. Time to rebuild the fragile understanding he had felt growing between them.

In a rare moment of indulgence, he found himself wishing for a different future. One where they walked companionably together through the gardens. One where Mara smiled at him again, her strange, lovely eyes sparkling with laughter.

Impossible. He shook his head to dispel such foolish thoughts.

He needed to focus on tactics and strategy. It was likely the Void would attack in force when it sensed Mara's presence at the barrier. Their best plan would be to pull all the patrols in, and concentrate on delivering a powerful blow directly through one of the breaches, striking at the heart of the Void with as much power as they could muster.

It was not enough for his people to simply continue defending their world. They must attack with the intent to wound as deeply as possible and drive the Void away from Elfhame, forever.

Bran. It was a whisper on the wind, carrying the glow of Hestil's magic. *Urgent. Contact now.*

He turned back toward the palace and lengthened his stride. As soon as he gained the privacy of his rooms, he assembled his scrying tools and summoned the magic to reach his second-in-command.

The surface of the water in the silver bowl shivered, then revealed Hestil's face.

"Bran—thank the moons." Her voice carried a raw edge. "The Void creatures have broken through and we can't hold any longer."

Fear coiled about his lungs, and he forced himself to breathe.

"Then you must retreat, as soon as possible. Try to limit the casualties, and use your magic to travel, if you have enough power to do so."

"We do, though it will take a heavy toll." Hestil's weary expression deepened. "But that's not the worst of it. Word has come from the Nightshade Court. They're under attack. I told them to evacuate to Hawthorne."

His blood ran cold at the news. Muck and mire. Things were coming to a head—and he and Mara *still* weren't married.

"Pull back to the palace," he said. "I'll alert the remaining guard, and contact the Nightshade Lady. Everyone must seek refuge here."

"She won't want to abandon her court."

"Stones can be rebuilt, but lost lives are gone forever. We cannot afford any more of our people's deaths."

Through the scrying bowl he heard screams and the clash of battle, and Hestil shot an anxious look over her shoulder.

"Retreat, before it's too late," Bran said, his stomach tightening. He should be there, helping hold back the Void. But he could not be in two places at once.

"Yes, commander. We will come, as quickly as we may."

It would be a grueling journey back to the Hawthorne Palace with the Void creatures on their heels. He prayed they would not sustain too many casualties.

"I'll ride out to meet you with whomever I can muster," he said, mentally calculating.

Garon would come, and the half-dozen other warriors left to defend the court. If they left within a turn, they would hopefully be able to reach Hestil and the others before the remaining fighters were cut down by the Void.

Yet they were still too far from Hawthorne. He feared he would not be able to reach them in time.

"Have you wed your mortal girl yet?" Hestil asked. She must have read the answer in his eyes, for she gave him a sharp look. "Do it. Now."

She was right. They had not a moment to waste, not with the Dark Elf warriors in full retreat and the Void creatures already attacking Nightshade.

"I will. Now clear the camp, quickly."

Hestil nodded, her image fading in the scrying bowl.

When the water was completely clear again, Bran scrubbed his hands over his face. They were out of time, and it took a massive effort of will to keep despair from settling on his shoulders. All his life he'd trusted to the prophecy.

He must believe it would not fail him now.

Bending over his bowl again, he contacted the ruler of Nightshade. Despite her reluctance, he extracted a promise from her to evacuate her court as soon as possible. The other courts were farther from the coming war—too far to send help or band together if Hawthorne fell. The fate of Elfhame truly was on his shoulders.

That task done, he sent a message to Garon to muster the soldiers left in the palace. Mara must be told of the change in plans, and his parents informed as well—a duty best done in person.

Anneth's rooms were closer than the lord and lady's suite. He knocked, then used a tendril of power to trip the lock.

"Bran—why are you back?" Anneth asked, coming to stand in the arched doorway of her bedroom. "Can't you let your mortal woman rest for a time? She is weary. Come back later."

"It is already far too late," he said. "Where's Mara?"

"Sleeping." Anneth glanced back into her bedroom.

A moment later his mortal came and peeked out the doorway. She was wearing an underdress, and her hair was in disarray. He did not mind marrying her in such a state, but no doubt *she* would. And the hastily-assembled court would be appalled.

"Dire news from the front," he said. "The Void has breached the barrier, and our warriors are in full retreat. Nightshade is under attack, and evacuating here. The creatures cannot be far behind."

"Oh, no." Anneth's eyes dilated in fear.

Mara looked pale, but she met Bran's gaze. "That changes things. I suppose we must marry right away."

He nodded, trying to ignore her flinch when she spoke the word *marry*. At least she'd grasped the situation immediately.

"I wanted to give you a little time to prepare," he said. "I must go inform the Hawthorne Lord and Lady, and do what I can to see that everything is ready for the ceremony."

"How much time?" Anneth asked.

"A turn, if we can manage it."

"Impossible," she said.

"I don't care if my hair's perfectly coiffed," Mara said. "Just put me in that silver gown, and we'll manage."

Bran shot her a grateful glance. It seemed that, once committed to a course of action, his mortal woman would not waver.

"Do you have the companion rings?" Anneth asked him.

"The jeweler will provide something adequate," Bran said, mentally adding a quick visit to the workshop to his list of critical items.

"Go finish the arrangements," Mara said. "We'll be ready in time."

Anneth did not look convinced, but Bran paid no heed to her sound of protest.

"I trust you," he said to Mara, then turned on his heel and strode back into the hallway.

It was true—he had every confidence that in a turn, Mara would arrive in the throne room, ready to marry him. Despite her clear distaste for doing so.

Of course, it was all so that she could go home. Perhaps she was glad of the escalated timetable, as it meant her return to the mortal world was that much closer.

Although first, they had the little matter of saving Elfhame.

Everything had shifted, but the prophecy *must* prove true. In a too soon a time, the moment he'd been waiting for since birth would arrive.

Unfortunately, it featured a reluctant bride, a promise he was not at all sure he could fulfill, and the threat of imminent annihilation by the Void.

When he'd envisioned his wedding, the few times he'd even thought of it at all, he'd assumed it would be a joyful event, as such things usually were.

But fate was ever playing cruel jokes. As long as Elfhame was saved, nothing else mattered. He'd learned long since to set aside his own happiness for the greater good. Clearly his future would be no exception.

CHAPTER 20

"We must go," Mara said, moving away from the mirror while Anneth still fussed over her hair. "I won't be late to my own wedding."

If she had to go through with this terrible event, she was resolved to do it with as much poise as possible. And in some ways, it was a relief to have the ceremony suddenly upon her. Better to take action than to spend the next few days miserably fretting over her upcoming marriage.

"Let me just put a few more flowers in," Anneth said.

"I look well enough." The irony was not lost upon Mara that she'd considered those exact words an insult mere hours earlier. But everything had changed.

It was fortunate that Dark Elf gowns were not tailor-made, but constructed more loosely. Anneth had done wonders with folding and tucking until the gauzy silver dress fit Mara comfortably, though the skirts were still too long. She picked them up and went into the sitting room to fetch her knife.

Anneth followed, managing to jam one last spray of sweet-scented white flowers into Mara's ornately braided hair.

"You look amazing," Anneth said. "I've never worked so quickly in my life."

"And I thank you for it." In another time and place, Mara suspected they might have become friends. "You've been very kind to me."

"Of course." Anneth gave her a look of mild surprise. "You're the woman—"

"Of the prophecy. Yes, I know. But you were under no obligation to take such care of me."

"Bran likes you," Anneth said, which made Mara blink in doubtful surprise. "And I like you as well. Now, do you remember everything I told you about the ceremony?"

"Let's review it while we walk," Mara said, opening the door.

The air in the hallway seemed to vibrate with urgency, and for once the corridor was well lit. A noble couple hurried past, pausing to bow and curtsey before going on their way. As she and Anneth went to the throne room, Mara listened closely, attempting to keep all of the Dark Elf's instructions fixed in her mind.

Normally, according to Anneth, the ceremony began with a procession and attendants waiting upon both the bride and groom, then moved to speeches from the heads of the families, and then a selection of poetry and song.

In this case, however, the wedding would be stripped down to its essentials. There would be no preliminaries: no procession, no speeches, no poems. She and Bran would stand together in front of the dais, before the lord and lady. With the Hawthorne rulers and the court bearing witness, they would exchange vows, give one another gifts, do something slightly unclear with a pair of rings, and speak the Rune of Binding together to finish the ceremony.

Mara mouthed the strange syllables silently to herself, desperately trying to imprint them on her tongue. That was the one thing she would've liked time to practice. Though Anneth had been encouraging, Mara knew she hadn't yet been able to pronounce the Rune correctly.

As they approached the court, she caught the scent of competing perfumes: musk and roses, cinnamon and burnt wine. The silver doors stood open, and a hubbub of urgent conversation poured out. The robed doorman bowed to them, then moved to stand just inside the doorway.

He raised his hand, and a chime rang through the air. Into the pause that followed, he spoke.

"Lady Anneth Ithilden Luthinor. And the Hawthorne Bride, Lady Mara Geary."

Every bone-pale face turned to Mara as she stepped over the threshold. Slitted eyes and sheathed claws, sharp-edged features and hair ranging from midnight to moonlight; all the nobles of the Hawthorne Court were there, arrayed in their finery. Watching her.

Fear leaped upon her like an attacking beast, but she stood her ground. It was not the first time today she had walked this path. Although, instead of having Bran at her back, he waited at the front of the court, before the dais where his parents sat.

She raised her chin and fixed her eyes on him. He wore a tunic of deep indigo with tiny white gems winking from the cuffs and neckline, and his expression was forbidding, as usual.

He turned to face her, and something flashed in his violet eyes. When his gaze dropped to her kitchen knife, stuck through the pearl-stitched belt of her gown, she saw the corner of his mouth twitch up.

A pang of regret went through her as she made her way past the waiting nobles. Just as she and Anneth might have been friends under different circumstances, so, too, might she and Bran have forged something more than a friendship. Given trust, and time.

But the shadow of war had swept quickly across Elfhame, and they did not have that luxury. Instead, duty and honor must carry the day.

When she reached Bran, she made him a curtsey, then turned and paid her respects to his parents. The Hawthorne Lord nodded his approval, but his Lady only gave her a narrow-eyed look from her hard violet eyes.

So be it. Mara would not dwell long enough among the Dark Elves for the Hawthorne Lady's opinion to matter overmuch.

"Members of the Hawthorne Court." Bran's father stood, his voice carrying through the room. "Every generation, a prophecy is pronounced over each heir to the ruling courts. Sometimes, fate treads lightly, or leave messages that cannot be clearly interpreted."

There were a few quiet snorts of laughter at this, and Mara guessed that in many instances, the prophecies were completely obscure or could be ignored altogether.

"In the case of our son, Prince Brannonilon Luthinor, his prophecy has guided him his entire life," the Hawthorne Lord continued. "And we are here to witness the fulfillment of his fate, as it was spoken on the day of his birth."

He drew in a breath, and then intoned in a deep, singsong voice,

"*Evil lurks and soon will fall,*
A door long closed must open wide,
Elfhame's greatest need will call,
A mortal woman as the bride
The Hawthorne Prince must surely wed,
Else all our kind shall perish, dead."

A hush fell over the court, and Mara swallowed, taking in the meaning of the words. She felt a twinge of sympathy for Bran, growing up with such a burden hanging over him, aware since childhood that the fate of his people was in his hands.

And, she had to admit, the prophecy was very clear as to her role as the mortal bride.

She shot Bran a glance, to find that he was watching her, his expression impassive. She narrowed her eyes slightly. If he'd told her everything from the first, instead of lying to her...

He dipped his head in the barest acknowledgement, but his brow rose in a question.

What would have happened, had he told her the truth? Would she have smiled sweetly and said, *Oh yes, of course I will marry you, you terrifying, hideous creature, since I have nothing better to do, and the fate of your world depends upon it?* Or would she have run screaming into the forest, desperate to find her way back home?

For a moment, Mara dropped her gaze to the patterned tile floor beneath her feet. Her boots had been enchanted to glitter with silver and pearls, but it was only an illusion.

And this was only a short-term marriage. Bran's prophecy was going to be fulfilled. First, the wedding, and then they'd somehow defeat the Void. And then he would reopen the doorway and she would go home, her terrible adventure over at last.

Holding that thought close, she lifted her head. Just a little while longer.

"Are you ready, Prince Brannonilon?" Bran's father asked.

"I am," Bran answered. Obviously, he'd been ready his whole life.

The Hawthorne Lord gave her an intent look. "And are you, Mara Geary?"

"Yes," Mara said, her throat tight. She cleared it and tried again, the word coming out more strongly the second time. "Yes, I am."

What other choice did she have?

"Then let the ceremony begin." The Hawthorne Lord seated himself on his throne one again, and the crowd murmured and shuffled, everyone trying for a better view of the bride and groom.

Bran turned to face her, and held his hands out, palms up.

Mara placed her hands over his, and he clasped her wrists. She could feel the prick of his claws against the delicate skin where her pulse ran.

"You clasp hands, like so," Anneth had demonstrated when she was explaining the ceremony. "And then extend your claws. Um. Well, dig your fingernails in, I suppose. It's to represent that you trust one another enough not to rip each other's throats out."

Mara pressed the tips of her fingers down, all too aware that her poor mortal fingernails were no weapon at all. The only way she could rip Bran's throat out was if she attacked him with her blade in the middle of the night, and even then she suspected his warrior's instincts would have him awake and her disarmed in a heartbeat.

Not that she would ever put it to the test. Nor did she want to. Despite his strange looks, Bran was not a terrible monster, and she did not wish him dead. She simply wished for him to be in his world, and her to be in hers, and all of this to finally be over.

"Mara Geary," he said, his violet-flecked eyes staring deep into her own, "I pledge my future to you, under star and shadow, by pale moon and bright, through fire and storm. I shall stand at your side, my blade yours to call upon, my magic at your command, until time and fate sunders our bond."

She could hear the sincerity resonating through his voice, and it made her feel unworthy. For her, this ceremony was a means to an end, but Bran was a man of unflinching honor. If he spoke the words, he meant them.

What if I stay? The thought whispered through her mind.

Then she considered all the ways she did not fit—could never fit—in the Dark Elves' world. There was only one path for her, and it led back to the mortal world.

Bran squeezed her hands lightly, a signal for her to say her part.

"Brannonilon Luthinor," she said, and oh, she'd practiced those syllables nearly as much as the Rune of Binding. Thank heavens her tongue did not trip over his name. "I pledge myself to you, under star and shadow, by pale moon and bright, through fire and storm. I shall stand at your side as we face the threat to your people, offering everything I can to help fulfill the prophecy, until our time together is at an end."

There was a restless murmur at how she'd changed the wording of the ceremony, but she had her own sense of honor to uphold. She could not, in good conscience, pledge to be Bran's companion for the rest of her life. All she could do was speak aloud the promise she'd made to him, and hope it would be enough.

His mouth tightened at her words, and she sensed the weight of the future settling heavily on his shoulders. He would have no one to share it with, once she was gone, for she knew deep in her heart that he would never seek out another to love. This marriage would bind him for the rest of his days.

The knowledge almost made her yank her hands away and implore him to find someone else to marry. Someone who could love him as he deserved, someone to share the rest of his life with.

But there was no one else. She was the woman of the prophecy, and she must see this through to the end. She wrapped her hands more firmly about his wrists. He gave her the slightest nod, then let go.

"As a token of my affection, I give you this bride-gift." He reached into his tunic and drew out an ornately twisted necklace glowing with starry gems, silver, and pearls.

It was the most stunning piece of jewelry she'd ever seen, fit for a queen, and she sucked in her breath as he held it up. From her place on the dais, Bran's mother made an annoyed sound, but he ignored her.

"Allow me?" he said softly.

Mara bent her head and let him fasten the necklace about her neck. It lay, rich and heavy, against her skin.

Her throat tight with thanks, with regret, she looked back up at him.

"And as a token of my respect, I give you this groom-gift," she said, unfastening her trusty kitchen knife from her belt.

She handed it to him, the only apology she could make for everything that was and could never be between them. This time the murmurs of the crowd were approving.

The look on Bran's face softened. He carefully took the knife, as if were made of the most precious metal, and slid it through his own belt.

"I thank you," he said.

She stood there awkwardly for a moment, trying to recall what came next. Then Bran reached into his pocket once more and drew out two rings, one small and one large. They were connected at one edge, two side-by-side circles.

"Just as the pale moon and the bright join together in the sky, so shall our lives join," he said.

He held up his right hand toward her, and belatedly, Mara mirrored the movement. When their palms touched, a flash of sensation moved through her, as though she'd passed her hand over a candle flame. Bran's eyes widened slightly, and she guessed he'd felt it, too.

Skin pressed to skin, he raised his other hand and slid the linked rings onto their middle fingers. For a moment, she felt trapped, and had to crush the urge to jerk her hand away. She could not have moved, at any rate—the rings were tightly connected, holding their hands fast.

Bran angled his hand, bending his fingers down to interlace with hers, and she did the same. They stood there, palm to palm, the rings tying them together.

"Ready?" he asked in a low voice.

Time to speak the Rune of Binding. She swallowed, trying to moisten her throat and recall the guttural syllables. This was the last step of the wedding. What if she could not say it correctly? Would the entire ceremony be a failure? Would the Void descend in a black wave and kill them all?

Her heart pounding, she nodded to Bran. She would do her best.

“When I squeeze your hand, we will say the Rune together,” he said softly. “Do not fear.”

Her gaze fixed on his, she made no reply, only waited. There was nothing but trust in his eyes.

He pressed her hand, and she opened her mouth, speaking the awkward syllables.

“Gwedhyocuilvorn!”

Their voices mingled, his strong tones overriding her slight mispronunciation. A searing light sprang from their clasped hands, and the air vibrated as though they stood within a giant bell that had just been struck. Mara squinted against the glare. Her hand felt as though it was on fire.

Then her skin prickled all over, and that strange feeling opened up inside her again: a rush of power filling her from her toes to the crown of her head. It spilled out, and bright azure flames leaped from her hand where it touched Bran’s.

His nostrils flared and he leaned forward.

“You must contain your power,” he said, his voice tight. “Pull it back in. I’m shielding the court, but I can’t continue for long.”

Mara dug her heels into the stone floor and concentrated on subduing the wild fire burning inside her. *Breathe. Calm.* Slowly, she felt the heat subside.

After what seemed like hours, but was probably only seconds, the blue flame winked out, and her power curled in and down, settling back to whatever shadowy place it inhabited. She swayed, and Bran caught her, pulling her in to lean against his broad chest.

Their hands were still linked. His heart beat strong under her cheek.

She drew in a shaky breath and slowly uncurled her fingers. He did the same.

To her great relief, their hands were no longer attached. She pulled hers away and glanced at the ring encircling her middle finger. Where it had been plain silver before, it now glowed a deep violet-blue. Bran’s was the same, and she didn’t know if they were supposed to look that way, or if the ceremony had indeed gone wrong in some way.

“That was unexpected,” Bran said, quietly enough that only she could hear. His breath was warm against her forehead "Are you unharmed?"

"I think so."

"Then you must stand beside me. Take my hand, like so. Now raise your ring so that all may see."

Mara obeyed, though she felt unsteady on her feet. Bran shifted toward her, bracing her unobtrusively against him.

Her vision was still blurred by the flash of power, but she could see shock and wonder on the faces of the assembled Dark Elves. She was pleased to note that the nasty Mireleth had lost her usual petulant expression, and Anneth was openly beaming.

"We have witnessed history in the making," the Hawthorne Lord said from the dais. Even he sounded a trifle amazed. "The union between Prince Brannonilon Luthinor and the mortal woman, Lady Mara Geary, is complete. Let us rejoice."

Anneth led the cheering, which was thin at first, then grew in volume until the entire court was calling out their approval.

Cutting above the noise, Mara became aware of a shrill, high keening. She glanced over at Bran, who looked exceedingly grim.

"To arms!" he cried, and the cheering abruptly cut off. "The Hawthorne Palace is under attack!"

CHAPTER 21

The palace alarm wailed, then finally ceased as the members of the Hawthorne Court scrambled for the doors. Bran set his hand on Mara's shoulder. His ring flared with blue light, reminding him that this woman was now, and always, his wife. Regret curled through him like smoke that they would never have a true partnership, or a future together.

For all her strangeness, and despite everything, he feared that he had learned to love his mortal woman. Not that he would ever speak such a thing to her. She would be disgusted, and presume he was only trying to hold her to Elfhame.

"What do we do?" she asked, turning to him. "Are Void creatures attacking?"

"Not quite yet," he said. "The alarm is set to ring when enemies cross the palace's outer boundary. We have less than a turn to prepare for battle before they are upon us."

"I'm fighting, too," Mara said, as if daring him to contradict her.

"Of course. We need you." *I need you.*

Anneth hurried up, and gave Mara a stern look.

"You're not going to war in *that.*" She gestured to Mara's silver gown.

"Then let's get back to your rooms and find me something suitable," his wife—*his wife!*—said.

Bran squeezed her shoulder and let go, though a part of him wanted to hold on to her and keep her safe, forever.

"I'll be in the courtyard just inside the main gate," he said. "Everyone willing to fight will muster there. Find me as soon as you're ready."

He did not bother telling her to hurry. It was clear that they had not a moment to waste.

She turned to go, and he caught her arm again.

"Take this." He drew his dagger from his belt and handed it to her, hilt first. "I don't want you to be unarmed."

"Are you giving back your groom-gift?" She made him a tight smile.

"Never. Merely lending it back to you for a time. Now go."

She and Anneth rushed off, and Bran turned to where Garon and a few members of the nobility waited beside the dais. To his surprise, his father stood there as well, though there was no sign of Tinnueth. No doubt she was busy barricading herself in her rooms.

"Father." He gave the Hawthorne Lord a nod of respect. The man had been a skilled swordsman in his day, and good enough with offensive magic. "Do you join us?"

"Of course I do," Lord Calithilon said. "This is still my court, and I will defend it til the end, if necessary."

Bran gave him a nod of respect, then turned to Garon. "How many fighters?"

"Ten. With yourself and Lady Mara and the Lord, that makes thirteen. A few defenders will stay behind, too. Cerreth and her brother will take to the towers with fiery arrows."

Bran surveyed the brave, grim faces staring back at him. "Put on your armor, fetch your weapons, and meet me by the gates as soon as possible."

They nodded and dispersed, leaving Bran alone with his father.

"Well done," Lord Calithilon said. "I am proud to call you my son."

"The battle's not yet won."

"But the prophecy is fulfilled, and I was wrong to ever doubt it. I am certain we'll win. Afterward, I'll ensure that your mother doesn't meddle with the mortal girl."

Bran gave him a short nod. This was not the time to explain that Mara would be leaving Elfhame. When Tinnueth learned of it, no doubt she would be delighted. As would Mireleth. The knowledge left a sour taste in his mouth.

"Off to prepare," Lord Calithilon said, a note of anticipation in his voice. He stepped onto the dais and headed for his private door.

For the first time, Bran wondered if perhaps his father was bored. He should have invited the Hawthorne Lord to come to the front, take part in a few skirmishes.

Well, there would be excitement enough just ahead. And, he feared, the worst parts of war as well: wounded warriors, pain. Death.

With those gloomy thoughts for company, he strode back to his rooms to don his leather armor and fetch his sword.

Garon and two other warriors were waiting when he entered the courtyard, and soon enough the rest of the fighters joined them. Lord Calithilon's eyes glowed, and Bran could feel his father gathering his magic in preparation.

Mara was the last to arrive, wearing a heavy tunic, leggings, and her mortal boots, which still shimmered slightly with Anneth's glamour. If his wife had chosen to stay in Elfhame, he would have commanded a set of the finest armor to be made for her.

Instead, he would be her shield and her sword.

"Something's coming," one of the fighters said, pointing at the pale road winding away from the palace gates.

The hiss of swords leaving scabbards filled the air, but Bran held up his hand. "Wait. Those are no Void creatures."

He sent a ball of glowing foxfire forward. Its blue light illuminated a line of Dark Elves straggling down the road. At the front strode the Nightshade Lady, her expression grim.

"We're here," she called back to her people. "Hurry—safety is just ahead."

Bran and the other fighters stood aside as the people of Nightshade came through the gates.

"Welcome." Lord Calithilon raised his hand in greeting. "Enter, friends, and seek food and shelter within. Our hospitality is yours for as long as you need it."

"My thanks, Hawthorne," the Nightshade Lady said, stopping beside Bran's father.

"You would do the same," he said. "How many?"

"Not enough." Her voice was hollow with weariness. "Our best fighters fell in the first attack. I fear Nightshade is lost to us."

"Not for long," Bran said.

Whatever happened, the war with the Void would be over soon. And if the Dark Elves were defeated, then the fate of the Nightshade Court mattered not at all, as all of Elfhame would be lost.

He watched the stream of refugees trickle in. Nightshade was a small court, smaller than their own, and after a dismayingly short time the road was empty again.

"The creatures are not far behind," the Nightshade Lady said. "I would stay with you and fight, but I fear my magic is spent."

"Recover as you can," Lord Calithilon said. "You traveled fast, to reach us this soon."

"The Rune of Quickness has its uses."

Bran shot her a look of respect. No wonder her powers were exhausted. To cast the Rune on one person was challenge enough. The Nightshade Lady had done so for all her court, and several times over, if he was any judge.

Hestil and the other warriors had a different magic. The ability to fold doors through the landscape was less taxing, but slower. By the moons, he prayed they would arrive soon.

A faint, chittering sound reached his ears, and he stiffened.

"The Void creatures come," he said. "Secure the gates behind us, and take your places. Mara, stay close to me."

He'd wanted to ride out and engage the enemy further from the palace walls, but it was too late. The creatures that had attacked Nightshade were too close. And there was still no sign of Hestil and her fighters.

It was up to their small band at the gates to throw back this first wave of enemies before the warriors from the front arrived.

With the wave of Voidspawn that would surely be on their heels

Between one breath and the next, the enemy was upon them. Red-eyed gyrewolves leaped and snapped, and one spiderkin leaped over them all, headed straight for the palace.

Bran shouted a warning, and saw his father blast the creature with a bolt of power before drawing his sword. Then all his attention turned to fighting the wolves swarming toward him and Mara.

As he'd guessed, somehow the Void sensed her presence. The battle soon became not a defense of the palace gates, but a circle of fighting around him and his bride.

A wolf came too close while he pushed back a spiderkin. Mara cried out and slashed at it with her dagger. The creature growled and prepared to leap, then was taken down by a swing of Garon's blade.

Bran's heart pumped furiously. That had been far too close.

He raised one hand, summoning his power, and let out a blast. It knocked back the current attackers, but by its light Bran could see more approaching, including two of the lumbering creatures. These ones were twice the size of the lumberer he and Lieth had dispatched, and he could not help a twinge of dismay at the sight.

"Now what?" Mara asked. One of her braids had come loose, and her mud-colored hair straggled across her face.

He gently tucked the strand behind her ear.

"We hold fast," he said. "This is a skirmish. I fear the real battle is yet to come."

"Something's happening yonder," Garon said, lifting his blade and staring toward the rise above the palace.

Bran looked, and saw the telltale glow of magic flickering against the starlit sky.

"It must be Hestil." He raised his voice in command. "Fighters, move position to the ridge!"

He sent another blast of power to keep the Void creatures at bay and give their small band enough time to scramble for the rise. As they ran, he caught Mara's hand. Despite Garon's lame leg, the old soldier kept pace on her other side. It seemed he'd appointed himself her bodyguard, and Bran was glad of it. As the small band of fighters vacated the area before the gates, arrows hissed from the towers toward their enemies, burning green and orange with magical flame.

They crested the ridge to see scores of Dark Elf warriors holding back a wave of gyrewolves and spiderkin. Lieth's bolts of magic flew true, and the glows of lesser magic users bloomed and faded over the trampled silvergrass. Bran scanned the fighters, finding Hestil in the process of dispatching a gyrewolf.

A spiderkin leaped to attack her. With a shout, he raised his hand and blasted it down. Hestil whirled and impaled the creature, dodging the green ichor spurting from its side.

"Bran," she called. "Thank the seven bright stars."

He'd opened his mouth to reply, when, with a deafening crack, the air above them split open.

CHAPTER 22

Bran pulled Mara to his side and stared up at the sundered sky. This was no mere breach. No—this was a portal torn into the very fabric of their world, blotting out the stars and pulsing with the malevolent energy of the Void. Somehow, the Dark Elves' ancient enemy had managed to bypass the barrier and push itself into the heart of Elfhame.

The final battle was upon them.

He glimpsed hundreds of red-eyed creatures massed and waiting to pour through the rift into Elfhame. And behind them, a devouring darkness that would not stop until it had eaten every shred of every world down to nothingness.

"Dear heavens," Mara whispered.

"If ever was a time to find your power, beloved, do it now," he said.

Letting go of her hand, he raised his arms high overhead, fingers pointing up toward the rip in their world. Already, Void creatures were spilling out, pressing the exhausted warriors.

But he could not pay heed to the desperate fights breaking out, the screams of pain, the wavering of Lieth's power, even his own father valiantly laying about with blade and flame.

Reaching deep into his wellspring, Bran sent pure power into the rift

—a sharp, fierce lance of magic aimed at the heart of the Void. It streamed forth from his fingertips as he poured every shred of his energy into the attack.

The Void resisted, its hunger stealing Bran's magic and blunting its force.

He swayed. It was not enough.

Then Mara caught his upraised right arm and pulled it down until their hands were clasped. Their rings met, and azure flame leaped through him, so strong it left him reeling. Before it could burn him to cinders, he channeled it up and out, renewing the attack.

His original bolt of power was now ten times stronger. Creatures sizzled and fell, screeching, through the air. The grasping touch of the Void could not hold back this new force of mortal and Dark Elf power combined. He felt the enemy shudder as the pure blue light struck deep into the darkness, burning clear and strong.

The Void bucked, spitting out more creatures, as if desperate to find him and cut off the attack. Still he kept the magic flowing.

Mara wrapped her other arm about his waist, and he felt her giving him all her strength. Too much, he feared, for her mortal body to endure. But they could not let up, not yet. Though his vision blurred and his lungs gasped for air, he must keep throwing their power at the enemy with all his might.

Something shriveled and cringed in the depths of the Void, and a horrible screeching cry wailed out between the worlds, scorching his ears, flaying his mind. It lashed out, a final black tendril of power that smote him to the bone. Freezing cold enveloped him for a heartbeat.

Then, with an earthshaking clap, the rift snapped shut. Bran and Mara's power splashed up into the sky, then faltered, the magic raining down like shooting stars.

The Void was gone.

All about the battlefield the red-eyed creatures stilled, slumping down into death. He shivered from the frigid touch of the Void's final attack, and prayed he'd taken the brunt of the blow, shielding Mara from it.

The Dark Elves had won—though his heart sank at the casualties scattered over the silvergrass.

Mara let out a shaky cry and pulled her hand from his. He turned to find her kneeling beside Garon. The old warrior lay surrounded by the carcasses of slain Void creatures, his heart's blood seeping out of a fatal wound to his chest.

While Bran and Mara had focused all their attention on attacking the Void, faithful Garon had kept the creatures at bay with more prowess than a fighter half his age.

"Do not weep, mortal girl," he said, his voice a weak thread. "It is a good death."

Bran went to his knees and took the old soldier's hand. "Garon. I could not have asked for a better, more loyal defender. Thank you, my friend."

"My honor to serve," Garon whispered.

Then he closed his eyes and let out his breath for the last time. Above them, the palemoon shone, steady and true.

"No," Mara said. Her cheeks glistened with tears.

"I am sorry." Bran's father came up to where they knelt, his shoulders bent with weariness. "The loss of a good man."

"One among many." Bran lifted his head and bleakly surveyed the causalities. To his great relief, he saw Hestil moving among the fighters, Avantor at her heels. But there were still too many fighters lost—companions he would never see again. His heart twisted with loss.

Yet the living must carry on.

"Come." He stood and offered Mara his hand. "We must tend to the wounded."

She wiped her face with her sleeve, then clasped his outstretched hand. Their rings glowed softly, but the fierce power was spent.

When she stood, she staggered forward a step. He caught her in his arms, worry spiking through him.

"Starting with yourself," he said.

"I'm not injured." Her voice rasped from her throat. "Just so very tired."

"I will watch over her," the Hawthorne Lord said. "You go tend to your warriors."

Mara nodded, and, reluctantly, Bran let her go.

"Guard her well," he said to his father. "I will not be long."

He'd bring Avantor back with him, of course, but he needed a moment to speak with Hestil and assess the full extent of their losses. The battle had taken a heavy toll—but the Void was gone. The small glow of victory kindled in his chest, pushing back some of the shadows left in the aftermath of war.

They would grieve, yes. Already he felt an empty space where Lieth ought to be, and feared she had drained her magic dry and fallen to the enemy. Garon, too, was a hole in his heart. And he feared that the greatest wound was yet to come, when he sent Mara back to her world.

But balancing that darkness was brilliant light, and cause for joy. The Void was defeated. It would not return for generations, if at all.

The prophecy had come true. Elfhame was saved.

CHAPTER 23

Mara opened her eyes and stared up at the golden curtains draping the bed. She knew exactly where she was: in Anneth's bedroom, in the Hawthorne Palace. In Elfhame.

But not for long.

Oh, how her siblings would exclaim when she told them of her adventures. The thought made her shake her head. Already, her time here was like a dream, the battle and the magic she had commanded more like something out of legend than an event that had truly happened.

"You're awake." Bran leaned forward from the chair he was occupying beside the bed. "How do you feel?"

Somehow, she was not surprised to find him there. She took a deep breath and wiggled her fingers and toes.

"Good. I feel good. And hungry."

A faint smile ghosted across his lips. "I'll send for food. Can you sit?"

She did, and before she could protest, he propped a few pillows behind her back.

"I'm not an invalid," she said.

"You slept for two palemoons. I feared..." A shadow crossed his face, then was gone. "No matter. Anneth will be delighted to hear you've woken. I'll fetch her, and return with food."

Her stomach gave an embarrassing gurgle, proof that it, too, was wide awake and in perfect health.

Bran left, and a moment later Anneth hurried into the room. She sat on the bed beside Mara and squeezed her hand.

"You are the heroine of the court," Anneth said. "Or more like the entire realm. You and Bran did it! You defeated the Void."

"I wasn't sure we could." Mara shivered, recalling that vast, devouring darkness.

"Father has declared a feast in your honor. This time, it might actually take place." Anneth smiled at her, her eyes shining. "We have a great deal to celebrate."

It seemed Bran had not told his sister that Mara was leaving. Probably it was for the best, since Anneth would only try to make her stay. No matter how much of a heroine Mara might be at the moment, she knew it would fade quickly.

Soon enough she'd be a stranger again, adrift in a sunless world she could barely navigate. Not only that, but married to the Hawthorne Prince, with not the slightest idea of what her new station entailed.

She could not be the Hawthorne Lady. Even if the court tolerated a mortal on the companion's throne, she had seen how rigid the Dark Elves were in their traditions and expectations. Once her notoriety wore off, she'd be a source of embarassment. Bran would be torn between his people and his wife, and she did not think she could bear the disappointment in his eyes when she failed to behave properly time and time again.

"A feast," she finally said, aware she'd been silent too long. "That sounds grand."

Anneth gave her a curious look. "Mara, is there something I ought to know?"

Bran strode in carrying a tray, and Mara was saved from answering. She vowed to be perfectly cheerful in front of Anneth. At least until she said goodbye.

"Save some room for the feast," Bran said, setting the tray on the nightstand beside the bed.

"I think I could probably eat two feasts worth of food." Mara reached for one of the Amaranth cakes.

"Knowing the kitchens, they will serve that much, and more," Anneth said. "Now, which gown will you choose this time?"

~

ONCE BRAN WAS REASSURED that Mara suffered no long-term ill effects from her prodigious use of magic, he took his leave. It had been easier to be in her company while she was asleep. He could gaze on her face and imagine to himself that she'd changed her mind.

But once she'd awoken, it was clear to him she still intended to go home. Back to her world.

He could not blame her. She had been thrust unexpectedly into a land and a fate not of her choosing. Not to mention a husband she didn't want. After the celebratory feast, he would fulfill his promise and send her back to the mortal world. Somehow.

The longer she stayed, the more it would hurt. A quick, sharp cut would be best. The kind that left a scar.

It would not be the first one he bore, nor the last. But he feared it would be the deepest.

He shook his head. What a sorry excuse for a warrior he was. It was useless to fill the hours with such thoughts. The future would bring what it would bring—although he felt strangely adrift without the prophecy guiding his steps.

Hands clasped behind his back, Bran turned toward his father's library, ignoring the bone-deep coldness that had settled inside him since the final battle. It was the aftereffect of using so much of his power that left him feeling dizzy at times, but he knew it would pass.

Meanwhile, there was work to do. The Hawthorne Lord had asked for his opinion in finalizing the plans to help Nightshade rebuild their broken court. Bran also wanted to broach the idea of sending a patrol around the entire circumference of Elfhame. They must ensure that the barrier was fully mended and secure.

In fact, he would volunteer to lead the party. It would remove him from the court and give him something to do other than dwell on the loss of Mara.

Working out the details of the aid they would provide the Nightshade Court, complete with arguments from his father and protests from the Nightshade Lady, kept him engaged until it was time to dress for the feast. Bran choose his formal tunic with care, picking a dark amethyst velvet that made him appear more like a prince than a warrior.

Not that it would do any good in Mara's eyes.

Mentally chastising himself for a fool, he went to fetch her from Anneth's rooms.

Although he thought he was prepared for the sight of his wife gowned and bejeweled, she never failed to steal his breath for a heartbeat. This time she wore deep emerald satin decorated with silver embroidery of twining leaves. The necklace he'd given her shone at her throat, and Anneth had woven pearls into her hair to match.

Her gaze went to his belt, and she laughed at the sight of her knife hanging there.

"Are you truly going to wear that to the feast?" she asked.

"Of course. Unless you would like to trade tokens?"

Her hand went to her necklace, and she shook her head. "I think you'd look a bit silly wearing this. Besides, it's too beautiful to part with."

Her obvious pleasure in his gift gave him a flash of warmth. At least he was not completely odious in her eyes.

With Mara on one side and Anneth on the other, he escorted them to the dining hall. As soon as they stepped into the room, everyone rose and began cheering. The tables were full to overflowing, the members of Nightshade and the fighters from the front making up for the empty places where fallen warriors ought to have been.

Garon. Lieth. His throat tightened at their loss.

At one of the near tables, Hestil raised her goblet in a toast to him. New lines were etched upon her face, but he saw peace there as well.

The Hawthorne Lord beckoned them to the head table, and insisted that Mara be seated on his right side, with Bran next to her, and then

Anneth. Tinnueth's mouth turned down at the corners, but she spoke not a word of protest.

Still, as the feast began, he caught her watching Mara, her sharp eyes cataloguing every misstep his mortal wife made. Mara used the wrong fork, reached too far for the salt cellar, and engaged in conversation all across the table as well as to either side. They were small things, but enough to begin a litany of errors that would only grow over time.

His mother was not the only one taking note. Mireleth was seated further down the table, and she sent frequent, narrow-eyed glances to where he and Mara sat. Partway through the meat course, he saw her lean aside and make some remark to her companion. The man looked at Mara and laughed unkindly.

Bran curled his fingers into his palm, feeling the stab of his own claws. Perhaps it was a good thing, after all, that Mara was departing. She had said so many times she did not belong in Elfhame.

But she belongs with me, his heart insisted.

Idiot organ. He hardened it to stone and continued eating, though he tasted not a bite.

At last the meal was over, the musicians played a final fanfare, and the Hawthorne Lord rose.

"Today, we celebrate victory," he said. "We owe it to the steadfast honor of the Hawthorne Heir, whose trust in the prophecy never wavered. And to Lady Mara, the mortal woman who opened the door between our worlds and used her newfound powers for the good of our land. We are eternally in your debt." He picked up his goblet and raised it high above the court. "Let us toast, to victory—and to Prince Brannonilon and his bride!"

Mara's cheeks colored and she nodded acknowledgment. Bran took up his goblet, full of rich elderberry wine, and raised his cup to her.

"Thank you, Mara," he said in a low voice. "You will be missed."

Freezing cold wormed through his bones, and he took a deep draught to dispel it. The wine tasted sweet and bitter in equal measure as he swallowed it down.

CHAPTER 24

The feast lasted forever, and yet was over too quickly. Despite her hunger, Mara took care not to eat too much of the rich food. She had a journey to make—not only through Elfhame to the doorway, but a second passage through the deep trees of the Darkwood. She hoped she would not become lost on her way back to Little Hazel.

Her pulse quickened at the thought of coming home at last, of seeing lights in the cottage windows, of stepping through the familiar doorway and at last embracing her parents.

And seeing the sun, and being surrounded by normal-sized beings whose eyes were not strangely slitted and whose features were not so strangely foreign.

Back in Anneth's rooms, however, an odd melancholy fell over her as Bran's sister helped her out of the satin gown. She had enjoyed playing the lady, though no doubt it would grow tiresome after a time. And the weight of the Dark Elves' expectations would bend her down to the ground.

"I'd like to wear the tunic and leggings from earlier," Mara said. She'd already run through the forest once wearing an impractical dress. No need to repeat the experience.

"Are you quite sure?" Anneth cocked her head. "This is your bridal night, after all. Don't you want something more..."

She waved her hand at one of the frothier gowns, but Mara shook her head.

"Bran is taking me riding," she said.

"Riding?" Anneth's brows rose.

"Anneth." Mara firmed her lips, then let out a breath. "I must tell you something. I'm not staying in Elfhame. Bran is sending me back through the doorway tonight."

"He's sending you away?" Anneth gave her a shocked look, brows drawn sharply together. "What an utter fool. Can't he see that's the most idiotic—"

"You misunderstand." Mara held up her hand. "I asked him to send me—I want to go. It was a condition I set before we wed, that he would use his magic to open the gateway back to my home, after we fulfilled the prophecy and defeated the Void."

"You *want* to leave?" There was a wounded look in Anneth's eyes. "But you saved Elfhame."

Mara let out a short, bitter laugh. "That doesn't mean I belong here. Truly, my mind is made up. Please don't ask me to stay."

Anneth stared at her a moment longer, then shook her head. "I don't understand you at all."

"No. And that proves my point. No one here ever will. We come from worlds that are too different. Even though I can speak your language, everything here is foreign. Your customs and thoughts, and even the way you tell time, make little sense to me."

"Bran would understand you. I think he already does."

Anneth's words sent a pang through Mara. But even if it were true, she and Bran had no real hope of a future together. No matter what the prophecy might think.

"I won't argue with you over this," she said. "I'm sorry, Anneth."

Bran's sister stood there a moment, lips tight. "I am sorry, too. But if you insist on going, I will help you prepare."

By the time Bran came to fetch her, Mara was wearing the sturdy tunic, her boots had returned to their original plain state, and her hair had been taken out of its elaborate coiffure and simply tied back from her face. She was Lady Mara no more.

"I see you are ready," he said, his features settling into his starkest expression. "Take the necklace. And this." He held out his jewel-hilted dagger.

"I can't. They're far too costly."

"That is precisely why I give them to you," he said. "Will such gems not serve you well in the mortal world?"

She tamped down her unexpected surge of disappointment. She should be grateful for his generosity, not sorry that he only had a practical reason for giving her such opulent gifts.

"If you insist," she said.

"Here." Anneth handed her the twisted strand of silver and gems she'd worn for her wedding.

Instead of slipping it into her pocket, Mara fastened it about her neck. *For safekeeping*, she told herself, but knew it was more than that.

She stuck Bran's dagger through her belt, then turned to Anneth, dismayed to see tears glinting in the Dark Elf's eyes.

"I always wanted a sister," Anneth said.

They're more trouble than they're worth, Mara almost replied, but instead she stepped forward into Anneth's embrace. When they parted, her throat was tight.

"Goodbye," she said. "And thank you."

Bran opened the door, and for the last time, Mara walked out of Anneth's rooms. She kept going and didn't look back. Bran paced behind her, and together they went to the end of the corridor, past the tower stairs, and under the arched doorway leading into the gardens.

The sweet smell of the flowers twined about her, and three glimglows swooped down, as if they'd been waiting for her. She took some comfort in the sight. Perhaps her journey back through the Darkwood would not be as dark and lonely as she'd feared.

A stablehand was waiting with Fuin. His eyes were full of questions, but he said nothing as Bran mounted and lifted Mara up to sit before him. This time she rode astride, which made her feel less like a helpless maiden and more like a woman taking charge of her own future.

Which she was.

They went silently, avoiding the ridge that had been the scene of their final battle with the Void. The warm wind swirled about them, and birds called softly as the large moon began to rise. The glimglows danced and darted above her head.

She breathed deeply of the warm air of Elfhame. Now that she was leaving, she felt a stab of regret. It was a beautiful land, in its own shadowed way. And though the Dark Elves were not beautiful to her eyes, they were powerful and magical. She would never forget her time among them.

And she would never forget Bran. Beneath that harsh-featured exterior was a man of integrity and honor.

Which was part of why she must leave. She could never be the consort he needed, though he was far too stubborn to admit it. It was better for both of them that she was going. If she stayed, if she admitted that she might have feelings for him, she would be nothing more than an anchor about his neck.

He deserved more than a flawed mortal bride. This way, both of them would be free to go forward into lives of their own choosing. With mates not dictated by the veiled whims of fate.

She did not know how to say such things to him, and so remained silent. As did he. His quiet was not angry or cold, but simply there, like the stars overhead or the leaves rustling on the trees.

It was not until the golden moon had lifted high into the sky that he spoke. "When we reach the doorway, I expect it will take our combined magics to open it."

She glanced down at the ring clasped around her finger. No doubt he was right.

She'd already rummaged about several times in the pockets of her tunic, but there was no secret glass key tucked there. It had done its work and disappeared, and she knew she would never see it again.

Perhaps it had gone to a new world, called by a different prophecy or quirk of fate to open another doorway that had been closed for too long.

They rode into a meadow filled with shimmering grass, and a shiver of familiarity went through her. This was the place she'd been attacked by the spider creature. And where Bran had saved her.

As if sensing her thoughts, his arm tightened about her waist, the ring sparking on his hand. Fuin went forward into the shadows under the trees, and the glimglows swirled up. Two more joined them, and they flitted ahead, bobbing between the dark trunks of the huge evergreens. Flowers glowed against the emerald-green mosses, scarlet and deep purple, veined with light. Ahead, she glimpsed the clearing where the two tall stones rose, their surfaces carved with mystic runes.

"The doorway," she said, breathing in the wild scent of herbs.

"Yes."

The horse halted, and Mara slid down before Bran could help her. She was nearly home, and her heart pounded with the knowledge. Home. Home.

Bran followed her into the clearing. The bright moonlight illuminated his fierce features, his strange eyes, his clawed fingertips.

"Are you certain you will not stay?" he asked.

Stay. The word echoed through her.

"I do care for you, Prince Brannonilon Luthinor," she admitted. "But to remain here, in the darkness among your people, would drive me mad."

He nodded once, the braids on either side of his face swinging. Then he stepped forward and cupped her cheek in his palm. His violet-flecked eyes stared down into hers.

"And I care for you, Mara Geary, more than you will ever know. Which is why I will honor the promise I made, and send you home."

Her vision clouded with unexpected tears. If only things were different. If only *she* were different, a Dark Elf lady, able to move confidently through the currents of their society. Able to be the wife this tall, stern warrior needed.

But she was a mortal, and as unsuited to Elfhame as a freshwater fish to the sea. She might swim there a short while, but soon enough it would sicken her beyond bearing.

His face came close, and then his lips pressed against hers, warm and fleeting.

By the time she blinked the moisture from her eyes, he had dropped his palm from where it cupped her face, and taken a step back, facing the space between the stones.

"Take my hand one more time," he said. "I will speak the Rune of

Opening. If we succeed, the door will appear, and you will be able to step through into your world."

She nodded and laced her fingers with his. Their rings clinked together, and a flicker of azure flame arose—but something was awry. She turned toward Bran, sensing a strange, cold darkness lodged deep within him.

"*Edro!*" he cried.

Blue fire leaped from their joined hands, covering the stones with a wash of flame. The air between the stones shimmered, then cleared to reveal the Darkwood. The trees beyond looked drab and colorless compared to the vividness of Elfhame. She hesitated and glanced at him a moment, searching his face.

"What is wrong?" she whispered.

The glimglows streamed through the doorway, and Bran released her hand.

"Go, Mara." His voice was tight. "Quickly, before it closes."

It was what she wanted. Why, then, was her heart so heavy, her steps so reluctant?

"Go!" He set his hand at her back and pushed her forward.

The doorway flickered. This was her last chance to return home. She must take it.

"Farewell, Bran," she said, then pulled in a breath and darted forward, passing between the stones.

The cool, moist air of the mortal world enfolded her, and the smell of cedars stung her nose. She turned around to see her husband outlined faintly in the doorway between the worlds.

He lifted his hand, and she mirrored his movement, the ring on her finger glowing dully.

Goodbye, my love. His words were a whisper on the wind.

The blue flame covering the stones winked out. The doorway closed, and Mara was left alone in the Darkwood, her cheeks wet with tears.

CHAPTER 25

As it turned out, the journey back through the Darkwood was not as difficult as the headlong flight that had first brought her to the stones. Mara had arrived back in her own world on the cusp of dawn. The grayness of the forest slowly faded, color seeping back into the world as the light grew stronger.

The glimglows darted ahead of her, marking the way, and this time there was no dark and feral beast pursuing her, no breathless dash through the trees with panic pulsing through her veins.

Dry needles crackled under her boots, and berries hung red on the bushes. She could not believe it, but somehow fall had come during the few short days she'd spent in Elfhame. What must her parents think? They would certainly be distraught at her long disappearance.

Urgency firing her steps, she began to run through the forest. The glimglows still danced ahead of her, but as the first rays of the sun streamed through the trees they began to fade, visible only in the shadows, then finally not at all.

No matter, though—Mara had reached the familiar part of the Darkwood where she'd often collected firewood. Side aching, she slowed her steps to catch her breath. A bright red cardinal flashed through the trees, brilliant as a drop of fresh blood in the sunlight.

The blessed, beloved sunlight.

Mara stopped in a patch of it, closing her eyes and lifting her face to feel its heat. Tears pricked behind her eyelids, but of gratitude this time, not grief. Despite the ache in her heart, she was home.

Joy settled in her belly, blossoming like a flower when she reached the edge of the trees and stepped out onto the lane leading to the cottage. The smell of baking bread and frying sausages hung in the air, and she could hear the high voices of children.

There had been no children in Elfhame, she belatedly realized, and she would never know why.

Then her younger sisters skipped out the door of their cottage, and Mara began to run, flying down the lane to her family.

"Pansy!" she called. "Lily!"

The girls looked up, squealed, and dropped their schoolbooks to pelt toward her.

"Mara, Mara!"

Drawn by the commotion, Mara's mother came out on the stoop, then yelled for the rest of the family. In moments Mara was engulfed in a flurry of hugs and exclamations and more hugs, right there in the lane outside the cottage.

"Step back, give her room," Mara's mother said, though she still kept her arm about Mara's shoulders. "Oh, heavens, we thought we'd lost you. Where have you been, child? And what is that about your neck?"

Mara lifted her hand. The necklace had traveled unscathed between the worlds. Her siblings stared at it with wide eyes, and her father frowned and leaned forward for a better look.

"I opened a door deep within the Darkwood," she said. "It led to the land of the Dark Elves, called Elfhame, and I had such adventures there."

Her mother shook her head in disbelief, and Pansy and Lily gasped. Her older sister, Seanna, glanced at the ring on Mara's finger.

"Hmph," her father said, though he could hardly say that magic didn't exist, now that she'd returned with the proof of it shining about her neck.

"Come inside, everyone." Mara's mother shooed them toward the door. "Mara can tell us all about it in the privacy of our own kitchen."

"How long was I gone?" Mara glanced at the yellowing leaves of the birch trees.

"Nearly five months," Seanna said. "And yet nothing at all has happened while you were away."

"That's not true." Mara's mother shut the door behind them, then went to fill the kettle with fresh water. "Thom the woodcutter's son got married to the fishmonger's daughter."

Mara blinked. Not that she was sorry to hear it, but clearly his affection for her had been fleeting, if he'd found another girl to marry after just a few months.

"His loss," Pansy said. "Mara's come back a rich woman. What are you going to do now?"

"I'm not sure."

Much as she loved her family, she still did not want to stay forever in Little Hazel—but somehow she could not imagine traveling the world without a tall, stern Dark Elf at her side. That was impossible, though. Bran was in Elfhame, and he could never fit in her world, just as she never had in his.

A great wave of weariness washed over her, and suddenly she wanted nothing more than to sleep. Sleep and forget.

Instead, she ate a bowl of porridge and drank the tea her mother brewed, and recounted her adventures to her family. Every word she spoke made the ache inside her grow. When she got to the part about her role in the prophecy, her sisters exclaimed.

"Never say you married him!" Pansy said. "That dreadful creature? Oh, Mara, how horrible for you."

"It wasn't, truly. The Dark Elves are not beasts, though they might look frightful to us. Prince Brannon always treated me with respect."

I care for you, more than you will ever know. The memory of his words pierced her heart.

She held her breath as the realization crept over her that, just possibly, she'd made a dreadful mistake. She'd been so set on returning home, on all the things she thought she could not bear to live without, that she'd missed what was blooming right beneath her nose. A strange, glowing flower under a sky filled with two moons.

Bran.

"Forgive me," she said to her family. "There is more to tell, but I'm tired beyond words. Once I've rested, I'll finish my tale."

Her mother murmured with concern, and her brother patted her back.

"Don't worry," he said. "If any of those Dark Elves come out of the forest, we'll defend you."

She did not waste her breath arguing that he had it all wrong. Instead, she gave her family a weary smile and headed up the stairs to her long-abandoned bed.

But despite her words, sleep would not come. Every time she closed her eyes, she saw visions of Elfhame: Bran battling the spider creature, Anneth smiling, blue flowers glowing with their own light. Bran again —always Bran, his stern, angular features printed in her memory.

"I could not stay," she whispered into her pillow, and it was true.

She was a stranger, an awkward mortal outsider. Even with Bran's support she would have pined away, yearning for her family, for the world she'd been torn from. But now that she was home, she yearned instead for Elfhame.

No, not quite. She did not long for the land of the Dark Elves, but for one Dark Elf in particular.

Brannonilon Luthinor. Her husband.

No matter how far she traveled in the mortal lands, or what new adventures she experienced, she knew it would never be enough to replace her memories of Elfhame, or of him.

At last sleep overtook her. Her dreams were full of starry flowers and a bone-piercing cold that sapped all her strength, until she lay down beneath the double moons and closed her eyes forever.

THE NEXT DAY she was no less melancholy. At breakfast, she finished recounting her story. When she ended her tale, her mother gave her a curious look, but said nothing.

Going out into the sunlight helped, but only a little. The strange coldness had settled inside her, along with a restless feeling that she'd forgotten something important. That night, as evening fell, Mara found herself looking toward the Darkwood and searching for glowing lights beneath the trees.

Again, she dreamed of searing cold, but this time it was Bran who suffered, his violet eyes leached of color, his skin growing pale as ice.

"Mara," he whispered.

She woke with a start in the early morning darkness, her heart pounding, the ring on her finger hot to the touch. Bran needed her. Somehow she knew it to the depths of her soul.

But how could she possibly reach him?

She had no appetite at breakfast. Her conviction that she must return to Elfhame grew with every passing hour.

At midmorning, once the family had all left, Mara's mother coaxed her out into the herb garden and sat her down amid the rosemary and thyme.

"I don't know what's amiss," her mother said, "but something surely is. Did you bring a wasting sickness with you out of the Darkwood?"

"I don't think so." Mara twisted the blue ring on her finger back and forth. Despite the sunshine, she shivered. "Perhaps I am heartsick, but it is nothing that will harm you."

"Do you love him, then?" Mara's mother gave her a long look. "You know that your father and I have never thought much of those tales of magic and such, but it's clear enough something strange has touched our family. Touched you. If you've fallen in love with a prince from a magical world then I think you must do something about it."

Hearing her mother speak the words out loud, Mara could no longer hide from the truth of it. She had, despite herself, fallen in love with Bran. It had taken her far too long to see it, to admit it. Fear had shadowed her eyes—fear of losing herself in the land of the Dark Elves, of never seeing the human world or her family again.

But now that she had returned, even though the sunlight was a honeyed balm to her soul, her heart would never recover. The mortal world was not enough.

Perhaps Elfhame wasn't either. She didn't know what the answer might be—but she would not find it here, in her family's cottage in Little Hazel, nor in the world beyond.

She would only find it at Bran's side.

"You're right." Mara drew in a deep breath of warm, herb-scented air. It did nothing to dispel the cold creeping through her. "I need to return to Elfhame. I fear something is very wrong, and I must go to Bran." Her husband.

Oh, she'd been a fool to turn her back on him so quickly, refusing to acknowledge what was right in front of her!

"I was afraid of that." Mara's mother shook her head, her face sad. "Did we regain you, only to lose you again so quickly?"

Mara drew in a ragged breath. Once again, her choices were tearing her in two. Yet she finally knew the path she must take.

"I hope not," she said. "But I'm going into the Darkwood tonight. I don't... I don't know if I'll ever be able to come back. But I will try."

"My darling child." Mara's mother leaned forward and enveloped her in a warm embrace. A single hot tear dripped down onto Mara's hand. "If that is what you must do, then we'd best make a fine supper and say a proper farewell. Just in case we never see you again."

CHAPTER 26

Mara's goodbyes to her family were tearful, but at least this time she had a chance to say farewell. They gathered at the door, her father looking stoic, her mother wiping her eyes on her apron.

"Who knows?" Mara said, forcing a lightness into her voice. "I've come out of Elfhame once before. Maybe I can do so again."

Indeed, she hoped so, for it was still true that she did not belong in that land. But Bran needed her—she felt it more strongly with every passing moment, the ring icy upon her finger. She could not remain in the mortal world while he suffered. And perhaps worse. She shivered.

"Be safe," Seanna said, giving her a final embrace.

Sean nodded, and Pansy and Lily would not let go of her arms until their mother bade them sharply to behave.

"Use the gemstones I left you," Mara said. She'd pried them out of the handle of Bran's jeweled dagger, seven in all. "One for each of you, and one left over."

She could not bear to dismantle the necklace, though, and had instead put it back on, the pearls and starry gems cool around her neck.

"Come back to us," Lily said mournfully.

"Hush." Mara's mother folded her arms about her youngest daughter and gave Mara a look. "Best be going now."

"I love you all," Mara said. Her voice caught on the words.

Wrapping her new woolen cloak about her, she hefted her small pack and stepped over the threshold. Her family crowded around the doorway, waving goodbye. The cottage windows shone a warm gold in the gathering twilight, and Mara glanced back over her shoulder.

Was she making yet another mistake?

No. The compass of her heart pointed into the Darkwood and the cold in her bones urged her to hurry. Bran needed her.

At the edge of the trees, three glowing motes bobbed up and down in greeting. Her steps sure, Mara walked under the whispering hemlocks, scarcely needing the glimglows to show her the way. The doorway pulled at her, and in a shorter time than she believed possible, she stood at the edge of the clearing.

Some magic of the forest had shortened the path, and her heart squeezed at the evidence that even the Darkwood knew she was running out of time.

Bran, she thought fiercely, *hold on. Whatever is wrong, I'm coming. I'm almost there.*

The standing stones rose against the stars—the familiar, beloved stars of her own world. She stared at them a moment, then stepped forward. If she never saw them again, then that was the choice she must make. The constellations of Elfhame would be her new sky, as long as Bran was there to share it with her.

The cold granite pillars of the gateway showed no flicker of blue fire, no silvery runes as she stood before them. Her heart squeezed with fear, with hope. There was no key in her pocket, no husband at her side to clasp her hand and link their powers.

Only herself, Mara Geary, a girl who had, all her life, yearned for more. And when she'd gotten it, she'd foolishly thrown it aside.

But deep in her belly was a wellspring of magic. And deep in her heart a shining love. Surely those would be enough to open the door.

Closing her eyes, she reached for the power she knew dwelt inside. It shimmered and surged, just out of reach. She clenched her hand about her ring, and thought fiercely of Bran.

For a moment she thought she touched her magic. She opened her eyes, and a blue spark shot from her hand to sizzle against the nearest stone.

"*Edro,*" she cried aloud, praying she'd recalled the Rune correctly.

The air between the stones wavered briefly, then faded again before she could take a single step. In that moment, though, she'd caught a glimpse of Bran lying in the clearing beneath the double moons, his eyes shut, his skin white as marble, his chest barely moving.

Her heart squeezed tight with the knowledge that he'd been waiting for her. And she had not come in time.

"No!" she yelled. The echo of it reverberated through the trees.

An owl hooted in the distance. The glimglows darted frantically back and forth. The doorway did not open.

On the other side of it, Bran lay dying.

"Please," she said, falling to her knees on the cool moss. She splayed her hand against the carved stone. "Please, open."

The air between the stones remained quiet and still.

Grief cracked her open, hot tears spilling down her cheeks to splash on the ground. She had not realized how much Bran meant to her, and now it was too late.

No.

She refused to give up.

She had not traveled twice through the doorway to let it defeat her a third time.

Slowly, Mara stood. She stared at the stones, letting her determination rise, pushing every willful ounce of herself to the fore. Making a fist, she beat it against the stone.

"Let me in." Her hand kept time with the words.

She said them louder. "Let me in!"

And louder still. "LET ME IN!"

The power sprang up from her belly in whoosh of blue flame. As it flowed from her to engulf the stones, she cried the Rune of Opening once more.

The doorway shimmered. Without hesitating, Mara sprang through.

The warm air of Elfhame wrapped around her as she scrambled

forward, every sense focused on reaching the man who lay cold and still at the edge of the clearing.

"Bran!" She dropped to her knees before him and grabbed his hand. His fingers were limp.

Desperately, she laced their hands together, willing her magic to reach him, willing him to open his eyes.

"Wake up," she said, her throat clogged with emotion.

He did not stir.

"I need you, Prince Brannonilon Luthinor. I am your wife, your woman of the prophecy, and I command you to hear me!"

A faint wind brushed the towering evergreen trees, but still Bran did not move. She placed her other hand on his cheek, as he had so often touched her. His skin was ice.

Her heart was breaking into a thousand pieces.

"Bran," she whispered, leaning over him. "I love you."

She pressed her lips to his, a last kiss for the Hawthorne Prince. A tear dripped down her cheek and landed on his face.

He flinched.

She pulled back, hope stabbing through her.

"I came back to Elfhame for you," she said, "and I refuse to let you go so easily. Now you *must* come back to me."

Warmth kindled in her ring. She glanced down to see it glowing softly, calling an answering light from Bran's.

She kissed him again, and this time felt the faintest flutter of breath against her lips.

"Did you hear me?" she asked. "I love you, you stupidly honorable man. How dare you come out here to die without me?"

He drew in a ragged breath and slowly opened his eyes. "Mara?"

"Yes."

"The Void," he whispered. "It marked me. Sapped me. It is too late."

"It is not," she said fiercely, holding up their linked hands. "Let me in, Bran."

"Too dangerous." He closed his eyes.

She pinched his arm, and he opened them again.

"I'm strong enough," she said. "And if I'm not, I'd rather die here with you than live the rest of my life—in any world—without you."

As she spoke the words, she realized how true they were. Seeing him again had made everything clear. How could she have abandoned him for the mortal realm? She'd been a fool.

Luckily, it was not too late. She hoped.

"You said... you love me." Even in a whisper, she heard the surprise in his voice.

She nodded, giving him a rueful smile. "I do. I love you. It took me far too long to appreciate the man inside this hideous exterior."

He weakly returned her smile, which had been her goal, but still he held his magic back from hers.

"Bran," she said, tightening her grasp. "Please. Trust me."

He let out a long breath, then nodded once. "I do."

He always had, she realized. Every time he'd had the choice, he had laid the power to act at her feet. And somehow, she'd always known that his strength would be there for her.

Now it was time to lend him hers.

"Are you ready?" he asked.

"Always," she said, bracing herself.

Bran opened his wellspring, and she shuddered at the coldness lacing itself through his power. But they had defeated the Void once, and they would do so again.

Squeezing his hand tightly, she fought back, sending waves of heat through their connected rings. The Void resisted, pushing back with emptiness, loneliness, rejection.

She countered with sunlight, family, and love. Boundless love. Love that would cross worlds to be together.

Begone, she thought fiercely to the sliver of the Void that had wormed its way into Bran's heart. *You cannot have him. He is mine. And I love him.*

Blue flame arced into the sky. Bran stiffened and let out a shout, and she felt the last of the coldness burn away.

They had done it. Together, they'd defeated the last of the Void.

The light of their magic faded and she slumped over, her power a mere trickle. Bran reached, his arms encircling her, and pulled her to rest against him. She wrapped herself about him and laid her head on his chest. Beneath her ear his heart beat strongly, and she nearly wept again to hear it.

"Did you know you were wounded, when you sent me back?" she asked softly.

"I suspected. And the moment you went through the doorway, the Void took the opportunity to attack. I collapsed here, and only the faint hope that you might return kept me fighting for my life."

"I was almost too late." Anguish for what might have been rose up in her.

He smoothed her hair. "Sh. You came, and it was enough."

"I'm never leaving you again."

"Nor I you."

They lay there silently for some time, breaths matching, hearts beating in unison. The flowers glowed about them, and high overhead the pale moon chased the bright one across the sky.

"Now what?" Mara finally asked, propping herself up on one elbow so she could see his face. His stern, terrifying, beloved face.

He smiled at her, his violet eyes glowing with promises. "Now, my love, we have worlds to explore."

She smiled back, then inched up to kiss him one more time. Her Hawthorne Prince. Her true love. She did not know how they would fit, mortal and Dark Elf, but whatever path lay before their feet—Darkwood or Erynvorn, court or battlefield, she trusted they would make their way.

Together.

~

HAWTHORNE

ACKNOWLEDGMENTS

A big thanks to my sibs; Colin, Jake, and Alexis, for their patience during our Alaska adventures (and a late-night final-chapter reading), and to Patrick at Northern Alaska Tour Company for driving the bus (literally). I finished this book while crossing the Arctic Circle on the Dalton Highway. Enjoy!

DEDICATION

For everyone persevering and thriving in long-distance relationships (especially B&A), this one goes out to you. Stay strong and true.

PROLOGUE

The twilight halls of the Hawthorne Court were filled with purple shadows and low whispers. The heir, Prince Brannonilon Luthinor, along with his strange mortal bride, had disappeared three palemoons ago, without a word to anyone in the court.

Except his sister, Lady Anneth.

Something was wrong—Anneth knew it deep in her bones. Knew it in the way the soft wind circled through the corridors. Knew it in how the glimglows had dimmed, the court gardens nearly deserted, lit with only a handful of their bobbing, light-filled forms.

Bran would never simply abandon Elfhame. Not after having defeated their ancient enemy, the Void, and making the realm safe for the Dark Elves once more.

As Anneth made her way to the dining hall for luncheon, she heard the whispers of the court, twisting and sibilant through the corridors.

Did you know? His horse returned to the stables, rider-less.

Now that the prophecy has been fulfilled, he ran away rather than face the truth that we are still doomed.

I heard the human murdered him. She destroyed the remains and fled back to her world.

Which was pure nonsense. Anneth knew the mortal girl, Mara

Geary, and knew that the love between her and Bran was unmistakable, no matter how much they both tried to deny it.

But perhaps their stubbornness had been their undoing.

Anneth stepped through the arched doorway to the dining hall, though her appetite had fled. She made her formal curtsey to the head table, where her parents sat, regal and uncaring. At least her mother certainly seemed unconcerned, wearing her usual cold, remote expression. The Hawthorne Lord had a slight furrow in his brow that *might* mean he was worried about his son and heir.

Or it might simply mean his elderberry wine had soured.

Anneth took a seat at a half-empty table. Glowing spheres of blue foxfire hovered overhead, illuminating the brocade tablecloth and platters of food.

Although the lord and lady presided, luncheon at court was an informal affair. Diners were free to summon whatever dish they wished from the kitchens, though most were content to eat the array of delicacies laid out.

She took a slice of moonmelon and some cheese, and poured a small measure of wine into the silver goblet at her place. Though she might not feel hungry, she must eat something. The hazy worry inside her was clearing, leaving a purpose behind.

She knew where Bran had gone. It was her task to attempt to find him. As soon as she finished her lunch—

"I don't understand how some people can eat in the face of this tragedy." A high-pitched voice broke into Anneth's thoughts.

Before she could protest, an ornately dressed lady took the place beside her, glancing at Anneth's plate with smug superiority.

"Lady Mireleth," Anneth said, offering no greeting or welcome.

"For myself, wine and honey is the only thing I can stomach." Mireleth let out a dramatic sigh. "Alas, the prince has abandoned us. That mortal woman he was forced to wed has lured him into her world. Or killed him with her treacherous human ways. Either way, we'll never see him again." She sighed again, then fixed Anneth with her hard, bright stare. "I suppose you're next in line for the Hawthorne Throne, ill-suited as you might be."

The words sent a stab of panic through Anneth. *Her*, inherit the throne? Oh, stars forefend. She understood the line of succession, of course, but had never considered that her brother would not take the throne. Of course he would—he had his prophecy to fulfill.

"Bran will return," she said. "And Mara too—you'll see. They didn't save Elfhame from destruction merely to abandon the realm. Besides, Bran is ever true to his duty."

"His duty." Mireleth sniffed in disapproval. "Better that he'd honored the betrothal bond he made with *me*. Dark Elf blood should not be tainted by associating with mortals. If that human woman never returns, none will miss her. Good riddance, I say. But we need the Hawthorne Prince."

Anneth's fingers tightened on the leaf-carved handle of her fork. Carefully, she set it down so that she would not stab Mireleth in the arm.

"You know as well as I do that your betrothal to Bran was a sham. A ploy, concocted by our fathers to activate the prophecy. And it worked."

Mireleth turned a wounded look on her. "I've loved Brannonilon all my life! I would have married him in an instant. But no—he spurned me for that hideous mortal creature."

There was no reasoning with Mireleth. Though Anneth strongly suspected the lady's "love" was motivated by a fondness for power and the title of Hawthorne Lady, rather than any true affection for Bran.

Anneth took a bite of melon, tasteless on her tongue, and forced herself to patience.

"And now he has deserted us," Mireleth said.

Anneth half expected her to fall into a despairing swoon so that she could be the center of attention, but Mireleth showed remarkable self-restraint, instead settling for yet another melancholy sigh.

"He'll be back soon," Anneth said, infusing her voice with a certainty she did not feel.

"I hope he returns, for all our sakes," Mireleth said. "What good is it to save the Hawthorne Court only to let it fall into disarray?"

Anneth shot a quick glance at her parents at the head table. As long as Calithilon and his unyielding wife ruled, the court would be stable.

But what if Bran never returned?

Anneth swallowed back the panic that tried to rise, hot and sickening, in her throat.

Whatever had happened, she could sit idle no longer. As soon as luncheon ended, she would pack a traveling bag, fetch supplies from the kitchen, and go out in search of her brother.

Unlike him, she would leave a note, telling her family where she was bound: a place where the edges of the mortal world and Elfhame brushed up against one another, full of magic and dangerous mystery. A place her people called Erynvorn.

The Darkwood.

CHAPTER 1

Prince Brannonilon Luthinor, heir to the Hawthorne throne, husband of the mortal woman Mara Geary, lay beneath the sheltering branches of an enormous cedar tree, his wife in his arms. Overhead, the palemoon was a bitten silver coin tossed against the dark. Stars flared in the sky, unthreatened by that half-light.

Exhaustion still pulled at him, tugging him down toward the blackness of sleep, but he fought it. Mara dreamed, and he would watch over her. A poor husband he would be indeed, to fall into slumber and let some enemy take them unawares.

Not that he trusted himself to be a particularly fine husband. He knew almost nothing of human ways and customs, and the strange girl sleeping in the shelter of his embrace was equal parts fascinating and confusing to him.

He let out a low, weary exhalation, echoed by the rustle of the wind through the feathery cedar branches. The prophecy was fulfilled, the great enemy of Elfhame defeated, and he felt like a boat unmoored, abandoned by captain and crew and left at the mercy of currents he could no longer chart.

Mara stirred sleepily, her fingers twined in the long, dark strands of his hair.

"Hush, love." He patted her shoulder lightly. "All is well. You are safe."

Even though his magic might be drained, his sharp sword was at the ready to defend her.

"Bran?" Her voice was hoarse with sleep.

"I am here."

Her grip on him tightened. "I thought I'd lost you forever."

"No, my heart. You saved me."

Barely. He had walked close enough to death to see his own reflection in the gray shadows of the Beyond.

"Don't ever go away again." There was an endearing fierceness in her voice.

"You must promise the same."

She sighed, warm against his neck. "I won't insist you send me away again, if that's what you mean. If I ever return to the mortal world, you must come with me."

He blinked at the palemoon through the lacework of branches. Leave Elfhame? The thought was cold and strange. He'd lived his entire life in service to the prophecy that demanded he save his land. The realm had been the heart of him for as long as he could remember.

"Why would I leave Elfhame?"

She shrugged, a curiously mortal gesture, felt more than seen. "You never know what will happen."

He gave a hollow laugh. "Once, I always knew. It was simply a matter of reaching that point."

"Poor love." She lifted her hand to cup his cheek. "It must be hard, now that your prophecy has been fulfilled."

It was so like her, to feel sympathy for him when *she* was the one trapped once more in his realm. A tremor of worry ran through him. A scant few moons ago, Mara had risked everything in order to return to her home world. Could she ever be happy here? Could she ever be happy with *him*?

He feared he knew the answer, and it was not kind.

"What will become of us?" he asked.

She slowly sat up and ran her fingers through her tousled brown hair.

"I don't know. I suppose you'll teach me more about the magic I carry, and the Hawthorne Court, and how to be a proper Dark Elf lady."

"You could never be one of them," he said, then cursed as he felt her stiffen beside him. He rose to his knees and placed his hands on her shoulders. "No, Mara, I did not mean that cruelly."

"You Dark Elves are ever cruel," she said, a bite in her voice, though he hoped she did not mean it. "In the fables we humans tell, it is part of your nature."

"Do you truly believe that?" He touched her face, careful to keep his claws sheathed. "I meant only that you are too kind and brave and strong to be a simpering court lady."

She stared at him a moment, her human features strange and lovely, lit by the soft purple glow of nearby dusk lilies. The hurt in her eyes faded, and a rueful smile crossed her face.

"And short-tempered and outspoken, too. You forgot to add those most admirable qualities of mine to your list."

She could make him smile as no other could. He gathered her against him, just to marvel at the feel of her in his arms. He dropped a kiss into her hair, breathing deeply of the smell of her: moss and flowers and joy.

"You know those attributes are prized beyond compare," he said.

"I'm lucky to have a moon-crazed Dark Elf for a husband, who believes such things." Her voice held laughter.

The moment was broken by the sound of a scream.

In an instant, Bran was on his feet, sword in his hand. His attempt to summon light resulted in a sickly, gaseous shimmer in the air, and even that much effort left him nauseated.

Then Mara stood and slipped her arm about his waist, and the deep power of her magical wellspring poured into him. He laid his arm across her shoulders and accepted the gift. The light steadied, and he cocked his head, listening.

"What is it?" Mara glanced at the tall cedar trees surrounding them. "Is someone in trouble? That sounded like a Dark Elf."

"Perhaps. Or perhaps it is another trap set by the Void."

"I don't think the Void is clever enough for that." She looked up at him, the reflection of their sphere of light sparking twin stars in her eyes. “It nearly succeeded in killing you—and would have, if I hadn’t returned. Why bother with more traps?”

He cocked up one shoulder and did not answer. Who knew the ways of the enemy? He had almost lost his life underestimating it. He would not make that mistake again.

Regardless, they must investigate. He drew on more of Mara’s magic, careful not to drain her overmuch, and sent a questing tendril into the dusky air.

It met a familiar energy, and he pulled in a quick breath. If he was not mistaken, his sister was roaming about Erynvorn—and she was in danger.

“Come, quickly.” He broke into a fast stride. Nearly a run, but if he sprinted away, he would leave Mara behind, and that, he refused to do.

“What? Where?” she asked, already breathing heavily as she followed his weaving path through the forest.

He could hear the edge of annoyance in her voice, but had neither the breath nor energy to answer. The compass in his mind was fixed at a bright point ahead, and the closer they drew, the more certain he was that Anneth was ahead. And engaged in some kind of battle.

Shadows take it, she was no battle mage. He prayed to the absent brightmoon that she still had the dagger he’d insisted she learn to use.

A spark of pain jabbed through him, and he winced at the evidence that his sister had been injured.

Mara drew in a sharp breath. She must have felt the same jolt through the magical bond they shared.

“Who?” she asked.

“Anneth.”

“Then hurry, Bran. Run!” He could not abandon his heart, his bride. But how could he leave his sister to face an enemy alone?

Anneth screamed again.

“Here.” Bran thrust Mara’s kitchen knife at her—her wedding gift to him, but he could not leave her unarmed.

She took it, then pushed him forward. “Go!”

Bran turned and ran, fleet-footed over the soft mosses. He must reach Anneth in time—and trust that Mara would come to no harm, and that she could fend for herself in her indomitable mortal way.

Poor husband, poor husband, his footsteps seemed to mock him.

Resolutely, he ignored them and sped through the silver-washed forest, fear and worry nearly breaking him in two.

CHAPTER 2

It was ridiculously easy to sneak out of the Hawthorne Court.

Anneth left the note concerning her whereabouts carefully folded on the embossed silver table in her quarters, then slipped out to the stables. She took one of the prepared travel packs kept ready for the scouts, checking to make sure there were supplies enough for several moons' worth of travel. Satisfied, she mounted on her mare, Silma, and rode out across the long-grassed meadows. Behind her, the elegant buildings of the Hawthorne Court shone faintly beneath the half-sphere of the palemoon.

After several turns of travel, she stopped and made camp, careful to cast protective wards about the small clearing. The night passed uneventfully, and the next moon, she approached the shadowy mass of Erynvorn. The forest reached up to cover the sky, and a shiver went through her. Her brother and Mara had entered that place moons ago—and never returned. She leaned back, and her mount halted obediently.

Despite Anneth's brave hopes to the contrary, what if Bran and Mara had, in fact, come to a dreadful end? She did not think she could bear to discover their broken bodies, or stare into their empty eyes. And yet, there was no one else willing to discover the truth of what had become of the Hawthorne Prince and his bride.

The huge, dark trees closed over her head, as though she'd plunged into a pool full of blackest night. Their branches whispered, either stirred by the wind or remarking upon her presence. Pine, cedar, hemlock—the scent of the forest imbued the air with a wild flavor.

As her vision adjusted to the dusky light, the flowers growing within Erynvorn brightened. Glowing white petals starred the mossy forest floor, and the nodding bells of *qille* shed violet light where they grew in clusters.

Even better, nearly a dozen glimglows flitted between the tall columns of the tree trunks. They darted to her in a flurry of sparks, weaving light-trailed patterns in the air, and came to hover just above her head. If she squinted, she could see the small, winged forms inside each ball of light.

"Hello," she said softly. "Have you seen my brother?"

To her immense relief, they seemed to understand her question. At least, she hoped their sudden whirl and rush into the forest meant they knew where to lead her.

General opinion was that the glimglows were not particularly intelligent, but Anneth had found that, if spoken to, they did respond. Not always in ways that made sense, however. She urged Silma forward and hoped that, in this case, the glimglows would not lead her astray.

They bobbed ahead, some darting off now and then, until only four remained. Those moved steadily forward, and Anneth followed, guiding her mount through the hushed and dim ranks of the trees. Her mare's steps were silent, muffled by the carpet of needle-strewn moss. The only sounds were the whisper of the wind high overhead and an occasional chiming—the noise of the glasslike stalks of *linque* rubbing together.

A sudden coldness moved through the air. The glimglows halted, then winked out as if extinguished. The smell of burnt iron scorched Anneth's nostrils, and she glanced, wide-eyed, at the shadows surrounding her.

Heart pounding, she drew the dagger at her belt.

"Who's there?" she asked. Her voice trembled on the words.

With a sudden rush, a dark form lunged at her—red eyes glowing malevolently, savage teeth bared. A gyrewolf!

Anneth screamed and kicked Silma into motion. The mare leaped forward. Snarling, the wolf gave chase.

Breath ragged in her throat, Anneth tried to guide her mount through the trees, but this was no wide road or grassland where they could run flat-out. The snarls of the gyrewolf sounded just behind them, and panic clouded her senses.

Silma stumbled, and the wolf sprang. Its sharp claws raked Anneth's back, and, with another scream, she tumbled to the ground.

Trying to ignore the pain, she jumped to her feet and faced the gyrewolf. It opened its jaws, as if laughing at her. Then it gathered its haunches and sprang.

"No!" she yelled, twisting to the side.

She thrust her dagger at the beast, wishing desperately she was better prepared—fully trained in weapons or magic to confront such a deadly foe. But no one had expected Princess Anneth to go into the forest unaccompanied, let alone face a gyrewolf.

It growled, low in its throat, and she saw her death reflected in its red eyes.

Then, as if from nowhere, a gleaming silver sword flashed out of the darkness, slashing the wolf across the flank.

With a screech of pain, the beast turned to meet its new foe.

"Bran!" Anneth cried, gratitude and love rushing hotly through her at the sight of her brother wielding the blade.

He was alive, thank the double moons. And there was none she would trust more to defeat the deadly beast.

"Get back," he said, his black hair flying as he pivoted away from the gyrewolf's attack.

She did, scurrying away to where Silma stood, nostrils flaring. Leaning for comfort against her mount's warm bulk, Anneth gritted her teeth against the pain in her back and tried to concentrate on the fight.

Something was wrong with Bran. His skin held a grayish hue, and despite being the best battle mage among the Dark Elves, he did not cast a single spell.

He slashed at the wolf, nimbly twisting away from its attacks, but his movements seemed weighted with weariness. Fear crawled through Anneth again. She must help.

Gripping her dagger tightly, she crept forward. The smell of the gyrewolf's blood hung rank in the air, its snarls interspersed with Bran's grunts as he tried to land a killing blow. Never had she seen her brother struggle so to dispatch an enemy.

Hoping the wolf was too focused on Bran to notice her approach, Anneth rushed forward and sank her dagger into the creature's back.

It let out a howl and whipped around to face her, adding distraction enough. With a mighty, two-handed blow, Bran cleaved through the gyrewolf's spine. It collapsed in a heap of blood-matted fur, the red light fading from its eyes.

Anneth drew in a shaky breath. The beast looked much smaller, now that it was dead.

"Are you unharmed?" Bran asked.

"No—it clawed my back. But what of you? And Mara?" A horrible thought stabbed through Anneth. "Did she truly leave you, and go back to her own world?"

It would explain why he looked barely better than a corpse. But she could not believe that, in the end, Mara would do such a thing.

Although—everything Anneth knew of humans was taken from books, and the few moons she'd spent in Mara's company. Perhaps Bran's mortal bride had, indeed, abandoned him.

His face softened. "No—she is here in the Erynvorn. I must go find her. If one of these Void-spawned creatures is about, there might be others."

With a look of distaste, he toed the corpse of the gyrewolf. Then, with two efficient swipes, he cleaned the blood from his sword on an unsullied patch of its hide.

The sound of something rustling through the forest made them both look up. Anneth wrenched her dagger out of the dead wolf and went to stand beside Bran. Her back burned, but she would face this new threat, undaunted.

"Bran?"

A smile broke over his face. "Mara. We are here."

He strode forward to meet his wife, and a moment later, she was in his arms. Even from where she stood, Anneth could feel the intensity of emotion swirling between them.

Then Mara peeked around his tall form and saw her.

"Anneth, thank goodness," she said. "We heard you scream and feared the worst."

"Hello, Mara." Anneth stepped forward to greet her, then winced as her back protested.

"But you're hurt!" Mara pushed out of Bran's embrace. "Where? What can we do?"

"The wolf caught my back," Anneth said. "It's not a grievous injury." At least, she hoped not.

"Turn around," Bran said sternly.

He lifted her cloak aside, and she heard Mara suck in a breath.

"Is it terrible?" Anneth asked, her heart pounding.

"No." Bran gently let the cloak fall back into place. "But you need tending."

"You can't heal her?" Mara asked, glancing up at Bran.

"I have not that skill," he said. "We must return to the Hawthorne Court."

Mara nodded, though Anneth could see the reluctance in her eyes. So far, the court had not treated the mortal girl kindly.

"You both need seeing to," Mara said. "The sooner, the better."

With Bran's help, Anneth mounted her horse and gratefully patted Silma's neck. The journey back would be easier than if she had to make it on her own two stumbling feet.

They made a slow, sorry procession through the Erynvorn. Bran kept his sword at the ready, and Mara kept glancing at him with a worried expression.

"What happened to you?" Anneth asked her brother. She swayed, fighting against the pain and weariness threatening to engulf her.

"The Void," he said shortly. "It seems, despite defeating our ancient enemy, they are not fully vanquished from our world."

"The gyrewolf," Anneth said.

"Yes." His voice was grim. "And I fear that other Void-spawned creatures remain in Elfhame, despite closing the rift between our worlds."

"There might be some shards, too," Mara said, giving her husband a troubled look. "Like the one that lodged in you."

Sudden despair washed over Anneth. "But we won the war."

"The Void is cunning," Bran said. "It will do anything to gain a foothold and spread into the realm. I must gather a band of warriors to root out any remaining traces."

"Not until you've regained your strength," Mara said sternly.

Bran made no reply—which meant he would pay no heed to her words. Anneth shook her head slightly. Her brother was ever stubborn, sometimes to the point of stupidity.

"Don't be a fool," Mara said, echoing Anneth's thoughts. "Besides, I need your help at court."

"Anneth can help you."

"She has injuries to recover from, too," Mara pointed out. "When you *both* are back to full strength, then you can abandon me, husband. Not before."

A faint smile pulled the corners of Bran's lips. "Very well, wife."

Anneth's brows rose. Very few people could make Bran listen. This mortal woman was a good match for him—even if the rest of the Hawthorne Court believed otherwise.

CHAPTER 3

Despite Mara's worry over her injured companions, she was sorry when they stepped from the shelter of the Darkwood. Although the realm of Elfhame was magical, the forest was particularly so, the mysterious shadows beneath the towering trees countered by the ethereal radiance of the flowers. And the glimglows, who had already proven themselves her allies.

Several of them floated overhead, their bobbing lights a small comfort against the ever-present night. She glanced over her shoulder into the lush darkness of the forest, her chest tightening with loss.

The gateway home is still there, she reminded herself—although she'd promised to remain with Bran in Elfhame.

Indeed, her heart demanded no less.

But still, it wasn't easy to imagine leaving her world behind forever. She missed her family, and the solid footing of knowing where she stood with everyone in the village of Little Hazel. And, perhaps most of all, she missed the sun.

After several turns, they made camp, all three of them teetering on the edge of exhaustion. Grateful for Anneth's supplies, they ate a hasty dinner and slept, then continued traveling the next day. Or what passed for day in Elfhame.

She glanced up at the palemoon riding low in the star-speckled sky. It was akin to the moon she knew in the human world, rising daily to mark the passage of time. At least Elfhame had the brightmoon, as well, to shed more light over the land. Now that she'd agreed to dwell in this realm, she must learn the cycles of the two moons, which did not move in tandem.

The motion of the moons, however, was the least of her worries.

Ahead lay the treacherous halls of the Hawthorne Court, which, she suspected, harbored more than one enemy. She scanned the rolling hills covered with purple grass, relieved to find no sight of the graceful palace. Yet.

"The palemoon sets," Bran said, a hint of strain in his voice. "We must make haste."

She gave him a sharp look, but bit her tongue. Although part of her wanted to plead her own mortal weakness and call a halt to rest, the sooner they arrived, the sooner Bran and Anneth could be tended to.

"Yes," Anneth said wearily. "Bran, take Silma and ride ahead—"

"I won't leave you." He gave her a stern look. "And you are in no condition to walk."

She gave him a crooked smile. "I thought you could summon help, while Mara and I rested."

"It's a good plan," Mara said. "You could come back with horses, maybe a litter for your sister." A thought occurred to her. "What happened to Fuin?"

She was a little embarrassed she hadn't remembered his beloved horse until that moment. Though, in her defense, all her attention had been on Bran, and then Anneth.

"He returned to the stables," Bran said, a thread of tension in his voice. "At least, that is my hope."

Neither of them voiced the very real possibility that the horse had been killed by Void creatures.

"In any case, we will stay together." Bran shot his sister a look. "All of us."

Anneth made an exasperated noise and toed the side of her mount. The horse increased its pace, and Mara forced herself to keep up, although the breath burned in her chest. Dratted Dark Elves and their long legs.

She shot a look at her husband, and found he was watching her, his black eyes hooded.

"I'm perfectly fine," she said, giving him a reassuring smile and ignoring the stitch developing in her side.

"Take care," he said, his voice almost a growl. "I'll carry you."

"I know." She found it touching, how solicitous he was of her—and a trifle annoying, that he did not take his own weakness seriously enough.

Just when she thought she might have to accept his offer, however unwise, they crested a rise and the shining spires of the Hawthorne Palace came into view. The arched doorways were framed by vines bearing white flowers, and even at this distance, their sweet scent reached her nose. Balls of foxfire illuminated the gardens and floated above the main gates. In spite of her worries, Mara let out a sigh at the beauty of the sight.

"Only a little further," Anneth said, though it sounded as if she was encouraging herself more than the others.

Bran gave a nod and lengthened his stride. Luckily, it was downhill, and Mara managed a half-trot to keep pace. The last thing she wanted was to trail behind like a fool as they entered the court.

When they reached the outer walls, however, Bran halted.

"Let us catch our breaths," he said.

Meaning her, of course, but Mara didn't have the energy to argue. In truth, she could use a moment to gather herself before stepping into the palace.

"Everyone will be pleased to see you," Anneth said, looking from her brother to Mara. "The rumors concerning your absence have been fierce."

"Glad to see Bran, you mean," Mara said. She had no illusions about her welcome at court.

"Well, *I'm* glad you're back," Anneth said staunchly.

"Thank you." Mara gave her a wry smile. "It's good to have at least one ally."

"And what am I?" Bran asked, sounding slightly offended.

"My husband, of course." Although in name only. Mara swallowed her rising apprehension about sharing living quarters with Bran. One thing at a time.

"Ready to go in?" He looked at her, his dark gaze intense.

"Yes." Mara straightened her shoulders. As ready as she'd ever be.

He sheathed his sword and led the way. Not to the front gates, she was glad to note, but to a smaller door facing the gardens. No matter which entrance he chose, however, she knew that word of his return would spread quickly.

The guards at the arched doorway stared a moment as Bran stepped forward.

"Your Highness?" one asked, a note of surprise in his voice.

Mara wondered what the nature of the court rumors had been. Judging by the man's reaction, they hadn't expected Bran to return at all. Worry seeped through her. Did the Dark Elves think she had stolen him away into her world? Or, worse yet, done him harm?

Neither thought was very comforting. Obviously, the denizens of Elfhame distrusted her—and all humans. It was a wonder Anneth had taken Mara under her wing at their first meeting.

"Jedry." Bran fixed the guard with a cool look. "Take Lady Anneth's horse to the stables and see to his care."

"Of course, milord." The man went to stand beside the gray mare, giving Bran room to assist his sister from the saddle.

As Bran set Anneth down, she winced. His expression hardening, he gestured to the other guard.

"Fetch Avantor at once," Bran said. "Tell him my sister is in need of healing. We will be in her rooms."

Mara opened her mouth to add that Bran, too, needed mending, but changed her mind at his grim expression. She would inform Avantor himself, after he'd seen to Anneth.

"And Jedry..." Bran straightened, as if bracing himself for the answer. "Is Fuin in the stables?"

"Aye, my lord," the guard said. "He returned two moons ago."

"Good." There was no hint of relief in Bran's voice, but Mara could see the tension ease in his shoulders.

"I will find the healer," the other guard said. He made Bran a bow, then hurried through the doorway into the blue-lit shadows of the corridor beyond.

They followed much more slowly. Mara could see Anneth clenching her jaw, and moved to offer her arm in support.

"Thank you," Anneth said, accepting the help.

Bran stepped up to her other side, and, between him and Mara, they managed to keep Anneth on her feet. With the wave of a hand, Bran summoned a globe of foxfire to bob above their heads.

The hallway made a T, and they turned right. A pair of elegantly garbed ladies occupied that corridor and, seeing Bran and Anneth, gasped. They curtsied to the royal siblings, their ornate jewelry and silken skirts gleaming under the light.

Mara could not help but notice that their narrow-eyed stares lingered on her. The ladies' whispers followed them down the hall.

"So much for quietly slipping back to my rooms," Anneth said as they reached the arched doorway to her suite. "Lady Niona is one of the worst gossips in the palace."

"The guards will have spread the word, too," Bran said, waving them to precede him into Anneth's parlor. "We could not have remained unseen. You know that."

"Yes." Anneth sighed. "But I don't particularly want to face our parents just yet."

Lips tight, Bran nodded. "They will give you time to recover. I'll see to it. Now, sit."

Anneth moved to one of the cushioned, backless chairs and slowly sank down upon it, her face drawn.

"What about you?" Mara shot Bran a look where he stood, arms folded, near the door. "At least sit down."

From her previous encounters with the Hawthorne Lord and his lady, she knew that they were rigid and demanding. And that Bran's mother, in particular, would be most displeased to discover Mara's continued presence in Elfhame.

"I must speak with them," he said.

"But surely not right away?" She wanted to go and wrap her arms about him, but the closeness they'd felt in the forest had faded the nearer they came to the Hawthorne Court.

Bran now had a stiffness about him, and she wondered if he regretted her return to Elfhame. She trusted their bond, but her presence represented so many complications. Not to mention that she was a constant reminder of the prophecy he'd fulfilled—and the fact that now he had no clear path to follow.

"My father must know that Void creatures still roam our realm," Bran said. "Precautions must be taken, with all haste."

Reluctantly, Mara nodded. His words made sense, though she did not like to see him go.

"Stay here with Anneth," he said to her. "I'll return as soon as I am able."

"Wait for Avantor, at least," his sister said. "Really, Bran. You know how difficult our parents can be. You'd do your cause—and Mara—the most good by meeting them with strength, rather than barely being able to stand."

He looked at Mara, something softening in his expression, and unfolded his arms. She did go to him then, wrapping her arms about his lean waist and letting her head rest against his chest.

"I am sorry, *indis*." His low voice vibrated beneath her cheek, and his long fingers stroked her hair. "I would wish your life here to be one of ease and comfort."

"That wouldn't be very exciting, though," she said. Although at the moment she wouldn't mind a bit of ease and comfort. For all of them.

A knock came at the door. "It's Avantor," the healer called.

"Come," Anneth said.

Mara stepped back from Bran as the healer entered. She had met Avantor before, when she first came to Elfhame, and recognized his lean features. A strand of silver wove through his hair, plaited and looped through the darker braids.

"Bran!" Avantor paused a moment, the surprise in his face quickly changing to concern. "You are unwell."

Bran shook his head and gestured to Anneth. "My sister is more injured than I. Look to her, while I attend to other business."

"Wait," Mara said, glancing at the healer. "Is Bran strong enough to go running off?"

"I am not some truant child—" her husband began, but Avantor held up his hand.

He frowned at Bran. "You are not well, either."

Bran made a sharp movement with one hand, and Mara glimpsed the points of his claws. "I am well enough."

"Let me at least sing a small healing upon you," Avantor said. "The moment your errands are finished, I expect to tend to you. Understood?"

"Is that an order?" Bran's voice was cool, but there was a glint of humor in his eyes.

"Yes, it is," the healer said. "Now, stand still."

He lifted his hands, palms facing Bran, and began humming. Mara watched, trying to sense Avantor's magic with her own newly awakened wellspring, but could detect little more than a faint glow about the healer. When he had finished, he gave Bran a serious look.

"Do not neglect to send for me," he said. "Whatever the nature of your injury, it is soul-deep. What I've done just now is only temporary."

Soul-deep. Mara shivered. Surely they had rooted out the Void fragment that had lodged in Bran. She could not bear to lose him again.

"I'll make sure to summon you," she said to Avantor.

The elf glanced at her. "Good."

He moved to where Anneth sat, and Bran reached for Mara's hand.

"Stay here," he said. "I know my sister will be glad of your company. I'll fetch you when I've finished speaking with my parents."

"I'll be waiting," she said. She was relieved to see that Avantor's spell had improved the papery texture of his skin and restored some of the spark to his eyes.

He squeezed her hand, then turned and strode out the ornately carved door.

She stood there a long moment, staring blindly at the carvings: sickle moons, and some flower she did not recognize. Hope and worry roiled through her. She'd made the right choice to return to Elfhame, for Bran would have died without her. But truly, she was a stranger here. An unwelcome one.

Oh, stop. She gave herself a shake and touched the violet ring encircling the middle finger of her right hand. Her wedding band. This was her choice, and she was not without allies. She was the woman of the prophecy, after all—the one who had helped turn the tide of battle and defeat the Void.

If the Dark Elves of the Hawthorne Court tried to treat her poorly, well, she would remind of them of the fact that, but for her, their realm would no longer exist. Mortal she might be, but she'd faced danger unflinchingly, and would do so again.

Chin high, she turned to see if there was anything she might do to help Avantor or comfort Anneth.

CHAPTER 4

Whispers followed Bran as he stalked through the halls. Formally garbed courtiers watched him, wide-eyed, as he passed. He paid them no heed. Whatever they chose to believe about his absence, and Mara's, both of them had both returned to the Hawthorne Court and all gossip could be put to rest.

Too soon, he reached the wing of the palace where his parents resided. The guard minding the hallway bowed to Bran and stepped aside to let him pass.

"Thank you, Sindor," Bran said. As commander of the Dark Elf forces of Hawthorne, he knew the names of all his soldiers, down to the lowliest trainee. "Is my father in his library?"

"I believe so, my lord."

With a nod of thanks, Bran strode down the corridor. Foxfire spheres bobbed at intervals, casting their cool light into the shadows. At the ebony doors of Lord Calithilon's library, he paused to take a breath. If he was fortunate, his father would be within. And alone. Despite the renewed strength Avantor had lent him, Bran had no taste for dealing with his mother, who had never held him in any particular favor.

He rapped at the door. "It's Bran."

"Enter," his father said.

Bran pushed open the door, then paused on the threshold. His mother, Lady Tinnueth, was seated across from her husband, two glasses of elderberry wine on the table between them. Starlight sifted in from the large window framing his parents, illuminating Lord Calithilon's haughty features and gilding his mother's silver hair.

"Don't stand there gawking, Brannonilon," Lady Tinnueth said. "It's most unbecoming behavior in a prince."

Schooling his features to register nothing of his feelings, Bran stepped into the room and made his parents a graceful bow.

"I'd heard you were back in the palace." His father rose. "Do you care to explain your absence?"

Bran hesitated a moment. He didn't want either of his parents to know that Mara had returned, briefly, to the human world, and then—impossibly—opened the gateway back to Elfhame.

"I felt a stirring of the Void within the Erynvorn," he said. True enough.

"So you went to investigate, by yourself?" Lord Calithilon raised one dark brow. "Unwise, at the very least."

"I was not alone," Bran said stiffly.

"Ah yes, the mortal girl." Lady Tinnueth's voice was cold. "I suppose it's too much to hope that she perished along the way."

He clenched his jaw, refusing to give her the angry response she sought. "I'm pleased to say that my wife is quite well."

"As to that..." His father waved to an empty chair, then moved to the sideboard to fetch another goblet. "Do join us for a cup of wine."

It would be the height of rudeness to refuse, and Bran needed his father's goodwill to offset his mother's enmity. Despite his reluctance, he took the proffered seat and accepted the goblet his father handed him.

"I must inform you both of a continuing danger," Bran said. "Creatures of the Void still roam our land. It's imperative that we form a company of warriors at the earliest—"

"Did you not close the rifts the Void had opened?" His mother leaned forward, a sharp gleam in her violet eyes. "Did you not beat back their assault upon our court, and save all Elfhame from invasion?"

With effort, Bran kept his claws sheathed. "I did. But there is still—"

"Then the prophecy of your birth has been fulfilled," she said. "Don't you agree?"

Giving himself time to regain his temper, Bran took a sip of the wine. There was something in his mother's expression he greatly distrusted. Yet what she said was true.

"The Void is not entirely vanquished from our world." He set down his goblet, the tart taste lingering in his mouth.

Lady Tinnueth waved a hand, the tips of her claws just visible. "I've no doubt you will manage to dispatch the creatures."

"Yes." His father gave him a pointed smile. "It should be easy, compared to the battle we waged for the Hawthorne Court. And the other courts will lend their assistance, of course—this threat concerns us all."

"Then I have your permission to form a coalition of warriors?" Bran gathered himself to rise. The sooner he was out from under Lady Tinnueth's scathing stare, the better.

"No need to be hasty," his father said. "Finish your wine."

Reluctantly, Bran remained in his chair and braced himself for whatever his father was about to say. He hadn't grown up in the Hawthorne Court without developing a highly attuned sense for trouble headed his way.

"I agree with your estimable mother," Lord Calithilon continued. "The prophecy foretold at your birth has been fulfilled. Despite the negligible cleanup that remains."

Bran bit his tongue. Voidspawn were never *negligible* to deal with, and it remained to be seen how many of the creatures still roamed Elfhame. But that was a topic better taken up with his warriors and battle mages. As soon as possible.

"What is your point?" He did not bother to hide his impatience.

"Why, that your marriage to the mortal can now be dissolved," Lady Tinnueth said, her voice like a honeyed blade. "Her purpose here has been served. Send her back through the gateway, and renew your promise to Lady Mireleth."

His mouth twisted. Of course—his mother would do anything to remove Mara and put the poisonous Mireleth in her place. He wondered what promises Mireleth's parents had made to the Hawthorne Lord and Lady in exchange for the sham betrothal.

A betrothal that, however unwillingly, he had agreed to. By the double moons, he'd been a fool to do so.

"It is the best course," his father added.

"It is the *only* course." Lady Tinnueth's eyes were as hard as the purple-hued marble columns gracing the room. "We no longer need that human abomination at court."

It was no secret that she regarded mortal blood as tainted, but Bran was taken aback by the viciousness of her words.

"No." He pushed his goblet away and stood. "I have wed Mara, and I stand by those vows. I'll hear no more of this. Good day."

He bowed curtly, then stalked to the door.

"We are not finished with the matter," his mother called after him. "The mortal does not belong here. You will come to see it, soon enough."

He closed the thick ebony wood on her words, and wished he could block them from his mind as effectively. For a part of him feared that Lady Tinnueth was right. Mara was out of place in the Hawthorne Court—and out of time as well. The longer she stayed in Elfhame, the more years would slip past in the mortal world.

At some point, even if she wanted to return, it would be far too late. Everyone she loved would have turned to dust, and she would be alone in her world. As she was alone now, in Elfhame.

Not alone, he reminded himself fiercely. Mara had him, no matter how flawed a mate he might be. Anneth would stand by her as well, he was certain. And there were others, who had seen her bravery upon the field of battle, who admired her calm strength. She was not without allies.

But would they be enough to shield her from the Hawthorne Lady's hatred?

CHAPTER 5

As Mara hovered discreetly in the background, Avantor tended to Anneth's wounds. She lay facedown upon her bed, her back bared. The bloody scores of the gyrewolf's claw marks looked raw, but the healer pronounced the injury, while painful, not grievous.

He held his hands over her. This time, instead of humming, he began to sing; a liquid, soothing melody. Pale light radiated from his palms. To Mara's amazement, Anneth's skin began to knit, though the gouges did not heal entirely.

"There should be no scarring," the healer said, giving Anneth a long look. "Provided you rest appropriately."

She turned her head and gave him a faint smile. "Unlike my brother, I'm sensible about such things. Though if you want Bran to rest, you'll have to chain him to his bed."

Avantor smiled ruefully. "He takes his duties seriously."

"Someone has to," Mara said. "The remaining Void creatures must be dealt with. Who knows who else they might attack, and what damage they'll do?"

From what she knew of his parents, she doubted the Hawthorne Lord and Lady would spring into action. Despite the recent battles against the Void, the elder Dark Elves did not seem to act particularly quickly.

Avantor glanced at her, his expression troubled. "It is worrisome, indeed. Nonetheless, our commander is in no condition to rush out and hunt the Voidspawn down. Please make him see sense until he's regained his strength."

"I'm not sure how much sway I have over Bran," she said. The powerful Dark Elf commander was not so easily handled.

Anneth let out a quiet snort. "He is your husband. You have more power than you think."

Maybe. But Bran had kept his promise to send her back to the mortal world. There were no more debts or obligations between them.

Only a marriage that was so new, she did not know if it would survive the Hawthorne Court's frosty disapproval.

"I'll try," she told Avantor. It was the best she could do.

The door swung open and Bran stepped inside. He looked worse than when he had left, his eyes full of shadows, his expression grim. He glanced at Mara, then away, his attention focusing on where his sister lay.

"How are you?" he asked, moving to Anneth's side.

"Well enough," she said. "Avantor says I'll heal completely, as long as I rest."

The healer looked Bran up and down. "I must recommend the same course for you. What happened while you were gone from the court, to drain you so?"

Bran flexed his hands, his claws bared for a moment, then re-sheathed, though with slow reluctance.

"In the final battle, the Void managed to slip a fragment of its darkness into me," he said. "It waited until I was weakened, then struck, sapping my life force. I would have died, but for Mara."

Anneth regarded him, eyes wide. Then she shot Mara a glance, as if to say that Bran owed her a great debt.

He did not, of course. Mara's insistence on returning to her own world had weakened his power to the point the Void could attack. Opening the gateway had taken almost all his strength. It was because of her that he'd been alone in the Darkwood and far from help when the darkness struck.

Avantor frowned. "You know as well as I that complete rest is the only way to refill a wellspring nearly drained dry."

"I have no time." Bran swung around and paced the length of Anneth's bedroom. "While I take to my bed, who else will be mauled and killed by the creatures? I cannot let that happen."

"Bran." Mara stepped forward and set her hand on his arm. The muscles were corded, as hard as steel. "Surely a warrior party will not be ready to set out immediately? Can't you let the other courts know to keep watch? Maybe even organize their own troops?"

She did not see why it all should fall on Bran's shoulders. True, he'd carried the destiny of his realm his whole life, but hadn't he paid enough price?

"Listen to your wife," Anneth said, her voice partially muffled by her pillow. "It's high time the other courts stepped up to face their own battles. Elfhame has relied on you long enough."

"Perhaps." Bran sounded far from convinced.

"Take a few days, at least," Mara said.

"At the *very* least," Avantor added. "Indeed, you should be resting right now. As should Anneth." He gestured Bran and Mara toward the door.

Bran hesitated at the threshold and glanced at his sister's prone form.

"Don't worry," the healer said. "A sound sleep, and she will be much restored. Now, go."

Bran let out a deep breath and ushered Mara from the room.

Luckily, his rooms were located only a short distance from his sister's, and before Mara could fret too much about him overtaxing himself, they reached his door.

With a somber expression, he ushered her through. In contrast to Anneth's warmly decorated rooms, draped with bright swaths of cloth and illuminated with foxfire chandeliers, Bran's rooms were austere. But, as Mara looked closely, she saw a few personal touches. A silver scrying bowl sat on a small wooden table, and cubbies filled with scrolls covered one side of the room beside a large map of Elfhame fixed to the wall in one corner. A stand held his ornate court sword, jewels gleaming on the handle, and another collection of weapons were racked nearby.

These were the rooms of a warrior, true, but also a prince, as the opulent materials proved. The few chairs and low couch, upholstered in a rich, velvety brocade, looked very comfortable. Thick, moss-colored rugs cushioned their footsteps, and while the lighting was not as ornate as Anneth's, foxfire balls were cradled in curved silver bowls polished to a high sheen.

Bran halted in the center of what she took to be the sitting room—at least, that was what she would call it in the mortal world. He gazed at her a long moment. Despite his stern expression, she thought she detected something stricken in his eyes.

"I did not think to make other arrangements for you," he said. "Forgive me. If you wish to stay elsewhere..."

Did he want her there? Did he want her to live somewhere else? The ground felt unstable beneath her feet.

She searched his gaze. "Among your people, is it usual for a husband and wife to share quarters?"

"It is. In most cases. However, if you do not wish—"

"I'd prefer to stay with you." She gave him a crooked smile. "I didn't come back to Elfhame and pull you from death's doorstep just so that we could live apart."

His expression eased. "I would not want to make you uncomfortable, wife."

"I'm not," she said. It was mostly true. "Although..." She could meet his eyes no longer.

"What is it?" He crossed the space between them in three short steps. Gently, claws sheathed, he raised her chin and studied her face. "What frightens you?"

"Not frightened, exactly, but—" She gave a small, wry laugh. "Among humans, the wedding night is, er... Well. The bride and groom share a bed."

He glanced over his shoulder at the next room, where the corner of the low bed was just visible.

"You are afraid I will roll over in the night and crush you in my sleep?" He shook his head. "Fear not. Your safety is my priority."

Heat rushed into her cheeks. Did she really have to explain such things to her new husband? She had assumed Dark Elves mated much like humans did, but perhaps she'd been mistaken. Not that she felt ready for such intimacy. Even with Bran.

"Then I won't worry." She mustered up a smile, privately resolving to speak with Anneth about the subject as soon as possible.

Bran swayed on his feet, and her embarrassment quickly transformed to concern for him.

"I think, speaking of beds, that you ought to lie down." She took his arm and led him to the next room.

It was, indeed, the bedroom. To her relief, she saw that the bed was quite large, and festooned with pillows. Bran sat with a grunt, tossed several pillows to the floor, and then lay back.

In mere moments, his eyes closed, and his breathing deepened to a faint snore. Sleep pulled him into its undertow, and Mara bit her lip at how weary he looked in repose. It reminded her too much of how she'd discovered him, lying all but lifeless in the Darkwood.

Carefully, trying not to disturb him, she sat beside him and reached out to cup his cheek. At her touch, his eyelids fluttered open.

"Mara," he murmured, reaching up to cover her hand with his.

"Rest now," she said. "I'll be here."

He nodded, his intensely purple eyes shuttering closed once more. For several long minutes she sat there, watching him breathe, etching his starkly handsome features into her memory. Brannonilon Luthinor, Prince of the Hawthorne Court, fearsome Dark Elf warrior mage.

Her husband.

CHAPTER 6

Once Bran had fallen into a deep slumber, Mara rose and went back into the sitting room. She settled on the low couch, her mind whirling. What had she done? And what was she to do now?

It was all very well to agree to dwell in Elfhame when she was saving Bran in the Darkwood, but the reality of her choice rose starkly before her. She was the only human in a land where, as far as she could tell, mortals were held in low esteem.

But though single-handedly changing the minds of the Dark Elves seemed a daunting task, it was where her path led. If she could eke out even a little respect, it would be enough to make her life bearable.

Power—that was what it came down to. Mara had a wellspring of magic, if she could learn to harness it. And she would, she vowed, closing her hands into fists. For her sake, and for Bran's.

Bran. There was a whole different problem. They came from such disparate worlds, and she had no idea what he expected of her. She had the unsettling feeling that he'd never looked past the prophecy and considered what it might mean to have a mortal wife.

Well. They'd muddle through together, she supposed.

In the meantime, he had a wellspring to recover, and she had a world to accustom herself to. In truth, Elfhame was magical and mysterious. Even with worries of the future weighing on her mind, the dreamlike wonder of her surroundings muted her fears. She had slipped into a fable and married a prince, and surely that was not such a terrible thing.

A knock sounded at the door, and she went to answer it. No doubt it was Avantor, coming to check on Bran.

She opened the door, and then wished she hadn't. The noble lady named Mireleth stood there, elegantly gowned and with a disdainful expression on her sharply drawn features. Seeing Mara, her lip curled.

"What are *you* doing, answering the prince's door?" she asked.

She made to step inside, but Mara didn't move, continuing to hold the door half closed. Nothing could entice her to step back and allow this woman into Bran's rooms.

"I'm his wife, as you might recall. And he's currently not seeing visitors."

"He will see me." Mireleth leaned forward, trying to peer past Mara. "Be a good little servant, and inform him I'm here."

Trying not to grind her teeth at the courtier's arrogance, Mara narrowed her eyes. "I'll tell him you called. Good day."

She made to close the door, but Mireleth inserted her foot in the jamb.

"Mortal girl," she said, her voice low and poisonous, "you have no place in our world, let alone marrying our prince."

The hateful words echoed Mara's earlier thoughts. Resolutely, she pushed them away.

Lifting her chin, she met the courtier's gaze steadily. "Nonetheless, here I am."

"It's not too late for you to leave." Mireleth modulated her tone, attempting sweetness. "Surely you miss the mortal realm, your family, your life. Don't you want to return?"

Mara had already gone back once—but she wasn't about to tell the Dark Elf her secrets.

"No," she said. "I am here to stay."

Mireleth's expression hardened as she dropped all pretense of politeness. "You will regret it. Prince Brannonilon will see his mistake soon enough. He has no more need of a human bride, and will cast you aside. Then you'll wish you'd gone when you had the chance."

The woman's motives were painfully obvious.

Mara shook her head in mock pity. "Believe me, even if I were gone, Bran would have no interest in wedding *you*. Goodbye."

She shoved the door and, reluctantly, Mireleth removed her foot rather than risk having it crushed.

"We are not finished, mortal," she spat.

"I am." Mara shut the door as forcefully as possible. For a moment she considered barring it—but she didn't want to prevent Avantor from entering if she were to fall asleep.

She let out a breath and leaned back against the carved wooden surface. Mireleth's threats had unsettled her, reminding her all too clearly that she had enemies in the Hawthorne Court.

I am the woman of the prophecy, she reminded herself. She had helped Bran beat back the Void and save Elfhame. Mireleth might try to intimidate and bully her, but Mara was strong. She would not let a poisonous elven courtier get the better of her.

Still, it would be good to start her magical training sooner, rather than later. So far, her use of power had simply been by instinct. It would be a very good thing to be able to direct her magic at will, the way Bran did.

Weariness shuddered through her, and she couldn't help yawning. Despite Bran's assurance he would not roll over onto her, she did not quite feel ready to share a bed with him. The couch was draped with a soft blanket. She pulled it over herself and settled in for a rest. Just a short one...

A KNOCK at the door roused her. She blinked sleepily, the foxfire lights in their curved bowls reminding her where she was. Elfhame. Bran's rooms.

"Who is it?" she called, pushing off her blanket. She wouldn't make her earlier mistake of simply opening the door.

"Avantor."

Good. She went to let him in.

"How is Bran?" the healer asked, stepping inside.

"Sleeping, I think." She glanced toward the bedroom. "I admit, I fell asleep out here."

Avantor nodded sagely. "You both need a good deal of rest. Your wellsprings are depleted, and Bran's life force is too low for my liking."

"How long does it take for wellsprings to refill?" she asked, trailing him into the bedroom. She was glad to see Bran was still deeply asleep.

"It depends on how much power you have, and how much you've used." The healer moved to stand beside the bed and held his hands out over Bran's prone form.

Mara watched him anxiously. Avantor's face remained calm, and she took that as a good sign.

"Is Bran recovering?"

Avantor frowned slightly. "Yes. Though, as usual, our beloved prince has pushed himself to the limits of his strength."

"When I found him, he was barely breathing." Her voice caught on the memory of how close she'd come to losing him.

"Do not worry." The healer dropped his hands and turned to her. "Bran is not currently in danger of dying. I predict a full recovery within a doublemoon."

She let out a relieved breath. "How long is that, precisely?"

The two moons of Elfhame danced about one another, the palemoon and the bright, but she had not yet spent enough time in that world to know how often they rose and set in tandem.

Avantor gave her a faint smile. "My apologies. I forget you are not accustomed to our realm. The next doublemoon will occur in roughly six risings of the palemoon."

Six days? "I don't think Bran will be happy about staying in bed that long."

"In that, I must agree with you." The healer shook his head. "I rely upon you to do what you can to keep him resting."

Mara folded her arms across her stomach. "I don't have that much sway with the prince."

"Of course you do." Avantor regarded her steadily. "He is married to you. What's more, he cares deeply about your opinion."

She wasn't so sure, but there was no point in arguing. Time would tell, she supposed.

"We should let him rest." She glanced down at Bran's sleeping form. Their conversation had not roused him in the least—proof of his soul-deep weariness.

"Yes." Avantor turned to the nearby bowl of foxfire. "*Gwath*," he murmured, and the light dimmed.

"Oh." Mara looked from him to the now-extinguished light. "Can you teach me to do that?"

"Of course. It takes no particular skill or magic. Just speak the word *gwath*." He gestured to the other bowl illuminating the room. "Try it."

Practicing the shape of the word in her mouth, Mara went to the light. It was all very well for Avantor to say it took no skill, but what if she could not do it? What if the foxfire only responded to Dark Elves? How humiliating that would be, having to ask anytime she wanted the lights off. Or on, for that matter.

"*Gwath*," she said softly.

The blue flame flickered, its reflection wavering in the silver curve of the bowl—but it did not go out. Her spirits plummeted. She could not even perform this one simple task.

Then the ball of foxfire slowly faded, and relief blossomed inside her.

Smiling widely, she turned to the healer. "I did it."

"I had no doubt."

She thought he smiled in return, but in the dimness, it was impossible to tell. The room was nearly dark, no light sifting through the curtains covering the tall, arched window on the far wall. The only illumination spilled from the sitting room.

"How do you summon the light again?" she asked.

"*Calya*," he said.

Immediately, a small blue glow kindled in the center of the bowl, growing in strength until it shed a steady radiance.

With a glance at Avantor, she moved to the other bowl and murmured the word. A ball of foxfire formed in answer, and a thrill went through her. Magic, at her command.

"Thank you," she said.

Avantor nodded. "I know this is not the life you are accustomed to, Mara Geary. Whenever you require assistance, please call on me. But for now, I recommend you rest. Perhaps..." He glanced at the bed where Bran lay, unmoving. "Perhaps near to your husband."

"And not on the couch?" She raised a brow.

"I do not know the customs of humans," he replied, a bit stuffily. "But it is advisable to remain close, in case he needs your help."

"Ah, yes." He did have a point. And though she would not promise to sleep beside Bran all night, she would not insist on bedding down in the sitting room, either.

"I will check on you both on the morrow," the healer said.

"I'll see you out," Mara said. "And practice turning on and off the lights."

Another faint smile crossed Avantor's face. "Good."

As soon as he'd gone, Mara spent a few minutes speaking the words he'd taught her. The foxfire went out and rekindled until she felt completely secure in her knowledge of *gwath* and *calya*.

She was eyeing the couch, and debating whether to pull the cushions into the bedroom, when Bran made a noise somewhere between a shout and a groan.

"Bran?" she called, running to the other room.

His eyes were closed, his face nearly chalk white. His hands clenched and unclenched over the covers, his half-extended claws leaving marks on the opulent fabric.

"Mara?" he whispered hoarsely.

She did not think he was quite awake.

"I'm here." She sat beside him and carefully took one of his hands in hers.

He quieted, his claws retracting, and let out a deep, shuddering breath. Watching him battle for sleep, a wave of weariness washed over her. When she tried to remove her hand from his, he clutched at her, murmuring something in elvish.

"It's all right." She smoothed a lock of his dark hair from his forehead. "I'll stay. But you have to move over."

Eyes still closed, he released her hand and half rolled. She lay down beside him, pulling the corner of the satiny quilt up to cover her. The bulk of his body was solid and comforting, and she recalled resting in his arms in the Darkwood. Half of her yearned to return there with him —to run away into the forest and dwell beneath the shadowy trees, far from the complexities of the court.

"*Gwath,*" she said quietly to the bowl of foxfire. It dimmed obediently, and she sighed into the dark. At least she'd mastered this small part of the Dark Elves' world.

One step at a time.

TWICE IN THE NIGHT—OR what Mara took to be night in the strange, dim world of Elfhame—Bran thrashed in the grip of dark dreams. When she touched him, his skin was cold to the touch, icier than even his usual coolness.

She put her arms around him and pulled him close, trying to warm him with her body. Both times, her presence seemed to ease him, and together they fell back into fitful sleep.

At last she opened her eyes, to discover the room was gently illuminated by a tiny ball of blue light hovering over the bed. She glanced at Bran, to find him awake and propped up on one elbow, regarding her.

"Good morning," she said, then blinked. "Do you even have mornings here?"

He laughed, a low chuckle that shook the bed slightly. "We do. Especially when the brightmoon rises, as it does today."

"How do you feel?" She studied his face, glad to see the strain about his eyes had eased.

"Better."

"Avantor gave me strict instructions that you rest until the next doublemoon," she said.

One of his brows rose, a slash of ebony. "We both know that's not possible."

"Yes, but please try." She reached over and gripped his arm. "I can't lose you."

His expression softened. "For your sake, then, I will rest—for half that time. But Elfhame requires me."

"Surely your warriors need some time to prepare before leaving the court," she said.

His lips firmed, but he gave a grudging nod. "I will send messages to the other courts to stay alert for Voidspawn, in the meantime."

With a graceful motion, he rolled from the bed and went to the window. He pushed the curtains open, letting a golden glow into the room, and Mara let out a breath. It was not sunlight—but the bright-moon's light was a welcome change from the cool silver of the palemoon.

"Are you hungry?" Bran asked, turning toward her.

"Yes. Should we eat in here?"

He glanced about the room, then shook his head, a regretful tilt to his mouth. "We will show ourselves at the midday meal in the dining hall. No doubt the court is rife with speculation about our return."

Mara bit her lip, and his gaze focused on her.

"Is there something I should know?" He raised one eyebrow in question.

"It's just... Mireleth called last evening."

His expression hardened. "Did she insult you?"

"Not too badly," Mara lied.

She could fend for herself, and didn't want to distract Bran with needless worry for her. He had his own burdens to bear. Once he'd returned from patrolling Elfhame, they could deal with any problems remaining at court.

"You will tell me if Mireleth is unbearably discourteous." He leaned forward, meeting her gaze.

"I'm not going to come running to you every time some courtier is rude to me," she said.

"Perhaps not. But you will wear a weapon." It was not a question.

"If you think it's wise." She didn't like the implication that she might be in physical danger—from Mireleth, or anyone else.

He nodded sharply and went to one of the weapons racks mounted on the wall. Slowly he moved past the wickedly curved swords, shaking his head until he reached a smaller dagger, its handle sparkling with green and blue gems.

"This one." He lifted it and brought it to the bed, where Mara still sat. “No one would dare attack my bride—but it is better if you are armed, all the same.”

She pushed the silken coverlet aside and rose, eyeing the ornate weapon. It seemed far too grand for the bumbling attempts of a beginner.

“Can’t I just use my kitchen knife?”

“No. You need a blade with balance and a good edge,” he said. “A weapon, not a tool. Take it, and wear it at all times.”

Reluctantly, she reached out and accepted the dagger. It was heavy, the gemstones cool to her touch. “I’ll need a sturdy belt.”

“We will have several made for you.” He looked at her, his slitted pupils narrowing. “As to that, we both ought to dress. Perhaps Anneth has something you might borrow.”

Mara glanced down at her homespun skirts, wrinkled and grubby, with a few spots of Anneth’s blood staining the cloth. No wonder Mireleth had been so dismissive.

“Maybe.” Mara didn’t want to disturb Bran’s sister, but she certainly couldn’t enter the dining hall in such a state.

Well, she *could*, but it would reflect badly on Bran. She owed it to him—to both of them—to take her new station seriously. After all, she was wed to the Hawthorne Prince.

And no matter the intricacies of court etiquette, the rumors and whispers, she would not change that fact for the world.

CHAPTER 7

An hour later, as Bran escorted Mara into the dining hall, she was not quite as confident. Everything in the Hawthorne Court seemed designed to make her feel small and inelegant, from the arched hallways to the ornately braided hairstyles of its inhabitants.

Despite Anneth's suggestions, issued from her propped-up position in bed, Mara had no hope of emulating the coiffures, let alone the poised grace, of the Dark Elf courtiers. She'd done what she could, but her wayward hair refused to stay in place, let alone fall like shining sheets of water about her shoulders, as Anneth's did.

At least Bran's sister had lent Mara a lovely silken azure gown, with jewelry to match. A tapestry belt wrapped about her waist, where her new dagger hung in its silver-scrolled sheath.

The moment she and Bran stepped into the room, heads turned and courtiers halted in the act of eating and drinking. A hush fell, then was quickly filled with the low buzz of speculation. Mara felt their sharp-eyed gazes, their sibilant whispers lodging just under her skin.

"Do not fear," Bran said in a low voice, his hand covering hers where it rested on his arm. "You look every bit a princess."

Up to a point, she supposed. But there was no disguising her blunt mortal features, round-pupiled eyes, and clawless hands, which were viewed with disgust by most of the Dark Elves.

Not all of them, however.

As Bran let her toward the high table where the Hawthorne rulers sat, Avantor caught her eye and gave her the faintest of smiles. Bran's lean second-in-command, Hestil, inclined her head in respect as they passed.

"My lord. My lady," she murmured.

Lord Calithilon and Lady Tinnueth watched Mara and Bran approach. Bran's father gazed at them impassively, but the cold hatred in his mother's eyes nearly made Mara miss a step. If Mireleth was a poisonous little spider, Lady Tinnueth was a sleek and deadly viper. Mara was suddenly glad for the weight of the weapon hanging from her belt.

They halted before the Hawthorne Lord and Lady, and Bran made them a formal bow. The weight of the courtier's regard heavy on her shoulders, Mara performed her best curtsey—careful not to make it too low. She was not some supplicant come groveling to the court, after all.

When she straightened, she caught a flash of amusement in Lord Calithilon's eyes. His wife's nostrils flared, and she kept her eyes upon her son, not deigning to glance Mara's way.

"You seem much recovered," Lord Calithilon said, nodding to Bran.

"Thank you, my lord. I am," Bran replied, as if he were in perfect health.

Mara resisted the urge to jab him with her elbow. Why must he be so stubborn? On the other hand, it didn't seem wise to show any weakness in front the Hawthorne rulers.

"Good." His mother's voice was cool. "Then you'll be delighted to hear that we have approved your plan to patrol Elfhame. You may depart as soon as your soldiers are ready."

Bran's eyebrows twitched, but he made her a small bow. "Thank you."

Mara wanted to protest, but it was not the time or place to voice her concerns. She hoped he would listen to reason—or at least to Avantor—when it came time to leave the Hawthorne Court. Which, no matter what Lady Tinnueth implied, would *not* be immediately.

"Sit," Lord Calithilon said, gesturing to the chair on his right. "I have messages for you to give the other courts."

"Of course." Bran settled Mara in the chair beyond, then took the indicated seat beside her.

The narrow-faced courtier on Mara's right gave her a swift glance, then looked pointedly away, lip curling.

"It's all very well for the prince to have saved our realm from the Void," he said to the lady seated next to him, clearly meaning for Mara to overhear. "But ultimately, it's of no use."

"Indeed," his companion replied, her voice melancholy. "Alas, we are doomed to perish."

Mara blinked, trying to absorb what they had just said. She looked at Bran, to see if he'd caught the words, but he was already engrossed in conversation with his father, discussing the Nightshade Court and the losses they'd sustained in the war against the Void.

A server paused beside her place, offering slices of melon and a dish of some unfamiliar grain. Mara accepted both, but after a few bites, her curiosity got the better of her.

"Pardon me," she said, turning to the courtier. "What did you mean, when you said defeating the Void was useless?"

He let out a sigh and gave her a sidelong glance. "Prince Bran prefers to keep you in ignorance, I suppose—and I cannot blame him. There's little you can do about it."

"About what?" She wanted to take the fellow by the shoulders and shake the information out of him.

"The prince pampers his new pet," the woman beside him said. "Unlike some of us, he chooses to ignore the fact that fulfilling his prophecy only prolongs our decline. Elfhame's enemy is defeated, true. Nonetheless, we are fated to die."

"To die? What do you mean?" Mara curled her fingers in her lap, her heartbeat accelerating.

Was some disease ravaging the courts, or a new invasion on the horizon? What fate had she consigned herself to, when she'd agreed to turn her back on the human world? And why hadn't Bran told her?

The woman gave her a pitying look. "Tell me, mortal creature. Do you see any children here?"

Mara glanced over the dining hall. The bobbing spheres of foxfire illuminated a crowd of Dark Elves that ranged from young adults to the elderly. No one appeared younger than perhaps twelve years of age, by mortal reckoning.

"I assumed your children took their meals elsewhere," she said.

Upon reflection, though, she realized she'd seen no youngsters dashing about the palace, heard no high-pitched laughter issuing from nurseries and schoolrooms.

The thin-faced courtier shook his head. "No Dark Elf child has been born for over two hundred doublemoons, when our people were struck barren by some mysterious malady."

"Prince Brannonilon might have beaten back the Void," the woman said, leaning forward and meeting Mara's eyes. "But perhaps it would have been better had he not. We are dying out. For myself, I prefer a quick end as opposed to a lingering decay. In a generation, only a handful of Dark Elves will remain, waiting for extinction."

"That's terrible," Mara said. She couldn't imagine living with the knowledge that humanity was destined to die out. "Surely some cure can be found?"

The woman slowly shook her head. "We have tried everything. Nothing has allowed us to once more conceive offspring."

Mara wanted to argue that surely there must be *something*. But it was not her place—and besides, the Dark Elves, with all their magic, must have done everything they could.

"It would have been better had you not come," the thin-faced courtier said, giving Mara a cold look. "It would be ended, now. Our people gone, devoured by the Void. Instead, we must gradually waste away."

"Yes," the woman said. "We have nothing to look forward to but a dreary future of loss and emptiness."

The Dark Elves had a taste for the overly dramatic, it seemed, and Mara's patience had worn thin. She'd grown up with two younger sisters, after all. The courtiers' fatalistic attitude, and their inability to honor Bran's victory, set her teeth on edge.

"Maybe fate has something else in store." She couldn't help the tartness of her tone. "Do you really think the prophecy is finished? That conviction seems foolish, to say the least."

The woman pulled in a sharp breath and turned pointedly away. The other courtier simply gave Mara a scornful look and went back to his food.

Well then. Mara poked at the melon upon her plate, her appetite gone. No wonder she'd had such a cold reception at court, if the majority of the courtiers still thought the Dark Elves were doomed. As soon as dinner was over, she and Bran were going to have a long talk.

At last, the meal came to an end. Bran turned to her, apology in his eyes.

"I fear I've neglected you," he said.

Mara squeezed his arm, the muscles hard beneath her hand. "You had much to discuss with the Hawthorne Lord."

After the narrow-faced courtier had gone back to ignoring her, she'd listened to Bran and his father. It seemed to her that Lord Calithilon was humoring his son instead of treating him with the respect that a warrior mage deserved. Especially one who'd won the war against the Void.

Did the rulers of Hawthorne also wish Bran had been unsuccessful?

Mara glanced at Lady Tinnueth, to find the woman watching her, catlike eyes narrowed in malice. Throat dry, Mara swallowed and refused to look away. Finally, Bran's mother gave a slow blink and turned to Bran.

"I believe Lady Mireleth would like a word with you," she said to her son.

"So I understand," Bran said stiffly.

"Do not treat her with discourtesy." Lady Tinnueth's voice held a note of warning.

"I will seek her out tomorrow." Bran stood. "And now, I must beg your leave. My wife is weary."

He held his hand out to Mara, who quickly rose. From the dark smudges beneath his eyes, it was Bran who needed to rest, but she would willingly bear the burden, if it meant they might depart the dining hall immediately.

"Yes," she said. "It's been a tiring day."

Lady Tinnueth's lip curled in disdain, but Lord Calithilon nodded.

"You have our permission to go," he said. "We know you have much to do to make ready for your departure, Prince Brannonilon."

"Thank you," Bran said.

Mara dipped another curtsey, and then took Bran's arm as they moved away from the head table. She could feel Lady Tinnueth's stare boring holes in her back, and forced herself not to shiver.

After what seemed like miles, they reached the silver doors and stepped out of the hall. Bran let out a breath, and she felt his steps drag the moment they were out of sight.

"You've pushed yourself too much," she chided him.

"It had to be done." His voice was hoarse with weariness.

"Bran," she said. "At lunch, I heard—"

"Prince Bran," Avantor called from behind them.

Bran paused, and the healer caught up to them, his brow creased with concern.

"I hope you are on your way to rest," Avantor said. "And not preparing to march out at moonrise tomorrow."

Bran slanted a look at the healer, then away. "I've duties to attend to."

"Then have one of your deputies arrange matters." Avantor's voice held a note of annoyance, and Mara sympathized.

"Please." She squeezed Bran's arm. "Let's go look in on your sister, and then you can send for Hestil. Surely it's her duty, as your second-in-command, to assist with such things?"

"It is," Bran said, giving her a look of reluctant agreement. "But if she organizes the patrols, she will expect to come. It was my intention to leave her here to watch over your safety."

"Isn't it more important to hunt down the Void creatures?" Mara asked. "Surely I don't need a personal guard here in the Hawthorne Court?"

"I will not leave you unprotected," he said, his tone uncompromising.

"You have other skilled warriors who might watch over your wife," Avantor said. "Take Hestil."

Bran made an exasperated sound. "Very well. I cannot stand against both of you."

Mara exchanged a glance with Avantor, glad of the support she saw in his eyes.

"Are you going, too, as healer?" she asked.

"I would prefer to." His words were measured. "If our commander agrees, of course. There is more need of me on the battlefield than in the court."

Bran shifted and began walking down the corridor once more. "It won't be a war, Avantor. I don't intend to put my soldiers in undue danger."

"But Void creatures are on the loose," Mara said. "Surely there is plenty of risk. Look what happened to Anneth." She glanced at the healer. "How is she feeling?"

"I am pleased to say she's recovering well so far," Avantor said. "Indeed, it's time for another visit from me. I will accompany you to see her."

"Good," Bran said. "And I warn you now, my sister needs your tending more than I need you to accompany my warriors into the field. If you insist I bring Hestil along, then you must remain at the Hawthorne Court. For all our sakes." Bran lengthened his stride, putting an end to the matter.

Avantor's expression soured, but Mara smiled at him, even as she was forced nearly into a trot to keep up with her husband.

"I'm glad you're staying," she said to the healer. "I find Hestil rather... severe." The warrior was downright intimidating, if she were honest.

"Sicil, the third-in-command, is just as formidable," he replied. "I do wish the prince would be more sensible and let me accompany him."

Mara shot him a rueful look. "We both know it's almost impossible to change his mind once it's made up." Witness her own inability to make him rest, let alone delay his departure until the doublemoon.

When they reached Anneth's rooms, Bran knocked on her door, then entered without waiting for an answer. Anneth lay propped on her side upon her low couch, a tray of partially eaten fruit on the table before her.

"Look who's charging in," she said, a lopsided grin softening her words. "A whole entourage come to visit. How lucky I am."

"Are you well?" Bran went to his sister and knelt, taking her hand.

He clearly was still wracked with guilt over her injuries, and Mara couldn't blame him. Anneth had come into the Darkwood looking for them, after all.

"I'm sore," Anneth said with a grimace. "Avantor tells me I'll be able to start moving about in another day, though."

"Not without some pain, I am sorry to say." The healer glanced from her to Bran. "At least one of my patients is wise enough to listen to me, and remain abed as advised."

Bran shook his head. "Our realm can't afford that luxury. I will not be damaged for life if I neglect my healing—but Elfhame may well bear scars if I fail to act."

"You've always put your people's needs before your own," Anneth said. "When will it be your turn, Bran?"

Mara couldn't help but agree. The Hawthorne Prince took his duties too seriously. But perhaps growing up under the shadow of the prophecy as he had, it was understandable.

"When our realm is safe." His tone was hard, and it was clear that no argument would sway him from his course. "I must go and meet with my second-in-command as soon as possible."

"Hestil is almost as bad as you are," Anneth said. "But what are you going to do about Mara's training?"

Bran glanced at Mara, his expression softening, and her annoyance with him faded. He was doing his best under trying circumstances. They all were.

"I've not forgotten you," he said. "My own tutor, Penluith, will meet with you in a half turn in my rooms."

"Will you be there?" Mara shifted, not wanting to sound demanding, but she had to admit that she was a bit apprehensive.

And more than a little excited. Who would ever have thought that she possessed magic? Back in Little Hazel, such things were the stuff of stories and fables, not reality.

"I will come, when I may," he said.

He took her hand, his claws sheathed, and dropped a quick kiss upon the back of it, then turned and strode from the room.

Avantor let out a sigh. "Our prince is ever single-minded."

"It's what allowed him to save Elfhame in the first place," Mara said in Bran's defense.

"He's not entirely focused on the realm," Anneth said. "He's clearly in love with you, and those divided loyalties make him more terse than usual."

Mara felt her brow quirk. "Maybe—but I don't want to stand in the way of him doing what he needs to."

"Don't forget *your* needs," Anneth said archly, and Mara felt her cheeks flush.

The words reminded her of the questions she meant to ask. Eventually. She flicked her gaze to Avantor, unwilling to broach the subject in his presence.

"I suppose I should go back to Bran's rooms," she said. "I don't want to be late for my first lesson in magic."

"Wait a bit." Anneth reached out, then winced as the motion pulled at her injury. "Distract me while Avantor changes my bandages. You have plenty of time before Penluith comes."

"What's he like, the tutor?" Mara settled in the low chair facing Anneth's couch. "Did you have him as a magic teacher, too?"

"Yes." Anneth's nostrils flared as Avantor began tending her injuries, but she staunchly continued speaking. "He's been the nobility's teacher for as long as anyone can remember. He even tutored my parents in the use of their wellsprings."

Mara blinked. "He must be very old."

How much longer did Dark Elves live than humans? Would she wither and age while Bran remained youthful? She shifted uncomfortably, not sure she wanted to know the answer.

"He has seen thousands of moons," Avantor said, glancing up at her as if sensing her worry. "But his wellspring also sustains him. Magic extends our lives. As it will yours."

Which reminded her...

"I heard something distressing in the dining hall," she said, taking a deep breath. "Is it true that no more Dark Elf children are being born?"

Avantor stilled, and Anneth's eyes turned sad.

"Yes," she said after a moment. "No one knows why."

"That's terrible." Mara swallowed. She did not know how to give condolences to a people destined to die out.

"You see why I'm annoyed with Bran, though." His sister smiled crookedly. "If we are all fated to fall to dust, why not enjoy what we have in life right now? Chasing the Void creatures won't save us."

Avantor cleared his throat. "Some think otherwise. Once the Void is entirely defeated and Bran's prophecy fulfilled, there are those who believe our fertility will return."

"Do you think so?" Mara glanced at him.

"I am not certain. The prince's prophecy *did* say he would save Elfhame. Surely that includes the people that dwell within the realm."

"Or maybe Bran and Mara will repopulate Elfhame." Anneth's grin turned impish.

Mara felt herself blushing again. "Surely we couldn't do that single-handedly."

"I'm only teasing."

"Um." Mara bit her lip, then looked at Avantor and charged ahead. "Can Dark Elves and humans even produce children together? Are we... compatible in that way?"

The healer looked at her over Anneth's shoulder, his expression thoughtful. "I believe that such pairings have resulted in offspring in the past. Dark Elves have been known to slip through the gateway, sometimes bringing mortals back with them, sometimes spending the span of a human life in your world before returning to Elfhame. There have been several instances of half-elf, half-human children."

"It's probably why you have magic," Anneth added. "Some Dark Elf ancestor passed the gift on to you."

"If I hadn't come here, I never would have known," Mara said. Although—that wasn't entirely true.

She pressed her lips together, recalling that a part of her had always been different. She'd felt the pull of the Darkwood, had seen the flitting lights of glimglows before she'd even known what secrets the forest contained.

Dark Elf magic ran in her blood. Why else had she found the magical key that opened the gateway to Elfhame? Why else had Bran's prophecy chosen her?

"Might it be possible to bring humans with Dark Elf blood into Elfhame, to help repopulate?"

She was grasping at straws now, she knew, but she couldn't bear the thought of her newly adopted people ceasing to exist. They, and their magic, could not simply fade away.

Anneth's expression turned melancholy. "Even if such a thing were possible, do you really think other humans would welcome the experience, knowing how the court has treated you? You are the woman of the prophecy, and it was difficult enough for you, in the beginning."

It was difficult still. Despite herself, Mara heard the echo of Mireleth's cruel words, recalled the hatred in Tinnueth's eyes. But there was no point in complaining. Anneth would only worry, and there was very little she—or anyone—could do about it. Mara would endure the animosity and hope that, in time, she would be accepted at the Hawthorne Court.

She had more questions to ask—but as Avantor hummed a song of healing, Anneth's eyes closed. Soon, she was fast asleep. Quietly, Avantor and Mara left the room, parting ways in the corridor.

"Good luck with Penluith," the healer said.

"Thank you." Mara bit her lip. It was probably too much to hope that learning magic would come easily.

CHAPTER 8

As it turned out, working with her wellspring was, indeed, more difficult than Mara had hoped. After returning to Bran's rooms —she supposed they were hers now, as well—she had distracted herself by turning on and off the lights until Penluith arrived.

He was a tall, elegant Dark Elf, his silver hair intricately braided, his eyes a deep indigo. The only signs of his age were the deep creases that formed about his eyes and mouth when he smiled. Which, thankfully, he did rather frequently. She was relieved that his personality was not as aloof as his appearance might indicate.

"Excellent," Penluith said after Mara demonstrated her ability to control the lighting. "Has Bran given you any other instruction in the use of your wellspring?"

"Not particularly—beyond helping me sense its presence." She set her hand to her chest, as if she could somehow feel the magic dwelling within her. "I tried summoning foxfire once, with no success."

No need to tell Penluith about helping Bran open the gateway back to the mortal world. Or her own struggle to return to Elfhame and those bleak moments when she feared she'd lost Bran forever.

"Then we shall begin with the basic lessons," the tutor said. "You have a strong natural ability—evidenced by your assistance during the battle against the Void—but a properly channeled wellspring will allow you to do much more."

Mara nodded. "Can I learn to create something like a magical cloak or shield?"

Having the ability to protect herself physically would make her feel much better whenever she encountered Mireleth about the court. Not to mention the Hawthorne Lady. From the thinly disguised hatred in Tinnueth's eyes, Mara wouldn't put it past Bran's mother to try slipping a dagger between her ribs while Bran was away.

The tutor pursed his mouth. "Do you feel unsafe here? I assure you, no one wishes you harm."

Clearly he hadn't been paying attention. Mara gave him a tight smile.

"Still, I wouldn't mind the knowledge, being so far from my own home as I am." She was careful not to ask about offensive spells. Implying she would attack members of the court, even in her own defense, was not something she wanted to share with the royal tutor.

Bran would show her something of battle magic if she asked. In fact, it might help ease his mind to know that his wife was equipped with some sort of ability to inflict damage. Just in case.

"Once you show satisfactory progress, I can teach you how to cast a ward about yourself," Penluith said solemnly. "It is a dangerous magic, however, as it drains your wellspring in proportion to the protection it gives. You must take care with its use."

"What happens if my wellspring is emptied?" Her mind flashed back to Bran, lying nearly lifeless in the embrace of the Darkwood. "Will it kill me?"

Penluith frowned. "Not kill you, no. The danger is that you will permanently lose your magic, or a large part of it. A wellspring, once drained, has difficulty regenerating. Not to mention that, if your power is depleted while you're under an active attack—say, from a Void creature—you will not be able to survive for long."

"I see." Mara pressed her lips together, thinking.

Perhaps it was different for her, as her wellspring had been dormant most of her life. And if she was drained of it, well, living without magic would be nothing new. She suppressed a pang at the thought that then she would, indeed, be nothing more than a mere human in the land of the Dark Elves.

"For now," the tutor said, "let us work on calling foxfire. Unlike kindling and extinguishing the lights, which are already summoned and tied to their chalices, creating foxfire uses a portion of your own magic." He gestured to the low couch. "When you succeed, you may well feel a bit tired. Now, settle yourself into a comfortable position and focus on your wellspring."

Mara stuck a pillow behind her, set her feet firmly on the floor, and closed her eyes, trying to sense her magic. After some concentration, she thought she detected a fizzy feeling in her chest. It was nothing like the fierce blue fire she'd felt before, first when she'd lent her power to Bran in battle, and later, when she'd forced the gateway between their worlds to open and let her back into Elfhame.

But perhaps a small fizziness, as opposed to a sheet of azure flame, was a good thing. There was no need to engulf half the palace in fire.

"Are you ready?" Penluith asked.

"I think so." She hoped so, at any rate.

"Watch closely." He leaned forward, one hand raised. "The word of summoning is *calma*."

As he spoke, a flickering ball of foxfire sprang into being above his fingertips. Mara studied it, trying to memorize the sound of the word in her mouth.

"Try it," Penluith said encouragingly.

She lifted her hand, mirroring his gesture, then squeezed her eyes shut, holding the image of foxfire steady in her thoughts.

"*Calma*," she said, and opened her eyes.

The air flickered slightly, but no hovering ball of light appeared over her hand. Spirits sinking, she glanced at Penluith, who regarded her steadily, no hint of disappointment in his lean face.

"Did I pronounce it wrong?" she asked. There was a subtle lilt to the word that perhaps she hadn't spoken correctly.

"Try saying it a few times, without attempting to summon foxfire." The tutor's tone was thoughtful. "I should have realized—you are not used to the cadence of our language. *Calma*."

Mara repeated the word after him several times, until he gave her a satisfied nod. Then she attempted to reach for her wellspring, and spoke the summoning again.

"*Calma*."

This time, there was not even a hint of shimmer in the air.

"Again," Penluith said patiently.

"*Calma*." She tried inflecting the word up.

Nothing.

After a dozen tries, Penluith held up his hand to stop her. "Let us try something else."

She nodded, swallowing back the bitter taste of failure. How could a word that sounded like "calm" be such a source of frustration?

"What other spells do Dark Elf children learn?" she asked, then winced as a desolate look crossed Penluith's face.

Of course—there were no children now. The tutor must feel that loss deeply.

"I mean," she hurriedly added, "perhaps I need to start with something simpler."

He nodded, grief still shadowing his eyes. "Yes—perhaps foxfire is too ambitious. Let me think..."

After several heavy, silent moments, he raised his head, held out his hand, and spoke a word she did not quite catch. A slender white flower appeared in his palm, the leaves furled closed.

"I will teach you the rune of opening," he said. "*Edro*. Try it."

She blinked, trying not to reveal that she already knew this word, and had used it to pry open the gateway between the mortal world and Elfhame. At the very least, she knew her pronunciation was correct.

"*Edro*," she said obediently.

"Very good. Now, concentrate on the flower, on coaxing the petals open. Breathe deeply, connect with your wellspring, and speak the rune."

Mara tried to do as he said, but the tickle of sensation she thought she'd felt in her chest seemed to have gone entirely. Still, she pursed her lips and narrowed her eyes, searching vainly for the fizz of her wellspring.

"*Edro*," she said, then tightened her hands and tried again. "*Edro*."

The flower lay motionless on Penluith's palm.

She attempted the rune of opening several more times, with no result. Finally, the tutor shook his head and banished the still-furled flower. He did not sigh, at least not audibly, but Mara thought she detected disappointment in his eyes.

"I'm sorry." She grimaced. "I didn't think I'd struggle this much. Maybe it's because I'm a human."

"Perhaps so. Learning to use one's wellspring does not always come easy," the tutor said. "Sometimes it takes longer than one hopes."

It was kind of him to say, but they both knew she'd had no trouble accessing her power to help combat the Void. Why was it now so difficult? Was Bran's presence somehow the key to her abilities?

She certainly hoped not—she was dependent enough on him as it was.

"We will meet again on the morrow," Penluith said. "In the meantime, practice sensing your wellspring."

"I will."

She also intended to spend as much time as possible trying to summon foxfire and open flowers. Surely it was not that difficult. She could master the use of her wellspring.

Indeed, if she meant to secure her place among the Dark Elves, she must.

CHAPTER 9

Bran bent over the map of Elfhame spread out across Hestil's table. He had the same maps in his rooms, of course, but it was better to do the planning at his second-in-command's and leave Mara undisturbed for her session with Penluith.

She would make a brilliant student, he was certain. Aside from his own power, he'd never felt such a strong wellspring, and he looked forward to hearing how her tutoring session had gone.

But for now, he must turn his attention to the realm. With one sheathed fingertip, he traced the road to the Nightshade Court.

"Our first stop," he said. "I have no doubt the Nightshade Lady will spare what warriors she can."

"It won't be many," Hestil warned.

Bran nodded grimly. Nightshade had sustained heavy losses during the last days of the Void attacks leading up to the final battle. "We must ask all the courts for assistance."

He frowned at the map. Moonflower and Rowan, as well as the inner courts, had not faced the Void directly—but it was imperative that the warriors of Elfhame scour the land and make sure their ancient enemy was eradicated.

"Our fighters will be ready to leave first thing tomorrow," Hestil said.

"Good." Bran lifted his hand, letting the map roll up.

The sooner they were gone, the sooner he could return to Mara and face his next challenge: becoming a worthy husband. In truth, fighting Voidspawn was a more appealing task. At least he knew how to vanquish such foes. But how could he even be sure of his mortal bride's love? She had wed him under duress and was a stranger to his land and his people.

She returned to save you, he reminded himself.

But what if her love was misguided? He could not help the premonition that she would be desperately unhappy in Elfhame. His emotions twisted at the thought. Mara was the only brightness in his life. But could he give her what she needed?

Perhaps he should spurn her, for her own good. Even though it would mean ripping his own heart from his chest and trampling upon it.

No. He shook his head. Such games were below him. When he returned from chasing down the last of the enemy, he would deal with his marriage as best he could.

"I wish you would remain here," he said, glancing at Hestil. "I trust no one better to look after my wife."

Hestil snorted. "You could no more leave me behind than you could leave your sword. Sicil will make a fine interim commander. And you know as well as I that your mortal wife is made of strong stuff. She will weather the Hawthorne Court until we return."

He hoped so. "I'll have Sicil give her some instruction in knife work."

"Wise." Hestil sent him a narrow-eyed look. "With all due respect, Commander—you should go rest. You look as wilted as a second-bloom moonflower."

Bran gave a reluctant nod. They had finished planning, and although he'd done his best to hide his weariness, his second was not so easily fooled.

"I'll see you at dinner," he said. "I'm certain my father will want to make some kind of inspiring speech before we set out."

The Hawthorne Lord was ever fond of such gestures, though Bran preferred action to talk.

"No doubt," Hestil said dryly. She was not overfond of court protocol, herself.

Bran took his leave and strode down the corridors. Pale moonlight flowed in through the high, arched windows to pool on the polished flagstones, providing enough illumination that he didn't bother summoning a light.

Unfortunately, the shadows were deep enough to hide the figure waiting for him until she stepped directly into his path.

"Bran," Mireleth said, her voice honey-smooth. "I was so hoping for a private word."

"I know what you hope for—and you must seek it elsewhere. Excuse me, my *wife* is waiting." He stepped around Mireleth.

She nimbly moved in front of him, forcing him to draw up short. Despite his urge to trample over her, he *was* the Hawthorne Prince. A certain etiquette must be maintained—though he let a scowl settle on his face.

"I understand you're leaving tomorrow." She shook her robe back, revealing the betrothal bracelet clamped around her wrist. "I was hoping to say farewell to the man I am pledged to."

He folded his arms. "Take that blasted thing off. I'm already wed."

It was a ridiculous show on her part. He had publicly broken the betrothal bond between them. The metal clamped about Mireleth's wrist was a desperate attempt to assert a connection that had been severed moons ago.

"Yes..." Her delicately arched brows rose. "But have you consummated that union?"

"That's none of your concern."

She gave a contrived shudder. "I cannot say that I blame you. The thought of lying with a mortal is quite distasteful."

"Step aside." He all but growled the words, trying to push down the hot anger threatening to fog his vision.

Ignoring the threat in his voice, she swayed closer and placed an elegant hand on his arm. "Whatever happens, I am here for you."

With a snarl, he brushed her away her. "Our foolish betrothal is over, Mireleth." He cursed the absent stars that he'd ever agreed to such a thing. "Begone. I am not changing my mind."

"Of course, my lord." She stepped away, a smug tilt to her lips. "You are a man of honor, after all. But the mortal cannot give you what you need. Remember that."

And with that, she was gone, slipping back into the shadows like a dark whisper.

Bran rubbed the back of his neck. The last thing he wanted to do was storm into his rooms prickling with anger at Mireleth. She was best put out of his mind—and his marriage—entirely.

CHAPTER 10

"*Calma*," Mara said, for what felt like the thousandth time.

Her throat was hoarse, and frustration gnawed at her, yet she persevered. Just one last time.

Or one more.

And one after that.

She'd vowed not to sleep until she conjured up a dratted ball of foxfire, no matter how tiny or misshapen.

Gritting her teeth, she held the image of flickering blue light in her mind. Her wellspring waited; she knew it did. Why wouldn't it respond? Irritation itched like sand under her skin.

"*Calma!*" She infused the word with an afternoon's worth of desperation.

Whoosh. A wind rushed through the room, pulling Mara's hair over her face. Then, with a force that knocked her back against the couch cushions, an immense ball of foxfire appeared in the center of the room.

Mara threw her arm up to shield her eyes from the brightness. Well! Triumph sang through her, and she grinned, though no one could see her. It seemed she'd succeeded beyond her wildest dreams.

"By the moons!" Bran's voice sounded from the door. "What are you doing, Mara?"

She jumped to her feet and went to where he stood in the doorway, his eyes narrowed against the blue inferno. The brightness made his skin look ashen, his hair black as polished onyx.

"I... summoned foxfire."

"So you did." He closed the door. "But why so much?"

"I wish I knew. I've been trying all day to conjure it up—and was only just now successful."

He glanced at the sphere of blue fire taking up his sitting room, then winced away from the light. "While I'm impressed with your display of power, perhaps you should dampen the foxfire—or dispel it altogether."

She bit her lip. "I don't know how."

"What?" His brow creased. "I thought Penluith would teach you better than that."

"Don't blame him. When he left, I hadn't succeeded in summoning anything, so there was no need to teach me how to un-summon it."

"That was careless." Bran shook his head. "Say *uscalma*, and imagine the light extinguishing."

Mara took a breath, then did as Bran instructed. Immediately, the foxfire went out. The room plunged into shadows, and Mara had to blink several times to adjust her vision. A sudden, sharp longing for sunshine made her nearly gasp, and she swallowed the sound. That bright, mortal fire was not for her. Not anymore.

"That's better," Bran said. "I'll have a word with Penluith. He's too accustomed to pupils who obey and don't think to practice on their own."

"Speaking of which..." Mara cleared her throat. "I understand that Dark Elves can no longer bear children."

He froze, then shot her a cautious look. "This is true."

"You didn't think to mention it before?" Exhaustion lent a sharp edge to her voice. "When we defeated the Void and closed the rift, I thought we'd saved your people! Imagine how it felt to learn that I was gravely mistaken and there is more to contend with. You should have told me."

He watched her warily. "It does not matter."

"Of course it matters." She clenched her hands and tried not to sound peevish. "How can I be the woman of the prophecy if we didn't actually save your people?"

Bran looked away from her, his expression suddenly weary. "My prophecy was to save Elfhame. Together, we accomplished that task."

She wanted to pound her hands on his chest. "What good does that do, if the Dark Elves are destined to die out as a people?"

"Mara." He reached and took her hands, gently unfolding her fists. "Who knows what else the future holds? It is enough that you are here, that we defeated the Void."

"Maybe for you." She tried to breathe past the tightness in her chest. "But apparently the rest of the Hawthorne Court feels differently."

His face tightened. "Pay the gossips no mind."

"How am I supposed to do that, when my own husband pays *me* no mind?"

Immediately, she wanted to bite her tongue, but the words were said. A small, sorry part of herself was glad of it, of the flash of momentary pain in his indigo eyes.

"There are others..." He hesitated, rubbing his cool fingers softly over her palms. "Others who believe the prophecy is only half fulfilled. That once the remaining Void creatures are dispatched, our fertility will return."

"Do you think it's true?"

"I hope it is." He stared down into her eyes. "I cannot believe that all of this has been in vain, Mara. Please, do not lose faith in me. In us."

Her heart squeezed, and she clasped his hands tightly. "I'm sorry for what I said. It's just... it's difficult for me here."

"I know." His voice was solemn. "And I, in turn, am sorry for that. You have an ally in Anneth, do not forget. And Avantor. I depart on the morrow, and when I return, everything will settle out as it should."

Her breath snagged. "And when will you return, Brannonilon Luthinor? How long will it take to vanquish the remnants of the Void?" *How long must I molder away in the Hawthorne Court, waiting for you to come back?* At least this time, she left the hurtful words unsaid.

Regret twisted his mouth. "I will not give you comfortable lies. It may well be several doublemoons."

She made a quick calculation, her dismay rising. "Months? What am I to do in the meantime?"

"Spend time with Anneth. Study magic with Penluith—and knife work with Sicil."

"I'll miss you." She felt hollow inside, the beginnings of panic shortening her breath. "I didn't come back from my world just to watch you ride off with your soldiers. I should come with you."

He cupped her cheek, his claws carefully sheathed. "Your magic is too untried—and you are too important."

"My magic was tried enough to help win the war!"

"Mara. We will be riding for long hours, hunting down the creatures. Even my best warriors will be hard-pressed to maintain the pace. And cornered Voidspawn are vicious. I will not risk you."

"Yet you risk yourself by not letting me come along. We are better together—we've proven that." Hot tears sprang to her eyes, and she turned away. She almost wished she'd never returned to Elfhame. Almost.

He set his hands on her shoulders, but did not force her to turn back toward him.

"I am a poor husband," he said, his voice low. "I know it—but I promise, when I come back, we will forge some happiness between us. I love you, my mortal wife."

She sighed, then pivoted. "And I love you, Bran."

For the first time, her traitorous heart wondered if that would be enough.

CHAPTER 11

It was all Mara could do to sit through another feast in the Hawthorne Court's dining hall. At least this time, Bran made a clear effort to include her in conversation with his parents—though Tinnueth markedly ignored every word she spoke, and Calithilon seemed only to humor her.

A different courtier was seated on Mara's right—a noblewoman who gave Mara a single, disdainful look, then pointedly turned away and only spoke to her companion for the rest of the meal.

Mireleth presided further down the table, a mocking smile upon her lips whenever she glanced toward Mara—which was too often for comfort.

"Bran," Mara said, when she'd finally had enough. "Will you give me a sip of your wine?"

He looked at her full cup, but said nothing, only raised his own goblet to her lips. When she finished drinking, he rotated the cup and placed his mouth where hers had just been. Warmth flashed through her, and she met his gaze.

"Thank you," she said softly.

"Always," he said. "Do not think I'm unaware of the difficulties you will face here." His eyes brightened with pride. "I know you are strong enough to prevail."

Her heart eased, and after that, Mara paid Mireleth no mind.

At the conclusion of the meal, the Hawthorne Lord stood. Quiet rippled into the room. Clearly everyone expected a speech from Bran's father.

"Tomorrow, our prince rides out," Calithilon said. "Our hopes and good wishes go with him as he seeks to finally put an end to our ancient enemy, and bring his prophecy to its ultimate fulfillment."

The listeners stirred, and Mara read dissatisfaction in the faces of several of the courtiers. Despite what Bran had said about his supporters, it was clear that many in the Hawthorne Court thought that he'd failed—that this final attempt at chasing down the Void was a useless gesture.

"I know that Brannonilon will succeed in this, as he has succeeded before," Calithilon continued. "And I know, too, that the brave warriors of Elfhame's courts will not rest until they have eradicated this threat."

However long that might take. Mara kept a smile on her lips, and pushed the thought into the background.

The Hawthorne Lord rested one hand on his son's shoulder and raised his ornate goblet in the other. "Join me in a toast. To victory. To Elfhame. To Prince Brannonilon Luthinor!"

"To Prince Brannonilon!" the court echoed.

The raised goblets winked with reflected light, and for a moment, Mara was reminded of the surface of a lake, chased with sunlit ripples. She thrust her cup in the air, then drank the sweet elderberry wine. To Bran. Her impossible, beloved husband.

"I will come back to you, as soon as I may," he murmured, slipping one arm about her waist.

"I know." She gave him a smile. "I'll be here. Waiting for you."

That night, Bran paced restlessly in the sitting area. Mara, her feet tucked up under her on the couch, watched him.

"Are you always so on edge before a campaign?" she asked.

She didn't know whether to be amused or annoyed. Annoyed, she decided. He needed his rest, after all.

"It helps me think." He tugged at the thin braids framing his stark cheekbones.

"I think... you'd do best with some sleep."

He gave a sharp shake of his head. "I'd only twist and turn, my mind filled with details. It's better this way. Eventually, I'll tire."

As if his words conjured up her own weariness, Mara tried to hide a yawn behind her hand.

Bran halted. "You don't have to stay awake and keep me company."

"I want to. It's my last chance to see you for... well, however long."

He came to sit beside her. "Tell Penluith to teach you how to scry. Do you know what that is?"

"I've seen you do it, I think. In a bowl of water, yes?"

A slight smile softened his mouth. "Yes. The first time I ever saw you was in my scrying bowl. You were running through the Darkwood."

"I was?" She tried to think back to the time before she'd met Bran. It seemed very long ago. "In my world, or yours?"

"It was not Elfhame—though there were glimglows."

"It must have been my birthday eve. I don't think I ever told you. Glimglows beckoned me out into the forest." To a magical destiny she would never have believed. Even now, it almost seemed a dream—except she was living it.

"I am glad." He enfolded her hands, his smile widening as she yawned again. "You should sleep now."

"I'll just curl up here," she said, pulling a pillow over to tuck under her head.

"If you wish." He brushed a kiss across her forehead, then stood. "But if my pacing disturbs you, I will not blame you for seeking the bed."

"You won't disturb me." In truth, she loved watching him move. Even in his weariness, every step was filled with elegant, powerful grace.

He nodded, then resumed his movements, concentration drawing his features taut.

Mara must have slept, for she was dimly aware of Bran gathering her up in his arms and carrying her into the dim bedroom. He set her down and drew a blanket over her.

"Sleep well, beloved," he said quietly.

She meant to wake more fully, to tell him not to worry, that she would not expire of frustration, or boredom, while waiting for him to return. But the blanket was soft, the room warm, and she slipped back into slumber.

When she next awoke, it was to find that she was still alone in the bed. Her questing hand found a warm hollow beside her, though, suggesting that Bran had risen only recently. She hoped he'd gotten enough sleep.

"Bran?" she called groggily.

"I am here." His voice came from the other room.

"Is it time?"

"Nearly," he replied. "We meet at the gates in a half turn."

"I'll get dressed, then." She certainly wasn't going to let her husband ride off without bidding him a proper—and public—farewell.

"*Calya,*" she said, rising on her elbows, and the foxfire obediently sprang to life within its silver bowl.

She hadn't realized how convenient that tethered magic was. Were there smaller lamps that could be used portably? Or was every Dark Elf capable of calling foxfire if they wished?

She glanced at the sand-filled glass on the low table beside the bed, wishing for the normalness of a human clock. The hourglasses the Dark Elves used were confusing—and, of course, they didn't count hours at all, only turns. One more thing reminding her how far she was from home.

She rose and surveyed the few outfits Anneth had lent her. It had been kind of Bran's sister, but it was increasingly imperative that Mara procure some clothing of her own. Silken wrap-dresses were well enough for formal court dinners, but seemed impractical beyond that. She wanted some sturdy homespun—though she was unsure if the Dark Elves even created such humble material.

After wrapping herself in a swath of gold-embroidered green, Mara went to join Bran in the sitting room. He set down the satchel he'd been packing with scrolls and strode over to envelop her in an embrace.

She leaned against him, breathing deeply of his spicy scent.

"I'll miss you," she said, trying not to sound too forlorn.

"My body might go, but my heart remains here."

It was one of the most romantic things he'd said to her, and she wanted to cling to him and beg him not to go. She had come back to Elfhame for him, and it was almost too much to bear that he was riding away.

But she *would* bear it—for his sake, as well as hers. And for the future of Elfhame.

A soft chime sounded, and his arms tightened about her for a moment before he let go.

"Stay safe, wife of mine." His voice was rough with emotion.

"I am not the one fighting gyrewolves and spiderkin," she replied. "You'd best return to me, Prince Brannonilon Luthinor. If you don't, I'll never forgive you."

"I swear it." He stared deeply into her eyes. "This is not goodbye, Mara."

The chime sounded again. Bran stepped back and scooped up his satchel.

"Is that all you're taking?" she asked.

"The servants already carried my bags out. Fuin and the other horses are saddled and waiting." He held out his arm. "Shall we?"

Lifting her chin, Mara laced her arm through his and let him lead her through the door. They went quietly down the silver-lit hall, but as they passed Anneth's rooms, her door opened and she stepped out.

"I was waiting for you," she said. "You're almost late."

"Are you certain you should be up?" Bran gave her a stern look.

She gave him a tilted smile. "I can't let my brother ride off without wishing him safe journeys. Besides, I thought Mara might like a bit of company once you go."

Mara sent her a grateful glance. "I would—thank you."

It would be far easier to bear the scathing looks of the court with Anneth at her side.

Bran firmed his mouth, but did not try to argue with his sister. Still, he slowed his pace slightly, and Anneth didn't urge them to hurry. The unspoken compromise carried them to the front doors of the palace.

In the courtyard before the gates, a dozen warriors were making their farewells to families and loved ones. Their mounts stamped restively, ready to be off. Calithilon stood there, his silver circlet resting regally on his dark hair. There was no sign of Tinnueth.

Mara was relieved not to have to bear the Hawthorne Lady's silent scorn, though she felt a pang for Bran, that his own mother didn't bother coming to see him off.

But his father was there, and Anneth, and a few others. The small crowd cheered as their prince descended the wide steps.

Bran nodded to his warriors, then turned to Hestil. "Is everyone ready?"

"Yes," his second-in-command said.

The groom brought Fuin, and Bran set his hand on his steed's shoulder, making ready to mount.

"Good luck," Anneth said, going on tiptoes to kiss her brother's cheek.

He nodded, his face stern, but his gaze softened as he looked at Mara.

"Bran," she said, then went into his arms.

She raised her face to his, and their lips met in a kiss she felt all the way down to her toes. A faint whisper ran through the onlookers, but she didn't care. This was her husband, her chosen one—no matter that the prophecy had forced them together.

"Beloved," he whispered against her lips.

Then he stepped away and swung up on Fuin. Mara's heart was hot with fierce love for him, heavy with sorrow.

"Fight well, my son." The Hawthorne Lord raised his hand. "We shall scry for you."

Bran gave him a short nod, then signaled to his riders. Almost as one, they wheeled their horses and rode out through the tall, pale gates of the Hawthorne Palace. As befitting warriors, none of them looked back.

CHAPTER 12

The arched gates of the Hawthorne Palace shone under the wan light of the palemoon, and the rising radiance of the brightmoon. The small crowd gathered there watched the warriors ride into the silver-misted air until they disappeared in the haze of distance.

Mara was the last to turn away, Anneth's hand on her shoulder.

"He'll be back soon," Bran's sister said in an encouraging tone.

"Or not." Mara faced the elegant palace. Knowing that Bran was no longer within made it seem a hollow, cheerless place.

"We have much to do while he's gone." Anneth smiled at her. "Starting with your wardrobe."

Mara glanced down at her silken dress. "That would be good. I wanted to thank you again for giving me a few things to wear."

Anneth waved a hand. "That's just a start. Come back with me to my rooms. I'll rest, and you can look through my wardrobe."

"I can't steal all your dresses!"

"I won't let you, don't worry. Whatever takes your fancy, we can ask the seamstresses to make something similar."

Mara nodded, then lent Anneth her arm for balance as they mounted the stairs. Bran's sister paused at the top, her breathing fast.

Mara gave her a sharp look. "How is your healing progressing?"

"Very well. Truly, it is—you don't need to frown at me as if you were Bran. By the morrow, Avantor says I can be up and around."

"But not today," Mara said pointedly. "You're my last ally here—I need you in good health."

Anneth tsked. "I would not have missed Bran's leave-taking. And as far as allies, plenty of people in the Hawthorne Palace support you."

"Who?" Mara glanced around the deserted courtyard. "Almost none of the courtiers, I'd wager."

She held the door for Anneth, then offered her arm again. Slowly, they made their way toward her sister-in-law's rooms.

"Perhaps not a great number of the nobles," Anneth conceded. "But some think well of you—Avantor, for one. And many of the craftspeople do, too. Of course, the soldiers are firmly with you."

"With Bran, you mean."

"And with you," Anneth said. "Everyone who was on the battlefield knows that without your help, Elfhame would have been lost."

"I've been informed by certain members of the court that our victory doesn't matter."

Anneth made an annoyed sound. "They are idiots. Or Mireleth's flunkies, who foolishly pinned their hopes on seeing her become the next Hawthorne Lady."

"She doesn't seem to have given up," Mara said as they stepped into Anneth's rooms. She was happy to have the solid door between their conversation and any listening ears.

"Mireleth is blind to anything but her own ambitions. Even the obvious fact that Bran loves you." Anneth sank down onto her couch with a sigh. "She's irritating, but harmless."

Even if that were so, it seemed to Mara that Tinnueth remained her most dangerous adversary. But how did she mention such things to the woman's daughter? Especially when Anneth was doing her best to help Mara navigate the intricacies of the court?

She didn't. Perhaps a better time would come, or perhaps her fears would amount to nothing. In the meantime, she had a wardrobe to select.

Anneth directed her to the tall, carved wardrobe in the corner, and bade her remove armloads of dresses. As Mara began sorting through them, her belly let out an inelegant rumble.

Anneth glanced at her. "I'd wager Bran didn't bother to feed you! Let me send for a tray."

The privileges of being a princess. Mara didn't argue—and she supposed she could do the same. Except for the fact that she needed magic to contact the kitchens. Which reminded her...

"Is it difficult to scry?"

"That depends." Anneth tilted her head. "How far apart the scrying parties are is a major factor, as is the strength of their bond."

"Bran told me he saw me in the mortal world."

Anneth's eyes widened. "Between the worlds! That's impressive. Of course, he's the strongest warrior mage we've had in eons. And the two of you are deeply connected via the prophecy."

The dratted prophecy. Mara was growing weary of bumping up against it at every turn.

"So, reaching the kitchens is simple," Mara reasoned. "But once Bran is several days away, it will be harder to contact him."

"Not for you, I don't think."

Mara wondered if the dreams she'd had of Bran dying, the ones that had drawn her back into Elfhame, had been a kind of scrying. She could ask Penluith—or no, she couldn't. The secret of her departure, and return, must remain between herself, Bran, and Anneth. If the knowledge became widespread, it would erode all sympathy among her handful of supporters, who were fiercely loyal to Bran. The mortal bride tried to abandon her prince? Unthinkable.

The fact that she'd returned would not matter to the rigid honor of the Dark Elves. One did not selfishly turn away from prophecy. Or the Hawthorne Prince.

The food arrived from the kitchens, providing a welcome distraction. Anneth joined her in nibbling a few honeycakes and a slice of moonmelon, but shook her head when Mara encouraged her to eat more.

"I had a large breakfast, I promise." Anneth covered her mouth, attempting to hide her yawn.

"And now you need a large nap."

"Yes." Bran's sister sounded suddenly weary. "Take the rest of the cakes with you, though. I can summon more when I'm hungry again."

Mara finished up her slice of melon, then wrapped a napkin about the remaining honeycakes. This way she could skip lunch—and uncomfortable interactions with the court. At least, until dinner.

"I'll check on you later," she said. "If you'd like."

"I would. And I'll make arrangements for the seamstress to send you a selection of clothing, based on the items you've picked out here. Meanwhile, take the purple dress—yes, that one. It looks well on you."

Mara scooped up the soft, billowing length of fabric. She wasn't sure she could arrange it around herself nearly as artfully as Anneth had, the first time Mara had worn it. But she'd manage.

"Rest well," she said, and left Bran's sister to her much-needed sleep.

Once again, Mara was thankful that Bran's rooms were nearby, and that the royal siblings were housed in a less-traveled hallway of the palace. She gained the safety of his rooms without meeting anyone, and added the purple gown to her small collection of clothing.

The rest of the day stretched before her. But Penluith would come after lunch, and she supposed that at some point Sicil would speak to her about the knife lessons Bran had insisted upon.

Still, loneliness ached beneath her ribs. She wished for her sisters, no matter how annoying they could be. And her books. Did the Hawthorne Palace have a library? She supposed she might explore—but she'd rather do that with a companion who knew the lay of the court. Once Anneth fully recovered, she'd prove a lively guide, Mara had no doubt.

The door to the gardens was nearby, if she recalled—but again, she hardly wanted to go wandering about the palace, opening random doors. That was a sure way to get herself into trouble, especially as she barely grasped the rudiments of court etiquette.

The unfamiliarity of everything hit her all at once, and she sank down on the low couch with an intake of breath that was close to a sob.

Stop it, she told herself, clenching her hands together. *I am strong enough for this.*

If only Elfhame was not so dim. Everything would be easier if the sun shone in this magical land.

Shutting her eyes, Mara conjured up memories of how it felt to stand in that warm light. She imagined the way brightness threaded through the green-leafed trees outside her family's cottage, the hot, dusty scent of the road in late afternoon, the sun-warmed stones of the low wall where she and her sisters would sit, braiding flower crowns.

After a while, the tightness in her chest eased. Yes, she no longer dwelt in the human world—but it still lived inside her, for as long as she could recall it.

CHAPTER 13

As Bran rode away from the Hawthorne Palace, he could feel Mara's gaze on his back. *I am sorry*, he thought, though he knew she could not sense it.

She was brave, his little mortal, and he knew she would face the future unflinchingly. He wished he could be beside her, but his duty called.

"Stay alert," he said to his warriors. "I will cast a net of sensing over the area. We must let no Void creatures escape our patrol."

The elves under his command nodded, and beside him, Hestil loosened her curved swords in their scabbards, as it was her preference to fight double-bladed.

Closing his eyes briefly, Bran spun his magic out, the tendrils of sensing similar to those guarding the borders of Elfhame, though not on such a grand scale. They formed an invisible net, moving out in a slow ripple over the countryside.

He turned to his second. "After we finish dealing with the Voidspawn, we must inspect the boundary wards and reinforce any thin places."

Hestil gave him a cool look. "Might I remind you that you promised to return to your wife as soon as possible?"

He winced slightly. "I am not succeeding very well at being her husband."

"Perhaps you do not need to carry the entirety of Elfhame's safety on your shoulders any longer," she said. "I am not one to give advice about love, but it seems to me that Lady Mara is equally deserving of your loyalty. Others can mend the wards, but you are the only one who can be husband to your wife."

But could he, truly, give Mara what she needed? For so long he'd been solely focused on his role in the prophecy—which meant focused on Elfhame's safety. He wasn't sure who he was without that driving force. Certainly not the kind of mate his brave, beautiful wife deserved.

"I lied to her," he said.

"Did you?" Hestil's tone was mild.

"I did not tell her that Dark Elves are now infertile. That many in the court think we are a doomed race."

"Do you believe it?"

"I cannot," he said fiercely. His legs tightened over Fuin's sides, and his horse danced forward a few startled steps. "I cannot believe that everything we have fought for is in vain."

Hestil glanced over at him, her expression calm. "And so you are here, scouring the land for answers."

"And for Voidspawn, don't forget. We still have a score to settle."

"I am with you, Commander." She shot him a tight smile. "Garon's death will be avenged with every gyrewolf I impale, every spiderkin who dies on my blade."

Bran bowed his head as a quick blast of grief for the old soldier blew through him. "We lost many good people on the field."

"And many more remain." She nodded at the warriors scattered before and behind them.

Bran was about to respond when he felt a quiver go through the sensing he'd cast. He held up his hand and brought Fuin to a halt. His warriors stopped a heartbeat later, and Hestil slid her blades free.

"That way," Bran said quietly, tipping his head toward a thicket of wireweed.

The fighters fanned out, weapons and spells at the ready. Their battle-trained mounts stepped softly through the underbrush.

They rounded the thicket, but no enemy awaited. Bran frowned as he focused on his magic.

"They are fleeing. Two... no, three Voidspawn. This way."

He nudged Fuin into a trot, then a loping canter. No use in trying for stealth when their quarry knew they'd been found. Up a silver-grassed hill, then down. Not much further now...

As he crested the next rise, he saw them: two red-eyed gyrewolves and a skittering spiderkin, heading toward the distant trees of the Eryn-vorn. Without urging, his mount broke into a gallop. The thud of his riders' hoofbeats sounded to either side.

As soon as the distance had closed enough, Bran conjured up a bolt of flame and flung it toward the rearmost gyrewolf. Sizzling blue fire scored its side. Snarling, it spun to face them, as did the spiderkin. The second wolf continued running.

"I'll take him," Hestil said, steering her mount on a course to intercept.

"Go with her," Bran directed two of the other warriors, keeping his eyes fixed on the enemy.

He raised his hand, readying another bolt, but held his fire as two of his younger fighters swooped in. Their swords flashed as they bent from their horses to strike the Void creatures. One hit the spiderkin, and green ichor spurted from the wound. The rider bit out a curse as the caustic liquid sizzled against his arm.

Then his warriors were clear, and Bran flung more azure flames at the spiderkin. The wolves were fast and dangerous, but spiderkin blood could maim even more quickly.

"Look out!" another of his fighters cried, a touch of panic in her voice.

Bran wheeled Fuin, his heart hardening into stone as he saw four more Void creatures bearing down upon them. Two lumberers—who could freeze the soul with a single touch—and two more of the blighted spiderkin, many-legged and poison-fanged.

It had been a trap—and he'd foolishly led his warriors into the heart of it. Instead of four fighters to an enemy creature, the odds had now tilted perilously against them. Somehow, the Voidspawn had been able to shield themselves from his magic. Very worrisome—but he had no time now to dwell upon it.

Drawing his blade, Bran urged Fuin forward. A lucky swipe damaged one of the lumberers, and his horse nimbly stepped away from the creature's counterattack.

All around him, blades slashed and blue fire sizzled. Bran's focus narrowed to the essentials—flame and fight, stab and swerve. The woman who had first sighted the ambush fought at his side, and together they brought down the lumberer.

Privately, Bran had to admit he was not at his best; his spells lacked their usual searing focus and his blade work was slow. Avantor would have scolded him mightily—another reason he was glad he'd left the healer behind. And while it might have been foolish for Bran to depart the Hawthorne Court before he was fully recovered, it was clear that the countryside was in danger. He could not have delayed another turn.

It was brutal, difficult fighting, but one by one, the Void creatures were vanquished. Hestil delivered a killing blow to the gyrewolf she'd chased at the same time as two of Bran's warriors cut down the last spiderkin.

In the aftermath, the silence was as loud as a ringing bell. Bran drew in a ragged breath and surveyed his troop. One warrior cradled her arm to her chest, and several of the fighters sported acid burns, but he was relieved to see that no one was gravely injured. Avantor's most gifted journeyman healer moved from person to person, humming softly as she performed quick spells of soothing and repair on burns, gashes, and bites.

"Well done," Bran said, pitching his voice to carry. "The creatures are growing clever, but you are all skilled enough to prevail against them. I am proud and pleased to number you among my very best."

He did not mention that, had they been one fewer, or the Voidspawn numbered any more, they might well have all fallen, their blood staining the silvergrass and seeping into the soil.

"Take a few moments more," he continued. "And then we make for Nightshade."

Where, he hoped, there would be enough time for his fighters to recuperate—and for him to regain the powers that were returning far too slowly.

"I could not help but notice that you have lost your edge," Hestil said softly as they regained the main road. "What happened?"

"Later," he said.

He had not wanted to admit to anyone but Mara how close he'd come to death—but his weakness on the field was a liability his second-in-command must be informed of. He blew out an annoyed breath. In truth, he should have told her earlier, but he had been hoping that his powers would return more quickly than they had. The Voidspawn had put him to the test, unfortunately, and there was no denying the weakness that still lay over him.

Still, telling Hestil was one thing, and letting his warriors overhear it, quite another. As Commander of the all Dark Elves' forces, it was imperative he project nothing but strength. Aware of Hestil's speculative gaze still resting on him, he forced himself to sit up straight and ignore the echoing ache of his wellspring.

CHAPTER 14

Several turns later, Bran and his troop reached the Nightshade Court. They were welcomed warmly, and the injured warriors immediately sent for additional healing. As Bran followed the Nightshade Lady through the mostly empty corridors of her palace, he could not help a shiver of premonition. If he could not find a way to make his people fruitful again, every court was doomed to waste away, the halls desolate, the rooms deserted.

No. He must not succumb to such despair. His prophecy was to save Elfhame, and he must believe that included the people that dwelt in the realm, as well as the land itself.

"It is quiet," the Nightshade Lady said, as if sensing his thoughts. "We lost many during the Void invasion."

"Your court has given much for the realm." Bran glanced down at her thin face. "I am sorry to ask for some of your warriors."

She waved away his words. "Hawthorne provided sanctuary when we most needed it. Whatever we have here is yours."

"I will only take a few fighters. You must have a force left to defend yourself from the remaining Voidspawn, should they attack."

He did not suggest that she evacuate the palace. That would be to surrender to fear. Besides, surely he and his warriors would be able to eradicate the last of the Void. Even if the enemy had grown surprisingly cunning.

"We will strengthen the wards about the palace," she said.

Bran gave her a short nod. "Scry to me, should you fall under attack again."

He hoped that would not be the case. Nightshade had borne too much.

They entered the dining hall, and he was relieved to see that, with the addition of his warriors, a respectable number of the tables were filled. Of course, the room was smaller than Hawthorne's, and when he looked closely, he could see that the tables were widely spaced, as though some had been removed and the room rearranged to close the gaps.

The meal was subdued, the courtiers discussing what it meant that a half-dozen Void creatures had been lurking in the area. Bran and the Nightshade Lady spoke of small things at first until, between the last courses, she mentioned Mara.

"I am surprised your wife is not with you," she said, regarding him steadily with her clear indigo eyes.

"I could not risk her," he said.

One of the lady's eyebrows tilted up. "She seemed capable enough of fending for herself on the battlefield."

"Still, she must have some tutoring in the use of her wellspring. She remained at Hawthorne to receive the proper training."

"Why don't you teach her?"

"I am not a skilled teacher."

He took a swallow of mead, trying to wash away the taste of failure. If anyone could guide Mara, it ought to have been him, but his attempts had been woefully inadequate.

"Perhaps humans learn our magic differently," the Nightshade Lady said. "Have her efforts with other teachers been successful?"

"Yes." He did not elaborate on the fact that Mara was struggling, even with the venerated and experienced Penluith as her tutor.

And he did not want to think too closely on Nightshade's words—for, if they were true, then he had no real reason to leave his wife behind. Except his own selfishness in trying to keep her safe.

"How long may we offer you our hospitality?" the lady asked.

Bran firmed his mouth. He'd meant to take a few hand-picked soldiers from among the Nightshade Court's fighters and depart for Moonflower as soon as they broke their fast. But the Voidspawn attack had taxed his troop, and they needed more than one sleep to recover.

"On the next brightmoon," he said reluctantly. "In the meantime, we can help strengthen the magical protections about the palace."

Too late, he remembered that his own powers were depleted. He'd have to fashion some reasonable excuse. That, or admit a portion of the truth.

He would have done so with no other ruler, but if anyone knew how to keep secrets, it was the Nightshade Lady. Her court had a long and troubled past, and he suspected the other courts, with the exception of the nearby Hawthorne, knew little of Nightshade's hidden history.

"We are glad to shelter you here as long as necessary," she said. "I will have my steward show your people to their rooms."

"Thank you." He had spent the last turn battling back his weariness, and knew that his warriors were in no better shape.

She rose, signaling that dinner was at an end, then turned to Bran. "Perhaps tomorrow we can speak more of the Void threat. And of the future."

"I would like that." He made her a slight bow—not a strictly necessary protocol between an heir and a ruler, but she had earned his respect several times over. Then, trying to keep his steps energetic, he followed his warriors from the room.

Mara ate her leftover honeycakes for lunch, but could not dispel the restless anxiety that settled on her shoulders. There was no need to worry for Bran—he was only traveling from the Hawthorne Court to the Nightshade—but a sense of foreboding seemed to linger in the shadows.

To banish it, she practiced summoning foxfire. Or tried to, at any rate. As before, her efforts amounted to nothing.

"Drat it!" she finally exclaimed, jumping to her feet.

When Penluith came, she'd ask him to teach her something else. Perhaps scrying, or the ward he had mentioned. What other magics did Dark Elves learn in the early stages? She had no idea what constituted the basics as opposed to more advanced spells.

A knock came at the door. Mara opened it cautiously, to find an unfamiliar Dark Elf woman standing there. She was garbed in the leathers of a warrior, with a long blade and short dagger belted on either side of her waist. Her black hair, braided back from her face, held glints of russet.

A scar ran down one of her cheekbones. Mara didn't realize she'd been staring at it until the woman spoke.

"I chose not to let the healers erase it," she said. "It is a badge of honor to me. I am Sicil."

"Hello. I'm Mara."

The elf nodded, as if it weren't obvious. "Are you ready to begin your knife training?"

Clearly Sicil wasn't one to mince words, or waste time on niceties. Which, Mara reflected, was a hallmark of most of the warriors under Bran's command. She was glad to see the warrior, despite Sicil's brusque manner. It brought Bran closer, somehow.

Mara glanced down at the length of scarlet silk draped, somewhat inexpertly, about her. "I suppose I should change."

"It is not necessary. May I enter?"

Mara stepped back, giving Sicil permission to stride into the sitting room. The elf took in the room with a glance.

"We'll need to move the couch back," she said, pushing the table out of the way.

Mara helped her move the furniture until the center of the room was cleared. With brisk efficiency, Sicil rolled up the ornately patterned rug, revealing smooth wooden planks the color of a pigeon's wing.

Did Elfhame even have pigeons? Mara thought not. The only flying things she'd encountered were the glimglows, and a dark-winged owl in the depths of the Darkwood. Of course, she hadn't seen very much of Elfhame. There might well be all kinds of creatures dwelling in the realm that she had no notion of.

"I understand you have a knife," Sicil said, glancing with disapproval at the lack of weapon at Mara's waist.

"It's in the other room. I'll fetch it."

Mara forced herself not to scurry to do Sicil's bidding. The woman had a forceful personality, but that didn't mean Mara should bow to the warrior's every command. She'd stood up to Bran, after all, and she could think of no one more forbidding than the Hawthorne Prince in one of his moods.

She returned from the bedroom with the dagger Bran had given her, the gemstones cool against her palm. It was a better weapon than her old, trusty kitchen knife, but she felt a pang of longing for the plain wooden handle and nicked blade.

Sicil held out her hand, and Mara gave her the weapon.

"Hm." The Dark Elf turned it back and forth, giving the haft a close inspection. She tested the blade with her thumb, and frowned.

"Needs a sharper edge, but the balance is good, the workmanship solid. You should wear it at all times." She handed the dagger back to Mara.

"Even when I'm alone in these rooms?"

"Of course." Sicil's voice held an impatient note. "What good is giving you lessons in blade work if you have no weapon handy when you need one?"

"And why shouldn't I change into something more practical?" Might as well ask all the annoying questions at once.

"If you are called upon to use your blade, it will not come at an opportune time. Your enemies will not wait for you to don proper fighting garb. You're not joining the ranks of the fighters." Sicil paused. "At least, that is not the instruction Prince Brannonilon gave me."

It was a somewhat laughable thought.

"He's right," Mara said. "I have no intention of becoming a warrior."

Sicil nodded. "Then we shall proceed as planned. Now, hold the dagger firmly, with your thumb wrapped about the handle, like so."

She demonstrated the proper grip, and Mara tried to emulate her. Sicil reached over and adjusted her fingers until she was satisfied with Mara's grasp.

"Now, your stance. Spread your feet wider and bend your knees."

Mara complied. At least the Dark Elf dresses were roomy enough to maneuver in. As long as she avoided tripping over her skirts, she supposed she could learn to fight in court clothes.

Sicil took her through a pattern of lunges and swipes, some high, some low, pausing at intervals to reposition Mara's arms.

"Where to strike depends on the size of your attacker," the elf said. "Whether they are wearing armor or silk, how skilled they are. A gut wound will slow your enemy, but a throat stab is better."

Mara halted, taking a moment to catch her breath.

"What kind of enemies do you think I'll face here, in the Hawthorne Court?" she asked.

And why hadn't Bran discussed such things with her, instead of informing her she'd be training to fight, and then leaving her behind?

Sicil's expression grew remote. "I cannot say, my lady. One never knows where danger lurks."

Wonderful. When Bran returned, Mara planned on having a serious discussion with him about the dangers of Elfhame.

"Do you think the prince is being overcautious?" She watched Sicil closely.

The Dark Elf's face remained impassive. "It is his duty—and mine—to ensure your safety, whether in the court or elsewhere. Shall we resume?"

"I suppose." Mara wiped her forehead with her sleeve, then took up her stance again and raised her blade.

By the time Sicil declared the practice session at an end, Mara was sticky with perspiration. She could tell her arms were going to be sore later, and probably her legs as well.

"Good work," the warrior elf said. "You will rest on the morrow, then alternate between working with me and lessons with Penluith."

Mara firmed her mouth. "I suppose Bran decreed this schedule?"

Without once discussing it with her. Clearly her husband had forgotten that theirs was supposed to be a partnership of equals.

Sicil must have heard the annoyance in Mara's tone, for her voice held a sympathetic note. "The commander sometimes forgets that we are not pieces to be moved about on a game board. If anyone can help remind him of that fact, my lady, it is you."

Mara blew out a breath. She hoped Sicil was right. And in his defense, Bran had been distracted, trying to recover from the edge of dying while also mustering his soldiers for their quest. Not to mention worrying about his sister and facing off against his parents.

"We shall see." And she would bide.

For now.

CHAPTER 15

It took longer for Bran and his warriors to recover than he would have liked. By the doublemoon, he was restless and impatient at the thought of Voidspawn loose throughout Elfhame.

He sat with the Nightshade Lady in her private study over breakfast, where they had taken to discussing the threat to Elfhame, and how best to face it.

"Sobering news," the lady said, pushing aside her plate. "There have been reports of a spiderkin spotted near Moonflower, a gyrewolf killed at the border."

"Nothing from the inner courts?"

"No." The Nightshade Lady sounded thoughtful. "Do you find that odd?"

"Not particularly. The main rifts were all in Hawthorne and Nightshade territory. Why should the Voidspawn disperse from the area?"

"Still, you intend to visit all the courts," she said.

Bran gave her a terse nod. "I must, to ensure the entire realm is free of our old enemy. I'll sweep the surrounding countryside as I go, of course."

"I have no doubt you'll succeed in your quest." She leaned forward, giving him a searching look. "And your wellspring? Is it replenished?"

"Well enough."

That had been a difficult conversation, admitting to the Nightshade Lady that the Void had injured him so deeply. But it was better than pretending all was well and continuing to drain himself dry. An exhausted commander did his warriors no good.

He shifted uncomfortably and changed the subject. "Once I've returned to the Hawthorne Court, I hope I might bring my wife here for a visit."

"I would like that very well." Her face softened. "What I saw of your lady, I admired."

Bran felt his lips lift in a slight smile. Yes, his wife was remarkable, and he was glad that Nightshade recognized her worth.

Unlike his own parents. His smile evaporated. "I hope that visit will come soon."

"As do I, Hawthorne Prince. But now, I see you are ready to depart." She pushed her chair back and rose. "I will not wish you a safe journey, for that would defeat its purpose, but I do wish you all success. May your sword fall true and your magic burn bright."

He bowed. "Thank you, my lady. Next we meet, the Voidspawn will be gone from our land, forever."

She nodded gravely, her fingers tight on the back of her chair. Neither of them spoke of the other threat hanging over the fate of the Dark Elves.

I will conquer that, too, Bran thought fiercely. *Our future depends on it.*

THE PALEMOON and the bright cast double shadows as Bran and his warriors—their party now numbering sixteen—rode out from the Nightshade Palace. The mood was cautiously cheerful, and he felt his spirits rise as they rode into the purple-hued meadows.

His wellspring, though still not at full strength, was recovered enough that he could once again wield his battle magic. His troop numbered enough to make up three scouting parties, so that they might cover more ground. And the Nightshade Lady respected his wife.

That, perhaps most of all, gave him heart.

The cold reception Mara had received at the Hawthorne Court angered him. He'd wanted to take the nobles by their collars and shake them hard, until they saw Mara's value. Wasn't it enough that she'd played a pivotal role in the battle against the Void? They were fools, all of them.

Especially Mireleth.

He gritted his teeth at the memory of his ex-betrothed waving her bracelet about as if it were some kind of promise, instead of a broken bond. She must have retrieved the bracelet after he'd severed that foolish betrothal. It was unheard of, for one party to continue to wear an empty promise, but then again, Mireleth was always looking for advantage and was happy to bend the rules to do so.

Once he returned to Hawthorne, he'd have to do something about her—and her ambitious father. There could be no more angling for a position at his side. Mara was the next Hawthorne Lady, and in his heart there could be no other.

At least Anneth understood. He knew that his sister would help Mara settle into the ways of the court. And once his wife mastered her wellspring, a greater acceptance must follow.

"Shall we break off?" Hestil asked, pulling him from his thoughts.

"Yes." He glanced at the five hand-picked warriors that would go with her, taking point as they made for Moonflower. "Contact me if you sense anything."

"Aye, commander."

She signaled to her fighters, and the six of them spurred their mounts forward. The moons illuminated them as they rode away—the bright glints of metal on their weapons and padded armor, the locks of raven and silver hair flying behind them from the wind of their passing.

"My lord." Turut, the leader of the second scout troop, guided his horse beside Fuin. "Shall we turn aside as well?"

"Not yet. We'll give Hestil some time to flush out our prey." If, indeed, any Void creatures lay in their path. Bran watched the riders until they disappeared over the crest of a purple-hazed hill.

He'd cast a net of sensing over the entire party. If his second-in-command engaged in a fight, the magic would alert him immediately. So far, all was quiet. Although, the Voidspawn had managed to elude his perceptions until the last moment during their previous encounter—further proof that they had grown in cunning.

"If she hasn't encountered any Voidspawn within two turns, I'll send you on your way," Bran said.

"Very good, my lord."

Turut fell back to ride with his scouts. Their party also numbered six, leaving Bran with three warriors. And his own powerful magic, of course. He planned to stay on the main road, while Turut and Hestil ranged ahead and to the sides. It would take them five sleeps to reach Moonflower, where he hoped to gather another half-dozen warriors, at least.

Then on to Rowan, which circled back to share a border with Hawthorne, though their courts lay almost as far apart as Hawthorne and Moonflower. The proximity of Nightshade to the Hawthorne Court was unusual.

But then, their two courts shared the Erynvorn and guarded the doorway within. Rowan and Moonflower had ever been removed from such things—and the inner courts even more so, preoccupied with etiquette and artistry rather than facing any threats at their borders.

No, the four outer courts had borne the brunt of shoring up the barrier that protected their small realm. Hawthorne and Nightshade most of all.

Bran flexed his hands, extending and retracting his claws. He was not certain what kind of reception he'd find once he turned to the center of Elfhame. His parents sat on the Courts' Council, as he would in turn, but the seven courts did not always agree.

At least they'd all sent warriors once the Void started breaking through in earnest. Bran had found no fault with their fighting skills.

The nobility, on the other hand...

He let out a heavy breath. He'd turn that glass when he came to it. Meantime, he had Voidspawn to hunt.

CHAPTER 16

As Mara had suspected, her arms were sore the next day from her training with Sicil. The ache helped distract her from the deeper pain of waking alone in Bran's bed. Did he miss her? How long would it be until he returned?

Such thoughts only served to hone the edge of her unhappiness, and she scolded herself for wallowing in them. Better to turn her mind to the new day. Determinedly, she rose, stretched, and decided to visit Anneth instead of going in search of breakfast.

But what to wear? Pursing her lips, she stared at the colorful lengths of silk hanging in the closet. Was it considered vulgar to don the same outfit twice in as many days? Probably. Good thing the seamstress was scheduled to deliver an assortment of new gowns after lunch.

She wrapped a length of turquoise silk around herself and tied the ends together behind her neck to anchor the garment. The skirts billowed about her legs, but despite the free-flowing fabric, the dress was not immodest. At the last minute, she recalled Sicil's instruction to wear her dagger at all times.

After a bit of searching through the wardrobe, Mara found a woven belt that seemed to match her dress. Or at least didn't clash with it. She looped the sash about her waist and slipped on the sheathed dagger. A polished silver mirror hung on the far wall of the bedroom, and she went over to inspect her reflection.

The turquoise fabric brought out the green of her eyes, and she thought she'd done an adequate job of dressing herself. She might yet master the knack of donning the Dark Elves' clothing, but it would never feel as familiar as her old homespun dress. She went back to the wardrobe and ran her hand down the coarse weave. It felt like home, and she couldn't help sighing before she closed the door and went to visit Anneth.

Bran's sister was delighted to see her, and Mara was glad to find that her friend was up and moving without apparent pain.

"Are you all better?" she asked, stepping into Anneth's sitting room.

"Avantor has pronounced me fit enough to resume my normal activities," Anneth said with a grin. "No vigorous riding for a bit longer, though. I must say, you've done a fair job with your dress. Let me just pull this bit out, here, and re-tuck it... Yes, like so. You see? And then this part goes over here."

Mara twisted about, trying to discern where Anneth had folded the fabric upon itself and where she had tucked it in. Whatever she'd done, the dress flowed more gracefully, and Mara felt a bit less like she was wearing her elder sister's castoff.

"I'm not sure I'll ever get it right," she said ruefully, meaning more than just the Dark Elves' style of dress.

"You will, with my help." Anneth gave her an encouraging look. "I was getting ready to go to breakfast. Come with me?"

Mara nodded. Truly, it was time to stop sulking in Bran's rooms. She could face the dining room with an ally by her side.

"How are the lessons going with Penluith?" Anneth asked as they stepped together into the hall.

"I am not the most talented of students," Mara said, unwilling to confess that she was, apparently, terrible at magic. Despite the fact that, according to Bran, she possessed an amazing wellspring. It did not seem to be a very obedient one, unfortunately.

"It will come." Anneth squeezed her arm, then glanced at the blade belted at Mara's waist. "I hear that Sicil is giving you weapons training."

"The rudiments of how to use a dagger, that's all. I'm not sure how useful it will be."

"Being able to wield a weapon of any kind is important," Anneth said, her voice somber. "After being attacked by the Voidspawn, I've vowed to work on my archery. Perhaps we can train together."

"Where?" Surely Anneth wasn't going to practice shooting her bow and arrows inside. "The gardens?"

"That's a marvelous idea. I'd thought the training arena, but the gardens are even better. There's a secluded corner near the old wall that will be perfect. When shall we start? After breakfast?"

Despite nearing the dining room's doors, and the no-doubt disapproving members of the court, Mara smiled. Clearly Anneth was feeling better, if her exuberance was any indication.

"Very well," Mara said. "As long as you don't laugh at me. I'm not very skilled."

"Of course you're not—you've just started. Whereas I am horrid with bows, despite having used them for years."

"That's not entirely true," Avantor said, catching up to them from behind, having clearly overheard Anneth's last words. "You just haven't cared to excel."

"Well, I care now," she replied.

The healer gave her a stern look. "You may practice your archery, but no sessions longer than a quarter turn until the next brightmoon."

Anneth made a face, but didn't argue. For her part, Mara was glad of the time constraint. She wasn't certain how much stabbing and lunging she could do, with the muscles in her arms and legs protesting with every movement.

The three of them entered the dining hall, and Mara was relieved to see it was not very full. The Hawthorne Lord and Lady's places were empty. A few nobles browsed the food set out on the long tables, and others clustered together, taking their meals.

"Is it always this quiet?" she asked Anneth in a low voice.

"Mostly—except when there's an event or special visitors." Bran's sister gave her a knowing look. "No one would remark upon it if you came to breakfast by yourself."

Mara firmed her lips. She supposed she could always fix a plate for herself and retreat, if the company became unpleasant. Meaning, if Mireleth or one of her cronies cornered her.

A quick glance around the room showed no sign of the Dark Elf lady in question, and a bit more of the tension drained from Mara's shoulders.

"It's not as formal as I'd expected," she said.

"Luncheon is similar," Avantor said. "Although perhaps you did not notice, having so recently come to the Hawthorne Palace. Our court protocols have been rather upended lately."

"Epic battles and prophecies fulfilled tend to shake things up." Anneth winked at Mara. "Come, I'll show you my favorite things to eat."

More than simple honeycakes and moonmelon awaited on the long tables. Anneth guided Mara through the array of fruits and pastries, the thinly sliced meats and baked grains. Even though she only took a small sample of the dishes, Mara's plate was nearly spilling over by the time they reached the end of the array.

Avantor, who had deftly made his selections, beckoned from a nearby table, and Anneth and Mara went to join him.

Once seated, Mara found that she was ravenous. Despite the unfamiliar flavors, she ate steadily while Avantor, after a series of questions to Anneth, decided she was sufficiently healed and released her from his care.

The talk turned to Bran and his route through Elfhame.

"He will be in Moonflower by now," Anneth said, glancing at Mara. "Our realm is not so large, truly. He'll be back at Hawthorne in a few more doublemoons."

"Provided he does not encounter unexpected complications," Avantor added.

Mara tried not to let the healer's doubts shadow her own mood, and instead turned to Anneth with a determined smile. "Where is he headed after Moonflower?"

"The inner courts, and then Rowan," Anneth said. "At least, I think that is his course."

It was time to study the maps in Bran's rooms again. Mara was not sure where Rowan lay in relation to Hawthorne. To the northwest, she thought, where the two courts shared a distant border.

As they finished their meal, Mireleth swept into the room, accompanied by her retinue. She surveyed her surroundings imperiously, and when her gaze landed on Mara, her eyes glittered with satisfaction.

"Brace yourselves," Avantor said softly, and took a sip of his tea. "She's headed this way."

Hidden by the table, Mara brushed her fingers over the handle of the weapon attached to her belt. Brandishing a dagger at Mireleth would probably not be within protocol, but she took comfort in the fact that she was armed, and at least had the option of drawing her blade.

"My dear Anneth," Mireleth said, arriving at their table in a swirl of skirts and smirking courtiers. "How marvelous that you've decided to grace us with your presence once more."

"Perhaps you're unaware that Lady Anneth was injured." Avantor's voice was cool. "She was resting, on my orders."

Mireleth widened her eyes in mock innocence. "Oh yes—supposedly the country is overrun with Void creatures, despite Prince Brannonilon's declaration that we vanquished the enemy."

One of the Dark Elves standing behind her tittered. "Not much of a triumph, then, was it?" she said in loud whisper to another of Mireleth's companions.

"I'd like to see you venture out from the Hawthorne Court," Mara said, swiveling in her seat to glare at the courtier. "Perhaps you'd like to fight one of the Void creatures yourself."

"No need for any of us to do so." Mireleth flicked her fingers dismissively. "I'm certain my prince has such matters well in hand. A pity he had to go running off so very quickly after your marriage. One might almost think he no longer wanted to remain at court."

Again a spate of laughter. Anger bubbling through her, Mara scraped her chair back and stood, confronting Mireleth directly. The Dark Elf's face tightened, and she took a small step back. Mara counted that as victory enough.

"I believe my *husband* is tired of the petty squabbles and silly maneuverings of the nobility," she said. "I can't say I blame him—I find such things tiresome, myself."

Lifting her chin in dismissal, she pushed past Mireleth and strode away, hoping somewhat desperately that Anneth and Avantor were right behind her.

"Well done," Bran's sister said at her shoulder.

Mara drew in a breath of relief, and glanced to her other side to find Avantor keeping pace. The three of them stepped into the hallway, and she paused a moment to gather herself.

"Thank you for following me," she said.

"Of course!" Anneth shot her a sly smile. "Mireleth deserves to be taken down a notch, and you're just the one to do it."

"Still, you must take care," Avantor said, his expression serious. "Lady Mireleth has many connections at court, and her family is powerful. You do not want to antagonize her too much."

"Spoken like a true courtier." Anneth shook her head. "What about Mara's connections, her power? She is to be the Hawthorne Lady. I believe she's right to put Mireleth in her place—and anyone else who insults her."

"I don't want to play such games," Mara said. "I just couldn't take another spiteful word."

Although she'd called such things *tiresome* mostly to irritate Mireleth, Mara found that the words were true. She was a village girl from Little Hazel, not a princess raised in a grand palace, groomed for the intricacies of rulership.

"Don't fret." Anneth reached over and squeezed her shoulder. "Bran will be back soon, the rest of the Void vanquished, and you will find solid footing at court. I know it."

Despite her friend's optimistic words, Mara was not so sure. The more time she spent at the Hawthorne Court, the more she knew she wasn't suited for such a life. But what else could she do?

She'd married the prince, after all, and abandoned her home world. The only place she had left was here, in the graceful prison of the Hawthorne Palace.

CHAPTER 17

As the doublemoons curved down toward the horizon, Bran's warriors came together to make camp. They had covered much ground in the last several turns and found no Voidspawn. Hestil reported a few blighted areas where it seemed the creatures had lingered, but beyond that, there was no sign.

"Do you think they are hiding from us?" she asked as they ate their rations of bread and dried meat.

Around them, the warriors pitched small tents, tended the mounts, and arranged for sentry duty. Bran watched them, chewing slowly and pondering Hestil's question.

"I would have said no, before that last skirmish," he said. "But something has changed. The creatures have grown cunning."

Hestil frowned. "I do not know how, or why, but it seems the Voidspawn have somehow become more than mindless minions. With the rifts closed, they should be simple to fight, but now..." She trailed off, her brow furrowed.

He had the same thoughts, and hearing Hestil confirm them sent a chill down his back. They knew so little about their ancient enemy—only that the Void was eager to devour new lands, sending its army in through rifts between the worlds to cut down any resistance, before slithering in to feast.

His people had legends of once-vibrant realms turned to dust, teeming worlds left arid and lifeless after the Void descended. Elfhame had stood fast, with magic and might. Until now.

"After the battle..." He paused. It was difficult to speak of his weakness, but in light of the Voidspawn's new behavior, he must tell his second some of what had transpired.

He would not share Mara's determination to return to her home world, and subsequent return, however. That secret would jeopardize her standing in the eyes of his soldiers. Even Hestil, although she might understand, would not think well of his mortal wife for attempting to abandon her husband.

Hestil watched him without demanding answers. She knew to let the silence lengthen, and that he would fill it when ready.

"Just before Mara and I struck at the heart of the Void and sealed the rift, something escaped," he finally said. "It lodged within me, depleting my wellspring and stealing my life force. I was very nearly dead. Mara saved me."

He suppressed a shiver at the memory of that icy malevolence.

"Did she kill it?" Hestil's eyes narrowed in concentration.

"I believed so. But my recollection of that time is hazy." He'd been exhausted, drained of hope, of magic.

"What if the Void shard survived?"

"And is directing the remaining Voidspawn?" he finished for her. "That would fit with what we've seen so far—the ambush, the ruined areas."

"And means the threat is far greater than we feared." Hestil's voice was hard.

"Indeed. We must redouble our tracking efforts." He frowned. "The Void shard, if that is truly what it is, would be seeking to strengthen itself, so that it could reopen a rift."

"It will find us difficult prey, as ever."

Bran took a bite of bread, letting his thoughts coalesce as he chewed. The stars overhead spread their soft radiance, and the night seemed peaceful—to those who didn't know of the dark threat roaming the land.

Every Dark Elf knew of the danger the Void and its creatures posed. As Hestil said, Elfhame and its people were capable of protecting themselves. Even, he hoped, with an inimical piece of the Void slithering about the realm.

But what if the Void sought easier victims? The bread he'd swallowed caught in his throat, and he coughed, trying to dislodge the uneasy thought along with his food.

Hestil thumped him on the back, and he nodded his thanks. Still, apprehension ran through him.

"What if the Void is making for the gateway in the Erynvorn?" he asked in a low voice, as if the enemy could overhear.

"How would it know to do so?" Hestil gave him an appraising look.

"Mara healed me there," he confessed.

His second raised a brow, clearly sensing there was more to the story, but she did not press him.

"Would it even be able to pass through into the mortal world?" she asked. "It takes great magical strength to open the gateway."

"Perhaps my fear is unfounded."

"And perhaps not." Her brows knitted together. "Do we split our fighters, sending some into the Erynvorn, while the rest continue on to Moonflower and Rowan?"

"It is not a decision to take lightly."

He set aside the rest of the bread, his hunger gone, and crossed his arms. Breaking the party up would be risky. They were under strength as it was, and if he'd guessed incorrectly, the odds would favor the now-clever Voidspawn. He suspected the only reason the party hadn't been attacked since leaving Nightshade was due to their numbers.

"We continue to Moonflower," he said, thinking aloud. "They should be able to lend us a dozen fighters, at least. There, we'll split into two parties. You will take half to the inner courts, scouring for the Void along the way."

Hestil's mouth tightened with displeasure.

"I will take the rest," he continued, "and make for Rowan. From there, we will close the circle of the outer courts and head into the Erynvorn."

Without more information—which he was unlikely to get—it was the best he could do. Even with his magic, there was no way to read the intent of the Voidspawn, or to know if their guess about its dark intentions was correct, or only fearful speculation.

A good commander did not make decisions out of fear. But neither did they ignore a possible threat. He did not like separating the warriors into two parties, but the Void could not be allowed to flow unchecked into the mortal world.

"I do not like it," Hestil said. "But I see no better way."

"If you find one, tell me."

The burdens of command lay heavy on his shoulders. He watched as the palemoon chased the brightmoon out of the sky, leaving faded twilight in their wake, and wished for answers he did not have.

CHAPTER 18

As promised, Anneth took Mara out to the far corner of the gardens for their weapons practice. A few glimglows trailed them, bobbing up and down like flames that had floated free of their candles, and the soft air carried the scent of flowers.

As they continued along the blossom-starred hedges, Mara's spirits rose. It took her several moments to realize why: the air was luminous with the light cast from both the brightmoon and the pale. Despite the strange double shadows cast by the moons, she smiled in relief.

It was a sheer pleasure to be out of the Hawthorne Palace—and the confines of Bran's rooms. When he returned, things would improve, she reminded herself. They must.

"Here." Anneth halted at a stretch of well-kept silvergrass.

The hedges continued on either side, giving them privacy. The spires of the palace were just visible over their dark leaves. A target had been set up at one end, and Anneth strode to it, leaving Mara to practice her knife drills.

The handle of her dagger felt awkward in her hand, and without Sicil's example, she went clumsily through the moves, but she persevered. For her sparring partner, she chose a dark-leaved bush with dangling blue flowers.

While Anneth sent arrows careening toward her target, Mara practiced slicing petals off the flowers. Neither of them were particularly successful. When their allotted time ended, Anneth set the end of her bow on the manicured grass and laughed.

"We are not very formidable, are we?"

"Not yet," Mara answered.

She was determined to master *something*, however—and since her magic was proving elusive, knife work seemed the better choice.

Anneth nodded. "I'm sure we'll improve, over time. Speaking of which, how are your lessons with Penluith going?"

"We have another session later today. I'm still working on summoning foxfire." Mara tried not to let her discouragement show in her voice.

"Perhaps it's difficult because you didn't grow up surrounded by such things." Anneth gave her a thoughtful look. "Once you become accustomed to life in our realm, magic should come easier."

"I hope so."

When she'd chosen to abandon the mortal world for Elfhame, Mara hadn't exactly envisioned spending her days failing at almost every task she was set. Or penned up in the Hawthorne Palace, waiting for her husband to return from his own quests.

As if reading her thoughts, Anneth patted Mara's shoulder. "I'm sure that once my brother returns, he will help. Are you ready to go in?"

Not particularly, but Mara recalled Avantor's instructions for Anneth to limit her training. So she nodded her assent and sheathed her blade, then helped Anneth gather up her stray arrows, and they left the gardens behind.

The corridors were depressingly dim, and Mara tried not to sigh as they moved deeper into the palace. She really must master the trick of summoning foxfire, and soon.

"I'll come visit after your lessons with Penluith," Anneth said encouragingly as Mara left her at her door. "Surely they'll go better this time."

Bran's sister was eternally optimistic—a quality as endearing as it was annoying.

"Thank you," Mara said, trying not to sound too glum.

Either her lessons would progress, or, more likely, they wouldn't.

Once she reached Bran's rooms, she stood and inhaled deeply, trying to catch a trace of his spicy scent. Trying to remember the wry crook of his lips when he smiled, the way his eyes narrowed when she perplexed him once again with her strange mortal ways. There was only the faintest hint of cloves in the air, and a pang of loneliness squeezed her heart.

How strange, that she should pine for the man she'd once thought monstrous—her clawed, pale warrior who wielded magic as easily as he did his fearsome curved sword. But fate had brought them together. Though she did not understand the Oracles and their divinations, she could not dispute that their prophecy had proven true. At least, so far.

Her ample breakfast carried her through lunch, and Mara spent the time before Penluith arrived trying to harness the power of her well-spring. When she closed her eyes and *reached* deep inside, she thought she felt it, like a quiet blue pool. But sensing it was one thing, and activating it quite another.

Penluith arrived, and once again demonstrated ample patience as Mara struggled to conjure foxfire. After half their time had run, with no success, she turned to him.

"What about casting a shield? Or, what did you call it—a ward?"

The tutor frowned faintly. "As I said earlier, it is a dangerous magic to harness."

"Well." Mara shrugged. "Since I probably won't be able to cast that magic either, it doesn't matter. Will you at least let me try?"

Penluith studied her a long moment. "Very well—but you must take care in its casting. The word is *turma*."

She practiced saying it aloud, without trying to summon any magic. Once the tutor nodded his approval, she concentrated on connecting with her magic.

"*Turma*," she said fiercely.

As usual, nothing happened. She swallowed the lump in her throat and lifted her chin defiantly, refusing to let Penluith see the despair creeping over her.

"Hm." He twisted his mouth in thought, then rose from his customary chair. "Let us see if a change of venue might help. Come."

Mara hoped he was leading her back into the gardens, but instead he took a circuitous route through the corridors. Despite her unfamiliarity with the palace, she thought he was leading her down hallways she'd never traversed before.

At last, they stepped through a graceful arch into a large, round room that shimmered with light. The center of the room held a pool filled with pale blue water, and the roof overhead was open to the sky.

"The Room of Reflection," Penluith said as Mara glanced about. "Some find that it helps focus the mind."

"So, the water's not for bathing?"

She didn't think so, and the tutor's shocked expression confirmed her guess.

"No," he said, sounding faintly horrified. "The pool is blessed by the Oracles. It symbolizes the wellspring, and the radiance that shines within us all."

Even humans? she wanted to ask, but bit her tongue on the words.

"Sit here," he said, leading her to a bench carved of pale stone.

Flat pillows adorned it, covered in blue silk that matched the water, and Mara settled, facing the pool. The water was as still as glass, the double spheres overhead just visible at the edge of the reflection.

"Breathe slowly," the tutor said. "Empty your mind of striving, of worry. Feel the peaceful center of your own wellspring."

It was surprisingly easy to follow his directions. The pool seemed to shimmer slightly, and Mara thought she felt an answering flutter deep inside.

"Call foxfire," Penluith said softly.

Trying to retain her fragile sense of peace, Mara opened her hands.

"*Calma*," she said.

A small blue spark ignited above her right palm, and she gasped in surprise.

"Look!" She lifted her hand to Penluith, only to see the tiny ball of foxfire snuff out.

Still, he gave her a nod of approval. "Try again."

She did, and succeeded about half the time. The tutor watched her closely, his indigo eyes inscrutable.

"Enough," he said, after Mara had failed a half-dozen times in a row. "I think I see part of the difficulty."

"What is it?" She folded her hands in her lap and tried not to hold her breath as she awaited his answer.

His lips quirked, possibly with annoyance. "You seem best able to call upon your wellspring when you do not try."

"But... how else am I supposed to do magic?"

"Without trying," he said dryly. "That is, let your wellspring open without attempting to open it."

It seemed quite contradictory. She stared at the pool, frowning, and tried to pick apart the why and how of her ability.

When Bran drew upon her power in battle, it was not an active attempt on her part to reach her wellspring, so she supposed that made sense. And when she opened the gateway, she'd been driven by desperation and panicked need. There had been no time to try—she'd simply had to act.

The time she called foxfire in Bran's rooms, she'd managed just as he entered—and she dimly recalled being distracted by his arrival. She supposed that, for a brief moment, she had not been pushing so hard to create it, and thus the foxfire came.

But having only intermittent access to her wellspring seemed worse than having no power at all. She needed to be able to rely on her own abilities.

"What if I must summon my magic right away—in case of emergency or attack?" she asked.

"If you know your runes by heart," Penluith said slowly, "then I would hope your casting would become automatic. In cases of emergency."

It was not the answer she hoped for—but the tutor had given her a key to why she was struggling. Now she must unlock the door. First, though, she had to find it—that elusive place in her being where her wellspring dwelt.

The twinned spheres of the palemoon and the bright floated serenely in the basin of the pool. Then, as Mara watched, they shivered as though a low wind moved over the water. The reflections broke into a half-dozen slivers of light, and she leaned forward, trying to make sense of what she saw.

Foxfire, flickering in a dark forest. No... torches. A glimpse of upraised swords and the rounded, blunt faces of human soldiers. Bran, turning with a look of surprise, as a black arrow flew out of the dark and lodged itself in his chest.

"No!" Mara cried.

The echo of her shout broke the peace of the room, and Penluith sprang to his feet.

"What is it?" He set his hands on her shoulders and peered into the water. "What did you see?"

"A battle. The Darkwood, and Bran in danger. I must go to him!" Leaving out the part about seeing her own kind, she sprang to her feet.

"Calm yourself," Penluith said. "What the water shows here is not events in the present."

She gave him an accusing look. "You didn't tell me this was a scrying pool."

"It is not." He shook his head at her. "At least, it is not used for such a purpose. But any reflection can be the vehicle for a scrying—and this water is Oracle-touched. You are not the first to see future visions within it."

"Who else has?" She sent a wary glance at the now-quiet pool.

"Prince Brannonilon."

"And what did he see?" She thought she could guess the answer, however.

"He saw you," Penluith replied, proving her right.

"He was being attacked." Her throat tightened. "I must warn him."

"He is commander of the Dark Elf forces and heir to the Hawthorne throne. Danger has always walked beside our prince. He knows to take care."

"But—"

"If the water has chosen to show you a vision, then you will be able to act in some way." He gave her a gentle look. "When that time comes, you will know. But for now, our lesson is at an end. Do not fret over Brannonilon, or what you have seen."

Very well—she would try not to dwell on it. But, for whatever reason, it seemed the prophecy was not yet done with them. Danger lurked, cloaked in the mists of the future.

As she left the Room of Reflection, she turned to give the water an accusing look. It did nothing more than placidly reflect the stars—but she could not escape the feeling that fate was laughing at her.

CHAPTER 19

Mara returned to Bran's rooms, her thoughts heavy. The chilling vision aside, there was the whole problem of how to access her magical power. It would be difficult to try to reach her wellspring without *trying*. Might as well ask a bird to fly without moving its wings.

She let out a gusty sigh and pushed open the door to Bran's rooms. At least the calm quiet of the reflecting room had given her a place to begin.

Just inside the door, an ornate chest sat, with a smaller box stacked on top. She blinked at them, confused, then cautiously lifted the lid of the box.

Jewelry, hairpins, and silver-shot woven belts gleamed up at her. It seemed her new wardrobe had arrived. Well, that would make a welcome distraction.

She was partway through sorting the jewelry when Anneth knocked at her door—a single rap, followed by three shorter ones. They had agreed on the signal, so that Mara would not have to worry about opening the door to unwanted visitors.

"Come in," she said, admitting Anneth. "Look—my clothing's here."

"Wonderful." Anneth clasped her hands. "You must try everything on, of course. What do you think of the gowns? Do they suit?"

"I haven't opened the chest yet," Mara admitted. "I was enjoying looking over the jewelry."

The low table was spread with winking jewels and intricately wrought metal. It was adornment fit for a queen, and Mara had to keep reminding herself that here, in Elfhame, she actually *was* a princess.

"Well, let's open it." Anneth took one end of the chest, and together they moved it to the center of the room, beside the low couch.

"I don't think there will be room enough for my gowns." Mara glanced at the heavy wardrobe set against one wall. "Bran's clothing and gear takes up most of the space."

Anneth shook her head. "You will need to move into a bigger suite, once he's done traipsing all over Elfhame. You'll each need a sitting room, and a place to store your clothing and personal items."

Not that Mara had many possessions. Certainly not enough to need an entire room of her own to house them. Although the chest of new dresses was a promising start. She pushed open the lid and drew out the first gown, a soft length of pearl-colored silk that seemed more like a dawn cloud than an item of clothing.

"That's lovely," Anneth said approvingly. "The cut will look very well on you."

Mara couldn't see that the garment was shaped at all. To her eye, it was all pleats and billows. But with Anneth's help, and one of the long belts, it began to make sense.

"Now go admire yourself in the mirror," Anneth said, after affixing an opaline comb in Mara's hair. "In fact, let's fetch it—there's one in the bedroom, is there not?"

There was: a tall, heavy thing that barely fit through the doorway. Once they'd positioned it to Anneth's liking, Mara took her place before the reflection. For an instant, the memory of her scrying overlaid the mirrored surface, and she shivered in memory.

Then the moment passed. Mara's vision cleared, to show an elegant woman garbed in a dress that seemed something from a legend. The shimmering fabric clung flatteringly about her chest and flowed into graceful skirts that did not hamper her movements in the least. Sicil would approve.

"Do you like it?" Anneth asked from her perch on the couch.

"I do. Though I still wouldn't wear it to pull weeds."

Anneth laughed. "That's what the gardeners are for. Though if you really wanted to do such a thing, I'm sure they'd let you join them."

"The warriors mostly wear trousers and tunics, I've noticed." Mara turned toward her friend. "Do you think I might have some of those made, as well?"

She didn't want to be too demanding, but, honestly, she couldn't imagine wearing nothing but the gossamer clothing of the Dark Elf nobility.

With an impish grin, Anneth waved at the chest. "I thought you might ask. There should be two sets of them, down at the bottom."

"Is it too eccentric of me?" Mara bent and began rifling through the silky, jewel-toned fabrics.

"No. You are a human, after all. It is probably a good thing, not to try to make yourself entirely into a Dark Elf courtier. A bit of oddity will go in your favor."

Mara's questing fingers found a heavier weave. She pulled out a dark blue tunic and shook it open.

"Ack!" Something scuttled over the cloth, and she hastily dropped the tunic. "There's a bug."

"There should be no insects in the clothing." Frowning, Anneth stood and nudged the cloth with her foot.

A white spider the size of a coin rushed out from the edge of the tunic, making for the shadows under the couch.

"Kill it!" Anneth shrieked, leaping back.

Mara grabbed a scroll from the table and whacked the spider, hard. It curled into a small ball and lay motionless on the carpet.

"Hit it again," Anneth said, her voice shaking.

Mara did, whacking until the spider was, without a doubt, dead.

"I didn't know you were afraid of spiders," she said, looking about for a kerchief or something to use to pick up the body and dispose of it.

"Don't touch it." Anneth let out a shaky breath. "It's an *unquale.* Deadly poisonous."

"Oh." Mara swallowed and eyed the lifeless spider. "Are they common?"

Anneth shook her head vigorously. "No. There never should have been one in your clothing. They dwell in the distant vales outside the Cereus Court. I have not once seen one in Hawthorne."

"Do you think... someone put it there on purpose?" Mara felt ill at the thought. If Anneth had not been there to warn her, she wouldn't have a known a deadly spider was loose in her rooms.

"It is the most likely explanation, though it distresses me greatly." Anneth shot her a worried look.

"Not a very foolproof plot, though. There was no guarantee the spider would remain in the chest, let alone leap out at an opportune moment." It seemed just the kind of thing Mireleth would do, though—a hasty, ill-conceived plan to inflict harm.

Not that Mara had any proof. Just a dead spider curled on one corner of the carpet.

"We must inspect the chest fully," Anneth said. "And each room. Then I will set a ward at the doors and windows, to keep any harmful person—or creature—from entering. I should have remembered that, without Bran here to renew them, the protections have faded."

Mara pressed her lips together. Anneth may have forgotten, but someone else surely had not.

"Show me how to cast the wards," she said.

She would not *try*, of course, but if her safety depended on it, she hoped her wellspring would respond.

To her relief, after Anneth showed her the simple protection spell, Mara was able to duplicate it. They scoured the rooms and, satisfied no more danger lurked, set the wards at the windows and doors. Anneth insisted on warding the door between the bedroom and sitting room, too. Just in case.

"I wish Bran were back," Anneth said when they were finished.

"I do too." Mara folded her arms across her chest, and tried not to think of black arrows flying out of the dark.

CHAPTER 20

As Bran had hoped, the Moonflower Court was able to provide enough warriors to swell their ranks to over thirty fighters. The rulers expressed dismay at the news that Voidspawn still roamed Elfhame, but did not seem unduly alarmed.

"You saw no sign of the creatures as you traveled here from Nightshade?" the Moonflower Lady asked, her voice holding only mild curiosity, as they lingered over their breakfast of fruit and cheese.

"We saw blighted areas," Bran said. "But none of the actual Voidspawn."

It had been worrisome, to suspect that the creatures were moving about Elfhame and yet managing to avoid the scouting parties.

The Moonflower Lord blinked sleepily at him. "Are you even certain that such blight is caused by the Void?"

"Not entirely." Bran bit out the words. "But I can see no other reason."

He wished he could inject more urgency into the languorous court, but Moonflower had ever held themselves slightly apart. Perhaps it was due to the proximity of the Oracles, who dwelt not far away, at the place where Moonflower and the lands of Cereus and Jessamin intersected.

He'd considered visiting the enigmatic seers, but they only ever spoke once to any single person, and that included saying the prophecy for each royal child. Belatedly, he realized that Mara was one of the few people in all of Elfhame whom the Oracles would see. As soon as he returned to Hawthorne, he'd plan a journey to take her to the place of prophecy.

"Perhaps there is a drought," the lady said. "Or an affliction of the soil. Such things have been known to occur."

Bran frowned. Not in his lifetime, or that of his parents, however. But there was no point in arguing with the rulers of Moonflower.

"Thank you for lending your support," he said instead, pushing aside his silver plate. "Your fighters are much appreciated."

"It is good for them to travel a bit," the Moonflower Lord said, as if Bran were taking the soldiers on a pleasure jaunt instead of a possibly deadly reconnoitering mission. "Gives them renewed perspective once they return home."

His wife nodded placidly. "Good journeys to you, Prince Brannonilon Luthinor."

With a tight smile, Bran took his leave. He did not envy Hestil her task of visiting the inner courts, though she'd protested his division of their forces.

"It's foolish for you to take fewer than ten warriors," she'd said, giving him a hard look.

"Rowan will give me more. If you keep the bulk of the force, you'll be able to patrol the inner courts that much more quickly, and then join me."

She'd frowned, but Bran knew his reasoning was sound—in this, at least.

In the light of the half-full palemoon, the soldiers gathered outside Moonflower's gates.

"We will come to you as soon as we may," Hestil said as they shared the traditional warrior's clasp, wrist to wrist. "Good luck, Commander."

"And to you, my second." He released her and raised his hand, signaling the riders to make ready.

For some reason, the lassitude of Moonflower made him want to make a show of this departure. Rather than simply riding out, he'd prepared the warriors for a battle charge across the open meadows surrounding the court.

It might do nothing but make him feel better, but perhaps the sight would stir Moonflower's blood. He could hope so, at any rate.

With a fierce yell, he swept his hand down.

The warriors echoed his cry, surging forward with their blades raised. After the initial charge, Hestil led her troop in a graceful curve to the southeast. They would enter Cereus near the Oracle's haven.

Bran's fighters continued north. He grinned at the sensation of the wind combing through his hair, the thud of hooves vibrating in his chest, the glint of blades sparking in his vision. He did not call a halt until the Moonflower Palace had receded behind them to a pale blur in the distance.

They made camp as the palemoon set, having encountered no trace of the Void. No corroded patches of bare ground marred the way, nor any hint of their presence in his magical sensing. The fighters were in good spirits, telling tales around the flickering campfire and sharing skins of mead. Still, Bran posted lookouts. Although the enemy didn't seem to be close, he'd learned caution early on. He would not risk his people by being lulled into a false sense of security.

After an uneventful sleep, they broke camp and continued on. They would reach the border with Rowan in a few turns, and the court itself on the morrow. As they rode, Bran practiced extending the range of his magical net. His wellspring was almost entirely restored after several moons of almost no spell casting.

Behind them, he could just barely sense the glow of Moonflower, and likewise with Rowan, ahead. To the west, his power brushed against the solidity of the barrier that enclosed Elfhame. It hummed softly, its protections unbroken.

East and north, the Erynvorn pulsed with living magic.

He could not discern the gateway, but knew it was there, tucked in a clearing hidden deep within the shelter of the ancient trees. The gate itself held no magic, and he hoped that would render it invisible to the Void. Even if the shard that had lodged within him had sensed the gateway opening and closing, perhaps it had been too embattled to understand what was happening.

It was a thin hope, and he knew he was foolish to cling to it. But the thought of the ravenous Void descending on the weak and unsuspecting mortal world made his stomach clench, and distracted him from his immediate purpose.

He turned his sensing away from the forest and back to the surrounding vicinity. For a moment, he thought he felt a flicker of black—but it was gone before he could reach for it.

Frowning, he turned in the saddle, but the silvergrass stretched calmly on either side of the road, broken by a few stands of pale birch trees where ashdoves cooed contentedly.

Still, he would set an extra watch that evening, and cast wards of protection about the camp himself.

Their sleep proved uneventful, and the palemoon dawned in a wash of lilac and silver. The party had just broken their fast and were packing up bedrolls, when the wards Bran had set blazed with blue fire.

"Gyrewolves!" one of his youngest fighters cried, scrambling for his bow.

Bran drew his sword and flung one hand out, casting a magebolt at the lead wolf. There were five of them against his seven. Not the best odds. His warriors would be victorious, but not without taking injuries. Luckily, they could count on their mounts, who were already lashing about with hooves and teeth.

Gyrewolves used the vicious tactic of attempting to separate a single fighter and tear them to bits. Already his archer, Brethil, was hard-pressed, one of the wolves facing him while a second circled behind, sharp teeth bared.

"To Brethil!" Bran cried, sprinting to the fighter's aid.

Two of his other warriors engaged the lead gyrewolf and were backing toward the embattled archer, who was slashing desperately with his short sword. The last three elves faced the two remaining wolves. One of the creatures rushed forward, snapping, and the other tried to slide between his fighters and the rest of the group.

"Stay together," Bran called.

Whirling, he struck at the beast menacing Brethil. The gyrewolf turned with a snarl, eyes glowing a menacing red.

"Bran, duck!" one of his warriors called.

He went to his knees, barely avoiding the lead wolf's flying leap. Vicious teeth snapped the air where Bran's neck would have been.

Brethil managed to score its side as it flew past. Hot blood spattered down onto Bran's hands. Luckily, gyrewolves did not secrete the same toxic compound as spiderkin.

A shout of pain came from the group of three. They'd beaten their attackers back, but one of the wolves had managed to charge in, sinking its teeth into one warrior's leg.

Time to end this.

"Keep them at bay," Bran said, then reached deep into his wellspring. "*Coronnar!*"

Flame shot from his fingertips, knocking the two closest gyrewolves back. They howled and twitched, no longer any danger to Bran or his men, and he turned to the remaining three. The lead wolf, again showing unexpected intelligence, had already taken flight, its companions trailing.

Bran invoked his fire again, sending a ball of flame at the fleeing creatures. It hit the back of the trailing gyrewolf, who yelped and redoubled its speed. An arrow, lofted from Brethil's bow, followed, but fell short.

The archer turned to Bran. "Do we pursue?"

"No. We've wounded to tend." Mouth set, he watched the gyrewolves flee into the distance, heading northeast.

Toward the Erynvorn.

The stink of scorched fur hung in the air. Bran toed one of the dead gyrewolves, then turned to his fighters.

"We need to incinerate them," he said. Though they were dead, he wanted to leave no stain of the Void upon Elfhame.

All but his injured warrior joined him in a rough circle around the bodies. Bran spoke the rune for cleansing fire, and the others added their magic—helpful, as his own wellspring had dipped with his use of battle magic. A clean white blaze sprang up, covering the gruesome bodies, and he watched them burn, narrow-eyed.

Fortune had favored his warriors, and he knew Hestil would not be pleased when he told her of the attack. Still, despite their small numbers, they had fought well.

Brethil, who had the most healing talent of those present, tended to the wounded fighter's leg, then performed soothing magics on the smaller injuries. Two of the horses bore claw marks, but they were mostly unscathed.

The fire burned until the gyrewolves were nothing but blackened ashes on the ground. Then, grimly, Bran and his fighters finished breaking camp, mounted their horses, and made for the Rowan Court.

CHAPTER 21

Mara dodged Sicil's dagger thrust, only to have the warrior pivot and bat the weapon from her hand. The little blade landed point-first in the deep moss of the garden, the hilt sticking up like a reprimand.

"Counterattack," Sicil said with a stern look. "Do not evade—it puts you at a constant disadvantage. You want your opponent to worry, not toy with you."

"I'm trying." With a sigh, Mara bent and plucked her dagger from the ground, then wiped the blade on her azure skirts.

"Back to lunge drills," her instructor said. "Take your stance. Now thrust."

At least the muscles of Mara's thighs didn't protest too much as she followed Sicil's instructions. Her body was toughening up, even though she wasn't yet performing to the warrior's exacting standards. A quiet life in Little Hazel and her stint as a chambermaid in Castle Raine hadn't given Mara much need to defend herself, let alone go on the offensive.

The magic was going better, at least. Although she failed more often than she succeeded, she could now call foxfire and cast rudimentary wards. Every night, she fell into bed exhausted in both mind and body. She welcomed the dark, dreamless embrace of sleep, and pushed herself during the day so that she would not have to think about her precarious place in the Hawthorne Court.

And to drive back the ache of missing Bran.

Anneth had promised to help Mara scry for him after her training session with Sicil was finished. Her own efforts along those lines had been fairly unsuccessful. She had not been able to summon Bran to a scrying. Once, she glimpsed her husband's face, set and unreadable, where he paced in an ornate courtyard ringed with pale flowers, and then the silver water had shimmered back into her own reflection.

"That is the Moonflower Court," Penluith had said, from where he was observing over her shoulder.

"He didn't seem happy."

The tutor pursed his mouth slightly--just the faintest thinning of his lips. "Moonflower is not quick to action."

Poor Bran. She hoped he met with less frustration as he continued on to the other courts.

"Where is he going next?" she asked, thinking of the maps hung in one corner of Bran's sitting room. "Rowan?"

"Likely," Penluith said. "But you would do better to inquire of Sicil about such things."

When asked, Sicil had given her a long look, then confirmed that Bran would be headed to Rowan. The knowledge comforted Mara. Instead of staring at the entirety of Elfhame, at least she'd have some notion of where in the land he was.

"Enough," Sicil said as Mara finished her last set of lunges. "On the morrow, we will resume sparring against one another."

Mara straightened and wiped her sleeve across her sweaty forehead.

Although at first it seemed ridiculous to train in court gowns, the dresses were surprisingly easy to maneuver in. The fabric had proven durable, despite its gossamer shimmer, and resistant to stains. Not quite as practical as homespun, but perhaps that was her own inability to imagine such garb as everyday wear. The rest of the Hawthorne Court seemed unbothered by such things.

Mara had seen them go for pleasure rides wearing ornate costumes, eat without a care for their exquisitely embroidered sleeves, and, in the case of the more simply clad warriors, spar without removing their elaborate jewelry. Such things were the Dark Elves' way.

After the encounter with the spiderkin, Anneth had insisted Mara send all her clothes for laundering. Since then, Mara had eyed the dark blue tunic, but not put it on. Perhaps she would do so on the morrow.

She bade Sicil farewell and returned to the rooms she was beginning to think of as hers. If one could fit themselves around the edges of a magic-wielding warrior prince, that was.

Still, Mara found that the ways of the Dark Elves had begun to seem less strange. The flavors of the food, though not what she'd grown up with, were now familiar on her tongue. She'd figured out the knack of winding her dresses about herself. And her progress in calling upon her wellspring was heartening.

As long as she did not imagine herself trapped in the Hawthorne Court for the rest of her life, she thought she could bear the future. If Bran ever came back...

The kitchens had sent a plate of fruit while she'd been training with Sicil. After freshening up, Mara took a slice of moonmelon and a handful of red berries. The tart berries provided a pleasant counterpoint to the sweet melon. As she chewed, she went to stare at the maps on Bran's wall.

Rowan shared a border with Hawthorne, but the courts were at opposite corners from one another. Her hopes that Bran might stop to see her were dashed as she traced the distance with one berry-stained fingertip.

A sharp cramp in her belly made her gasp and double over. It passed quickly, but was followed by a wave of nausea that had her running to the commode.

Several shaky minutes later, after emptying the contents of her stomach, she felt better. She rose, washed out her mouth, and went back to the sitting room. The couch felt particularly comfortable, and she sank back into the pillows. She'd just rest until Anneth came.

Anneth's knock at the door woke Mara from a light doze.

"Yes?" she called out sleepily, the tatters of a restless dream still misting her mind.

"It's Anneth."

"Come in." Mara sat up and rubbed her eyes. She felt strangely drained, her limbs numb and heavy.

Bran's sister opened the door and stepped in, the smile falling from her face when her gaze fell upon Mara.

"Whatever is wrong? You're quite pale."

"Am I?" Mara looked down at her hands, which seemed normal, despite the slight tingling in her fingertips. "I think maybe the fruit went bad."

She gestured at the silver platter set on the table, noting that the red berries had, strangely, turned to black. That would explain her sudden illness and the lingering aftereffects.

Anneth glanced at the fruit, then gasped, a sharp inhalation edged with fear. "Where did this come from?"

Anneth's fright was contagious, and Mara shivered at the stark look on her friend's face.

"It was here when I returned from training—I assumed the kitchen sent it up. Why?"

"Did you eat any of the berries?"

"A few. Anneth, what—"

"I must fetch Avantor." Anneth whirled to the door. "Those are marlock berries. And they're deadly."

She was gone before Mara could ask anything more. Shaken, Mara slumped back on the couch. Someone had tried to poison her—and very nearly succeeded. But how had they managed to pass the wards?

Someone at the Hawthorne Court wanted her dead. The knowledge was like shards of ice through her belly. As to whom it might be? Both Mireleth's threats and Tinnueth's hatred were tangible, and Mara knew that one, or both of them, must be at the heart of the attacks.

She closed her eyes as a wave of weary bitterness washed over her. If only she could return home. She would give almost anything to be in her own bed, her mother's warm hand on her forehead.

The sound of the door opening roused her again. Avantor entered first and sprinted to her side, Anneth following. Mara noticed that she locked the door behind her.

"Lie still," the healer said, taking Mara's hands in his. "This is not going to be comfortable, I'm afraid. But I must drive the poison out of your system as quickly as possible."

"That's all right," Mara mumbled, her tongue thick in her mouth.

Avantor began chanting, and the tingling in Mara's hands intensified. The sensation turned to a blazing fire, sweeping up her arms and into her chest. It took all her self-control to keep from crying out in pain as her body was engulfed in magical flames. Tears sprang to her eyes and she pressed her lips tightly together. Surely it would be over soon.

Finally, the heat faded. She pulled in a wavering breath.

"Done?" she asked.

Avantor nodded, his expression grave. "The marlock has been purged from your system, but you will feel weak and listless for at least another day."

The tear tracks on her face itched, and she pulled her hands from the healer's grasp in order to swipe her palms over her cheeks. "Someone is trying to kill me."

Anneth let out a squeak of dismay, but neither she nor Avantor tried to argue otherwise.

"How did they come into the room?" Mara continued, looking at Anneth. "I thought the wards prevented such things."

"They protect from malice and threatening creatures," Avantor said. "But if an innocent person entered, even bearing such poison, the wards would not be activated."

"And marlock berries could be made to look like something perfectly innocent, with a small illusion spell," Anneth said.

That would explain the color shift.

"I'm not safe here," Mara said. "I have to leave."

"Not... back to the human world?" Anneth's voice was desolate.

"No." Not yet, anyway. She had promised Bran she would stay.

"Perhaps Nightshade," Avantor began.

"Not there." Conviction crystallized inside Mara. "I'll go join Bran."

"I don't think that is advisable," Avantor said.

"Why?" Mara scowled at him. "Don't try telling me it's too dangerous. Obviously the Hawthorne Court is worse."

He tucked his chin back, affronted. "I only meant that you should not depart immediately. The marlock poison—"

"Then come with me, to make sure I don't fall off my horse."

"Take Sicil, too," Anneth said. "You need a warrior with you."

Avantor shook his head. "Bran placed her in charge here. She will not abandon her post. But perhaps Ondo, the leader of the scouts, will come."

"I will see to your provisions myself," Anneth said, giving the fruit platter another wary glance.

"How soon can we leave?" Mara asked. "I don't want to spend another night within these walls."

Avantor gave a sigh of disapproval. "I will speak with Ondo, and scry to Bran, asking him to wait for us at the Rowan Court. I warn you, he will not be pleased."

Mara struggled to sit up, her mind already racing with plans—and relief.

"Trust me, he'd be even less pleased to return to Hawthorne and find me dead. Anneth, help me change into that tunic and trousers, if you would."

"And I will take this away." Gingerly, Avantor scooped up the platter, keeping his fingers well away from the marlock berries. "I will return as soon as I speak with Ondo."

Mara nodded at him. Soon enough, she would leave the Hawthorne Court behind. She could hardly wait.

CHAPTER 22

As Bran and his troop approached the Rowan Court, the summons for a scrying tugged at his attention. He glanced at the pale walls of the palace ahead, then sent out a quick sensing. This close to the court, he was satisfied there was no danger.

"Go on without me," he said to his warriors, turning off the roadway and reining Fuin in. "I must take a moment to scry."

"I will keep watch," Brethil said, lifting his bow.

Bran nodded his assent, and the archer rode a short distance away, giving his commander a modicum of privacy. Wind riffled the tall silvergrass around Fuin's legs. As soon as the small party had ridden on, Bran quieted his mind and focused on the summons.

Avantor's face shimmered in the air before him, and the sight of the healer sent a stab of apprehension into his gut.

"What is it?" Bran demanded. "Is Mara well? Anneth?"

"Both are... well enough."

Bran frowned at Avantor's hesitation. "Tell me."

"Someone slipped marlock berries to Mara." The healer held up his hand, stilling Bran's startled interruption. "Her own body knew enough to rid itself of what it could, and my healing did the rest. She is recovering and will be back to full health soon."

"Someone tried to poison my wife?" Bran tensed with anger. "I will return immediately."

"No. We are coming to you. Mara wants to leave the Hawthorne Court, and I cannot persuade her otherwise."

Despite the black tide of anger rising in him, Bran could not hold back a tight smile. His beloved was strong-willed—one of the things he cherished about her. "In that case, come to Rowan. We've just arrived. She will be safe here." And with him.

"We will be on our way soon." Avantor's image faded.

Frowning, Bran turned to survey the graceful pillars of the Rowan Court rising from the meadows ahead. Behind the palace, a grove of birch trees whispered. The sight was not enough to ease the tight knot from his throat.

Marlock berries. He had not imagined needing to warn Mara about them. What other dangers had he overlooked?

He'd been a fool to leave her behind. Would she forgive him for believing that the Hawthorne Court was safer than traveling with him? He should have listened to her.

"I won't fail you again, Mara Geary," he said softly into the breeze. "That, I promise you."

THE PALEMOON HAD SET by the time Mara felt well enough to leave the Hawthorne Court. Despite her strong words to Avantor, she was not fool enough to set out while her body still trembled and fatigue fogged her mind. Still, she was resolved not to sleep again within the treacherous walls of the palace.

In any case, it was better to depart while most of the courtiers were asleep. The fewer people who knew she'd left, the safer she would be.

She'd considered staying at the court and coming up with some intricate plot to unmask her enemy. But, in truth, she did not have the allies or resources to do so. Her naivety about Elfhame had already put her in mortal danger, first with the spider and second with the berries. What else was she unaware of that might be her undoing?

Avantor had suggested she remain in Bran's rooms under heavy guard until the prince returned. She'd quickly rejected that idea. The Hawthorne Court was prison enough. Being trapped in a small set of rooms for who knew how long would surely drive her mad.

Besides, Bran had been informed she was coming to Rowan. Surprisingly, according to Avantor, he hadn't argued.

So she had rested for a time under the healer's watchful eye, and then, with Anneth's aid, gathered a small bundle of her belongings, donned the tunic and trousers, and belted on her dagger. After helping her, Anneth had slipped down to the kitchens to fetch them provisions.

"Go make ready," Mara told Avantor, who was hovering about her in an annoyingly solicitous manner. "I've got my dagger, and I promise not to open the door to anyone but you or Anneth."

"Keep it locked," the healer said, clearly reluctant to leave her alone.

"I will." She let a touch of exasperation edge her voice. "Now, go. The sooner we are away from here, the better."

He gave her a tight nod, then cracked the door open and surveyed the hallway. Satisfied that no one was lurking, he slipped out. Mara shot the bolt home as soon as the door closed.

Despite her brave words, she did not feel entirely comfortable being alone in the palace. But whoever was trying to kill her had used subtle means, thus far. Surely she was not in any immediate danger.

She spent the minutes looking at the map of Elfhame mounted on the far wall. The Darkwood covered the northeast section, depicted on the map in deep purple. The parchment did not hint at the fact that the gateway back to her world lay hidden in the depths of the forest.

And although it seemed all of Elfhame knew of the portal, mostly they did not care. The human world was of little interest to Dark Elves—all except Anneth, who had made a study of all things mortal. A hobby that was, apparently, mocked by the denizens of Hawthorne.

A flame of anger flickered in Mara's chest. Without that gate, and her own presence, Elfhame would have been consumed by the darkness of the Void.

Her temper cooled as she recalled that they were still a doomed people. The end was coming. Slowly, but inexorably, until the last of the Dark Elves grew old and faded away.

No. She clenched her hands into fists. It was not right, that she had given up her world in order to save Bran's, just so that he could watch his people die. The prophecy could not be finished yet.

Though she had no notion how to reverse the infertility of an entire population. If it could be done by magic, surely the Dark Elves would have done so. But what else was left?

Avantor's return pulled her from such unhappy musings, and Anneth followed soon after. She distributed the neatly wrapped packets of food, along with three full water skins.

"This should be enough to get you to Rowan, with extra to spare," she said. "Is Ondo meeting you here?"

"No," Avantor replied, tucking away the extra provisions. "He is gathering the horses. We are to meet him behind the stables when we're ready to depart."

"Which we are." Mara looked to Avantor. "Yes?"

The healer gave her a short nod, and Anneth stepped forward to embrace Mara.

"I'll miss you," she said, her eyes bright with unshed tears. "Please, be careful."

"I will—and it's not that far to Rowan. Avantor can scry you with our progress." At least, Mara assumed he could.

Quietly, they walked down the dimly lit corridors. Mara warily eyed the patches of shadow between the foxfire balls, but no one skulked there, waiting to leap out at her.

When they reached Anneth's rooms, she squeezed Mara's hand, then slipped inside. The fewer people moving about the halls, the better chance they'd go undetected. Mara felt even more lonely once she was gone. Avantor was not poor company, exactly, but she would sorely miss Anneth's light spirits and the impish sweetness of her smile.

Silently, Mara and Avantor made their way to the door leading to the gardens. Outside, a faint wash of starlight lay silver on the closed buds of the flowers, and a soft breeze murmured in the leaves.

A single glimglow roused as Mara passed, rising to bob in the air like a small beacon. Avantor gave her a wide-eyed glance. They could not risk discovery.

"Shh," Mara told it, waving the glowing creature away.

As if understanding their urgency, the glimglow sank back and tucked itself under a spray of ferns, its light dimming to a soft golden pulse.

Swallowing with relief, Mara followed Avantor past the furled blossoms and dark-leaved hedges until they reached the back of the stables. Ondo awaited them, as promised, with three mounts.

Her heartbeat echoing in her ears, Mara glanced up at the tall creature meant as her mount. Sudden yearning for Bran stabbed through her as she recalled her first ride to the Hawthorne Court, perched before him on Fuin. It had not been comfortable, riding with a forbidding warrior mage, but now she missed his strong, taciturn presence with every inch of her body.

Soon. She would see him in a few moons, according to Avantor.

Ondo made quick work of stowing their bags and provisions behind the saddles, then glanced at her.

"Milady," he said in a quiet voice, indicating that she should mount.

Clenching her jaw, Mara took hold of the pommel and, with a boost from the scout, managed to land atop her horse. Unlike riding in the human world, the Dark Elves used no reins or bridle. Mara set her hands on the pommel and hoped her mount knew what to do. Mostly, it just needed to follow Ondo, who guided his horse ahead of hers. Avantor, expression unhappy, took up the rear.

The scout led them single file through the hushed grounds to an arch in the wall. It was high enough for them to ride beneath, and between one breath and the next, they were through.

As she emerged beyond the walls, tension ebbed from Mara, and she looked back over her shoulder at the shimmering stones of the palace. The arched windows, curved columns, and graceful towers rose into the star-speckled sky like an enchanted dream.

With a poisoned heart.

Letting out a low breath, she turned her back on the Hawthorne Court and let the stillness of the realm of Elfhame enfold her.

CHAPTER 23

"Prince Brannonilon." Pharne, the primary Rowan Lord, greeted Bran with a weary smile. "We have been expecting you. Welcome."

"Is all well?" Bran glanced at the party who had gathered to greet him at Rowan's gates.

The black-haired Lords, their quiet daughter, who had been born to Pharne's mistress just before the Dark Elves became unable to conceive, and a handful of warriors. Even here, in the court, their stances were wary.

"My scouts have encountered Voidspawn recently." Lord Pharne shook his head. "It is troubling, to say the least."

"Very," Lord Indil agreed.

"Are the creatures behaving strangely?" Bran asked. At least he wouldn't have to try to convince Rowan of the danger, unlike his experience with the leaders of Moonflower.

"Yes." Rowan's commander, Nehta, stepped forward—a soft-voiced woman who was reputedly fearsome in battle. "Twice now, they have set ambushes for our scouts—but if outnumbered, they disengage and flee."

"Toward the Erynvorn?" Bran asked, though he knew the answer.

"Aye."

Unease settled on his shoulders. "Troubling, indeed. I have received word from my second-in-command—and confirmed it with my own magic—that the inner courts are free of all traces of the Void. Whatever creatures remained after the Void's defeat, they seem to be gathering in the forest."

"To mount another attack?" Nehta asked, fingers tightening on the pommel of her sword.

"Perhaps." Bran looked from her to the Rowan Lords. "We should speak more of this, privately. Also, my wife will be arriving in three moons."

Lord Indil's dark brows rose, perfect arches of surprise. "The mortal woman?"

"Her name is Mara. I expect you to treat her with all courtesy."

"Of course we will." Lord Pharne glanced at his husband, then back to Bran. "Is there... any particular reason she is joining you?"

"It is time for her to leave Hawthorne, but she is not coming here because we expect a battle at Rowan," Bran said, offering what reassurance he could. "The Void rift has been closed, beyond a doubt. And there are not enough remaining Voidspawn to overrun a court." He hoped.

Lord Pharne gave him a tight nod, but the Rowan commander's pale blue eyes slitted thoughtfully. Nehta was a clever woman, and Bran could see her coming to the same conclusion he had: there might not be a fight coming to the Rowan Court, but nonetheless, one loomed.

It was up to him to eradicate the Void creatures, with whatever reinforcements Rowan could lend. Hestil was on her way too, but it would be at least a doublemoon before she arrived—which might well be too late.

He hated to think of Mara's reaction when he told her of the threat to her world. There would be no stopping her from riding into battle with him—and, in truth, he was glad of it. They had been too long apart.

"Come, refresh yourselves," Lord Indil said, gesturing Bran and his party forward. "Prince Brannonilon, let us meet in the royal library in a turn, if that suits?"

"A half turn will suffice." The sooner they discussed strategy, the better.

The Rowan Lord nodded and held his arm out to his partner. The couple led their guests through the arched entrance of the Rowan Court. As they strode the foxfire-lit halls, Bran took note of the difference between Rowan and Hawthorne.

In keeping with its namesake, the ceilings of the Rowan Court featured carvings of bright berries and branched leaves, the sprays trailing down to wind about the foxfire sconces. The corridors were a hand span narrower than those of Hawthorne, and as they walked, Bran calculated the distance of his sword swing.

If pressed, there would be just enough room to fight. Not that he was anticipating needing to do so. And he always had his magic, of course, but a warrior's training kept him on the alert.

Nehta led Bran's soldiers to their guest quarters, and the Rowan Lords ushered him deeper into the palace.

"We hope you are comfortable here." Lord Indil halted, indicating a door inlaid with silver moons.

"I'm certain I will be." Bran nodded his thanks.

"Then we'll see you in a half turn." Lord Pharne gave him a tight smile. "I look forward to discussing how to deal with this current threat."

"As do I."

~

"I AM NOT certain it is necessary to pursue the Voidspawn into the Erynvorn," Lord Indil said, leaning forward with an earnest look on his face. "As long as they are not attacking the courts, why risk our warriors?"

With effort, Bran kept his claws from extending, though he wanted to shred the plush upholstery on the armchair he was occupying. The Rowan Lords' library was full of opulent furnishings and gilded scrolls—too soft a place to be discussing strategy, in Bran's opinion. But there was nothing he could do about it, except try to rein in his temper.

"It is our duty to eradicate the remaining Voidspawn," he said tightly. "Elfhame is not safe until they are gone."

"That is the point," Lord Pharne said. "If we wait, the problem may well take care of itself."

Bran frowned at him. "Are you honestly suggesting we let the creatures roam freely, until they expire?"

A sly expression crossed Lord Pharne's face. "We both know there is another way to expel the creatures from Elfhame, without sustaining more losses."

Surely the Rowan Lord wasn't implying they let the Voidspawn invade the human world? Yet, as Bran studied his face, it was clear that Lord Pharne meant precisely that.

"No." Bran clenched his hands. "I cannot believe you are suggesting such a thing. The gateway between our realm and the human world must remain closed."

"We cannot lose more of our people," Lord Indil said, leaning forward. "Prince Brannonilon, you know as well as I that we are doomed. The life of every Dark Elf is more precious than ever, now. Why not open the gateway and let the Voidspawn depart?"

"Because humans are completely unprepared for an incursion of the Void," Bran said tightly. "We have magic to keep the darkness from tearing another rift into our world—but the mortals do not. They would have no idea how to combat the Void."

Lord Pharne shrugged slightly. "The Void has eaten many realms. What happens outside of Elfhame is not our concern."

His husband nodded. "We cannot save every world. It is enough that Elfhame is safe, no matter that our people might be dying out. Prince Brannonilon, surely you see that the Dark Elves cannot be protectors of all other realms?"

Bran clamped his mouth closed on the shouts of protest thundering in his chest. The Rowan Lords were right... and wrong.

"If the Void overruns the human world," he argued, "they will gain enough strength to force the gateway open into our world once more. Elfhame will not be safe."

"But how long will that take?" Lord Indil asked, his voice mild. "The last of us may well be gone by that point, and thus it will not matter if our realm falls into shadow."

Unable to sit a moment longer, Bran rose, breaking protocol. He didn't care if he loomed over the lords. They should be glad he wasn't sending mage bolts sizzling into the shelves.

"This is the thanks you give me, and my human wife, for saving our world?" He didn't bother to control his temper any longer. "I thought you had more honor than that."

Lord Indil had the grace to look ashamed, but Lord Pharne simply cocked a brow. "We are not saved, Hawthorne Prince. The end is simply delayed."

"Are you saying you no longer trust the Oracles?"

Lord Pharne rose, his graceful movements marred by tension in his shoulders. "Your prophecy promised to save Elfhame, Prince Brannonilon. It did not explicitly say you would keep our people from perishing."

"Surely the prophecy meant the Dark Elves as well as our lands!"

"We cannot know that." Lord Indil stood, joining his partner in facing Bran. "You are welcome to our hospitality, but we will not send our warriors with you into the Erynvorn."

Bran narrowed his eyes. He wanted to throw their so-called hospitality back in the Rowan Lords' faces and storm out immediately, but he must think of his own soldiers. They needed a respite from the road. A pity it would be shorter then they'd anticipated.

"We will not overstay your hospitality," he said stiffly. "On the morrow, we will depart."

He and his warriors would rendezvous with Mara on the road. If he could, he would keep the information from her that Rowan was content to let the Voidspawn loose on the mortal world. She was already unhappy in Elfhame, and knowing that the Dark Elves cared nothing for the plight of humans would not make her any more kindly disposed toward his world. Rather the opposite.

"As you wish," Lord Pharne said. "Your party is, of course, welcome to join us for the evening meal."

Although Bran was inclined to sulk in his rooms, his position as Hawthorne Prince dictated otherwise. He inclined his head in an attempt at graciousness. "We will."

The food would be tasteless, the conversation strained, but he and his soldiers would take what nourishment they could before setting out once more in pursuit of the Voidspawn.

CHAPTER 24

The palemoon rose as Mara and her companions rode through dappled birch groves and meadows of silvergrass. Ondo led, following a narrow trail just wide enough for the horses to traverse. It seemed traveled enough that no branches crossed the pathway, no underbrush covered the trail.

Mostly, they rode in silence. The scout was a quiet fellow, and although Avantor answered Mara's questions about various foliage and the small animals they encountered, such things did not lead to long conversations.

She supposed they were worried about the attempt on her life—as was she.

"Do you think Anneth is safe, remaining in Hawthorne?" she asked, craning her neck back to address Avantor.

The healer lifted one shoulder in a half shrug. "I see no reason why she would be in danger."

Mara pressed her lips together. He was probably correct, but she still did not like leaving her friend behind.

She'd asked Anneth to come with them, but Bran's sister had shaken her head.

"One of us must stay and try to uncover who it is that means you harm," she said. "I am the best candidate. After all, no one else knows that I'm aware of the attempts on your life."

She'd pressed Mara's hand and told her not to worry, and nothing Mara said would sway her.

And now, the court was several hours' ride behind them and all questions of staying or going were past answering. Mara took a deep breath of the flower-scented air and tried not to fret. Elfhame was not the human world, but its ethereal beauty was soothing.

"Are you weary?" Ondo glanced back at her. "We can make camp soon."

She shook her head, denying the wave of exhaustion washing through her. "I'll ride as long as you think necessary."

His eyebrows drew together slightly. From behind her, Avantor let out a short laugh.

"Do not wait for Mara to call a halt, Ondo. She is as tough as a stone, and will ride until the brightmoon rises, if you let her."

"Hm." The warrior's brow smoothed. "We'll take a short rest to eat, then, before continuing on. The more time we make now, the shorter our journey will be."

That didn't quite make sense to Mara, but she didn't argue as Ondo led them to a small clearing beside the path. She slipped down from her mount without help, though her legs protested as she jarred down to earth. It seemed riding called for different muscles than dagger training, and she winced at the thought of the aches ahead.

It was worth it, though. Not only to be free of the Hawthorne Court, but to be riding toward Bran. The prospect of seeing him again lifted her spirits.

"I need to relieve myself," she told Avantor, a bit shyly. "Is there a place...?"

"Behind that coppice," the healer said, gesturing to a small grouping of trees. "Do not stray too far, however."

She nodded and went into the trees. To her surprise, there was a tiny building tucked in the shadows, with adequate, though limited, facilities. The Dark Elves must use the clearing as a regular stopping point, she guessed. No matter how tiny the trail seemed, it was the main road between Hawthorne and Rowan, after all.

When she was finished, she stepped outside and took a moment to stretch, relishing the solitude of the woods.

A twig broke, and she whirled.

"Who's there?"

Only silence greeted her. The birds had fallen silent. A shiver crawled up her back, and she dropped her hand to the handle of her dagger.

Between one breath and the next, a figure draped in gray charged at her from the left, sharp blades flashing in each hand.

Mara yelled and whirled to meet the attack, pulling her own blade free. Everything slowed, and with terrible clarity, she saw the sharp-edged steel descending.

Clang! Against all reason, she was able to parry the first blow with her own dagger, though her arm felt almost numb from the impact. But the attacker's other knife was sweeping in, and she had only an empty hand to meet it with.

Blue flame gathered in her belly, and without conscious thought she flung up her palm.

"*Turma!*" she cried, invoking the shielding spell Penluith had drilled into her.

Unlike the weak flicker that was all she'd been able to cast previously, the air around her ignited, the light so bright that Mara had to squint to see anything. Although heat poured from her hands, nothing but coolness enveloped her.

Her attacker let out a cry and dropped his now-burning blades. The gray cloak he wore wisped away into flame, then smoke, revealing a figure Mara did not recognize.

"Mara!" Ondo burst from the trees, Avantor close behind.

Mara's attacker glanced at them, then fled, melting into the woods as fluidly as he'd appeared.

As suddenly as the shield had flared to life, it extinguished. Mara's legs went out. With a gasp, she toppled, managing at the last moment to turn her fall into an inelegant cross-legged sprawl upon the leaf-strewn ground.

"Are you injured?" Avantor went to his knees beside her and hastily waved his hands over her body.

"No." She sucked in a shaky breath. "At least, I don't think so. He didn't land a blow."

Avantor exchanged a quick look with Ondo.

"Go after him," the healer said.

The warrior pivoted and ran, fleet-footed, in the direction her attacker had gone. Despite Ondo's speed, Mara doubted he would be able to catch her would-be assassin.

"How was he able to follow us?" Mara asked as Avantor finished checking her over.

His face hardened. "Strong magic. Both Ondo and I should have sensed him. And we never should have let you go alone. I beg your forgiveness, Lady Mara."

"There's nothing to forgive. How could you have known?" She pulled her knees up to her chest. "We took all care to leave the court undetected. Who would have magic so strong that they could shadow us for hours, undetected?"

The healer looked at the ground and would not meet her eyes when he spoke. "The rulers of the courts."

A chill moved through her. "That wasn't the Hawthorne Lord or Lady. Are you saying there are other heirs? Or that my attacker was someone from Rowan?"

"No." Avantor was quick to correct her. "It is possible to imbue a talisman with magic. A spell of concealment, in this case. But only those of royal blood have the power to create such things."

She wanted to bury her head in her hands. The more time she spent in Elfhame, the less she knew.

"So it probably was someone from Hawthorne," she mused aloud. "Someone sent by Bran's parents."

His expression troubled, Avantor's gaze once again went to the scuffed soil.

"How were you able to summon such a shield?" he asked, clearly changing the subject.

Mara didn't press him. How could he admit that at least one of his rulers wanted her dead? Tinnueth seemed the obvious choice. Had the Hawthorne Lady been behind the other attacks on her? Somehow, Mara didn't think so. If Tinnueth wanted a thing done, she succeeded. The only reason Mara's assailant had failed was because of her unexpected ability to conjure a mighty shield—something that no one, herself included, knew she was capable of.

"Penluith taught me the rune," she said, answering the healer's question. "Although it was... a little more intense than I'd planned."

"That intensity saved your life." He gave her a long look. "Most attacks can be blunted by casting *turma*, but in your case, you turned it into weapon of its own. At least, from what I could see. And from those."

He nodded at the blackened blades discarded upon the ground. The metal still smoked. When he prodded one knife with a nearby stick, the blade flaked away into ash.

Mara swallowed. It was gratifying that she could, in fact, protect herself so powerfully. Gratifying, and a bit disturbing. Fighting the Void was one thing. Being able to turn weapons, and potentially, people, into a crisp was something altogether different.

"When I was working with Penluith, I could barely cast the shield." She spoke slowly, searching for more answers to her wayward manifestations of power. Even after her visit to the pool, that particular spell had proven elusive. "I suppose... if my wellspring had responded fully, it would have been extremely dangerous."

She winced at the thought of the royal tutor on the receiving end of that magical blaze.

Avantor nodded thoughtfully. "Bran told me your wellspring is one of the deepest he's ever felt. It makes sense that it must be called upon carefully. Even if you did not realize that you were doing so."

"Are you saying my power is smarter than I am?" She gave him a rueful smile. "I suppose we should all be grateful for the fact."

Ondo reappeared, his expression harsh.

"I pursued, but was not able to catch the attacker," he said. "He had a horse waiting, and I did not want to leave the two of you. Seeing you safely to the Hawthorne Prince is my sworn duty."

Avantor gave him a terse nod. "Then we had best be on our way. And on our guard."

He offered Mara a hand up, and soon they were mounted and riding the forest trail—though this time with far more caution.

CHAPTER 25

That evening, after the Rowan Court's feast, Bran accompanied his warriors back to their quarters and informed them they'd be departing Rowan on the morrow. They sent him curious looks, but made no argument.

He was sorry to deprive them of their well-earned rest, but there was no help for it. As soon as they had some distance from the court, he would explain—but he knew all too well that walls had ears, and courtiers' whispered gossip was seldom still.

He made his way back through the halls to his own room, mulling over the fate of the realm. Both Elfhame and the mortal world were intertwined, no matter how much the Rowan Lords might deny it. Perhaps the answer to his people's infertility lay beyond the gate, as strange as that notion was.

Despite being deep in thought, he sensed someone waiting in a shadowed alcove ahead. He dropped his hand to his sword.

"Who's there?" he demanded. "I have little patience for games."

"Your pardon, prince." Nehta stepped forward, hands open before her to show she held no weapon. "I wanted a word."

He raised a brow. "And skulking in the corridors is the best way to get one?"

"In this instance, yes." Her lips tightened. "I understand you plan to depart Rowan in the morning and make for the Erynvorn."

Word traveled fast in the Rowan Court. Too fast. He scowled at her, but she did not flinch from his gaze. Strong—as all good commanders should be.

"It does not concern you," he said.

"Anything that threatens Rowan's domain—and all of Elfhame—is my concern. When you go, I and a small cohort of warriors will join you."

He blinked, not expecting her answer. "I do not think your lords look kindly upon my mission."

"They have not spoken against my course of action." Her voice was bland.

Which meant that she had not told the Rowan Lords of her plans, and they had not thought to expressly forbid it. Bran bit the inside of his lip, whether to hold back a smile or a reprimand, he was not certain. Perhaps both.

"I see. In that case, I will not forbid it, either."

She tilted her head. "I shall see you on the morrow, my lord."

As silently as she had appeared, Nehta was gone. Bran narrowed his eyes. He didn't want the commander to jeopardize her position with Rowan, but all the same, he was glad of the support. At least *someone* in the blighted place was being sensible.

Back in the privacy of his guest room, he set out his scrying bowl and summoned an image of Avantor. The healer's face wavered in the water, and he looked tired. From the pattern of interlaced branches moving against the stars behind his head, it was clear the party was still on the move.

"Why have you not made camp?" Bran asked, after exchanging a short greeting.

Avantor glanced away a moment. "It seemed best to continue. Your wife wishes to see you with all possible haste."

Bran peered at Avantor's dim image, wishing he could see the healer more clearly. Unease prickled the back of his neck. "What's wrong?"

Avantor hesitated a heartbeat. "Nothing."

Clearly it was more than nothing, but Bran trusted Avantor's discretion. He let the matter drop—for the time being.

"You will need to adjust your direction," he said. "Tell Ondo to make for the western edge of the Erynvorn, where the Dragon Stones lie." It was a solid landmark, and he knew the experienced scout would be able to lead his party there without difficulty.

"Why the change in plans?" Avantor gave him a close look. "Is anything amiss?"

"No."

Clearly they were both hiding information—but soon enough they would be face to face, away from unfriendly allies and the machinations of court, and able to speak freely.

"Let me see him." Mara's voice.

Bran smiled to hear it, though he let no trace of emotions show on his face. Growing up under Tinnueth's baleful scrutiny, he'd learned that lesson long ago.

"It is not easy to shift a scrying," Avantor said, glancing to one side—presumably at Mara.

"I don't care," she said. "Try it anyway."

"Bran?" Avantor turned to him.

"One moment."

He closed his eyes, calling up the image of his wife's face. *Mara.*

"Now," he said, opening his eyes.

The water in his silver scrying bowl shimmered, and then Mara was there, staring intently back at him. She looked weary, and with alarm, he noted the pallor in her usually ruddy human face, the heavy shadows under her eyes.

"You should rest," he said curtly.

Her lips twitched with amusement. "I'm glad to see you too, husband."

It went without saying that he felt the same, of course. He shook his head slightly. He'd never understand his human wife.

"We have been too long apart," he admitted.

"Yes." There was a weight of meaning in that single word, and Bran wondered if she would ever forgive him for leaving her behind.

He had an apology to make, for certain—but it was best done in person.

"I will not keep you longer," he said. "Travel safely."

She winced slightly at his words, and he leaned forward, suspicion flaring. Something had happened while they were upon the road.

"We will," she said quickly. "How soon until we meet?"

He firmed his lips, calculating. "Two moons for my party to reach the Erynvorn. Tell Ondo he must be reasonable, and not push you too quickly."

"I'll tell him." She regarded him a moment longer with her clear blue-green eyes—a color unknown among his people.

Bran wished he could reach through the scrying bowl and gather her into his arms, smooth the exhaustion from her face, inhale her scent of dew-dappled mint.

Her reflection shivered, then disappeared.

"I love you," he said, to the now-silent water.

Despite Mara's urging to press on, Ondo was maddeningly obedient to his commander's wishes.

"We will make camp here," the warrior said, after they had ridden less than an hour from the place they'd spoken with Bran.

Mara opened her mouth to protest, but Avantor shot her a pained look, and she subsided. Very well. The sooner they rested, the sooner they could set off once more. Grimly, she dismounted and tried to make herself useful as they tended the horses and set up camp.

Once the tents were pitched and a small supper consumed, Ondo seemed satisfied.

"I will take the first watch," he said. "Get what sleep you can, Avantor. I'll wake you when it is time."

"What about me?" Mara glanced between them. "I can watch, or keep you company."

"No." Avantor's tone was firm. "You must replenish your wellspring. Not to mention finish recovering from the marlock poison."

She wanted to argue that she felt perfectly fine, but she knew the healer wouldn't believe the blatant lie. In truth, she wanted nothing more than to roll into her tent and sleep. And wake in Bran's arms. Unfortunately, that last wish would have to wait. *Soon*, she reminded herself.

"Very well," she said. "But I want to depart at moonrise." Would she ever accustom herself to the fact that, in Elfhame, the palemoon replaced the sun?

The elves exchanged a look, and she tried not to scowl at both of them.

"We will depart when ready," Ondo said, which was no kind of promise at all.

Under Avantor's watchful eye, she made ready for bed and crawled into the first tent. At least the Dark Elves understood comfort, even when on the road. The bedroll that had been attached behind her saddle turned out, through some enchantment, to grow into a reasonable mattress, and the thin coverlet was surprisingly warm.

Despite the weariness running through her, though, she could not sleep.

She replayed her short conversation with Bran, smiling into the darkness as she recalled the sharp planes of his features. And the expression on his face, just as their scrying ended. It seemed clear her husband had missed her as much as she'd longed for him.

What had happened at Rowan, though, for him to depart so quickly? And, even more troubling, why were they headed for the Darkwood?

When Mara awoke, a silvery wash of moonlight shone brightly through the sloping fabric over her head. Blinking, she scooted out of the tent to find that the palemoon had climbed several hand spans into the star-specked sky.

"You should have woken me." She frowned at Ondo, who was tending a small, smokeless fire.

"Avantor needed to rest, as much as you," he said, nodding to the second tent where, presumably, the healer still slumbered.

"Did you sleep at all?" She peered at the warrior. He didn't seem unduly exhausted, but with his impassive bearing, it was hard to tell.

Instead of answering, he offered her a mug of strong tea and a hunk of bread studded with seeds and dried fruits.

"Break your fast," he said. "Avantor will rouse soon."

She had not yet finished her bread when the healer emerged from his tent, proving Ondo correct. He shot the warrior a sharp look, but said nothing.

"You seem well rested," Mara observed as Avantor settled beside her on a mossy log. Though the healer would never admit it, it had been clear that tending to her and then scrying with Bran had taken a toll on his powers.

He looked her up and down. "As do you. And though we might both take issue with Ondo's decisions, you must admit they are well made."

She sighed into her mug, then drained the last bit of the warm beverage. There was nothing more annoying than being proven wrong. At least Ondo, if he overheard, showed no sign of gloating.

In the time it took for Avantor to eat his breakfast, Ondo packed up the camp, loaded the horses, and brushed away the obvious traces of their presence.

"Do you think the assassin is still following us?" Mara asked.

Ondo lifted one shoulder. "Whether or not he is, there's no need to draw undue attention to our passage. Elfhame holds other dangers."

Like the renegade Voidspawn. Mara tried not to shiver at the thought of encountering a gyrewolf or spiderkin. Although, unlike her first experience with the creatures, she now had a wellspring of magic to draw upon.

Which reminded her...

"Avantor," she said, as they set out on the path, "will you teach me the words to cast a fireball?"

He shot her a startled glance. "I think such things are better left to the tutor. Didn't Penluith—"

"No. He was waiting for me to control simple things, like the shield and summoning foxfire—but we now know that my power operates rather differently."

Which was an understatement. In fact, would summoning foxfire work as an offensive spell, given the force of her wellspring? If Avantor refused to teach her, she would try that instead, the next time they were attacked.

Her heart gave an uncomfortable bump at the thought. There *would* be a next time—she was, unfortunately, certain of the fact. Whatever reason Bran wanted to meet them at the border of the Darkwood, it couldn't be good.

Avantor took a moment to respond. Mara guessed he was wrestling with the answer, but at last he spoke.

"I will," he said. "Against my better judgment, might I add."

"A wise choice," Ondo remarked from his position in the lead.

Mara exchanged a look with the healer. Apparently Ondo's ears were sharp enough to catch even their quietest conversations.

"To summon a ball of flame, the casting is *coronnar*," Avantor said.

Mara tasted the word under her breath, fixing the shape of it in her mouth. *Coronnar*.

"I pray you, do not practice it now," Avantor added, somewhat dryly.

"Don't worry," Mara said. "I'm not planning to set the grass on fire. Once cast, how do I banish the fireball?"

"In the event that it has served its purpose and not yet burned out, the word is *firnar*."

She filed that word away, too, hoping she wouldn't be called upon to cast the spell too soon. It felt good, knowing she had the ability to do more than lend the strength of her wellspring to Bran. Being a source of power for his admittedly more advanced magic had been essential in defeating the Void, but she liked being more than a stick of firewood waiting passively for the flame.

The rounded edge of the palemoon curved against the sky, and the unfamiliar stars overhead sent a pang of homesickness through her. Ah, but she missed the sun.

"When does the brightmoon rise again?" she asked.

"In two more passes of the palemoon," Avantor said.

"After we meet Bran, then." Her heart warmed at the thought.

Not only would she be reunited with her husband, she would have light enough to not feel so drab-spirited. At least for a short time.

"If we are entering the Erynvorn, the doublemoon will be a good thing," Ondo said. "The forest is well named."

The Darkwood.

His words made Mara's thoughts skitter to the one thing she'd been trying to avoid. The gateway back to her world, and her growing suspicion that the Void was hungry to force it open.

Surely she and Bran could stop it, though. The fragment she had cast from him had not been so very large.

That makes it no less dangerous, her thoughts warned, and she found she could not quiet them.

CHAPTER 26

Bran woke, restless, in the starlit quiet hours of the slumbering Rowan court. Nothing external had roused him—only his mounting concern over the destination of the Voidspawn.

Still abed, he reached into his wellspring and summoned a sensing spell. His strength had returned enough that he could send the casting out to the edges of Elfhame. The magic skimmed along the boundary protecting the realm, then circled, sweeping up from Moonflower through the inner courts. Eyes closed, he stayed alert for the slightest ripple of malice that would signal the presence of the Void and its creatures.

Nothing...

Until he encountered the blot of malignancy gathering near the Erynvorn.

The presence of a few dozen Voidspawn was unmistakable. And festering beneath, the coldness warning him that a shard of the Void still remained in Elfhame.

Suppressing a shiver, Bran rose and set out his scrying bowl. Although Hestil could not match his range or power, she would be able to confirm that the southern part of the realm was clear of Voidspawn.

She answered the scrying clear-eyed, her braids neatly binding her hair back. If he'd roused her, she gave no sign of it.

"Commander," she said. "What news?"

"Have you found any trace of the Void in the inner courts?"

"None at all—and not for lack of looking." She firmed her mouth, then continued. "There are troubling reports of Voidspawn moving northeast, however."

"I'm afraid it's true." He frowned. "My sensing confirms that the Void is gathering just inside the Erynvorn."

Her eyes widened in immediate comprehension. "Do you think they plan to mount an attack on the gateway to the human world?"

"Yes—and do everything they can to force their way through." His throat was tight on the words. "Make all haste to meet me. We are under strength and need your fighters."

"What of Rowan?"

He gave a quick shake of his head, trying to rein in his anger at the court's inaction. Thank the stars for Nehta and her handful of trusted warriors.

"We depart the court here in a few turns," he said. "How long will it take you to reach the Erynvorn?"

She tilted her brows together, and he could see her making some quick calculations. "One rising after the doublemoon, if we push hard."

"Come find us, when you reach the forest. I will try to delay the fight until then." They needed Hestil's forces to keep from being seriously outmatched, but if the Void attempted to open the gate, he would have to act.

"Understood. I will rouse the warriors now and make haste for the Erynvorn."

He gave her a terse nod, then waved his hand over the scrying bowl, dismissing her image. Before picking it up to pour out the water, however, he paused.

"Show me Mara," he said, once more passing his hand across the still water.

The silver reflection of his own face shimmered, then re-formed to show the image of his wife, fast asleep.

The cords of tension winding about him eased as he watched her. No matter what happened, they would be together soon.

"I'm coming," he murmured, then banished the scrying.

Despite the early hour, he suspected his warriors would be awake and making ready to go. It would not hurt for their commander to join them. Bran quickly gathered up his few belongings, then sent a quick magical summons to the kitchen, requesting a hearty breakfast be delivered to the warrior's quarters.

Outside the guest chambers, he was unsurprised to meet Nehta, accompanied by a half-dozen warriors.

"Prince." She made him a half bow in greeting.

"Commander. Thank you for joining us." He waved her to precede him into the soldiers' quarters. "Have you yet eaten? You are welcome to join us."

"Thank you—we will." She lifted her brows slightly, acknowledging the fact that warriors who broke bread together shared a deeper kinship in battle.

It was probably why they'd arrived at that hour, which reinforced Bran's already high estimation of Rowan's commander. If joining him resulted in her losing her position at the Rowan Court, he would find a place for her, and her warriors, at Hawthorne.

Provided they all survived.

~

Mara woke from dreams of her husband.

"Bran?" She rolled over, for a moment certain he was there beside her, but found only the empty pallet and the cold fabric of the tent.

Outside, she heard Ondo's quiet movements, the hiss of water boiling over his conjured fire, the shuffle of a horse shifting position. They had ridden well past moonset before making camp. She had no idea what time it might be—not that the passage of time in Elfhame made much sense to her human notions of day and night.

But based on what Bran had said, she thought they would arrive at the meeting point by the end of the day. The thought was enough to get her up and moving, despite the weary protest of her muscles.

Avantor and Ondo both looked up as she emerged from the tent.

"Did you rest well?" the healer asked.

"Yes." She stretched, surprised to find that the words were true, then shot Ondo a suspicious glance. "You didn't let me sleep too long, did you? I intend to see Bran today."

The warrior gave her a pointed look. "You rested as much as necessary. And do not fret—we will reach the Dragon Stones before the palemoon leaves the sky."

"Good." She blew out a breath, then twisted her tangled hair into a makeshift bun, uncomfortably aware of the stickiness of her skin, the smudges of grime on her hands. "Is there any way I might wash up?"

It would be nice to make herself presentable before reuniting with her husband.

Avantor gave her a half-smile, as if aware of her thoughts. "I believe our path leads beside the Celebronen—the silver lake—for a time today. Perhaps there might be time for all of us to bathe."

Ondo frowned, but nodded a grudging assent. "One at a time, of course."

"Of course," Mara echoed. None of them wanted a repeat of the assassination attempt.

While she ate, Ondo packed away her bedroll and tent, and soon they were on the move once more. Perhaps it was the knowledge she would see Bran soon, but the air seemed lighter, the beauty of Elfhame striking her to the core.

The sky overhead was dark purple at the edges, the lilac palemoon washing out the nearby stars. Glowing flowers peeped from dark-leaved thickets as they passed, and the silvergrass waved in the light breeze.

As promised, after about an hour of riding, the trail rounded the crest of a hill to reveal a shining expanse of water below. The lake, Celebronen. Mara smiled at the sight of the moon reflected on its rippled surface.

The trail descended to curve along the shore. Wavelets lapped the stone-strewn beach, making a gentle hushing noise. A wild, sweet scent reached Mara's nose, and she sniffed appreciatively.

"Lissalma," Ondo said, gesturing to a bush laden with pale yellow blossoms. "It blooms by the waterside."

"It smells lovely." A thought struck her and she eyed the flowers askance. "They're not... poisonous, are they?" She'd learned her lesson about appreciating the apparent bounty of her new land.

"No," Avantor said. "Sometimes, during celebrations, we weave the blossoms into our hair."

It was a lovely thought. Perhaps, once she'd bathed, she'd do the same.

They followed the water for what felt like hours. The soft air and quiet sound of the waves lulled Mara into a waking doze. When Ondo called a halt, she was surprised to find that the palemoon had begun to dip toward the horizon.

"Lunch," the warrior said.

"And then a bath, I hope." She glanced longingly at the lake.

"Aye."

She was first to finish the small meal of dried fruit, cheese, and seed bread. Ondo directed her to where a spit of grassland jutted out into the water.

"We cannot give you privacy," he said apologetically. "But I will avert my eyes."

"I understand. I'll be fast."

He gave her a short nod, then unsheathed his sword. Just in case—though unless the assassin could breathe under water, Mara did not see how she could be in danger. Still, she had no idea what magics the Dark Elves were capable of. Better to be safe, than dead.

Avantor brought her a square of cloth to use as a towel, and a thin disc of soap. She supposed, as a healer, he'd be prepared with such things.

"Thank you," she said.

The water was chilly, which helped speed her bathing process. She tried not to yelp as she dunked her head under and finger-combed out the worst of the tangles. Avantor's soap smelled medicinal, but it did its job. She emerged feeling much cleaner, then quickly dried off and donned the fresh tunic she'd had the foresight to pack.

"That's better," she said, rejoining her companions.

"I'm next," Avantor said, twisting his hair into a bun high atop his head.

Ondo gave him a curt nod. "Do not linger. Prince Brannonilon waits."

Mara pulled in a breath, aware of a prickling excitement running through her. While Avantor bathed, she plucked a few of the lissalma flowers. Unlike the Dark Elves, she did not sport intricate braids to tuck the blossoms into. Instead, she settled on braiding the long stalks together to fashion a makeshift crown.

"Most fitting," Avantor said, donning his clothing and shaking his hair free. "You are a princess now. Never forget."

She gave him a strained smile. "I'm not sure I want to be. Especially not within the walls of the Hawthorne Court."

He sobered. "Your husband will not allow you to step back into danger. Once we meet with Bran, we will make a firm plan for your safe return to the Hawthorne Court."

"We must defeat the remaining Voidspawn first," Ondo reminded them.

He swung up on his horse and gave them an expectant look. Trying not to groan with stiffness, Mara let Avantor boost her onto her own mount. Single file, with Mara again in the middle, they set off once more.

The path curved away from the water, and she was sorry to leave the shimmering expanse of the Celebronen behind. Not only had the quiet ripples of the water soothed her, but the reflected light had offset the encroaching darkness as the palemoon set.

Now, lavender shadows sifted over the land. The tall grasses shone purple, and in the distance, a dark mass of trees arose, just visible on the horizon.

The edge of the Darkwood.

CHAPTER 27

Bran's spirits rose as his party approached the Dragon Stones. The sliver of the palemoon was nothing more than a sharp tip slipping below the horizon. Despite the hulking shadow of the nearby Erynvorn, and the battle that surely awaited within, he was filled with anticipation. Soon, he would be reunited with Mara.

Their time apart had been a dull ache in his side, a sense of missing a part of himself. He did not want to experience it again. Whatever happened in the next few moons—and beyond—he would spend them by his wife's side.

"There," Nehta said from where she rode beside him. She gestured at the ridged rock of the meeting place. "I see movement."

He closed his eyes and sent out a searching tendril of thought. His magic sensed two Dark Elves—and the unmistakable feel of a human presence. Mara. He leaned forward, and Fuin responded to the movement by picking up his pace.

"Prince," Nehta said, urging her mount into a trot. "Do not go alone."

"It is not Voidspawn."

She gave no response, merely pressing her lips into a line and loosening the spear strapped in its holder beside her saddle.

"Your caution is commendable," he said dryly. "But there is no need for your weapon."

He kindled a small ball of foxfire and sent it to hover just above his shoulder, so that his dark-blind wife might see who approached.

Not that there should be any question. Her wellspring was attuned to him, and he was certain she knew of his presence, just as he sensed hers. But something had made her and her companions wary, and he wanted to reassure Avantor and Ondo that no danger approached.

The movement near the jagged spine of stones stilled for a long moment as he and Nehta rode forward. Then foxfire blossomed ahead, shedding light over the three figures gathered there.

"Bran!" A glad cry burst from Mara's lips and she nudged her mount forward.

In turn, he urged Fuin into a faster pace. Just as they met, he guided his horse slightly to the side and plucked Mara off her mount, pulling her into his arms.

"What are you doing?" she asked, a scolding laugh in her voice as she laced her arms around his neck to secure her perch.

"Greeting you properly." He bent his head and breathed deeply of her human scent and the flowers woven into her hair.

"Well, don't drop me."

She looked up at him, her strange round-pupil eyes smiling, even as she tried to keep her features stern. Ah, would she ever know how precious she was to him? Once again, he cursed himself for leaving her behind.

In a few short paces, they reached the rest of her party. Bran, still holding his wife, threw one leg over Fuin and gracefully slid to the ground.

"You should put me down," she said, though she still held tightly to him.

Reluctantly, he set her gently upon her feet, but could not help keeping one arm around her shoulder. Deep inside, his wellspring sighed, then settled.

"Commander." Ondo made him a bow, then turned to acknowledge Nehta.

Avantor, his expression carefully blank, made his greeting, and Bran narrowed his eyes. The healer was clearly hiding something.

"What happened?" he demanded, his gaze fixed on Avantor's face.

Avantor winced and opened his mouth to answer, but Ondo stepped forward.

"The fault is mine, my lord," he said. "I carelessly allowed your wife out of the campsite, and she was attacked."

Fear and anger swept hotly over Bran, and his hand went to his sword.

"Attacked? By all the stars, you should have told me! Was it Voidspawn?"

"No." Ondo's mouth screwed up in repentance. "It was an assassin."

The fear won, then, and he whirled to Mara. "Is he dead?"

She shook her head, and Ondo grimly continued.

"We were fortunate that Mara's magic repelled her attacker, but he was able to escape. Since then, we've kept a close watch."

Bran's thoughts raced. He did not ask how Ondo had failed in his duties so miserably, for clearly a greater magic had been at work. A power that could only be wielded by one of the rulers. But who wanted Mara dead?

For a moment, his mind skittered to his parents, but he could not begin to think of what that might mean. Not now, with another fight looming. And surely even Tinnueth would not be so cruel.

She would, though—he'd known since birth that his mother cared for little but herself and her own power.

"Forgive me." He took Mara's hands in his, anguish tightening his throat. "I placed you in more danger than I ever would have guessed."

"You didn't mean to," she said softly, and her lack of recrimination made his guilt twist all the more tightly inside him.

"I will not lose you," he vowed.

In answer to the strength of his words, the azure rings of binding on both their hands flared to life. The blue light limned her hair and sparked in her eyes, turning her into an ethereal creature. His heart ached at the sight of her, and he nearly wanted to weep at the thought of losing her once more.

Then the rings returned to their quiescent state, and she was back to being his beloved human wife.

"Just don't leave me behind ever again," she said, a tart note creeping into her voice. "Where you go, I go."

"Aye." He glanced down at their linked hands, steeling himself for what he must say next. "I must tell you. The Void is gathering here, in the Erynvorn."

She drew in a quick breath, as though she'd guessed the same. "All of them, in the whole realm?"

He gave a single nod. "My sensing says it is so—and Hestil has confirmed it."

"What about..." She leaned close and lowered her voice. "What about the fragment we drove out of you?"

"It is... elusive, but I believe it is directing the Voidspawn. They are acting with a purpose and intelligence I cannot otherwise explain."

"Then..." She locked gazes with him. "Then they mean to force the gate open and invade my world." Her voice shook, ever so slightly.

"It seems so."

A flash of panic crossed her face. "We have to stop them!"

"We will." He tried to project more confidence than he felt.

She leaned to the side and peered around him. "How many soldiers have you brought?"

"Hestil is on the way to meet us, with her forces," he said, evading her question. "And we have the best of the Rowan Court's warriors with us, as well as their commander."

He nodded at Nehta, who had been watching the interaction between him and Mara with quiet interest. She stepped forward and made Mara a short bow.

"I am pleased to meet you, Hawthorne Princess."

Mara winced at the title, but, to Bran's relief, did not try to deny it.

"Thank you for coming," Mara said, then glanced back at Bran. "How soon until Hestil arrives?"

He let out a relieved breath that his wife understood the danger of charging immediately into the forest.

"After the doublemoons rise. I will scry her once we make camp."

"Not until tomorrow?" Mara was clearly dismayed by the delay.

He could not blame her—he knew the soul-clenching fear of the Void threatening his world and all he held dear, and wished she could be spared that particular horror.

"The Voidspawn have not yet reached the gateway," he said. "Let alone attempted to interact with it. And the passage between our worlds is not without its protections."

He gave her a significant look, a reminder of the immense strength needed to open the portal, let alone hold it for more than a few heartbeats.

"Very well," she said unhappily. "I suppose we'd best make camp."

"There is a sheltered place at the far side of the rocks," Ondo offered. "And a spring nearby."

"Show me," Bran said. He would sweep the entire area with his magic, to ensure that no Void creatures waited to ambush them.

Or assassins.

By the moons, his troubles mounted on either side, and he could not help the cold certainty that a battle lay ahead.

Then Mara slipped her hand into his. The warmth of her human touch steadied him, beat back the foreboding icing his blood. They would triumph once more. He could believe nothing less.

CHAPTER 28

Delight over being reunited with Bran warred with Mara's fear for her own world, mixing uncomfortably in her belly. They settled into the camp, quickly pitched on the far side of the Dragon Stones, but she had little appetite for the simple stew Ondo fixed for their supper. Every few bites she would pause and stare at the huge shadow of the Darkwood ahead, panic tickling the back of her neck.

The village of Little Hazel lay on the other side of the gate.

Not right outside it, but it was the closest human habitation to the center of the forest, tucked as it was on the outskirts of the Darkwood. If the Void creatures forced their way through...

She shuddered, unable to banish the terrible image of the gyre-wolves and spiderkin descending on her unsuspecting family. Her sisters, her brother. Their village devoured.

"We will stop them," Bran said, sensing her thoughts. "Here, drink." He held out his goblet of wine to her.

"It won't make me forget the danger," she said, eyeing the silver cup. "Unless you've bespelled it—in which case I won't drink."

She did not need her husband cosseting her, and ever since the marlock berries, she was wary about what she let pass through her lips.

"I would not attempt to enchant you without your knowledge." He sounded affronted. "It is only wine, but perhaps it will help blunt your worries."

"I'm not one to drown my sorrows in drink," she said, but she accepted the goblet and took a swallow anyway.

The tart, flowery taste lay on her tongue, and she tried to think of other things. The quiet beauty of Celebronen's waters, the tilt of Anneth's grin.

"Tell me of your studies with Penluith," Bran said. "I expect you have proven an apt student."

"Somewhat." She blew out a breath and went on to describe her troubles harnessing her magic reliably. "I don't know whether it's because I'm human or something else, but even the simple magics don't always work for me," she finished.

"They protected you well enough when needed," he said grimly. "I have never heard of a simple shielding spell behaving in such a fashion as you described, when that assassin attacked. I will work with you to harness your wellspring once the realm is safe once more."

"Both our realms, Bran." She took another swallow of wine, her gaze once more drawn to the waiting Darkwood.

"Of course." He touched her shoulder. "I would not leave the human world in danger."

He said no more, as if voicing the thought that the Void might enter her world would make it come true.

"What did Hestil say?" Mara asked. "Will she be here on the morrow?"

He glanced at her, then away. "No."

"Why not?" Mara clenched her fingers around the silver goblet. "We have to catch the Void! I'll go alone, if necessary."

"You will not. And Hestil is making all speed, but she cannot wear her forces ragged if we wish them to be any use in the coming fight."

Misery tightened Mara's throat. "You can't force me to stay in the camp—not when the enemy is mounting an attack on the gate."

"I will not make you stay here," he said quietly. "I only said you will not go alone."

"Oh." She took a gulp of wine, then handed the goblet back to him. "Then will we go, tomorrow?"

He glanced at the web of stars stitched overhead—constellations Mara had yet to learn—then drained the goblet.

"When the brightmoon rises on the morrow," he said, "we will strike camp and follow the Void into the Erynvorn."

"Good."

It wasn't good, of course, but the knowledge that Bran was with her eased the knot in her stomach.

"We should rest," he said, rising gracefully and offering his hand. "My lady, will you join me in my tent?"

"Yes." She managed the wisp of a smile for him and let him draw her to her feet.

Despite the comfort of Bran's solid body beside her, Mara slept fitfully. After the third time she woke and lay rigid, staring up at the fabric of the tent, Bran reached over and stroked her hair.

He offered her no empty words of comfort or promises of victory. Just the simple reassurance of his touch, his presence. She pulled in several deep, wavering breaths. Then, finally, she went into the dreamless dark.

When she woke, brightness filtered through the tent. *The sun!* She sat up, filled with joy for a fleeting moment—then realized her mistake. To her light-starved eyes and homesick heart, she had mistaken the rising brightmoon for the light of her home world.

She was not surprised to find the tent empty, the spot where Bran had lain cool to her touch. No lying abed for the commander. She felt a twinge of remorse that her insistence on entering the Darkwood had no doubt drawn him to his duties at first light.

Despite his assurances that he was fully healed, she saw the faint shadows in his eyes, and had noticed that he had summoned only the smallest balls of foxfire the night before. Perhaps he was conserving his strength for the battle to come, but she feared that his wellspring was not yet returned to its full power.

She was with him, though, and her wellspring seemed as potent as ever. As before, he could draw on her magic if necessary.

And she feared it would be necessary.

With a grimace, she pushed back the soft blue coverlet, shook out her tunic, and twisted her hair into a messy bun at the back of her head. Anneth had given her a hairpin fashioned of silver and inlaid with a flat, shining purple stone. It seemed too fine to wear into battle, but Mara had nothing else to keep her hair in place.

Well, she supposed she could jam a stick through her bun, as she'd used to do when rambling about the woods, but that was equally foolish.

With a fortifying breath, she ducked out of the tent. The camp was all but struck. A few of the warriors sat on the tumbled rocks, finishing their meals. She turned slowly, making a count by the golden illumination of the brightmoon, and her heart clenched as she numbered the soldiers. There were so few!

"Mara!" Avantor hailed her from a nearby jut of stone. "I have porridge for you."

She joined him, bidding him good morning. Despite her lack of hunger, she set herself to scooping up the spiced grains from the bowl with a flat wooden spoon. At least Bran and his warriors had their healer with them once again. Avantor's skills would be a welcome, and necessary, addition when the fighting began.

As she chewed, Mara watched Bran stride about the camp. He paused to speak with Nehta, the Rowan commander, and her pitifully small force.

"Why so few?" Mara asked Avantor in a low voice. "I know that Nightshade could not send many fighters, after losing so many in the last battle. But why did Rowan not provide more?"

The healer shifted uncomfortably. "You must ask Bran."

"I will." She set her bowl down and met Avantor's gaze. "But I'm also asking you. Why do you think there are only a handful of fighters from Rowan?"

He frowned, his gaze going to the Rowan contingent, then back to Mara. "At a guess—and it is only a supposition, nothing more—I would say the Rowan Lords did not think it necessary."

Lords? She noted that bit of interesting information, then tucked it away to puzzle over later.

"Not necessary?" She looked quizzically at Avantor.

When he said nothing more, she made herself think, and the answer dawned, cold and awful.

"They are content to let the Void invade my world if it means the enemy is gone from Elfhame?" The words were bitter in her mouth.

Avantor hunched his shoulders and could scarcely meet her eyes. "Aye. But not all Dark Elves—"

"Let them hang!"

She rose and grabbed the empty bowl, then stalked over to where Ondo was finishing the washing up and deposited the dish with him. Part of her wanted to condemn all Dark Elves for consigning her world to the Void without a fight—but that was unfair.

Bran's forces might number only two dozen warriors, but he was here, ready to pursue the Voidspawn into the forest. And, if Avantor's guess was true, Nehta and her fighters had gone against the wishes of her rulers to accompany him.

Mara blew out a breath, letting some of her anger go. Not all Dark Elves were so careless of human lives. A grudging part of her even understood why the rulers of Elfhame might turn their backs, as long as their own people were safe. Wouldn't many human kings do the same?

Bran strode toward her, his tall form outlined in the warm golden glow of the brightmoon, and the last of her temper ebbed away. She could not afford it—not now, when their whole focus must be turned to the task ahead.

"Are you ready to ride into the Erynvorn?" he asked. His hand rested on his sword, and he looked every bit the warrior commander he was.

Mara checked that her own blade rested comfortably at her waist, then lifted her chin and met her husband's inhuman gaze.

"Yes, my Hawthorne Prince. I am."

CHAPTER 29

They did not make a triumphant charge into the shadows of the Darkwood, however. Mara reminded herself there was nothing to charge *at*, after all. Not yet. And despite the driving need to protect her home, she was not eager to meet the fierce gyre-wolves and skittering spiderkin the Void used for its army.

Bran and his warriors filtered through the forest. Mara was in the middle of a rough circle, fighters to either side of her riding swiftly and silently through the trees. Bran led the party, and Nehta rode at the back, scanning constantly for danger that might come upon them from behind.

To Mara's relief, Avantor and Ondo stayed near. While they traveled deeper into the Darkwood, she silently reviewed her small store of spells. Foremost among them was *coronnar*, the fireball. The shielding ward would be useful as well, and possibly calling foxfire. That, and the dagger at her side, were the sum of her weapons.

She hoped they would be enough.

After what felt like hours, Bran halted, holding up one hand. The rest of the warriors brought their mounts to a soundless stop, and Mara belatedly followed suit. Without a word, Bran pointed ahead and to the right, then pulled his sword.

The hiss of blades leaving scabbards made the back of Mara's neck prickle with apprehension. She scrambled to pull her dagger, then nudged her horse to follow as the entire party veered in the direction Bran had indicated.

One moment there was nothing but the dimly lit underbrush on all sides. Then, with an ominous rustle, a dozen Void creatures emerged from the trees and swarmed toward them.

"Guard Mara," Bran called over his shoulder at Ondo, then raised his sword and urged Fuin forward.

Mara watched, her heart clenching, as he beat back a gyrewolf leaping for his throat. Then the soldiers surrounding her blocked her view as two spiderkin scuttled forward in attack. The forest was suddenly loud with the sounds of battle: the Void creatures snarling and screeching, the thud of blows falling, the grunts and cries of the Dark Elf warriors.

"Stay back," Ondo said, maneuvering his mount between Mara and a gyrewolf that had sprung from a nearby thicket.

He was hard-pressed, the wolf nearly biting his arm several times. Pulse pounding, Mara gripped her dagger tightly, preparing to rush to his aid if she saw an opening. She did not trust her ability to cast a firebolt at such a close range without scorching Ondo into the bargain.

Then Nehta was there, deftly blocking the wolf's attack with her spear. It snarled and turned to face her, and Ondo managed to stab it in the side. Together, they dispatched the creature, short, brutal work that made Mara flinch, despite her experience on the battlefield.

All around them, small, desperate fights were being waged. But where was Bran?

Mara turned her horse in a tight circle, searching desperately for a glimpse of her husband. Blue fire flared, and she tracked it to where he and two other warriors were battling one of the spiderkin.

She closed her eyes briefly, thankful to see him unharmed.

A rustling overhead made her open her eyes and look up, even as she drew her dagger. What came hurtling down at her from the sturdy limb was not a Void creature, however, but the dark-cloaked figure of the assassin.

Her mount shied. She managed to slide off, then stumbled over a protruding root and dropped her dagger. Her attacker gave a soundless laugh and flowed forward like ink spilled in water, bright blades flashing.

Mara flung up her hand and cried, almost without thinking, "*Coronnar!*"

Even as the knife descended to her throat, a jagged bolt of blue flame struck the assassin square in the chest. His eyes widened as he fell backward, fire coruscating over his body. The deadly knife landed point-first in the soft loam, and a tendril of Mara's hair, neatly sliced from beside her neck, floated down beside it.

"Mara!" Bran yelled, full-throated and full of anguish.

She brought her hand up to her throat and pulled it away, expecting to see blood. The assassin twitched and shuddered, thrashing beneath the trees, then stilled. Mara blinked at her unstained fingers, at the unmoving body.

Then Bran was there, gathering her against him. She pulled in a shuddering breath and clung fiercely to him. Death had stared her in the face once more, and she had barely escaped it this time.

"Are you hurt?" Bran thrust her away and scanned her, head to toe. Satisfied she bore no injury, he clasped her close again.

"I'm all right," she said, even as a wave of shivering gripped her.

Ondo had arrived moments after Bran. He toed the body, assuring himself the assassin was dead.

"Do you recognize him?" Bran asked.

The scout shook his head. "No—but those who choose the deadly blade are careful not to be known, especially among fighters."

Shouts broke out at the vanguard of the fighting, and Bran's mouth twisted.

"I must help my warriors," he said, then gave Ondo a fierce look. "Do not stir from her side."

"I swear it." He drew his sword.

"Let me help," Mara said, looking up at Bran. "My strength—"

"Will be needed later," he said grimly. "Look. The creatures are already on the run."

It was true. The Dark Elves had beaten back their attackers. Even as Bran ran to lend his aid, the spiderkin skittered back into the depths of the forest. He sent a bolt of fire after a fleeing gyrewolf, and the creature yelped and collapsed.

A hush followed the fighting, thick silence where Mara could hear her heartbeat still thudding frantically in her chest. The fighters were cleaning blades, taking stock of injuries—which, thankfully, seemed few.

Bran directed them to collect the two bodies of the fallen Voidspawn, then tramped back to where Mara stood.

"We will burn the assassin, as well," he said. "A cleaner end than he deserves." He gestured at Ondo. "Check the body for anything that will help us identify who sent him, and from where."

"There is probably nothing," Ondo said, grimly bending to his task.

"Aye. But we must look."

Mara turned away from the gruesome sight of the person she had killed. Yes, it had been to save her own life, but it still shook her deeply.

"Once again, I have failed you," Bran said, his eyes full of self-recrimination.

She met his gaze. "You can't be all places at once. And, as you can see, I can protect myself."

"I do not want you to have to." He cupped her cheek briefly.

"I know." She managed a wan smile. "We'll just keep muddling through."

It was all anyone could do, she supposed. At least they were together.

Ondo straightened from checking the body.

"Nothing to identify it, Commander," he said.

"Disappointing, but not unexpected."

Bran motioned for Ondo to grab the body's feet, and together they moved it to where the dead Voidspawn lay. Mara followed—not too close, but near enough so that Bran would stop fretting.

Once the bodies were magically ablaze, she turned to her husband.

"How far are we from the gate?" she asked in a low voice.

He peered into the depths of the Darkwood for a moment, eyes narrowed. "Less than a turn—provided we are not set upon again."

She looked at the small group of fighters. How many more attacks would they be able to face before their strength flagged and they began to fall? Dark Elf warriors were hardy, she knew, but they could not fight endlessly.

"Hestil?" she asked.

From the shadow that crossed Bran's face, she knew that his second was too far away to aid them.

"Given the choice, I would wait for her, but..." His gaze unfocused for a moment, then snapped back to her. "The Void is at the gate."

CHAPTER 30

A look of anguish crossed Mara's face. Bran wished he could gather her into his arms again, murmur reassurances into her hair—but there was no time. His sensing had shown the remainder of the Voidspawn gathered at the gateway to the mortal world, along with an oily black shadow that could only be the Void shard.

The enemy might not be strong enough to crack open the gate. But he could not take that chance.

"Ride!" he called to his warriors, then boosted Mara into her saddle.

The formation was not pretty as his small troop raced through the forest. But despite navigating thickets and fallen logs, the party kept Mara safely in the middle, surrounded on all sides by keen-eyed fighters.

There was little time for speech, not that there was any need for elaborate planning. They would charge into the clearing holding the runed gateway and battle whatever Voidspawn were present.

As for the shard, all he could think of was to focus the might of his magebolt upon it, in hopes he could incinerate it to nothingness. If that were not enough, he must then draw upon Mara's wellspring.

And if that was still not sufficient?

He thrust the thought away and bent low over Fuin's neck, urging his horse to greater speed. The glowing bells of *qille* flashed beneath his mount's hooves, and the radiance of the doublemoon fell in shafts between the trees.

The sensing he had cast thrummed with danger, and with gut-wrenching dismay he realized that the Void had begun to cast its malignant magic over the gateway.

With every breath, his urgency grew. The fabric of Elfhame shivered under the Void's assault.

"Faster!" he called.

Their pace was already reckless, but thanks to the doublemoon, there was enough light to avoid the tangling briars and treacherous dips. Mostly. Mounts still stumbled, and even surefooted Fuin had a moment of unsteadiness—but they could not slow.

The brightness increased, and Bran glanced up in surprise to see dozens of glimglows streaming overhead. Their light evened out the crooked shadows and illuminated obstacles in the path ahead.

Mara rode slightly behind him, and he glanced back every few paces to make sure she was not falling behind. She stared up at the glimglows in wonder, then met his gaze, her eyes wide.

Whatever impulse had called them forth, the glowing sparks continued to light their way until, ahead, the huge trunks of the Eryn-vorn thinned.

Without slowing Fuin, Bran drew his sword. Around him, his warriors followed suit. Nehta grasped her spear tightly, teeth bared, and Brethil nocked an arrow to his bow.

They burst into the clearing housing the gateway.

Fewer than a dozen Voidspawn clustered around the standing stones marking the gateway. Two of them were the hulking lumberers, however—the most formidable of the Void's creatures.

Three gyrewolves turned, snarling, and launched themselves at Bran's party, while the spiderkin spread out, skittering to position themselves at intervals around the gateway. Bran's warriors slowed to meet the enemy, and Bran pulled Fuin to a halt, his attention fixed on the gateway ahead. Mara drew up beside him, her breath coming in small gasps.

The space between the stones glowed, and Bran's heart clenched. Slowly, the Void was forcing the gate open. A shadowy presence hovered over the stones, and he felt its malignant intelligence as it tried to insinuate itself into the mortal world.

"No!" Mara cried.

She flung out her hand and cast *coronnar* at the darkness.

It flinched as the fire flew at it, then somehow opened itself and extinguished the blaze of blue flame, sucking it down into the icy blackness of the Void.

Mara stretched her fingers out to cast again, but Bran caught her hand.

"Do not spend your power recklessly," he said. "It will only devour whatever we send at it."

"But—we drove it out once before," she said, her eyes wild.

"It was weaker then—don't you sense its renewed strength? I do not know what will stop it now."

"We will," she said grimly.

About them, his warriors fought. One of the wolves was dead, and a spiderkin as well, but his troops were hard-pressed. Avantor sang a continuous song of healing, keeping the worst of the injuries at bay—but his power would run dry soon, and the odds were still against them.

The gateway flickered, and Bran glimpsed the fierce light of the mortal world beyond. Strangely, the landscape was covered in white, as though a blight had settled. Had the Void already begun to sap the human world's strength?

One lumberer broke off its attack and, ignoring the arrows Brethil sent after it, shambled to the glowing gateway. The darkness roared soundlessly, and between one moment and the next, the lumberer passed through into the mortal world.

"Stop!" Mara called, too late, and urged her mount toward the gate.

Bran chased after, dimly aware of his fighters redoubling their efforts. A spiderkin skittered forward to block his path.

He reached deeply into his wellspring, bringing all his fear, all his determination to the fore.

"*Coronnar!*" he yelled.

The spiderkin ignited, spraying its toxic blood in a wide arc.

Bran ducked, cursing as a few specks spattered his hands. He hastily wiped them on his cloak, then veered Fuin around his downed foe.

Ahead, Mara dismounted beside one of the tall stones marking the gate. A dark tendril lashed out at her, but she stood fast, summoning *turma*.

The shield blazed with light, and the Void shard recoiled. Even under attack, though, its magic held the gate open, allowing a gyrewolf to dart into Mara's world. Bran slipped nimbly from Fuin's back and joined his wife, sword raised.

"Bran." Her voice was heavy with heartbreak. "They're getting through."

The remaining gyrewolf made a dash for the gate, but Nehta sprinted forward. With a mighty throw, her spear went through the creature's shoulder, throwing it off course. Three of Bran's warriors sprang forward, and the malignant shard of the Void howled as the wolf perished under their blows.

That victory was offset by a spiderkin scuttling furiously toward the gateway. Bran lunged in front of it, landing a blow to its carapace. It let out a chittering cry, then gathered itself and leaped over him. He stabbed upward, felt his sword connect, but even as he ducked away from the toxic blood, the spiderkin passed through the gate.

"We will fight them on the other side," he said. Under no circumstances could he allow the threat of the Void to run loose in Mara's world. She had helped him save Elfhame—a debt that he could never repay. But he could try.

Mara stared at him, tears tracking down her cheeks. "You can't cross. I saw a vision... you were attacked by humans. I must go alone."

"Never." He would save her world—even if it meant his death.

The Void pulsed overhead, and he knew that he must forge his own way through the gate. To pass through the sticky blackness of the Void would be sheer folly.

"*Edro!*" he shouted. The clean blue light of his magic sliced through the doorway, opening a thin path for him to follow.

"Bran, no!" Mara reached to stop him, but he stepped into the whirl beyond her grasp.

He could feel the clash of his own power against the Void—a

humming instability that vibrated through his bones. The gateway wavered, threatening to disintegrate and trap him between the realms.

Then he was through. The cold air of the mortal world pierced his lungs, and he blinked, closing his inner eyelids against the painful brightness.

Light flashed, and with a thunderclap, the door between the worlds closed—leaving Mara on the other side.

CHAPTER 31

"Bran!" Mara cried as the gateway clapped shut.

She threw her hands up, ready to call upon the rune of opening, when Ondo thrust her aside.

"Back, my lady!" he cried, raising his sword to defend her against the huge Voidspawn lunging toward them.

She took a single step, then summoned a ball of flame to fling against the lumberer. It staggered, but continued to attack. Overhead, she was aware of the pulsing black blot of the Void shard.

Whether it was gathering itself to attack them, or to reopen the gateway, she did not know. Her heart squeezed tight in her chest, but she could not voice her sobs.

Bran.

She must believe that his death by human hands was not imminent. Her vision had shown a full-leafed forest, at night, and she clung to the fact that she'd glimpsed a daylit winter landscape through the portal.

Nehta joined the fight, nimbly wielding her spear, and slowly she and Ondo beat the lumberer back. In the corner of her vision, Mara saw the last spiderkin expire, and then the rest of Bran's fighters rushed to help them battle the lumberer.

With a sound like metal scraping on stone, the creature shivered, then folded in on itself and collapsed.

The black cloud of the Void shrieked.

Not only at the demise of its minions, but at the swarm of glimglows descending upon it. One of Bran's archers shot an arrow at the Void, but it passed through the oily shadow, doing no harm.

Despite Bran's earlier failure with casting magic against the thing, Mara took a deep breath and spoke the rune of fire.

"*Coronnar!*"

She poured her heart, her love, her fear into the spell, blasting the darkness with light and power. The warriors shaded their eyes, and the glimglows whirled like a golden vortex about the fragment of the Void.

A dark malevolence pushed back, and she felt the drain upon her wellspring as she continued to channel fire through her outstretched hands. Behind the Void shard a vast hunger seethed, driven by a malignant intelligence.

"No," she said fiercely. "This realm is mine, and you may not have it."

The darkness shuddered, and she redoubled her efforts. For Anneth, for her sisters, for the beauty of both their worlds, her magic blazed. And, most of all, for Bran. Her beloved. She would not let his world fall, even as he protected hers. Together, they would vanquish the dark.

The Void shard withered under the onslaught, the darkness dimming until, with a last shrill screech, it was gone. A moment later, Mara's spell winked out.

She swayed, feeling like a vessel with all the water poured out. It seemed her wellspring was not inexhaustible after all.

"Mara!" Avantor was at her side in an instant, propping her up.

Ondo took her other arm, and she sagged between them.

"I must go to Bran," she said, her voice a hoarse croak.

Avantor glanced at the portal, then back to her, his expression tight with worry. "The gate is closed."

"I will reopen it." Even as she spoke the words, she knew they were foolish. She had not the strength to cast a wisp of foxfire, let alone open the gateway back to the mortal world.

"He will come back to you, my lady," Ondo said.

"The vision." She looked at Avantor. "In the Room of Reflection, I saw Bran attacked in the mortal world. We cannot wait."

"You must," Avantor said gently. "You are in no condition to work magic."

"How soon?"

"One sleep, at least."

She sighed, her head heavy, as though she wore a crown of iron. "I will rest for one night only. And then, will you help me open the gate?"

"I will," Avantor said.

"As will I," Ondo added.

"All of us," Nehta said, clearly having overheard. "We cannot leave the commander to battle the Voidspawn alone in the mortal world."

The other fighters nodded in agreement. No one pointed out that by the time they opened the gateway, Bran might well have been defeated.

No. Mara refused to even consider it.

"Sit." Avantor guided her to a moss-covered stone at the edge of the clearing.

She stumbled to it without complaint and watched in a daze as the Dark Elves burned the Voidspawn corpses and made a hurried camp just within the shelter of the trees.

In the center of the clearing, the two gateway stones stood, silver runes shining in the light of the setting doublemoons. Had the day run already?

She blinked. and ate the stew Ondo brought her. Blinked again, and crawled into the shelter of her tent. The bedding smelled like Bran, and she wept into the starlit dark.

Bran stared at the closed gateway for one stark moment. Then he whirled, sword raised, to meet the leaping attack of the gyrewolf. He beat it back with magebolt and blade, drawing upon all his formidable skill. Thankfully, the spiderkin had crawled some distance away, writhing in its death throes.

Of the lumberer there was no sign, but Bran did not have a moment to spare wondering at its fate. Twisting, he parried the savage snap of the gyrewolf's jaws. The power of his wellspring faltered, already depleted by opening the gate and crossing over. Gritting his teeth, he reached deep and flung a last, mighty bolt at his foe.

The gyrewolf collapsed mid-leap, the red light fading from its eyes.

Panting, Bran turned in a slow circle. The clearing stank of burned fur and spiderkin ichor, but both the Voidspawn were dead.

The lumberer, though—where had it gone?

Ice crunched beneath his boots, and he glanced down, perplexed. In Elfhame, the mountains at the far edge of Rowan bore frost, but the cold stayed in its place and did not venture forth into the summerlands of the courts.

At least the frost bore the sign of the lumberer's passage. The brushed trail led into the forest. Bran cleaned his sword on the dead gyrewolf's body, then headed into the trees of the mortal Darkwood. Their trunks grew thinner than those in his realm, their reaching branches not quite as majestic.

A cold wind stirred the branches, and a dark shadow seemed to flow past. Bran glanced up, unable to suppress a shiver. Had that been the Void shard, loosed into the mortal world? If so, it must be seeking the last of its creatures.

Despite the weariness wrapping him head to foot, foreboding pushed him forward. The intense brightness of the mortal world faded, and he sighed in relief as dimness descended. Small creatures chirped and rustled, seemingly unconcerned by his passing. There were no flowers, as he was used to in the Erynvorn. Only frost-edged leaves of darkest green, and brown tangles of dormant thickets.

Too late, he realized he had lost the lumberer's trail.

Exhaustion dragged at his limbs and blurred his vision as he scouted back and forth. Finally, he admitted defeat, if only temporarily. He must rest—but on the morrow, he would find and dispatch the creature, and return to Elfhame.

As he slipped into slumber, however, his fate whispered that it would not be that simple...

CHAPTER 32

To Mara's dismay, it took two more days for her wellspring to regenerate to the point where Avantor agreed to attempt opening the gateway. In truth, though, she'd barely had the energy to argue with him. The first palemoon had slipped away in slumber, and it was only on the second that she roused enough to mark the passage of time.

The bustle of the camp around her had increased so much that she poked her head out of her tent in alarm. Ondo sat cross-legged just outside. He looked up in relief when she spoke his name.

"What is happening?" She gestured at the commotion.

"Hestil has arrived," he said.

"Finally." Mara scanned the camp. "Could you bring her to me, please?"

"I will send for her," he said, clearly unwilling to leave his post. "And Avantor, as well."

She nodded, then ducked back inside to make herself presentable. Urgency simmered just under her skin, but she was now clearheaded enough to know that they must make plans.

No matter how much she wanted to go charging back into her world to find her husband.

There was just time enough for her to settle outside with a cup of hot tea before Hestil arrived.

"My lady." The hard-faced warrior made her a bow. "Avantor has told me what happened. We owe you another great debt, for vanquishing the Void once more. It is my deepest regret that I was too late to join the battle."

"But not too late to help open the gateway," Mara said. "I am going after Bran."

If he could draw upon her strength, she reasoned, then why could she not do the same with the other Dark Elves? It was worth a try, at any rate.

"I will go with you into the mortal world," Hestil said, just as Avantor arrived.

"That is not wise." The healer frowned. "Would Bran agree to rob Hawthorne of both its commander and its second? What if you never return?"

Hestil's eyes narrowed, but she did not argue. "I could say the same for you, Avantor. If I stay behind, then you must as well."

"Bran must have a healer—"

"Then we will send Brethil," Hestil said.

"And Ondo," Avantor replied. "And perhaps—"

"Stop." Mara held up her hands. "I'm not taking an entire troop with me. Who knows what we'll find once we open the gate? With luck, Bran will be waiting to step back into Elfhame."

The memory of her vision rose, and she clenched her jaw to keep her fear from spilling forth.

Avantor and Hestil exchanged a look, and then the warrior offered her a hand up.

"Our people are gathering at the gateway stones," she said. "Let us make the attempt and, as you said, see what lies on the other side."

Mara gulped the last of her tea and then took Hestil's calloused hand, glad of the assistance.

Nearly two dozen Dark Elves stood in a loose circle around the gateway. They bowed to Mara as she passed, and some offered words of thanks and encouragement. Hestil and Avantor strode beside her, Ondo just behind, and all too soon, she stood before the stones marking the gateway.

A hush fell. Mara bit her lip, then turned to Avantor.

"Everyone must take hands," she said, with far more confidence than she felt.

What if her plan failed? What if it did not, only to reveal tragedy on the other side?

Avantor reached to Hestil, who linked hands with Ondo, and on down the line to the last warrior. Once they were all connected, Mara took a deep breath and set her hand on Hestil's shoulder. She had no notion if this idea would work.

True, she'd opened the gateway by herself once before, but that was after weeks of letting her wellspring lie quiescent in the mortal world. She did not have that depth of power now.

Now, she and the rest of the Dark Elves stood arrayed before the silent gray stones of the portal. The air between was still, showing only the clearing beyond. Three glimglows flitted overhead, and Mara sent them a grateful glance. They had always been her allies.

With a deep breath, she held her free hand, palm open, toward the gateway. Recalling Penluith's admonition not to *try*, she focused instead on the thought of Bran there, beyond the gate. The azure ring on her finger pulsed with her heartbeat.

"*Edro!*" she cried.

Blue light flared, and the runes inscribed on the portal stones blazed to life. The view of the clearing between the stones flickered, but did not change.

She squeezed her eyes shut and poured herself into channeling the spell of opening. Already, she could feel her wellspring's power dipping.

"Open!" she yelled, and tightened her grip on Hestil's shoulder.

A surge of power flowed through her, and the wavering strength of her wellspring roared back to fullness. The gateway shimmered, then cleared to show the trees of the mortal Darkwood.

Mara sucked in a breath of dismay. Instead of the frosted winter landscape she'd glimpsed when Bran went through, the fresh green of spring brightened the forest beyond.

Still holding the portal open, she glanced at Avantor. "It is a different season than before."

She'd forgotten that time moved differently between the realms, and panic tightened her throat. How many months had passed in the mortal world, while she had rested? At least two, judging by the season.

"Look." Avantor nodded to the clearing in the human world. A glowing scroll lay on a flat rock just outside the gate. "Can you reach it?"

Mara reached, her hand coruscating with light as it passed between the stones. Her fingertips brushed the curl of paper, and she strained forward, managing to grasp one edge.

The gateway crackled as she pulled the scroll through. Once it was in her hands, she realized that it was not paper, after all, but bark. She guessed Bran had fashioned it somehow, using magic and ingenuity.

"What does it say?" Hestil asked.

One-handed, Mara held the scroll up. It unrolled, and for a moment, the elvish markings were unintelligible. Then the writing blurred and re-formed, and she read the message aloud.

"*Beloved. I must pursue the Void further into your world. Find me.*"

"To the point," Hestil said dryly. "How much longer can you hold the doorway?"

"A bit," Mara said, though she felt the strain of channeling their combined power. "I am going through it, of course."

"I am with you," Ondo said, and Mara noted the pack of supplies at his feet. "I swore to our commander that I would protect you, and I will not break that vow."

She could not argue with him, though she'd prefer to go alone.

"Very well," she said.

"Take Brethil, too," Avantor urged, but Mara shook her head.

"You're lucky I've agreed to Ondo." Her hand trembled, the gateway wavering. "We have no time to argue. Besides, I'm not certain I can transport even the two of us safely through." She glanced at the scout. "Are you ready?"

He nodded and stepped forward.

"Be careful," Avantor said, his expression sober. "Return to us safely, Princess Mara Geary of the Hawthorne Court, and bring our prince home."

"I will." She could feel her strength ebbing.

"Now," she cried, letting go of Hestil and grabbing Ondo's hand. She dashed forward, pulling him behind her into the fading light of the mortal world.

CHAPTER 33

Breathless, Mara stumbled into the clearing. The surrounding evergreens rustled, as if in surprise. Ondo gripped her hand tightly—the only sign of his apprehension.

She glanced over her shoulder. For a heartbeat, she glimpsed the glowing violet sky of Elfhame, the stars of the flowers scattered beneath the huge trees. Then the gate closed, a sigh of blossom-scented air brushing past them. Mara's connection with the linked elves cut off, and she swayed as exhaustion slammed into her.

"My lady!" Ondo dropped her hand and rushed to prop her up.

"I'm all right," she said through gritted teeth. "Help me sit."

She must rest—but first she must attempt to locate Bran.

"Did you bring a scrying bowl?" She glanced at the pack of supplies Ondo had brought. Thank goodness he had been thinking ahead, even if she had not.

He helped her settle with her back against one of the portal stones, then fetched a small silver bowl and poured a measure of water into it. The scrying bowl shook in Mara's hands, the liquid shivering. But no matter her exhaustion, she must reach her husband.

Bending over the bowl, she spoke the rune of scrying. "Show me Bran," she whispered.

Her wellspring responded sluggishly, and the surface of the water continued to reflect the dusk sky overhead. A stab of fear went through her. What if she were too late? What if her vision had come true, and she had lost him?

No. She took a steadying breath. Bran lived—she felt it, a steady glow deep inside.

She touched her wedding ring with the tip of her thumb. Instead of trying to force the scrying, she focused on her yearning for her husband, the bright, steady warmth of the love they shared between them.

"Bran," she said again, her voice taut.

The silvery water shimmered, then an image formed in the center. Bran's face, gazing back at her, his features shaded by a deep hood. She slumped in relief.

"Mara." His voice was thick with emotion. "I knew you would come. Are you well?"

"Well enough. Ondo is with me. Where can we find you?"

A crease formed between his brows, and he glanced over his shoulder. "I have traveled a distance, beloved. It will be no easy thing for us to meet."

"I would go through fire and flood for you," she said, her heart clenching. "But where are you?"

"Far beyond the borders of Raine, I fear. In a place called Parnese."

Parnese? She frowned, trying to place it on a map. Didn't it lie beyond the sea, to the south?

"What of the Void?" She curved her shoulders forward and shot the forest an apprehensive glance.

He frowned. "I am still following its trail. It eluded me, easily crossing the great water while I had to search for a passage over."

The surface of the bowl flickered back to reflecting the sky for a moment, then cleared again.

"The scrying is fading," he said urgently. "Ondo must remain in the forest, guarding the gateway. Our kind is much feared in your world."

"Yes." Her throat dried with fear. "Are you safe? Unharmed?"

"I am managing." He gave her a crooked smile. "The sight of you heartens me greatly."

"We will speak again, soon," she said. "After I rest."

"Take care, my heart. I cannot bear to lose you again."

His image blurred, until only the tree-edged sky remained. Mara swallowed back tears and looked at Ondo.

"You will find him." The scout sounded certain of the fact.

"Yes. And together we'll banish the Void."

She and Bran had faced impossible odds before. And this was her world. She would fight fiercely to defend it.

"Must I remain in the forest?" Ondo asked, a stubborn look in his eyes.

"You heard the prince's command," she reminded him. "You must stay in the Darkwood. But, perhaps, you can escort me to where the forest ends before returning here."

She rose, one hand braced on the rough granite portal stone.

I'm coming, Bran, she thought into the descending dusk.

Three glimglows swooped overhead, then danced to the edge of the forest. They bobbed up down impatiently, as if expecting her to follow. Gathering herself, she stepped forward.

"Where are we going?" Ondo asked her. "You must replenish your strength."

"I will." She glanced up, to where the first familiar stars were beginning to twinkle in the sky.

The Darkwood hushed and rustled, but she was not afraid.

She was home.

CHAPTER 34

Bran drew his hand across his face, tasting dust.

At last, Mara had crossed back into the human realm. His spirits felt lighter than they had in moons. Although he had known it would take time, he'd begun to wonder, with an edge of despair, how long he would have to wander the mortal world alone.

No longer.

The tight band of worry about his ribs eased. Mara would be with him soon.

He settled his sword more firmly over his hip, then strode from the quiet alleyway back out into the busy marketplace he'd been browsing when the scrying summons came. The scent of spices tickled his nose, and the heat of the lowering sun beat through his cloak.

Despite that warmth, he kept the hood drawn up. He'd learned to misdirect his true appearance with magic, but it took some effort. Easier to let the shadows aid the softer blur he cast over his features.

It had not been easy, learning to navigate the human world.

His first encounter with a human had left them both shaken. He hadn't meant to take the woodcutter by surprise, but the man had yelled and charged at Bran with his axe.

Startled, Bran had tried to speak to him, but the woodcutter continued to brandish his weapon, yelling, "Away with you, monster! I swear I'll hew you limb from limb unless you return to the place you sprang from. Demon!"

Despite the man's bold words, his eyes had been wide with fright, his skin pale. It seemed more prudent for Bran to withdraw than to try to convince the fellow he meant no harm. Belatedly, he recalled Mara telling him that humans did not dwell within the forest, but at its edges. He had not realized that a Dark Elf was a frightful thing for a human to behold.

His respect for Mara grew even greater as he realized how much of her own fear she'd had to battle upon their first meeting.

After that, Bran had lingered in the forest and worried about how he might pass for human. If he hunched over, he could make himself appear shorter, and draw his hood over his head for concealment—but that would not be enough.

A rune of misdirection, he decided. If he channeled that power, humans would see what they expected within the shadows of his cloak. That should do, though he would have to test it before venturing into the wider world.

He had no supplies except his sword, the small eating knife at his belt, and, of course, his magic. It had been enough to keep him fed and sheltered for the night and day he spent within the Darkwood.

Finally, he had the chance to use his rune when he discovered a huntsman moving stealthily through the forest in search of game. Not quietly enough for Bran's ears, however.

Humming loudly, so that the bowman wouldn't shoot him by mistake, Bran circled around the man and emerged behind him on the small trail he followed.

"Hush," the man said, whirling with a frown. "Do you want to frighten all the deer between here and the coast?"

Bran dipped his head.

"Sorry," he mumbled.

"Who are you?" The man's hand tightened over his weapon.

"Lost my way," Bran said, thinking furiously as he replayed the hunter's words in his mind. "From the coast."

The man frowned. "That's some distance. Though not the strangest thing to ever happen in these woods, I'd wager. Turn around and when you see the road, follow it to the left-hand branching. Though Portknowe is at least a day's walk, if not further."

He gestured with his bow.

"Thank you." Bran lifted a hand and pivoted, smiling grimly to himself. It seemed his disguise was a success.

Whether it was his magic or his marriage, he was grateful he could speak and understand the human tongue. Just to be safe, as he made his way through the forest he concocted a story of being from a far-off village and becoming lost in the woods.

As the fearsomely bright blaze of the sun was at last fading, he reached a mid-sized village. There, was able to barter most of his jewelry—all except his azure wedding band, which he would never part with—for the supplies he needed. Including a horse, though the chestnut gelding was no match for Fuin.

A nudge of spell-work kept those he met from questioning his story too closely. He followed the Voidspawn's trail, able to track it with a spell of sensing once his wellspring regenerated. The creature was moving southward and east, and he pursued, gaining ground.

Until he reached the shore, where the strange, endless waves lapped. The lumberer's path led directly into the water. Frustrated, Bran rode back and forth along the shoreline. His mount balked when he tried to ride it into the waves, and he quickly abandoned that notion. But how to follow?

It was not until he spied the strange wooden contraption floating against the horizon that he understood there was a way for him to cross the wide waters.

The next day, he reached the town of Portknowe, where the waterborne vessels came and went.

After a few mishaps, he'd learned how to enchant small items into the appearance of coin, and traded some for passage aboard a ship—a strange experience, to journey borne by wood and wave. When he once more stood upon land, the Voidspawn's trail was faint.

With much effort, he traced the creature to the city of Parnese, where the trail once again faded. He'd been desperately trying to find it again when the scrying from Mara had come.

Now, half of him wanted to turn back to the cool green land of Raine. He wanted nothing more than to take his wife in his arms, inhale the scent of her, and remind himself of everything good in both their worlds.

But, as ever, duty and honor bound him to a different course. No matter how much his heart might cry otherwise.

Mara would find him, he had no doubt, even as he continued his pursuit of the Voidspawn. It would be easier for her, moving through her own, familiar, world—and their ability to scry with one another would make it that much simpler for her to catch up and find him.

Soon, my love, he thought, sending his love flying northward, across the water.

Soon.

With a deep breath, he strode from the marketplace to the small inn where he'd taken rooms. The sun was setting, and in the blessed dimness of the human world's twilight, he vowed to turn all his power to tracking the Void, and eliminating it.

Meanwhile, he must content himself with the memory of Mara's sweetly human face, the light in her eyes, the steadfastness of her spirit.

On the far horizon, the sun of the mortal realm sank slowly in a blaze of crimson and gold. Surely, in all the worlds, light would prevail, and vanquish the darkness of the Void.

He could believe nothing less.

~

RAINE

DEDICATION

This one goes out to everyone working on building bridges between worlds.
You know who you are.
Keep the light burning bright~

CHAPTER 1

In the overheated back corner of a Parnesian wine house, Brannon Luthinor, heir to the Hawthorne Throne, Prince of the Dark Elves, warrior-mage and prophecy-born, was losing at dice. Rather spectacularly. And not on purpose.

"Pity," said the olive-skinned man seated across the table as he swept the last of Bran's coin into his pile. "Got any more stake?"

The silver gleamed mockingly against the pitted wooden tabletop. Bran, trying not to clench his teeth, shook his head. While surveilling the wine house, he'd thought to plump up his purse with a simple game of chance. He'd thought wrong.

For a moment, the leashed wellspring of his magic flared.

Just a little nudge of the dice, and the tables would turn...

No. That was not his way, no matter how much the mortal world might tax his patience. He glanced over at the man who had taken the last of his coin.

"I am finished," Bran said.

"Tsk." The man sucked his teeth. "Another coin or two, and you might win it all back."

"I have no more."

"I could lend you a bit." The gambler smiled, his expression all kindness with not one drop of sincerity.

Bran regarded him steadily from within the shelter of his hooded cloak. "I think not."

"Eh. Your loss." The man scooped the coins into his purse with a sweet, metallic clink of farewell. "Better luck tomorrow, then."

"Perhaps," Bran replied, though he had no intention of frequenting that particular wine house. The Soiled Cockerel. It seemed aptly named.

"Ciao." The man flashed a cheeky smile and slid out from the bench to spend his ill-gotten gains elsewhere. He eeled his way into the crowd around the bar, leaving Bran to his tangled thoughts and his empty purse.

The Hawthorne Prince let out an irritated breath. It was only money, after all. He would sleep beneath the bridges tonight, and manufacture more coin on the morrow. The flat white stones along the riverbed were easy enough to enchant into silver florins, and they spent as well as any mortal coin.

Although the whole concept of money was strange to him. They did not use such a system of commerce in Elfhame. It had taken him some time to understand its use, and longer still to take advantage of it.

"Another glass?" the barmaid asked, coasting past his table with a half-dozen empty goblets blooming like a crystal bouquet from her hand.

"Thank you, but no." Bran pushed aside his goblet, still half-full of harsh red wine.

There were no answers here, no hint of the enemy he was chasing. A wasted evening, and it was his own fault for thinking drink and a bit of gambling would help ease the tight twist of yearning in his heart.

His own fault, too, for being worlds away from his beloved, Mara.

When he'd leaped through the gateway from Elfhame into the mortal realm, it had been the only course of action. The Void, his people's ancient enemy, could not be allowed to escape and wreak havoc upon the humans.

But he'd lost the trail of the Voidspawn here, in the bustling city of Parnese. The lumberer, that fearsome creature of the Void, had somehow vanished. Now, disquieting rumors were surfacing about strange deaths in the poorer quarters: withered corpses found floating beneath the piers, beggars who disappeared, only for the husks of their bodies to be discovered in dank alleyways and abandoned buildings.

He was certain it was the Void, gaining in strength. Yet, despite Bran's formidable powers, he was unable to discover where the creature had gone to ground.

Did the Void still maintain the aspect of the lumberer? He doubted it. But what form had it taken, and where was it? The questions kept him restless and on edge.

It did not help matters that he must draw upon his magic at all times in order to appear human, which honed his already sharp temper. He could not alter his height, and did not choose to change the dark plaits of his warrior's braids, although his enchantment of misdirection softened the angles of his face and rounded his pupils. The mortal world was frustrating, and the fact that he dared not show his true self or perform any obvious acts of magic made it all the more so.

He'd thought Mara difficult to understand—but here, in the heart of the human city, he felt like a creature of the air thrust underwater and expected to swim. Was that how his mortal bride had felt, trapped in the realm of the Dark Elves?

It was not a pleasant sensation in the least, and once again he acknowledged what a poor husband he'd been to her. Poor husband and —so far—failed hero.

But enough of these desperate thoughts.

He gave himself a mental shake. At least Mara had finally been able to contact him via the magic of scrying, though she was a kingdom and an ocean away. It would not do for her to find him lost in self-pity and at his wits' end.

Even if he felt that way daily.

Day.

That was part of the problem, too. In his own land, there was no fireball scorching its way across the sky, blinding and burning the people beneath. The Dark Elves were made for moonlight, the soft radiance of their doublemoons twining through the shadowed hours. Sometimes both moons shone, sometimes one, and rarely none at all.

Thus, his people had developed the ability to moderate their vision to the amount of available light.

Thank all the bright stars that he could do so with the sun as well, sliding a protective membrane over his catlike eyes in order to reduce its terrible glare. That, plus the deep-hooded cloak he wore, made the refracted brilliance bearable.

Night was a relief, and so he had become a denizen of that darker time. Mostly, it was a wise choice. Unless, while trying to distract himself, he lost all his coin in an unlucky game of chance.

Fingering his now-empty purse, Bran rose. It was past time for him to leave the Soiled Cockerel. Too bad he'd not paid in advance for lodgings—but he'd learned his lesson. Despite his distaste for moving about in the day, on the morrow he would secure a place for the next fortnight.

How long would it take Mara to reach him?

He longed to scry to her—but without a private room and a lock on the door, it would be utter folly. He must not run the risk of discovery, no matter how much he longed to see his wife's face and hear her voice.

For now, he must content himself with the knowledge that she'd managed to open the gate and step from Elfhame into the mortal world. She was on her way to him—and surely, as a native of this world, she would not find it so difficult to come to Parnese.

Not nearly as difficult as he had.

As soon as they were reunited, he felt certain that, with their joined powers, they'd be able to track down the Void. No matter where it had hidden itself, or how well guarded it might be.

He clenched his hands, his partially sheathed nails biting into his palms. He would keep searching, of course—prying relentlessly into the scum-infested areas of Parnese, like the Soiled Cockerel—and pray to the doublemoons that the Void would not take too many more victims.

CHAPTER 2

The Darkwood stirred, a cold wind whispering through the tall hemlocks as Mara Geary and the Dark Elf scout, Ondo, trod the paths beneath the trees. The gateway between the worlds lay far behind them, the standing stones hidden in their secret glade in the center of the forest.

Shafts of sunlight sifted down, illuminating patches of pale blossoms, and Mara could not help sighing at the sight of the sun. She had missed it dreadfully during her time in Elfhame. Even a few hours back in her world had helped ease her heart. Not to mention that she was in the same realm as Bran, and on her way to him. She let out another long breath.

"Are you well, my lady?" Ondo asked, casting a look over his shoulder. "Should we call a rest?"

"No need. We're almost at the edge of the forest."

Almost to the wide meadow where the road to the village of Little Hazel began—and her family's cottage stood.

"I do not think it wise to leave you," the scout said.

"Coming with me would be more foolish. My magic is too unreliable to disguise you. And besides, I'll make better time traveling alone."

He frowned, the gaunt lines of his face tightening, but turned back to the path. They both knew that she was right—he would only slow her down with his lack of knowledge of the human world, and if anyone guessed what he was, they would both be in danger.

Beyond those arguments, though, was the simple fact that his prince had ordered him to remain in the Darkwood and guard the gateway between the worlds. Ondo would not disobey.

The trees thinned, and Mara caught a whiff of wood smoke drifting on the breeze. Soon she would see her family again. Her pace quickened, anticipation pushing her forward.

Her sisters, Lily and Pansy, would be older, of course; everyone would. Time ran differently in the land of the Dark Elves, and where a few months had passed for her, she knew that equaled almost two years in the mortal world. How strange, to think that Pansy would now be older than she was, and Lily nearly her same age.

Would they be courting? Pansy had wanted nothing more than to marry a rich merchant and leave Little Hazel behind. Lily had expressed no opinion either way.

And as for the twins, Sean and Seanna, Mara couldn't imagine them making separate lives apart from one another—but perhaps they had.

She and Ondo reached the last stand of cedar trees, the feathery branches marking the edge of the Darkwood.

"Thank you," she said, turning to him. "I know you wish only to keep me safe, as you have done before. But this is my world, now. I'll come to no harm."

His lips twisted, as though he wished to argue, but he merely shook his head. "I wish you safe travels, my lady. Find Prince Bran, dispatch the Voidspawn, and return to us, as soon as you may."

"I will."

By her calculations, it was a two-day ride to the coast of Raine and then a journey of four days by ship to Parnese. So, a fortnight's worth of travel there and back—but that did not include helping Bran track down the elusive Voidspawn and then dispatching it. At the very least, they would not return for a month.

Her family deserved more than one day's visit from her, as well, and she must provision for the journey ahead, by land and by sea.

How had Bran managed? Were there even oceans in Elfhame? How strange it all must have seemed to him.

"Bide—and we will scry to you," she told Ondo. "Meanwhile, take care not to be seen."

"I am adept at woodcraft," he said in an injured tone.

She set her hand on his arm. "I know—but you would appear monstrously frightening to any human who might catch a glimpse of you."

"Monstrous?" His dark brows drew together. "But you do not find us so, my lady."

"No." Her mouth twisted in a wry smile at the memory of how dreadful she'd found Bran on their first meeting. "Not any longer."

"I will be cautious," he said.

She nodded. "I don't doubt it. Farewell, Ondo."

"May the moons shine upon your path," he said, bowing.

"And the sun upon yours." She smiled, then strode out of the forest into the crisp light of spring.

New shoots of green were emerging from the brown hummocks of meadow grass, and the first hardy yellow flowers bloomed beside the road. The meadow gave way to fenced fields and thickets, and soon she caught sight of the stone-walled cottages scattered ahead.

Without meaning to, she began to run, flying toward the second cottage on the left. Home.

She drew up at the front step, heart pounding. The lilac bush beside the door had grown into a tree, the first new buds swelling beneath the bark. The scent of fresh-baked bread permeated the air, and from inside the cottage she could hear laughter.

Suddenly tearful, she lifted her hand and knocked.

"Coming!" her mother called.

The door opened, revealing Mara's mother, whose mouth fell open when she caught sight of her daughter. "Mara—dear heavens."

She opened her arms, and with a sniffle, Mara stepped into her mother's embrace.

With an ear-splitting screech, Lily joined them, wrapping her arms tightly around Mara's shoulders. At least, Mara thought it must be her youngest sister, but her eyes were so blurred with tears it was difficult to tell.

When her mother let her go, Mara rubbed her vision clear and took a shaky breath. She knew she'd missed her family, but she'd tried to ignore how very fiercely her longing to see them had burned through her. Now, standing on the scrubbed wooden floorboards of their cottage, with her mother and sister before her, she could scarcely breathe past the happiness filling her chest.

"Come in, take off your cloak," her mother said, closing the door.

"I can't believe it," Lily said, looking Mara up and down. "I'm taller than you! Did you shrink there in the magical land of the elves? Are they all ridiculously short?"

"Far from it," Mara said, laughing. "But look at you—you're all grown up."

Her sister's brown hair, the same shade as her own, was coiled into a neat bun, her hazel eyes bright with curiosity.

"Alas," their mother said with a mock sigh. "Lily might be a young woman now, but she has no suitors."

"But I have a kitten," Lily said proudly, going to scoop up a ball of fluff from the chair before the hearth and holding the kitten out for inspection. "Isn't she beautiful?"

"Very." Mara hung up her cloak beside the door, then went to admire her sister's new pet.

The kitten's marmalade-colored fur was soft as silk. It blinked up at her with green eyes, then yawned.

"You've missed Pansy's monthly visit," their mother said, bustling to the hearth to put the kettle on. "Dare I ask whether you'll be staying?"

Sobering, Mara looked at her mother. The fine lines about her eyes had deepened, and new streaks of gray threaded her brown hair. The cost of staying in Elfhame, Mara realized with a pang, was that she would have to see her family grow old without her.

Unless she stayed forever in that dark land—but that thought squeezed her heart with too much pain.

"I can't stay," she said, wishing she could erase the sorrow from her mother's eyes.

"Surely you're not stepping right out the door again?" Lily asked, cuddling her kitten beneath her chin. "You must see Papa."

"And the twins," their mother added. "We'll have them over for supper."

"They don't live here anymore?" Mara glanced at the steep stairway leading to the bedrooms upstairs. It was strange to think of the house emptying out, her siblings moving away and going on with lives she knew nothing about. "Where has Pansy gone?"

Their mother shook her head fondly. "She did what she always said she would... married a rich fellow and moved to Meriton."

"Is she happy?" Mara asked.

"Ridiculously so!" Lily rolled her eyes, and Mara smiled to see the echo of the child still within the young woman. "We all thought her a fool for leaving Little Hazel, but she lives in a mansion now. I'm to spend a month with her, come autumn, and she'll show me all the sights of the city."

"As long as you keep out of trouble," their mother said.

Lily snorted in response and went to deposit her fluffball back on the cushion.

"And Sean and Seanna?" Mara asked, going to sit in her favorite chair.

She paused, brushing orange cat hair off the worn green upholstery, then settled. Things had changed, but not too terribly. The cottage was still home.

Her mother fetched the teapot from its shelf and strewed a handful of leaves inside, then set out three mugs.

"Old Soraya passed this last winter," she said. "The twins were studying with her, as you recall."

Mara nodded. Her oldest siblings had always shown a penchant for herbcraft, and the whole village knew that they would inherit the herb-wife's mantle.

"They moved into her cottage," her mother continued, "and seem well content."

"They have a suitor, though," Lily said, giggling.

"Both of them?"

Mara's mother firmed her lips. "We don't know for certain which one young Orion is courting—and it's no business of ours. Eventually, they'll make some sort of announcement."

Considering the fact that their middle daughter was married to a Dark Elf prince, Mara supposed that a human, of any persuasion, was nothing for her parents to concern themselves over.

"Lily, run tell the twins that Mara's here and bid them come for supper this evening," their mother said.

Without protest, Lily jumped up and grabbed her cloak from its spot by the door. She paused a moment to finger Mara's finely woven Dark Elf garment.

"This is lovely workmanship," she said. "Did you bring us more jewels this time?"

"Shoo," their mother said, flapping her apron at Lily.

Grinning, Lily slipped out the door.

"I don't know what I'm going to do with that child," Mara's mother said.

"Ship her off to Meriton?" Mara smiled at her mother. "I think she'll have a grand time with Pansy."

"Hopefully not *too* grand." Her mother poured hot water from the kettle into the teapot, then came to sit across from Mara. "But speaking of changed circumstances, how is your life as a princess?"

Mara picked up her empty earthenware mug and rolled it thoughtfully between her hands. There was a fine line between putting a good face on things and confessing all her troubles to her mother.

"Complicated," she finally said. "And not at all settled. I'm sure you're wondering why I'm here."

Her mother gently removed the mug from Mara's grasp and poured out their tea. "You've a good reason, I'm sure."

"Bran—my husband—is here in the human world."

"Here?" Her mother set the teapot down with a thump and glanced at the door.

"Don't worry, he's not about to come striding in," Mara said. "He's in Parnese."

"Parnese—across the sea?"

"That is the place, yes," Mara said dryly.

"And he went all that way without you! Whatever for?" Concern shone in her mother's eyes.

Mara shifted in the chair. Much as she wanted to tell her mother everything, she didn't want to unduly alarm her, either.

"Something... escaped from Elfhame, and Bran is tracking it down. As I said, things are complicated. I was delayed, and am only now able to follow him."

"Well. He might have stopped here for help, you know," her mother said.

Mara could imagine how *that* might have gone. Screams and consternation, her father laying about with his sharp axe, Bran trying to defend himself with magic. The cottage would have been flattened, at the very least.

"Ah, well," she said, trying to sound noncommittal, "it's probably best if I introduce you the first time you meet."

Her mother took a sip of tea, studying Mara's face, then nodded.

"I fully expect both of you to make a stop here on your return journey," she said. "I'm not sure we could forgive you for depriving us of the chance to get to know our son-in-law. I assume you're going to fetch him, yes?"

"Yes."

"And that the whatever-it-is that's running free poses no danger." Her mother gave her a sharp look. "It's not some poor runaway child, is it, going to be hauled back in chains?"

"Of course not!" Mara covered her mother's hand with her own. "And Bran is more than a match for the bit of... I suppose we can call it *stray energy* that got into our world."

She neglected to add that it was the fragment of an inimical force that wanted to devour any world it came into contact with. After all, she and Bran would be able to find and extinguish the Void shard.

Mara clung to that firm belief and sipped her minty tea.

"You're leaving tomorrow, I take it," her mother said, ever observant.

"First thing in the morning. Could I borrow the donkey cart? And maybe Lily, to drive it home from Portknowe?"

"Better yet, your father has to make a delivery of ale tomorrow. He must stop at the castle, but then he'd be glad to take you to the coast."

And if he wasn't, well, Mara's mother would see to it that he'd drive her there anyway.

"Thank you, Mama. I don't want to be any trouble."

Her mother rose and took the now-empty teapot to the sink. "I'll tell you what's trouble—those muddy roads. The donkey cart's too small. You'd get stuck every mile. The ale dray will make better time, and your father will see to it that the innkeepers give you a warm welcome. Half the country drinks his ale now, you know."

"I'm glad to hear the brewing is going so well. And thank you."

Her mother waved the dishtowel at her. "You're family, silly girl. Leave those princess manners at the door, and come help me with the washing up."

With a wry smile, Mara joined her mother. For now, she was a daughter of the house—but later that night, she would scry to Bran and reassure him she was on her way.

For a moment, her thoughts went to the Hawthorne Court. She cared little for the machinations of the courtiers, but her one friend in Elfhame, Bran's sister, Anneth, must surely be wondering how her brother fared. Mara was not strong enough to scry between the worlds—she doubted anyone could, except perhaps Bran.

Whatever transpired in Elfhame, the worlds turned their separate ways, and, on the whole, she was glad to have left Hawthorne behind.

CHAPTER 3

Owen Mallory, Crown Prince of Raine, stared somberly at his mother's mausoleum. The white stone was freshly cut, carved with twining leaves, the doorway sealed where her body had been interred.

Overhead, the sky was closed with clouds, a spring drizzle spitting down. Spring. It had used to be his favorite time of year. Owen braced his legs as though the damp ground might give him some solidity.

It didn't.

Nothing was firm any longer—not with his mother suddenly dead, and his father wounded in the carriage accident that had taken the queen's life.

"You must marry," his father said, leaning heavily upon his cane with his good hand. "I am old and infirm, and the people must cheer themselves with the prospect of a hale young king and new queen."

"You're not old," Owen said, blinking rain out of his eyes. Or tears. Probably both.

"The last few weeks have aged me." King Philip let out a low sigh that matched the cold wind blowing through Owen's heart. "We shall find you a bride."

Owen clenched his hand, the fine leather of his riding glove straining at the knuckles. "I have no desire to marry."

He had loved, once. Foolishly, as it turned out.

"It needn't be for love," his father said, correctly reading his expression. "The stability of the kingdom is paramount, what with the Athraig making veiled threats and the Fiorlanders too busy with their own troubles to lend us aid. A pity Princess Jutta is a mere babe. But perhaps—"

"I am not marrying a child twenty years my junior," Owen said sharply. "And, as you said, Fiorland is preoccupied at the moment."

The king stood silently, shoulders bowed, his cloak darkened with rain. Behind them, the horses stamped restively, jingling the harness that attached them to the royal coach. Owen couldn't bear the thought of being cooped up in the gloomy interior, and had taken his own mount, who stood patiently under the hand of the coachman.

"The Athraig princess..." his father said.

"We both know that would be the first step in their annexation of Raine," Owen said. "They've long wanted control of our shores."

For over a century, the small island nation of Raine had, with their superior navy, kept incursions at bay. But now that the kingdom was unsettled by the death of their queen, the Athraig would take full advantage.

"All the more reason to get you married to a Rainish girl, then," his father said. "And soon."

The only Rainish girl Owen had been inclined to marry had left his heart in tatters. He'd truly thought Lady Elisa loved him. He had fallen deep into the clear blue of her eyes and the sweetness of her smile—only to discover that she had another lover, and wanted him only for his throne.

All those pretty words of love she'd spoken were like flower petals. Beautiful, but quick to shrivel and blacken once the truth was out.

"Let's go back," Owen said, turning away from the white-slicked marble of the tomb.

"A ball," the king said thoughtfully, making his slow way back to the coach. "A joyous event, to give everyone something to anticipate. We'll invite all the eligible young ladies in the kingdom. Surely you'll be able to find one that suits."

Owen glanced at his father. “I hardly think I’ll find the right girl by sifting through hundreds of women in the space of a single night.”

“It won’t be hundreds,” the king said. “The census last summer was very thorough. If we narrow the age range, I believe it will be fewer than fifty.”

“That’s still several dozen too many—and I can’t believe I’m even considering this mad idea.”

But, much as Owen hated to admit it, his father was right. He *did* need to find a bride, despite the fact it would be a loveless marriage. And the kingdom needed something to distract it from its grief.

“Surely a few young ladies will catch your eye,” the king went on, undeterred. “We can invite them to stay on at the castle so you might get to know them better. It’s not as though you need to make a decision right away. Now, help me into the coach. I need to speak with the council so we might set things in motion. An early summer ball, I think—that will give us enough time.”

Owen shook his head and assisted his father up the unfolded coach steps. He gently tucked the lap blanket about the king, taking care not to jar his leg.

A fresh gust of raindrops pattered on the coach windows, and Owen let out a low sigh. Despite the unmistakable signs of spring burgeoning through the forest, it seemed to him that winter would never end.

CHAPTER 4

Lady Anneth Luthinor paused before the arched entrance to the Hawthorne Palace's dining hall and tucked her dark plaits back behind her pointed ears. From the murmured gossip she'd heard in the corridors, it seemed that, once again, the Hawthorne Lord was absent from the evening meal.

Her first clue that something was wrong had been a few moons earlier, when Lord Calithilon had suffered a bout of coughing at dinner. Seated as she was at the high table, she'd seen blood flecking her father's napkin, a spatter of red against the white cloth, before he quickly folded it into his lap. After that, she'd noticed things. Small things, to be sure—his too-slow response to a question, his sunken-eyed gaze—but worrying when taken all together.

When Anneth stepped into the vaulted hall, she saw that the head table was indeed occupied only by her mother, the sternly elegant Lady Tinnueth. For a moment, all Anneth wanted to do was flee back to the quiet safety of her own rooms, but it was too late. Her mother had spotted her, and beckoned her forward with one twist of a bejeweled hand.

Pasting a smile on her face, Anneth obeyed her mother's summons. A trail of whispers eddied in her wake: speculation about the

Hawthorne Lord's continued absence from meals, concerns that the Hawthorne Heir had once again gone missing, and sidelong glances that spoke all too clearly of the court's unease at the possibility that Anneth might eventually take the throne.

Stars forbid! The last thing she wanted to do was preside over the intricacies of a Dark Elf court. She'd deliberately shunned that path, instead taking up the unlikely, and much scoffed-at, study of mortals and their world.

Now that her brother, Bran, had wed a human, however, her knowledge was coming in handy. Provided that said human actually was in residence at the Hawthorne Court...

"Anneth." Her mother raised one arched brow as Anneth stepped onto the dais. "How good of you to join me."

Not as if she had a choice, but Anneth inclined her head and took the seat to her mother's right. Her presence seemed to underscore the emptiness of the chair on Lady Tinnueth's left, where her husband should be sitting.

"Where is Father?" Anneth asked, unfolding the silken napkin over her lap.

The magical dome of silence permanently cast over the head table ensured that the rulers of the court could discuss anything without fear of being overheard. Perhaps Lady Tinnueth would finally speak freely about her husband's wellbeing.

"Is there any news of your brother?" Lady Tinnueth asked instead—as usual, paying no heed to anyone's needs but her own.

"You would know better than I."

Her mother's lips thinned. "I have heard nothing. A pity your strange little hobby isn't of more use."

"Knowing about the mortal world doesn't mean I'm able to scry between the realms." Anneth kept her tone even, denying Lady Tinnueth the pleasure of making her lose her temper. "Even Bran can't do that."

Though he'd confided, once, that he'd seen Mara in a scrying, before she'd opened the gate between the worlds and entered Elfhame. Of course, a cross-world vision was rather different from an actual two-way communication.

The servers came with the fruit course, providing a temporary distraction, but soon enough, Anneth and her mother were alone again. The head table was enough removed from the other diners that a sea of space seemed to spread out around them.

"What good is it that Brannonilon is the most powerful magic user in history, if I can't even communicate with my own son?" Lady Tinnueth did not sound like a distraught mother—she had never been maternal—but rather, annoyed that Bran was out of her reach.

Anneth twisted the napkin between her fingers, wishing that she, too, could escape into the mortal world. Would it be as fascinating as she thought? Oh, why hadn't she asked Mara more questions about life among humans, before she'd left the Hawthorne Court?

"Bran and Mara will be back soon, I'm sure," she said, trying to reassure herself more than her mother. "Time flows differently in the human world, after all. Chasing down the last of the Void might take several moon-turnings there, but only a short time in our world."

"A doublemoon has already come and gone," Lady Tinnueth said. "Bran must be fetched from that other place. He is needed here."

No mention of his wife, of course. Lady Tinnueth would prefer that Mara didn't exist, despite the fact she was wed to Bran—and that the Dark Elves would never have been able to defeat the Void's invasion of Elfhame without her help.

"The gateway between the worlds isn't a simple door that can be opened and closed at will," Anneth said, trying to keep the irritation from her voice.

"Hestil knows how it's done," her mother continued heedlessly. "I'll send her into the Erynvorn, and the others who were there when Bran went through, to help her open the gate. She can go through and find Bran."

"How will she get back?"

Lady Tinnueth waved a hand. "She will tell Bran to return immediately, and accompany him home."

There were so many problems with that plan that Anneth didn't know where to begin—but she resolved to try to make her mother see sense.

"Don't you think that, with Bran gone, his second should stay at the

Hawthorne Court instead of being dispatched to the mortal realm? And what about Healer Avantor? He helped open the gate, but perhaps you have need of him here. Don't you?"

It was an obvious attempt to pry information about her father's state of health from Lady Tinnueth. Too obvious, of course. But the fact that Bran's presence was deemed necessary was... worrisome.

"I will send them at the next brightmoon," Lady Tinnueth said, then turned to Anneth, her cold gaze filled with intensity. "But now let us discuss your betrothal."

Anneth stared at her mother, a shiver running through her. "My... betrothal? But I don't have one."

"Precisely. It is time we addressed the situation. I was thinking perhaps Prince Deldarinnon of Cereus. Your destiny is to wed a prince, after all."

A cold wash of fear went through Anneth. Was her father's health so very fragile, then? Things must be bad indeed if Lady Tinnueth was thinking of marrying her off. Anneth knew she was a pawn in the Hawthorne Court, but for most of her life, she'd been an overlooked one.

"Surely there's no need to hurry my birth prophecy along," Anneth told her mother, scrambling for some excuse, however flimsy. "Besides, I've never met the Cereus Heir."

Lady Tinnueth's mouth curled. "Of course you have—but Prince Deldarinnon is not the heir. His older brother, Prince Garithilon, is. Which you would know if you'd spent a quarter of the time paying attention to the affairs of Elfhame that you've spent in your ridiculous study of the humans. At any rate, you are to meet him soon. He arrives tomorrow."

"Tomorrow?" Anneth dropped her fork with a clatter that pierced the silence surrounding the head table.

The nearby diners glanced their way, and Anneth saw Lady Mireleth bring a hand up to her mouth—a gesture supposedly meant to hide her titter of amusement, but actually designed to bring attention to the fact she was laughing at Anneth.

Trust Mireleth to always enjoy someone else's discomfort.

Lady Tinnueth ignored her daughter's reaction. "There will be a reception tomorrow to welcome him, three turns before moonset. I expect you to dress accordingly."

Meaning, as a Princess of Elfhame. And, Anneth supposed, throne-bait. For that was the deeper message: with her father possibly quite ill—though Tinnueth hadn't admitted it—and Bran missing, Anneth was next in line for the Hawthorne Throne, should Lady Tinnueth choose to step down.

But that was Bran's future, Anneth knew. Not hers. Even though both of them had been schooled in the duties and responsibilities of their station, she'd always known that she was an afterthought. And she'd never desired that power—or burden.

She'd never imagined being married off, either—at least, not so soon! Dark Elves were very long-lived, and she'd had every confidence her parents would continue to rule the Hawthorne Court for decades.

Certainly, in the rare moments she'd contemplated her potential futures, Anneth had assumed she'd have plenty of time before the issue of her betrothal arose. In truth, she'd imagined Bran on the throne at that point, and he would never force her onto a path she did not choose.

Unlike their mother.

But it seemed fate—and Lady Tinnueth—had other plans, whether Anneth willed it or no.

CHAPTER 5

Mara gripped the water-glazed rail of the sailing ship with both hands and kept her eyes fixed on the distant shore of Parnese. That hazy line did not seem nearly close enough, and her stomach gave another uneasy lurch.

Sea travel, she'd discovered, did not agree with her. The past four days aboard the vessel had been, while not exactly miserable, not terribly comfortable, either. After the first night, she'd only eaten bread and water, which seemed to keep her stomach as settled as it could be under the circumstances.

Was there a magical cure for seasickness? She let out a low breath. Even if there were, with the unpredictability of her powers, who could say if she would not end up enchanting herself with some sort of unforeseen consequence, like a raging thirst that couldn't be quenched? Or turning herself into a fish, for that matter.

Once she reached Bran, she would resume practicing the handful of runes she'd been taught. But on the middle of the sea, she'd judged it unwise to try even the simplest spells, like calling foxfire, for fear of incinerating the boat or wreaking some other havoc.

The captain of the vessel had said they should arrive in port just after dark. A wave sent spray into Mara's face, and she tasted salt on her lips. Her skin was sticky from it, and she was looking forward to a bath almost as much as seeing her husband.

Bran had promised to meet her when the ship docked, then show her to the rooms he'd rented at a nearby inn. There, they would make their plans to hunt down the Void, which seemed to be preying upon the citizens of Parnese. It was imperative they find it as soon as possible.

The longer the Void spent in her world, the stronger and more dangerous it grew. They must vanquish it at all costs.

And then what? The thought made her nearly as queasy as the motion of the ship. *Return to Elfhame?*

Someone in the Hawthorne Court wanted her dead. Her magic was unpredictable, at best. And she and Bran had a new marriage to navigate, not to mention two worlds to try to bridge.

She could not ask him to stay in the human world with her. He was heir to Hawthorne, his destiny proclaimed by the Oracles—and she was certain that his destiny did not include a quiet existence in the village of Little Hazel, pretending to be human.

But she was not at all certain she wanted to return to Elfhame and live out her days among a dying people. Especially not when her own life was in danger.

Yet she loved Bran, with all her heart and soul.

Heart tangled with doubt, she faced the salt-flavored breeze and clung to the hope that, together, they would find their way forward.

Bran leaned against the stone warehouse wall at the dock, watching the lights kindle through the port district of Parnese. The smell of the sea was rank—old fish, bitter salt, and the black tar the mortals used to coat their ships and make them watertight.

Watercraft of all sizes bobbed at anchor, the sea restless beneath them. Watching them, he thought back on the novel experience of journeying across the sea.

When the trail of the Voidspawn he'd been tracking through Raine disappeared into the water, he hadn't known what to do. His first impulse had been to shed his clothing and swim after it, yet as far as he could see, there was only water. It would be sheer folly to jump into a lake that had no distant shore. Not to mention the inadvisability of leaving his weapons behind.

Yet he could not abandon the trail.

Frustrated, he'd made camp nearby and begun scouting the woods for materials to make something that would carry him over the waves. He could stitch it together with magic, he supposed, yet he'd no idea how long the journey might take, or how many provisions he should bring.

It was a daunting prospect, even for Elfhame's strongest battle-mage. His powers were better suited to attack and defense, not envisioning how to build a floating craft.

His human wife would know what to do, and he berated himself for dashing so precipitously through the gateway, leaving her behind. He'd been entirely focused on pursuing the Voidspawn that slipped into the mortal world. Who could have guessed that the gate would close the moment he stepped through?

After a frustrating day spent trying to bind sticks together with magic, he'd spotted a large craft passing by, floating on the water, and understood that the humans had already invented what he was trying to create. Quickly, he'd abandoned his efforts, broken camp, and followed the shoreline in the direction he'd seen the vessel go.

The next morning brought him to a human town built beside the water. Several vessels floated in the curving bay, many of them only big enough for one or two people.

Mindful of the first mortal he'd encountered, and the woodcutter's horrified reaction to his appearance, Bran had spent some time crafting a spell that would make him appear human. It was complex, involving taking the perceptions of those around him at any given moment and bending them, showing them what they expected to see. But he had power enough to sustain it while he moved about in the mortal world.

He cast the magic once more, then stepped out onto the road leading into the port town—Portknowe, according to the rough-hewn sign. Despite an earlier test, with a hunter in the forest, he wasn't entirely certain how well the rune would work in a more populated environment. The people he met didn't cry out in fear or cower away, however, and the tightness in his lungs eased. The rune worked, though he must feed it a small, constant trickle of power.

The road turned to a stone-paved street, and Bran tried not to reveal his curiosity as he strode through Portknowe. Unlike the measured elegance of the courts of Elfhame, or the deliberate construction of the few Dark Elf towns, this human place seemed to have grown any which way.

Streets curved around and deposited him back into the very square he'd just left. Buildings of varied size, color, and materials stood shoulder to shoulder. Some seemed to be dwelling places; others displayed a variety of goods in their windows. Strange smells wafted from open doorways: bitter herbal scents, unfamiliar spices, thick floral perfumes.

Whatever magic had allowed Mara to understand him and his people seemed to be working in reverse. He caught snippets of conversation as he wended his way through the town, and was even able to ask for directions to the water when yet another twisty lane took him the opposite direction.

At last he emerged from a narrow alley onto a wide stone causeway. Wooden structures jutted out into the water, enabling access to the vessels—boats, as he now understood from overhearing, and he was now at an area called *the docks*.

Making sure his hood was drawn high, he stepped into the bright light, made even worse by the reflections off the water, and made for the largest boat.

A big, well-muscled man, nearly as tall as Bran, stood guard at the wooden plank leading up to the boat. Clearly, not just anyone could saunter onto the craft.

"Are you going across the water?" Bran asked, halting before the man.

"To Parnese?" The man scowled. "Aye, if the waters be clear of Athraig ships. Buggers have been raiding."

His words made little sense, but Bran nodded as if he understood. "May I join you?"

"As a sailor? Captain doesn't need new hands. But he'll take your coin if you're seeking passage."

"Coin?"

"Ten silvers." The man took a flat, round piece of metal and flipped it into the air. It winked as it turned. Then he deftly caught it and slipped it back into his pocket. "Do you dice?"

"No." Whatever dice might be. Nor did he have any coin.

"Pity." The man eyed him up and down. "You look like a fellow with a goodly purse. At any rate, you'll find the captain over a pint at the Staggering Gull, yonder."

He pointed to a building with a bird painted inexpertly beside the open door. Even at a distance, Bran could hear raucous laughter issuing from within, and the sound of dishware clinking.

"I thank you," he told the man, then turned toward the Staggering Gull.

"I'll teach you how to gamble," the fellow called after him. "It'll be good sport."

Bran merely nodded. His first task was to procure silver coins, and he had no idea how to go about it.

He wandered a bit more, observing how the humans exchanged coin for food and goods. It was a clever system, he supposed. His own people simply traded value for value, but in a land of strangers, it would be nearly impossible to know what to offer.

He could go back into the forest and trap animals, but he didn't have the time. It would be far easier to find some small objects, pebbles or leaves, perhaps, that he could bespell into the appearance of coin.

Making his way down to the water, he discovered a small cache of shells that had washed up against one of the dock supports. Perfect. He stepped into the shadows and, after a moment's thought, crafted a rune of illusion that turned them, he hoped, into a fair approximation of the silver coin the man had tossed into the air.

Then he'd gone to seek the captain of the boat. It was not difficult to find the fellow, as he seemed to be holding court at a large table in the center of the Staggering Gull, regaling his audience with tales of adventure upon the sea.

After quickly surveying the room and its occupants, Bran made his way to the counter and exchanged one of his coins for a glass of foamy ale. The serving man studied the silver a moment, then shrugged and handed Bran back a handful of smaller copper-colored coins. Apparently, beer did not cost a great deal.

Bran took his glass and settled at the edge of the captain's enthralled crowd. There was a wealth of information to be teased from his tales, and Bran gathered that the crossing to the land of Parnese took several days, that a warlike people from further north were menacing the ships, and that the life of a sailor was filled with ease and carefree adventure.

Judging by the captain's callused hands and the scar upon his cheek, Bran rather doubted that last bit.

Finally, the man finished entertaining his audience and Bran approached him.

"I enjoyed your stories," he said. "And I would like to buy passage on your boat to travel to Parnese."

The captain tilted his head and scrutinized Bran. "Twelve silvers."

"Ten," Bran countered.

"Eleven, and that's final. We leave with tomorrow's tide."

Realizing he should have offered eight, Bran nodded. He had much to learn. But at least he could now continue pursuing the Voidspawn.

As it turned out, his time among the sailors aboard the *Pride of Clundy* was highly educational. He had use of a cramped cabin, but spent much of his time out on deck. Eik, the first man he'd met, taught him how to play dice, and gleefully scooped up Bran's store of coin every time he lost.

He grew accustomed to the rough fare of the sailors, and learned the words for most things nautical, as well as the various creatures that inhabited the sea, the term for a woman whom one could pay for physical favors (a very odd concept), and the various types of alcohol the men consumed, or wished they could consume.

At night, in the privacy of his cabin, he scried for the Voidspawn. The lumberer's trail was faint, but as the ship came closer to the shore, Bran was certain the creature had emerged from the sea somewhere along the coast.

The traces of shadow seemed to indicate that it was further south, and still on the move. Once they reached Parnese, he would bend all his power upon seeking it out.

He cursed himself for his inability to do so thus far. But now that Mara was about to come ashore, he had faith that, together, they would be able to track down the Void and eradicate it from the mortal world.

CHAPTER 6

As promised, Prince Deldarinnon arrived at the Hawthorne Court with his retinue from Cereus, and the palace was abuzz with gossip over his visit. Anneth stayed in her rooms, trying to avoid the inevitable. No matter how much she wanted to, she couldn't forgo attending his welcome reception—and she still hadn't decided what to wear.

The pale silver gown spread across her bed was elegant and refined, and seemed far too close to a wedding garment for Anneth's comfort. She whirled, mouth screwed up with frustration, and rifled through the large armoire taking up most of the opposite wall.

What about the scarlet dress? No, too forward. Purple? She lingered, stroking the smooth fabric, then shook her head. She'd lent that gown to Mara, and those memories would distract her from the purpose at hand.

Perhaps the indigo blue...

A knock came at the door, and she blew out a breath, grateful for the interruption.

"Who is it?" she called, striding into her sitting room.

"It is I, Lady Mireleth."

Anneth paused. She truly did not want to spend any time with her least-favorite courtier. Still, Mireleth had a good eye for fashion, in her flamboyant way, and Anneth was at an impasse. Much as she hated to admit it, she could use some help. Even if it came from Mireleth. With an inward sigh, Anneth went to open the door.

"Oh, my," Mireleth said, eyeing Anneth up and down. "You aren't ready?"

"I almost am," she lied, wishing she could wipe the superior smirk off Mireleth's face. This hadn't been a good idea at all. "I'll see you at the recep—"

"Have you not summoned a maid to help you?" Mireleth asked, pushing past Anneth and peering into the bedroom. "Really, Anneth, there's no need to live like a lowly human, no matter how much you might admire them. Now, what have you picked out to wear?"

"I'll show you, but you must share all the gossip about Prince Deldarinnon," Anneth said. She might as well get some use out of Mireleth's little visit and discover as much as she could about the prince.

"He's come to find a bride," Mireleth said, pausing to admire her own reflection in the mirrored panels of the armoire. "I intend to catch his eye, of course."

Anneth blinked. So, the courtiers hadn't yet heard that she was supposed to be the prince's intended. And at least Mireleth was *finally* setting her sights on someone other than Bran.

"Is he handsome, then?" Anneth asked, pulling out the indigo gown and shoving the silver one back among the other dresses.

"Of course. He's a prince, after all."

Anneth stifled her smile. The fellow could be ugly as a tree stump, and Mireleth would overlook it due to his pedigree.

"He arrived with a chef, you know," the courtier continued. "And a troupe of dancers and musicians. And so many trunks of clothing that a separate set of rooms had to be found just to house his wardrobe. Can you imagine?" She let out a trill of laughter.

"Marvelous," Anneth said, her mood plummeting. It sounded as though Prince Deldarinnon was planning on a rather lengthy stay. So much for her hopes that he'd come, she'd stall for some time, and then he'd depart.

"Although," Mireleth said with a touch of annoyance, "it isn't as if we're uncivilized in the outer courts. He needn't have brought the chef."

Or the dancers, *or* the enormous amounts of clothing, Anneth privately added. "I suppose we'll change his mind," she said.

"Oh, I intend to," Mireleth said, brightening. She patted her elaborately braided hair, the dark strands almost entirely hidden by an array of multicolored gems. "And you ought to make an effort too, Anneth. Try to do justice to your station. In fact..."

She turned and rifled through the armoire. While Mireleth was occupied, Anneth took the opportunity to shed her comfortable dressing robe and don the indigo silk. She adjusted the length of fabric about her, wrapping it a bit more tightly about her waist.

"Here." Mireleth thrust a silvery overskirt at her. "Try this, with the sapphires. Oh, don't give me that blank look—you know the ones I mean. Platinum settings, in the shape of flowers."

"I hadn't realized you knew my jewelry collection so well," Anneth said dryly.

Mireleth sniffed. "You might not care about your gems, but some of us make it a habit to observe such things."

A soft, bell-like chime rang through the air: the signal that the reception was about to begin. Anneth fastened the overskirt on, admitting that Mireleth had chosen well, then went to don her sapphires.

"A pity about your hair," Mireleth said, trailing her to the dressing table. "There's no time to do anything about it, though. We'll be late as it is."

Anneth shrugged and pulled a brush through her own dark hair. Her few braids shone with faint russet highlights, and she coiled them atop her head, fixing them with a gemmed hairpin. Adequate, perhaps even understatedly elegant, in contrast to the colorful riot blazing atop Mireleth's head.

"Why did you stop by to see me?" Anneth asked as she and Mireleth stepped down the corridor toward the throne room. The courtier never did anything unless she could benefit from it in some way.

"I thought we might go in together," Mireleth said, with an insincere smile. "Seeing as how we're such good friends."

"Mm."

Clearly, Mireleth wanted the prince to think she was favored by the rulers of the Hawthorne Court, with the princess as her bosom companion. No doubt she'd casually drop the fact that she and Bran had been betrothed in the past—and leave out that the entire thing had been a sham, meant to trigger the prophecy that Bran would wed a mortal woman.

There was a short line at the entrance to the throne room, since the court was observing the formality of announcing each of the attendees as they arrived. As Anneth approached the doorway, she craned her neck, hoping to catch a glimpse of her father.

The courtiers in front of her stepped into the room, and Anneth was relieved to see the Hawthorne Lord seated upon his throne, his wife by his side. From a distance, he looked well enough.

"Princess Anneth Luthinor, Lady Mireleth Andion," the herald called, and Anneth stopped looking at her parents and belatedly followed Mireleth into the silver-lit room.

It was impossible to miss Prince Deldarinnon. Garbed in a dark green that was nearly black and sporting a thin silver circlet over his dark hair, he stood near the door, surveying everyone who entered. Two pale-haired warriors flanked him, one female, one male, similar enough in looks and bearing to be siblings.

Lady Mireleth hastened up to him immediately, of course, and sank into a pretty curtsey. Anneth trailed behind her, trying not to show her amusement. She would meet the prince, then go and speak with her father. Perhaps he would be honest with her, even if Lady Tinnueth refused to be.

"My Lord Deldarinnon," Mireleth said to the prince. "It is indeed a great pleasure to meet you."

"Rise, Princess Anneth," he said, extending his hand to her. "A lady of your beauty and station should not prostate herself so."

"Oh," Mireleth said, glancing over her shoulder at Anneth, a touch of panic in her eyes. "I'm not... That is..."

Remarkably, she seemed at a loss for words.

"Your pardon, prince," Anneth said, stepping forward. "My tardy entrance into the room seems to have caused some confusion. I am Lady Anneth."

"Ah." The prince pivoted smoothly and made her a slight bow. "My apologies to both you and your lovely companion. Lady... Mireleth, was it not?" He turned back to Mireleth with a polite smile.

Well. Anneth had to give him points for diplomacy, at any rate.

"Yes," Mireleth said, looking coyly up at him. She seemed to have quickly recovered her equilibrium. "Welcome to the Hawthorne Court, my lord."

"Thank you," he said, a hint of coolness in his tone.

The three of them stood together awkwardly for a moment, Mireleth gazing at the prince, and him looking at Anneth. She knew she ought to make small talk, but across the room, she noticed the Hawthorne Lord rising from his seat. She could not lose the opportunity to catch her father, even if it made her appear rude.

"Yes," she said to the prince, "welcome. I look forward to making your further acquaintance, Prince Deldarinnon. But I must go have a word with my father. If you will excuse me?"

"Of course." Face impassive, he inclined his head.

As she strode away, she heard Mireleth say, "Not everyone in Hawthorne is quite so standoffish, my lord—I assure you of that. Perhaps you might let me show you about the gardens later?"

The prince's reply was lost in the general noise of conversation, and Anneth was sorry she'd given Mireleth an excuse to make veiled insults. Or not so veiled, as the case may be. The next time Anneth encountered the prince, she'd have to be extra-charming, to make up for her first impression—otherwise she was certain Lady Tinnueth would hear of it, and she was already weary of her mother's scorn.

But now, her father was about to slip out of the room using one of the secret doors concealed behind a long, silver-embroidered tapestry. They were for the Hawthorne Lord and Lady's exclusive use, and opened only at their command. Anneth ran the last few paces and caught his arm.

"Father," she said brightly. "I've been wanting to see you."

This close to him, she was taken aback by how dark and sunken his eyes were, how weary his face. Under her grip, his arm trembled faintly.

"Anneth." He gave her the whisper of a smile. "I must go now. Perhaps tomorrow we might speak."

"No!" A few courtiers looked their way, and she lowered her voice. "What is wrong? You can't keep avoiding me—or the court—forever. I'm worried about you, and Tinnueth—"

"Your mother is doing what's best for Hawthorne," he said. "Have you met Prince Deldarinnon?"

"Yes, but—"

"Excellent." He pulled out of her grasp and, with a complicated gesture, opened the door. "Good evening, Anneth."

"Wait! Father..."

She was left speaking to a blank wall, the tapestry swinging gently back and forth where her father had brushed past.

For a moment, she wanted to stamp her feet in frustration. She did not want to be married off to some prince she didn't know. She wanted honesty from her father, not the constant maneuverings of the court.

"Anneth."

A touch on her shoulder brought her around to see the healer, Avantor, a concerned look on his already-serious face.

She counted the healer among her friends, but clearly he was deeply embroiled in whatever was going on. For the past several moons, he'd been avoiding her altogether.

"You've been nearly as scarce as my father," she said. "Who, quite frankly, doesn't seem in the best of health. I'm concerned about him, Avantor."

"We need to speak." He scanned the room, then shook his head. "Later. You're already drawing undue attention."

"Doesn't Hawthorne deserve to know if their lord is mysteriously ill?"

Sickness was all but unknown among the Dark Elves. The rest of the court seemed content to believe Lady Tinnueth's excuses that the Hawthorne Lord was immersed in a deep period of quiet and contemplation in preparation for a journey to the Oracles. But Anneth hadn't been satisfied with Lady Tinnueth's official reasons why the Hawthorne Lord was suddenly absent from almost every court function.

And now, seeing her father, it was clear that something was very, very wrong.

"I'll go dance with Prince Deldarinnon," she told Avantor. "But I expect you at my rooms just after moonset."

He nodded and strode away into the crowd. With a deep breath, Anneth went to find the prince and, hopefully, repair whatever damage Mireleth had done.

CHAPTER 7

The bustle of the Parnesian docks flowed about Bran as he stood in the shadows, watching the ship weigh anchor. It was not the *Pride of Clundy*, but a different boat that bore Mara to him. He spared a moment's thought to hope that the captain and crew of that vessel were well, and that his rough acquaintances were staying out of trouble.

Then anticipation swept through him, and it was all he could do not to fling himself up the gangway and seek his wife out that very moment. But it was best not to draw undue attention, and so he waited, hands clenching and unclenching.

Finally, after what felt like hours, her slight figure appeared, a bulging satchel slung over one shoulder. He strode forward and met her as her foot touched the quay then swept her up in his arms.

"Mara," he murmured, inhaling deeply of her scent—mint and the smell of the sea.

She felt perfectly right in his arms, and he cursed himself again for so precipitously charging off and forcing them worlds apart.

"I missed you," she said, drawing back to study his face, though she kept her tight grip on his shoulders. "You don't look human. Are you not wearing an illusion?"

"I've cast an expectation," he said. "People see what they wish to see."

She nodded and lifted a hand to his cheek. There was a trace of sorrow in her eyes, and his heart clenched at the sight.

"Forgive me," he said. "I should never have abandoned you."

"You went to save my world," she said softly. "I don't begrudge you that one bit."

He shook his head. "And yet here we both are, and the fragment of the Void is still unvanquished."

"We will find it." She gave him a weary smile and stepped back.

"Here." He took her bag, which he assumed contained clothing and a few supplies. "I have a set of rooms at a nearby inn."

"I wouldn't mind a bite of supper. Now that I'm finally on land and not constantly bobbing up and down, my appetite seems to be returning." She sent him a curious look and fell into step beside him. "Did sea travel affect you much?"

"No. I spent my journey across the water learning to play dice, and at night seeking out the Voidspawn's trail."

"Which led here." She glanced about the docks, still bustling, despite the late hour, with cargo being loaded and unloaded and boisterous groups of sailors going to and from the ships. "This is nothing like Raine's port."

"I've learned that Parnese trades in goods up and down the entire coast, and throughout the continent. It is a busy place, indeed—and you have not yet seen the half of it."

The city that spread out inland had amazed Bran at first, with its sprawling and diverse areas—trade districts and several large markets, places where the residents barely scraped out a living, contrasted with opulent homes, temples, and, of course, the Parnesian royal palace set on the hill overlooking the city.

Unfortunately, the sheer size of Parnese made it all the more difficult to track the Void. As they walked, he told Mara of his suspicions: that the Void had taken a new form and was preying upon those least likely to be missed.

"Although there have been no new bodies discovered in the past few days," he said.

Brow creased with worry, she sent him a glance. "What do you think that means?"

He'd been giving it a great deal of unhappy thought. "I fear that the Void has gone to ground. If it no longer needs to hunt, then it has found a way to bring victims to it. I fear..." He let out a breath. "It may soon be strong enough to begin opening rifts into this world."

She clutched his arm. "Dear heavens, no."

"It is only speculation," he said, wishing he could offer her more reassurance. "Now that you are here, we will be able to track it down, wherever its lair might be."

"I hope so." Her voice was tight with apprehension.

They arrived at the side street where the inn lay—a place that catered to traveling merchants and visitors to the city. The common room was peaceful, unlike the rougher lodgings the sailors frequented. He ushered her through and up the stairs to the two small rooms he'd rented—a sitting area connected to a bedroom.

"I hope this will do." He watched her anxiously. "It's smaller than our rooms in the Hawthorne Palace."

"Oh, Bran." She turned to face him. "I don't care about such things. I'm just glad to be with you—no matter the circumstances."

She removed her cloak and hung it beside the door, then went to look out the window, which showed a view of the courtyard and one corner of the palace perched above the city.

He draped his cloak beside hers, then paced to stand beside her. She was like the brightmoon, and he the pale, drawn by her brightness.

"We will find the Void," he said, circling his arms about her waist. "I swear to you, I will not let your world fall to the enemy."

She sighed and leaned back against him. "We've always been stronger together."

"Yes."

He tried not to show how much of a failure he felt. It would almost be better if she berated him for incompetence rather than meet his lack of success with such calm confidence.

"But we will not search tonight," he said. "You are weary from your journey. Eat, rest, and tomorrow we will begin anew."

And this time, he swore fiercely to himself, he would not fail.

Mara slept soundly, descending quickly into the grateful slumber of a body and mind no longer tossed about on the surface of the sea. She was dimly aware of Bran's solid bulk beside her throughout the night, and his presence reassured her all the more.

When she finally awoke, the late-morning sun was filtering in through the drawn curtains. Bran sat at the small table in the other room, his scrying bowl before him. A frown creased his forehead, and she wanted to smooth it from between his brows.

Instead, she watched him, marveling at the severe features that had grown so dear to her—the sharp cheekbones and angular planes of his face, the strangeness of his eyes.

He glanced up, and, seeing her, his expression gentled.

"You're awake."

She sat, pushing her hair out of her face. "It's hard to believe I'm here with you. We've spent so much time apart." She gave him a lopsided smile. "Are you done running away from me yet?"

"You ran from me first."

"Yes," she said. "But I came back. You didn't have to keep chasing me." Even as she said the words, a pang went through her.

Did Bran regret marrying her? She had thought that, despite the prophecy's demand that he wed a mortal, what they felt between them was strong and true.

Was love.

Her mother had always told her to judge a man by his actions, not his words. Bran was a man of few words, which certainly didn't help matters. And his actions, so far, had been to send her away—which, yes, she had insisted he do—and then, when she came back, depart the Hawthorne Court almost immediately in search of the remaining Void in Elfhame.

Then, once she had rejoined him, he had leaped through the gateway, leaving her behind once more.

Expression solemn, he rose and came to sit on the edge of the bed. "I do not want to force you to any course of action against your will. It was unwise of me to follow the Void through the gateway. I thought only of the threat to your world."

He paused, staring down at the covers, a hint of anguish in his eyes. She set her hand over his, hating to see her bold warrior look unsure.

"I know," she said, "and I honor you for it. Your entire life's purpose has been fighting the Void. How could you do anything except pursue?"

He gave a grudging nod. This close, she noted the shadows under his eyes, his too-pale complexion. Alarm skittered through her.

"Bran—is something the matter with you?"

"My wellspring is somewhat depleted," he admitted. "I did not take time to fully recover, and am drawing upon my power daily so that I can move about your world without detection. It is... tiring."

"There must be another way." She pursed her mouth in thought. "Is there a rune that you can use to cast a spell, rather than constantly channeling your magic?"

"What kind of spell?" He shook his head, his long hair swinging beneath the intricate warrior's braids. "We have no need of appearing human. As far as I know, I'm the first Dark Elf to come so far into your world."

"Parnese is the farthest I've ever been from home, too," she said dryly. "With the exception of Elfhame, I suppose. But what about the illusions your people cast? Can one be modified in some way?"

"Hm." He cocked his head and was silent a moment, a faraway look in his eyes.

She sat still, trying not to distract him. Maybe part of his difficulty in finding the Void was because he was siphoning his own power in order to function in the human world. It was so like him to push himself to his limits.

But now there were two of them, and he didn't have to bear the entire burden of tracking down the Void alone.

"There might be a way," he said. "I will attempt to merge the rune of illusion with a command to appear human."

"Try it," she said, pressing his hand. "Do you think it will work?"

"I've no idea." He lifted a dark eyebrow. "No new runes have been created for centuries."

"Let me lend you my strength. Maybe being linked with a mortal will help."

"I do not wish to tax your power."

"You won't." She didn't add that she was more worried about him running his wellspring dangerously dry.

"Very well," he said.

It was a grudging agreement, but Mara smiled at him. Getting Bran to accept help of any kind was a victory, no matter how small. She interlaced her fingers with his and leaned forward.

"I'm ready." She imagined her power flowing to him, filling his wellspring, giving the new spell enough strength to succeed.

He drew in a deep breath, paused, then spoke the rune. "*Firyanem*."

Leaning forward, she studied his face. "I don't see any change."

His expression hardened. "Again. *Firyanem*."

Power moved between them, and his features flickered, but still did not look human.

"It almost worked that time," she said. "Try once more."

"It's taking too much power," he said. "The rune should not be so difficult to cast. There's no point in trading one energy-draining magic for another."

"Is there another rune you could try instead?" Surely there was a solution—she could almost taste it.

"Hm." He frowned in concentration. "Perhaps. But this is the last attempt."

For now, anyway. She nodded.

"Ready?" His gaze met hers.

"Yes." Once again she funneled power through their clasped hands.

"*Nemfirya!*" he called. The rings they both wore flared azure, and she felt the rush of their combined magic blow through the room like a sudden breeze.

She looked up at him and grinned with delight. "It worked. You appear completely human—which is very strange."

The man who sat beside her did not look in the least like a Dark Elf. She studied his face, looking for traces of her beloved in the rounded cheeks and square chin, the mortal eyes and lips. She knew that her husband sat before her—yet he did not look like the man she'd married.

"Am I... hideous to you?" he asked, with uncharacteristic hesitancy.

"Never. You will always be my Bran." She leaned forward and kissed him. "Your hair didn't change, nor your height. How long do you think the illusion will hold?"

"I cannot say."

"Well then, I suppose we'll find out. Meanwhile, I ought to get up. Have you eaten yet?"

"No."

"A hearty breakfast will do us both good. And then, husband of mine, I think you should rest." She held up her hand to still his protest. "I'll go about the marketplace and see if I can discover any bits of news. Women gossip, you know. Maybe I'll hear something that will give us an idea of where to look next."

"I'll come with you."

"No—even with human features, you're far too intimidating. I'll learn more on my own." It was true, even if her primary motivation was to force Bran to rest.

He scowled at her, but didn't argue—which, in itself, told her he was far wearier than he would admit. Her foolish, beloved prince.

Smiling, she kissed him again, feeling love sweep from her toes to the crown of her head. He returned her kiss, and for a moment she felt as though they stood alone in a clearing in the Darkwood, the bright-edged stars whirling above them.

Then the sound of someone shouting in the street outside their window broke the spell. She drew back and they gazed at one another.

"We will find the Void," she said.

Truly, they had no other choice—not if the future was to be anything more than an endless quest in search of their dark enemy. Or a world consumed to nothing.

CHAPTER 8

As soon as the palemoon had slipped from the sky, a soft knock came at Anneth's door. She opened it and ushered Avantor in. After a glance down the hallway to ensure they were unseen, she quietly shut the door and gestured the healer to her sitting area.

"How was the rest of your evening at the welcome reception?" Avantor asked, settling on one of the low couches.

Anneth pressed her lips together. "It's clear the Cereus Prince knows very well why he's been invited to Hawthorne. We didn't take to each other, especially, but he's quite taken with the idea of becoming Hawthorne Lord."

Indeed, after her unsuccessful attempt to speak with her father, Prince Deldarinnon had rejoined her and spent the remainder of the event at her side. They had begun with a stilted conversation about his journey from Cereus to Hawthorne, which soon trailed off into awkward silence. She truly had no intention of encouraging him. Despite this, he was attentive, in a formal kind of way, as if going through a checklist of how to woo a princess. Bring her a glass of blackberry wine. Dance with her. Compliment her gown.

Too soon, however, he began to make little comments about what he would change in the Hawthorne Court.

"The throne room is a bit small, compared to the one I'm used to," he'd said, glancing about the vaulted space. "It wouldn't be difficult to expand, I imagine."

Then, later, he'd mentioned how much nicer the gardens would be if they planted a more diverse array of flowers.

"Night-blooming cereus would be appropriate." He looked down at her, all but smirking. "Don't you think?"

"What a lovely idea," she'd said, pretending to misunderstand. "You're right, my parents should plant an homage to all the courts. The cereus can go behind the nightshade. Or no... perhaps the moonflower."

She'd tilted her head up at him and smiled innocently, ignoring the annoyance in his expression. He lifted his goblet of wine and turned to survey the room from their vantage point off to one side.

"What is the entertainment for the morrow?" he asked. "This is all very pleasant, of course, though rather subdued."

"Subdued?" She blinked at him. "I don't think there is anything specifically planned, beyond the welcome reception."

He turned back to her with a disdainful lift of his eyebrow. "In Cereus we have daily events. It helps with the monotony."

She couldn't help laughing at him. "You sound like an elder of a thousand moons! Is your court so terribly boring, then?"

Perhaps it was. Prince Deldarinnon was not preparing to take on the duties of the Cereus Lord, after all, since he had an older brother, and a sister after that. And clearly he hadn't cultivated an area of study, as she had, or been driven by prophecy, like Bran.

"For those with refined sensibilities, yes," he said.

"Too refined to take up a sport or hobby?" she asked, too curious to take offense at his implied insult.

"I have blade training, of course. And I flatter myself that I'm an accomplished illusionist. I almost always win the contests of fancy we hold at court."

Anneth tilted her head up at him. She'd heard of such things, though Hawthorne had never held contests of fancy. "Perhaps you can give us a demonstration. I haven't seen much illusion work, I must admit."

Part of her magical training had included learning to summon small displays, like a shimmering flower or a miniature castle she could cup in the palm of her hand. But Penluith, the mage tutor, had not spent much time on that particular skill.

"How can that be?" Prince Deldarinnon gave her an incredulous look. "Isn't the point of magic to create beautiful illusions for our amusement and pleasure?"

She took a sip of blackberry wine to cool the tart reply on her tongue. She might be outspoken, but she'd already been rather blunt with the prince. And this last statement of his was so outrageous that she needed to consider her response.

"I see there are, indeed, some differences between the inner courts and the outer," she said after a moment. "Here, near the barrier, we focus more on battle magic."

For the first time, true interest sparked in the prince's eyes. "We learn some defensive spells too, of course," he said. "But does everyone here truly study the art of magical combat?"

"Considering that until very recently the Void was opening rifts into our world and sending its creatures through to attack, yes," she said dryly. "Though some of us are more skilled than others. My brother Bran, for instance, is Hawthorne's strongest warrior-mage."

And even then, they wouldn't have been able to defeat the Void without Mara's help.

Prince Deldarinnon glanced at the dais holding the Hawthorne thrones. "I understand your brother is... away."

"He is currently in the mortal world. But he'll be returning soon, I've no doubt." She smiled at him, trying to hide the fact that she worried a great deal over her brother's return.

"Then I will be glad to meet him. And discuss the details of magical combat." There was an eager note in the prince's voice. "I'd like to have had the chance to fight the Voidspawn."

"No, you wouldn't," she said without thinking. "They're dangerous, nasty enemies."

Stung, he drew back. "As if you have such knowledge, Princess Anneth."

"Oh, I do." She shivered, her back prickling with the memory of a gyrewolf's claws raking down her spine. "I was attacked by one in the Erynvorn."

"You were? What happened?" The prince had dropped his world-weary tone and his eyes were wide with interest.

"It was a few days after we won the battle against the Void, and we didn't suspect that some of the creatures still lingered in Elfhame. I was riding to meet my brother, and a gyrewolf leaped from the underbrush at me."

"How did you vanquish it?"

"It was Bran," she admitted. "I held it off, but he arrived in time to dispatch it. And save my life."

Prince Deldarinnon gave her a concerned look. "Has your injury fully healed?

"Yes." She moved her shoulders slightly beneath the silken gown. "Though I bear faint scars."

He took a sip of his wine, then gave her a rueful look. "I know it was unpleasant for you, but nothing so interesting ever happens in the inner courts."

"I could do without things being quite so lively."

It had been a trying time, compounded by the assassination attempts against Mara, and Bran leaving to chase the Voidspawn all over the realm. And now they were both gone, and her father was not well...

"Perhaps, during my time at Hawthorne, a bit of adventure might come my way," the prince said, sounding so eager at the thought that Anneth did not have the heart to say that she wished the opposite—that her life at court would cease being so disrupted. Peaceful monotony would be welcome, though under the present circumstances, very unlikely.

It was a tiring evening, all told, and she was glad when she could make her excuses to the prince and seek the privacy of her rooms.

Her private thoughts, however, were in turmoil. Hopefully, Avantor would be able to give her answers, even if they were uncomfortable ones.

Now she leaned forward, hands clasped.

"Tell me what ails my father," she said to the healer. Might as well get the issue directly out into the open. She was tired of evasions and misdirection.

"Your father. Yes. Well..." Avantor's gaze darted to the foxfire chandelier illumining the room, skimmed the ornate mirror on the wall, and finally settled back on her.

"The truth," she said.

He hesitated a moment, then acquiesced with a sigh. "What I tell you must be held in strict confidence. If your mother discovers I've spoken, I fear what she might do."

Anneth nodded in sympathy. They both knew that Lady Tinnueth was as hard and unyielding as a diamond. "I won't say anything, I swear it."

"Then, bluntly, Lord Calithilon is, indeed, ill—but with some sickness I am unable to diagnose, let alone cure. All I am able to do at this time is hold it at bay—but I fear even that reprieve will be brief. It was all I could do to give him enough strength to make an appearance at the welcome reception this eve."

Anneth slowly leaned back, breath hissing out through her teeth. "You've no sense of what's wrong? How can that be? You're the most skilled healer in Elfhame."

"Not skilled enough, I fear." He grimaced. "You see why Bran must be returned to our world as quickly as possible. I cannot say how long your father will be..."

He faltered to a stop, and Anneth couldn't blame him. The thought of the strong and powerful Hawthorne Lord wasting away, and so quickly, was almost impossible to contemplate.

"I'll go after Bran," she said. As soon as she spoke the thought aloud, she realized it had been budding inside her for some time, waiting for the proper moment to flower. Perhaps her earlier conversation with Prince Deldarinnon had catalyzed her decision. "Of anyone, I know the most about the world of the humans. I'm the perfect choice."

Avantor's eyes widened with alarm. "With Bran gone, you are the next heir! If you leave, there is no clear successor to the throne."

"I suspect my mother plans to continue to rule Hawthorne for hundreds of moons yet," Anneth said dryly. "Certainly I don't want to be the one to make her step aside. And although my father is ill, I trust you to keep him alive."

"I will continue to do what I can." Avantor glanced down at the ornately patterned carpet. "I received a cryptic message from the Oracles that made me wonder... What if this is a new manifestation of our fate, and your father is only the first to be stricken?"

That was a chilling thought. Was the end of the Dark Elves coming so quickly?

Anneth refused to believe it.

"Our fate is not to disappear forever," she said. "It can't be. Perhaps... perhaps there are medicines in the human world that can help?" The thought took hold inside her, and she warmed to the idea. "Once I reach Bran and Mara, she can tell me what we should bring back. Herbs and such grow there that we don't have in Elfhame. That must be the answer to our current troubles!"

"It might be." Avantor did not look convinced. "But the humans are not necessarily skilled in such things."

Anneth scowled at him. She was well accustomed to the disdain that even the most well-read Dark Elves had for mortals—though she'd hoped for better from Avantor. He'd accepted Mara well enough. But then, that was easy to do when she was the prophesied bride of the Hawthorne Prince, and the only mortal in Elfhame.

"The mortal world is not hopelessly backward or filled entirely with peasants," Anneth said. "They have healers, and scholars, and scribes. Kings and queens, merchants and explorers. And probably things that we have never seen in our world."

Her pulse fluttered with anticipation and the conviction that she was right. Somehow they would open the gate, she was certain of it. And then she would, at last, set foot in the human realm.

Avantor rose and began pacing. "I cannot advise it."

"As long as you don't oppose the idea, I'm going."

He pivoted and gave her a long look. "Lady Tinnueth must grant permission for you to depart."

"She'd be happy to see me go." Anneth tried to keep the sour edge from her voice.

Both she and Bran had never known warmth from their mother.

Indeed, most of the time, the Hawthorne Lady seemed to actively dislike her offspring. And although she had arranged for Prince Deldarinnon to come from the Cereus Court to woo Anneth, it seemed more like an afterthought. Bran, as the true heir, was the priority. If Anneth, with her knowledge of the human world, volunteered to go after him, she knew her mother would agree.

Tellingly, Avantor switched tactics. "Hestil will not approve. As acting commander of the Hawthorne warriors, her job is to keep you safe."

"She will not be able to deny me, if I have the ruler's blessing."

"Then what about Prince Deldarinnon?" The healer sounded a bit desperate. "Isn't it a diplomatic misstep for you to go running off when he's come to court you?"

"Hm." Anneth folded her arms and drummed her fingers on her elbows, thinking.

That was a bit of a tangle. The betrothal was her mother's backup plan in the unlikely event that all other options had been exhausted—and a way to dispose of Anneth's future. Even when Bran returned, she knew the Hawthorne Lady would try to push her into the match.

But maybe, if she spoke further with him, Prince Deldarinnon would understand. At the very least, she hoped she could make him see that her departing on this quest was not an insult directed at him. Plans had been made to reopen the gate before anyone—with the exception of Lady Tinnueth—even knew the prince was arriving at the court.

"What does Cereus know about the gate in the Erynvorn?" she asked the healer.

Avantor shrugged. "The inner courts are not as concerned about such things. Certainly, they know of its existence, and that Mara was destined to come through from the mortal world to help save Elfhame."

"It's not in his best interest for Bran to return, or my father to recover," she said quietly.

"The prince does not strike me as one to maliciously plot for his own advancement. He might well be happy here in Hawthorne as part of the noble family, without the guarantee of a throne."

Anneth winced at the thought. "Well, I wouldn't be happy to wed him."

"You are young, yet." Avantor gave her a paternal look. "In time, you might find that Prince Deldarinnon is not as annoying as you first thought."

"Yes, but what if he is?" She jumped up, tired of watching Avantor pace the length of her sitting room. "Anyway, I'll speak with him."

She had no idea what she would say, but it seemed the best course.

Avantor gave her a skeptical look, but made no more arguments about why she must stay in Elfhame. Instead, he glanced at the silver sand running through the turnglass.

"It is late," he said, moving to the door. "And you've much to do on the morrow, if you truly intend to pursue this course of action."

"I do," she said firmly. "Rest well, Avantor."

"And you." He gave her a nod, then slipped out.

Anneth locked her door behind him. Ever since the attempts on Mara's life, she'd become far less trusting. Sometimes a little caution was a good thing, even though it might go against her nature.

She didn't intend to sleep, though—at least not yet. There was so much planning to do, and so little time! It was imperative that they set out for the Erynvorn as soon as possible. And then—she shivered with excitement at the thought—she would at long last set foot in the human world.

CHAPTER 9

As the royal tailor buzzed about Owen, he was sorry he hadn't put up more of an argument against the royal ball. Too late now.

The time had sped by, and in just a handful of days, the event would be upon him. And still, he was no more prepared to choose a wife than he had been on that rain-spattered day beside his mother's tomb. But there was no help for it. Plans were in motion and he could not hold them back, no matter how he felt about the matter.

"You've lost a bit more weight," the tailor said, clicking his tongue against the roof of his mouth. "Really, Prince Owen, you must cultivate a better appetite. I can't keep making adjustments to your coat."

Owen wanted to tell the man to leave it be. So what if the coat didn't hug his waist and shoulders to perfection?

"You are the crown prince." He heard his mother's voice in memory, the day he'd arrived in the throne room with mud across one knee and leaves in his hair. "Owen, always remember that you carry the dignity of the kingdom on your shoulders."

"He's just a boy," his father had said, brushing the leaves away.

"A boy who will soon be a man," the queen had said, a sad note in her voice.

And so, as a man, he kept silent and let the tailor pinch in the waist of his coat a bit more. He'd wanted to remain in black, but his father had overridden Owen's objections.

"We have mourned," the king said, "and now it is time to move forward into the future of the kingdom. You could wear the uniform of the navy, perhaps."

Owen had shaken his head sharply at that suggestion. He could not veer from somber to festive so quickly.

"No?" His father had given him a mournful look. "If not red, at least something with color. A sky-blue coat would look well on you."

They had settled for dark blue, neither of them happy. Which was the sign of a successful agreement, Owen knew. Especially when both parties wanted completely different things.

"That should do," the tailor said, standing back with a satisfied expression. "You look very well, your highness. A credit to the throne."

"Thank you." Owen gave him a tight smile along with a nod of dismissal.

When he was alone, he turned to survey himself in the full-length mirror installed in his royal dressing room. The tailor was right—he looked gaunt, shadows haunting his lean cheeks. His green eyes blazed brightly from his winter-pale face, and the tawny streaks that sunlight had painted in his brown hair had all but faded.

The sun was out now, though, banishing the last clammy days of spring.

He should go riding, at the very least.

And he should practice his dancing, too, though he had little taste for the thought of squiring blushing young ladies about the dance floor. Despite his father's hopes, Owen thought it extremely unlikely that any of them would spark his interest—but he was the Crown Prince of Raine, and he would do his duty.

CHAPTER 10

The dark bulk of the Erynvorn rose from the silvergrass plain, trees reaching up toward the dimming scythe of the palemoon. As their party approached that shadowed expanse, Anneth shivered.

She had gone into the forbidding forest alone once before, and had barely escaped with her life.

Now, though, she was flanked by warriors. Commander Hestil rode at the front of their group, hand resting reassuringly on the pommel of her sword. The soldiers who had previously helped Bran and Mara open the gateway between the worlds had come, too. Plus, surprisingly, Prince Deldarinnon.

Or perhaps not so surprisingly, given their conversations. After the welcome reception, she'd arranged for a private luncheon between the two of them. They had eaten at a table set in the far corner of the gardens, away from prying eyes and ears. A few glimglows flitted overhead, and the pale blooms of flowers scented the air.

As soon as the servants delivered their food and departed, Anneth leaned forward.

"I wanted to tell you that I am going in search of my brother and his wife," she said. "Please don't take it as an affront—it was my intention to go before I even learned of your visit." Which was almost the truth.

"You are going into the mortal world?" he'd asked incredulously, setting down the spoonful of chilled soup he'd lifted to his mouth. "Alone?"

"Not alone—there is a Dark Elf scout who will meet me in the forest. And all I need to do is scry to Bran. It won't be difficult to reach him once we're in the same world."

Prince Deldarinnon sat back, his food forgotten, and studied her. "What if it's not that simple? What if your brother doesn't intend to return? What if you come to harm?"

"It won't come to any of that," she said, though his words sent a jab of anxiety through her.

"Let me come with you. I can help protect you from any threats you encounter. It will be an adventure!"

Oh dear—she hadn't anticipated that reaction, though she supposed she should have. The prince was desperate for novelty, and there were few things more thrilling than the thought of crossing between worlds. She couldn't begrudge him his excitement, as she felt the same.

But it was a delicate undertaking, not without some danger, and she couldn't imagine that anything good would come from his presence in the mortal world.

"I truly appreciate your offer," she said, searching for the words that would convince him to abandon the idea. "But the Hawthorne rulers could not, in good conscience, allow you to cross between worlds. In the unlikely event something goes awry, they cannot risk incurring a blood debt to Cereus."

He frowned, his expression almost a pout. Then some thought occurred to him, and his face brightened.

"Let me go into the Erynvorn with you, to the gateway. At least I could say I've seen it, which is more than most."

It was hard to deny the hope in his eyes. There was something endearing about Prince Deldarinnon, once he dropped his condescending air. Endearing, that was, in a somewhat annoying, childlike fashion.

Anneth folded her arms, considering. "You would still need my parents' permission. And Commander Hestil's, even more. She's in charge of the escort into the forest."

He nodded. "Opening the gateway takes considerable power, I understand. Don't forget, I'm of royal blood."

It took her a moment to follow his argument, until she recalled that royalty often possessed deeper wellsprings of power than other Dark Elves.

"I suppose any additional magic to help open the gate would be beneficial," she said. It was an argument that would sway Hestil, whom she knew was concerned about their ability to conjure the doorway.

"I am quite magically talented," he said, back to his usual arrogance. "You might think illusion work is frivolous, but it takes a skillful use of power."

"I never said it was frivolous."

"Princess Anneth—has no one told you that your thoughts are written plainly on your face for all to read?"

She blinked in consternation. Surely she was not as transparent as that. "Perhaps it is only that you inner court dwellers are used to hiding your feelings, and must scrutinize one another's expressions, searching for a hint of meaning."

One brow quirked up, but he didn't argue. "Nevertheless, I wish to accompany you into the Erynvorn. I will go speak to your commander after we finish our luncheon. It should not take long to win her permission."

Anneth tried to swallow her skepticism, along with a bite of berry-laden cake.

Hestil hadn't been easy to convince. Anneth had spent some time considering how best to strategically approach the people whose objections she would need to overcome: first her mother, then the commander, and now the prince. One by one, she had managed to succeed.

With Lady Tinnueth, it had been as simple as Anneth had hoped. It took only a short conversation for the Hawthorne Lady to grant her daughter permission to go in search of Bran, especially after Anneth reassured her she would smooth things over with Prince Deldarinnon.

Anneth tried to tell herself that her mother's quick capitulation didn't sting—but of course it did. Lady Tinnueth hadn't seemed to care if Anneth put herself in danger, as long as Bran returned.

With her mother's consent in hand, it had been a matter of winning over Hestil. Finally, eyes narrowed in displeasure, the commander had agreed.

"Only because the Hawthorne Lady wills it," Hestil had said. "I very much dislike having both you and Bran out of reach beyond the gate. What if you put yourself in danger?"

"Ondo is there still, is he not?" Anneth countered. "And I'm not defenseless. My archery has improved a great deal, you have to admit."

After Mara had departed the Hawthorne Court, Anneth had dedicated herself to honing her skills with the bow. She'd spent hours at archery practice, forcing herself to improve. It was satisfying to hear the thunk of an arrow into her target and imagine it was piercing the heart of the assassin who had dared to threaten her friend.

Grudgingly, Hestil had admitted that Anneth's bow work was passable enough, though she still was clearly unhappy with the thought of letting Anneth cross into the mortal world.

But unhappy or not, the commander would obey the dictates of her ruler.

Which had left Prince Deldarinnon—and that had gone well, if in a somewhat unexpected direction.

"If you hope to encounter any Void creatures in the Erynvorn, you'll be disappointed," she told him. "Bran and Hestil dispatched them all."

All but the ones who had slipped through the gateway into the mortal world... but the prince didn't need to know that.

"There are other dangers, though, aren't there?" he asked hopefully. "Wild creatures, treacherous mazes of briars, the chance I might get lost?"

"All of those, I suppose." She shook her head at him. "I don't recommend you get lost, though. The Erynvorn is not some garden folly to amuse yourself within."

"I'm aware of the fact," he said, too lightly.

Anneth swallowed a sigh. She would have to tell Hestil to keep a sharp eye on the prince and keep him from wandering off.

And now, here they were, with the trees rising before them like the walls of a dark fortress. A breeze moved the branches, and she could not decide if they were beckoning the party forward, or waving them away in warning.

Prince Deldarinnon spurred his mount up beside hers and flashed a quick smile before returning his attention to the forest. “I had no idea the trees would be so enormous. We’ve nothing like this in Cereus.”

“There is only one Erynvorn in all of Elfhame.”

The prince nodded, craning his neck as they rode into the cedar-scented shadows. Tall trunks rose about them, and the hushing sound of the ceaseless wind whispered overhead. The horses’ hooves were muffled by the soft carpet of mosses, starred here and there with white flowers.

No one spoke. The quiet of the forest held a certain ancient quality, and Anneth felt suddenly very small and inconsequential.

Then, one by one, a half-dozen glimglows drifted through the trees to range themselves above the party’s heads. They shed a soft light, and for some reason Anneth was comforted by their presence—perhaps because they were even smaller creatures than herself.

“There are glimglows here?” the prince asked softly, glancing at the hovering balls of light. “I thought they only dwelt in our gardens.”

“I think they come from the Erynvorn,” Anneth said. “Or are somehow connected to it.”

Many Dark Elves were of the opinion that the small, winged figures had no more intelligence than a moth, but she had seen them behave in ways that suggested otherwise. And Mara had said the glimglows led her through the forest to the gateway when she first came to Elfhame.

It was not all dim shadows beneath the trees. *Qille* grew in scattered clumps, their bell-like flowers shedding a soft radiance. Anneth and the prince rode through a small clearing where starlight sifted down, and she drew in a deep breath.

Something eased inside her, a sense that whatever happened, it was meant to be. Hawthorne lay behind her, and the human world ahead.

“How long until we reach the gate?” Prince Deldarinnon asked.

They had already spent one night on the road, the warriors billeted upon the ground while Anneth and the prince each had a tent of their own.

"We will make camp once more," Hestil said over her shoulder, clearly overhearing his question. "It's possible to push forward and reach the gate in a few more turns, but there is no need. We are better served to arrive fresh and well rested. Opening the gate between the worlds is no easy task."

The prince looked disappointed, but he nodded and went back to surveying the mysterious depths of the forest around them. No doubt he was hoping some wild beast would come rushing from the underbrush so that he might leap from his horse and combat it.

Anneth suspected their party was too large and noisy, however. Any sensible creature would stay far away. Except the glimglows, of course.

It was not long before Hestil led them into a glade and directed her warriors to set up camp. After the evening meal, Anneth found herself weary from a full day of riding. Sleep came swift and easy, and the next day, as the palemoon rose, she swung up on her mount with renewed excitement.

Prince Deldarinnon bade her a good morn, his eyes bright with enthusiasm, and she thought that perhaps he was not as tedious as she'd first found him. As long as he had something interesting to do, he seemed a pleasant enough fellow.

But for now she would set aside her opinion of him and concentrate on the matter at hand: the gate, and whether they would be able to open it. She'd forgotten, within the walls of the Hawthorne Palace, what a wild and unpredictable place the Erynvorn was.

Perhaps the forest did not want to allow them passage into the mortal world, and then what?

"We're almost there," Hestil said. "I ask everyone to use caution when we reach the gate stones. I don't expect anything to happen, but stay well back until we are ready to act."

The other soldiers nodded, clearly knowing what to expect. Anneth glanced at their faces, seeing a hint of worry here, a restless anticipation there.

The prince leaned close to her. "What are the gate stones?" he asked quietly.

"From what I understand, they form the doorway."

His gaze sharpened. "You've never seen it, and yet you plan to go through?"

"I almost came this far before," she said, trying to keep her brief annoyance from showing. "And Mara and Bran have both described the place to me." Although, she had to admit, not nearly in as much detail as she would've liked.

The gate, once they reached it, was a bit of a disappointment. The stones were scarcely taller than her head, and made of plain gray rock. There was no crosspiece marking a doorway, just the two slender stones arising from the center of a clearing, with enough space between them for a person to pass through.

Granted, there was a secretive sense to the place, hidden as it was in the Erynvorn, but she felt that the gateway between worlds should be more... majestic, perhaps. Or at the very least impressive.

"This is the place?" Prince Deldarinnon asked, sounding as underwhelmed as she.

Hestil shot him a glance. "Do not take it lightly, my lord. It might look unassuming, but once the gateway opens, it is almost overwhelming. Provided we can muster the power to do so."

The assembled warriors nodded, and Anneth had to content herself with the fact that all of them, except herself, had seen the gate in action.

"Everyone, dismount," Hestil said. "Ziat, take charge of the horses —and keep them at the edge of the clearing. Everyone else, follow me."

She arranged the party in a circle around the standing stones, with Anneth facing the space between. This close, Anneth thought she could make out silvery runes inscribed on the rock. The moss underfoot was lush, and the scent of crushed herbs scented the air as the party spread out.

"Princess," Hestil said, turning to her, "do you have everything at the ready?"

"I believe so." Anneth patted the pack she'd removed from her horse.

It contained a small tent made of lightweight silk, a cloak and a few changes of clothing, a canteen of water, and supplies enough for several meals. And, of course, her scrying bowl. Her bow and quiver were slung across her back, and she had a dagger attached to her belt.

"Scry to Bran as soon as you are able," the commander said. "And look for Ondo."

"I will." Anneth bit her tongue to keep from reminding Hestil that they'd gone over the plan several times in great detail. She was completely prepared for her arrival in the mortal world.

The commander was still unhappy about sending Anneth across the gate, and her concern made her brusque—but complaining about it would do no one any good. They must all stay focused on the task at hand. Namely, opening the gate.

During the ride, Prince Deldarinnon had asked why Anneth was going alone.

"Surely it makes sense to send a few warriors with you," he'd said. "You are the Hawthorne Princess, after all."

"According to Hestil, it requires a great deal of power to send even one person through the gate—and we don't know if, even with all our combined power, I'll be able to cross. Mara managed to take Ondo, the scout, with her, but she is very powerful. It must have sapped her well-spring a great deal. Once I'm there, Bran and Mara will have to bring me back with them, and Ondo too. We can't risk transporting more people between the worlds."

The prince had nodded thoughtfully. "I suppose that makes sense. And this scout will be there, to watch over you?"

"I believe so. Indeed, it may well be that Bran and Mara will be nearby, and we'll return to Elfhame right away."

"If that's the case, then why haven't they come back already?" he asked.

She had no good answer for him.

Now, facing the blank expanse of air between the standing stones, Anneth tried to shake off her fear. So much could go wrong—starting with the gate refusing to open, and ending with her trapped in the mortal world with no sign of Bran and Mara.

But she must not give in to such dark contemplations. Surely fate would not allow their tale to end so grimly.

"Link hands," Hestil said to the assembled warriors. "We must channel our power to Anneth."

It was new, this linking of power, but Mara had been able to draw upon the combined strength of the Dark Elves in order to open the gate. Surely Anneth could do the same. She bit her lip, battling back the panic that threatened to overwhelm her.

"Steady," Hestil said, placing a reassuring hand on her shoulder.

Prince Deldarinnon stood on the other side of the commander, one hand clasped in hers, the other linked to Brethil.

"When you feel ready," Hestil said to Anneth, "speak the rune of opening. When you see the mortal world between the stones, take up your pack and run through."

Anneth nodded, heartbeat pounding in her ears.

"Ready?" Hestil called.

The assembled warriors nodded. and Prince Deldarinnon gave her a grin. He was the only one truly enjoying this adventure. Anneth would have liked to, but her mind was too clenched with fear. Everything rested on her shoulders.

At first, she felt nothing. She closed her eyes, summoning her own wellspring of power.

Unlike Bran, she had not spent years honing her use of magic, and she now regretted it. Although her brother had been single-mindedly focused on his prophecy to the point of obsession.

Warmth trickled into her from where Hestil's hand rested, and with a brief thrill, Anneth realized it was the sensation of the others' power flowing to her.

But would it be enough?

She opened her eyes and focused on the gateway. It looked no different than before. The glimglows that had accompanied them through the forest floated overhead, and then suddenly descended. They whirled about the stones, top to bottom, and back up, a golden blaze of sparks trailing in their wake.

When they rose again, Anneth gasped to see that the faint, silvery runes inscribed on the rock were now glowing brightly. A humming noise rose around her, and she realized it was the sound of their combined magics.

Her body flushed with heat, Anneth drew in a deep breath. It was time.

"*Edro!*" she cried, speaking the rune of opening.

The air between the stones flickered, and for an instant, she caught sight of a different forest. Then the image faded, and Anneth's heart sank.

"More!" Hestil commanded. "We must not fail."

Prince Deldarinnon furrowed his brow. A moment later, Anneth felt a bright zing of power fill her.

"*Edro!*" she called again.

The strange forest appeared once more. This time, it held. The glimglows danced in a wild, erratic flurry above that dark doorway.

"Quickly, my lady," Hestil said, her voice strained. "Go."

Anneth took a firm grip on her pack and dashed forward. As she entered the space between the stones, her entire body shivered—first with flame, then frost. Her breath caught, and for an interminable moment she was falling, impaled by shards of ice, scorched with heat...

Then, miraculously, she was through, sprawling on hands and knees while the pack went tumbling to the ground before her.

She turned her head and tried to call her thanks back through the stones. Her voice came out a weary croak, and she was certain they could not hear her.

For a moment she saw the trees of the Erynvorn reaching majestically into the star-streaked sky, Hestil's expression of exhausted triumph, Prince Deldarinnon cheering. And then the gateway closed with a thunderous clap, cutting her off from Elfhame and everything she had ever known.

Leaving her alone in the strangeness of the mortal world.

CHAPTER 11

The Parnesian sunlight was warm, the air scented with herbs as Mara made her way through the crowded marketplace square. She was glad to leave the fish smell of the harbor behind. Bran didn't seem to mind it, but the aroma made her slightly queasy.

She'd left him behind, too, with stern instructions to rest. Whether or not he'd comply, at least he'd agreed to stay inside instead of stalking the streets.

Besides, she'd meant it when she said he was too intimidating. His features might appear human now, but there was no disguising his height or the breadth of his shoulders, or the princely way he carried himself. There would be no casual gossip to overhear if he were striding at her side.

The Parnesians spoke with a slight, lisping accent, but she had no problem understanding. In one corner of the market, a knot of women were discussing possible suitors for their daughters, while at a nearby stall filled with ceramics, the conversation centered on the more sobering subject of Athraig pirates.

"Come summer, the Strait will be more dangerous," said a man with a short-clipped beard. "Their ships will be hiding behind every island, waiting to pounce."

"I'm not worried about our trade," the merchant said. "The Athraig have their eyes on Raine. Ever since their queen died—"

"I wager that wasn't an accident," his young assistant said, but the merchant continued as if the boy hadn't spoken.

"—the country has been ripe for a coup. The king isn't the leader his wife was, and the prince is untried. No, any Athraig incursions will be focused on that kingdom."

Mara shivered at his dire prediction. She hadn't even known the queen was dead. Was her country truly in danger? Could she and Bran do anything to help?

No.

Not while the Void shard was unaccounted for somewhere in the depths of Parnese. Despite the lovely, warm day, she pulled her cloak tighter about her shoulders.

She paused at a spice seller's to admire the bright yellows and reds and vibrant greens of flavorings she had no name for, let alone their uses. In the center of the square, a troupe of acrobats were performing to the shouts and applause of the crowd. She dropped a copper in their basket, then moved on, drawn by the scent of fresh-baked bread.

She'd purchase a loaf or two to take back to Bran to add to their dinner.

Outside the bakery, she joined the line of women waiting with their market baskets slung over their arms.

"The power came down from the Twin Gods themselves," the stout woman in front of her was saying, her voice full of earnest fervor. "It's a mark of divine favor."

A gray-haired woman further up the line shook her head. "So say the priests—but they spin whatever tales they think will draw people to their temple."

"It's true, though," a third lady commented as the line shuffled forward. "My Alejandro saw the relic with his own eyes. It glowed, he said, with the light of the Gods."

Mara leaned forward, her attention caught. Objects glowing with divine power? She didn't think such things were usual, even in Parnese. Could it be connected to the Void? Was it possible for that dark force to lodge itself inside an object?

She supposed so. If it could animate creatures like spiderkin and lumberers, and insinuate itself as a tiny sliver of ice into her husband's wellspring, of course the Void could imbue an inanimate thing.

"Excuse me," she said, touching the stout woman's elbow. "May I ask where this relic is located?"

The woman turned and eyed Mara up and down. "Are you a believer?"

"I've only just arrived in Parnese," Mara said. "I'm a... seeker. I'd like to view this glowing relic you're talking about."

The group moved into the bakery, but Mara's attention was focused on the women ahead of her, not the plump golden loaves on display.

"Only the followers of the Twin Gods are allowed into the temple's inner sanctum," the third woman said, her voice pious. "For the nonbelievers to behold the relic would profane its sacred power."

The first woman nodded emphatically, but the gray-haired one gave her companions an exasperated look. "Not everyone is as enamored of the priests as you two. If this object is so powerful, you'd think they'd let everyone see it, so that they could convert even more followers."

"The priests follow the will of the Twin Gods," the devout woman said. "It is not ours to question."

She made a sign with her fingers, and the woman in front of Mara mirrored the gesture. Then they reached the counter and turned to give the clerk their orders, dismissing her from the conversation.

They had said enough, though, for Mara to piece together the basics. Somewhere in Parnese was a temple dedicated to the Twin Gods, and hidden inside was some object that glowed with magical power.

According to rumor, at any rate. It was a thin clue, but it was better than nothing. And it made a kind of twisted sense. The Void was gathering its powers. Why not place itself where willing supplicants would come to it, instead of hunting the streets?

Mara paid for two loaves and headed back to the inn, and Bran, mulling over what she'd heard. She knew little of the Twin Gods—just that they were worshipped on the continent and, presumably, there were two of them.

It seemed a visit to the temple was in order.

When she returned to their rooms, Bran sat up groggily from the bed, and she was glad to see that his mortal illusion hadn't yet faded. With luck, it would last the rest of the day, if not longer.

"Is everything well?" he asked, his voice heavy with sleep.

"Yes." She tucked the loaves with the rest of their supplies. "How are you feeling?"

"Better." He stretched, then rose.

The light sleeping tunic and pants he wore revealed his muscular body, and she blushed and busied herself with the foodstuffs.

"I discovered something," she finally said, glancing up at him. "At least, I think so."

He grabbed a water skin and took a long drink, then slung himself into the closest chair, his raised brow inviting her to explain.

"According to street gossip, one of the religious temples here has acquired some kind of powerful relic. The timing is... suspicious."

"You think it might be the Void shard?"

"Well, I certainly think we need to investigate further. Apparently they keep it hidden away in the depths of the sanctuary."

"Hm." He rubbed his chin. "Probably well guarded. When we reconnoiter, I'll bring my sword."

"We can't just charge into the temple, fight our way past the guards, and grab the relic." She shook her head. "For one thing, we don't even know if it *is* the Void. And for another, we'd need an escape plan. The priests won't be happy to have their object of power stolen."

"We could simply destroy it in place."

"Maybe." She frowned and rubbed her eyes as weariness tugged at her. "But that means we'll both be distracted while potentially surrounded by enemies. No—we don't know enough at this point."

He gave her a close look, concerning shadowing his expression. "Rest, beloved. Recover your strength. I have a feeling we'll need it when we discover whatever awaits us at the Temple of the Twin Gods."

The words rang true, and Mara couldn't repress a shiver. Peril lay ahead. For them, and for her entire world.

CHAPTER 12

The ground of the mortal world felt foreign under Anneth's hands—coarse with grass, and cool to the touch. Slowly, fighting off dizziness, she pushed herself up until she was kneeling before the gateway stones. Two glimglows circled her head, their light casting wavering shadows on the hummocks of plants growing all around her.

Strange—the clearing on Elfhame's side was smoothly carpeted with moss. She hadn't expected to arrive in the middle of a meadow filled with foliage. Tentatively, she reached out and brushed a nearby leaf with her finger.

A sweet scent rose from even that light contact. Anneth brought her hand up to her face and sniffed. Perhaps this was one of the herbs she should bring to Avantor. Mara would know.

And speaking of Mara...

Anneth reached for her pack, surprised to see her hands were trembling. The effort to cross through the gate had taken its toll. Indeed, when she closed her eyes and attempted to draw upon her wellspring, all she felt was a hollowness where her magic ought to be.

It was not dangerously drained, she could tell that much. But there would be no scrying to Bran and Mara until she regained her strength.

She glanced up. The sky seemed far away, the stars distant, cold specks making patterns she did not recognize. A sharp-edged moon silvered the forest around her, and things rustled in the underbrush. Small scuttlings, but she couldn't help a twinge of alarm. Using the nearest stone for balance, she rose unsteadily to her feet, then pulled her bow off her back.

"Is anyone there?" she asked, her voice raspy. "Ondo?"

No answer, except the insistent thud of her heartbeat as she retrieved an arrow from her quiver.

She stood quietly, arrow nocked to the string, but nothing rushed out at her from the darkness beneath the trees. After several moments, she decided there was nothing to fear from the shadows. At least, not imminently.

Keeping her bow close to hand, she pulled her pack over and rummaged through it for a bit of hard bread and smoked cheese. Even though she didn't feel hungry, she knew she must eat and drink in order to help replenish her wellspring.

And sleep.

Mouth set, she turned to survey the clearing. The plants grew thickly clustered nearest the standing stones of the gateway, but near the edge of the forest, there seemed to be clear spaces where she might pitch her small tent.

Where was Ondo?

She turned, scanning her surroundings once more, but there was no sign that anyone, Dark Elf or human, had passed by recently. Let alone taken up residence nearby.

Her chest squeezed with a sudden pang of fear. What if something had happened to Ondo? And Bran and Mara? Was that why they hadn't returned? What would become of Lord Calithilon then? And herself, if she could never return to Elfhame?

Stop it, she told herself. There was no point in letting fear muddle her thinking.

The tent was awkward to set up by herself, but she managed. There was just enough room for her to pull the pack and her bow in. Unfortunately, casting wards of protection wasn't possible with her depleted power. But she would sleep lightly, with her weapons at the ready.

She wrapped her cloak around her and used a spare tunic for a pillow, then lay staring up at the dark green silk of the tent.

It was not the arrival she had hoped for, tumbling exhausted and alone into the human realm. But on the morrow, surely things would be better.

Fierce brightness woke her. She blinked, sliding her shadow-lids across her eyes to protect them from the glare.

According to Mara, the Dark Elves' ability to modify their vision depending on the amount of available light was a trait unheard of in humans. Mortals had eyes and eyelids, and no inner membranes that could regulate brightness. Perhaps it was because Elfhame was sometimes darkly moonless and at other times the doublemoons shed brilliance over the land, that the Dark Elves had developed this ability.

Anneth was grateful for it. Even the strongest foxfire could not match the intensity of the illumination she now encountered. This, then, must be the *day* that Mara had spoken of so fondly. If it was so light inside the tent, what must it be like outside?

Carefully, she pulled open the flap, then let out a yelp when she caught sight of someone sitting cross-legged on the ground outside. Quickly, she dropped the fabric and scooted back, catching up her knife.

"Who's there?" So much for sleeping lightly.

"Your pardon, my lady. It is I, Scout Ondo. I did not wish to disturb your slumber."

Ondo. She let out a relieved breath. "When did you arrive?"

"A few turns before sunrise. I am sorry I was not here to greet you when you passed through the gateway. I came as soon as I was aware of a disturbance."

"You had no way of knowing I was coming," she said, lifting the tent flap and crawling outside. "I'm glad to see you."

It was good not to be alone, though she was proud that she'd made her own camp. And even if Ondo had sneaked up on her in the night, he was a scout. It was his job to be stealthy.

She pulled her cloak over her shoulders, then settled beside him.

After a few moments, her eyes fully adjusted to the light, and she glanced about eagerly.

The clearing by day was a different place than the strange, uncomfortable meadow she'd fallen into. The plants were a rich green hue, with the beginnings of flower buds showing between the leaves. A soft wind whispered through the branches, bringing intriguing new scents to her nose.

But the most amazing thing was the sky overhead. A great, blazing orb took up one part of it, so intensely bright that she could not even look directly at it. And the rest of the sky was a vivid blue! She'd never imagined such a thing.

"Where have the stars gone?" she asked, squinting. It was disorienting to not have those pinpricks of light shining above. "Did the sun burn them away?"

"Lady Mara told me they are still there, behind the sun's brightness. Once it sets, the stars will return. I have seen it myself."

"How strange." She stopped looking for the invisible stars and returned her attention to Ondo. "What of Bran and Mara? They are nearby, I hope?"

"Sadly, no."

Her spirits plummeted at this news. "Please, tell me they've come to no harm."

Ondo shifted uncomfortably. "They are across the water, in another land. Unharmed, to the best of my knowledge. I believe the final Void fragment is proving elusive, thus the delay."

Anneth swallowed back her rising panic. "But they're needed in Elfhame! That's why I came—to tell them the news and bring them home."

This was dreadful. How could Bran and Mara not have eliminated the Void threat yet? She certainly could not ask them to abandon their quest and leave the human world to the mercy of the darkness. And yet every moment that passed took a greater toll on Lord Calithilon, and threatened the stability of the Hawthorne Court.

Time runs differently here, she reminded herself. Days in the mortal world were but a handful of turns in Elfhame. Surely, even if Bran and

Mara were delayed, they would come back in time to save the Hawthorne Lord.

Ondo watched her with a worried frown. "What is the news of Hawthorne, my lady?"

"Lord Calithilon has fallen gravely ill," she said, hating how the admission made the fact of her father's failing health all too real. "Not only is my brother, as the Hawthorne Heir, needed back at court immediately, I promised to return with medicines from the human world that could aid in my father's recovery."

"Is it that dire, then?" The scout sounded shaken.

"I'm afraid so. Avantor is doing what he can, but..."

"We must scry to the prince and his bride at once." Ondo shot her a look. "Is your wellspring regenerating?"

"I... don't know." A weary emptiness filled her, her worry for her father compounded by the disorientation of crossing between the worlds.

How long did it take for one's power to return? She felt like a fool for not asking earlier. Well, perhaps a night's sleep had been enough.

She held out her hand and attempted to summon foxfire.

"*Calya,*" she said, then tried again. Not even a weak flicker shone at her fingertips.

Ondo nodded. "It will be another few days until your wellspring refills—provided you rest comfortably."

"Comfortably." She gave him a wry look.

A tiny tent at the edge of the forest, with a cloak for a blanket and a wadded-up tunic serving as her pillow—but this had been her choice. And surely it wouldn't be long before Bran and Mara arrived and they could hurry back to Hawthorne to save Lord Calithilon.

"I am sorry I cannot provide better for you," Ondo said. "I am used to living wild—but, of course, that is not sufficient for a princess. My apologies."

"You could hardly expect my arrival." A pity she hadn't been able to haul more supplies through the gate with her. But if Ondo was subsisting on twig tea and broiled rabbit, she would do the same. "And I've camped before."

Although perhaps not in quite such primitive conditions. Still, despite the urgency, she must look upon this as an adventure. She was in the mortal world, after all. Even if she never saw a human, at least she had seen the sun.

"Let me contact your brother," Ondo said, opening his pack.

He set his scrying bowl and a skin of water on the matted grasses before them and made the preparations. Once poured into the silver bowl, the water reflected the peculiar sky above in a perfect circle of blue.

The scout passed his hand over the water and spoke the rune of scrying.

"Show me Prince Brannon," he commanded.

The blue shivered. Holding her breath, Anneth leaned forward, eager for a glimpse of her brother's face.

The water darkened. Slowly, an image formed on the surface: the stern expression and keen eyes of the Hawthorne Prince.

"Ondo," he said sharply. "What is it?"

"All is well," the scout said, with a swift glance at Anneth. "However... your sister has come through the gate."

"Anneth? In the mortal world?" Bran's brows drew together. "Is she well? Why did she not scry to me?"

Bran turned his head, as though listening to someone. When he turned back to the scrying, his frown had smoothed somewhat.

"Mara reminds me that my sister's wellspring is depleted from the crossing."

"Yes," Ondo replied. "I told Anneth that several days of rest will help restore it."

Bran nodded. "My wife also bids me ask if you've built a shelter in the forest during our time away."

The scout's brow furrowed. "I have no need of one."

"You might not, but Anneth does. One moment." Bran looked aside again, and Anneth could almost hear the murmur of Mara's voice.

"It is a good thought," he said. "But what of her appearance... Ah, of course."

"What are you talking about?" Anneth demanded, leaning over the scrying bowl. She knew Bran couldn't hear her, so instead she poked Ondo. "Ask him. But first, tell him about Lord Calithilon."

"My lord," the scout said. "Questions of your sister's lodging aside, she brings dire news from the Hawthorne Court."

"What is it?" Bran's gaze sharpened.

"Your father has fallen ill, and you are needed in Elfhame as soon as possible."

Worry flashed through Bran's eyes. "We've not yet dealt with the Void. But surely Lord Calithilon is hardy enough to weather a bout of sickness."

"I fear it is worse than that," the scout said. "Lady Anneth says he is fading quickly, and that you must bring whatever mortal remedies you can with you when you return to Elfhame. Time is of the essence."

"I understand," Bran said grimly. "We're doing what we can."

"I do not doubt it, Commander. But please, make haste."

"We will." Bran glanced to the side again and nodded. "While you wait for us, Mara suggests that her family might take Anneth in until she regains her strength. Their cottage lies a short distance outside the Darkwood. Anneth will recover faster if she can sleep in a real bed and eat regular meals instead of making do with a scout's camp. And all of us will need to be at peak power in order to open the gateway home."

While Anneth wanted to argue that of course she was capable of regenerating her wellspring while camping in the forest, the thought of actually living among humans made her pulse leap with nervous delight.

"I agree," Ondo said grudgingly, "it would be better for the princess. But how does she hide the fact she is a Dark Elf and not a mortal?"

"The same way I do." Bran gave a tight smile. "After some missteps, and with Mara's help, we've crafted a rune of disguise."

"A new rune?" the scout asked, clearly shocked.

Anneth shared his surprise. It had never occurred to her that new magic could be created. Then again, it wasn't commonplace for Dark Elves to run about the human world, either. New situations must call for new ways of thinking.

"A rune of illusion," Bran said, "to make me appear human. I'll teach it to you and Anneth—but you'll have to cast it upon her until her power returns."

"How long will such a seeming last?" Ondo asked.

"Every morning, I summon it afresh. The illusion fades by midnight."

"And if you are not in concealment by the time your true features return, what then?"

Bran gave him a crooked smile. "Then I pull up my hood and let Mara take the lead. It's an unnecessary waste of power to recast the rune, when I know I will need to invoke it again in a matter of hours."

The scout nodded. "Teach it to me."

"First, you must fix the thought of human-seeming features in your mind. Then gather your wellspring and speak this rune: *nemfirya.*"

Nemfirya. Anneth turned the syllables on her tongue. *Appear mortal.* It was a simple enough construction, and she must trust that it would work as planned.

"I will cast it upon Lady Anneth now," Ondo said. He turned to her, his expression serious. "Are you ready?"

She nodded. "It won't hurt, will it?"

"Prince Bran did not say anything to that effect." The scout hesitated in the act of lifting his hands. "Shall I ask?"

"No, no. Whether it causes pain or not, it still must be invoked. Go ahead."

She squeezed her eyes closed. Ondo cleared his throat.

"*Nemfirya!*" he cried.

A wave of heat, not unpleasant, washed over her, lasting but a moment.

"Is it done?" she asked, opening one eye.

"Indeed." Ondo sounded a bit awed. "You look very human, milady."

She opened her other eye. "I don't suppose you have a reflecting glass?"

"Alas, I do not. But believe me when I say that there is no trace of Dark Elf about your appearance." He shook his head. "It is odd. I know you are still Princess Anneth, but you do not look it."

"I suppose that's good." She'd never imagined what she might look like as a human, and curiosity burned through her.

"Did you summon the rune?" Bran demanded from the scrying bowl.

"I did," Ondo said.

"And?"

"Lady Anneth appears very human."

"Strange, isn't it?" Bran gave him a wry look. "You'll have to refresh the casting upon her until her wellspring is restored. Mara suggests you meet Anneth in the woods at dawn each day to set the spell."

"What if her family sees me as I am?" Anneth asked, a spike of apprehension going through her. "Will they... harm me?"

Ondo relayed her question, and they waited while Bran asked his wife.

"Humans fear us," Ondo said. "I believe your brother was attacked when he first arrived."

Anneth bit her lip. She hadn't realized how perilous her mission might be. But it was far too late to turn back now—not that she would have, in any case.

The reflection rippled, and Bran's image returned.

"Mara says they will be startled if your illusion slips, but you have nothing to fear. However, it is better for everyone's sake that you maintain the disguise as best you can."

"I understand," Anneth said, wishing her brother could hear her.

Although if staying with Mara's family would help restore her wellspring more quickly, she'd soon be able to scry to him herself.

"We must go," Bran said. "Keep us informed daily, Ondo. And watch over Anneth, even if it must be from the edge of the Darkwood."

"I will," the scout said fiercely. "Fare well."

Bran's image faded, the water showing the dome of blue above.

"Wait," Anneth said as the scout reached for his scrying bowl.

Edging him aside, she knelt over it and peered down, trying to assess her appearance. It was a difficult angle, but even so, she blinked at what she saw.

Her face was softer, her cheekbones far less pronounced, and her skin had taken on a rosy tint. The biggest change was to her eyes, which now bore the strange, round pupils of a mortal girl. Her ears were rounded, too, but when she lifted her hands to them, she could still feel the pointed tips. Instead of claws, her fingers were blunt and weak-nailed—yet she could still sheathe and unsheathe her claws.

It was one of the very oddest experiences of her life. And from the way Ondo was looking at her, he was equally disoriented.

"I'm still me," she said, "so you needn't act strangely. Now, do you have anything to eat?"

The scout blinked, then dropped his gaze. "Of course, milady—I've a bit of rabbit and some nuts. Then you must rest. Later, we will travel to the edge of the forest. With tomorrow's dawn I will cast the rune upon you again, before you seek Lady Mara's home."

It was a reasonable plan, and Anneth pushed back her desire to leap up and go in search of humans immediately. Nuts and rabbit meat would have to do for the time being. Besides, she was undeniably weary. She would bide, and the morrow would come soon enough.

As she chewed her sparse breakfast, though, she couldn't help smiling. After so much time studying the ways of humans and daydreaming about their world, she would finally have the chance to dwell among them.

No matter how terrible the circumstances that had brought her to Raine, and the burden of worry she carried for her father, there could be no denying—she was about to embark upon the adventure of a lifetime.

CHAPTER 13

The tug of a scrying summons had pulled Bran from restless dreams after a night spent mostly awake. He'd spent the dark hours staring at the pattern of shadows on the wall and listening to the city of Parnese quiet as the hours deepened. Finally, his thoughts, too, had quieted enough to let him rest.

Now, however, his worries had come roaring back—with the additional burden of fear for his father. And his sister.

He sat stiffly in the inn's small chair, trying to absorb everything Ondo's scrying had revealed while his mind reeled from the implications. On the table in front of him, the water in his silver bowl lay quiet and still.

Lord Calithilon's illness, while deeply troubling, was not as immediately upsetting as Anneth's presence in the mortal world. She was not a warrior-mage, and despite her knowledge of the human realm, wasn't well equipped to fend for herself. Even with Ondo to watch over her.

Seated beside him, Mara shot him an anxious look.

"That's not good news," she said. "Your father, unwell—and Anneth here, in Raine."

"I know." His stomach tightened with tension. "Are you certain it was a good idea to send her to your family?"

"She'll fare better with them than remaining in the forest, no matter how hard Ondo works to make her comfortable. And when we return to the Darkwood, the gateway awaits. It won't be easy to reopen that door."

He sighed, acknowledging the truth of it. "We must deal with the Void as soon as possible. And then we will all return to Elfhame." She stiffened almost imperceptibly, and he turned to her. "What is it?"

"I... Nothing." She looked away. "We must go to the Temple of the Twin Gods today, and discover whatever we can about that relic."

"If the Void is there, we will destroy it and depart immediately for Raine." Yet even as he spoke the words, he knew they were overly optimistic.

Ships only sailed for Raine once every few days—if they were fortunate. As a seasoned commander, he knew it was beyond foolish for them to charge into the Temple of the Twin Gods without a plan of escape. A magical battle would not go unnoticed by the priests, especially if the relic housing the Void's power was sacred to their sect.

They would have to arrange passage back to Raine, and then make plans for how to defeat the Void. Provided it was even housed at the temple.

He folded his arms, frustrated by the necessary delay. He needed to get to Anneth, and then see to his father.

"If the Void is in the relic of the Twin Gods' inner sanctum, it will be guarded," Mara said, clearly thinking along similar lines. "How do we reach it without the priests stopping us?"

"We must enter the temple unseen."

Her brows rose. "Can you do that? I thought one had to remain stationary for a rune of invisibility to work."

"That is generally true. It takes a great deal more power to maintain the rune while also moving. But it is not beyond my ability."

She nodded. "And you have my wellspring to call upon as needed. I'm only sorry I can't control my magic well enough to be of more help."

"Don't worry." He reached over and took her hand. "You told me you were making progress when you were studying with Penluith in the Hawthorne Court. When we return, you can resume your work with him."

"Bran, I..." She looked out the window a moment, then back at him. "I'm not sure I want to go back."

His heart squeezed with cold apprehension. "To Hawthorne? We could go elsewhere than the court—"

"To Elfhame." She held his gaze, her expression troubled. "I don't belong in your world. And don't forget, there's assassins out there, waiting for me. Someone in the Hawthorne Court wants me dead."

"I know," he said grimly. "And I promise not to leave your side until we find them and eradicate the threat to you."

She remained silent, regarding him with sorrow-filled eyes. He could scarcely bear the pain ripping through him at the thought of losing her.

"Please, Mara. Give Elfhame—give *me*—another chance. I swear I won't fail you again."

She let out a low breath. "I know you will try, but... I need to spend time with my family. I need to feel the sun on my face—"

"We can open the gate any time you desire."

It wasn't true, though. Opening the doorway was no simple thing, but he felt as though he were trying to keep the waves from slipping through his fingers, desperately trying to hold on. And failing. He was losing Mara. Losing his father. Losing their battle against the Void.

In the end, would he have anything left?

Unhappiness shone in her eyes as she squeezed his hand, then let go. "I haven't decided yet, one way or the other. I just... I need time to think."

Do you not love me any longer? He could not voice the words, could not expose the anguish ripping through him. Instead he rose and paced the room, wishing he could fight something, anything.

At least there were plenty of enemies at hand—most especially the Void.

And after that? No matter how much he wanted to demand that Mara return with him to Elfhame, he could not force her to make that choice. He could not trade her happiness for his.

Bleakly, he stared out the window at the unrelenting light of the mortal sun, wishing with all his heart that he was back beneath the palemoon.

"Bran." Quietly, Mara came up behind him and slipped her arms around his waist.

He stood rigidly as she laid her head against his back, the human warmth of her slowly seeping into him.

"I cannot bear to lose you again," he finally said, the words coming out ragged and low.

"You could stay with me?" Even as she asked, he could hear the hopeless tone in her voice. They both knew he could never abandon his duty as the Hawthorne Heir.

"Is our fate to be miserable, then?" He let out an unhappy sound. "I can see no way forward, Mara."

Dampness at his back, and he realized that she was crying. He turned and took her into his arms.

"I love you," she said, holding tightly to him. "And I don't know what to do. I can't imagine myself being happy in your world. Or in mine, if you aren't with me."

He stroked her hair with the palm of his hand, his thoughts whirling as he tried to find a solution. "At one time, I had thought we might visit the Oracles—that they could have an answer for you. Would you be willing to go to them before you make a final decision? They would have the power to send you back to your world, should you desire it. A power I would insist they use on your behalf."

She was quiet a long moment, the silence pressing about them. Bran tried not to hold his breath as he waited for her answer. A spice-scented breeze moved through the partially open window, and finally she spoke.

"As long as I don't have to go back to the Hawthorne Court, I will go to your Oracles." She looked up, her expression fierce. "But you are required to spend every moment in Elfhame beside me, Prince Brannonilon Luthinor."

"I swear to it," he said solemnly. "By the seven bright stars, by the palemoon and the bright, I will protect you with my life."

This time, he vowed, it would be enough to win her heart. Permanently.

THE PAIN in Bran's eyes smote Mara to the heart—yet she had told him the truth. She didn't know where she belonged.

But it was too soon to make an irrevocable decision. If they didn't act *now*, she wouldn't have a world of her own to choose. The Void threatened everything.

She pulled in a long, shuddering breath. "First, we need to destroy the Void."

"Of course." He squeezed her shoulders. "The temple awaits."

He stepped away from her, going to gather his cloak and boots, and she gave him a sharp look.

"We need to break our fast. Have you been in the habit of skipping meals, Bran?"

He raised one shoulder in a half shrug, which was answer enough. Foolish man.

"It's no good for you to tell me to regain my strength if you keep neglecting yours." She gave him a chastising look. "I know we need to hurry, but we've bread and cheese. Breakfast won't take long. Then we can find out where the Temple of the Twin Gods is."

"It's on the hill below the palace," he said, pulling on a boot. "My time roaming the city hasn't been entirely wasted. But I'm unsure of who the Twin Gods are, or what powers they're rumored to possess."

She fetched the bread, trying to dredge up anything she could recall.

"The people of Raine don't follow that sect," she said, sawing thick slices from the loaf. "If I remember aright, the Twins are not particularly kind. Something about fire and darkness?" She furrowed her brow. "I don't really know."

Boots donned, he came and stroked her hair. "Let me resummon my rune of illusion."

She set down the knife and leaned against his solid bulk for a moment. "Yes—the last thing we need is for you to be harried through the streets."

"I haven't yet been." A wry look flashed across his face. "And with you at my side, no one will notice me."

"Your height and the length of your sword aren't easily overlooked," she said dryly. "I'm just an ordinary human woman."

"Parnese is full of many peoples. I have seen one or two men taller than myself. And plenty of them wear weapons."

"I suppose." She handed him a slice of bread and cheese.

They ate, then made ready to go. Bran insisted she belt on her knife, and she didn't argue. To be honest, she should get into the habit of wearing it constantly. He draped his cloak over his shoulders, but left the hood down as they departed the inn and strode into the cobbled streets.

She let him take the lead, as the way twisted and turned unexpectedly. They passed through several small squares, one with a fountain in the center where children laughed and splashed, another filled with tables along the sides where men and women drank tea or glasses of pale yellow wine.

The further they went from the port area, the more ornate the buildings became. Many of the façades were covered in painted blue-and-white tiles, while small statues of animals posed beside the doors or paraded along the cornices.

They reached a broad street with a drop-off along one side, and Mara paused to catch her breath and admire the view.

"Nearly there," Bran said, glancing at the marble-clad palace perched atop the hill.

"I hadn't realized Parnese was so steep," Mara said. "Or that we'd be able to see so much from up here."

The city curved down to the blue water of the Strait, a sweep of red-tiled roofs descending to where the waves sparkled, dotted with tiny boats. Somewhere out there, far beyond the blue horizon, lay Raine.

She frowned, thinking again of her overheard conversations. If the gossip was right, Raine was in danger from the Athraig—but surely the king and his advisors were aware of such things. The fate of the kingdom wasn't hers to worry about.

As she and Bran resumed climbing, bells began to ring, tolling the hour. She'd heard them earlier in the day, but here, in the heights of the city, the air carried the sound—a rich clang and clamor that made her smile.

"The temple," Bran said, halting within the shadow of an alleyway.

Mara drew up beside him and stared thoughtfully at the high-roofed building across the square from where they stood. It was made of reddish stone, a series of broad stairs hewn of the same material rising to the huge, double-arched entry.

Over each door was mounted a statue in an ornate niche. The left-hand one held the likeness of a young man wearing a dark robe. His curling, shoulder-length hair was painted bright red, and his face bore a remote expression as he stared out over the crowds moving up and down the stairs. One hand was raised, holding a stylized flame gilded with gold that caught the light.

The other statue was, presumably, his twin. Her robe covered a female body, though she had the same cold face and curling scarlet hair. She held a sword aloft. It was not covered in bright gold, however, but some kind of black material that seemed to absorb the light.

"The Twin Gods," Mara said softly. "They don't look very friendly."

"From what I understand, gods are not supposed to be." There was a wry edge in Bran's voice. "I admit, I don't quite comprehend their purpose. In Elfhame, we have the Oracles, and that is more than enough."

"Best not to speak of it." She set a hand on his arm.

There didn't seem to be listeners nearby, but one couldn't be too careful. Especially in a foreign land.

And most especially outside the temple of two fierce-looking gods who were potentially guarding a dangerous fragment of the Void.

"What now?" Bran glanced at her.

"I wonder if we can just... go in." She watched the ebb and flow of visitors for a moment. "There doesn't seem to be a line, or a gate. At least, not that I can see from here."

"Then we shall try."

"Wait." She caught a handful of his cloak as he was about to stride out into the plaza. "Let me look at you."

He turned obediently, and she studied his face, trying to determine if the illusion was at risk of fading.

"Well?" He cocked an eyebrow.

"It seems to be holding."

"I will keep my hood up, just in case."

"If they let you." She looked at the temple entrance once more. What secrets did that shadowed interior hold?

Well, they were about to find out.

They joined the dozen or so people mounting the stairs to the arched doors. As they got closer, Mara could see a priest standing to the side of each open doorway. They didn't seem to be wearing any visible weapons, but those large black robes could easily conceal any number of blades.

It didn't seem to make a difference which of the Twin Gods one entered beneath. She made for the left-hand arch guarded by the flame-bearing twin. Bran followed silently behind.

The priest at the door looked them up and down and stepped forward, questions in his eyes. Quickly, Mara held up her hands and made the sign she'd seen the women at the bakery use—fingers to palm.

The priest nodded, the questions in his eyes fading, and moved back to his post. As they crossed the threshold, Bran shot her a look of admiration. She sent him a small smile in return.

It was cool and shadowy inside, and her husband gave a quiet sigh of relief. Soft murmurs echoed between the columned cloisters lining the walls. In the center of the large space, rows of benches faced a stone altar. There, a flame burned in a golden bowl and a black sword stood upright, pointing to the high, rounded ceiling hundreds of feet overhead.

Behind the altar was an enormous painting showing the Twin Gods. Their implacable stares looked out over the benches, the flickering lamps mounted on the walls, and, presumably, into the city beyond.

Bran touched her elbow and nodded to an empty bench at the back. Together they took their seats on the hard wood, although it didn't seem as though any ceremony was imminent. People came in, sat with their heads bowed in prayer, and then, after a time, left.

Some of the worshippers approached the altar and left coins or other offerings in the polished bowls set out before the flame and sword. Mara kept her head down, mimicking the other supplicants, and surveyed what she could of the huge space.

Windows high up on the walls let in soft light, but the room was mostly lit by lamps along the side walls and the flame on the altar. On either side of the large central space, behind the arched hallways, were smaller sub-temples. Judging by the statuary and symbols, the one on the left was dedicated to the male twin, the one on the right to his sister.

"I am going to try to sense the Void," Bran said softly.

She nodded and laced her fingers with his. The two of them bowed their heads, and she sent him a small flow of power.

After a moment, he stiffened. She shot him a quick glance. His eyes were closed, a look of fierce concentration on his face. A droplet of sweat trickled down his mortal-seeming cheek. Despite the curiosity flowing through her, she held her questions and fed him more power through their joined hands.

Several heartbeats later, he let out a breath and opened his eyes. Frustration and triumph simmered there in equal measure.

"You found it?" she asked in a low voice.

He gave a nod, then sent a meaningful glance at the arched doors behind them.

As they sidled out from the row of benches, a new group of supplicants entered. Mara watched as they approached the altar. Before taking their seats, each one laid two fingers of their right hand across their left palms in some kind of worshipful sign. She recalled the women at the bakery making such gestures, too.

Then Bran was at the doors, and she had to hurry to catch up to him. The priests watched impassively as they strode out of the temple into the bright sun. Bran immediately tugged the hood of his cloak further over his face, and she knew the light was an assault on his sensitive vision.

Without speaking, they made their way down the stairs and back into the twisty cobbled streets.

"It is there," Bran finally said. "Somehow, the Void shard has been shielding its presence from me. But with your added power, and perhaps because we were so close, I finally sensed it."

"So it *is* in the temple." Mara pondered this information. "Could you tell precisely where?"

"Behind the main altar—likely in whatever room lies beyond the main place of worship."

"The women at the bakery mentioned an inner sanctum," Mara said. "I wonder how we get into it."

He laid his hand on his sword, but she gave him a warning look.

"We can't fight our way through. Yes, I know you're an amazingly skilled warrior-mage—but you can't reveal your power, at least not openly. And we can't leave a trail of innocent bodies in our wake."

"The Void will do more than that." His voice was tight with tension.

"I know—and I want to protect my world as much as you do. But we need to come up with a solid plan." She shot him a look. "One that doesn't involve undue bloodshed and mayhem."

They would have to breach the inner sanctum without being captured, or killed, and extract the relic housing the Void—whatever that object might be. She prayed the thing would be small enough to transport easily.

If not, and Bran had to destroy it in the temple, that opened them up to a host of other problems.

At least the illusion spell seemed to have solved the constant drain on his wellspring. She could tell by the brisk pace he set as they headed back to their rooms that his energy was already returning.

"We'll go back to the temple tonight," he said, sending her a wry look when she opened her mouth to object. "Only to observe—don't worry. I would like to see what time they close the doors."

"If they do at all."

She needed to teach Bran the hand gesture, too, before they returned. Appearing to be a devout follower of the Twin Gods had already proven useful, and she suspected they'd need every advantage they could find if there were to gain the depths of the temple and, at last, defeat the Void.

CHAPTER 14

The next morning—and what a curious thing that was, to see the fiery orb of the sun ascend the sky—Anneth and Ondo made their way to the edge of the Darkwood. It took several turns of walking, and she found the forest rather plain compared to the glowing opulence of the Erynvorn. All the radiance of the mortal world had seeped up into the sky, it seemed, leaving the land below dull and unshining.

At last, after traversing a series of meandering paths for what felt like forever, the trees began to thin.

"Are you certain you wish to attempt this?" Ondo asked, shooting a concerned glance over his shoulder.

Anneth frowned at him. "I know you're worried about me, but truly, I'll be careful. And of course I want to."

She'd been wondering about the human world all her life, and she certainly wasn't going to waste her chance to experience it now—especially since she even *appeared* to be human. Ondo had cast the spell upon her, and on himself, before they reached the edge of the forest.

"Mortals generally do not come this far into the Darkwood," he said. "But we must take care, as we are about to travel the areas they frequent."

It was strange to see his features transform to the blunt and rounded shape of a human face, but he was still recognizable. And beneath the façade, they were still both Dark Elves to the core. Or she would be, once her wellspring regenerated and she was able to summon runes again.

More and more light filtered through the whispering branches, and the damp, needle-strewn soil gave way to grass and flowers. Anneth slowed her steps, looking at the blooms. One plant bore bright orange petals that curved gracefully back on themselves, while another boasted blue flowers shaped like stars.

She was glad to see that the human world was not as plain as she'd originally thought.

Then a small lane and the first cottage walls came in sight, and all thoughts of flora were thrust away by her excitement—and sudden sense of trepidation.

"There is the path," Ondo said, pointing. "Follow it. Lady Mara's family lives in the second cottage on the left-hand side. She showed me the place when first we arrived in the human world."

"What if they cannot understand me?" Anneth caught his arm, pulling him to a halt. "I didn't even consider that!"

She had a sudden, horrified vision of standing in front of Mara's family and babbling incomprehensibly until they turned her away.

"Do not fear," Ondo said. "Whatever magic that enables Lady Mara to understand our speech, the reverse seems to be true here in the mortal realm. Prince Bran has had no difficulty with human speech."

"That's all very well for my brother. But what if it doesn't work for me?"

"You are of royal blood," Ondo said, as if that answered everything.

Perhaps it did. She dearly hoped so, at any rate. There was no way to know until she'd tried.

"You'll wait for me?" she asked, pulling in an unsteady breath. "Just in case?"

"Yes." Ondo gave her hand a reassuring pat. "Although I still would prefer to escort you to the door."

"But then you'd have to go back into the forest, and that would raise too many questions about who you are and why you're here in the first place. No—it's better if you wait. Just... don't leave right away."

"I will bide, milady."

Anneth gave him a smile she hoped didn't tremble at the edges. "I'm sure everything will be fine."

Bran was the brave one, not her.

I went after him into the Erynvorn, she reminded herself. And even fought off a gyrewolf. Surely meeting Mara's family wouldn't be half as terrifying, no matter how much her heart pounded at the prospect.

She hoisted her pack, much lighter since she'd left her tent and most of her supplies with Ondo, then stepped onto the small track leading out of the forest.

"Meet me here next morning," the scout said.

She glanced back at him, momentarily startled at the sight of his human features. "I will. I hope my wellspring regenerates soon."

"As do I. Be safe, Lady Anneth."

She patted the knife at her belt. Both she and Ondo had decided it was more prudent to leave her bow and arrows with him for the time being. The bow was a long-range weapon, and would do her little good on this foray into the village. Little Hazel, that was what it was called. Surely, with such a name, it could not be too dangerous a place.

As she walked, her senses drank in her surroundings: the smell of wood smoke drifting on the quiet breeze, the strange, hot feeling of sunshine on her body, the sharp cry of some animal. She reached the first wall and brushed her fingers over the mortared gray stones. *Humans built this.*

That cottage stood quiet, and she recalled Ondo's directions. Second cottage on the left.

Pulse pounding in time to her steps, Anneth continued down the lane. It widened as she went, and she wondered if, by the time it reached the center of the village, it would be a full-blown road.

She passed the first cottage without a second glance. Only a short distance up the lane lay Mara's home. A tree grew beside the door, and beds of herbs edged the front of the building. The windows held sparkling, diamond-shaped panes of glass, and the door itself was painted a cheerful green.

Anneth slowed as she approached, then halted a few paces from the front stoop.

Maybe this was a foolish idea, after all. Maybe she would be better off returning to the forest, no matter how uncomfortable. Maybe—

The door was flung wide by a young woman with the same earth-hued hair and rounded cheeks as Mara.

"Hello," she said, giving Anneth a glance, head to toe. "Are you from Elfhame?"

"I... Yes. I am. How did you know?" This was not at all how Anneth had imagined her arrival.

The girl grinned. "Nobody in Little Hazel—or even the castle—wears clothing like that. How did you get here? Is Mara with you?" She craned, looking over Anneth's head.

"I am alone," Anneth lied. "Are you Mara's sister?"

It seemed a reasonable guess, from what Mara had said of her family. Not to mention the strong resemblance.

"Yes, I'm Lily. Come in." The girl stepped back and nodded for Anneth to enter. "Mother's in to town for some shopping, but she'll be home soon."

"Thank you. I am Anneth."

She knew she ought to explain a bit more, but all her attention was taken up by her first glimpse of the inside of a human's home. Large windows let in a great deal of light, and the furnishings were rustic, yet cozy. A colorful braided rug covered most of the wide-planked wooden floor. A portion of the room was clearly the kitchen, with a large table on one side. A narrow hallway held a few doors leading to more rooms. Stairs ran up from the center of the living area, and Anneth gave them a curious glance.

"Would you like some tea?" Lily asked, closing the door and coming around to the kitchen. "Maybe a scone? Mother would scold me if I didn't offer our hospitality."

"That would be lovely." Though Anneth wasn't entirely sure what a scone might be. She had so much to discover.

Lily directed Anneth to one of the backless wooden stools pulled up on the near side of the counter, then commenced opening cupboards and setting items on the wooden countertop. Trying not to be obvious,

Anneth watched with great interest. How curious, to not have a separate kitchen where one could summon food with a simple spell.

Of course, the food was prepared by chefs and under-cooks. She was somewhat chagrined to realize that she'd never put much thought into how her food was created—only that it was there to be called for whenever she liked.

"I'm biting my tongue on a thousand questions," Lily said. "Mother will have the same, and I don't want to make you repeat yourself. Oh, but it's hard! Why are you here? Do you know Mara? Silly me, of course you do—otherwise you wouldn't have come to the cottage. Does that mean you know this mysterious husband of hers, too? Wait—don't answer any of that."

Anneth had to grin at the deluge. Lily was endearing: a girl on the cusp of womanhood, who veered wildly between the two. Not so long ago, Anneth had been the same. But in recent moons, maturity had settled more firmly on her shoulders.

"Of course I know Mara," she said. "As you yourself have guessed. I am her—how do you put it here—her sister-in-law."

"Oh!" Lily paused from sifting dried herbs into a spouted pot and stared at Anneth. "Then the mysterious husband is your brother?"

"Indeed."

"That's all right, then. You don't seem so terrible." Then, as if belatedly realizing what she'd just said, Lily blushed and returned to her task.

"I'll take that as a compliment," Anneth said dryly. "Although my brother is generally considered more fearsome than I am."

"Well, brothers," Lily said, re-capping the container of herbs and shooting Anneth a grin. "I have one myself, you know. Is yours older?"

"Yes."

"I'm the youngest. Then Pansy, Mara, and the twins. Did she tell you about us?"

"She did. She misses you all a great deal."

Lily made a face. "Then she should have stayed longer than a day before running off after your brother. Why is it the women always have to help the men out of trouble?"

It did not seem like a question Anneth was meant to answer, and so she kept silent. She was finding it a little difficult to grasp the flow of conversation with a human. Or perhaps it was simply Lily's way, to leap from topic to topic.

"What is his name again?" Lily asked. "Brandon or some such?"

"Brannonilon Luthinor," Anneth said.

"That's so ornate." Lily shook her head, then stilled, eyes widening. "But wait—isn't he a prince? So that makes you a princess! I can't believe I'm hosting an actual princess from another world. Here, in our cottage in Little Hazel."

"I… am not sure what being a princess means, in your world."

"Why, that you're nobility." Seeing Anneth's confusion, Lily continued, "You're rich, and refined, and have handsome suitors falling at your feet. Why would Elfhame send you here?"

"It is a delicate situation," Anneth said, weighing how much to say.

"Wait, wait—Mother's not here yet." Lily heaved a sigh, then rummaged about in the cupboard again, emerging with a plate of some kind of baked good. "At least we can eat to pass the time. Oh, and since you're a princess, let me tell you about our prince."

"You have a prince here?" Anneth glanced about the living area.

Lily burst out laughing. "Not in the cottage, silly. Not even in Little Hazel—but in the castle, beyond. I suppose you live in a castle? No, don't answer that. Anyway, the prince is very handsome, in a tragic way. His mother died recently, and—"

The door opened, and Lily broke off to jump up and help relieve the older woman who entered of some of her bundles.

"Who is this?" the woman, who surely must be Lily's mother, asked.

Anneth rose and made her a slight curtsey. "I am Lady Anneth Luthinor, from the realm of Elfhame. Lily has been most kindly entertaining me while we waited for your return."

There. She could be as polished and diplomatic as any courtier, if she chose.

"Heavens. How unexpected." Lily's mother set down the basket she'd been carrying. "Welcome to our home. I'm Deirdre Geary, and you've met Lily. My husband, Padraig, will be home in time for supper. I see Lily's offered you tea and scones."

"And the tea's just ready." Lily set out a third mug and poured a fragrant, steaming liquid from the teapot.

"Let me tuck these things away," Mrs. Geary said. "Please, make yourself comfortable—no need to perch on the kitchen stools. I recommend the green armchair, myself."

She gestured toward the sitting area, then picked up her basket and bustled away down the short hallway. Anneth obediently slid off the stool and went to the green chair, to find it was already occupied by some small orange creature made of fluff.

The thing opened green eyes and yawned at her, showing sharp little teeth in a pointed face. It was endearing, and a tiny bit frightening —but surely it wasn't dangerous, or Lily would have said something.

"Oh, just move the cat," Lily said, coming over with two mugs of tea. "She thinks that's her chair."

Anneth wasn't sure how to *move the cat*. Did she pick it up? Or shoo it away? Was there a certain request that one made of the cat, first? Oh, why didn't she know anything about this creature that Lily seemed to take for granted?

There were felines in Elfhame, great star-colored leopards that hunted the wide plains of Moonflower—but no one in their right mind would ever invite one into their home. They were wild creatures, feral and deadly. Nothing like the little animal napping in the chair.

She leaned over, one hand outstretched. The cat jumped up, revealing a long tail, and brushed its head and side against her palm. Her fur was soft as thistledown. Anneth could have stood there, marveling, but the cat hopped down off the chair and scampered into the kitchen.

Perhaps it would come back later, so that she might study it further. And pet it, if the creature permitted.

Lily handed her a cup of tea, seeming not to notice Anneth's distracted fascination with the cat.

"Hurry up, Mother," she called. "I've kept from pestering Anneth with questions, but I'm about to perish from curiosity!"

A moment later, Mrs. Geary emerged from the back of the house. She took up the plate of scones from the kitchen counter and delivered it to the low table centered between the armchair Anneth was currently inhabiting and the one where Lily perched.

"A bit of waiting will do you good," Mrs. Geary said to her daughter.

She settled on the couch across from the chairs and pulled over a basket filled with spun fiber and two pointed sticks. Anneth watched curiously as Mrs. Geary looped the yarn through itself, using the sticks. She seemed to be partway through a work in progress, and her hands moved rapidly, manipulating the sticks and yarn. There was something magical about the way she transformed the single length of fiber into a piece of cloth.

"Do you knit?" Mrs. Geary asked, clearly noting Anneth's stare.

"No," Anneth said. "Is it difficult?"

"Well, it depends on the pattern." Mrs. Geary twitched the piece of fabric on her lap, revealing a complex weaving of ridges and dips. "This one, for example—"

"Please," Lily said, "could we wait to discuss your knitting until *after* Princess Anneth tells us why she's here?"

"Princess?" Mrs. Geary shot Anneth a look, brows raised. "I thought you hadn't asked her anything, Lily."

"We conversed a little," Anneth admitted. "I told her that my brother, Bran, is married to Mara."

"And you worked out the implications, aye." Mrs. Geary shook her head fondly at her daughter, then turned back to Anneth. "Very well, Princess Anneth—why are you here?"

"Just call me Anneth, please. You are family." She was already different enough. No need to let her title create another layer of formality.

Mrs. Geary nodded, her hands busy with her knitting.

"I came to find my brother and deliver an important message," Anneth continued. "Our father is ill, and Bran must return as soon as possible. I was hoping to bring some medicine from your world, as well." She gave Mara's mother a hopeful glance.

"Of a surety, we can spare some tisanes and poultices," Mrs. Geary said. "My twins, Sean and Seanna, will be able to provide you a good sampling. I'm sorry to hear your father is not well."

Perhaps later, when Anneth knew the family better, she would reveal how dire things were in Elfhame—but for now, she would have to bear the burden of her worry alone.

She inclined her head. “Thank you for your condolences.”

“My, you *are* fancy,” Lily said, her eyes wide. “Is your brother the same way?”

“Don’t be rude,” Mrs. Geary said to her daughter, then nodded to the plate of pastry. “Do have a scone, Anneth.”

It was like a moon cake, Anneth thought after her first bite, but a bit saltier, with a lighter texture.

“Delicious,” she said.

“They’re even better with honey,” Lily said. “I’ll fetch some.”

She jumped to her feet, then paused, looking out the wide window.

“Mother,” she said, somewhat breathlessly, “someone’s coming—and oh my! It’s a carriage from the castle. Do they know Princess Anneth is here, and have they come to welcome her?”

“Surely not.” Mrs. Geary hurriedly set her knitting aside and glanced at Anneth. “Would they have any reason to know about your presence here?”

“No.” Anneth’s shoulders tightened and she glanced at the hallway, then the stairs.

Should she hide? Should she flee? It was imperative she not be discovered, especially not by anyone in a position of authority. The secret of Elfhame was a perilous one, and belatedly she realized she’d put Mara’s entire family in danger by her visit.

No kingdom wanted to learn that there was a gateway to another world hidden in the depths of the nearby forest. Especially not a world inhabited by magic-wielding monsters. Anneth knew from her study of mortal history that humans were quick to attack what they did not understand.

“I am sorry,” she said softly.

“Don’t fret.” Mrs. Geary rose to her feet. “Lily, fetch the big apron. We must cover Anneth’s dress. And a kerchief for her hair. Those intricate braids are not any kind of usual hairstyle.”

Lily sprang into action, and in a matter of moments Anneth was transformed—she hoped—into a regular-looking mortal girl.

“Into the kitchen,” Mrs. Geary said, shooing her behind the counter.

"You're so pale, but we can say we're baking, and the flour can account for it."

Lily was already pulling supplies from the cupboards, and her mother clanged several loaf-shaped pans down beside the stove. Outside, Anneth heard hoofbeats stop, then a creak and jingle.

"They're here," Lily whispered.

"Don't say a word," her mother said sternly. "Either of you."

She wrapped a faded apron about her ample middle and strode to the door, just as a self-assured knock sounded.

"Pour out some flour on the counter," Lily said hurriedly. Then, when Anneth simply blinked at her, she pulled a few handfuls of white powder from one of the canisters ranged on the counter and piled them before Anneth. A puff of dust rose up, and Anneth sneezed.

Mrs. Geary shot them a quelling look, then opened the door.

A finely dressed man stood at the threshold. He wore a plumed hat, his vest was decorated with silver buttons, and his long cloak was swept back at the shoulder with a gleaming brooch. In one gloved hand he carried a roll of parchment.

"I am the royal emissary," he said importantly. "Is this the Geary household?"

"It is, indeed," Mrs. Geary said. "What business does the palace have with us? My husband is already planning to provide ales for the upcoming festivities, if that's—"

"No, no." The man waved his parchment at her. "Surely you're aware that every eligible young lady in the land is required to attend the ball. Even the commoners."

He glanced into the simple cottage with a frown, and Anneth tried to make herself look small and inconsequential.

"According to the records, you have two unmarried daughters still in residence beneath your roof," he continued, with a quick look down at his paper. "By the names of Lily and Mara. Correct?"

Mrs. Geary hesitated a moment, and the man gave her an impatient look.

"Yes, of course," she said, gesturing behind her. "There they are now, doing a bit of baking, as you can see. My daughters."

"Hmph." The man tucked his parchment away. "Make sure they

arrive tomorrow afternoon at the castle, three hours before sunset. I presume your girls will not arrive bedecked in flour."

Mrs. Geary drew back, insulted. "Of course not, sir. Though you might've given us a bit more notice."

He let out a heavy sigh. "I have been up and down the length of Raine for the past fortnight, informing every family with daughters of the prince's decree. Your village is the last on my route—and it's a wonder you haven't heard the news before now."

"I have," Lily called cheerfully. "But I didn't truly think we'd be invited."

"You are *commanded*," the emissary said, a bit sourly. "When you enter the castle, your names will be noted against the list of attendees. I encourage you to arrive early. Good day, madam."

"And to you, sir."

The moment he turned back to his coach, Mrs. Geary shut the door. She walked slowly to the kitchen, a frown scoring a line between her eyebrows.

"He was rather puffed up, wasn't he?" Lily said.

"I'd have offered him a scone if he'd shown even a degree of politeness," Mrs. Geary said. "Imagine, implying you'd go to the ball covered in flour! We may be commoners, but we aren't ignorant of the ways of the castle. Why, Mara was even employed there for a short time."

"She was?" Anneth shot her an eager look. Mara had said so little about herself, and she welcomed the chance to learn more.

"Aye. It was a few years back, after Castle Raine was built and the king and queen and their court took up residence. They needed servants, so Mara took a job there as a maid. She didn't much like it, though, and ended up coming back home."

"And then she went into the Darkwood, and we thought she'd been eaten by wolves," Lily said in a dramatic tone.

Mrs. Geary shot her daughter a look. "Perhaps not that, but we feared something terrible had happened to her. The forest isn't safe."

Then, as if recalling where Anneth had come from, she cleared her throat and began bustling about the kitchen, brushing the worst of the flour off the counter and putting away the pans.

"But just think, we get to go to the ball," Lily said, grinning at Anneth. "How lucky that they thought you were Mara."

Anneth drew a circle on the flour-dusted counter with her fingertip.

"I am grateful that the misconception saved me from discovery, but why would they make that mistake?" she asked.

"A year after someone disappears, you report them as dead," Lily said—rather cheerfully, considering the subject matter. "But then Mara came back and told us where she'd been, and we couldn't very well tell people that she'd gone through a magical doorway and married an elf prince."

"Indeed." Mrs. Geary put the canisters back in their place. "And we also couldn't say that she'd left town to get married, for whenever she returns, it will be from the forest, not through the village driving a cart filled with her luggage. It would raise too many questions."

"So you let people believe she was still here?" Anneth frowned. "Didn't anyone notice that she wasn't?"

"Little Hazel might be a small village," Mrs. Geary said, "but people know how to be discreet. And when not to ask questions."

"But won't people wonder, when they see me using her name?" Anneth drew another circle beside the first.

"Nobody will, though!" Lily grinned at her. "After they check your attendance as Mara, you can just be yourself."

"Although perhaps leave off the princess part," Mrs. Geary added.

Anneth swiped her hand across the counter, erasing her circles. No matter what name she used, Mara or Anneth, she still would not be attending the ball.

"I don't think it's wise for me to go," she said with a pang.

"Why ever not?" Lily clasped her hands and gave her a pleading look. "You must come! It won't be any fun without you."

"I am a stranger here—and I don't wish to bring trouble upon your home."

Mrs. Geary gave Anneth a long look. "It seems to me that the trouble would arise if you *don't* go. The emissary made that clear enough."

"I could... suddenly feel unwell?"

"I'd think they would come to check, seeing as we're so near the castle," Mrs. Geary said. "And clearly you're feeling just fine today. If you're looking to avoid awkward questions, it's for the best if you simply go. Go, enjoy yourselves, and return here with none the wiser."

Apprehension wrestled with excitement in Anneth's belly. "But I've never attended a ball in your world. What if I make some dreadful mistake?"

"Don't be silly." Lily waved a flour-dusted hand at her. "I've never been to a ball either, obviously. But at least you know what it's like to be in a castle."

Mrs. Geary nodded. "You saw what the emissary thought of us. As long as you don't behave outlandishly, no one will scrutinize the behavior of two lowborn girls."

"Well..." Anneth let out a sigh, weighing Mrs. Geary's words.

"Please, *please* come," Lily said, with a soulful look.

Whatever Anneth chose, there was some danger. But now that the officials in the castle believed her to be Mara and expected her attendance at the ball, going to the event was probably the best course.

As Lily had said, Anneth knew how to behave at court—not that she'd be called upon to do so.

"I suppose I'll attend," she said. "Provided we don't draw attention to ourselves, there's no harm in it."

"Good girl," Mrs. Geary said, as Lily let out a shriek of glee.

"We're going to the ball," Lily sang, dancing about the kitchen in excitement. Then she halted, eyes wide. "But whatever shall we wear?"

Anneth wiped her floury hand on the apron she wore. "I admit, I didn't bring any formal court gowns with me."

"Probably a good thing," Mrs. Geary said dryly. "Untie your apron, and we'll go up to Lily's room and see what's in the closet."

Anneth did, hanging the large apron on the nearby hook, then followed her hosts to the staircase.

"It's not fair," Lily said, marching ahead of them up the stairs. "We have no time to even sew new dresses, while the rest of the girls in the kingdom have had months."

"Only a fortnight, according to the emissary," her mother reminded her. "And it's not the gown that makes the girl. Beauty comes from within."

Lily only rolled her eyes, and Anneth filed the words away. They had the ring of a mortal saying about them, although not one she'd ever seen written down in the books she'd studied.

If beauty came from within, then would they forgive her if she let her illusion spell drop? Not right away, that was certain. To learn someone's true self took time.

"Surely it's important to make a good impression," she said. "This is the prince we're meeting, after all."

"I can't imagine how he plans to converse with every eligible young lady in Raine in the course of one evening," Mrs. Geary said.

"A very long evening, though." Lily led them into her bedroom, and Anneth tried to listen to her while taking in every detail of the room. "Three hours before sunset? Whatever will we do about dinner?"

A trio of narrow beds ranged between the windows on the opposite wall, each bed covered with a colorful quilt. A shelf took up the left-hand wall, which contained a few books, shiny rocks, and a carved wooden box. The room smelled faintly of wood smoke, and a braided rug softened the floor.

"The castle will feed everyone," Mrs. Geary said. "They've ordered two dozen barrels of ale from your father, and goodness knows what else from the rest of the country. I'm sure no one will go hungry."

Lily opened a door on the right-hand wall, and Anneth was surprised to see it led to a small room filled with clothing. A closet, Mrs. Geary had called it. Dark Elves had nothing of the kind in Elfhame, only large wardrobes and armoires where they kept their clothing. It seemed rather a waste of space, until Anneth considered that the bedroom itself was quite small. Then the notion of a closet made sense.

"Good thing Pansy sent me some gowns from the city," Lily said, gathering up an armful of dresses and dumping them on the near bed. "Anneth, you're so tall, though—I'm not sure any of these will fit."

"I can let out the hem." Mrs. Geary fingered the fabric of one: a green material that was stiffer than the silks Anneth was accustomed to.

"If she only wears one petticoat, it might be long enough," Lily said, nodding.

Anneth smiled, as if she understood what a petticoat was.

"So, the green for Anneth, and perhaps the rose for you, Lily," Mrs.

Geary said. She held up the dresses side by side, and Anneth studied them.

Unlike the flowing silks of Elfhame, which could be wrapped and tucked in many ways, these dresses were formed with specific arms and waistlines. Lily's concerns about fit suddenly made sense to Anneth, for when a gown was so exact, it would be difficult for many wearers to share the same garment, or adjust it for mood, or changes in the body. How curious mortals were, to restrict the boundaries of their clothing so tightly.

Both gowns had puffed sleeves, scooped necklines leading to gathered waists, and voluminous skirts. The green dress featured sparkling beads sewn upon the bodice, while the rose-colored one boasted gold embroidery.

"I know they're probably not as grand as you're used to," Lily said apologetically. "But they're the best we can do."

"I think they're both lovely," Anneth said. "We've nothing like them where I come from, and I look forward to wearing such a gown."

"Provided we can get the length right," Mrs. Geary said. "Why don't you two change, and I'll see about that hem. Let me fetch my sewing basket."

She stepped out of the room, and Lily thrust a frilly white skirt at Anneth.

"Start with the one," she said. "Though I usually wear three or four, depending."

In a matter of minutes, Lily had removed her everyday dress and put on the rose gown. Anneth watched out of the corner of her eye, trying to understand how to don the unfamiliar clothing. The white skirt went on before the dress, which seemed strange. Why even wear it, if it wasn't going to be seen?

The gown's armholes seemed straightforward enough, but once it was on, Anneth had no notion of how to fasten the garment. This must have been how Mara had felt, donning elvish clothing for the first time, and Anneth felt a stab of sympathy.

She smiled at the memory of helping Mara prepare to meet the Hawthorne Court. How strange that now their places were reversed!

Right down to sisterly assistance in dressing for an event at an unfamiliar royal palace.

"Turn around, and I'll lace you up," Lily said. "Then you can do the same for me."

Anneth obediently swiveled in place, trying to work out exactly what Lily was doing. Surely it couldn't be that difficult to lace up a gown. It certainly felt simple, if a bit constricting.

Confronted with the back of Lily's dress, however, Anneth fumbled with the long, gold-colored laces. Presumably they went back and forth, crisscross, but she was unused to threading cords through small holes, and it took her some time to do up the entire back.

"Can't you pull any tighter?" Lily asked, once Anneth finished. "There can't be any gaps."

"I will try, but we do not fasten our clothing so, in Elfhame."

Lily turned to face her, the pink skirts belling out with the motion.

"How do you do it?" she asked. "Do your dresses stay up by magic?"

"Not at all." Anneth had to smile at the notion. "We have belts and clips, and we tuck fabric in, just so."

"It sounds rather strange," Lily said.

Mrs. Geary arrived, carrying a basket in one hand. "Look at the both of you," she said. "A picture of loveliness. But yes, that hem is too short for you, Anneth. Your petticoat's showing."

Anneth gathered that was not a good thing. She obediently rotated in place as Mrs. Geary knelt and made tearing sounds at the bottom of the skirt.

"That should do." Mrs. Geary clambered to her feet. "I'll need to finish the edge, but the length is acceptable."

"Thank you," Anneth said. The neckline of the gown was a trifle itchy, but she would not be so rude as to mention it.

"Back into your regular clothes, and we'll have a bit of lunch," Mrs. Geary said. "Anneth, we can put you in here, or upstairs in the loft, where Sean used to sleep."

Oh. Anneth blinked, assessing her options. It hadn't occurred to her that she wouldn't have a private room.

She'd glimpsed the loft as they'd come up the stairs, and there wasn't even a door, just an open space with a sleeping pallet and a chest of drawers. Anyone might see her, and she'd have to traverse two flights of stairs on her way out of the house.

"I will share with Lily," she said.

It would make sneaking out the next morning a bit more difficult. But not impossible. She would just have to rise early and take care not be seen.

CHAPTER 15

The kingdom of Raine's round council chamber was located midway up the southernmost turret of Castle Raine. Morning light slanted through the windows, casting diamond-shaped patterns on the wide oaken planks of the central table and falling on the map of Raine spread out in the middle.

This was not, of course, the first council meeting Owen had attended, but it was certainly the most fraught with tension. The handful of people seated around the table all sported grim expressions, himself included.

"I received this missive last night, by special courier," King Philip said, holding up a folded parchment, the elaborate red seal broken.

Owen recognized the design. It seemed that, once again, their enemies to the east were proving eager to meddle in Raine's affairs.

"From the Athraig?" Captain Crane, the commander of the castle's warriors, leaned forward, eyes narrowed. "It's not enough that their warships are nosing about our northern coast?"

"Admiral Byrne is dealing with them." The king looked to the admiral's second, who sat across the table from Owen.

"Aye," the woman said. "The navy will send them running home soon enough, tails between their legs."

Owen certainly hoped so. Raine's naval strength had always been superior, and their sources of intelligence within the Athraig government hadn't indicated anything had changed.

He nodded at the parchment in his father's hands. "What do the Athraig have to say?"

Expression grim, the king unfolded the paper. Bits of wax scattered like dried blood on the tabletop before him.

"They are sending an official delegation to Raine," he said. "Led by Lord Jensen, Greve of Sonderborg—a distant cousin to the king, I believe."

"Turn them away at Portknowe," the under-admiral said. "We can deny them landing. Fire the shore cannons if they refuse."

The king shook his head. "Under the terms of our truce with the Athraig, that would be interpreted as an act of war—which would play into their hands. They sent those ships north for a reason."

He tapped the far shore of Raine—a place with few villages, dominated by the Darkwood. It would take an intrepid group indeed to make their way through the leagues of forest and arrive at the castle.

"Surely they don't think to invade us from that direction?" Owen asked. "It would take them at least a week to come through the forest. That's no terrain to march any army through."

"I cannot say." King Philip sighed and sat back in his chair. "Perhaps Lord Jensen will answer that question. At any rate, I trust Admiral Byrne to keep them from our shores."

"When's this delegation due to appear?" the under-admiral asked.

The king glanced at the parchment. "Within the week. Owen, I want you betrothed by the time they arrive. We must not give them any opportunity to thrust their own princess forward."

"Can't they get eaten by bears on their way up from Portknowe?" Owen asked, only half in jest.

King Philip shook his head. "That would cause a diplomatic incident, I'm afraid."

"Another thing the Athraig would seize upon as an excuse for war," the captain said, his dour expression deepening. "Though it's almost worth the risk."

"No." The king swept them with his gaze. "Raine cannot afford a war. Not now. Far better that we show the envoy that all is well and stable within our kingdom, and send him on his way as soon as possible."

"It's good we delayed the official announcement of the ball for so long," Captain Crane said. "No doubt the Athraig were hoping to get here in time to cause trouble."

"Your advice to let rumors circulate, but not send the royal emissary out until a fortnight before the event, was sound," the king told him. "It bought us enough time, I believe, to avoid the Athraig's intervention."

They all looked at Owen: his father, Captain Crane, the under-admiral, even the secretary taking notes. The weight of their expectations pressed against him. But he knew what he must do.

"I understand," he said. "I'll select some suitable prospects tomorrow, and choose between them shortly."

That was the whole point of the ball, after all.

"Good." His father smiled at him. "I trust you'll make the very best choice possible."

For the kingdom, of course. Owen didn't think there would be any best choice for himself—but he'd resigned himself to that fact. Love was not for him. Duty must suffice.

CHAPTER 16

Once they'd finished lunch, Anneth's excitement could no longer mask her weariness. Much as she disliked admitting it, crossing through the gateway had sapped her strength. After her third bout of yawning, Mrs. Geary sent her to rest, and Anneth didn't argue. Despite the unfamiliar feel of the mattress and pillow, she was soon fast asleep.

When she awoke, the brightness of the day was gone, replaced by a welcome dimness. The unrelenting light had contributed to her exhaustion, Anneth realized. Hopefully, she would adapt to it, as surely her brother had.

She wished she could contact Bran and Mara, but until her wellspring refilled, she would have to be content with looking over Ondo's shoulder as he scried. Hopefully they would be on their way back very soon. Time was precious, especially for the Hawthorne Lord.

Once again she reminded herself that time was working in their favor as long as they remained in the mortal world. There was nothing she could do to speed or slow things, or aid her brother in his quest.

What she could do was rest, recover, and graciously accept the Gearys' hospitality. Constant worry about her family would not be helpful to anyone.

Delicious scents drifted up to where she lay, and in the rooms below she heard the murmur of conversation. A lower-pitched voice joined, and she guessed that Mara's father had returned. Anneth rose and smoothed her hair, hoping she was somewhat presentable, then went downstairs.

"And there she is now," Mrs. Geary said as Anneth stepped into the living room. "Anneth, come meet my husband, Padraig."

Mara's father was shorter than Anneth, though still taller than his wife and daughters, with a wide belly and kind eyes. His sandy hair was just a fringe around his bare scalp, and Anneth wondered if that was the effect of some calamity or whether such a thing was normal in humans.

She could think of no way she might ask the question, so she simply smiled and made him a curtsey. "A pleasure to meet you, sir."

Mr. Geary nodded, openly studying her. "So, your brother's the one what married our girl. I'd like to clap eyes on the fellow someday."

"I'm sure you will," Anneth said, resolving to force the issue, even if Bran wanted to simply hide in the forest when he and Mara returned. "My brother means no discourtesy, but he is single-minded, and allows very little distraction when he's on a mission."

"Tell us more about why he and Mara are back in our world," Mr. Geary said.

"She will," his wife put in. "But supper's ready, and we can continue this conversation at the table."

They did, and Anneth recited her tale in between bites of strange food. It was not without flavor, but the mashed white roots had an unfamiliar creamy texture, and the meat—some kind of fowl, she thought—was spiced with herbs her tongue could not name.

Instead of wine or clear water, as Anneth was used to, the Gearys served mugs of a foamy, amber-colored brew. She took a cautious sip, eyebrows going up at the bittersweet flavor. She thought she detected a bit of fermentation in the drink, as well.

"My newest batch of ale," Mr. Geary said. "A bit fresh, yet, and could use more hops, but it'll do."

"Father's beer is sent all over the kingdom," Lily said. "He's the best brewer in Raine. Geary's Ales are famous."

He laughed and hoisted his mug. "Not quite. But the castle likes them well enough, and it's a good living."

"Speaking of the castle," Mrs. Geary said, "the girls are invited to the ball tomorrow."

Mr. Geary set down his ale. "Is that wise? I mean, Anneth is a foreign princess in disguise. P'raps she should stay home."

"We've discussed it." Mrs. Geary shot Anneth a glance. "But the castle believes Mara is still living here, and after the emissary got a look at both girls, it would cause questions if Lily showed up alone."

"Yes," Anneth said. "It is best if I attend."

"Well enough." Mr. Geary nodded. "I suppose you know your way around balls, Anneth. We'll trust you in this."

Certainly she was accustomed to official events at the Hawthorne Palace, but they did not actually have such things as formal balls. From her study of humans, she understood that dancing was a key part of such events.

"I am not sure what kind of dancing will be required," she said. "We do things differently in Elfhame."

"Do you even know how to dance?" Lily turned a concerned gaze on her.

"Yes—but what we call dancing, and what you do... I don't know if it's the same thing."

"I haven't been to many balls," Lily said, then made a face at her mother's snort of amusement. "Of course, none at the castle—but Pansy took me to a cotillion when I visited her in the city. And we dance here at the harvest fair every fall. So I do know a thing or two. What kind of dancing do you do, Anneth?"

Anneth was silent a moment. It was strange, thinking of how to describe the formal dances of court as if she were an outsider to them.

"We stand in a circle, or sometimes in lines across from one another, and move back and forth—a step up, two behind, turn in place, with the arms raised."

"Do you have partners?" Lily asked.

"If you mean dancing two by two, no. Sometimes the lines pass closely by one another, and then you take a moment to mirror the moves with whomever is across from you."

"So you've never waltzed? Or danced a polka?" Lily sounded shocked.

Mrs. Geary patted her daughter's hand. "Even in our world, customs differ. I hear that in Parnese they do a twirling dance that would make you fall down dizzy if you tried."

"It sounds like you need to teach Anneth to waltz." Mr. Geary scraped back his chair and rose. "I'm back to the brewery to finish readying the barrels for the castle."

"Try not to be out too late, dear." Mrs. Geary stood and kissed his cheek, then began clearing the table.

Anneth took up her plate, but her hostess removed it from her hand with a tsk.

"You're our guest," Mrs. Geary said. "I'll do the cleaning up, while Lily teaches you to waltz."

"Thank you," Anneth said. "I hope I'll be able to learn the steps quickly."

"You will." Lily caught her hand and towed her to the living room. "Help me push the couch back and roll up the rug, so we have room."

Anneth assisted in clearing the space, then stood facing Lily. "What now?"

"Take my hand, here," Lily said, "and put the other one on my shoulder—yes, like so. Now, I am the lead, so when I step forward, you step back. Oh, and count to three. Ready?"

Anneth nodded, not sure what counting to three had to do with it. Lily stepped forward, and Anneth hopped back to keep her toes from being stepped on.

"Not like that," Lily said, laughing. "Here, I'll dance without you."

Anneth stood aside, and Lily, holding her arms out to her imaginary partner, began dancing around the room.

"*One*, two, three. *One*, two, three," she chanted. "See, watch my feet. The big step is on the one, then two and three are smaller. And you can turn about, too."

She pivoted on the bigger step, and Anneth watched Lily's feet closely until she came to a halt.

"I think I understand," Anneth said. "Shall we try?"

It took several false starts and a few stumbles but finally Anneth had the feel of the waltz. Lily then went on to show her the simpler allemande, which was similar to the Dark Elves' processionals, although a bit quicker in movement.

"Don't worry," Lily said, as she walked Anneth through yet another hand clasp and turn. "The same moves go over and over, just with different partners. I'll stand beside you in the line, and you can watch me."

"Or perhaps I will sprain my ankle and be unable to dance," Anneth said. She was not at all sure she was up for the attempt, after all.

"Don't fret," Mrs. Geary called from the kitchen. "I've been watching, and you're graceful, Anneth, even though you don't quite know the steps. Not every girl in the kingdom is an accomplished dancer, after all. You'll do well enough."

"We'll practice more tomorrow, in our gowns," Lily said. "You'll be ready."

"Thank you for showing me the waltz," Anneth said, keeping her misgivings to herself. She only hoped she wouldn't embarrass herself too badly.

THAT NIGHT, as she and Lily went to their respective beds, Anneth told herself to wake just before dawn. As soon as the strange, silvery light of the approaching sun filtered into the sky, she would go find Ondo in the forest.

It wasn't easy for her to fall asleep, however. Her thoughts swung between the ever-present fear for her father, worry for Bran, and the guilty pleasure she felt at the thought of attending the mortal ball. In the end, she fell into dreaming as she imagined herself waltzing. *One*, two, three, *one*, two, three...

She woke several times in the night, listening to Lily's slow, steady breathing and checking the sky outside the window for any sign of change. Only the strange stars of the mortal world stared back at her, unblinking.

At last, a faint sifting of radiance dusted the sky. Silently, Anneth rose and crept to the door. There was no need to don her clothing, as she'd told Lily that her people slept in their clothes. It was a lie, but a convenient one for her purposes.

She glanced over her shoulder at Lily, who was fast asleep, then slipped out of the room and down the stairs. One of the treads creaked underfoot, and she froze, heart pounding. After a long moment, the house still and slumbering about her, Anneth continued, her steps careful.

Reaching the front door without mishap, she slipped on her boots and grabbed her cloak, then let herself out into the cool air.

A few birds were rousing, letting out sleepy chirps. Dew drops glistened on the leaves and blades of grass, shining like gems to Anneth's enhanced vision. Swiftly, she went down the lane toward the looming trees of the Darkwood.

Ondo met her just inside the sheltering shadows. He wore the hood of his cloak drawn up, hiding his face from human eyes. Anneth smiled to see his familiar Dark Elf features.

"Everything is well, my lady?" he asked, giving her a close look. "Your true visage has returned. You were able to leave the house unseen?"

"Yes, I was careful. And I do feel better." A night in a bed and a hearty meal had certainly helped.

"I spoke with your brother earlier," the scout said. "He and Mara are still in the land across the sea, but they have located the Void and will soon destroy it. He bids you take care until he and Mara reach Raine, and hopes that your power regenerates soon."

"So do I."

She felt within her for the stirring of her wellspring, then held out her hand and spoke the summoning for foxfire. A faint flicker of blue light appeared, and her heart rose at the sight—only to fall again as the light snuffed out.

"Soon," Ondo said, laying a reassuring hand on her shoulder. "That you were able to conjure even a glimmer is a good sign."

"I suppose." She sighed and faced him. "Cast the illusion, and I will meet you here again tomorrow."

"I do not like it. Come back with me into the forest. What if something happens and you are discovered?"

"You worry too much." Now it was her turn to pat his shoulder. "I'm safe and well cared for at the Gearys'."

He bowed his head. "I trust you are correct, my lady."

"I am."

She did not add that she was going to attend a ball at the castle that very evening.

Ondo would certainly protest, then insist on accompanying her, and truly, she was not a child needing an escort. Even though she might not have magic at her fingertips at the moment, everything would be fine.

CHAPTER 17

Anneth quietly let herself back into the Gearys' house. The kitten, curled up into a ball of orange fluff by the hearth, opened its eyes a crack, gave her an incurious look, then went back to sleep.

Avoiding the creaky stair, Anneth crept back to the bedroom and slipped beneath the colorful quilt. In the bed beside hers, Lily snored softly. No one had witnessed Anneth's departure and return, and she snuggled down under the covers, secure in the knowledge that her secret was safe—at least for another day.

When she roused again, the sun's brilliance filled the room. Lily's bed was neatly made, and the sound of dishes clinking drifted up the stairs, along with the delicious scent of baking bread. She lay for a moment, staring up at the plaster ceiling. It was a cozy little house, and so unlike the elegant rooms of the Hawthorne Palace.

She liked it very much.

Not that Anneth disliked her suite—but she'd never had the chance to look at her home from a different perspective. Some in the Hawthorne Court, Mireleth among them, would certainly disdain the quaint comforts of the Gearys' home, but Anneth found it charming.

Footsteps sounded on the stairs, and Anneth glanced over as Lily appeared in the doorway.

"You're awake," she said cheerfully. "Mother sent me up to see if you'd like some breakfast."

"Certainly." Anneth sat up and scooted herself out of bed. "I hope you didn't wait for me."

"Father ate ages ago and is off to the brewery to load the barrels up to the castle for the ball tonight. Oh, I can hardly wait!" Lily clasped her hands under her chin. "After breakfast, we can go out and gather flowers for our hair."

"Is that what one usually wears to a ball?" Anneth asked, following Lily downstairs.

"Only the girls who can't afford jewelry," Lily said. "Which is us."

Mrs. Geary looked up from making tea, clearly catching the end of their conversation. "We are rich enough, Lily, in the things that matter. And you are both welcome to look through my jewelry box. Perhaps something there will suit."

"Thank you." Lily dropped a kiss on her mother's cheek, then took the basket of sliced bread from the counter over to the table.

"You thought I should change my hair." Anneth ran one hand over her intricately braided locks. "What do you suggest?"

"Braids, still," Lily said. "Just not quite so fancy. What do you think, Mother?"

Mrs. Geary studied Anneth's head for a moment. "The looped braids are a lovely effect. We can keep the same feeling, without all the between rows. Provided you agree, Anneth?"

"I don't want to stand out as being too different," Anneth said. "I defer to your judgment in this."

Mrs. Geary nodded and finished bringing breakfast to the table. Coddled eggs, crisp fruits unfamiliar to Anneth, with smooth red skins and tangy white flesh, and fresh-baked bread with a variety of jams to spread upon them.

Suddenly ravenous, Anneth ate and did not speak much. She was content to listen to Lily talk about the other village girls who would be at the ball.

"Don't forget that your sister Seanna will be there, too," Mrs. Geary said. "You should take Anneth over to meet the twins on your flower-gathering expedition this morning, since they weren't able to come for dinner last night."

"I'd like that," Anneth said, when Lily glanced at her for confirmation. "But might I have another piece of bread first?"

"My stars, you eat like a starving creature," Mrs. Geary said, passing her the basket. "Don't they feed you there, in your land?" She smiled, showing she meant the words kindly.

"It's only because your bread is so delicious." Lily snatched a piece from the basket as it went by. "Nobody can refuse it."

"It is excellent," Anneth said. "Indeed, every meal I've had with you has been marvelous. You are an excellent cook."

Mrs. Geary blushed slightly. "Coming from a princess, that's high praise indeed. I expect you're used to finer things than what we serve."

"Different, that is all," Anneth said. "But to answer your question about my appetite—the crossing between worlds is intensely draining."

Lily gave her a stricken look. "Oh, no! Are you strong enough to attend the prince's ball?"

"Don't worry," Anneth said, smiling at her. "Good food and rest is making all the difference. I feel nearly recovered now. And I expect going to the ball will be the highlight of my visit—after meeting all of you, of course."

"Speaking of which..." Mrs. Geary rose and made a shooing motion. "You'd best go and see if you can catch the twins. I know they'd love to meet Anneth."

In a matter of minutes, Lily was leading Anneth through a nearby field, stopping occasionally to pluck a few blooms and stick them in the metal bucket she carried.

"It's not heavy," Lily had assured her as they set out. "There's only a little water in the bottom, and flowers don't weigh that much. Besides, it's not far to Sean and Seanna's."

Anneth was relieved that Lily's siblings didn't dwell in the middle of the village. She wanted to save her energy for the ball, but she knew that if they set foot in Little Hazel, she would not be able to resist exploring every part of it.

Later, she reminded herself. There would be opportunities to do so in the coming days, since Bran and Mara had not yet begun their journey back to Raine. And surely, since the hours ran more quickly in the human world, her father was not—yet—running out of time. She hoped.

At any rate, there was nothing she could do except wait.

And learn what she could of the mortal world—including any healing remedies the twins might be able to provide.

She followed Lily through a meadow of yellow-green grasses stitched with flowers. Ahead lay a low dwelling with white walls and a roof that seemed to be made of hay.

"Old Soraya's cottage," Lily said, gesturing. "Of course, it's Sean and Seanna's now. Look—they're in the garden."

She ran forward, calling a greeting, and the two figures kneeling in the beds of greenery rose and waved. At first glance, it was difficult to tell them apart. Both were garbed in long tunics and leggings made of gray cloth. Both had shoulder-length auburn hair pulled back from their faces. But as Anneth approached, she saw that Sean's features were more angular, while Seanna's figure was clearly that of a woman.

Lily made breathless introductions, and Sean and Seanna shook Anneth's hand, both regarding her steadily with their gray-green eyes.

"Your brother married Mara," Sean said. "Will we ever meet him?"

"Yes—I mean, I hope so," Anneth said. "He and Mara should be returning shortly, as he's needed in Elfhame. But before we go, I was hoping you might provide me some mortal medicines. My father is ill."

"Describe the symptoms," Seanna said, brow creasing.

Anneth did, including his cough, sunken eyes, and general weakness. Both twins gave her a sharp nod at the exact same moment.

"Vervain, comfrey, rue," Seanna said, ticking the list off on her fingers.

"Willow and valerian, for comfort," Sean added.

"Oregano to strengthen the constitution." Seanna pursed her lips. "We have all that in store, plus a few Parnesian herbs that may be of help."

"It will take two days to formulate the possible remedies," Sean said.

"At least," his sister added.

"We have the time," Anneth said. "I thank you for your aid." And prayed that whatever the twins concocted would be able to help the Hawthorne Lord.

"Are you going to the ball tonight?" Lily asked, lifting the bucket of flowers. "We're collecting blooms for our hair."

Seanna made a face. "I suppose I must—but I don't intend to stay a moment more than is necessary. I've more important things to do."

"Don't you want to come with us, though, to gather flowers?" Lily asked. "You ought to at least make *some* effort with your appearance."

Seanna shook her head. "It isn't necessary. I've no interest in making an impression upon Prince Owen, and neither should you, Lily."

Owen. Anneth filed the name away. It was a very mortal name, and so much shorter than what she was accustomed to. In Elfhame, it would be something like Owennelthinor. She smiled at her own flight of fancy.

"Princes don't marry commoners," Seanna continued. "No matter what the fables say."

"I know that," Lily said, eyes flashing. "But you needn't take all the fun out of it."

"Seanna's being practical," her twin said. "Now, we've much to do, especially if we're going to have Anneth's medicines ready within the next few days. Good day to you both."

"Don't bother trying to find us at the castle," Lily said. "I wouldn't want to stand in the way of your hasty departure."

"I won't," Seanna said calmly.

"Hmph." Swinging her bucket, Lily turned away. "Come on, Anneth."

Anneth began to make the twins a bow of farewell, but they were leaning together in close conversation and not even looking at her. Clearly the visit was already out of their minds. Well then. With a mental shrug, she went to join Lily, who waited for her at the edge of the lane running past the cottage.

"They are so rude," Lily said, obviously not caring if her siblings overheard. "We don't need them, anyway. More flowers for us."

"I suppose."

To Anneth, the twins had seemed blunt and straightforward, but not in a deliberately impolite way. More as though their thoughts marched in a slightly different time, and they saw no need to adjust their steps to match everyone around them.

She and Lily wandered the lane and meadows gathering flowers for the next turn—*hour,* Anneth corrected herself. She must start thinking of time in human terms.

Here, they had devices with gears and markers, the hours inscribed with numbers that repeated twice in one day. It was very confusing.

The Dark Elf way of marking such things was to use doubled spheres of glass fused together with a small opening between. Every turnglass measured the same stretch of time, no matter how large or small the glass might be—she had a palm-sized one tucked away in the pack she'd left with Ondo, while there was one nearly twice her height in the Hawthorne Palace throne room.

One side of the turnglass was filled with carefully calibrated gemstones. Flip it upside down, and the gems would trickle into the empty glass sphere. When that side filled up, one turned it over again. None of this cutting up pieces of the day into numbered portions.

Although she supposed that, since the sun rose and set at regular intervals, it made sense.

Her people measured such things by the gleaming arcs of the palemoon and the bright as they danced about one another in the star-stitched sky. The brightmoon trailed its smaller companion, and every few rotations of the palemoon they would join together in a doublemoon, casting their gold and silver radiance over the land.

Anneth tucked a few more bright blue flowers into the full bucket, which was a blaze of color beneath the bright mortal sun.

"That should be enough," Lily said.

"I'll carry it back," Anneth offered. "I'm not one of those princesses who never do a bit of work, you know."

Lily hesitated a moment, but then handed the bucket over. "Are you interested in catching the prince's eye?" she asked. "Seeing as how you're actually of royal blood."

"Not at all," Anneth said, surprised. "I already have a prince as a suitor, and that is one too many."

"You do?" Lily's eyes shone with excitement. "You must tell me all about him. Where is he from? Is he handsome? Do you think he misses you terribly?"

"Prince Deldarinnon is from the Cereus Court, in Elfhame. I suppose he is handsome enough. And we hardly know one another."

Indeed, Anneth had spared little thought for the Cereus Prince since she'd stepped through the gateway. If she had to guess, she supposed he'd either foolishly ridden off alone into the Erynvorn in search of adventure, or was back at the Hawthorne Palace, flirting with all the court ladies and making jaded remarks about how provincial Hawthorne was compared to Cereus.

"Do you think you'll marry him?" Lily asked.

"No." Anneth said the word without thinking—very undiplomatic of her. She was supposed to be entertaining the idea of their betrothal, after all.

"Why ever not?"

Anneth switched the bucket to her other hand and continued down the lane. Ahead, she glimpsed the Gearys' cottage.

"Because my mother wants me to, for one thing," she said. "What I want is of no consequence—I'm just a piece upon her playing board."

"But would you, if you loved him?" Lily pressed.

"I don't know. I've never felt that kind of love." Not like Bran and Mara, who would risk everything and cross worlds for one another.

They reached the front door, and Anneth was grateful to let the conversation drop.

Mrs. Geary insisted on feeding them a hearty lunch, then sent Anneth upstairs to rest.

"Not for too long, though," Lily said. "We've a ball to get ready for!"

CHAPTER 18

Bran and Mara spent the entire day surveilling the Temple of the Twin Gods. They tracked the priests' schedules, and noted that a male priest guarded the door of flame while a woman watched that of the blade. The temple was open to worshippers from dawn until dusk, when the bells of the city pealed out in a cacophony that made Bran wince, though Mara seemed to find the sound joyful.

She had, during one of her stints "praying" before the main altar, spotted a small doorway to one side of the huge painting of the Twin Gods, though none of the priests seemed to use that door. At least not during the hours Bran and Mara spent observing.

He also believed the ornate wooden paneling lining the walls in the smaller shrines held secret openings leading to the areas beyond. But to verify his guess, he would need to cast a rune of revealing, and there was too much risk during the daylit hours.

That night, he and Mara solidified their plans for reaching the inner sanctum—and the relic holding the Void.

"We'll go in before dark, while the temple doors are still open," Bran said. "Then we can find an out-of-the-way spot to wait, and I'll cast invisibility over us. Once they close the temple, we'll find our way to the inner sanctum."

"I think the priests keep count of who enters and leaves," Mara said. "They'd search the temple if we didn't come back out, and maybe even send in the city guards."

"Then I'll have to hold the rune of invisibility while we go into the temple." As he'd told her earlier, such a thing was not beyond his powers. Though it also wasn't easy.

She frowned, as if reading his thoughts. "We have no idea what lies beyond the main area of the temple, though. We should try to conserve our magic as much as necessary. What if..."

She trailed off, frowning in thought. He didn't interrupt her. Already her ability to imagine different ways of using magic had allowed them to create a new spell. Who knew what else his clever wife would think of?

"Could you create the illusion of us leaving the temple?" she finally asked. "It might be simpler that way, instead of trying to sneak in unseen. We could find a hiding place and then mislead the priests into thinking we left. Is that possible?"

"Indeed." He smiled at her. "That should work very well." Invisibility worked best in stillness and shadow—two things the hushed and dim temple had in abundance.

The final battle approached, and his pulse notched up in anticipation. Another day, perhaps two...

"I'll inquire at the harbor first thing in the morning," he said. "With luck, there will be a ship departing shortly for Raine."

Indeed, as the fierce fire of the sun broke above the horizon the next day, Bran was already at the docks. After asking over a dozen captains, he finally found passage on a merchant vessel, the *Pridewell*, bound across the Strait to Raine. It was a smaller ship than he would've liked, but it was the soonest departure available from Parnese. Under the circumstances, it would do.

Especially considering the worrisome whispers at the docks that the Athraig were planning to invade Raine. Fear for Anneth itched constantly at the back of his mind, despite Ondo's reassurance that she was safe at the Gearys', and recovering her power. That worry was small, however, compared to the problem of infiltrating the temple and locating the Void shard.

Not to mention the question of his future with Mara.

Even though she'd agreed to see the Oracles, that was no guarantee she'd remain in Elfhame. Whatever her choice, though, he vowed to track down whoever was plotting to kill his wife, and ensure they called off their assassins. And then faced the consequences of his wrath.

Finally, he could not escape the looming fear for his father and what would become of Hawthorne once Lady Tinnueth took the reins of power.

The weight of so many burdens was nearly unbearable.

But he was Prince Brannonilon Luthinor, and he had won against impossible odds before.

As he strode from the harbor, he forced his pain and worry aside and narrowed his concentration to the task at hand. His intention and power must be focused on finding and destroying the Void, and nothing more. The future would bring what it may.

Mara glanced up as he stepped into their small rooms at the inn. She stood at the table, their traveling packs before her, which she was filling with essential supplies—food, a change of clothing, and the last of their coin.

He had paid for their passage already. If fate and fortune were with them, he'd have no more need of enchanting stones to silver before they left the mortal world behind.

"Any luck?" Mara asked.

He came and dropped a kiss on her herb-scented hair. "We sail first thing tomorrow, with the dawn tide."

She inhaled sharply. "So, tonight we invade the temple."

"Yes. This evening, we'll go in before they close the doors for the night. Soon after, I'll create the illusion of the two of us departing."

"While we hide in the shadows." She glanced down at her dark trousers and tunic. "Just in case it was tonight, I've dressed for the occasion."

"My clever wife." He wanted to pull her tightly against him and never let her go. Instead he drew in a deep breath and gripped the pommel of his sword.

Either by might or by magic, they would find their way to the inner sanctum of the Twin Gods' temple and do whatever was necessary to destroy the Void. This time, they would not fail.

CHAPTER 19

The moment Anneth lay down atop the bed for her post-lunch nap, weariness washed the bright pulse of her excitement away. It seemed like no time at all had passed before Lily was there, gently shaking her shoulder.

"Wake up," Lily said, grinning. "It's time to put on our gowns and do our hair."

Anneth sat up, trying to shake the grogginess from her head. Tentatively, she reached for her wellspring. It stirred sluggishly in response, and she was glad to feel the first trickles of magical energy seeping through her. Another day more and it was quite likely she'd be back to, if not full power, enough to cast the rune of illusion without Ondo's help.

"I'll bring you up some tea," Lily said. "That will help. And then we can go through Mother's jewelry box."

She skipped off, and Anneth resisted the urge to lie back down. *The ball,* she reminded herself. *Castle Raine, up close. Dancing with mortals.*

This last thought was enough to pull her upright with a jolt of mild anxiety. Then Lily returned, a cup of tea in one hand and a carved wooden box under her arm. She perched on her neatly made bed and patted the quilt.

"Sit," she said. "You can put your tea on the windowsill and lean against the pillow until you're awake."

"I'm awake now," Anneth replied, but she tucked herself at the head of the bed anyway.

Lily placed the small chest between them and opened the lid. "Let's see what we can use."

The chest held a tray of rings on top, which Lily set aside. Beneath it gleamed a handful of necklaces, some plain silver chains, others bearing simple gems. A prismatic glint caught Anneth's eye, and she reached forward, setting a finger on the gemstone.

"This is from Elfhame," she said, a sudden pang going through her.

Much as she was enjoying the human world, so much strangeness was taxing, and for a moment she wished she were back in her rooms in the Hawthorne Palace, surrounded by everything known.

"Yes." Lily plucked the gem out and held it up. "Mara left us with seven jewels, after she came back and then went away again. We all got one, and this must be the extra. Pansy had hers set into a wedding ring."

"What did the others do with theirs?"

Lily shrugged. "Father used his to expand the brewery, and Mother turned hers into coin to save and spend. With Sean and Seanna, who knows? I'm keeping mine as part of my dowry."

"I should have brought you more," Anneth said. How selfish she'd been, not thinking of what she might bring into the mortal world that might be of value.

"We don't need more." Lily smiled at her. "My family's practically rich these days, especially now that I'm the only one still at home."

All the same, Anneth resolved that the next time she came, she'd bring them a satchel stuffed full of jewels.

If there *was* a next time.

"I think there's a necklace in here that would suit you." Lily tucked the shining gem back into the box, then stirred the jewelry with one finger. "Here it is."

She pulled out a silver chain bearing a pendant made of some cloudy green stone. The teardrop shape was simple, yet elegant.

"What about you?" Anneth asked, accepting the necklace.

"This one." Lily produced a thick braid of gold. "It should match the embroidery on my dress, and if it doesn't, I'll wear the rosebud cameo."

Anneth nodded, though she didn't know what a cameo was. At least she knew a rose was a type of mortal flower, the same shade as the gown Lily planned to wear.

"Dresses now," Lily said, a trill in her voice. "Mother said she's just finishing up the hem of yours. And then, our hair."

Mrs. Geary appeared with the green gown, and soon Anneth and Lily were laced into their finery. Anneth glanced down at her skirt, which did not pouf out nearly as widely as Lily's. Of course, Lily had pulled on four petticoats beneath it.

"That's one too many," her mother said, with a pointed look. "I can see the ruffle peeking out from underneath."

"I hear that's the fashion in Meriton," Lily said.

Mrs. Geary's brow rose. "It's not the fashion in Little Hazel, however. I won't have my daughter appearing improperly dressed at the ball."

Lily blew out a sigh that lifted the hair over her eyes, but stripped the fourth petticoat off.

The necklace choices proved to go well with their gowns, though Anneth was a trifle disappointed she wouldn't get to see what a cameo was. She should have asked when she had the chance.

"Sit, Lil, and I'll do up your hair," Mrs. Geary said, indicating the low stool tucked in the corner. "And I'll let you borrow my gold earbobs."

"Thank you, mother!" Lily's frown smoothed away, and she gave her mother an embrace, though she had to lean awkwardly over her full skirts to do so.

"Would you like earrings, as well?" Mrs. Geary asked Anneth, as Lily dragged the stool into the center of the bedroom.

"I don't think so," Anneth said. The dress made her uncomfortable enough without having to worry about strange jewelry hanging off her ears.

Lily picked up her skirts and dropped them over the stool, then sat, surrounded by a circle of pink.

"I can't reach very well," Mrs. Geary said dryly.

"I don't want to crinkle the gown," Lily said. "Especially not on my behind. Think of how that will look."

"I highly doubt that everyone is going to walk to the castle simply to preserve the lay of their skirts," her mother replied.

"Where are all the guests staying?" Anneth asked.

"Some are at the inn at Little Hazel," Mrs. Geary said. "Some in the tents raised to house guests, outside the castle. And the highborn in the castle itself, of course."

With expert fingers, Mrs. Geary wove together strands of Lily's hair then wrapped the braid around her head and fixed it in place with hairpins. At least the pins were recognizable to Anneth, and she was relieved that not everything between the worlds was strange and different.

"Your turn," Mrs. Geary said, beckoning Anneth to take Lily's place on the stool. "I plan to keep some of your braids in, but soften the effect around your face, if you agree."

"Certainly. I want to blend in."

"You're a bit too tall for that," Lily said with a laugh. "And honestly, there's something mysterious about your features."

"Yes, and we want to emphasize that," Mrs. Geary said, gently tugging at Anneth's hair as she unplaited and rewove the strands. "Without, of course, being too outlandish."

"I'll bring the flowers up," Lily said, glancing at herself in the oval-shaped mirror hung beside the door. "I can weave in a lovely crown, don't you think?"

She didn't wait for an answer, and soon was back, setting the bucket down on the floor beneath the mirror. It sloshed quietly, and the flowers nodded, as if agreeing with Lily's previous question.

"Fetch a towel," Mrs. Geary said. "We don't need water dripping all over the floorboards."

"I brought one." Lily waved the red-striped cloth at her mother.

Then, humming under her breath, she plucked a few blooms from the bouquet. She wiped the moisture from their stems and held them up over her ear, turning her head back and forth to study the effect.

"Cornflowers, or sweet pea?" she asked. "Or both?"

"I like how the blue and pink look together," Anneth said. "Add a bit of green or white for contrast, perhaps."

"Oh, I like that." Lily continued picking through the bucket, wiping up the occasional drip from the floor.

"Shake your head gently," Mrs. Geary told Anneth. "I want to make sure the loops are secure."

Anneth obeyed. It was an odd sensation, to feel her hair moving back and forth when she was accustomed to plaits woven tightly against her scalp.

"Good." Mrs. Geary squeezed Anneth's shoulders to signal she was done. "Lily, move back so Anneth can see herself in the mirror."

Lily turned, her eyes widening in approval as she studied Anneth's hair.

"That's lovely," she said. "The same, except different."

Curious to see what her hostess had wrought, Anneth stepped up to the mirror. It took a moment for her to recognize herself in the soft-faced woman looking back at her. Part of the effect was the braids, she realized. Instead of being pulled back severely from her temples, loose loops of dark hair framed her features.

"It's lovely," she said. "Thank you."

"Now for flowers." Lily poked a long-stemmed daisy through one of the braids.

It bent, tickling Anneth's nose, and they both laughed.

"Perhaps something smaller," Anneth said.

Lily nodded and sorted through the flowers, choosing a few sprays of starry yellow blossoms and a handful of ferns. She began weaving them through Anneth's hair. Watching in the mirror, Anneth thought the effect was surprisingly elegant. In Elfhame, they sometimes wore flowers in their hair as well, although she was more accustomed to jewels.

Mrs. Geary put her palm in the small of her back and stretched. "Don't take too long. The emissary did caution you to arrive early."

Lily glanced out the window at the wash of afternoon sunlight, then bounced up and down on her toes. "I'm done—unless you want more blooms in your hair, Anneth?"

"Then I'd resemble a garden." Anneth smiled at her. "No—this is perfect as it is."

"You'll need your cloaks," Mrs. Geary said, then glanced at Anneth's feet. “Oh dear—I didn’t think about shoes. I don’t suppose you brought dancing slippers with you from Elfhame?”

“Only my boots.” Anneth felt a pang for her lost magic. With it, she could have enchanted her shoes to resemble anything—slippers made of satin, or silver, or even crystal.

“I think there’s an old pair of Pansy’s,” Lily said, going to the closet. “The ones she decorated herself, for the Spring Fair that one year.”

“Those?” Mrs. Geary sounded doubtful. “Didn’t the fabric stretch out?”

“Yes, which is why she didn’t take them to Meriton.”

Lily began rummaging through the closet. She had to lean over very far, as her wide skirts wouldn’t fit through the door. After a few moments she emerged, face flushed with exertion.

“Here they are!” She triumphantly held up a pair of the most highly decorated footwear Anneth had ever seen.

They were made of white velvet, but the fabric was almost entirely obscured by hundreds of shimmering glass beads sewn into complicated patterns. Moons and stars of bright silver swirled above a shining jet-black background, with ice-white beads interspersed between. The slippers caught the light, casting tiny prisms across the wall.

Mrs. Geary smiled at the sight. “Remember how many hours she spent sewing on each bead?”

“Ages.” Lily made an exasperated face. “And just when it seemed she was done, she’d decide to add something else. Look at the miniature forget-me-nots embroidered on the inside soles.”

She thrust the slippers out for Anneth’s inspection. They were heavier than they looked, and Anneth carefully lifted one, to see a slightly worn pattern of blue flowers adorning the interior.

“Your sister danced in these?” she asked.

“Until they fell right off her feet.” Lily laughed. “All that beadwork was too heavy. But try them on, see if they fit!”

“Are you certain?” Even if Pansy had used them, Anneth wasn’t certain she’d be able to dance in the slippers. The weight was not as much of a concern as the thought of ruining them.

Mrs. Geary must have seen the doubt on her face, for she nodded. “If Pansy had wanted them, she would’ve taken them to Meriton. They’re made to be worn to a ball, Anneth, and this will be the grandest one of the decade, at least. Please, give them a try."

Anneth resumed her seat on the stool. She couldn't refuse her hostess, despite her misgivings. Gently, she pulled one of the slippers on.

It fit well enough, surprisingly. Perhaps the tiniest bit too big, but not enough to present a problem. She moved her ankle back and forth to see if the slipper was easily dislodged, but it stayed in place.

"You look grand," Lily said. "Do the other one."

It fit equally well, and Anneth stood. "I suppose we should attempt the waltz," she said to Lily. "I'll try not to fall on you if the slippers come off."

"I'll catch you," Lily said, with a grin.

Anneth would probably crush Lily if she tried, but she bit her tongue on her doubts and held her arms up in waltz position. Lily grabbed her hand and began guiding her about the small space, counting under her breath.

To Anneth's surprise, the slippers were not as hazardous as she'd feared. And, since she couldn't enchant her boots to appear delicate and graceful, they were her only option.

"They'll do." Mrs. Geary nodded, watching Anneth's feet. "If you like, we can sew some ribbons on to tie about your ankles and keep the slippers more secure."

"Is that commonly done?"

"Only for little girls," Lily said.

"Then I will endeavor to keep them on my feet without help from ribbons." And perhaps enough of Anneth's magic had returned that she could cast a tiny spell of binding to help.

"Well then." Mrs. Geary looked them both up and down and pursed her lips in satisfaction. "Fasten on your necklaces, and then I believe you two lovely ladies are ready to depart. The ball awaits!"

In what felt like a heartbeat, she'd ushered them out the door and into the waiting donkey cart.

As Lily expertly guided the cart down the lane, Anneth twisted around on the small bench to watch the Gearys' house recede. A strange pang went through her, as though she might not ever see it again. But that was foolish—they would be returning in a few hours.

"I wonder what Seanna's going to wear," Lily said, then launched into a catalogue of all the dresses she'd ever seen her sister in—which were, admittedly, not many.

A response didn't seem required, so Anneth made appropriate noises as Lily went on to speculate about the rest of the village, and then moved on to the prince.

"I suppose he'll be the best dressed," Lily said. "Probably with a crown."

She turned to Anneth, and the donkey continued to plod obediently past the low stone walls and white-walled cottages of Little Hazel.

"Do you wear a crown?" Lily asked.

"Only on the most formal occasions," Anneth answered.

"Like what?"

"Most recently, the arrival of Prince Deldarinnon." It seemed like forever ago.

"Your suitor." Lily nodded sagely. "I suppose it will feel strange to you, meeting our prince without him knowing that you're actually a princess."

"At present, I'm enjoying being a simple mortal girl," Anneth said. "Sometimes the crown is heavier than it looks."

Ahead, a line of horses, carts, and larger conveyances snaked toward the castle. Anneth raised her brows at Lily. They must mind their words from here on, until they were safely back at the Gearys' cottage.

Lily gave her a nod of understanding as they joined the slow procession winding through the edge of the woods. The road met up with a wider way and their progress slowed even further.

It was an excellent opportunity to inspect the other guests, not all of whom were young women and their families. Anneth guessed that anyone who was able to had made the journey. Mostly, though, she was interested in observing the girls who were obviously there as prospective brides for the prince.

A few of them glittered with jewels, their skirts made of brocade and satin, while others wore plain woolen dresses and, like Anneth and Lily, had flowers in their hair.

Other than her slippers, Anneth thought she and Lily were about in the middle: not finely dressed nobility, but not the poorest of the lot, either. It felt like a safe place to be, despite Lily's envious looks at the grandly gowned young ladies.

While Lily concentrated on steering the donkey cart, Anneth closed her eyes and reached for her wellspring. A surge of warmth greeted her, and she let out a silent breath of thanks. She was not yet at full power, but there was enough magic pooled within her to cast the small magic that would keep her borrowed slippers on her feet.

Under pretense of bending to adjust her skirts, she laid her hands upon her footwear and whispered a rune of attachment. Faint silver light glowed about her feet, then faded. Excellent—she would not be in danger of injuring herself while dancing. Or breaking her neck while walking up the stairs, for that matter.

"We'll be able to see the castle when we clear these trees," Lily said, oblivious to Anneth's rune casting.

Even as she spoke, the cart passed out of the trees, and Castle Raine was revealed.

Heavy stone walls enclosed the castle, and behind the walls rose four towers, with crenellated walls between, all made of the same hard gray rock. Anneth stared at the castle, a bit taken aback. It looked like a fortress or prison, with no resemblance to the airy, graceful palaces of the elven courts.

The road led beneath an iron-spiked portcullis in the wall. For a moment, alarm gripped her, and she stiffened with the knowledge that she was entering enemy territory in disguise.

Humans are not my enemy, she reminded herself, forcing a breath past her tight lungs. If anything, most Dark Elves thought mortals were weak and inept, more to be laughed at than feared.

Besides, her power was returning. She was in no danger.

Slowly, the line moved forward. She tried not to shiver as they passed under the portcullis and into a large enclosed courtyard.

A liveried groom stepped up to take the donkey's reins.

"Good day," he said. "When you're ready to leave, ask for Timmy, in the east pasture. I'll bring the donkey and cart back here to you.

Lily nodded and handed over the reins. "Thank you."

She and Anneth gathered their cloaks and disembarked at the base of a wide staircase leading up to tall double doors. The doors were open, manned by relaxed-looking guards, and beyond them Anneth could see the beams of the high vaulted ceiling.

"Invited young ladies to the right," a uniformed fellow called, gesturing. "Everyone else, to the left."

"Another line," Lily said, an exasperated edge to her voice as they joined the back of the queue. "I hope we won't spend the rest of the evening inching along here and there."

"It must be better inside," Anneth said. "The castle seems quite large."

"Larger than—" Lily caught herself, but Anneth knew what she'd meant to ask.

"I look forward to seeing it," she said, which wasn't an answer.

Truly, Anneth wasn't sure how to judge the space. As they moved up the steps, she caught glimpses of what looked to be a very large hall. It was dim, lit by scattered high windows and branches of candlesticks, both mounted along the walls and suspended overhead.

The smell of perfume and savory foods wafted out the doors, along with the sound of music, played on unfamiliar instruments. Excitement tingled up Anneth's spine, replacing her earlier apprehension.

She was here, at Castle Raine. She was going to a mortal ball. For a moment it seemed completely unreal.

They reached the top of the stairs, where the royal emissary sat at a table, a roll of parchment spread out before him.

"Names?" he asked as they stepped up.

"Lily and... Mara Geary," Lily said, fidgeting with the edge of her cloak.

The emissary didn't seem to notice her nervousness, or perhaps he ascribed it to the fact that she was attending the prince's ball.

"Good," he said, dipping what looked like a feather into a jar of black ink and using it to make a note beside where their names were inscribed. "Wait a moment for your numbers."

He turned to another, smaller page, with numbers running down the side and a name written beside each. The names ended a little more than halfway down, and Anneth observed there were forty-five spaces in all.

"Twenty-six, for you." He pointed his feather at Anneth. "And twenty-seven for your sister. Don't forget."

"Thank you," Anneth said, but he was already turning his attention to the next girl in line.

"We're here!" Lily said, all her line-induced aggravation gone as they faced the doorway. "The prince's ball. Isn't it grand?"

"Indeed." Anneth held out her arm. "Shall we, milady?"

With a giggle, Lily slipped her elbow through Anneth's, and together they stepped into the imposing great hall of Castle Raine.

Prince Owen tried not to fidget as his valet Antoine buzzed about him, tugging his coat sleeves down and fussing with the white neckcloth tied at his throat.

"Are you certain you will not wear the lace-edged one?" Antoine asked, a note of entreaty in his voice.

"No, Antoine." Owen held up his hand. "And don't ask me again about the circlet, or the cologne."

"But you are the crown prince! You must make an impression upon all the lovely young ladies who have gathered here to meet you."

"I thought it was the other way around," Owen said dryly. "Aren't *they* supposed to impress me?"

Not that he was counting on any such thing happening.

"Your highness—"

Antoine's plea was cut short by the arrival of King Philip, accompanied by Captain Crane.

"Excuse the interruption," the king said, nodding to the valet. "I must have a word with my son."

"Of course, your majesty." Antoine bowed and, with one last mournful glance at Owen, left the room.

"What is it?" Owen asked softly. The look on the king's face was grim.

"The Athraig delegation has made faster time than we thought," his father said, leaning heavily on his cane.

"Curse those white-haired bas—" Captain Crane cut himself off at a look of reproach from the king.

Owen's fingers curled into his palms as a cold stab of worry went through him. "They're not arriving tonight, are they?"

"Thankfully, no," his father said. "We have at least another day until we must play host to our enemies."

"Barely enough time," the captain muttered.

"At any rate, I came to wish you well tonight," the king said, giving Owen a quick look up and down. "You look well. Handsome—your mother would be proud. Don't forget your circlet."

Owen swallowed past the lump in his throat. "Thank you, Father."

He could not argue, and Antoine would be pleased. Thank all the trees in the forest, however, that the king hadn't insisted Owen wear the cream-and-red uniform of the navy. No matter the occasion, gold braid and tassels felt frivolous.

As did the thought of selecting a prospective bride.

Not frivolous, precisely, but with the shadow of grief still clinging to him, it was difficult to imagine some kind of future happiness with a girl he'd never even met. But surely there would be some agreeable young ladies in attendance at the ball.

He hoped.

The king gave him a quick embrace, and then he and Captain Crane took their leave. Antoine returned, delighted that the prince had shown some sense, at last. He fetched the thin silver circlet and placed it atop Owen's head, rotating it until it settled firmly over his thick, dark hair.

"Now you are ready," the valet said with a nod of satisfaction. "Although perhaps there is a smudge on your boot..."

He grabbed the polishing cloth, but Owen waved him away. "Five minutes of wear and you know the boots will have a mark or two. Do you really plan to follow me about all evening, tucking my hair back into place and swiping at my footwear?"

Antoine frowned. "Someone must be willing to make the effort, your highness."

"I am aware of what's at stake." Owen drew his shoulders back and summoned his most haughty expression, which he fixed upon his valet.

"Yes, yes, that is more like it." Antoine pursed his lips. "You will be irresistible. Now go, watch your guests arriving!"

Privately, Owen thought he looked far too full of himself. The moment he stepped outside his rooms, he let the expression drop. However, Antoine's thought that he observe the arrivals was a good one.

Quickly, Owen made his way to the musician's balcony situated on one side of the great hall. The players turned to look at him as he stepped in, but he waved at them to continue their tuning up.

Seeing the lutes gave him a pang. His mother had insisted on lessons, saying that part of a royal education included learning to play an instrument. After several years of study, he was a passable lute player, but nothing special—not like the court musicians, who could make magic with the flick of their fingers.

He stationed himself near the front of the balcony, near the wall, where he could look down on the arrivals without being too obvious. Already the hall was filling with attendees. He scanned them, noting with relief that the floor didn't seem awash in a sea of young ladies waiting to drown him.

Families, older couples, nobles, merchants, and farmers milled about. Some perused the refreshment tables; others clustered in knots of conversation. Owen saw several young women who were no doubt there by royal invite, but none of them stood out particularly.

Still, the afternoon was young, and the ball wasn't due to officially begin for another half-hour yet. A steady trickle of guests flowed in, briefly silhouetted against the summer's afternoon as they entered.

One tall, graceful figure caught his eye: a woman, judging by the outline of her skirts and long hair. He waited, watching her as she moved further into the hall, to see what the filtered light might reveal.

Her black hair was wound with a delicate array of flowers, and her green dress was of a simple cut and fabric. Not nobility, then. He stuffed back his twinge of disappointment.

There was nothing that forbade him from courting a young woman of any social class. His father's parents had been merchants, after all. But he knew from watching his parents how heavy the crown could be, and how it would help, having a partner versed in the ways of the court.

His father had learned, of course—but there had still been times, up until the queen's death, when she'd had to explain something that seemed quite clear to Owen's eyes. Perhaps that was why his father was pushing for a marriage now, so that Owen might take the kingship and remove that burden from King Philip's shoulders.

It was not a comfortable thought. He did not feel ready to steer the kingdom, regardless who might stand by his side.

The young woman he'd been watching bent her head and smiled at something her companion said. Something about the lay of the light across her cheek lent a foreign cast to her features. Owen blinked at the sudden air of mystery about her. Then she moved past the flickering candelabra and the impression faded.

She was simply a Rainish girl, albeit a bit tall.

The musicians finished tuning and conferring amongst themselves, then struck up a lilting jig. Owen stepped back as faces turned toward the balcony. Time to mingle with the crowds upon the floor, whether he wished to or not.

He cast a last glance about the hall, trying to locate the young woman he'd been studying. There, near the middle of the room. Then a fresh batch of guests surged through the doors, and a moment later she was caught up in the swirl of the crowd and was gone.

CHAPTER 20

The sunlight was folding into the reddish hue of late afternoon when Bran and Mara stepped out of the inn together. They had left only empty rooms behind them—nothing to give any clue to their whereabouts or destination.

If all went well, their activities that evening at the Temple of the Twin Gods would go unnoticed, but Bran had long ago learned to plan for the worst. There was every chance the priests would discover them, or the city guard. He'd already planned the most secretive route back down to the harbor, and had paid extra for the ship's captain to keep a dinghy moored beside the far pier. Whatever the hour, he and Mara would be able to reach the *Pridewell*, hopefully unnoticed, and remain under cover until they were well away from Parnese.

They moved through the streets in silence, and reached the Temple of the Twin Gods as the lowering sun struck bronze sparks from the windows of the palace above. Bran led the way to the arched entrance beneath the flame-bearing twin, but, to his dismay, the priest on duty moved to block their entrance.

"Only true believers are allowed to enter this evening," the priest said. "Come back tomorrow if you wish to pray to the Twin Gods."

"But we are devout followers," Mara said, stepping forward and making the gesture she'd shown Bran—two fingers touching the middle of her palm.

The priest's stance relaxed. "You must be new to the gathering. Next time, wear your medallions openly and no one will stop you from entering."

"Our medallions." Mara lifted one hand to her throat, then turned to Bran, her expression urgent. "You did bring them, did you not?"

"No—you said you would." He did his best to sound aggrieved. "I specifically remember you saying you'd make sure we had them."

She set her hands on her hips. "By telling you not to forget! What are we to do now?" Her voice turned pleading and she looked at the priest. "Perhaps you might let us in, this once? I promise we'll wear them next time."

The man shook his head. "I'm sorry, but the rules make no exceptions. Next time, don't forget your medallions. It's that simple."

He waved them away, and slowly Bran and Mara retreated down the stairs.

"The sun's about to set," she said, grasping his sleeve. "Now what?"

"Around the corner." He whisked her into the shelter of the nearest wall. "I'll cast the rune of invisibility, and we must hurry back before they close the doors. Go before me, and I will hold your shoulder."

Expression anxious, she nodded. "Draw on my wellspring, too."

"If necessary." He closed his eyes, summoned his power, and spoke the rune: "*Ucenima*."

Blue light flared, then faded to the fog-like shadow that signaled the spell was cast. He squeezed Mara's shoulder, and she moved forward, steps quick and silent on the broad red stone. In the light of the setting sun, the temple seemed washed in blood.

They were several paces away when the priest guarding the flame entrance stepped back into the dimness of the temple. Slowly, the tall arched door swung closed. Bran heard Mara's quick intake of breath, and he matched his pace to hers as she hurried forward to the archway beneath the sword-bearing Twin God.

That door was already swinging closed. Holding Mara against him, Bran flung them sideways through the narrowing gap. They nearly crashed into the second priest, and Bran wrenched them around in the parody of a dance, barely avoiding the woman.

He and Mara collided with the wall just inside the door, and she gave a soft gasp at the impact.

"What was that?" The priest turned in a circle, peering about the temple.

Her gaze landed on them, and Mara stiffened in Bran's arms. He pulled more power from his wellspring, and the priest's attention slid over them like a coin across a grease-coated table.

"Are you jumping at shadows again, Doria?" her companion asked.

"I thought I heard something." There was an edge to her voice. "You know the importance of the ceremony tonight. We can't be too careful. No one must know the power of the relic except those sworn to the Twin Gods."

"The wardens will ensure there are no infiltrators," the first priest said. "Now, lock your door. I don't want to be late, and you know we must go together."

Scowling, she slid a heavy bar across the door, locking it in place with a key made of the same dark iron. The other priest gave the bar a shake and then, apparently satisfied, the two of them turned and went into the main temple.

Still holding Mara against him, Bran adjusted his vision to the lack of light. He watched as the priests made their way behind the altar and opened the small door Mara had spotted there. It closed behind them with a thud that echoed softly through the large space.

For several heartbeats, he and Mara stood unmoving. Then, carefully, he let the spell of invisibility dissolve. He might need to recast it later, but it would take as much power, or more, to maintain the rune as they moved about the empty temple, and he was mindful of the cost to his wellspring.

Mara stepped away and, eyes wide, nodded to the altar area. Silently, they walked past the rows of empty benches. The cold, watchful stares of the Twin Gods followed them as they approached.

It was simple enough to step over the low railing surrounding the altar, though Bran's senses were alert for any hint of alarm. They passed the huge painting, and he heard Mara let out a relieved breath once they were beyond the Twin Gods' view.

The door was decorated with scarlet and gold filigree, and at first glance there was no obvious handle. He felt about for a moment, recalling that one of the priests had reached to the right before the entryway opened.

There—his questing fingers found a small lever set into the wall. He toggled it, and the door sprang open a bare inch.

Mara was ready, though, and caught the panel, coaxing it wider. The two of them peered inside to see a short hallway illuminated by a red-shaded lamp mounted at shoulder height on the stone wall.

He paced carefully forward, one hand on his sword. There seemed to be no immediate danger, but his nerves sang with the need for caution. They were going deeper into enemy territory now, and the risks mounted with every step.

Satisfied the passageway was safe, he beckoned Mara to join him. She pulled the door closed with the handle mounted on the back side, and the latch clicked back into place. The lever on their side of the doorway was easier to spot. He was glad they weren't trapped there, sealed in the inner recesses of the temple.

The passage led a short distance, ending in another door. From beyond came the sound of chanting, and Bran frowned.

"Invisibility rune?" Mara whispered.

"Not yet. But stay back."

This door had a regular knob—no need to hide it from curious eyes, he supposed. Anyone who came this far into the building presumably knew the secrets of the Temple of the Twin Gods.

Excruciatingly slowly, he turned the handle and cracked the door open, just wide enough to give him the sliver of a view.

A cloying scent filled the air, and the chanting voices were louder, though he still could not make out the words.

More importantly, though, he jerked as the sense of the Void's presence hit him like a physical blow. It was nearby, and his pulse leaped with readiness. This time, he would destroy that darkness once and for all.

Luck was with them; the door opened into a small, cloistered hall providing a reasonable amount of cover. The Twin Gods were fond of their arched hallways, and he was glad of the fact. Nodding at Mara, he opened the door wide enough to slip through, and held it open for her to follow.

She moved into the shadow beneath the nearest arch. He silently closed the door and followed.

From there, they had a view of the room beyond. It was filled with roughly two dozen priests and acolytes garbed in black robes. At the far end of the room stood an altar, a red-robed priest on either side of the raised stone plinth.

It was much smaller than the altar in the main temple, though the painted visages of the Twin Gods looked down upon the gathering with the same pitiless gaze.

Most important of all, however, was the cloth-covered object in the center of the altar. It was roughly the size of his two fists placed together. The air around it shivered with the Void's power, and it was all Bran could do to keep from drawing his sword and leaping forward.

The red-robed figure on the left held up his hands, and the chanting ceased.

"True worshippers of the Twin Gods," he called, "behold the Esfera! A mighty relic handed down from warden to warden since the founding of the temple—and now the repository of the Twin Gods' power."

With a flourish, he pulled away the cloth to reveal the item beneath. It was a sphere of deep red stone set upon an ornate golden stand—and it pulsed with malevolence.

Could the priests not feel the threat? Bran glanced at the man who'd revealed the Esfera, and shivered. These humans were playing with power far beyond their comprehension. A dark force that would destroy their world utterly.

The Void was strong, and growing stronger. He was only surprised it had not yet acted.

"Who will be the first to receive the Esfera's blessing?" the priest asked, sweeping his gaze over the gathered worshippers.

Several of them fell to their knees, and the priest on the other side of the altar pointed to a woman near the front.

"Violetta Ramundi," she said. "In gratitude for your service to the temple, you have been chosen. Rise and approach the altar."

Tears of gratitude streamed down Violetta's cheeks as she stood and went forward. The first priest used the cloth to pick up the Esfera, avoiding touching it with his bare skin, and a prickle of unease went up the back of Bran's neck.

Beside him, he felt Mara tense. She glanced up at him, dismay in her eyes. Whatever was about to occur, it would not bode well for the chosen victim.

And there was nothing they could do to stop it.

He'd promised not to leave a trail of blood and mayhem behind—but his chest burned with the need to act. Clenching his jaw, he forced himself to stillness.

"Set your hands upon the stone," the priest said, holding the Esfera toward the woman. "The Twin Gods will mark you as their own."

Mara shuddered, her throat moving as she swallowed. Bran briefly brushed a hand across her shoulder, silently urging her to be strong.

Before the altar, the woman reached forward and touched the red stone housing the Void.

The lamps lining the walls guttered, flames flickering desperately for air. The woman screamed, a sound equal parts agony and ecstasy. And within the Esfera, the hungry power of the Void grew as it eagerly drained the woman's life force.

"Enough!" The priest pulled the stone away. "Violetta's soul has touched the power of the gods—she must be taken away to recover from encountering the divine."

He nodded at two black-robed priests, who quickly gathered the limp woman up and carried her out of the room—fortunately in the opposite direction from where Bran and Mara stood.

Dark power flickered around the Esfera, and Bran wondered if the humans could see it. By the look of dread on Mara's face, it seemed she could.

"We can't let it take another," she said softly.

He gave a short nod, then drew deep on his wellspring. He must incapacitate the priests. Taking a step forward so he could see the entire room, he lifted one hand.

"*Lornatala!*" he cried, hoping the simple rune of slumber would work.

Thank the moons, the magic leaped in a wave over the crowed. The gathered worshippers all slumped down where they stood, fast asleep.

All except the red-robed priest who still held the Esfera.

He jerked his head toward their hiding place, his fanatical gaze locking with Bran's.

"Infiltrators!" he shouted. "Take them!"

There was no one awake to respond.

"How long will it last?" Mara asked softly.

"With so many, I must keep the power channeled," Bran admitted. "The force of the initial casting was diluted by the number of people affected."

"So when your wellspring runs out, they'll wake up?" She caught his arm. "Draw upon mine."

"Not yet." He gave a sharp nod toward the priest, who was stumbling toward them, the Esfera in his hands. "We must take the Void first."

Bran drew his sword and, ignoring the fear pressing heavily on his chest, stepped forward to meet his ancient enemy.

CHAPTER 21

Anneth let Lily tow her about the large hall of Castle Raine, smiling as her companion exclaimed over the ornate silver candlesticks and the tempting array of food spread out upon the refreshment tables. Her uncomplicated delight was contagious, and Anneth felt the last bits of her apprehension melt away.

She would not be discovered—the illusion spell would hold until well after dark. Meanwhile, here she was, attending a human ball.

Perhaps she ought to write her own study of her time amongst the mortals, so that in the future some other inquisitive Dark Elf could benefit from what she'd learned. It could join the handful of similar scrolls in the Hawthorne Court library. Perhaps she would title it *A Visit to Raine.*

The notion pleased her, and that warm glow, plus Lily's enthusiasm, carried her along for some time before Anneth realized something was wrong. Despite the lilting music drifting down from the balcony on one side of the hall, despite the cheerful babble of conversation, something darker moved through the crowd.

Anneth turned a slow circle, trying to pinpoint the sensation.

"Look over here!" Lily exclaimed. Oblivious to Anneth's preoccupation, she took her arm and pulled her to a table filled with wooden tankards brimming with amber liquid. “It’s my father’s ale—you must try some.”

Lily scooped up two of the tankards and pressed one into Anneth’s hands then watched her with an expectant look.

Anneth obediently lifted the ale to her mouth. It smelled like dusty bread and honey, and tasted the same, with a slight tingle upon her tongue.

“Very good,” she said. “More refreshing than the blackberry wine my—”

She caught herself before saying anything more. Too many listening ears surrounded her.

“Geary’s Ales are renowned throughout Raine,” Lily said with a satisfied nod. “Shall we get some food? Others are filling their plates.”

Anneth wasn’t particularly hungry, but she took her place behind Lily in yet another line. As they moved down the table, she selected a few tidbits—a stuffed mushroom cap, a slice of fruit—but mostly she contemplated the other guests.

Was she simply imagining that slight edge of threat present in the great hall?

Perhaps so. Humans and Dark Elves were different, after all. Still, she would not assume that everything was as it seemed. Her hand went to her waist before she realized she hadn’t brought her dagger. And her bow, of course, was safely secured with Ondo in the forest.

She might not have her weapons, but she did have her wits. And, hopefully, a bit of magic, should anything go awry.

She and Lily found a place at one of the crowded tables and enjoyed their food.

“It’s probably not what you’re used to,” Lily said, brandishing a piece of cheese, “but the cheese is excellent.”

“It’s all quite delicious,” Anneth assured her. “And the castle has to feed so many—clearly the kitchens have done a fine job.”

The musicians in the balcony overhead struck up a fanfare, and those seated at the tables sprang up so they could see what was happening at the end of the hall.

“It’s the king and prince,” Lily said, craning her neck. “Oh, I wish I had your height. What do you see? Don't you think Prince Owen is incredibly handsome?"

Anneth watched the two finely dressed men, the older one using a cane, step onto the dais. The younger man, presumably the prince, held his father's elbow as the king took his seat in the ornate throne dominating the space. Once he was settled, the prince moved to the smaller throne on his father's right.

Mindful of Lily's question, Anneth studied the prince.

He was somberly dressed, with a plain silver circlet placed over his thick brown hair. His green eyes flicked over the crowd, and for a moment he seemed to gaze directly at her. Then his attention moved on, and she took a breath.

"Well?" Lily demanded.

"He is very handsome," she said. Provided one found mortals' strange, round-pupilled eyes and blunt features fascinating instead of outlandish.

Which she did.

"I think he looked at you," Lily said, with a smug note in her voice. "He could tell you're a prin—"

"Have you spotted your sister yet?" Anneth interrupted.

"Oh!" Lily belatedly covered her mouth with her hand, then glanced about. "No, I haven't seen her—she'll probably come late and leave early. But I think the dancing's about to begin. Come to the floor with me. Do you remember how to waltz?"

"I hope so."

As it transpired, though, the first dance was not a waltz. Servants moved the tables back while someone Lily said was the dancing master organized the guests into a series of concentric circles. Anneth took hands with Lily and the older gentleman on her other side, and they stepped back and forth, circled left and right, then wove in and out of the other dancers.

It was quite easy to follow the dancing master's deep-voiced instructions, and by the time the dance finished, everyone was flushed and smiling.

"Clear the space," the dancing master called. "Ladies numbered one through eight, make ready and line up here." He indicated a spot beside the dais.

At the mention of yet another queue, Lily and Anneth shared a quick look. Anneth could see her companion holding back laughter. She felt a similar amusement, along with gratitude that formal events at the Hawthorne Court were never quite so unwieldy.

"After this first group of eligible young women finishes, we will take a break for general dancing," the dancing master continued. "And now, ladies and gentlemen of the land, please welcome His Highness Owen Mallory, Crown Prince of Raine!"

Cheers and applause filled the room as the prince stood. He bowed, acknowledging the crowd. Then, unsmiling, he descended to the dance floor, and Anneth felt a pang of sympathy. Clearly he was not thrilled at the prospect of dancing with dozens of young ladies, but he would do his duty to the kingdom.

She understood royal duty all too well.

The indicated young women clustered beside the dais, and Anneth could feel the nervousness and excitement rising like heat from where they gathered. Two of them wore ornate gowns—one with a gauzy pink overskirt, the other sparkling with purple gems. The remaining girls were dressed more plainly, Anneth was glad to see.

"Do you know any of them?" she asked Lily.

"No. Let's see how their dancing is."

Anneth nodded, and they found a place against the wall where they could watch. Many of the guests did the same, some clearly there to evaluate their competition, others with more genial expressions who were simply enjoying the spectacle.

"I'm glad we're not in the first batch," Anneth said softly, grateful for the opportunity to watch people waltzing.

"But I'm just going to get more and more nervous," Lily said. "I wish I were first."

The music began, and the dancing master beckoned the first young lady to the floor. Judging from the near-panic in her eyes, she didn't share Lily's sentiments.

The prince strode to meet her and bowed over her hand. He murmured something, she replied, and they began to waltz. To Anneth's inexperienced eye, both dancers moved stiffly, but she supposed nerves played a part, even for a prince. After all, he was on display for the entire crowd, and would be all evening—his every look and word and smile weighed and measured. She didn't envy him in the least.

Once the couple had stepped around the circumference of the dance floor twice, Lily shook her head. "Maybe the next one will be a better dancer."

"Perhaps—though how do you know it's not the prince who's the problem?" Anneth asked.

Lily shot her a glance. "Of course he knows how to dance. He's the prince, after all."

"Knowing how to waltz isn't necessarily a talent that royalty is born with." Anneth lifted a brow in reminder.

Lily simply rolled her eyes and went back to watching the dancers. After three times around the floor, the music slowed. Prince Owen spun his partner in a gentle circle, then bowed and stepped back.

"Two!" the dancing master called.

With a brilliant smile, the gauzy-skirted young lady stepped forward. She made the prince a graceful curtsey, then flowed into his arms without a trace of awkwardness.

"Lady Fiona Waterford," a woman standing near Anneth said. "She has the best chance of all of them, I'd say."

"Wager on it?" asked her companion, a stout fellow wearing a bright yellow coat.

"Certainly." The woman grinned at him. "I'll gladly be taking all your ale money for a fortnight."

The prince and Lady Fiona began to dance, and Lily elbowed Anneth lightly in the ribs.

"See? I told you he knows how to dance."

"Apparently so," Anneth said.

The difference from the last waltz was remarkable. The prince and his new partner swept elegantly about the floor, spinning in wide arcs that made Lady Fiona's skirts flare out. Anneth spared a sympathetic glance for the first young lady, who was looking down at her feet with an expression that suggested she wished the ground would open and swallow her up.

Poor girl. Anneth knew that when her own turn to dance with Prince Owen came, her skills would far more closely resemble his first partner than his second. Still, she studied how Lady Fiona moved her feet, and tried to imagine herself in the lady's place.

The couple even appeared to be conversing. Lady Fiona let out a laugh, seeming oblivious to the watching crowd.

"Aye, you've the right of it," the yellow-coated man said sourly to his friend. "I shouldn't have made that bet."

"Well, the evening's just begun," the woman said. "I might yet be proven wrong. Though I doubt it."

The prince twirled Lady Fiona about as the music came to a close. He bowed, and she smiled at him, and Anneth rather agreed that the yellow-coated fellow was going to lose his wager.

"Three!" called the dancing master, and the next girl stepped forward.

She was not as stiff as the first girl, but not nearly as confident as Lady Fiona. The watching crowd ebbed as people went to refill their tankards and plates.

"We should sit," Lily said. "I don't want my feet too tired from standing about when it comes time to dance. At this rate, it will be hours yet."

Probably not hours, Anneth thought, but their assigned numbers seemed rather distant. Especially if the dancing master was going to lead the crowd in social dances between the groups of young ladies. In truth, what she most desired was to find a quiet corner where she might practice the footwork she'd just seen Lady Fiona perform.

"Go sit," Anneth said to Lily. "I'll find you when the general dancing starts—I just want to refresh myself on the waltz."

Lily glanced about the crowded hall, brows raised. "Good luck. Oh, there's Seanna! Come have a tankard with us when you're done."

Anneth nodded, though she intended to forgo the drink. It was always best to keep a clear head—especially with the strange undercurrent she'd sensed in the room. Meanwhile, she had the more pressing problem of finding someplace to practice her dancing unobserved.

She'd grown up in a palace, however, and knew all the tucked-away doors and hidden hallways of Hawthorne. Surely Castle Raine could not be all that different. Chin high, she set out to find a place to waltz in private.

Eight young ladies down, Owen thought as he bowed farewell to his latest dancing partner, a shy girl with brown hair who had not said more than two words the entire dance. *How many more to go?* At this rate, the evening would drag on for a hundred years.

"Thank you, Miss Iona," he said, keeping a pleasant expression on his face.

She blushed, as though his remembering her name was a mark of particular favor. "It was... The pleasure was mine, sir... your highness."

He nodded, then strode back to the dais. It was common courtesy to recall his dancing partners' names—at least until their brief waltz was over. The only one who'd made any impression at all so far, however, had been Lady Fiona.

They were acquainted, of course, which made it easier. Her mother held lands to the southwest, near the coast, and their wealth primarily came from the raising of sheep. Lady Fiona was a pleasant girl, well spoken, and understood the responsibilities of nobility.

He could do worse, he supposed.

Trying not to frown—a prince shouldn't frown at his own ball—he settled on the throne beside his father's. On the floor below, the dancing master was organizing the crowd into long lines in preparation for a reel.

"You could join them," the king suggested, leaning toward Owen. "I know you enjoy the faster dances."

"Perhaps later. How many girls are there, again?"

"Upwards of forty."

"Six groups." Owen let out a silent sigh. He greatly feared they would all blur together by the end of the night. Perhaps he should simply settle on Lady Fiona and be done.

But that would dash the hopes of all the other young women in attendance, and he knew better than to do such a thing. No matter what his private decision might be.

He brought his hand to his face, massaging the slight ache at his temples.

"Have you eaten anything?" His father's voice sharpened. "Tonight, of all nights, is no time to forgo dinner. Your mother would say you're too slender."

King Philip's expression grew shadowed, and they were both silent for a few heartbeats. Then Owen stood.

"You're right. I'll go find some nourishment."

Along with a bit of quiet. The great hall echoed with the sounds of music, and voices raised in conversation to compete with it, so that he could scarcely hear his own thoughts.

The king nodded, and Owen slipped behind the thrones to the small door at the back of the hall. The guard there pulled the door open for him, and he gratefully stepped into the cool quiet of the hallway.

It led toward the dining room in one direction, and the library and kingdom's offices in the other. Most times it was busy with servants and courtiers going about their business, but now it was soothingly private. Owen pulled in a deep breath and removed his circlet.

When he returned to the great hall he'd put it back on, but it was a relief to set the crown aside for a moment.

The smell of bread and grilled meat drifted from the direction of the dining hall and kitchens beyond. It wasn't protocol, of course, for him to sneak into the kitchen and beg a meal, but Mrs. Henley, the cook, had spoiled him with treats ever since he was a boy. She wouldn't begrudge him a bite of dinner, no matter how the servants' brows might rise.

As he passed the dining room, movement through the half-open doors caught his eye. He halted, peering into the room. The evening sun cast bars of light through the high windows, but back at the shadowed end, beyond the long dining table, he saw a woman.

Her back was to him, her arms upraised. She seemed to be dancing, all alone. Somehow, she'd managed to sneak into the forbidden areas of the castle. How had the guards not stopped her?

"Excuse me," he said coldly, stepping into the room. "Who are you, and what are you doing here?"

She stopped abruptly and whirled to face him. Owen recognized her by her height and jet-black hair as the tall young lady he'd observed earlier.

"I'm sorry," she said. "I'm La— My name is Anneth. The door was unlocked and I needed a place to practice. I'm afraid I'm not very good at waltzing, and I didn't want to trip the prince during our dance."

He could hear the self-deprecating smile in her voice, and his mood softened—although clearly he'd need to have a word with Captain Crane about his men's watchfulness.

"You're not allowed in here without permission," he said.

"I understand. I'll just go, shall I?"

She gathered up her green skirts in one hand and stepped around the long dining table. The beadwork on her bodice picked up glints of light, flashing emerald as she breathed, and her face was slightly flushed with exertion.

As she made to pass him by, he held out a hand.

"Wait." He couldn't simply let her leave to wander about the castle unescorted, and yet he wasn't ready to return to the hubbub of the ball himself.

Besides, something about Anneth piqued his interest. She had an intriguing lilt to her speech and a confident bearing that made him wonder if she were related to nobility.

"It's not easy to practice waltzing by yourself," he said. "Would you like a partner?"

She halted, sending him a startled look. "I would... but aren't you Prince Owen? My apologies that I didn't recognize you right away, your highness."

He waved her words away and held up the silver circlet in his other hand. "You're forgiven, as I'm not wearing my crown, and we haven't yet been formally introduced. I'm Owen Mallory."

"A pleasure to meet you." She dropped into a very elegant curtsey. "Anneth, as I said before."

"Just Anneth?"

"Anneth Geary," she said, then blinked, as if momentarily startled. Whatever thought had flickered behind her eyes, however, was quickly hidden.

"And where are you from, Anneth?" He strode forward and offered his hand.

Slowly, she placed her palm over his, and a strange shock went through him. Their gazes locked, and he realized she was only an inch shorter than he, if that.

"I have family nearby," she said, "but I live on the other side of the Darkwood."

"Are all the girls there so tall?" he asked in jest.

She tilted her head thoughtfully, the yellow flowers shining in her hair. "Many of us, yes."

"I'd like to see your town full of giantesses someday."

Her eyes widened briefly, and he wondered why the idea made her uneasy. He nearly pressed the matter, then thought better of it. No need to frighten her off. He could always quiz her about her upbringing when they met officially on the dance floor.

"Let us attempt the waltz," he said, pulling her gently into dance position and slipping one arm about her waist. "I'll count to three, and then we'll start. Ready?"

Her eyebrows twitched together, but she nodded. This close, he could see her pulse beating in her throat. Her hand was cold in his.

"Begin slowly, if you would," she said. "I've only ever waltzed once."

Only once? Her town must be very small indeed. He frowned, calling to mind the maps of Raine he'd studied and trying to remember the names of the hamlets and villages on the far side of the forest.

"Perhaps not quite this slowly," she said, giving him a crooked smile, and he abruptly recalled that they were supposed to be dancing.

"Forgive my distraction," he said, then counted to three.

They started off a bit haltingly. Anneth bit her lip in a rather endearing way, and snuck several glances down at their feet, but soon she relaxed and the dance began to flow. Owen stopped counting aloud, and they moved together in the sunlit silence of the dining room.

He steered her in a wide loop about the table, mindful of the chairs, and she followed, her steps light. When they reached the space at the head of the table, she met his gaze.

"Perhaps we might try a turn," she said. "I was watching earlier, and think I can manage it."

"If you'd like. It's true that the dance can be rather monotonous, otherwise."

She nodded slightly, and on the next beat of one, he rotated them about in a swooping arc. Her skirt belled out, and she tipped her head back and laughed. The sound made something ease in his chest. In order to hear it again, he pivoted them a second time.

She followed, her movements growing in confidence.

"You're right," she said, grinning at him. "This is much more fun."

Flecks of gold shone in her eyes, and for a moment he was lost in the mystery of her gaze. Who *was* this woman, and why had he never met her until this day?

"Ahem." The sound of someone clearing his throat in the doorway broke the spell. "There you are, your highness."

Owen halted and looked over to see the captain of the guard standing at the threshold. Guilt crept over him at being caught dancing with a stranger in the dining room, but he brushed it aside.

"What is it, Captain Crane?" he asked.

"The next batch of young ladies is assembled and waiting." The captain shot Anneth a suspicious glance.

"Of course." Owen bent over Anneth's hand. "Thank you for the dance, milady. I look forward to our next one."

"As do I," she said.

Snatching up his circlet from where he'd set it on the table, Owen strode to the door. "See our guest to the great hall, if you please," he said to the captain, before stepping into the hallway.

He wasn't certain what had just happened—but he did know that reentering the ball with Anneth on his arm would cause more gossip than he was ready for. What a curious young woman she was, and full of contradictions. She didn't know how to waltz, yet was poised in his presence, not fumbling or tongue-tied like so many girls he met. But not over-polished like Lady Fiona, whom he always felt was holding up a mirror to hide her true thoughts.

Indeed, as Owen hurried down the stone corridor back to the hall, he couldn't deny the warm glow of anticipation at the knowledge that he and Anneth would share another dance that very evening.

CHAPTER 22

Under the stony gaze of the captain of the guard, Anneth moved to the door of the dining room.

"Who are you, and where are you from?" he asked suspiciously, one hand going to the sword at his belt.

"My name is Anneth," she said, doing her best to sound like a mortal girl and not an elven princess. "I'm from the far side of the Darkwood."

It was true, after all. The man grunted, which she took to mean he had no further questions—at least, not yet.

"Back to the hall with you, and no more sneaking about, you hear?" He gave her a hard look. "Follow me closely."

Meekly, Anneth bowed her head and trailed him. The corridor was cool and dim, and she felt her pulse settle as they walked through the shadows. Her escort was silent, which gave her the opportunity to mull over what had just happened.

She'd danced with Prince Owen.

That was rather extraordinary—but even more unexpected was how comfortable she'd felt with him, and how quickly. The waltz, which she'd been apprehensive about, had turned out to be such fun. And the prince himself had a certain quiet reserve that she hadn't expected.

She wasn't quite sure what she *had* expected in a mortal prince. Cocksure arrogance, perhaps, or an inflated sense of himself.

With a wry inward smile, she shook her head. No, Prince Owen did not possess those qualities, but the Cereus Prince certainly did. It was a little disconcerting to realize that the Dark Elf prince did not compare well with his mortal counterpart. Perhaps she, too, was guilty of the same assumptions about mortals that she'd found so objectionable in her own people.

The guardsman led her to a large arched doorway instead of taking her to the small, out-of-the-way door she'd discovered behind a tapestry in the great hall. He pushed it open, meeting the startled young guard on the other side with a frown.

"Kavan," the captain said, "explain to me how you let this intruder slip past your guard."

Wide-eyed, Kavan glanced from his superior to Anneth. "Sir! I never did. I've been at this door all evening. Nobody has come in or out during that time, I swear it."

"Hmph." The captain turned his grim gaze on Anneth.

She gave him an innocent look in return, and no answers.

"Stay out of trouble, young woman," he said. "I'll be watching you."

"Yes, sir." She dropped him a quick curtsey, remembering at the last moment to bob up and down like a village girl and not perform the elegant movements drilled into her at the Hawthorne Court.

Then, clearly dismissed, she edged away. She scanned the crowd for a sight of Lily, but didn't spot her.

The prince, however, was hard to miss. He was dancing with a young lady in a light blue gown. From the set of his mouth, he was not enjoying himself nearly as much as when Anneth had waltzed with him, and that knowledge kindled a warm glow in her chest.

Ah, but she oughtn't to be foolish. There was no point in feeling even a shred of interest for a human prince—their paths were not destined to run together in any way.

Conscious of the guardsman's gaze at her back, Anneth headed to the refreshment tables, now rather depleted. Servants were clearing the emptied platters and sweeping up crumbs, but there still seemed to be plenty of ale.

Anneth scooped up a fresh tankard. Even though she had no intention of drinking more ale, holding it would give her something to do, and hopefully make her seem less suspicious. Quietly, she stepped back into a nearby alcove and set her shoulders against the cool stone wall. There was nothing to do now but keep watching for a glimpse of Lily, and wait until the current batch of ladies finished their dances and her group was finally called.

Furtive movement on the other side of the ale cask drew her attention.

A man in servant's livery drew a vial from his pocket and, back turned to the hall, poured a small measure of its contents into a half-dozen tankards. Holding her breath, Anneth watched him. Surely there could be no innocent intent to such an act.

She reached for her wellspring, feeling the magic stir sluggishly. It was still far too weak to summon any of the greater spells, but perhaps she might cast a small sensing to try to determine precisely what the man had put into the ale.

Closing her eyes for a moment, she focused her power. When she opened them again, the man had already hoisted the tankards onto a tray and was moving into the middle of the hall.

"*Nanhalya.*" She murmured the rune of unveiling, flexing her fingers and staring at the serving man.

Slowly, her magic responded, revealing a sullen red cloud of betrayal about him, and a sickly green glow clinging to the cups. Poison!

And the man was headed directly for the dais where the king sat.

"Stop," she cried, pushing her way through the crowd.

Her use of magic had weakened her, though—her panicked cry went unheard, her body trembling as she forced herself forward. To her horror, the servant bowed, offering the tray to the king. Smiling, the monarch selected a tankard.

"No!" Anneth forced herself into a run.

She cut through the cleared dance floor, glimpsing Prince Owen's surprised expression as she stumbled quickly past. Saving her breath for one final sprint, she flung herself up the dais and crashed into the servant, knocking his tray to the floor, and the drink from the king's hand.

The music stopped, Prince Owen halted, and she heard a collective gasp from the watching guests.

"What on earth?" The king grabbed his cane and stood, his ornate coat dripping. "Guards!"

"It's him." Anneth pointed to the servant, who was already melting into the crowd. "He tried to poison you."

She swayed, and someone slipped a hand under her elbow, steadying her. She gratefully turned to see Prince Owen at her side, his expression grim.

"Explain," he said.

"I saw that man pour poison into the cups," she said.

"Catch him!" the prince called.

The watching guests stirred, glancing about, but it seemed the traitor had already disappeared. It would have been simple enough for him to tear off his servant's tunic, don a neckcloth, and blend with the guests in a matter of moments. Oh, why hadn't she gotten a closer look at the fellow?

Servants hurried to the dais and busily began mopping up the spilled ale. Captain Crane and several of his guardsmen arrived hard on their heels.

Once the captain had determined the king was unharmed, he pulled Anneth roughly away from the prince.

"You," he said. "Come with me."

"Why?" She shivered—not from fear, though he would think so, but from the aftermath of her use of magic. Her wellspring was back down to a bare flicker of power.

"For questioning."

Prince Owen stepped forward. "Surely you don't think she's involved in a plot to murder the king?"

"How did she know it was poison?" Captain Crane shook his head. "Your highness, this woman is very suspicious. You must allow me to do my job."

The prince glanced from the captain to Anneth, expression sober. "Very well—but don't hurt her."

Hurt her? Anneth shot the guard a wide-eyed look. What kind of barbaric place had she come to?

"Of course not," the captain said stiffly. "I'm taking her to the gold parlor, not the dungeon."

Her stab of panic ebbed, though the knowledge that Castle Raine possessed a dungeon did not set her at ease.

"I'm going to change my clothing," the king said, glancing down at his sodden garments. "I'll join you shortly."

"As will I," Prince Owen said, but the king shook his head.

"The ball must continue," he said. "Everyone is unsettled enough without making an undue fuss."

"Undue?" the prince asked, his voice low and urgent. "Father, someone just tried to poison you. We should close the gates immediately and question everyone until the traitor is found."

The captain's grip on Anneth's arm tightened. "We'll have answers soon enough, never fear."

"But I don't know anything," she said.

"Music!" the king called, gesturing to the players in the balcony. As soon as a somewhat ragged melody started up, he looked at his son. "Finish dancing with your current crop of young ladies. We will know more at the break—after Captain Crane questions our guest."

Prince Owen's mouth tightened into a grimace, but he didn't argue with his father. And despite her own precarious position in the chain of events, Anneth had to agree that continuing the ball was the best choice, strictly from a court protocol perspective.

Already the mood was growing less fraught as the prince stepped back down to the floor and bowed to the young lady he'd abandoned mid-waltz. The servants finished their cleanup, and the king, escorted by two guards, exited through the small door tucked behind the dais.

"Come." Captain Crane tugged her arm.

She didn't have much choice in the matter, and there was no point in trying to escape. After all, she was innocent.

Of trying to poison the king, at least. As for her other secrets, the captain of the guard had no way of guessing she was a Dark Elf—and she certainly had no intention of revealing the truth about herself.

CHAPTER 23

Mara watched, stomach clenched with fear, as Bran drew his sword and stalked toward the red-robed priest. The black-cloaked figures lying about the Twin Gods' altar looked more like strewn corpses than sleeping bodies—but if Bran's magic faltered, they would awaken, and she and her husband would be horribly outnumbered.

Through her connection to him, she could feel his wellspring's power seeping away. Her azure ring, linked to his, ached with bone-chilling cold.

She could not fight the priest, who had halted just beyond the reach of Bran's sword, the Void-infused relic in his hands. But perhaps she could shift the rune of slumber to herself, leaving Bran free to fight.

Concentrate! What had the syllables been? Lorn-something...

Cursing her lack of familiarity with the language of the Dark Elves, Mara shaped the word in her mouth. *Lorna...Lornatala.* Surely that was it.

The priest, face set in a grimace, raised the Esfera.

"I call upon your power, Twin Gods," he cried. "Let your divine relic smite these infidels who have dared to violate your temple!"

Dark power pulsed within the stone, gathering to strike. Black tendrils whipped out, aiming for Bran. He ducked, his sword low as he held up his other hand and summoned a shield of blue power. The Void's attack struck sparks, and with each hit, Mara could feel Bran's power dip.

The sleeping worshippers began to stir and moan as the rune of slumber faltered.

"*Lornatala!*" she cried, flinging her arms wide. Like a wave crashing upon the shore, her power surged forward, breaking over everyone in the inner sanctum.

Bran staggered. The priest fell to his knees, losing his grip on the Esfera. And the slumbering bodies went deathly still.

Crack! The stone sphere hit the marble floor. At the point of impact, the floor split into jagged lines. The priest's eyes rolled back in his head and he tumbled forward, one arm outstretched.

The fault lines spread across the marble, fast as fire. One ran under the priest's hand, which glowed and began to sizzle with the sickening smell of burning flesh. He twitched in agony, but did not awaken.

"Stay back," Bran cautioned her, leaping over a snaking crack that seemed determined to catch his feet.

The Esfera sent more seeking tendrils toward the fallen figures. With each one it touched, Mara could feel its inimical power increase.

Bran sent bolt after bolt of blue fire at the stone. Each blast made the sphere shake, but it did not break. Somehow, they had to get it out of the inner sanctum, away from the bodies it was feeding upon.

Still pouring her power into the rune of slumber, Mara stumbled away from the cracks. They followed Bran as he darted back and forth, never able to get close enough to land a blow from his sword.

"Watch out!" she shouted, as three lines etched the floor behind him.

He whirled and barely managed to jump clear, fetching up against the wall. As if sensing he was trapped, the Esfera pulsed with malevolent magic. A web of lines advanced toward him, and Mara cried out in denial and prepared to shift the force of her magic to attack the sphere. It seemed only their combined magic could defeat the Void.

Bran whipped off his cloak.

"*Astagar!*" he yelled, and flung it over the Esfera.

The cracking floor froze, the room shuddering with the force of the contained sphere.

"Run!" Bran called, scooping up the cloak-covered Esfera.

Mara turned and dashed for the hallway leading back into the main temple. Bran followed at her heels, the Esfera pulsing in its fabric prison. Tendrils of acrid smoke rose from the cloak. They raced through the passage and burst through the door into the hushed dimness of the main temple.

For a moment Mara thought they might be able to fight the Void there—but confused shouts echoed from the room they'd just left. The priests and worshippers were waking. While some of them might not regain consciousness, enough would to pose a threat. She and Bran must flee the temple immediately.

They ran past the benches, their footsteps ringing loudly. Halfway to the tall arched doors, and freedom, Mara recalled they were barred and locked.

"Bran," she gasped, "can you unlock the doors?"

He groaned. "It is taking all my power to keep the Esfera trapped."

Behind them, the first red-cloaked pursuer burst into the temple.

"Catch them!" he shouted, and his followers responded, surging forward.

Mara and Bran were almost to the doors. If they didn't open...

She stretched out one hand toward the barred archways.

"*Edro,*" she called, praying the rune of opening would work.

The doors creaked, the bars straining, but they remained closed.

"Halt!" the priest shouted behind them. "Halt or face the Twin Gods' wrath!"

Mara summoned all her desperation, all her horror at what the Void was capable of, all the determination that they would win free, and wound it into a searing ball of azure light.

"*Edro!*" she cried again.

The doors exploded in a blaze of blue fire.

She and Bran plunged through into the Parnesian twilight. There was just enough light remaining at the far edge of the sky that she was not in danger of breaking her neck.

"This way," he said, veering sharply to the right.

She pelted behind him, rounding the sharp corner, then followed him down to the next alley. Then the next, and up a twisty cobbled walkway that was more stairs than street.

Finally, lungs burning for breath, they fetched up against a high wall made of pale stone. Mara glanced at Bran, dismayed to see the strain on his face. In his arms, the cloak-wrapped sphere shuddered, the fabric beginning to smolder.

"I can't hold it much longer," he said, his voice harsh with effort.

Wildly, Mara glanced up and down the street. Rows of shuttered shops, with lamp-lit apartments above. This was not a place they could unleash the Void. She turned, her gaze going to the top of the wall they sheltered beside.

A leafy canopy of trees rose beyond, barely visible against the dark sky. A garden of some sort, if the fates were kind.

"On the other side of the wall," she said. "Stay here—I'll find a way through."

He nodded, face taut.

Though she had scarcely caught her breath, Mara ran up the street bordering the wall. Just when she was about to give up, she spotted a small doorway set into that blank expanse of stone. Quickly, she went back to where Bran could see her and waved at him to come.

This time, she swore she'd use far less power to cast the rune of opening.

When Bran arrived, chest heaving with effort, she'd coaxed the door open without blasting it to pieces. As she'd hoped, a park spread out behind the wall, the short-cut grass extending beneath tall trees.

"Good," he said, stepping through.

She closed the door behind them, wedging it with a nearby stick. Bran lurched forward, and she hurried to catch him by the elbow. The darkness of the Void hummed through him with bone-shaking intensity, and she marveled that he was able to stand, let alone carry that evil burden.

Together, they lurched toward the shelter of a hedge clipped into fanciful shapes: pyramids, squares, circles.

"Here," Bran said once they'd put the foliage between themselves and the door in the wall.

He went to his knees, dropping the cloak-wrapped Esfera to the ground, and drew a long, ragged breath.

She immediately came to stand behind him and placed her hands on his shoulders. Though they were both exhausted, the hardest task of all lay before them.

"I'm ready," she said in a soft voice, reaching for her wellspring.

He brought one hand up to cover hers. Their rings touched, blazing momentarily with blue fire.

"Together, beloved, we are strong," he said. "Hold fast. We must not let it escape again."

As if his words were a signal, the Esfera began to rock back and forth. Flames kindled from Bran's cloak where it covered the sphere, and Mara could feel the dark power of the Void on the verge of breaking free.

She closed her eyes against the faint silhouettes of the trees, against the fear trying to wash over her, and summoned up all her hope, all her love. With each breath, she released power to Bran through their linked hands.

The wildness of his Dark Elf magic met hers, and together their wellsprings mingled, streams of joy and sorrow, laughter and longing. Everything that made them different, everything that bound them together.

A sweet wind blew Mara's hair from her face as their power twined, higher and higher. She could taste the combined light of the double-moons and the sun, smell mingled roses and the glowing *qille* blossoms of Elfhame.

Darkwood.

Erynvorn.

Two worlds, standing together.

The power streamed from them. Mara opened her eyes to see it glowing, a whirlwind of blue magic, of gold, illuminating the garden with eerie light.

The Void screeched, flinging itself at them, then reversing direction to charge against the bonds of their power, desperate to escape. Each attack stung, stealing her breath, burning her skin.

No, she shouted at it with all her might. *You cannot have these worlds.*

Still the joined magic built, until Mara felt as though she were nearly drowning in the intensity of their power.

Bran rose to his feet, his hand still tightly clasped with hers. He pulled in a breath, then, in a deep voice that rang like a bell, spoke a final rune.

"*Lacarina Oiale Morgoth.*"

Begone forever, dark enemy.

The ground beneath their feet shuddered, the wind whipping in a frenzy of light, dark, light.

Bran intoned the words again. The Void responded with a surge of searing pain that made them both scream aloud.

"Together," Mara whispered, her throat raw.

Bran's gaze met hers, and he nodded.

"*Lacarina Oiale Morgoth,*" they cried in unison.

Blue light streaked high into the sky, then turned and plummeted like an arrow. It struck the Esfera with a sound like a thunderclap, found the heart of the Void lodged inside, and unmade it. Utterly.

The night went dark around them. Weakly, Mara leaned against Bran and scrubbed her wet cheek with her palm. She hadn't even realized she'd been weeping—tears of pain, tears of exertion.

A quiet breeze stirred the shrubs about them. Some insect gave a single, tentative chirp.

"Is the Void truly defeated?" she whispered, glancing up at Bran—her beloved husband. Her heart.

He nodded, exhaustion shadowing his eyes. "It is gone. From your world, and mine—forever."

They could have stood there another hour, supporting one another in the dark garden, but slowly Mara became aware of a commotion on the far side of the wall. Shouts and the flickering lights of torches, the shrill whistle of the city guards.

Of course. Even in Parnese, a tower of glowing light and strange, otherworldly winds, not to mention the sound of the Void shard's final destruction, would not go unnoticed.

"We must go," Bran said, scooping up the remains of his cloak. "If there is a gate into this garden, surely we can find another one out."

She nodded. Wearily, they stepped into the shadows beneath the trees.

In the harbor below, the ship waited to take them home.

The red-robed warden sat in the center of the cracked floor in the ruined inner sanctum of the Twin Gods, cradling his maimed hand. Waves of pain ran through him, leaving him sweating and trembling. He would never use that hand again.

The agony he endured meant nothing, though, compared with the knowledge that the Twin Gods had granted him.

Their power was real.

And sorcery was not something imagined, to be found only in fanciful tales. He had seen it with his own eyes, how the tall man had cast bolts of blue flame from his hands. How the woman had swept everyone in the room up in a wave of irresistible slumber.

They had been sent by the Twin Gods to show him the way. Perhaps they had been avatars, to wield such power, and he an unwitting bystander to the struggles of the gods themselves.

He would never know where they had come from, or why, but he knew enough. From now until the moment of his death, he would work to unlock the secrets of sorcery. He would form a clandestine sect within the wardens of the Twin Gods, made up of others who had seen the power, and knew.

It might take years. Centuries.

But one day, the priests of the Twin Gods would possess such magic that the entire world would bow beneath their feet.

CHAPTER 24

As the captain of the guard towed Anneth through Castle Raine's great hall, she glanced about, looking for Lily. Thankfully, there was no sign of her.

The last thing Anneth wanted was to drag the Gearys into trouble. Plus, the fewer different versions of her origins the captain heard, the better, and she didn't trust Lily not to babble if she were questioned.

Anneth's stomach knotted while her mind worked furiously. She was in trouble now, no doubt about it. She only hoped it wouldn't grow worse—but surely, after questioning her, the castle would let her go.

Without a last dance with their prince, however. One didn't allow suspects, no matter how innocent, to consort with the crown prince.

At least he'd argued in her defense, despite knowing almost nothing about her. She was glad that he'd seemed to believe she was blameless—or, at least, he hadn't thought the worst of her. She'd saved the King of Raine, after all, no matter who believed it.

Captain Crane escorted her a short distance down another corridor, then yanked open a door and propelled her into what must be the gold parlor. The room was dim, but a moment later a servant hurried in to light the sconces lining the walls and the lanterns set upon the low tables.

It was far less convenient than simply speaking the rune for light and seeing foxfire spring up to illuminate the room. Anneth supposed it was the best a people without magic could do, and truly, whoever had first discovered the ability to create fire had been very clever indeed.

Who, she wondered absently, had been the first Dark Elf to speak the word for light?

"Sit." The captain thrust her at a chair upholstered in yellow fabric.

Slowly, she sat and folded her hands in her lap. He remained standing, a scowl on his face.

"What's your name, girl?" he demanded. "Your full name."

With a stab of horror, she recalled that she'd told the prince she was a Geary. A misstep indeed, and one that she must rectify. Yet she must keep her lies from tangling together, or matters would only become worse, especially if the captain and prince compared stories.

But no matter what, she must protect Mara's family from falling afoul of the castle.

"Anneth... Cleary." Please, by the brightmoon, let that be a well-used Rainish surname. With luck, the prince he would think he'd misheard.

Her false answer seemed to pass muster, as Captain Crane loomed over her with his next question. "And where, precisely, are you from?"

She'd known he'd ask, and this time he wouldn't accept a vague answer about hailing from the other side of the forest. As he'd led her from the hall, she'd scoured her memory of the scrolls she'd read, trying to dredge up any mention of towns near the northern edge of the Darkwood.

One had come to mind, and she desperately hoped it was still inhabited. Claiming to come from a long-abandoned village would not go over well with the captain, but refusing to say where she was from would be even worse.

"Shallowstrae," she said, burying her fear and meeting his gaze calmly. "As I said, on the far side of the forest."

He scowled. "Convenient, that. Too far for me to send a man and hear back tonight whether you're lying. Make no mistake, though, I'll have a guard on the way shortly. And you'll be enjoying our hospitality in the castle until he returns with an answer on the morrow."

Oh, no. She swallowed. There was no possible way she could spend the night at Castle Raine. She must return to Ondo so he could recast the human illusion over her.

If only she hadn't taxed her magic earlier by summoning the rune of revealing...

But she would not change what she'd done. If not for her actions, the King of Raine would be dead, and quite possibly the prince as well.

"Sir," she said, "have you found the man posing as a servant? I fear there's a plot in motion against the throne of Raine."

"Do you?" He narrowed his eyes at her. "And what would a country girl from Shallowstrae know about such things?"

"I saw the man put poison in the ale," she said, her temper rising. "He was trying to kill the king."

"We have only your word for it. Too bad that the entire tray of ale spilled." His tone implied he didn't believe that had been by accident.

"Squeeze out the servant's rags, then, if you want proof—but you must believe me. Why would I lie?"

The captain crossed his arms. "Because you're an agent of the Athraig, here to disrupt the ball and create confusion."

She had no idea who the Athraig might be, but now was not the time to reveal her ignorance. Frustrated, she put her hands in her lap and laced her fingers together, to keep from squeezing them into fists of annoyance. Any tension she revealed to the captain would only be taken as a sign of her guilt.

"I am not an agent of the Athraig," she said steadily. "I was invited to the ball to dance with the prince."

"Then why were you skulking about earlier in the private areas of the castle? No—I'm afraid we're keeping you under lock and key for the time being."

He glanced up as the king limped in, accompanied by his guards. Anneth looked down at her hands and took a breath, trying to calm herself. For a moment her illusion of humanity wavered, revealing her long, clawed fingers.

She froze, heart clenching in sudden panic. Why was the spell fading? It was too early! She must get away immediately. Her gaze darted about the room, going to the tall windows. They were black with night, showing only the blurred reflections of the parlor lamps.

The captain was telling the king about his suspicions, his attention momentarily diverted. Tensing, Anneth sprang to her feet.

"Look!" she cried, pointing at the open doorway. "The traitor just went past."

The king's guards moved to the door. Quickly, she spun and dashed to the window, knocking over the chairs between her and the captain.

"Stop," he shouted, lunging at her as she scrabbled to open the window.

The catch released and she flung herself through. A leafy bush caught her headlong fall, and she managed to roll free and gain her feet. Gasping, she pointed at the window and whispered the rune of closing. By all the stars, let her have enough dregs of magic left that the spell would work.

The casement slammed shut just as the captain reached it.

She didn't wait to see how long the window held, but took her skirts up in both hands and ran. After two steps she realized that the magic binding her slippers on had faded, too. With every other step, her bare sole met the cold ground. In her rush to escape, she'd left one of the beaded slippers behind.

Too late now.

Blessing her ability to see in the dimness, Anneth pulled off her remaining slipper. Clutching it tightly, she fled toward the sheltering darkness of the trees rising behind the castle. The sound of breaking glass and confused shouts followed her into the night.

Owen endured his next six dances, each one passing in a blur. Finally, after what felt like an eternity, he was free to go see what the captain of the guard had decided to do about Anneth.

She wasn't a traitor; Owen was sure of that. But there was no denying there was something unusual about her. Beyond her unusual name and height, she carried herself like one of the nobility and spoke with the air of someone accustomed to having others listen and obey.

Yet she had come to Castle Raine dressed like a commoner, claiming no title.

He also couldn't overlook the fact that somehow she'd found her way into the deeper confines of the castle without any guardsmen apprehending her. It was all quite suspicious—but unlike Captain Crane, Owen didn't think Anneth was a traitor or a spy.

Although why he thought her innocent of plotting, he couldn't say.

Perhaps it was her touch of naiveté, or the genuine joy in her laughter. Both of which could be feigned by an accomplished saboteur, he knew, but still he could not believe ill of her. Despite their very short acquaintance.

The moment he finished his waltz with the last girl in the current group, he made her a short bow and strode out of the great hall. The corridors of the castle were full of hurrying guards, and Owen's chest tightened with unease. He lengthened his steps, almost running until he reached the gold parlor.

At the threshold, he paused. His heart sank when he saw the captain with a thunderous expression on his face, and the king, looking equally troubled, in urgent conversation in the middle of the room.

There was no sign of Anneth.

"What happened?" Owen asked, stepping into the parlor.

"Your traitor girl escaped." Captain Crane gave him a grim look. "Jumped out the window and ran into the night. We're in pursuit, of course. She can't get far—there's only forest on one side, and we're preparing to conduct a house-to-house search in the village."

Owen pressed his lips together. Voicing his opinion that Anneth was innocent would not be well received at the moment. Especially as the evidence seemed to prove otherwise. Why had she run?

"Did she tell you anything?" the king asked Captain Crane.

"Nothing. She claimed to come from Shallowstrae, across the forest, but I doubt it. I've sent a man to confirm." The captain scowled at Owen. "You danced with her. Did she let anything slip?"

He shook his head. "She told me the same—that she was from the other side of the Darkwood."

A cool breeze blew in from the broken window at the far side of the room. Avoiding the shattered glass on the floor, Owen went to peer out into the night.

"One of my guards went after her," his father said. "They'll catch her soon, I've no doubt."

"And then it's the dungeons," Captain Crane said, a satisfied note in his voice. "We can't have Athraig agents roaming freely about."

A glint of silver caught Owen's eye: the edge of a beaded slipper winking from beneath the wind-tossed curtain. He reached and tugged it free from where it was wedged at the corner of the sill. Surely it belonged to Anneth. He recalled the light catching the ornate beadwork as they danced.

Silently, he tucked the slipper beneath his coat, then turned back to his father and the captain. Neither of them seemed to have noticed.

"I'll have the royal emissary go over the roll of invitees, immediately," the king said. "Anneth is an unusual enough name that it will stand out."

"Provided that's her actual name." The captain frowned. "More likely she's under an alias—or came in that way. But don't fear, your majesty. We'll find the girl and get to the bottom of this Athraig plot."

"Meanwhile," Owen said, "we must stay vigilant. Clearly someone tried to poison you, Father. I doubt that's the work of one person acting alone."

If Anneth was innocent, as he still believed, that meant the true enemy was still at large. And that his father was in grave danger.

CHAPTER 25

Anneth dashed through the underbrush and wove between the rough trunks of cedar and hemlock, her toes digging for purchase into the soft loam underfoot. Slowly, the sounds of pursuit faded, the flickering torchlight growing dimmer behind her.

A shape moved between the trees, and she drew up short, heart pounding with exertion and fear.

"Who's there?" she asked sharply, wishing for her blade and bow.

"It is I, my lady." Ondo stepped from behind the sheltering branches.

"Thank the moons." She sagged in relief. "We must travel deeper into the Darkwood, and leave no trace."

He nodded. "Follow in my steps."

"Why are you here? Not that I'm disappointed to see you."

The scout frowned. "It is my duty to look after you, milady. I could not enter the castle, but I have been following your movements and keeping watch. Just in case anything were to happen."

And happen it had. She let out a deep breath, then fell into line behind Ondo, carefully placing her feet where his had been. They traversed fallen logs and leaped across the bracken, leaving no broken ferns or imprints of their footsteps in the soft loam.

"We must remain hidden until Prince Bran and Mara return," Ondo said.

Anneth was about to agree, before realization hit her. She paused, throat tight.

"I cannot. The castle will be looking for me."

"Exactly." Ondo glanced over his shoulder. "That is why we must go to ground. I don't think the humans will think to search deep into the forest, but we cannot be sure. Come, princess."

"No." She wrapped her arms about herself. "I've put the Gearys in danger. The castle will trace me to them, and I refuse to let them bear the punishment. Whatever it might be."

Despite her subterfuge, she knew the captain would scan the records and speak with the prince. It was only a matter of time before the Gearys were questioned. She didn't trust the grim captain of the guard not to toss the entire family into the dungeon, and then what would become of them and their livelihood? She simply couldn't allow it.

"You are a princess of Elfhame," Ondo said. "Your safety is paramount."

"I can't let Mara's family suffer because of my actions." Even though she *had* saved the king. "I must return and surrender."

"No." Ondo's tone was fierce. "You would endanger all of Elfhame, should you be discovered."

"My magic is nearly restored," she said. "I was even able to summon a few runes today. Another night's rest, and I should be able to hold the illusion." She hoped. "As your princess, I command you to obey."

The scout said nothing for a long while as they moved carefully through the forest. Finally he stopped in a clearing silvered by starlight, and faced her.

"Tomorrow, when the sun rises, I will scry your brother," he said. "If the prince agrees, then I will have to allow it—but I have no liking for this mad scheme."

"I'm not terribly happy about it myself." She was careful not to mention the prospect of the dungeon awaiting her. "But Mara's family cannot be punished for helping me. If anything, it's my fault for wanting to attend the ball."

She should have stayed in the forest with Ondo. Or at least remained in the Gearys' cottage. But no—her curiosity had been her undoing, and now she must pay the price.

"I'll let them detain me in the castle," she continued. "As soon as Bran and Mara return—which shouldn't be long—I'll use my power to escape. We can warn the Gearys to go into hiding before we return to Elfhame."

It was the best solution she could see to her predicament. She hoped her brother would feel the same.

Ondo ceased arguing with her, maintaining a stony silence until they finally reached his simple camp. Anneth sighed at the prospect of a night spent on the hard ground, but at least, since Ondo had the bulk of her belongings with him, she could change out of her much-abused gown and sleep in her own tent.

Even if Bran agreed with her plan to return to Castle Raine, there was no point in charging back until she could cast the illusion spell upon herself.

She had every hope that when the blazing ball of fire ascended the sky on the morrow, she would be able to assume her mortal appearance on her own. Despite her confident words to Ondo, though, she had to admit to a twist of apprehension when she thought of Captain Crane and his talk of the castle dungeons.

I have magic, she reminded herself. It would be enough.

When the first light of the rising sun filtered into her small tent, Anneth awoke. She felt surprisingly rested, under the circumstances. Perhaps the quiet hushing of the cedar boughs in the dark had soothed her, the peace of the night forest seeping into her mind. In any case, when she reached for her wellspring, she was relieved to feel it spark in response.

Rising, she glanced at the much-abused ball gown she'd folded and set aside, then down at the comfortable leggings and tunic she'd donned before bed. She wasn't looking forward to putting the dress back on—but she must return to the castle in the same state she'd left it. Bare feet, muddy gown, and all.

With a sigh, she changed back into the gown and then ducked out of her tent.

Ondo, of course, was already awake. He squatted before the nearly smokeless fire, stirring a pot of porridge. Two mugs of herbal brew sat steeping on the flat rock he used as a table.

"Good morning," Anneth said, pulling her hair back into a twist to keep it out of her way as she joined him at the fire.

The scout gave her an intent look. "How do you fare, princess?"

"Watch." She inhaled, focused her magic, and spoke the rune of illusion.

Her wellspring was a touch slow to respond, but then the power flared, and she felt the spell take hold.

"You are recovered." He didn't sound pleased at the fact.

"I am," she said, scooping up her mug and settling beside him. "Are you ready to contact my brother?"

He frowned, but after a moment took out his small silver scrying bowl and poured a measure of water into it. He settled back on his heels, then shot her a reluctant look.

"I know you'd rather keep me coddled in the forest," she said. "And if Bran agrees with you, then I'll stay."

Though she was nearly certain her brother would concur that she must surrender herself to the castle in order to keep Mara's family safe. It seemed the only honorable choice.

With a barely audible sigh, Ondo spoke the words of scrying. The water at the bottom of the bowl shimmered, then cleared to reveal Bran's face. His reflection moved oddly up and down, and Anneth leaned forward, trying to determine where he was. In a conveyance of some sort?

"Ondo," Bran said. "It is well you called upon me—Mara and I have destroyed the last of the Void, and are even now on our way back to Raine. We'll arrive in a matter of days."

"That's wonderful," Anneth said, though she knew Bran couldn't hear her.

Not only did it mean they could return to Elfhame soon with remedies for Lord Calithilon, it also ensured that her imprisonment in Castle Raine would be short.

"That is good news," the scout said in a somber tone. "But I am unhappy to report that your sister has stirred up trouble."

Bran frowned. "What kind of trouble? Is Mara's family involved? Is Anneth there with you?"

"The princess is here, and safe—unless she embarks on the foolish plan she's concocted."

Anneth poked Ondo with her elbow. "Just tell him what happened."

"Princess Anneth attended a ball at Castle Raine," Ondo continued. "She drew unwanted attention to herself. My advice is that we remain hidden until you arrive."

"No." Anneth caught the scout's arm. "I can't just abandon the Gearys."

"You didn't answer my question," Bran said with a stern look. "If my sister has brought trouble to Mara's family, then you cannot hide from it in the forest. You must protect them from whatever Anneth has wrought."

"See?" Anneth gave Ondo's arm a shake, then let go.

"My prince..." The scout's words trailed into a heavy sigh. "I am reluctant to put your sister in danger."

"I'll be perfectly safe," she said loudly. "My magic will enable me to escape the castle when it's time. Once I turn myself in, they'll stop looking for me—and, more importantly, stop asking awkward questions that will lead to Mara's family."

"Her wellspring hasn't yet fully regenerated," Ondo said to Bran.

"Lies!" Oh, she wanted to take Ondo by the shoulders and rattle his teeth. "I'll scry to Bran myself, then."

She began to rise, but Ondo looked over at her. "Be still, princess. I haven't finished."

Folding her arms, she let out a snort of impatience. "I *will* scry him, and it will be your fault that my wellspring is that much more diminished."

The scout narrowed his eyes in annoyance, then bent over the bowl once more. "Princess Anneth is, however, able to summon the rune of illusion, and other small magics."

"What is this plan of hers that you deem so foolhardy?" Bran asked.

"She believes that, by returning to the castle, she will draw suspicion upon herself and away from Mara's family. She fears they'll be in danger if it's discovered she was sheltering with them."

"What did my sister *do*, to become a hunted fugitive?"

"Apparently she snuck into the private areas of the castle, danced with the mortal prince, foiled a plot to assassinate the king, and then escaped when the castle guard began questioning her."

"All that, in one evening?" Bran sounded both irritated and amazed.

"I'm afraid so. I'm sorry, my prince, for failing so miserably in my duty to protect her."

The reflection swayed, and the scrying was silent a long moment, presumably while Bran consulted with Mara.

When he reappeared, his expression was weary. Surely defeating the Void had taken a great deal of power. He should not be wasting his energy on endless scrying.

"My power is waning," he said, confirming Anneth's impression. "I've spoken with Mara, and we are in agreement. As your prince, I command you to let Anneth set matters straight. Whatever the danger, she can defend herself better than the Gearys. In my time among the mortals, I have learned that they only see what they want to."

"Tell Bran they already think me a foreign spy," Anneth said. "I'll pretend to admit to being an agent of... the Athraig, I think it was. That will keep suspicion focused squarely on me, and away from Mara's family."

Ondo gave her an unhappy look. "What if they attempt to extract further information from you, by... indelicate means?"

She laid a hand on his shoulder. "Then I'll leave the castle immediately and join you in the forest until Bran and Mara arrive. It won't be long. Besides, I can always scry to you for help. Together, we are more than a match for a few guardsmen."

Now that her magic was returning, she would be able to slip out of the castle undetected whenever the moment came. And her power *was* coming back. Even now, she could feel the quiet ripples of her wellspring regenerating, despite her earlier summoning of the rune of illusion.

Bran's reflection flickered, and he glanced away again.

"I must end the scrying," he said. "Let Anneth take whatever action she feels is best. We will be there soon enough."

Then he was gone, the shivering surface of the water showing only the cloud-scattered sky and tops of the breeze-stirred trees.

Ondo blew out a breath and settled back on his heels, his gaze fixed on the forest.

"I know you're trying to protect me," Anneth said in a conciliatory tone. "But this is truly the best course. Now, how about that porridge—it must be well cooked by now."

"I do not like this plan," he said, returning his attention to the fire. "At least take your knife when you return to the castle."

"They would only confiscate it. No, my magic will be enough. And I'll scry to you when I can—but if you don't hear from me regularly, don't be alarmed."

There was no way of knowing where they would imprison her, or how much privacy she'd have. She wouldn't make Ondo promises she couldn't keep, for fear of him storming into the castle to make an unnecessary rescue.

He scowled at the porridge as he ladled it into the folded bark bowls he'd made, then added a bit of honeycomb and a scattering of berries to each portion.

"You'd best take an extra helping of honey," Anneth said lightly.

"Nothing will sweeten my mood."

"I know." She relented, shooting him a rueful smile. "I'll contact you as soon as I'm able. I promise."

It was the best she could do, and they both knew it. He gave a terse nod, and they finished their breakfast in silence, Anneth pondering what, if anything, she might take with her back to Castle Raine.

She would leave her remaining slipper with Ondo—and pray that the castle guards hadn't yet traced its mate back to the Gearys.

With a jolt, she recalled that her boots and clothing were still in their cottage, and she had no way to send word that they should dispose of them. By all the stars, she hoped they kept their heads down and didn't do anything rash. Especially Lily.

"You must cast your human illusion," she said to Ondo, "and go to the Gearys' right away. Fetch my things, and tell them not to worry. Or to get involved."

He frowned, the expression carving deep lines beside his mouth. "Then they will know there are two of us."

"That's better than them going to the castle and bringing trouble upon themselves. If the captain of the guard thinks I'm a spy, then surely he'll suspect them of the same." She pulled in a quick, apprehensive breath. "In fact, they might think Mr. Geary is behind the poisoning, as he's the one who brewed the ale."

"After I accompany you back to—"

"No." Anneth cut him off. "We must both depart, immediately."

She scraped the last bits of porridge up with the carved wooden spoon, took a few more hasty swigs of her tea, and stood.

"At least wear some shoes." Ondo glanced at her bare feet.

"I can't." She frowned at the scratches marring her feet, but there was no help for it. "The castle must believe I have no allies nearby. No handy source of extra footwear."

There was very little to say after that. Ondo cast his own rune of illusion, and they parted ways a short distance from the camp.

Like all of her people, Anneth possessed an unerring sense of direction. Mindful of how she placed her feet, she made her way back through the Darkwood, heading toward Castle Raine. The slanted rays of sunshine filtering through the trees and the colorful bursts of flowers did little to cheer her. Despite her optimistic words to Ondo, she was afraid.

What if the humans harmed her? She had read of the barbaric practice of torturing enemies, either to extract information, or out of pure spite. The Dark Elves did not do such things.

Well, that was not entirely true—but they had magic. There was no need to inflict physical pain when a carefully focused spell would yield the same results.

Captain Crane seemed the sort to employ bloody methods. She hoped that her prompt confession, no matter how false, would appease him. And Prince Owen had seemed to be, if not her friend, then a cautious ally.

Would he still be, once she claimed she was a spy?

She bit her lip as doubts hammered at her heart. The closer she came to capture, the more foolish her plan seemed.

And then it was too late for second thoughts.

"There!" a man cried. "I think I saw her."

"Where?" several others called, and the man shouted directions.

Anneth paused, then turned and started to run, heading for where she sensed the edge of the forest lay. No point in leading them deeper into the Darkwood.

As she wove through the thickets and dodged fallen logs, it was easy to keep her pace slow enough for them to catch her. Despite her care, she had a gouge on one foot and a bloody scrape on her ankle.

"Halt! Surrender yourself, or we'll shoot."

Slowly, pulse pounding, she turned. Four men were arrayed behind her, each with drawn bows, their arrows pointing at her chest. Briefly, she noted they were of the type called crossbows, which she'd only seen in pictures. Faced with the deadly points of their bolts, the weapons were suddenly all too real.

"I..." She swallowed past the sudden dryness in her throat. "I surrender."

"Keep your hands out," the leader said. "Matt, run tell the captain we've got her. Kavan, Ian, bind her."

Anneth waited, trying not to tremble, as the men lowered their bows and came to take her prisoner.

CHAPTER 26

Directly after breakfast, Owen met with his father in the king's private study.

"Sit." His father gestured to the chair on the other side of his wide desk.

Owen took it, noting the lines of weariness on the king's face.

"Were you awake all night?" he asked. "Any news of the fugitive?"

"No word, but Captain Crane assures me she'll be taken into custody soon. His soldiers began searching the forest at first light for any clues as to her whereabouts. If they don't find her soon, they'll move on to the village."

The thought of the glass-beaded slipper tucked deep in the trunk beneath his bed gave Owen an uncomfortable twinge. He was not certain why he was hiding it—other than the fact that he still believed Anneth to be innocent.

"The girl is only one of our concerns, however. The Athraig are due to arrive tonight." The king rubbed his eyes, then straightened. "But let us speak of happier things. Certainly you must have found some of the young ladies last night agreeable and worthy of further acquaintance. Tell me who, and we'll invite them to stay at the castle."

Foremost in Owen's thoughts was Anneth—but if she were to

return to Castle Raine, her stay would not be in one of the well-appointed guest rooms, but the cold stone of the cellar dungeon.

"Lady Fiona," he said, noting his father's nod of agreement. "Miss Rinna Thompson of Meriton, Lady Laura Wakefield, and Miss Chassily Dupont."

"The Duponts with ties to the nobility of Parnese?" His father gave him an approving look. "That's a wise choice as well. We could stand to strengthen our foreign connections now that the Athraig are circling Raine. Too bad the Fiorlander princess is only a babe."

"Yes, they ought to have timed their heir production to match yours," Owen said dryly.

The words elicited a wry laugh, as he'd meant them to.

"Anyone else?" the king asked.

Owen shook his head, just as a loud knock sounded on the paneled door.

"It's Captain Crane," the man announced. "I've news."

"Enter," the king said.

The captain strode in and made King Philip a short bow, then glanced at Owen. "Glad you're both here, majesties. We've apprehended the Athraig spy. One of my runners just brought word."

Owen kept his face carefully blank at the news.

The king smiled at his captain. "Where did they find her?"

"In the forest, not too far off. Obviously she tried to go to ground and wait for the rest of the Athraig delegation to arrive. She'll be escorted to the dungeon for questioning when she arrives."

"I want to be there," Owen said, surprising them all.

"Why?" Captain Crane turned to him. "We won't hurt the girl."

Owen wasn't entirely convinced that the captain's zealous loyalty wouldn't result in some injury to Anneth. But the king had complete confidence in the man, and now was not the time for Owen to raise his concerns.

"I feel as though she trusted me, at least somewhat," he said. "Let me speak with her."

"We're not bringing her up into any of the main castle rooms," the captain said with a scowl. "She'll be marched right down to the cells. It's not a comfortable place, your highness."

"You needn't be unduly concerned with my comfort," Owen said. "I'm the crown prince, and in this case it's my duty to confront the prisoner. And keep the king out of harm's way."

"True enough," his father said. "You can report back to me after you question her. The both of you. Meanwhile, I'll have the royal emissary inform your chosen young ladies and their families that they are invited to remain at Castle Raine for the time being."

"Good," the captain said. "High time we sent everyone else home. Less chance of infiltrators within our walls."

"At least until the Athraig delegation arrives." The weariness had returned to King Philip's face.

"I say we refuse to let them into the castle." Captain Crane clenched his fist. "Truce or no, I don't trust those cold bastards."

"We cannot afford to spark a war," the king said heavily. "Now, go and speak with this spy. And bring me back some good news."

Owen rose, bowed to his father, then followed Captain Crane from the room.

THE CASTLE DUNGEON was cold and damp. And dim, but at least Anneth didn't mind that part.

After hauling her back to the castle, the guardsmen had brought her down a steep flight of stone steps to the cellars and locked her in one of the three cells located at the very back. They smelled faintly of onions, and were not often used, judging by the spider webs the guards had to brush aside as they thrust her into the middle cell.

"Captain's on his way," the leader said to the other guards. "Keep a sharp watch on her while I light the torches."

Well, that answered Anneth's unspoken question of what was to happen now. She retreated to the stone bench running along the back wall, which she supposed served as a bed. A scattering of old straw provided little cushion as she sat and wrapped her arms about herself for warmth. Her gown, now ruined beyond repair, would do little to keep the cold at bay.

Her feet were chilly, the bare stone leaching the warmth from her soles. She drew her toes up under her skirts, and watched the guard strike sparks onto the pitch-soaked torches stuck at intervals along the wall.

They sullenly came to life, casting ruddy light and dark streams of smoke into the air. It wasn't long before the approaching sound of booted footsteps echoed into the cellar. Anneth unwrapped her arms from about her knees and set her feet back on the floor. No matter how apprehensive she might be about her imprisonment, her pride wouldn't allow her to present herself as a dejected huddle to the captain of the guard.

The captain strode into sight, and she was somewhat heartened to see Prince Owen at his side. In contrast to the captain's scowl, the prince gave her a thoughtful look.

"Good work," Captain Crane said to his men. "I want the three of you in rotating shifts to guard the prisoner. Ian, you're first."

The russet-haired man nodded and set his hand on the dagger at his belt while the other two gathered themselves to leave.

Prince Owen's gaze sharpened as he surveyed her cell, and then he rounded on the soldier. "Bring her some water, at least. And a blanket. She might be a prisoner, but she's not an animal to be locked in a pen and left untended."

The captain frowned, but nodded at his man. "Do as the prince says. Bring a bucket, too, for waste."

How undignified that would be, but Anneth had little choice in the matter. The reality of her imprisonment settled heavily upon her shoulders. If she were to be constantly guarded, escape would be more difficult. And she hadn't bargained for her surroundings to be quite so dire.

But there was no changing her plan now. She only hoped the Gearys had managed to keep themselves out of the castle's scrutiny.

"So, spy." Captain Crane faced her through the thick iron bars of her cell. "What do you have to say for yourself?"

She lifted her chin, but remained sitting, so as not to remind the captain of her unusual height.

"I admit to being an agent of the Athraig," she lied. "But I had no part in the attempt upon the king's life. That is another faction's work."

"What faction? Are they part of the delegation that's about to arrive?"

The Athraig were coming? That certainly changed things, and made her story more plausible—she hoped. It also brought a new host of complications, but she would deal with those as they arose. No point in borrowing trouble from the future. She had more than enough at present.

In answer to the captain's question, she shook her head. "All I know is that when word of the ball reached us, my masters chose to send me as a candidate. My task was to catch the prince's eye and secure an invitation to the castle, so that I could provide information about the royal family's movements to my superiors. I was not aware of any assassination plot."

She sent Prince Own a look of apology. The lie certainly didn't paint her in a good light, but she hadn't been able to think of a better explanation.

Captain Crane grunted and turned to the prince. "I told you she was suspicious."

"At least she didn't try to kill my father." Prince Owen frowned at her. "That explains your air of mystery, I suppose. Is your name really Anneth?"

"It is."

"You gave me a last name, as well." The prince stepped forward. "Geary?"

She swallowed, her throat tight with apprehension. "I chose a common surname, to avoid suspicion. And I believe it was Cleary."

Prince Owen's eyebrows drew together, but he didn't challenge her.

"I think she knows more than she's telling," the captain said. "I'll ask the king if I might try some further methods of questioning—"

"Not yet," the prince said. "We'll wait to see what the Athraig delegation does once they learn we have one of their spies in our dungeon."

Anneth shuddered at the implication of the captain's words.

"If we can get the truth from her, we can compare her story with what the other Athraig have to say."

"We already have her story," Prince Owen said. "She was sent to infiltrate the castle, not kill my father. If she's lying about that, I'm sure the truth will come out soon enough."

The captain scowled but, to Anneth's relief, didn't press the matter. The sound of someone approaching caught his attention, and he set a hand to his sword.

It was the russet-haired guard, returning with a blanket, skin of water, and bucket. Under the captain's watchful eye, he unlocked Anneth's cell and set the items just inside.

Careful to appear harmless, she sat very still, not moving even when the barred door clanged shut again and the man turned the key in the lock.

"Go ahead." Prince Owen glanced at the blanket and gave her an encouraging nod. "Have you eaten anything today?"

Porridge—but she could hardly admit that she'd shared a decent breakfast with a Dark Elf scout hiding deep in the forest. Mutely, she shook her head.

"I'll have the kitchen send down some bread and cheese," the prince said.

"She's not some court lady to pamper." The captain scowled. "A little hunger won't hurt her."

"We will show her common courtesy." Prince Owen turned a cold look upon the captain. "At least until she proves unworthy of that trust."

"Thank you." She inclined her head.

The prince regarded her, their gazes locking. "Do not abuse our hospitality."

"I'll endeavor not to." Still, she couldn't promise not to escape.

"Enough." Captain Crane pointed to his man. "Ian, remain on guard. I'll send Kavan to relieve you at the end of your shift. Don't leave her unwatched."

"No, sir." The guard drew himself up.

Prince Owen sent Anneth a final, unreadable glance, then turned and followed the captain to the stairs. No one had mentioned the slipper.

If it were found, could they trace it back to the Gearys? It certainly bore an unusual pattern. Eventually, someone would know where the slipper had come from. She could only hope it would remain mysteriously missing.

The guardsmen had confiscated her small scrying bowl, which she should have anticipated. She wondered if she would ever get it back. It complicated matters somewhat in terms of contacting Ondo, but she would find a way, even if she must cup water in the palm of her hand.

Slowly, keeping a wary eye on the guard, she rose and picked up the blanket and water skin. The cell wasn't comfortable, but at least she could keep the chill from her back and sip away the apprehension that insisted on drying her throat. Beyond that, all she could do was wait.

Wait for the guard to grow weary and perhaps sleep. Wait for a moment that she might lie down and turn her back to the bars, and send a message to Ondo. Most of all, wait for Bran and Mara to arrive, so that she could end this grim, self-imposed imprisonment.

CHAPTER 27

That evening, the Athraig arrived at Castle Raine. Owen and his father, seated upon their thrones, received them in the great hall.

"Your majesty." The leader of the delegation bowed to King Philip. "As my letter of introduction states, I am Lord Alvar Jensen, Greve of Sonderborg. On behalf of the Athraig, we are delighted to be here in Raine."

Behind him were arrayed a pair of minor nobles and a retinue of personal guards. In all, a dozen of the fair-haired foreigners had disembarked from the coaches hired at Portknowe to take them through the Darkwood to the castle. Accompanied, of course, by an honor escort of Captain Crane's men.

Owen had watched them arrive earlier from the hidden peephole over the courtyard. There had seemed, to his mind, a disproportionate number of fighters among the Athraig.

Then again, they weren't exactly entering friendly territory. Raine and Athraig upheld an uneasy truce, but there was a history of conflict between their two countries. Still, as the delegation bowed and made their greetings, he was grimly aware of the number of sword-bearers among the group.

What are you up to? he wanted to demand of the greve. But he was afraid he already knew. They were there to test Raine's weakness and try to force an alliance—one that would not benefit his country. He shifted on his throne and shot a glance at his father.

"I bid you welcome," the king said with a bland smile. "The servants will show you and your people to their rooms, Lord Jensen. Once you're settled, perhaps you might join us in the study for a glass of wine, and we may speak further as to the intent of your visit."

The greve made a flourishing hand gesture more suited to the court of Parnese than Raine's simple protocols. "As to that, your majesty, we make no secret of it. You have a prince; we have a princess. It would benefit both our kingdoms if they wed one another."

The king's lips tightened, and Owen had the unpleasant satisfaction of knowing he'd been right. They meant to convince him to marry the Athraig princess.

It would be disastrous for Raine, of course. Every country the warlike Athraig made "alliances" with ended up becoming vassal states in short order. They could not be allowed a toehold in Raine—and Owen wondered that they even would try.

Perhaps the Athraig leaders thought the kingdom was unsettled and vulnerable after the queen's death—and, if Anneth was right, they plotted to kill the king. Did they think Owen would be so overcome with grief at that point that he would agree to marry their princess?

He would never consent to it.

"The Athraig will be under close guard at all times," Captain Crane had said, when word of the delegation's imminent arrival reached the castle. "My soldiers are a match for any of those pale-haired bastards. We'll let no harm come to you, your majesty. Or yourself, Prince Owen."

"I rely upon you and your men, of course," the king had said. "But do remind them that the Athraig are our guests. We don't want to incite violence."

The captain had nodded, though Owen thought he looked a bit disappointed at the king's reminder to be civil. For himself, he found he was in sympathy with the captain for once. He'd rather they boot the Athraig from the castle, and damn the consequences.

"When should we let them know we have their spy in the dungeon?" Captain Crane asked.

"Not immediately." The king rubbed his forehead. "I'd like to see what they have to say first, and how they comport themselves. Perhaps they'll slip up and reveal something they shouldn't."

Now, watching the greve bow and smile, Owen thought the fellow was unlikely to put a foot wrong. He was too much the polished court diplomat—much like the Parnesian nobles Owen had encountered during his educational visits abroad.

For a moment he regretted the straightforward nature of Raine's court. The running of their small country did not lend itself to intrigues and machinations, beyond simple attempts to curry favor with the king and catch the prince's eye.

Perhaps, if the court were more skilled at subterfuge, they would not be at quite so much of a disadvantage.

Owen squared his shoulders, vowing to himself that Raine would never bow to the Athraig. No matter what schemes they might try in order to seize power.

"I see," King Philip said, replying to the greve's suggestion. "My son is all but betrothed, however, so we must decline your generous proposal of an alliance. Still, we offer you the hospitality of the castle."

Lord Jensen's mouth twisted in an unpleasant expression, quickly smoothed away.

"I understand," he said. "Nonetheless, we look forward to further conversations along these lines."

"No doubt." The king's voice was dry. He gestured to the waiting servants. "You must be tired from your long journey. Allow my people to see you to your rooms, Lord Jensen. Food will be sent up, and your needs tended to."

Teeth bared in something that passed for a smile, the greve bowed. "Until tomorrow, your majesty."

The rest of the delegation bobbed their farewells and, under the watchful eyes of Captain Crane's guards, were escorted from the hall.

When the last of their footfalls had faded in the distance, King Philip turned to Owen.

"You must make your choice," he said in a low voice. "Tonight."

Owen stiffened in his seat—but he couldn't deny he'd seen this moment coming.

"If I must select a bride, then it will be Lady Fiona," he said. She was the least objectionable of the bunch.

"Good." The king gave a sharp nod. "We'll announce it tomorrow at breakfast. Go, now, and make your intentions known."

"Yes, Father." Owen stood.

He would speak with Lady Fiona—but first, he would pay a visit to the dungeon.

In the clammy dimness of her cell, Anneth turned her back to the guard and poured a small measure of water into her cupped palm. She had no idea if it would be enough to cast a scrying to Ondo, but she must try.

Despite her assurances to him not to worry, she had no doubt he was stationed just outside the castle, ready to charge to her rescue.

Holding her palm close to her face, she whispered the rune of scrying, directing it toward Ondo. It was difficult to make out any reflection at all, but she held very still, concentrating. The water in her hand caught the light of one of the greasy torches, and a moment later, Ondo's face appeared.

"Princess," he said urgently, "are you well?"

"Shh," she whispered. "Well enough, under the circumstance. They are holding me in the dungeon, but I am unharmed, and my illusion is holding strong."

"Hey!" the guard, who'd recently taken over from the russet-haired man, rose to his feet. "What're you doing?"

Hastily, Anneth gulped the water in her cupped hand, bringing the scrying to a quick end. She hoped Ondo would not be unduly alarmed.

"Taking a drink," she said, turning toward the guard and lifting the skin of water.

"You were talking." He scowled at her through the bars of the cell.

"Simply saying a prayer." She smiled innocently at him, then poured more water into her hand and drank.

"You Athraig." He spat into the dirty straw strewn across the floor.

"We'll never make an alliance with you, you know. No matter how much you might threaten our kingdom."

"I mean no threat." She kept her expression mild.

"Your man upstairs does." He jerked his head toward the ceiling. "I can hardly wait til it's my watch on them. I'll piss in their ale, I will."

Anneth blinked, casting a suspicious glance at her water skin. It didn't taste foul—but perhaps she wouldn't drink too much more. Just in case.

The guard resumed his seat, and she pulled the blanket up around her shoulders. It was going to be a chilly night upon the hard stone, and she did not look forward to it. But Bran and Mara would reach Raine soon, and she would be free.

Soft light filtered into the dungeon as someone approached, carrying a lantern.

"Who's there?" The guard stood, one hand going to the sword at his belt.

"Prince Owen," the answer came.

Anneth's heartbeat accelerated. Why was the prince coming to visit at this hour?

A moment later, he stepped into the dungeon, his lantern held high. His expression was set, his green eyes clouded with worry.

"Your highness." The guardsman made a rough bow.

"Has the prisoner been any trouble?"

"Only that she's polluting our air with her Athraig breath," the guard mumbled. Then, as the prince's expression hardened, cleared his throat. "No, my lord."

"Good." Prince Owen peered into her cell. Anneth met his gaze defiantly.

She might be a captive, but she was still a princess. There was no need to grovel.

"Are you well?" he asked softly, stepping toward the bars.

"Take care, my lord." The guard joined him, giving Anneth a wary look. "These Athraig are slippery. Don't stand too close—she might have a concealed dagger."

"Didn't you search her?" the prince asked mildly, obviously not overly concerned that Anneth might leap up and stab him.

"Of course we did." The guardsman sounded affronted. "But you never know with these foreigners."

"I trust you with my safety." Prince Owen set his lantern down. "In fact, I'm happy to relieve you for a short time. Go fetch yourself a late dinner."

The guard hesitated. "My lord, are you sure?"

"Go." The prince waved his hand. "I can mind the prisoner for a short time. I'll answer to Captain Crane, should there be any trouble."

"If you don't mind. I'll be back in a trice, your highness." The man bobbed another quick bow, then headed for the stairs, leaving Anneth alone with Prince Owen.

They regarded one another in silence for a long moment.

"Are you acquainted with Lord Jensen?" the prince asked.

Anneth shook her head. "If you're here to interrogate me further, I've nothing more to say."

"No." He let out a low breath. "I was only wondering if you could give me insight into the man—and how long we might put him off before I must announce my betrothal."

Prince Owen sounded unhappy, and grudging sympathy moved through Anneth. She knew how it felt to be forced into making a match because of one's royal blood. At least she could say no to Prince Deldarinnon, whereas it seemed this prince had no choice at all.

"You've picked a bride, then?" Why did the thought give her a little stab of pain? Prince Owen meant nothing to her.

"Yes." He wrapped his fingers around one of the bars of her cell. "I've decided upon Lady Fiona."

Of course. Anneth let out a breath. "I'm sure she was delighted at your proposal."

He glanced away. "I haven't told her yet."

"Oh?" Her brows rose. "Honestly, she seems the best option—not that I'm very familiar with your prospects. The people at the ball seemed to think she'd be the one."

She didn't tell him they'd been laying bets on the matter.

He looked back at her, frowning. "But where are you from, mysterious Anneth? You don't look like any Athraig I've ever met. You're too tall, and your hair is too dark."

"I… I colored it, as a disguise." Even as she spoke, she could tell how unconvincing she sounded.

He studied her intently, and she glanced at her hands to make sure her human semblance was still firmly in place. Why was he suddenly so curious about her?

"The Daroese in the far south are quite tall," he said. "With black hair—but their skin is much darker-hued than yours."

"Shouldn't you be visiting your soon-to-be betrothed rather than indulging in wild speculation about where I'm from?"

"And that's another thing—you don't speak like any commoner I've ever heard. Or Athraig, for that matter."

There was truly no response she could make to that, so she folded her arms and narrowed her eyes.

"I think you're avoiding doing your duty to your kingdom, Prince Owen," she said, trying to needle him into leaving—or at least stop trying to guess where she was from. "You're distracting yourself with foolish speculations so you don't have to think about marrying Lady Fiona."

Instead of becoming annoyed, as she'd hoped, he let out a low sigh and leaned his forehead against the bars.

"You're the only one I can talk to," he said, so simply it left her breathless. "My father doesn't understand, Captain Crane thinks every problem can be solved with a sword, and my mother—" His voice caught. He paused, swallowing. "My mother isn't here anymore."

"I'm sorry," she said, truly meaning it. Although she'd never had a sympathetic mother of her own, she knew they existed.

"Sometimes…" He trailed off, shaking his head, but Anneth recognized the expression on his face. She'd seen it on her own, in the polished silver mirrors of the Hawthorne Court.

"Sometimes you wish you weren't the Crown Prince of Raine," she said.

He jerked his head up, gaze meeting hers. "I can't admit that, to anyone."

For a moment they stared at one another, and she had to resist the sudden urge to reveal herself to him. She gave a sharp shake of her head. How could she even contemplate doing such a thing?

"Don't worry," she said. "I'm not going to tell your secrets." Or her own. "Besides, who would listen to a stranger in your dungeon?"

"A very perceptive, intelligent stranger," he said softly. "Anneth—"

Footsteps on the stairway signaled the imminent return of the guardsman, and Prince Owen straightened.

"Well." He glanced at the stone bench that would serve as her bed. "I'll send down another blanket, though I'm afraid I can't do much more."

She lifted one shoulder in acknowledgement. "I understand. Thank you."

"I'll visit you again tomorrow. Good night."

He turned to go, and she called softly after him, "Good luck."

He looked back over his shoulder, a flicker of gratitude crossing his face. Then the soldier was there, and Prince Owen strode away, the oily torches sputtering behind him.

CHAPTER 28

Although he knew he could not delay much longer, Owen couldn't quite bring himself to call upon Lady Fiona that evening. He told himself it was late, and besides, he hadn't rehearsed what he was going to say. A lady of her station would have certain expectations about how a prince's proposal should go, and a halfhearted declaration was hardly the way to begin a lifelong alliance. Whether he loved her or not.

First thing in the morning, he vowed he'd do his duty. And he would *not* go see Anneth in the dungeon—no matter how much he might wish to. Against all reason, she felt like a kindred spirit, and he had the strangest suspicion that she carried royal blood.

The castle halls were quiet as he returned to his suite. He nodded to the pair of guardsmen posted outside his father's door, and to the man standing sentry at his own.

Inside, the lamps were lit, and Antoine waited to help remove his coat and boots. As soon as those tasks were done, Owen dismissed his valet. He had no taste for further conversation that night.

It took him a long while to go to sleep, and he was roused before dawn by the sound of shouting coming from his father's rooms.

Heart racing, he leaped out of bed and hastily pulled on his clothing.

Grabbing his sword, he wrenched open the door. With a clatter, his blade was struck from his hands. He lunged to retrieve it, but drew up short at the sword pointed at his chest, wielded by one of Lord Jensen's fair-haired soldiers.

The greve himself stood a pace back, another of his men beside him. All three had bared swords, though only the one man had his turned upon Owen.

"Prince Owen," Lord Jensen said with sly smile, "we were just coming to fetch you. How obliging of you to awaken and join us."

"What's going on?" Owen asked, though he had the sick feeling he knew. "If you've hurt my father..."

He glanced up the hall to the king's door. There was no sign of the king's guardsmen, though a smear of blood on the wall made Owen's heart sink even further.

"King Philip is unharmed. For now." Lord Jensen nodded to his men. "Let's escort the prince to meet his father."

He gestured for Owen to proceed down the empty corridor. Wary of the sharp steel surrounding him, Owen kept his arms at his sides. If he'd been thinking more clearly, he would've shoved a knife in his boot. But all his thoughts had been on reaching his father.

"Where's Captain Crane?" he demanded as the soldiers herded him down the stairs to the main floor of the castle.

"If you're thinking of calling for help, don't bother," the greve said. "He is at this very moment telling his men to stand down."

Owen sent Lord Jensen a sharp glance. "The captain would never betray his king."

"Of course not—he would do anything to keep King Philip from harm. Which is why, as long as we hold a blade to your father's throat—or an arrow to his heart—the captain will do as we tell him."

"You can't hope to hold the castle for long," Owen said, thinking frantically. Wherever they were keeping the king, there had to be a way to win free and stop the Athraig coup.

"We don't need to hold it." The greve gave him a cold smile. "Our ships are standing just off the coast. On second thought, they're probably landing soldiers by now. At a fast march, they'll be here by tomorrow. We only need to keep your overzealous captain at bay for one day."

"The navy—"

"Has been decoyed to the opposite shore. By the time your Rainish fleet understands they've been led astray, it will be too late. Castle Raine, and the kingdom, will be under our control."

"And then what?" Owen forced his breath out through tight lungs.

"Why, we'll celebrate your marriage to Princess Rella—who just happens to be with the flotilla. Nothing like the festivities of a royal wedding to hearten a country."

"I won't marry her." Owen's voice was rough with leashed anger. They'd been fools to welcome the Athraig into the castle, too blind to the danger of treachery.

"To keep your father safe, of course you will." Lord Jensen gestured to the stairwell leading down to the cellars. "Mind your footing."

"You're keeping us in the dungeon?"

"Yes. Very convenient of you to have a few cells handy," the greve said, and one of his soldiers laughed.

"What about Anneth?" Owen asked. No use waiting for the Athraig to slip and mention their spy, as presumably they'd already discovered and freed her.

"Who?" Lord Jensen asked.

"Your informant in the dungeon."

The greve's upper lip curled into a condescending sneer. "If you mean the young woman occupying one of the cells, she's still there. Whoever she's working for, it's not the Athraig. Your intelligence is not the best, I have to say. Our man completely escaped your detection."

Anneth wasn't an Athraig agent? Owen paused, trying to digest this new information, and the soldier shoved his shoulder.

"Keep going," the man said.

Mind whirling, Owen descended the stairs to the cellar. So, Anneth was innocent, and there was a different agent of the Athraig still on the loose, as she'd claimed.

But why had she lied and told them she was working with their enemy?

Two more men stood guard at the bottom of the stairwell. They stood stiffly at attention as Lord Jensen passed.

Surely, if Captain Crane's men rushed the stairs, they could overwhelm the guards. There weren't that many Athraig, after all. Fight the remaining soldiers, get to the cells and free the king...

As they stepped into the dungeon, Owen's rising hopes were dashed by the sight of two men, crossbows trained on the figure of the king, who occupied the right-hand cell. The archers were stationed so that even if Captain Crane's soldiers could take out one, the other would still be able to fire his bolt. At such a close range, it would easily pierce the king's heart.

"My two best marksmen," Lord Jensen said, then nodded to the man prodding Owen. "Lock him in the last cell."

Despite the soldier's sword at his back, Owen stubbornly halted. "Put me with my father."

"And let you take the bolt meant for him?" The greve shook his head. "I can't abide heroics."

A sharp prick against his ribs made Owen step forward, and the greve's soldiers thrust him into the cell on the left. The clang of the closing door sent a chill through him, and he stared at the heavy length of chain the men threaded through the bars.

"Just in case," Lord Jensen said, closing the chain with a heavy iron padlock, then pocketing the key.

Owen narrowed his eyes. The man had thought of everything, and once again he cursed himself for not taking a firmer stand against letting the Athraig set foot in Castle Raine.

"All the comforts of home," Lord Jensen said. He nodded to the blanket, bucket, and plate of bread and dried meat set on the wide stone bench running along the back of the cell. "Try not to look too disreputable by the time Princess Rella arrives."

Then he turned and, his men behind him, strode out of the dungeon. The two archers never glanced up, each of them entirely focused on keeping their crossbows squarely trained upon the king.

"Are you all right?" Owen's father called from his cell.

Slowly, Owen turned to face the king. And, of course, Anneth, who occupied the cell between them. She sat on the bench, her feet drawn up beneath her blankets, watching him with wide eyes.

Beyond her, King Philip stood in his own cell, peering at Owen through the rows of bars. He still wore his dressing robe, and Owen was dismayed to see his bare feet beneath. They hadn't even given him the common courtesy of letting him don footwear, and that fact was chilling.

The Athraig weren't intending for the king to survive. As soon as Owen was married to their princess, the king's life wouldn't be worth a copper coin.

"I'm well enough," Owen told his father. "Given the circumstances. And you?"

"The same." King Philip let out a heavy sigh. "I am sorry—I should have listened to you and Captain Crane concerning the Athraig's intentions. Now look at us." He spread his hands, then lurched slightly and grabbed the nearest bar for balance.

Alarmed, Owen strode to the edge of his cell, where it bordered Anneth's. "Did they hurt you?"

"My leg pains me. They didn't allow me to bring my cane, and were not patient." The king grimaced. "I'm afraid our enemies don't plan for my reign to continue much longer."

Grimly, Owen nodded. "I fear the same." He pitched his voice low. "We must escape."

Anneth's head jerked up. "I might be able to help," she said softly.

Casting a wary glance at the archers, Owen gestured for her to come closer. She stood, and Owen was reminded that her feet, too, were bare. He spared a single thought for the ornate slipper upstairs, then gave a mental shrug.

Since she wasn't an Athraig spy, and seemed to mean the king no harm, Owen was willing to listen to any plan she might have. The mystery of who she was paled in comparison with their current situation.

Once they were free of the dungeons, however, he had some hard questions for her.

Anneth came close beside him, only the cold bars separating them. Despite her time in the dungeon, she seemed composed. She'd twisted her hair into a series of intricate braids, presumably to keep it from tangling, and brushed the bits of hay from her crumpled green dress.

"My allies are on the way," she said, pitching her words barely above a whisper.

A bright spark leaped through him. “Can they storm the castle and free us?”

Presumably her people—whoever they might be—would mount an effort to reach the dungeon. Between them and Captain Crane, there was a chance the Athraig could be defeated and King Philip safely restored to the throne. The tightness in his chest eased.

The dark wings of her brows drew together. “Possibly—though they are fewer in number than the Athraig.”

“How many?”

She hesitated, her gaze going to the cobweb-festooned corner before returning to him. The torchlight flickered and for a moment the shadows lay sharply against the planes of her face, reflected in eyes that seemed strangely inhuman.

Then he blinked, and the impression was gone.

“Well?” He leaned forward, awaiting her answer.

“Three,” she reluctantly said.

He stared at her, his brief flare of hope extinguished. “Three people? They have no chance.”

She swallowed, then drew in a breath. “There is something I must tell you—”

“You there!” one of the archers called. “No talking. Step apart.”

He gestured with his crossbow. Giving Owen a pained look, Anneth moved back to her stone bench.

Owen regarded her a long minute. What had she been about to tell him? And how could it possibly make any difference?

His gaze moved past her to his father, and his heart clenched in fear and sorrow. The reality of their predicament descended, cold and heavy, on his shoulders.

They were trapped in the dungeon, the fate of Raine hanging in the balance.

For a wild instant, he imagined goading the archers into shooting him. It was one way to escape the forced marriage to the Athraig princess. But it would solve nothing.

Bending his head, he turned away from the sight of his father, one hand clutching the bars. Away from Anneth, her face pale and worried.

His mother would tell him to never give up—that even in overwhelming darkness, light was possible. The memory of her smile, the lines crinkling at the corners of her eyes, made him straighten.

Somehow, no matter how dire the odds, he must believe there was a way forward that did not include a coerced alliance with the enemy. Or his father's death.

CHAPTER 29

At the prow of the ship, Bran faced into the wind, flicking his vision light to dark. No matter how hard he looked, however, he could catch no glimpse of the shore of Raine.

Beside him, Mara clutched the railing and took shallow breaths. It was difficult for her to tolerate the motion of traveling over the waves. Being outside helped, and eating small bites of bread every few hours, followed by cool water.

"No sign of the shore?" she asked miserably.

He slipped one arm about her shoulders, and she leaned against him with a sigh. "Not yet," he said.

Luckily, the winds had propelled them quickly across the Strait, taking nearly a full day off their return journey. He sent Mara a concerned glance. The sooner they reached solid ground, the better. For her sake, and for Anneth's.

According to Ondo, Anneth had been able to reach him briefly and assure him she was unharmed—but Bran very much disliked the thought of his sister held captive in Castle Raine's dungeon. Even if it seemed to have kept Mara's family safe from suspicion.

He cast one last look at the blue-gray horizon, then turned to his wife.

"Are you ready to return to our cabin?" he asked.

She nodded, smiling weakly. "Time to scry Ondo, I suppose—since you did insist on daily communication. Which I wholeheartedly agree with." She set her hand on his arm. "I don't like Anneth being imprisoned any better than you do. But we'll be there soon."

Not soon enough, he wanted to say. Despite the urgency burning through him, he forced patience as he helped Mara through the hatch and down the ladder. A breeze lifted his cloak then swirled down the corridor, leaving a faint scrim of salt behind.

Their cabin was the first door on the left. Although cramped and dim, it boasted a porthole with a teetering view of the water and sky.

While Mara lay down, Bran sat on the edge of the bed and poured water into his silver scrying bowl. The liquid undulated with the motion of the ship. Bracing himself, he spoke the rune of scrying. A moment later, Ondo's face appeared in the sloshing reflection.

"Any news?" Bran asked.

The scout frowned. "I am worried, my lord. Last night there was a disturbance at the castle. I do not yet know what it means."

"What kind of disturbance?"

"Shouting, people moving about. It was difficult to determine what was occurring, as I am keeping to the edge of the forest."

"Stay hidden," Bran said shortly. "We don't need you to join Anneth in the dungeon. Has she scried to you?"

"Only the once." Ondo leaned forward, his image looming in the water. "I would like to enter the castle. Something is not right."

Bran shook his head. "Don't set foot inside, unless Anneth calls for your help. Or unless you sense the use of magic. Mara and I will be there soon. The captain of the ship says we'll make port tonight. From there, we'll procure horses and come as quickly as we can."

"I do not like it." Ondo's brow creased with worry.

"Neither do I. But unless my sister makes a direct cry for help, I command you to wait. Try to discover what you can, but don't risk discovery by entering the castle. Three of us will be better able to rescue Anneth should something go awry. I don't want you falling into trouble."

"I do not *fall into trouble*," the scout said. "But I understand, your highness."

"Thank you." Bran softened his tone. "I'll scry again as soon as we reach Raine. And you can always cast a sending, should the situation change."

"I will," Ondo said. "Hurry."

Bran ended the scrying, and turned to find Mara propped up on one elbow, watching him.

"I hope your father is holding," she said softly.

"As do I." He frowned down at the empty water, but there was no way to scry between the worlds.

And even if there were, it would take a tremendous amount of power—magic that he needed to conserve in order to open the gateway.

"Do you think, before we go, we'll have time for you to meet my parents?" she asked.

He set the bowl down, then lay on his side upon the thin mattress, facing his wife.

"If we're able to get Anneth away without raising an outcry, yes," he said.

Although he found the thought of meeting Mara's parents nearly as daunting as facing the Void. Perhaps even more so, as he'd been preparing to fight the enemy his entire life, while the notion that he would one day encounter his human wife's kin had not even crossed his mind until recently. He feared that all his inadequacies as a husband would be mirrored in their eyes—that they would see him and immediately know he was unworthy of their daughter.

"Don't worry." Mara laid a hand against his cheek. "They will accept you as part of the family."

"Even though I have stolen their daughter from them?"

Her lips tilted in a wry smile. "I'd have left Little Hazel, whether I'd set foot in Elfhame or not. Parents are destined to lose their children. My sister Pansy moved to the city, and they scarcely see her at all."

"At least she inhabits the same world."

"And I might, still." Her smile faded. "It's not an easy thing, trying to choose."

He had no answer for that, so he pulled her against him. She sighed and rested her head against his shoulder. For a long moment they lay there, breathing in unison. His heart ached with the thought of losing her.

"I know I am not much able to show it," he said softly, "but I love you, Mara."

"And I love you. But I am not sure where I belong."

At my side, he wanted to say—but he could not force her to dwell in Elfhame if everything else there brought her bitter unhappiness.

"The Oracles will provide an answer." They must, or he would go mad with grief.

ANNETH WATCHED Prince Owen pace back and forth behind the bars separating them. Every so often he'd pause to glance at his father, who sat slumped on the cold stone bench in his own cell. Then, expression set, he'd resume pacing.

Earlier that night, she'd awoken when the man guarding her had been summoned away by a shout from the cellar. Her heart had leaped; she thought Bran and Mara had arrived and her rescue was at hand.

But then two well-dressed Athraig stepped into the dungeon, roughly herding the king before them. He stumbled, and she winced as they'd shoved him into the right-hand cell. They were closely followed by two soldiers carrying the strange-looking crossbows armed with lethally sharp bolts.

The archers took up stations at either side of the dungeon, then trained their weapons on the king. He leaned weakly against the bars by the locked cell door, and she watched in horror, thinking he was going to be murdered before her eyes.

"Guard him," the more ornately garbed of the Athraig said to the bowmen. Then he turned to face Anneth, looking her up and down with a haughty expression. "You must be the one who interrupted the attempt to poison King Philip."

"Don't you know your own spy, Lord Jensen?" the king asked weakly.

The Athraig let out a cold laugh. "She's not ours. How delicious that you threw the wrong suspect into your dungeon, while our agent went undetected."

The king looked from Lord Jensen to Anneth. "You're not an Athraig spy?"

Mutely, she shook her head.

"You were right about the poison attempt," the king said, a frown bracketing his mouth. "We should have listened."

Lord Jensen's lip curled. "You Rainish have no judgment. Look at this girl! She doesn't resemble an Athraig in the least."

Anneth turned to him. "Will you let me out?"

"I don't think so. You're clearly *someone's* spy. Once we finish dealing with the royal family, we'll consider what to do with you."

That wasn't promising—but his lack of immediate curiosity meant that Mara's family was likely out of danger. Unfortunately, the king was in grave peril, judging by the Athraig's treatment so far.

Lord Jensen turned his back on the cells and strode out of the dungeon, accompanied by the other nobleman. The archers remained, never removing their attention—or their aim—from the king.

Anneth swallowed, then went to the bars separating herself from King Philip. He limped to the stone bench along the back wall of the cell and sat, staring down at his hands.

"Your majesty, what is happening?" she asked softly, casting a wary glance at the nearest bowman.

The king gave her a pained look. "Isn't it plain? The Athraig are taking over the castle."

Her lungs tightened in fear. She'd stumbled into a far worse situation than she'd imagined when she first agreed to go with Lily to the prince's ball. And while Anneth was skilled at smaller court intrigues, she'd never thought to find herself caught between two warring kingdoms.

"What about the prince?" she asked, wrapping her fingers around the cold metal bars.

"They're going for him now." The king gave a sorrowful shake of his head. "I should have known better."

"Maybe Prince Owen has escaped."

"No. He would never leave me in danger." He slumped further back on the stone, a look of desolation in his eyes.

Anneth could offer no reassurances, so she returned to her own bench and waited in tense silence until, as the king had guessed, Prince Owen was brought to the dungeon.

Now, watching him stride back and forth, she wished the archer hadn't interrupted her earlier. The prince might have dismissed her information that she had a handful of allies outside the castle, but he didn't know how powerful they—and she—were.

There was only one clear course of action. She must escape. And take the king and prince with her—even though it meant revealing her magic.

She would need to draw upon her wellspring to scry to Ondo, at the very least. Most likely, she would have to cast several runes: slumber for the guards, opening for the cell doors, and probably some kind of shielding or invisibility so that they could make their way unseen out of the castle.

With a sudden shock, she realized that in the turmoil she hadn't refreshed her rune of illusion. Hurriedly, she lay down, turned her face toward the clammy stones, and pulled the blanket over her. With luck, the guards would be too busy watching the king and prince to notice her casting the small illusion.

Focusing her power, she softly spoke the rune Bran and Mara had created. The wall was momentarily illuminated by a flash of blue. By the brightmoon, she hoped that telltale light had been concealed by the glow of the ever-burning torches.

"What was that?" one of the archers asked.

"Dunno," the other said. "I didn't notice anything. Someone coming?"

The first man shook his head. "My eyes getting tired, that's all. Grinar and Folie better come relieve us soon."

His companion grunted, and that seemed to be the end of it.

After a long moment, Anneth cautiously rolled over. She was startled to see Prince Owen, arms folded, leaning against the bars nearest where she lay.

"Who *are* you?" he whispered, his eyes filled with wary curiosity.

She sat up and scooted closer. "I'm not sure you'd believe me if I told you."

"Try."

"I..." She hesitated. Perhaps there was still a way out of their predicament without using magic. Or at least without admitting to the prince who, and *what*, she truly was.

"Have you heard the tales of the Darkwood?"

During her study of the human world, she'd found the handful of stories the mortals told about magical monsters dwelling in the forest humorous. Especially as she knew the truth.

Now, though, they did not seem laughable in the least.

"I grew up in Raine," the prince said. "Everyone knows those fables. But there are no monsters or mysteries in the Darkwood. Those are just stories to frighten children."

Anneth glanced down at the dirty straw covering the floor, then back up, meeting the prince's green eyes.

"What if the stories are true?" She held his gaze.

He stared at her a long moment, frowning. "How could they be?"

"Watch."

She turned her back on the archers, then cupped her hands and, with a whisper, called up a tiny ball of foxfire. It glowed between her fingers, and she heard Prince Owen's inhalation of surprise.

She flattened her palms, revealing the foxfire. Then, before the guards noticed, quickly extinguished the light. When she turned back to the prince, his eyes were wide, and she could see him struggling to reconcile what he'd just seen with his lifelong belief that magic didn't exist.

"It can't be some sleight of hand," he said, half to himself. "There's nothing here for you to use to create such trickery. And so..." He paused, giving her a penetrating look. "You are somehow able to summon light."

"Yes," she said softly. "And much more. As can my allies."

His brows drew together in thought. "Are they nearby? Can you summon them?"

"They will contact me as soon as they are close."

"When will that be?"

She shook her head. "I'm not sure—but I will try to find out."

"Soon, I hope." He glanced at his father, who was now fast asleep on his stone bench. "The Athraig are sending troops to take the castle, though it will take them a day to arrive. We must win freedom and regain control of Castle Raine before that, or the kingdom is lost."

Her body prickled with tension.

"Give me a moment," she said. "I will attempt to make contact."

She went and scooped up her water skin, giving the archers a quick, sideways glance. One of them was watching her, his eyes narrowed, though his bow was still trained upon the slumbering form of the king.

Clearly she couldn't cast a scrying without raising the guard's suspicion. Instead, she retreated back to her ledge, throwing the prince an apologetic look.

He gave a nearly imperceptible nod.

Weariness tugging at her senses, she leaned her head back against the unyielding stone. It was impossible to tell what time it might be, though judging by her exhaustion, the flaming sun was probably well-risen in the mortal sky.

Bran and Mara will come tonight. She clung to the thought, hoping desperately, for all their sakes, that they would be there soon.

CHAPTER 30

The rocking motion of the *Pridewell* sent Bran, still holding Mara close, into an uneasy slumber. When he woke, dusk was filtering silver shadows through the porthole. Mara still slept, and he was glad to see her resting comfortably. For a long while he lay there, gazing at his wife's beautiful mortal face.

How many more times would they wake in one another's arms?

The question twisted inside him. To distract himself, he gently disentangled himself from Mara, pulled the blanket up over her shoulders, then sought the deck. Perhaps the wind of their passage would clear away his melancholy, and he would finally spot the dark bulk of Raine over the rippling backs of the waves.

When he reached the forward deck, however, he discovered the captain and several of the crew gathered at the railing. The captain was peering through a long tube, pointed ahead and slightly to the left. Bran squinted, trying to determine what the man was looking at. At first he saw nothing, but after flicking on his dark vision, he could make out a cluster of lights floating above the water. Another ship?

Behind it, the shadowy shape of Raine's coastline rose from the sea. As he watched, the lights drew apart, separating into two groups. Two ships, their silhouettes visible in the fading twilight.

That certainly didn't bode well. Around him, the sailors moved restlessly.

"Pirates," one said, in a low voice.

"Athraig?" another suggested.

"They be one and the same," the first man replied.

"How far, cap'n?" the mate asked, gripping the rail with calloused hands.

"Close—and getting closer." The captain lowered the tube, frowning. "They carry too much sail for us to outrun."

"Can we make harbor before they catch us?" the mate asked.

"They're between us and land." The captain lifted the tube to his eye again. "No chance we can slip by—they're on a direct course to intercept."

For an instant, Bran considered casting a rune to raise the wind—but he was not adept at weather spells. And even if the ship could escape whoever was on the water with them, he did not want to turn them away from Raine. Not when they were so close.

He moved to stand at the captain's shoulder.

"My sword is at the ready," he told the man. "Will there be a fight?"

The captain lowered his device and turned to Bran. "My men aren't soldiers, and those are Athraig warships coming to meet us. We don't stand a chance."

"What do they want?" Bran cast a glance at the quickly approaching ships.

"Our goods, likely. The hold is full of Parnesian cloth and spices." The captain grimaced. "It'll be a hard loss—but at least I'll be able to bring back a load of lumber to help recoup the cost."

"Once they empty the ship, they will let us go?" Bran asked, his pulse spiking as the shadowy forms of the other boats grew larger and larger.

"Aye." The captain turned to his men. "Prepare for boarding. Hide anything you value, and let the others know. Fall off!"

The sailors scurried away, and the ship turned, the sails beginning to flap as they lost wind. The slap of the waves against the sides quieted from a hiss to a hush as they slowed.

"Best go stash your coin," the captain said to Bran. "And keep that sword sheathed. No need for bloodshed."

Bran gave him a tight nod, then strode back to the ladder leading to the cabins below. He swiftly descended, then pushed open the cabin door to see Mara awake and looking out the twilight-illuminated port-hole mounted beside the bed.

"Other ships," she said, turning toward him. "Trouble?"

"The captain thinks they're Athraig raiders, come to steal our cargo. They'll board and be gone soon enough. He advised we conceal anything of value."

Her gaze went to his sword, the jewels gleaming on the pommel. Bran covered it protectively with his hand and bared his teeth. "I dare anyone to try."

She shook her head, but didn't argue. "At the very least, we need to recast your illusion."

"That, I can agree to."

He sat on the edge of the bed and spoke the rune. A quick flare of blue light, and his human semblance was refreshed. It would last through the night, and, if all went well, they would be nearly to Castle Raine by the time he'd need to summon it again.

A moment later, they heard the clunk of metal meeting wood and the thud of running footsteps overhead.

"I want to go up." Mara rose and grabbed her cloak from the hook by the door. "Do you think it's safe? The thought of being trapped down here..." She shivered.

He frowned in thought. "Even if we were pursued from Parnese, which is unlikely, word of what happened there would not yet have traveled this far. It should be safe enough to go above. According to the captain, the raiders will not shed blood as long as the *Pridewell* surrenders."

And he'd rather have room to swing his sword if things turned ugly.

He went first up the ladder, then gave Mara a hand up. The deck swirled with motion, but no one was fighting. A much larger ship rode beside them, their vessel tethered to it with ropes and grappling hooks, and a long plank had been shoved across the watery chasm between.

Several fair-haired soldiers in dark uniforms were herding the sailors together. At the prow, the captain was arguing fiercely with a woman who, by her proud bearing, was the leader of the Athraig.

Mara glanced at Bran. “Shouldn’t they be unloading the cargo?”

“Something is wrong. Come—we need answers.”

He headed toward the captain, Mara beside him. They received a few curious looks as they made their way past the sailors and soldiers, but no one stopped them.

“And these are our passengers,” the captain said as Bran and Mara halted before him.

“Bound for Raine?” The Athraig leader’s cold blue gaze swept them up and down.

“Yes,” Mara said. “I’m going to visit my family. Is there a problem?”

“Aye,” the captain said, a bitter edge to his voice. “We’re being taken hostage.”

“What! Why?” Bran demanded, narrowing his eyes at the Athraig woman.

She met his stare without flinching. “No ships are allowed to land upon Raine at this time.”

“For what reason?”

“Not your business to know,” she said.

“I could make it my business,” he said, resting his hand on his sword.

“Bran.” Mara caught his arm and nodded to the armed soldiers closing in around them.

Bran clenched his teeth and slowly removed his hand, letting his cloak fall closed over his weapon. Mara was right—it was not the time to fight. Yet.

Although it was clear the Athraig were trying to isolate Raine. Whatever their intentions, they couldn’t be good.

“How long will you be keeping us?” the captain asked.

“Two days,” the Athraig told him. “You’d best ration your stores.”

“What happens after two days?” Bran asked, casting a look at the large ship. It was large enough to carry several dozen soldiers, at least.

The woman ignored his question, and Mara stepped forward. “Even if you must keep the ship, can’t you just put us ashore?”

The woman cut her hand through the air. “No more questions. Unless you’d like to be confined to your quarters.”

When they remained silent, the Athraig leader turned back to the captain. “My pilot will take the helm, and I’ll be leaving a detail of soldiers aboard. We’ll escort you to the flotilla. Don’t try anything clever. Our cannons will be trained on your ship.”

The man grimaced. “I understand.”

“Good.” She swept them all with a last, icy glance, then turned on her heel and strode to where the plank spanned the two ships.

Bran wished he could make the vessel lurch as she went up the length of wood. Unfortunately, despite the movement of waves and wind, she was surefooted, and gained her ship without mishap.

“Damnation,” the captain said in a low voice. “Wish I’d listened to the rumors.”

“At least they didn’t take your cargo,” Mara said.

“Yet.” The man gave her a dark look. “I won’t count my blessings until I’m back in Parnese, that’s for certain. What are those devils planning?”

Invasion, Bran thought, though he didn’t say it aloud. His gut clenched at the thought of the danger to Anneth, trapped in Castle Raine’s dungeon.

Bran and Mara stayed on deck as the *Pridewell*, escorted by the Athraig leader’s ship, set off on a course parallel to the dark bulk of Raine’s shoreline. The other warship stayed behind, presumably to intercept any other vessels bound for harbor in Portknowe.

Grimly, Bran watched as they moved away from the port. The ships rounded a long, rocky promontory, and Mara let out a breath at the sight of another two Athraig warships anchored some distance out, surrounded by a few small fishing vessels.

“Four warships,” she said softly. “They plan to attack Raine. But where is our navy?”

“They likely lured your country’s ships away. But even four ships’ worth of soldiers isn’t enough to capture an entire country, no matter how skilled in battle those warriors might be.” He narrowed his eyes at the small flotilla. “They have some other scheme in mind.”

"Look." Mara leaned over the rail. "Do you see something on the beach, up near the trees?"

He caught the back of her cloak, not liking to see his wife lean so far over the water, then turned his attention toward the distant shore. The gray stones on the curve of beach shone very faintly in the last light. Bran flicked his dark vision on, then bit back a curse.

"Empty boats," he said. "The soldiers have already landed."

She turned to him, face pale, and grabbed his hands. "We have to get ashore. My family, and yours, are in terrible danger. We must warn them, and rescue Anneth."

The same urgency burned through him, but much as he wanted to leap overboard that instant, they must come up with a plan.

"To our cabin," he said tersely.

She gave him a short nod, and together they left the darkening deck as the first bleak mortal stars emerged overhead.

CHAPTER 31

In the confines of their cabin, Mara folded her arms about herself, trying to contain her fear for her family and, looming behind that, worry for her entire country. Raine, under attack by the Athraig! The rumors in Parnese had been right. Even if she'd known they were true, however, there was nothing she could have done about it at the time.

Now, though, her tension notched up at the knowledge that rumors had become reality—and Little Hazel lay far too close to Castle Raine to provide any safety.

"Tell Ondo to warn my family," she said as Bran poured a measure of water into his scrying bowl.

"His first duty is to free Anneth," he said tightly.

"Surely he can stop at the cottage on the way to the castle. Once my family leaves home, we can meet them in the forest."

The forest... For a moment, the vision she'd had in the Pool of Reflection at Hawthorne swam to mind. They'd been fleeing through the Darkwood at night, Bran turning as a black arrow flew from the shadows and struck him full in the chest. She shuddered at the recollection.

Yet they must pass through the forest to reach the gateway.

Just because I saw it, doesn't mean it will come to pass. The tutor, Penluith, had said as much at the time. But what if he'd been wrong?

"And then what?" Bran asked, unaware of the turn of her thoughts. "Your family will be even more reluctant to abandon the mortal world than you are. Will you really tell them to flee Raine without first trying to help your country?"

She let out an unhappy breath. "What can we do, Bran? You're a powerful warrior, but you can't push back this assault—especially if the Athraig already have taken the castle."

"Together, we defeated the Void invasion," he reminded her, setting his water-filled silver bowl on the tiny table.

"Yes, but that was with over a hundred warriors keeping the Void creatures at bay while we focused our magic. And even though the Athraig are Raine's enemy, we can't just destroy them with magic. Those soldiers are guilty only of loyalty to their commanders and country."

"You are too soft-hearted."

"And you can't just murder dozens of people!" She stared at him, heart pounding.

He held her gaze, his expression shadowed. Finally he blew out a long breath.

"I cannot promise not to spill mortal blood," he said. "Especially with Anneth's safety at stake. But I will do everything I can to minimize that bloodshed."

"I know." She shut her eyes briefly. "We must take things as they come."

He settled at the table, scrying bowl before him. "Perhaps Ondo has discovered something more."

Biting her lip, she moved to stand behind her husband. He passed his hand over the shimmering surface and spoke the rune of scrying. A moment later, Ondo's face appeared, worry carving long lines beside his mouth.

"What news?" Bran asked. "Have you spoken with Anneth?"

"No. I fear for her safety. Please, give me leave to enter the castle."

"You have it." Bran's tone was grim. "Athraig soldiers are on their way, and she must win free of the dungeon before they arrive."

"Are you near?" Ondo asked. "I will wait until you come."

Bran gave a sharp shake of his head. "No. We're being held off the coast. There's no hope of us reaching Castle Raine before the soldiers. You and Anneth will have to accomplish her escape, and hide in the forest until we come."

Gently, Mara set her hands on Bran's shoulders. "Remind him to warn my family. They don't have to leave Raine, but if they know what's coming, they can at least make the choice to remove themselves from harm's way."

He gave a tight nod, and did as she asked.

"I will tell them," Ondo said. "And I will attempt to scry to Princess Anneth—though they keep her under close watch."

"If you can't reach her, you'll need to find your way to the dungeon, and do whatever is necessary to get her out."

"I will, my lord." Ondo bowed his head. "You have my word."

"We will come as soon as possible." Bran's voice was taut with leashed frustration.

Mara felt the same. By now, they should have been riding toward Castle Raine—not trapped in an Athraig-controlled flotilla.

Bran dismissed the scrying and sat back with a sharp exhalation.

"As soon as the ship quiets, we'll leave," Mara said, rubbing the tension from his neck. "Cast the rune of invisibility, find a dinghy, and get to shore."

"What then?" he asked tightly. "A half-day, at least, lies between us and the castle. We will arrive too late."

She swallowed back a stab of panic at the thought.

Everything was happening too quickly—and too slowly. Every few minutes, panic would try to steal her breath, and she'd stuff it back down, only for it to rise again.

Save her family. Save Raine, if she could—though she had no idea how she might accomplish such a thing. Free Anneth. Open the gateway, and leave the mortal world. Save Lord Calithilon. Then what? Stay in Elfhame, or return to Raine forever?

The thought of losing Bran made her heart twist with foreshadowed grief.

But so did the thought of never seeing her family again.

"Could we not make a rune of some kind?" she asked. "Haste, to move us quickly through the forest?"

Bran frowned. "We have such castings—children use them in play. But without a direct line between where you are and where you wish to go, terrible things happen. The first branch we encounter would impale us, or we would drown in a pond, or—"

"I understand," she said, interrupting his gruesome description. "Flight? What if we went above the treetops?"

He shook his head. "Our magic is connected to the earth, even here in the mortal world. If I could have soared across Raine and the sea in pursuit of the Voidspawn, believe me, I would've done so."

"Then there's nothing else we might try?" Tears caught in her throat.

Gently, he squeezed her hands, though his expression mirrored her own desolation. "Once night falls, we'll slip off the *Pridewell* and make what haste we can. That is our only course."

ANNETH PLUCKED straw out of her hair by the light of the sullen torches lining the dungeon walls. She'd slept fitfully, eaten when an Athraig guard had shoved bowls of cold porridge into the cells, and waited for a moment when she might attempt a scrying to Ondo.

Unfortunately, hours had passed without such an opportunity. In addition to the archers keeping the king under constant threat, two other guards had taken up posts just outside the cells.

Every time Anneth tried to speak with Prince Owen, she'd been harshly told to keep her silence, and her distance.

The prince grew increasingly agitated as the day wore on. He rose and paced at frequent intervals, shooting worried glances at his father. For his part, King Philip seemed diminished. Lines of pain scored his forehead whenever he moved, and Anneth feared the Athraig's rough treatment had grievously damaged his already weak constitution.

Three times since waking she'd felt the tug of a scrying, but had no way to safely respond. With each missed attempt, her worry mounted.

How could she plan her escape when communication with her allies was impossible?

Finally, when the tense silence in the dungeon had reached suffocating levels, Lord Jensen strode in. He faced the king, hands on his hips. His usual sneer had been replaced by taut-mouthed anger.

"Well, your majesty," he said, the title dripping with sarcasm, "it seems your captain of the guard needs a demonstration of our sincerity."

Prince Owen rushed to the front of his cell.

"What do you mean?" he demanded, gripping the bars with white-knuckled hands.

Lord Jensen spared the prince a glance. "Captain Crane thinks he can incite his soldiers into retaking the castle. I intend to dissuade him from that idea."

"How?" the prince asked in a choked voice.

Alarm singing through her, Anneth moved to the door of her cell. Although it was locked, there was no additional chain holding it closed, like the others. Silently, she reached for her wellspring, focusing her power.

Lord Jensen jerked his head at the guards. "Remove King Philip from his cell."

"Take me," the prince said. "If you must make an example—"

"Your wedding is imminent," the Athraig leader said. "Princess Rella arrives tonight, and on the morrow, the marriage will take place. She would not be happy to find her bridegroom missing a limb."

His words sent a cold clutch of fear into Anneth's stomach. Her gaze darted from Lord Jensen to the guards and archers. The prisoners were outnumbered five to three—or two, since the king was in no condition to fight. Judging from his pained movements, he would need assistance fleeing the dungeon, which made their odds of escape even worse.

With a jingle of keys, the guards undid the chain fastened across the door of King Philip's cell.

"No," the prince said, the word a low moan.

Anneth held herself still, her mind racing. When Lord Jensen took the king, he would need at least one of the archers and one of the guards to accompany him, which made her and Prince Owen's chances of escape better.

The king's pace would be slow, too. Even if the guards had to carry him, Anneth and the prince could catch up—hopefully before Lord Jensen inflicted further harm.

The two guards moved into the king's cell and took him by the arms. For a moment, King Philip resisted. Then one of the Athraig kicked his leg, and he let out a yelp of pain. Only the guards' grip kept him from collapsing to the straw-scattered floor.

"Stop," Prince Owen said sharply, pressing himself against the bars.

The Athraig ignored him as they hauled the king from his cell.

"Folie, with us," Lord Jensen said, gesturing to the nearest archer. "Grinar, keep a close eye on these two. If they try anything, shoot the girl."

"What?" the prince cried in horror.

Lord Jensen glanced at him. "As I said, you won't be harmed. Not before you're wed, at least."

The implication chilled Anneth to the bone. Unless she acted soon, none of them would escape Castle Raine with their lives.

The guards dragged King Philip forward. As they passed the prince's cell, he stretched his hands through the bars.

"Father," he said brokenly, reaching for the king.

"Take heart." King Philip gave a weary smile and met his son's anguished gaze. "You will make a good king—your mother would be proud."

"No!" the prince cried as the guards, led by Lord Jensen, took the wounded monarch away.

Her throat dry with sorrow, with fear, Anneth watched as the archer took up the rear, his crossbow trained on the king's back.

Prince Owen shot her a desperate look. Tears shone against his cheeks, eerily resembling blood as they reflected the ruddy torchlight.

"Please," he whispered. "Do something."

Anneth glanced at him, then leaned forward as far as she could, peering into what she could see of the cellar. The metal bars were cold against her cheeks, but after a few ragged breaths, she was all but certain that Lord Jensen and his miserable retinue had gone.

"Back to your bench," the remaining archer said, jerking his bow at Anneth.

She widened her eyes at the prince, giving him a nearly imperceptible nod. Then, drawing on her power, she lifted her hands. One palm pointing at her cell door, the other at Prince Owen's, she shouted the rune of opening.

"*Edro!*"

CHAPTER 32

Blue light exploded from Anneth's hands. The sharp clang of metal on metal resounded through the dungeon as the cell doors burst open, followed by the clinking of shattered chain links hitting the stone floor.

"Look out!" Prince Owen cried, leaping for the archer, even as a bolt whizzed past Anneth's ear.

She jerked away, and a black braid drifted to the ground, shorn from her head. Fear grabbed her heart and squeezed. Any closer, and instead of that plait of hair it would have been her body lying there, bleeding her life out on the dirty straw.

She ducked, readying her next rune, but the prince was faster. He collided with the archer, and she heard a dull thunk as the man's head hit the wall.

The archer's eyes rolled back in his head. Prince Owen yanked the crossbow from his hands and grabbed one of the scattered bolts. He cranked back the string and managed to jam the bolt into place just as the two guards stationed in the cellar came running.

The first received a bolt to the chest. The other halted, then slumped to the ground as Anneth's rune of slumber took him.

Prince Owen dropped the bow and bent to snatch the sword from his fallen foe. She stepped forward and scooped up the abandoned crossbow and a handful of bolts. Their wickedly sharp points would serve as makeshift daggers, if it came to close fighting. There wasn't time to unbuckle the quiver from the unconscious archer, so she jabbed the bolts through the material of her sleeve, mentally apologizing to Mrs. Geary. Although, in truth, the dress was already ruined beyond repair.

"Hurry." Urgency burned in Prince Owen's voice as he straightened, weapon in hand, and turned toward the cellar.

"Wait." She awkwardly shouldered the short-stringed bow. "Let me cast shadow upon us."

Invisibility would be better, but that rune took intense concentration, and she could already feel the strain upon her wellspring. Shadow, though imperfect, was easier to summon, and at least would help conceal them from sight.

The prince paused, impatience flashing in his eyes.

Hastily, Anneth spread her fingers and spoke the rune.

"*Unuhuine.*"

Patchy darkness shrouded her face and settled about her shoulders like a tattered cloak.

Prince Owen peered at her. "When we are free, Anneth, you have a great deal of explaining to do."

There were still far too many obstacles ahead for her to worry about answering to Prince Owen. Without replying, she cast shadow upon him in turn. The moment it was done, he whirled and ran for the cellar stairs. She was right behind him as they dashed up the stairway, and was barely able to stop herself from colliding with him when he halted at the closed door at the top.

With excruciating slowness, he lifted the latch and pushed the door open a crack. The room beyond was dim. The kitchen, if she remembered correctly.

Flicking on her dark vision, Anneth took the unfamiliar weapon and tried to recall how the prince had armed it. Cautiously she cranked back the string and set a new bolt along the wooden shaft, taking care to keep her fingers away from the trigger on the underside.

What a strange contraption—but she did not have time to examine at it further, as Prince Owen pushed open the door and motioned her forward.

They crept out into the deserted kitchen. The scent of meat and cooked onions lingered in the air, and a long counter next to the sinks held rows of drying dishes. Dinner must be over, and the servants dismissed until it was time to prepare for the next meal.

Motioning her to stay behind him, the prince led the way past the cavernous hearths and the huge table, stained and pitted from kitchen work. At the end of the room, he paused at the short run of stairs, listening.

"A moment," Anneth whispered, veering toward the sinks.

She grabbed the nearest bowl—a dented metal thing—and splashed some water into it. Not even bothering to set it on the table, she angled it to catch the slice of sunset coming in from the single window high overhead.

Ondo, she thought fiercely, as she intoned the rune of scrying.

"Princess!" His concerned visage stared up at her from the bowl. "Are you safe?"

"Shh. I have little time, but are you near? We need your help."

"I am just inside the castle wall, near the herb gardens," he said. "Even though it's nearly sunset, there is much activity—it's difficult to move about unseen."

Her heart leaped with hope, that he was so close. "Bran and Mara, too?"

"No," he said, and her spirits plummeted back into shadow as he continued. "They are detained at the coast by the Athraig. But where are you?"

"The kitchen."

"Very near." His voice tightened with urgency. "There is a door at the side. I will wait for you there, and we will make for the Darkwood. You are almost free."

She glanced at Prince Owen, who was watching her. Despair crept over his face, and she could tell he thought she was going to abandon him. With a deep breath, she looked back at Ondo.

"No." The word abraded her throat. "I must help rescue the king."

"I forbid it." The scout's voice rose, and she gestured him to quiet.

"I must," she said. "Where are the Athraig gathering?"

He remained stubbornly silent.

"Ondo," she said, bringing all her regal training to bear, "I command you to tell me. If you refuse to help me now, my death is upon your head."

The scout squeezed his eyes shut. When he opened them, his expression was resigned.

"They are in the courtyard," he said. "I will meet you there."

Without responding, she dashed the water out into the sink, set the bowl back on the counter, and turned to Prince Owen. His eyes burned with fierce emotion.

"I am in your debt," he said.

"Your father's not free yet." She nodded to the stairs.

He pivoted, and she followed him up, both of them staying close to the wall. Anneth kept her bow pointed low, so she wouldn't accidentally shoot him if she stumbled. The sound of her heartbeat was like a drum in her ears as she tried to think of what runes she might need.

She wasn't strong enough to cast slumber on a large gathering, and even if she could, it wouldn't last long. In fact, the guard in the dungeon would awaken soon, and then they'd have enemies at their front *and* back.

If only Bran were there! He was skilled at battle magic, and she and Prince Owen were desperately overmatched. Ondo knew some runes of attack, but his wellspring wasn't terribly strong. Certainly he wasn't as powerful as the Hawthorne Prince.

But he was all they had.

The short stairwell opened into the great hall of Castle Raine. Anneth blinked to see it dark and empty. Only a few lanterns shed radiance, leaving lonely pools of light on the flagstones. How long ago the motion and hubbub of the prince's ball now seemed. It was hard to believe it had only been... She frowned.

Time passed strangely in captivity, and she'd been careful to recast her illusion rune after every sleep—but she guessed it had been two mortal days. Not long, and even shorter in Elfhame, thank the moons. Surely Lord Calithilon still lived.

And here she was, going to the aid of another ruler.

She would give almost anything to save them both.

A shout sounded from outside the doors at the end of the hall. Exchanging alarmed glances, she and the prince began to run. Their footsteps echoed softly in the deserted room as they dashed between rows of benches—no doubt set up for Prince Owen's imminent, and involuntary, wedding.

Breathing heavily, they fetched up at the tall doors. The prince adjusted his grip on his sword, then opened the door just enough for them to peer out.

The red-orange light of the setting sun illuminated a grim scene.

At the bottom of the hewn stone steps stood King Philip, held upright by an Athraig guard. Lord Jensen was next to him, facing a furious-looking Captain Crane, who had his arms pinioned behind his back by two other Athraig. Two more of Lord Jensen's men stood behind the imprisoned captain, their blades drawn.

"I'll control my men," Captain Crane said, his voice fierce. "Just don't harm the king."

"Rather too late for that, isn't it?" Lord Jensen said. "On both counts. A pity you didn't take us more seriously." He beckoned to the nearest soldier. "Demonstrate to the captain that we are true to our bargains—especially when they are broken."

The man stepped forward, lifting his gleaming sword over the king. "Where shall I strike him, my lord?"

"No!" Prince Owen cried, shoving the door wide.

Anneth gave him an alarmed glance as he dashed out. Forcing her hand to remain steady, she lifted the bow, sighted the swordsman, and depressed the trigger mechanism. By the brightmoon, she hoped she'd set the arrow correctly.

Thwack!

The bolt flew true. It buried itself in the guard's chest, and he stumbled back, his sword clanging to the cobbles.

Prince Owen reached the man holding his father and drove his blade into the guard's side. With a gurgle of pain, the guard released King Philip. The prince hastily caught his father, but now was hampered in his fighting.

Lord Jensen called for more soldiers, a note of panic in his voice. With a vicious kick to the knee, Captain Crane sent one of the guards holding him to the ground, then whirled and jabbed the other one in the throat.

Quick as thought, he scooped up the sword and sprang toward Lord Jensen, now guarded by the two other swordsmen.

Halfway down the stairs, Anneth paused. There wasn't time to pick off each soldier individually. Already the remaining guards were advancing on Prince Owen and the king.

Squinting against the last rays of sunlight, she reached for all the power in her wellspring and held up her hand, palm toward the fighting.

"*Calya!*" she yelled, the rune for summoning light, then turned her head away, squeezing her eyes closed.

A brilliant flash blasted down the stairs, brighter than the sun. The power of it scorched her skin. From the yelps of consternation below, the rune had done its job.

It was not a bolt of magic, but even foxfire could temporarily blind.

She opened her eyes, wincing at the afterimage of light seared across her vision, and sprang down the stairs. The soldiers scrubbed at their eyes. She had bought a little time, but not much.

They must disappear before their enemies could see again.

"This way," she whispered urgently, grabbing Prince Owen by the arm and hauling him toward the corner of the castle.

The prince resisted her pull, lagging to help support his father. Anneth quickly took the king's other arm and, with as much haste as possible, they hobbled toward safely.

"What about Captain Crane?" the prince asked softly.

"I can't guide you all." She cast a distressed glance over her shoulder. She didn't much like the captain, but how could they abandon him? They needed every ally they had.

Then a lithe form darted into the courtyard. Ondo!

He took Captain Crane's shoulder, then ducked as the man made a wild swing with his sword. Leaning forward, the scout whispered in the captain's ear.

A moment later, they were heading toward Anneth at a rapid pace. Even though Captain Crane couldn't see, he moved with efficient ease under Ondo's guidance.

"Help the king," Anneth said as soon as they were near. "We're almost to the corner. I'll go first, to make sure it's safe." And to cast a rune of slumber, if necessary.

"Take hold of my cloak," Ondo told the captain.

He thrust his garment at the man, then turned and took Anneth's place, slipping his arm around the ailing king's waist.

Captain Crane grabbed a handful of Ondo's cloak and cocked his head. "Who are you?"

"One of my allies," Anneth said.

"Helping us escape?" the captain asked, directing the words in her general direction. "Strange behavior for an Athraig spy."

"Later," Prince Owen said.

She could tell the captain wasn't satisfied, but he was wise enough to hold his tongue—for the moment.

"Halt a moment," she said, peering around the corner of the castle.

No one was in sight, thank the seven stars, and she urged her companions forward. As soon as the bulk of the stone wall lay between them and the Athraig, she let out a ragged breath. They weren't safe yet, but at least they had a chance.

"That way," Ondo said, jerking his head to the right, as his hands were full with the king. "Past the kitchen gardens. There's a small door in the outer wall."

"Can any of you see yet?" she asked.

"A little." The prince blinked several times. "Shapes—dark and light."

"Move faster," the captain said. "If we're recovering our vision, so are they."

No one argued.

The smell of bruised herbs stung Anneth's nose as they made their way through the gardens. It was painfully obvious that the king would not be able to flee into the forest. He was barely able to stagger along, even supported on both sides.

But they could not leave him.

A shout came from behind them, and Anneth glanced back to see the guard from the dungeon.

"Here!" he called, presumably to Lord Jensen and his remaining soldiers.

Anneth grabbed Prince Owen's arm, but there was no use urging him to speed up. Not while he and Ondo still supported the king.

Captain Crane frowned. "We must make a stand."

"No—we must get my father to safety," Prince Owen argued.

"Do both," Ondo said. "Two of us take the king out the side door and flee. The others defend, giving them time to escape."

Although surely the captain couldn't see Ondo's face, he and the scout exchanged a glance.

"No," Anneth said, with a shiver of understanding. "I refuse to let you sacrifice yourself so that I can escape."

"It is my duty, my lady," Ondo said gently. "And my privilege to serve the Hawthorne Court."

The prince's expression grew bleak. "Captain Crane, I forbid—"

"No time." The captain released his grip on Ondo's cloak. "I can almost see well enough to fight. Get to the door. Now!"

He turned to face their pursuers, sword raised. Ondo coaxed the king to go faster. Face twisted in pain, King Philip increased his hobbling steps. The outer wall loomed ahead, the small wooden door dwarfed against the high stone.

"Take my place," Ondo said to Anneth as they reached the door. "We will buy you enough time to reach the Darkwood. Farewell, Princess Anneth. Tell your brother I am sorry."

Throat tight with unvoiced sobs, Anneth reached for the latch. She pulled open the door, helped Prince Owen carry his father through, then froze in disbelief.

Facing them, only a few paces from the wall, stood over a hundred Athraig soldiers. They carried torches, the light reflecting off bits of metal on their stiff leather armor.

And off the diamond crown of the fair-haired young woman borne on a palanquin in their midst.

Her ice-blue gaze skidded from Anneth to the king, then fixed on Prince Owen.

"Ah," she said, with a small, cold smile. "My intended groom, Prince Owen of Raine. How thoughtful of you to come out and meet me."

CHAPTER 33

Owen stared at the Athraig princess, his thoughts freezing. Their hard-won escape had been for naught. His hopes squeezed down to dregs, a bitter wine he could scarcely stomach.

His father, one arm draped heavily across Owen's shoulders, made a sound of dismay.

"Too late to ask Lady Fiona now," he said, his voice rasping with misery.

Behind them came the sound of fighting, and the princess snapped her fingers. Ten men in black armor stepped forward, presumably her personal guard.

"Take them," she said, nodding to where Owen stood with his father and Anneth. "And see what's happening behind that wall. Signal if you need reinforcements."

Owen looked as his father's bowed head, and despair flooded him. There was no use trying to run.

As the Athraig soldiers advanced, Anneth shot him an intent look.

"Prince Owen," she said with soft urgency. "If you must be betrothed, then marry me."

He blinked at her a moment before comprehension dawned. As his father had reminded him, Rainish law forbade an already-engaged person to wed someone else. That had been the entire point of the ball, after all.

"Anneth," he said hurriedly. "Will you consent to be my bride?"

"Yes," she said, without a moment's hesitation.

Their gazes locked. A strange sensation rang through Owen, as though he had just been struck by a pulse of inaudible sound, dashed by a wave that carried no water.

The Athraig guard reached them. Three of them roughly took charge of Owen, Anneth, and the king. The others dashed through the door into the castle grounds beyond.

A few shouts rang out, a final clang of swords meeting. Owen held his breath, hoping the bravely loyal Captain Crane, as well as Anneth's man, still lived.

A taut silence fell, finally broken by Lord Jensen's appearance. As he stepped through the doorway, he shot Owen a triumphant look. Then his attention turned to Princess Rella, and he swept her an ostentatious bow.

"Your highness," he said, "how wise—and fortuitous—of you to come to the side door in the castle walls."

She gazed haughtily down at him. "Credit me with some sense, Jensen. Our reconnaissance showed that your control of Castle Raine was less than complete—which I'm sure my father will find... disappointing."

The greve flinched slightly, but stood his ground. "We've quashed the momentary uprising, my lady, and taken the dissidents back into custody."

Owen briefly shut his eyes in gratitude. Their loyal defenders had survived.

"And the escaped prisoners?" Princess Rella tipped her head toward Owen. "It seems we're needed here to mop up your careless spills."

"My soldiers were on the verge of retaking them."

"They never should have gotten free in the first place!" Her tone was sharp. "Indeed, I don't trust you to not botch things further. We shall hold the wedding without delay. No more of your ineptitude will be tolerated."

Her warriors murmured in agreement, and Lord Jensen went pale at the rebuke.

"Of course, my lady," he said. "I will prepare the great hall—"

"No." She glanced about the dusk-filled stretch of meadow where they stood, fitfully illuminated by torchlight and lantern. "We will not give my intended any more opportunities for flight. The ceremony will take place here. Fetch the cleric. And more light."

"As you wish." Lord Jensen made her another bow, then spun and stalked back to the door in the castle wall.

"Bring the dissidents," the princess called after him. "After the ceremony, we'll make an example of them."

Anneth's head jerked up at that. She glanced at Owen, her eyes wide with fearful questions. All he could do was shake his head. At the moment, there was nothing they could do to save their men. Or themselves.

And now that they weren't fleeing for their lives, he recalled what her man had called her. Brows knitting, Owen turned his head to stare at her.

"You're a princess?" he asked in a bare whisper.

Her mouth tightened, but she jerked her head in affirmation.

So, his intuition had been right—she was no commoner. But what country would send their princess, unescorted, into such a perilous situation?

Not completely alone, however. In the dungeon, which felt like an eternity ago, she'd told him she had three allies. The first, arms tightly bound, was even now being escorted through the doorway, Captain Crane behind him.

But where were Anneth's other supporters?

By the light of the oil lantern mounted on their cabin wall, Mara finished tucking the last of their provisions into her bag. Straightening, she glanced out the porthole. Night had finally descended, the last shimmering reflection of daylight fading from the sea. It was time for them to leave the *Pridewell.*

Grimly silent, except for a few whispered consultations about who would carry what, she and Bran had made ready. All the while, she'd been thinking furiously, trying to find a solution to the problem of their distance from Castle Raine.

They couldn't travel any faster, as Bran had already made clear. But perhaps there was a different answer...

"Ready?" he asked, turning from his packing to face her. "Once I cast the rune of invisibility, we must not speak until we're safely ashore."

She lifted her hand, forestalling him. "There might be another way."

His brows rose, but he waited patiently to hear what she would say.

Speaking slowly, she tried to put her glimmer of inspiration into words. "Could we craft another rune? One that would transport us across Raine to the Darkwood—not with speed but..." She paused, searching for the concept.

Bran watched her intently. "A door?" he suggested.

"Yes." She smiled at him, hope blossoming inside her. "If magic can create a gate between worlds, certainly it can create a doorway from one place to another within the *same* world."

"Another gateway," Bran said, dawning hope in his eyes. He took her hands in his. "Your mortal perspective is sorely needed in Elfhame, my love. Until this journey of ours, creating new magics was unthought of among my people."

Her shoulders twitched uncomfortably. Just because she'd helped invent new runes didn't mean she ought to dwell among the Dark Elves forever. The question of her future loomed ever closer, and with effort, she set it aside. Their first priority must be to reach Anneth, and then her family. The rest would follow as it may.

"How would we know where to arrive, though, without any gateway stones to mark the way?" she asked, frowning. "It will do us no good to wind up in some featureless tract of forest, with no idea which direction to go."

"If you can envision it, then I believe I can transport us there," he said, pressing her hands. "I have little memory of Raine, other than the coast, but you must know the area around your family's cottage well."

"Of course." She'd lived there her whole life, after all, until she'd been magically whisked into Elfhame. "There's a place where the forest clears to meadow, just at the edge of the Darkwood."

"Then you will be our guide." He let go of her hands and began to pace with excitement. "We must think of the rune."

"Door, or gate?"

"*Fende,*" he said. "Combined with the word for travel... Perhaps *lelyafende* will work."

"If it does, we won't even need to attempt to sneak ashore." Her pulse rose with renewed hope. "We can cast the rune from here, inside the cabin, and be there in a matter of moments!"

"It will take a great deal of power," he said, coming to a halt before her. "We'll need time to recover after such a casting."

"Yes, but at least we'll be at the edge of the forest."

"The forest..." His expression darkened. "Neither Ondo nor Anneth have sent a scrying. They would if they'd reached the safety of the Darkwood."

"You think she hasn't been able to escape?" The heady sensation of hope drained from her.

"Not yet," he said grimly.

She brought her knuckles to her mouth, thinking, then met his turbulent gaze. "We can travel directly to Castle Raine. I served as a maid there for a short time. I'm sure I can recall the courtyard well enough."

"Too dangerous. We cannot arrive weakened in the middle of enemy territory, with no way of knowing if it's safe."

He was right. The courtyard was too public, even at night.

She let out a frustrated breath, mouth twisting as she wracked her memory. Where could they land?

The smell of smoke tickled her nose, and she suddenly knew.

"There's a small door in the outer wall, near the kitchen gardens. We used to empty the fireplace ashes on the compost heap next to the wall. I could take us there—and it's completely out of the way."

"Hm." He narrowed his eyes, clearly weighing the idea.

"The maids only go there during the day. I'm certain we'd arrive unobserved."

After a moment, he gave a sharp nod. "Very well. Let us try."

Swallowing back her tremble of nerves, Mara grabbed her pack, then stood beside Bran. They took hands, twining their fingers so that their azure rings touched.

"Fix the place in your mind," he said. "Then open your wellspring. I will direct the casting through you."

Praying it would work, Mara closed her eyes and recalled the tall outer wall of Castle Raine, moss clinging between the cracks in the stone. The small wooden door, dwarfed beneath the shadow of the castle. The smell of damp ashes and rotting onions.

"I'm ready," she said, opening her eyes.

He glanced at her with a half-smile, then pulled in a deep breath and spoke the new rune.

"*Lelyafende.*"

Their power flared, the cabin blurring around them. She felt Bran's magic pushing them forward...

With a jolt, they arrived.

Mara's elation quickly turned to dismay to see they were back in the cramped cabin aboard the *Pridewell.*

"It didn't work," she said softly. At least their wellsprings weren't too much diminished. Perhaps only a successful casting would drain their power.

Bran's mouth tightened.

"I could almost see the place," he said. "And almost reach it—but not quite. It seems that whoever is holding the destination must cast the rune."

It made brutal sense, and alarm surged through her at the thought. "But Bran, my magic's too unstable! Half the time I can't summon a spell, and when I do, the power is all out of proportion."

He studied her intently. "I thought your work with Penluith—"

"I let you believe I was making progress because I couldn't bear your disappointment." She looked down at the floor.

"But your rune of slumber in the temple was well cast. All the priests fell instantly back asleep."

"Which was a good thing, yes." She looked back up at him. "But I couldn't control the intensity. If I needed to only put one person to sleep, who knows what might happen? I could just as easily kill them."

His brows drew together. "I understand. Nonetheless, you must try to transport us to Castle Raine."

"What if I fail?"

He raised their joined hands and kissed her knuckles. "Then at least we made the attempt. I have faith in you, beloved. And you do not disappoint me. Ever."

Tears stung her eyes, and the tightness gripping her heart eased. She would try. She must.

"Say the word again," she told him.

He did, several times, and she watched his face carefully, shaping the syllables with her own mouth.

"Lelya..." she said after a moment. "Fendi. Fendae. Fende."

"Good," he said. "The last time was correct."

Repeating the sound under her breath, she once again pulled up her memory of the doorway in the castle wall. Glancing at her husband for support, she took a deep breath.

"*Lelyafende,*" she said fiercely.

Blue light flashed around them as the rune took hold. The cabin flickered once, twice...

And then reappeared around them as the spell ebbed.

She had failed.

With a sob, she pulled her hand from Bran's and sat heavily on the edge of the bed. It was no use. Her power was too unpredictable. And without being able to control it, she would never be able to dwell easily among the Dark Elves.

"I'm sorry," she whispered.

He knelt beside her, cupping her cheek in his palm. "Do not cry, love. We'll go back to our original plan."

He did not add what they both knew: that they would arrive at Castle Raine far too late.

CHAPTER 34

Wrists bound before her, the cold stones of the castle wall at her back, Anneth watched as the Athraig prepared for their princess's marriage to Prince Owen. Her heart beat fast in her chest, a glimglow fluttering for escape. But there was no escape.

In a very short time, the stretch of meadow outside the walls had been illuminated with a flickering array of lanterns and torches. Under other circumstances it might have been lovely, but in her current predicament the light cast ominous shadows, glinting off naked swords and sharp-tipped arrows. The flames cast grotesque shadows over the watching Athraig, and she shivered.

A small man holding an ornate book waited in the space readied for the marriage ceremony: a cleared semicircle outside the small door set in the wall. His bald head glistened with sweat, and every few moments he darted an anxious glance at the mass of gathered soldiers.

Princess Rella had disappeared somewhere behind her troops. Presumably she would return imminently, ready to marry the prince and seize control of the kingdom.

On either side of Anneth stood the Athraig's prisoners, all of them bound as she was. To her left, King Philip slumped against the wall, barely conscious, his face drawn with pain. Beyond him, closely guarded by two of the princess's men, was Captain Crane, rage sparking from his eyes.

Ondo, on her right, merited only one guard. A bruise had risen on his cheek, and blood darkened the sleeve of his forearm, but other than that, he seemed unharmed—thank the moons.

Standing at the edge of the semicircle of torches surrounding the nervous cleric, Prince Owen had fallen under the less-than-tender hand of Lord Jensen. The Athraig nobleman held a wickedly sharp dagger point-first against Owen's ribs, even as a flustered man hovered over the prince, attempting to transform him from prisoner to bridegroom.

"Enough," Lord Jensen said as the fellow brushed the prince's hair out of his eyes for the third time. "He's presentable enough. You're dismissed."

"Thank you, Antoine," Owen said in a low voice. "I do appreciate the attempt."

The man jumped back, bobbed a quick bow—aimed at the prince, not the Athraig lord—and made to scurry away. He was quickly stopped by an armored soldier and brought to stand against the wall with the rest of the captives.

Their sorry line was bracketed by Lord Jensen's archers, crossbows at the ready in case any of the prisoners managed to wrest free. Anneth knew all too well the power of those short bolts, and how quickly they flew from their strange, sideways bows.

Lord Jensen nodded at one of the black-clad guards. "Inform the princess we're ready," he said, his dagger never wavering from its place against the prince's side.

The soldier hastened away, and Owen shot Anneth a glance. She raised her brows. When was he going to reveal their hasty agreement?

It had been a wild impulse, spurred by the king's words about Lady Fiona. But anything they could do to forestall the Athraig from taking power gave Bran and Mara more time to reach them.

Anneth hadn't been prepared for the result of her impromptu suggestion. When Owen asked and she'd said yes, her wellspring had surged, power flaring as though a solemn binding had just been made.

But what did it mean? Even among Dark Elves, not every betrothal resulted in a bond-spark. And certainly not one that sent out such a forceful ripple of magic.

Cautiously, she tapped her wellspring, amazed to find it partially restored. Their earlier attempt to escape had left her drained. Now, though, they had a chance. Not much of one, but she guessed—hoped—that Ondo still had a reserve of power. Between the two of them, they might be able to win free yet again.

If the opportunity arose, which was not a certainty by any means.

Soon enough, she supposed, the prince would announce he could not marry the Athraig princess. Most likely he'd bide his time until all attention was upon him during the ceremony. A loud public declaration would have the most impact.

Her gaze flicked to Lord Jensen and his dagger, and anxiety cinched her lungs. Surely he wouldn't slay the prince. The point of the forced marriage was to lend legitimacy to the Athraig's takeover, quelling any attempts at rebellion.

And despite Lord Jensen's previously veiled threats, she didn't think the Athraig would kill Owen immediately after the wedding. No, they would make sure he sired an heir before doing away with him.

Gruesome thoughts, but she'd grown up in a court and had learned the machinations of power from watching her own mother's manipulations.

There was a stir among the soldiers as the princess's black-armored guards cleared a path. Someone among the crowd began to play the flute—a breathy thread of sound that wove eerily through the air.

At the far end of the makeshift aisle, Princess Rella appeared, wearing a silvery gown and long cape. She paced forward accompanied by sparks of faceted fire, and Anneth realized the edges of her cape and gown were sewn with diamonds. Each gem caught the reflection of the passing flames and amplified it. Combined with the crown blazing atop her pale hair, the Athraig princess was a glittering sight.

She reached the cleric, and Lord Jensen prodded Owen forward to stand before his supposed bride.

The cleric cleared his throat and, after a quick glance at Lord Jensen, began to speak.

"Dear friends and companions, we are here today gathered—"

"Skip the preamble," Princess Rella said coldly. "Begin on page four of the ceremony."

The man ducked his head and shuffled through the pages of his book, anxiously turning them back and forth beneath the princess's imperious gaze.

"Ah, yes, here," he mumbled, setting his finger on the text. "Princess Rella Jansdotter, Princess of the Daneric Inlands and... um..."

"The titles don't matter," she said, with a slash of her hand. "Go on."

"Is there any reason known to you which prohibits your marriage to this man, Prince Owen Mallory?"

"No. I am free to wed as I choose."

The cleric bobbed a nod and turned to Owen. "Prince Owen Mallory, heir to the throne and only son of his majesty Philip Mallory, King of—"

The princess skewered the man with her pointed gaze. "Faster."

"Yes, your majesty.... Prince Owen isthereanyreasonknowntoyou." The cleric gulped for breath, then plunged back in. "Whichprohibitsyourmarriageto this woman, Princess Rella Jansdotter? Then, if there is no objection—"

"I am not free to marry the princess," Owen declared in a loud, ringing voice.

A shocked silence spread over the crowd. The cleric paused, mouth open.

Princess Rella slowly turned to Owen. The anger in her eyes was sharper than the dagger Lord Jensen held to his side—and just as lethal.

"You lie," she hissed. "Lord Jensen assures me you weren't able to make a formal offer of betrothal before you were imprisoned."

"Nonetheless, I am promised to another." The prince held his head high, calmly meeting Princess Rella's stare.

"To whom are you betrothed?" she asked.

Owen gave no answer, but Lord Jensen's head swiveled to where Anneth stood. She could see the cold calculation in his eyes as he worked his way to the inevitable conclusion.

"Her," he said, tipping his chin at Anneth. "The foreign spy."

Princess Rella looked Anneth up and down and let out a sharp, disbelieving laugh. "That bedraggled commoner? Prince Owen, you are in desperate straits, indeed, to contemplate marrying so low. I am a much better match. Break off your engagement, immediately."

Owen's gaze locked with Anneth's, and again she felt the chiming ripple of magic.

"I will not undo my promise," he said. "She is the woman I will marry."

Rumbling whispers spread through the watching soldiers. Beside her, Anneth felt Ondo tense.

"Are you quite certain?" Lord Jensen asked.

"Yes." Owen held her gaze.

"Then the solution is clear." The Athraig lord gestured to his nearest archer. "Kill her."

Heartbeat slowing to a dull thud, Anneth turned. She threw up one hand, mind scrabbling desperately for a rune of protection. Too slow. Too slow. The archer sighted down his bow. Tightened his grip.

"No!" Ondo cried, flinging himself forward.

The bolt flew—straight toward his heart.

DESPITE BRAN'S words of encouragement, desolation swept through Mara. The porthole was a dark mirror now, reflecting the cramped cabin. She bowed her head, shutting out the sight.

Beside her, Bran jerked in surprise. "Did you sense that?" he asked, voice startled.

"Sense what?" She glanced about the room in confusion.

For a moment there was only the gentle rocking of the ship at anchor. Then she felt it too—a shiver of magic in the air, far distant, but unmistakable.

She turned to Bran. "What was that? It reminded me of something..."

"You felt it when we married," he said. "That was the echo of a *vestalevere*."

"A vestale...?"

"There is no exact word in your language. It is the moment of a pledge of bonding that creates a resonance between two people."

No exact word in your language. His statement lodged in her mind. She stared at him as enormous understanding began to dawn.

No exact word...

"We've been so foolish," she said softly.

"Many times." His lips twisted in a rueful smile. "But which particular instance do you refer to?"

"All of them. All the times I've done magic—don't you see?" She rose, a fire of disbelief, of hope, glowing in her belly. "Crossing the gateway in either direction allows us to understand the other world's language; we know that. Except your runes don't translate, as the words are the way you summon your magic. So of course I've been trying to cast runes as you do, in your native tongue."

He nodded, clearly trying to follow her thoughts. "Yet you do not speak the language of the Dark Elves."

"That's just it! No wonder I've struggled. The pronunciation, even the very concepts, are foreign to me."

"Yet you have had some success."

She grimaced at him. "Barely. The times my power has flowed best is when I lend it to you—or at moments of all-encompassing need."

"When the sheer might of your wellspring overwhelms the errors in casting." His eyes widened. "We've been going about this all wrong."

She shot him a wry look. "Well, it's not like you've had many humans in Elfhame who can do magic."

"Or any at all," he said, with a gesture of frustration. "Still, we should have thought of this far earlier."

"Perhaps—but we've no time now for recriminations." Her nerves tingled with anticipation. "If I'm right, then we still have a chance to reach the castle—immediately. The word I need to speak is not in your language, but mine. And I know exactly the one to use."

"Then, beloved, do so." He caught up their bags and reached for her hand.

Fingers laced together, she closed her eyes and concentrated: the small door in the outer wall of Castle Raine, the night sky overhead, the damp smell of the earth and compost heap.

She was ready.

Heart racing, she reached for the power of her wellspring. It leaped at her touch, as if eager to pour its magic through her.

"*Portal!*" she cried, drawing upon that blaze at the center of her being.

An eldritch wind whirled through the room as she and Bran were enveloped in blue fire. The door to the cabin slammed open, startling a passing sailor, who cautiously peered inside.

But the room was empty.

CHAPTER 35

Bran braced himself as the overwhelming vortex of his wife's power engulfed them. He had only a moment to marvel at the ease of her casting before her magic spat them out beside a tall stone wall.

But instead of a silent, night-swept meadow, his senses reeled with confusion to see an array of flickering lights, a small army of warriors, and, just ahead, a strange ceremony underway.

Motion caught his eye, and he watched in horror as Ondo flung himself in front of Anneth...

"*Ustavanwa!*" Bran yelled, throwing a blazing ball of white fire from his palm.

It sped forward, incinerating the arrow about to bury itself in Ondo's chest. The scout, his arms bound before him, flinched away, then turned his stumble into a graceful roll and regained his feet.

"What is this?" a richly dressed woman cried from the center of the semicircle of torches. "Guards, take them!"

Judging from the sparkling crown atop her head, she was royalty of some sort, but Bran didn't care. He flung out his hands and, mindful of Mara's aversion to shedding human blood, cast a sweeping spell of slumber over the throng. He didn't have time to select their allies by name, so as he cried the rune, he targeted it toward anyone who was an enemy to Raine.

The soldiers slumped, falling where they stood, and he turned to see Mara had already dealt with the guards surrounding the prisoners. He strode forward, taking in the scene: fallen guardsmen, flickering torches, bound prisoners.

Foremost among them, Anneth.

Alive, tears tracking her face.

"Bran," she said, her voice breaking.

He freed her in a matter of moments, then folded her in his arms. "I was so worried for you," he said.

Belatedly, he became aware of a dark-haired young man staring hotly at him. Anneth took a step back and swiped her sleeve across her face, drying her tears. Then she glanced at the young man and gave a crooked smile.

"Bran," she said, "this is Owen."

Stony-faced, the man nodded.

Bran glanced about. Everyone still awake was an ally—including, presumably, the nervous fellow who had bolted back inside the walls—but all too soon, their slumbering enemies would awaken. They must have a plan in place before that moment occurred.

He was glad to see that Mara had already freed Ondo and a hard-faced guardsman who'd also been among the prisoners. Now she supported an older man slumped against the wall, his head hanging low.

"Can you heal him?" she asked Bran. "He seems very weak."

Owen leaped forward with a gasp of dismay.

"Father," he said, slipping his arm around the other man's waist. "Father—wake up."

"We have no time." Bran glanced at the sea of bodies around them, some of them already beginning to stir.

"I'll fetch reinforcements," the guardsman said, brusquely hurrying to the door.

"We must retreat," Anneth said. "Stay inside the walls and defend the castle. All the Athraig are out here."

"They will lay a siege," Owen said. "One we're not equipped to withstand."

"Kill them?" Bran suggested.

"That would surely incite a war," Anneth said. She gestured to the crowned woman sprawled upon the grass. "That's Princess Rella of the Athraig. We can't simply murder her and her men."

"We will send them away," Mara said decisively. "Back to their ships lying off the coast. But I will need all your help."

She beckoned, and they gathered around her. Anneth, her face drawn with exhaustion but her head held high. Ondo, loyalty and relief shining from his eyes. The human man, Owen, who kept shooting Bran narrow-eyed looks.

And Bran himself, who came to stand behind his mortal wife, his hands laid gently upon her shoulders.

"Are you strong enough?" he asked softly, guessing at what she was about to do.

"I hope so. With your help." She pulled in a breath. "Can you muddle their memories? I want them to have no thought of magic, or revenge."

"Only of defeat at the hands of a superior enemy?" He nodded. "I will do my best."

"Then lend me your power." She held out her hands. "All of you."

Anneth grasped her left hand, Ondo her right, and Owen gripped Anneth's arm, confusion in his eyes.

The enemy soldiers surrounding them began to wake, sitting up and reaching for their weapons.

"Princess!" one of them shouted.

Mara's magic surged, and Bran opened his wellspring to her. A whirling circle of blue light appeared, hovering above the grass. Through it he glimpsed the dark sea, the silhouette of the Athraig warship. He clenched his jaw and threw up a veil of confusion and defeat, hazy memories of battle outside the castle, that each of their enemies must pass through.

"*Portal!*" Mara shouted.

The gateway expanded, sucking the nearby bodies through. Some of the soldiers rose and tried to attack, but they could not withstand the pull of the magic.

The princess, fair hair whipped by the wind, hung for a moment in the eye of the storm, then was gone. One by one, the Athraig were disappearing from the meadow. But over half of them—fifty at least—remained.

With a terrible, piercing clarity, Bran understood that his small group would be overwhelmed. Their magic was not enough.

Mara began to tremble, and he poured all his strength, all his love into her. He felt the thin thread of Anneth's nearly depleted wellspring, the staunch trickle of Ondo's power.

The awakening soldiers stumbled forward. One, sword swinging, came too close. Ondo managed to kick the man away, and he was sucked through the doorway.

The portal shuddered, contracted. Mara gasped with effort.

"Hold fast, beloved," Bran murmured.

A new source of energy joined their efforts—a faint touch of magic that, shockingly, could only have come from the human, Owen.

Two more Athraig stumbled through the portal.

Again, Mara's spell faltered, and this time there was no reprieve. Like the brightmoon setting, the doorway waned, fading to a smear of light in the air.

Leaving their exhausted party facing dozens of infuriated Athraig.

Bran released Mara, stepped forward, and drew his sword. It weighed a thousand pounds, but he raised it, arms burning with effort. It had taken everything in him to channel his power to Mara, while also holding the confusion veil.

He would defend her to the death.

Beside him, Ondo pulled a knife from his boot, and at his other side, Owen scooped up an abandoned sword, looking dazed.

"Charge them!" one of the black-armored soldiers called.

The Athraig surged forward. Baring his teeth, Bran braced himself for a short, but brutal, battle.

He managed to incapacitate the first man to reach him, sidestepping the warrior's blow and clouting him on the side of the head—but there was another just behind him.

The new enemy swung his broadsword at Bran's chest. He parried, the shock ringing through him, and was slow to counterstrike, barely nicking his opponent's arm. The man pivoted, blade arcing out, and Bran realized, with detached horror, that he was watching his death blow descend.

Dimly, he heard Mara cry out.

And then the Athraig crumpled as a strangely fletched bolt pierced his forehead. Blinking, Bran saw two more of the enemy go down in the same fashion.

Suddenly, they were surrounded by soldiers, led by the hard-faced guardsman Mara had freed. Yet they were still terribly outnumbered.

One of the castle's men fell, then another.

Sobbing, Mara fell to her knees and splayed her hands wide in the air.

"*Portal,*" she cried, her voice raw with grief.

There was a pause, like a great ingathering of breath.

Then enchantment rushed up from the very ground—a deep magic full of the whispers of wildness. The splash of a streamlet over rocks, the seed-bright eye of a wren, the thin purple petal of an aster. The power grew, strengthened by the snap of a sharp tooth, the creak of wind-tossed branches, the cry of a raptor plummeting from the sky. Silver runes crackled to life in a dark clearing.

The Darkwood. And the Erynvorn.

The nearly vanished portal flared to eye-searing brightness. With startling quickness, the rest of the invading Athraig were pulled through.

Then, as abruptly as it had opened, the portal closed, winking out like a flame doused in water. Bran swayed, shaking his head. What they had just witnessed was unbelievable. How could the forest have woken, let alone called to the Erynvorn?

And yet, the Athraig were gone.

The human realm. Elfhame. Two separate worlds, more tightly twined than he had ever guessed.

Owen stumbled to his father, who had collapsed at the base of the wall.

"Can you help him?" Owen asked, looking up at Mara. "Please?"

He clutched the man's limp hand in his, desperation etched on his face. Mara stood, swayed on her feet, then managed to make her way over to the wall. With a heavy breath, she went to her knees. Bran joined her, forcing the weary haze from his vision.

They had so nearly failed.

"I have no power left," she said, but reached out a trembling hand and laid it on the fallen man's head.

Bran sent her a worried look.

They were both spent, with only the barest dregs of magic remaining. He wished he could forbid her from draining her wellspring completely dry—but this was her world, and it was her choice.

Anneth knelt beside Owen, taking his other hand in hers. Watching them, Bran suddenly knew the source of the *vestalevere* he and Mara had sensed. Improbable as it seemed, his sister and this human shared a life-bond.

Mara's face grew pale as she forced the last of her power into trying to revive the older man. After a strained moment, his eyelids fluttered open, and he gazed weakly up at them.

"Owen," he said, his voice a mere creak, like wind rubbing two branches together. "You survived."

"Yes." Owen's voice trembled with grief.

"Strong. You will make a good king."

King? Bran glanced from father to son, further understanding the connection between his sister and Owen. Princess... and prince.

"Don't leave me, father." Owen clutched the dying king's hand. "I need you. I can't—"

His voice broke and he turned his head away, tears brimming in his eyes.

"You can. My blessing upon you." The king turned his gaze on Anneth. "On you both."

Then, with a look of weary serenity, he closed his eyes. They did not open again.

"No," Owen gasped, folding over his father's body.

Anneth slid her arms around his shoulders, holding him as he wept. She glanced up at Bran, fear in her eyes, and he knew she was thinking of their father, lying ill in the Hawthorne Court.

As soon as they recovered a semblance of their strength, they must return to Elfhame.

They'd lost one king. But, Bran vowed to himself, they would not lose another.

CHAPTER 36

Despite the need to see her family and then enter Elfhame, Mara slept heavily through the night and most of the next day. She awoke in an ornate, unfamiliar bed, blinking at the afternoon sunlight sneaking in through imperfectly drawn velvet curtains.

It took a moment for her to recollect where she was: in one of the guest rooms at Castle Raine. What a strange turn her life had taken. She never would have predicted she'd be an honored guest of the crown prince in the very castle where she'd once scrubbed out fireplaces.

In the course of that journey, she'd helped save two worlds, finally mastered her magic, and, most importantly, married a horribly handsome, and astonishingly stubborn, Dark Elf warrior-prince.

Speaking of Bran, where was he?

She levered herself up on her elbows, scanning the room. The only signs of her husband were his pack in the corner and his cloak flung over one chair. The garment was ragged at the edges—much like both of them, after their recent adventures.

Suddenly ravenous, she rose and opened the curtains, letting golden summer light flood the room. To her relief, she discovered her freshly laundered clothing folded in a neat pile on the table near the door.

Although she had a change of clothes in her pack, they were wrinkled and a bit grubby. It was difficult to keep up with laundering while escaping from temples and voyaging across the turbulent sea.

As she finished dressing, the door opened and Bran poked his head into the room.

"Mara." He smiled and entered, quickly coming to her side.

She slipped her arms about his waist. He made a contented sound and pulled her close. For a long moment they stood there, hearts beating in unison, savoring the simple fact that they were alive. That they were whole, and safe.

"Did you rest well?" His breath was warm against the top of her head.

"I did."

She looked up at him, studying his face in the strong light. The lines of tension and worry on his forehead had eased, she was glad to see—though there was now a strand of silver threading through his hair. It gleamed against the blackness of his braids, a testament to their hard-won victories.

"How long have you been awake?" she asked.

"Not long," he said. "I had something to eat, and the maid is bringing up a tray for you. I've also been making arrangements for our travel into the Darkwood."

The responsibilities of the world came rushing back—along with the choice she must make—and she heaved a sigh. "Won't we just portal to the gateway?"

"No portal," he said. "We must conserve our power to open the gateway between our worlds. Horses will take us to the stones—we'll bring a few riders, who can return the mounts to the castle while you, I, Anneth, and Ondo continue into Elfhame."

She nodded slowly. "That seems the wise choice."

"Besides," he said, quirking one eyebrow, "this way we can make a quick stop at your cottage. I have a certain family to meet."

Her heart thumped, and she squeezed him tightly. "Thank you."

"I did promise," he reminded her, bending to drop a kiss on her hair.

"Yes." And she hoped her family would be on their best behavior, though with Lily, one never knew. “We should leave today. Your father...”

“Time is short, but we’ll depart tomorrow, after breakfast.”

“I slept too late.” She frowned, wishing she could call back those lost hours.

“No—we both needed to recover. Especially if we’re to succeed in opening the gate.” He scrutinized her face. “Is your wellspring regenerating?”

Closing her eyes briefly, she reached for her power. It stirred sluggishly, without the sparkling blaze of magic she’d grown used to.

“You’re right,” she said. “We’re not yet strong enough to return to Elfhame.”

She could only hope that by tomorrow, they would be.

Or perhaps the forest would, yet again, lend its aid.

She glanced out the window at the shadowy expanse of the Darkwood. Wind stirred the branches into motion, and a bird darted overhead, a bright streak of blue, before diving back into the dimness. Already the sun was lowering, the light slanting to warm gold.

Melancholy stirred through her, bittersweet.

This might well be her last afternoon in the mortal world.

The stone hallways of Castle Raine were pleasingly dim, Anneth thought, as she walked beside Prince Owen. Wall sconces shed light at distant intervals, leaving pools of shadow between. She found it comforting rather than oppressive.

Although the escort of Captain Crane, striding a pace behind them, was less reassuring.

The prince—or rather, the new king—had knocked on her door after she’d taken luncheon in her room, and asked if she would like to see the castle. His intent gaze carried the unspoken message that they had much to discuss.

“Yes,” she’d said, stepping out, then drew up at the sight of the captain of the guard.

"Captain Crane insists on accompanying me," Owen said. "Even though he's apprehended the Athraig agent. The *true* one, this time."

She raised her brows at the captain.

"My duty is to protect the rulers of Raine," he said, without apology. "And you still owe us an explanation of your part in all this. Not to mention your strange allies, and the fact that his highness says you're a princess of some foreign land—"

"No need to interrogate her," Owen said. "I'm certain Lady Anneth will reveal everything, as soon as she may. But for now, let our tour of Castle Raine commence."

With a bow, he offered his arm. She rested her hand on his forearm, conscious of the little prickle of warmth the contact sparked.

It was overpowered, however, by a rush of nervousness. Owen was confident that she would share all her secrets with him. And she wanted to, but...

Even the fact she was a Dark Elf?

Despite their undeniable connection, if she showed him her true face, she knew he would recoil, thinking her hideous or terrifying. The prospect sent a wrench of pain through her.

For a brief time, earlier that day, she'd considered trying to live the lie. Invent a distant kingdom, constantly maintain her rune of illusion—anything, so that she could continue to be with him. Owen would invite her to stay at the castle; she knew it, as surely as the stars filled the sky.

They would talk, and flirt, and friendship would lead to more. If, that was, he thought her a mortal woman. One of his own kind.

The temptation to continue the charade pulled at her. *You will be so happy,* her treacherous heart insisted. *Just keep pretending to be human.*

But that was a sure route to misery. She'd seen it in her own parents' marriage: the brittle façades, the pretenses that neither could admit to. The strain of ruling together had only made it worse, fracturing what had once been a true union. Even as a girl, she'd vowed never to follow that path.

No matter how much her emotions might try to lead her astray.

Sorrow swamped her. She knew that her friendship with Owen was drawing to its inevitable end. She'd face it bravely, just as she'd faced certain death in the moment before the crossbow fired.

This time, however, there would be no reprieve.

No matter how wounded her heart, she wouldn't die of it—though she would never fully recover. Her time in the mortal world had permanently marked her, for good and for ill.

She had decided she'd go back to Elfhame and, if Prince Deldarinnon still wanted an alliance, she would tell him yes, making it plain that it would be for purely political reasons.

There was no point in thinking she would find love. Not when a green-eyed mortal prince was all she'd ever yearn for.

Enough, she told herself firmly. She must leave the dark clouds of misery on the horizon and turn her face to the present—to the precious time she had with Owen before the storm arrived.

Despite his sorrow over his father's death, Owen seemed to take comfort in her company. He showed her the parlor full of musical instruments, the study, the balcony behind the gardens.

Lastly, he took her to the vaulted library of Castle Raine, full of enough books to lighten anyone's mood. Captain Crane watched, arms folded, as she explored the banks of shelves, running her delighted fingers over the spines of the books: fat volumes, slim tomes with elegant embossing, squat histories, tall books filled with enticing pictures. Finally, smiling, Owen drew her away.

"I'd no idea you'd find the library so fascinating," he said.

"I am somewhat of a scholar back home." She couldn't tell him that this room, packed with so much knowledge of the human world, made her dizzy just contemplating what she might learn. Had she the time.

But that was another life—one she could not live.

He slanted a glance at her. "And will you tell me where home might be?"

"Yes." She looked over at the brooding captain of the guard. "It there a place where we might speak privately?"

Owen nodded. "I'd been planning to show you my secret hideaway next."

"That sounds intriguing, as long as it's not in the cellar. I think I've seen more than enough of the underside of the castle."

He shot her a wry look. "As have I. No, I'm taking you in the opposite direction."

As promised, he led her up several staircases and down a long hallway, Captain Crane trailing them. At the end of the hall, Owen stopped in front of a heavy door with a rounded top that reminded her of the arched doorways of the Hawthorne Palace.

He turned to his guardsman. "I request that you remain here, captain."

"I'll come with you, my lord—"

"Let me rephrase." Owen gave the captain a stern look. "I *require* you to remain here. We both know this is the only door leading in or out of the tower."

Captain Crane's expression darkened. "If you insist—but only if I clear the area first. Wait here."

He loosened his sword then pulled the door open. Instead of leading into another room, stone steps spiraled up the circular wall. She and Owen waited while the captain strode up them, soon disappearing from sight.

He returned shortly and gave Owen a terse nod. "Don't stay too long, or I'll come up and get you."

"We'll descend when we're ready." Owen's voice was steel, and Anneth smiled to herself to see him winning the battle of wills with his captain.

Without waiting for Captain Crane's response, he stepped into the round stairwell. She joined him and peered up, realizing they stood at the base of one of the turreted towers of the castle.

"Are you afraid of heights?" Owen shot her a glance. "I should have asked earlier."

"Not at all." She grinned at him. "As a child, my brother and I dared one another to see who could climb highest in the trees near our palace. I usually won."

"I'd like to meet your brother someday."

"Oh." She paused with one foot on the stair. "But you have. I introduced you."

"You did?"

"Yes—you met Bran the other night."

"Wait." He blinked with astonishment. "Bran is your *brother*?"

"Of course. Didn't I say so?"

"No." He let out a sharp laugh. "No, you didn't. He's your brother."

"Who else would he be?" She stared at him in confusion.

"Come." He caught her hand, elation dancing in his eyes. "The view from the top is amazing."

Anneth was slightly winded by the time they gained the top of the tower. It was enclosed in rough stone, but two windows were set in the walls. Owen pulled her to the first, which looked back over the castle. She recognized the small green squares of the kitchen garden and the long run of the great hall, opening to the wide courtyard.

From there, the road began. It ducked under the portcullis and wound out through the trees, and she glimpsed the cottages of Little Hazel beyond.

"It seems so long ago since I first came up that road," she said. "I arrived by donkey cart to attend your ball."

"I saw you," he said, turning toward her and leaning his hip against the windowsill. "I was watching all the prospective young ladies come into the great hall. And you caught my eye."

"Probably because I'm so tall." She gave him a mock frown.

"That is the only reason," he agreed. "Your grace and humor and smile have nothing to do with it."

She felt her cheeks heat and looked away.

"Anneth." He leaned toward her. "Where are you from?"

When she remained silent, he reached into the pocket of his tailored coat and pulled out the slipper she'd left behind, the night she'd fled the ball.

"You have it!" she exclaimed.

"I do—and I was hoping it would provide a clue to who you really are."

He lifted it and turned it back and forth, studying the pattern. The beads caught the sunlight, sparkling with a blaze of color.

She shook her head. "The slipper's not mine, I'm afraid. I only borrowed the pair for the night, as I didn't have anything to wear except my boots."

He lowered the slipper, one brow twitching up in question. "It doesn't seem you were very well prepared to attend a royal ball. I wonder why?"

So. Now they came to it.

Anneth let out a sigh. "I didn't know you were having a ball. I didn't, in truth, know much about the current state of affairs in Raine. Except that it was inhabited by humans."

He tilted his head at her. "By... humans?"

There was only one answer she could give him.

Slowly, still holding his gaze, she spoke a quiet rune of banishment and let her illusion fade.

His eyes widened. The slipper fell from his hand, landing on the floor with a slap as his attention darted to her mouth, her pointed ears and claw-tipped fingers, then back to her eyes.

For a tense moment she waited for him to push her back and shout for Captain Crane to come dispatch the monster that had materialized in her place. At the very least, she expected him to shudder and turn away.

Instead, he leaned closer. So close she could feel the warmth of his breath.

"So the stories are true," he said softly. "The Darkwood holds magical creatures... What are you, Anneth?"

"I am a Dark Elf."

"You're rather frightening looking." His gaze grew intent. "And also very beautiful."

For a long moment they stared, unmoving, into one another's eyes. The depth of Owen's regard left her trembling and breathless. Then, slowly, he closed the distance between them.

Their lips met, and a shock of sensation flashed down to her toes. It was too sweet, too strong—too impossible to bear. With a sharp inhalation, she drew away.

"Why aren't you afraid of me?" she asked.

"I saw your face, once," he said. "In the dungeon. I thought it a trick of the light."

"There's more I must tell you." She glanced out the window. "My people do not actually dwell in the Darkwood, but in a world that can only be reached through an enchanted gateway deep in the forest."

"Extraordinary." His brows drew together. "It seems unbelievable—except that you are sitting before me, and the night we defeated the

Athraig, I witnessed magic with my own eyes. What is the name of your world?"

"Elfhame. And my parents are the rulers of the Hawthorne Court."

"So, despite looking human, all of you are actually Dark Elves? Bran, and your man Ondo, and Mara?" He shook his head. "I never would have guessed it."

"Actually..." She swallowed, hoping she wasn't about to put the Gearys back in danger. "Mara is human."

His gaze sharpened. "What is she doing with the Dark Elves? Does she know what you are?"

"Of course she does. She's married to Bran."

Owen let out a soft, incredulous laugh. "I wager that's quite some tale."

"It is. One that's long in the telling."

"What are you all doing here? You said you had no idea I was giving a ball, or what you'd find in Raine. Did the others? Did Mara?"

Anneth pressed her lips together and stared out the window again. "Mara is from the village yonder. I took shelter with her family when I arrived in your world, and the royal emissary assumed me to be part of the family. Had I known what attending the ball would set in motion..."

She let out a breath. It left a soft mist on the window glass, blurring the scene beyond.

"You wouldn't have come?" he asked, a vulnerable note in his voice.

"No." She turned back to him, trying to engrave his features in her memory. "For then I wouldn't have met you."

They stared at one another for a long moment.

"But you did come," he said softly. "More importantly—will you stay?"

The question hung in the air between them, an impossible, fragile thing. She was afraid to speak, to breathe, for then it would be broken, and all their possibilities gone.

"Your highness." Captain Crane's voice echoed up the stairs. "Is all well?"

Frowning, Owen turned away from the window. "Yes," he called back. "We'll be down soon."

When he looked back at Anneth, she knew what her choice must be.

"I can't stay," she said, trying to keep the misery from her voice. "I don't belong in your world."

She recalled how desperately unhappy Mara was dwelling in Elfhame. There was every chance that she would not, in fact, remain with Bran, but instead choose to live in her own world, among her own people. Anneth could not fault her.

Indeed, faced with the identical choice, Anneth's decision was the same. It had to be.

"Are you certain?" Owen asked, his voice catching.

She looked toward the curving staircase. "Captain Crane would never accept me. Nor would your people. I would be seen as a monster."

Instead of answering, he pushed away from the window.

"Captain, attend me," he called down the stairwell.

"Wait." Anneth raised her hand to her face. "What are you doing? Let me recast—"

"No." Owen returned to stand before her. "My soldiers saw extraordinary magic performed the other night. Bolts of blue fire, the invading Athraig falling into an enchanted slumber, then disappearing into thin air. Strange and marvelous things, and yet they have all taken it remarkably well. There's been no fear, no worry, no awkward questions. It makes me think that perhaps you are meant to be here."

Captain Crane's footsteps grew nearer, and she glanced apprehensively at the curving stairs, waiting for him to appear.

His head cleared the stairwell. Catching sight of her, he paused for the barest moment, then continued up into the room.

"Captain Crane," Owen said, "may I introduce her highness, Lady Anneth..." He shot her a questioning look.

"Luthinor," she hastily supplied.

"Lady Anneth Luthinor, princess of the Hawthorne Court of Elfhame—the land of the Dark Elves."

The captain's eyes narrowed, but he made her a formal bow. Straightening, he scrutinized her face.

"Well," he said brusquely. "That explains a great deal."

When he said no more, she tilted her head. "Don't I appear strange to you?"

He shrugged. "I can't say, my lady. You're exceedingly tall, that's for certain."

Confusion twisting through her, she turned to Owen.

"Magic," he said simply. "If you're welcome in this world, then you will be seen as belonging."

Mouth dry, she looked from him to Captain Crane. Could it be true?

"What if your subjects fear me? What if—"

"Trust." Owen took her hands in his. "My mother told me not to fear the future, but to embrace it. No matter what happens. I'm not certain I could stand a future without you in it, Anneth. Once more, I'll ask. Will you stay?"

Tears hot in her eyes, she nodded.

"It won't be easy," she whispered.

He gave her a crooked smile. "The best things never are."

CHAPTER 37

Despite his projected assurance, Bran couldn't help the nerves clenching his stomach as their party rode out from Castle Raine to the village of Little Hazel.

He was going to meet Mara's family.

Despite the mortal illusion he wore, he feared they would find him unworthy, at best. And despise him utterly, at worst. Which would give Mara that much more reason to leave Elfhame behind forever.

The day was bright, the air warmed by the fire of the sun. The road was edged with sweet-smelling grasses that riffled in the breeze, gold and green. Dust rose in soft puffs from beneath their horses' hooves as they traveled, two by two, away from the hulking stone walls of the castle.

He and Mara rode in front, followed by Anneth and Owen, who were giving one another small, secret smiles that solidified his suspicions that they had come to an understanding. Behind them came Ondo and Captain Crane. The soldier had insisted on accompanying his king into the Darkwood when Owen had announced his intention to accompany them to the gate. And finally, two guards brought up the rear. They would take the extra mounts back to the castle once the Dark Elves and Mara stepped through the doorway.

Bran was more than ready to return to the graceful white arches of the Hawthorne Palace, the soothing, violet-tinged shadows cast by the moons of Elfhame—yet he suspected he would miss the vivid, brash human world.

Especially if it was where Mara chose to dwell.

He glanced to where she rode beside him, and found her watching him, concern in her clear-eyed gaze.

"Try not to worry," she said softly. "My family will accept you."

He gave a nod, unwilling to speak his fears aloud.

Mara guided them around the edge of the village, as their little procession would surely invite speculation. Not to mention the risk that some curious child would follow them into the forest. All too soon they left the cluster of whitewashed buildings behind, and the road turned toward the Darkwood and the handful of homes built on its periphery.

And then they were there.

Mara pulled her mount to a stop in front of a two-story cottage with gleaming multi-paned windows and bright red flowers planted about the front stoop. No sooner had they dismounted than the door banged open and a young woman raced out.

"Mara!" she cried, enveloping her sister in a fierce embrace.

"Lily." Mara smiled widely. "Is everyone home? Are you well?"

"Of course!" Lily stepped back. "We only hid in the forest for a few days. We were more worried for you, and for Anneth."

Lily rounded on Bran's sister and hugged her, too. Then, a bit more subdued, she turned to Bran.

"Are you the prince?" she asked.

"I am." He gave her a solemn bow. "Pleased to meet you, Miss Lily."

She blushed and curtsied, then scanned the rest of the group. When she saw Owen, she dipped him an even lower curtsey.

"Your majesty," she said. "Welcome. Oh, won't Mother be in a tizzy."

"I will not," said an older woman, stepping out through the front door. "But I will certainly offer them tea, if they so desire."

"Thank you, Mother." Mara gave her mother a brief hug. "I know you weren't expecting a gaggle of royalty on your doorstep this morning."

"Perhaps not—but I expected you'd show up soon. Which is why I hid the honeycakes from Lily last night." Smiling, Mara's mother held the door open and bowed to the group. "Please, make yourselves welcome."

Mara took Bran's arm—perhaps worrying he might run away into the forest if she didn't hold on to him. While he might have the urge to do just that, he tried not to frown as she pulled him into the house.

Bran tried to take it all in with a glance. This was where his beloved had grown up, after all.

The kitchen and eating area lay to the left of the door, a cozy living room to the right, furnished with slightly threadbare armchairs and a couch. Despite the lack of grandeur, the space was warm and inviting. Bright rugs were spread over a spotless wooden floor, and a vase of meadow flowers adorned the table.

A man with a fringe of sandy hair stood waiting to greet them, with two people who could only be the twins Mara had spoken of.

"Is Pansy here?" Mara asked her mother.

"No, we had thought it best she stay in Meriton. Just in case."

Nobody mentioned that alternative outcome: a kingdom in turmoil from the Athraig takeover.

The room grew crowded as Anneth, Ondo, Owen, and Captain Crane followed them into the cottage. Mara's mother bustled about, directing the twins to bring over a bench from the table, and seating the guests.

"Lily," she said, nodding to the ball of orange fur ensconced in the green armchair, "remove your cat from the best chair at once, if you please."

Lily went to scoop up the creature and cuddle it beneath her chin.

"Your majesty, please sit." Mrs. Geary attempted to brush the stray hairs from the chair, then offered it to King Owen.

Captain Crane, looking every inch the royal guardsman, went to stand behind his monarch.

"Your kitten has grown," Mara said, smiling at her sister.

"Her name's Marigold." Lily stepped over and held the cat up for Bran's approval.

It yawned, showing very sharp teeth, and he eyed it warily. The creature resembled the great felines of Moonflower, in miniature. Yet, despite its size, he'd no doubt that even such a small thing could inflict plenty of damage, if it so desired.

"Are you afraid of her?" Lily blinked at him.

"No," he said stiffly.

"There are no housecats in Elfhame," Mara said, running her fingers over the feline's back. "Perhaps we ought to bring some with us."

Bran glanced at his wife, unsure if she were simply teasing him. She smiled back, and he supposed that she was.

Mrs. Geary pressed them all to sit, then brought out a plate of crumbly golden cakes. As she handed the plate around, they finished making the introductions. Sean and Seanna nodded somewhat coolly to Bran, but greeted Anneth with more warmth. Mr. Geary thanked Ondo for his part in protecting their family.

"We're grateful to all of you," Mara's father continued. "I don't know the full of it, but clearly you saved the castle, and the kingdom." He rose and went to Bran, holding out his hand. "I'm Padraig."

After a moment, Bran realized he wanted to clasp palms in greeting. He extended his own hand. "Bran."

Mr. Geary's handshake was firm, his gaze direct as he looked Bran over. "Pleased to finally meet you."

"Can you stay?" Mrs. Geary asked, looking to Mara.

"I'm afraid we can't," Mara said gently. "We must return to Elfhame shortly and deliver what medicines we may to Bran's father."

"We've made up some tinctures," Seanna said, then elbowed her brother. "Go get them." He frowned at her, but stood and went to the door.

Owen had provided some remedies from the castle's stores as well, and Bran's pack now clinked with a half-dozen carefully labeled bottles. Between those, and whatever the twins provided, surely they'd find a cure for his father.

Yet lords of the realm died. The knowledge left a hollow in the pit of his stomach as he looked at the new King of Raine. Was Owen ready to shoulder the burden of running the kingdom?

Am I? Bran brushed the question away. They were not yet in Elfhame. Whatever awaited them there, he could not give in to the possibility of anguish.

Owen's face was weary, a shadow of desolation in his eyes. Even as Bran watched, that grief faded as Anneth, seated next to him, reached over and took his hand.

"I'm going to tell them," she said, and a hush fell over the crowded room.

"Tell us what?" Bran asked.

She met his gaze without flinching. "I'm not going back with you to Elfhame."

Mara pulled in a breath of surprise, and Ondo rose from his seat.

"My lady," he said, going to his knees before Anneth and raising his fists in supplication. "I failed you, I know—but please do not abandon our world!"

Bran couldn't help glancing at Mara. All too soon, he would hear her declare her intention to return to the mortal world—and he was not certain he'd be able to bear that pain.

"Why stay?" Mara asked.

Owen raised Anneth's hand and brushed a kiss across it. "Because I intend to make Anneth my queen."

"You can't." Bran sent his sister an urgent look. "Think this through. What happens when—"

"When it's discovered I'm a Dark Elf?" Anneth gave him a slight smile. "Watch."

She spoke a quiet rune of dissolution under her breath. Half rising, Bran moved to stop her, to shield her, but she gave him a sharp shake of her head.

Her illusion of humanity fell away, like a gossamer cloak dropping to the ground. Her eyes slitted, her cheekbones sharpened as her face lost its roundness. The tips of her claws became visible, and the points of her ears.

Fraught silence descended. Adrenaline burning through him, Bran set his hand to his sword and glanced at Captain Crane. If the man lifted so much as a finger toward Anneth, Bran wouldn't hesitate to strike.

But instead of fear and horror, the soldier merely stood there calmly.

Bran's gaze went to Owen, who held Anneth's hand, love still shining from his eyes.

"You knew it would not be a calamity," Mara said to Anneth, a note of accusation in her voice. "You'd already revealed yourself."

"Yes," Owen said.

"I don't understand." Bran glanced from the king to his sister. "Mortals find us hideous, fearsome creatures."

"Not any longer," Anneth said.

"It changed," Mara said, her voice thoughtful. "When the Darkwood came to our aid and helped oust the Athraig, Raine accepted the Dark Elves."

"Magic," Owen said. "My kingdom needed you, and thus, you belong."

Brow furrowed, Bran glanced once more at Captain Crane. Despite the evidence before him, he still didn't trust the explanation. Didn't trust the captain not to pull his weapon and attack.

As if sensing his thoughts, Mara placed her hand on his arm. "Why don't you show your true face?"

No. What if Anneth was accepted only because of the king's love for her? Bran didn't think he could bear to see Mara's family struck with horror when they looked upon his Dark Elf visage. The last thing he wanted was to fight his way free of the cottage and flee into the Darkwood.

"I don't think that would be wise," he said.

Mara regarded him, her clear gaze full of acceptance. Faith in him shone from her eyes.

As he stared back at her, his heart wrenched with the knowledge that, whatever happened, he would always love her. Even if they ended up worlds apart, and time, the ocean of the present giving way to a sea of memories—he would carry her with him always.

Always.

And she would always love him. Their connection was as true as the stars in the sky, and he'd been a fool to doubt it. No matter where she chose to belong.

Bran took a deep breath, his heart, at last, steadying. He undid the clasp of his stifling cloak of fear and let it fall away, though he felt bare and unprotected without it.

Then, with a fleeting prayer to the brightmoon, he banished the spell of illusion hiding his face.

Slowly, Mara smiled.

"My husband," she said, going on tiptoes to brush a kiss across his lips.

"Why, he's even more handsome than before," Lily said, crossing her arms. "I don't understand why he'd want to conceal it."

"To keep young ladies from swooning over him," Mr. Geary said dryly.

His wife cuffed him lightly on the arm. "As if you knew anything about it, you gadabout."

He waggled his brows at her. "You and I both know I was a charmer back in the day."

Bemused, Bran looked at his sister. It couldn't be that simple. Could it?

She grinned back at him. With a shrug, Ondo also dispelled his rune, with a similar lack of reaction among the humans.

Bran bent close to Mara. "Would that Elfhame had granted you the same acceptance," he said in a low voice. "It doesn't seem fair that you had to struggle so."

She gave him a wry look. "That would have made things easier... but then again, your people are far more magical than mine. And perhaps it was meant to be."

He searched her eyes. Letting her go would be the most painful thing he'd ever done—but if that was what she wanted, what she needed, he had no choice.

"It has been hard for you, in my world," he said softly. "I understand if you want to stay with your family."

"I do, Bran."

His heart plummeted, and he had to turn his face away to hide the devastation coursing through him.

"Look at me." She touched his cheek, then gently pulled his chin around until he faced her again. "Part of me wants to remain with my family—but that's not the choice I'm making. I'll never stop missing them, but I belong with you, Bran. I'm going to dwell in Elfhame."

Her words fell into stillness, and he was dimly aware that the entire gathering watched them. But they didn't matter, nothing mattered, except for the lovely, courageous woman before him.

"Are you certain?" He all but whispered the words.

Her lips curved in a smile as she held his gaze. "Yes."

His heart broke and mended in that moment, stronger than ever before.

"You're leaving us forever?" With a little sob, Lily flung herself toward Mara.

One arm about her sister, Mara met her mother's gaze. "I'm sorry."

Mrs. Geary shook her head. "Don't be. At least we got to say a proper farewell. And meet your husband." She looked over at Bran, a fierce light in her eyes. "Treat her well, you hear?"

"With everything I am." He looked at Anneth. "But is this our good-bye, too?"

He could scarcely believe it, and his emotions teetered from joy to grief, and back again.

"We'll ride with you to the gateway," she said, blinking back tears. "And you can always come visit, can't you?"

It wasn't that simple, of course. The door between the worlds could only be opened by a great expenditure of power, and possibly only at moments of great need. Bran doubted they would be able to traipse through it for a cup of wine now and again.

"We will try," he said, keeping his doubts to himself. He knew Anneth understood the limitations as well as he did.

The cottage door swung wide, and Sean came in, carrying a bulging satchel.

"I've brought every remedy I could think of," he said, holding the bag out to Mara. "Plus a sheaf of instructions. I hope something works."

"Thank you," Mara said.

She rose to embrace her brother, and everyone else stood as well. Mr. Geary brushed cake crumbs from his lap, Lily wiped her face with her sleeve, and Seanna went to confer with Mara and her brother.

Bran moved to Anneth and folded her in his embrace. Growing up with a cold mother and a distant father, it had always been the two of them against the world—despite the driving force of his prophecy. And now he was losing her.

Trading Anneth for Mara. His heart broke either way.

Owen gave Bran a serious look. “I promise I will care for her with my soul, my sword, and every power at my command.”

Bran gave him a gruff nod. “See that you do.”

Reluctantly, he opened his arms, and Anneth went to hug Mara. Both their faces were wet with tears when they parted.

“We’ll miss your wedding,” Mara said. “I’m sorry. And the coronation, and... well, everything.”

“But we will hold you in our thoughts, always,” Anneth said, mustering up a smile.

Owen slipped his arm around her, and the affection between them was so clear that Bran’s sorrow was blunted the tiniest bit. There was pain, yes—but also, in due time, happiness.

For now, however, the doorway to Elfhame awaited.

CHAPTER 38

As they rode in single file through the Darkwood, Mara tried to absorb as much of the mortal world as she could: the stray sunbeams filtering through the dark trees, the flit of a yellow-and-black-striped butterfly, the liquid call of a thrush hidden by summer foliage.

It was beautiful. But so was the Erynvorn beyond the gate.

Most importantly, Bran would be there. She glanced ahead to where he led their small party through the forest. He sat his mount with graceful ease, his dark hair lifted slightly by the breeze, where it was not gathered into warrior's braids.

She'd made her decision to stay in Elfhame, arriving at that place like a person moving through a dark room. Small steps, going by instinct, her hands held before her until, at last, she'd found the door.

Bran was that door, for her—the place her heart belonged.

His decision to drop his illusion before her parents was, perhaps, the bravest thing he'd ever done. After all, he'd been raised a warrior and a mage. Confronting dire enemies, while not an easy task, was what he'd been born for.

Facing his own fears and insecurities was the much harder challenge. But if he could do that for her, she could do the same for him. And even though an assassin might await her on the other side of the gateway, she would trust that, together, they would be safe.

She let out a quiet sigh, just a puff of air, but her husband swiveled to look at her, concern in his eyes.

"Is everything well?" he asked.

"Yes." She held his gaze.

"We will be there soon."

"Already?" She glanced at the tall hemlocks and cedars around them. "We haven't been riding nearly long enough."

"The Darkwood makes way for us." Bran looked behind her, to where Owen rode. "And, I think, for the king of the land."

That made sense, though her heart clenched at the thought of their imminent next round of farewells.

"We will open the doorway and go through quickly," Bran said, as if he, too, dreaded saying goodbye to Anneth one final time.

The horses descended a gentle slope, picking their footing with ease, and Mara shook her head. She suspected it was the same ravine that had opened beneath her feet the night she'd fled through the forest and found the clearing.

This time, though, instead of rolling in a precipitous tumble to arrive at the gateway between worlds, she brought her mount to a gentle stop at the edge of the meadow. A meadow inexplicably filled with golden flowers that seemed to shed a soft radiance. In the center of the clearing, rising as if from a shining sea, the two gray stones stood, marking the doorway.

Marking the finality of her decision. And the rightness of it. She breathed out the last of her doubts.

Bran dismounted and, along with Ondo, began carefully unloading their stores of medicines, seemingly unconcerned by the profusion of flowers.

"What are those?" Anneth asked, guiding her horse beside Mara's and nodding to the blooms. "Is that usual?"

Mara shook her head and dismounted. "I don't think I've ever seen those flowers before."

"Are they... glowing?" Owen slid off his mount and, accompanied by the ever-watchful Captain Crane, went to stand at the edge of the meadow.

"Not to my eye," the guardsman said, squinting at the blooms. "But that doesn't mean they aren't. Magic's a strange thing."

He turned his narrow-eyed gaze on Anneth, but there was no malice in his look—just recognition of how his world had changed.

"Magic, indeed." Bran frowned at the meadow. "The blossoms are infused with an essence of power I don't quite understand."

"You've never seen them in Elfhame?" Mara shot him a quick look, just to make sure.

"Ondo?" Bran turned to the scout. "You've more woodcraft than I. Do you know these flowers?"

"No, my lord."

"We must take some back with us," Mara said, handing her mount's reins to one of the soldiers who had accompanied them.

"My thoughts as well," Anneth said, going to rummage behind her saddle. "You can fill my bag. It's empty."

"How many should we take?" Ondo asked, drawing a small blade from his boot.

Bran set his hands on his hips and surveyed the meadow. "We'll cut a path to the stones, and leave the rest untouched."

The scout set to work, and Bran quickly joined him. A harvest of shining blossoms fell in their wake. Anneth carried the saddlebag, holding it open while Owen and Mara heaped the flowers inside. Captain Crane followed, muttering that at least one of them must stay on guard.

He did bend and scoop up the occasional stray blossom, however, and fling it in among the others.

Just when it seemed they could carry no more, they reached the center of the clearing.

"Look," Anneth said, a smile in her voice.

Three glimglows danced among the stones, darting back and forth. Their light reflected the soft radiance of the flowers.

"There is power enough here to open the gateway easily," Bran said, a hint of wonder in his tone.

"Is that why the forest produced the flowers?" Owen asked, lacing his fingers with Anneth's.

Mara turned slowly, her gaze sweeping over the golden-hued clearing. "I don't know. I wonder if they're also growing on the other side of the doorway."

"We'll find out, soon enough." Bran adjusted the satchel of medicines he was carrying. "Are you ready?"

"To share the rest of my life with you?" Mara clasped his hand, so that their azure rings touched. "Yes. Always."

Anneth gave a choked sob and stepped forward. "I'll miss you both so much."

The three of them embraced one last time.

Letting go of family was one of the hardest things in any world, and Mara's eyes pricked with tears. But she and Anneth had both chosen a future where the bonds of a heartmate, a companion and lover, outweighed the ties of kinship.

It wasn't easy. But it was right.

Bran was the first to step back. With a final squeeze, Mara let go of Anneth and picked up the saddlebag brimming with mysterious flowers.

She cradled it in one arm and caught Bran's hand. Their gazes met and, together, they raised their voices in the rune of opening.

"*Edro!*"

As simply as a door swinging open, the gateway shimmered, revealing the soft darkness of the Erynvorn, the immense trees gilded with the light of the palemoon. A wild, sweet scent swirled through the air.

Palm to palm with her husband, Ondo at their heels, Mara strode through. She didn't look back.

As the gateway between worlds closed, Anneth turned her head into Owen's neck. His arms tightened about her.

"You could still go," he said, his breath warm against her skin.

"No." She lifted her face, blinking the tears from her eyes. "I will miss my brother and Mara—but the Hawthorne Court was never truly home, for all that I grew up there. And the fate of Elfhame..."

"Yes," he said gently.

During one of their discussions, she'd told him she would not be able to bear him an heir to the throne.

"Some calamity struck my people, and we are now barren," she'd said, her earlier joy fading. "I am among the last generation of Dark Elves. Even if the people of Raine accept me, I cannot consign you to a childless union."

He'd given her a long, serious look. "I trust in the magic that brought us together. Perhaps your affliction will be lifted simply by being in the mortal world."

"But you can't know that. Your kingdom must have an heir." Her throat tight, she'd turned her face away. She'd been a fool to think their story might end happily.

He'd leaned forward. "If the fates are unkind to us, I have cousins—or we could foster a child. There are other answers, Anneth."

"I can't make you—"

"It's not your choice." He'd made the wry expression of a ruler faced with hard decisions. "I'd rather be happy, with you, than raise a child in a miserable marriage. And what kind of future monarch would that make?"

She'd given him a half-smile. "My brother Bran will do well enough, I've no doubt."

"I think he's the exception." Owen had leaned forward and brushed a kiss across her lips. "Stay, if that's what you desire. We will take each problem as it comes. Together."

Now they stood in a field of golden flowers, Captain Crane and his soldiers waiting impatiently behind them. Anneth took a deep breath and turned away from the gate stones.

"Ready?" the captain asked in his usual brusque fashion.

Owen nodded, but Anneth bent to pluck a handful of the strange blossoms.

"We'll take these to the castle's herbalists," she said. "Who knows what remedies they might contain?"

"A good thought." Owen gathered up his own bunch, the flowers spilling soft light across his hand.

"Enough time spent picking daisies," Captain Crane said. "You've a coronation to plan, your majesty. The sooner the better."

Owen was the king now, as he'd explained to Anneth, and had been at the moment of his father's passing. But it was customary in Raine to celebrate the new monarch with a formal crowning.

"Give us a moment," Owen said to his captain, waving for him to precede them from the clearing. "And you needn't scowl so."

The captain grudgingly stalked away, and Owen turned to Anneth. To her surprise, he went to one knee before her and held out his small bouquet.

"We didn't do this quite properly before," he said, smiling up at her. "Princess Anneth Luthinor, of the Hawthorne Court of Elfhame, would you do me the very great honor of becoming my queen?"

She began to cry in earnest, her grief at seeing the doorway close now spinning to joy—the emotions two sides of a coin. Of a heart.

"Yes," she managed to say. "Yes, King Owen Mallory of Raine. Nothing would make me happier."

"Then why are you crying?"

The question didn't need an answer as he rose and enfolded her in his arms.

Finally, she was home.

CHAPTER 39

Bran, Mara, and Ondo emerged into Elfhame—and into the middle of a busy encampment. Flicking on his dark vision, Bran put his hand to his sword, then checked the motion to draw it as Hestil strode forward.

"Prince Bran," she said, her normally reserved expression breaking into a smile. "Thank the doublemoons, you're back."

"We are." Bran clasped wrists with her in the warrior's greeting.

Now that they'd returned, his first concern was for his father. Did the Hawthorne Lord still live? Surely he must. Even between the worlds, Bran would have felt Lord Calithilon's death, as the mantle of Hawthorne Lord fell upon his own shoulders.

A moment he certainly wished to prevent. His heart clenched with urgency.

"What news of my father?" he asked softly.

"He is... well enough. But let us speak in my tent." Hestil's gaze went past him to Ondo, and her brows drew together. "Where is Anneth?"

Bran raised his hand to forestall the fear rising in her eyes. "My sister is safe and happy."

"And chose to stay behind in my world," Mara said.

Hestil blinked. "Why?"

"For the same reason I'm here." Mara slanted a smile up at Bran. "She found her prince."

Hestil's frown deepened, but she turned and gestured to the large tent set up near the edge of the clearing. "I look forward to hearing of what transpired in the human world. It sounds like quite a tale."

"It is."

Bran strode forward, Mara at his side. Ondo trailed them, carrying the pack full of medicines from the castle.

Foxfire flickered in silver bowls at intervals around the camp. Activity had ceased at the prince's arrival, and while the soldiers were too disciplined to rush forward in greeting, they all bowed or raised a hand, welcoming their commander home.

"How long have you been camped here?" Bran asked, noting established cooking areas, roughly constructed tables, and weapons racks.

"Since Lady Anneth went through the gateway," Hestil said. "And we mislaid Prince Deldarinnon."

Alarm spiked through Bran. "You lost the Cereus Prince?"

"Only temporarily," Hestil said.

In one of their spare moments together, Anneth had told Bran of Prince Deldarinnon's visit, and their mother's attempt to force an alliance.

"Tell him I'm sorry," Anneth had said, unable to hide her grin. "I wish him all the best—but it turns out he was not, in fact, the prince for me."

Now, though, it seemed Bran had a diplomatic incident on his hands.

"Don't look so fierce," Mara said. "I'm sure Hestil resolved the situation in a satisfactory manner."

"Indeed," Hestil said dryly. "We recovered Prince Deldarinnon, and he's safely on his way back to Cereus even now."

"What happened?" Mara asked.

"Another tale, and long in the telling," Hestil said. "We have more pressing concerns at the moment, I'm afraid."

"Yes," Bran said as they reached the tent.

Hestil went in and lifted the door flap. Bran ducked inside, followed by Mara and Ondo. As they settled about the small table taking up half the space, one of the soldiers brought them cups of strongly brewed tea.

"Lord Calithilon is fading," Hestil said bluntly, as soon as the soldier departed. "Avantor updates me regularly. Since the brightmoon's rising, the Hawthorne Lord has taken a turn for the worse."

Bran's claws dented the wooden table. "We must depart immediately for the palace."

"I fear it will be too late." Hestil's expression grew shadowed. "Even taking a change of horses, the ride—"

"There's another way," Mara said. "And thankfully, our magic is not too depleted to use it."

Bran rose. "We have remedies from the mortal world—we must get them to Avantor immediately."

"And these." Mara lifted the saddlebag filled with golden flowers. She glanced at Ondo. "Give your pack to Bran—I'm not sure we can manage to transport three people plus all the medicines."

"Better not to risk it," the scout agreed gravely, rising and handing Bran the pack. "I will stay and help Hestil decamp."

"And provide a full debriefing," Hestil said. She looked back at Bran. "We will join you as soon as possible."

"Of course. And I will scry to you after we reach the palace." He hefted Ondo's pack, checked that his own satchel of remedies was secure, then reached and took Mara's hand.

She nodded at him.

Holding the thought of his rooms at the Hawthorne Palace clear in his mind, he pulled deeply on his wellspring, and spoke the rune in the human tongue.

"*Portal.*"

The tent whirled away, and for a moment there was nothing solid beneath his feet. Mara gripped him tightly, her magic mingling with his.

Then they arrived, standing a bit breathlessly before the low couch in his darkened living area.

"*Calya,*" he said, summoning light.

Foxfire lanterns sprang to life in their curved silver bowls, and he looked at Mara. Despite the evidence of strain in her expression, she gave him a brief smile.

"Definitely faster than riding." She set the saddlebag down, then scooped out a handful of the flowers, surprisingly unwilted after their magical journeys. "Let's go see about saving your father."

Bran nodded and strode to the door, the vials and tinctures clinking as he adjusted the pack and satchel.

Their appearance in the halls of the Hawthorne Court was met with wide eyes and exclamations, but whenever a courtier approached them, Bran waved them away. Later, there would be time enough to announce their return—though considering the speed at which gossip traveled through the palace, an official proclamation would probably prove unnecessary.

He went quickly through the corridors, making for his parents' private rooms. At his side, Mara was nearly trotting in a valiant effort to keep up. As soon as they were in view of the Hawthorne Lord's suite, Bran slowed, giving Mara time to catch her breath.

And himself time to marshal his emotions. He must be prepared for the worst, even as he hoped for the best.

The warrior at the door bowed at their approach, quickly mastering his surprise—but then, Sindor had held this particular post for quite some time. Very little surprised him.

"Commander," he said, "welcome home."

He turned and opened the door, and Bran, with a nod of thanks, stepped into his parents' suite. The scent of blackberry wine and his mother's floral perfume made a swirl of memories, mostly unhappy, rise within him.

How many times had he been scolded while standing just there, before the hearth? How many times had his mother's cold gaze moved past him, his father's frown judged him unworthy?

Mara touched his arm, and Bran straightened. The past was done. It was the future that mattered now.

"Bran!" Avantor rose from the armchair positioned beside the door to the bedroom. The healer looked exhausted, deep shadows beneath his eyes, his braids a rough tangle.

"Am I in time?" Bran asked softly, glancing at the half-open door.

"Barely." Avantor's voice was grim. "I do not expect your father to live much past moonset."

"We've brought medicine," Mara said. "And these."

She held out the handful of golden flowers, while Bran rummaged through the pack, setting the various bottles out on the side table.

"Mara." The healer managed a weary smile. "I'm so glad you and Bran are here. What do those blossoms do?"

She shook her head. "I've never seen them before. Have you? They were growing all around the gateway, but only on the human side."

Bran's brow twitched up. He hadn't noticed that detail in his single-minded desire to reach Hawthorne in time.

Avantor took one of the flowers from Mara's outstretched hand. He brought it to his mouth and closed his eyes, whispering a rune Bran didn't catch. The petals stirred and Avantor opened his eyes abruptly, jerking as if in shock.

"Extraordinary," he said. "We must brew a tisane—there might still be a chance."

He whirled, summoning up a large bowl of steaming hot water and an empty mug. Murmuring softly, he plucked the petals of the flowers and strewed them over the water. They spun, tiny golden boats, then gently drifted beneath the surface, leaving sparkling trails in their wake.

The desire for answers pricked Bran, but he held his tongue as the healer worked. This was no time for distractions—Lord Calithilon's life was at stake.

Mara watched Avantor intently, her arms folded about herself. After what felt like a hundred turns, the healer nodded to himself, then poured a measure of the brew into the mug he'd conjured up.

The smell of sunshine-warmed grass filled the room, a scent few Dark Elves would even know, but the recognition of it tickled Bran's senses. There was an underlying resonance, something he felt he should recognize. But what?

"Salt," Avantor said, answering Bran's unspoken question.

"Tears," Mara said softly, amazement stealing over her face. "My tears, when the gateway would not open. But how could they be the seeds of flowers?" She glanced at Bran, as if he had answers.

"I do not know, beloved."

"We will have time for this mystery later." Mug in hand, Avantor pushed the bedroom door open. "I have a patient to tend."

Bran hesitated a moment, then followed the healer in.

The sight of his father lying gaunt and listless in the wide bed sent a spike of pain through Bran. He'd thought he was prepared to see the Hawthorne Lord at the edge of death.

He wasn't.

Gulping back his fear-tinged grief, Bran came to stand at the foot of the bed.

"Father," he said quietly. "I am here."

"And not a moment too soon," came the sharp reply, as Lady Tinnueth stood from her vigil at the far side of the bed. "So, you finally decided to grace Elfhame with your presence. How noble of you."

The spite in his mother's voice was a lash against his raw emotions. Bran clenched his fists, feeling the sharp prick of claws against his palm. *She is grieving,* he told himself, wishing it were true.

More likely, she was waiting for her husband to die so she could take up the mantle of sole ruler. Bran's return clearly brought her no joy.

"I hope you left that odious creature you married behind in the mortal world, at least," Lady Tinnueth said. "Although I'm sorry to say that Lady Mireleth tired of waiting for you to come to your senses."

Bran kept himself from glancing over his shoulder to the room where Mara waited. There was no point in telling his mother that his wife had returned with him to Elfhame. The Hawthorne Lady would discover it soon enough.

"Please," Avantor said as he slipped an arm around his patient's shoulders. "Be quiet, or leave. The both of you."

Lady Tinnueth glared at her son a moment longer, then turned to the healer, watching impassively as Avantor coaxed Lord Calithilon partially upright.

"Drink this." Avantor held the cup to the dying lord's lips.

Lord Calithilon's eyes remained closed. He made no movement, except the labored rise and fall of his chest as he breathed.

"Drink, my lord," Avantor pleaded.

Bran rounded the bed and joined the healer. He went down on his knees and took his father's hand. It felt fragile in his grasp, the once-powerful sinews and muscle now as breakable as a glass goblet.

"Father," he said, leaning forward. "I've brought you medicines from the human world. I'm home. Please, do as Avantor asks."

Lord Calithilon took a deep breath. Let it out.

For a stark moment, he lay perfectly still. Then his eyelids fluttered open and he inhaled raggedly. He blinked at Bran, then, as slowly as the motion of the moons in the sky, turned his gaze to Avantor.

The healer held the mug up once more. This time, the Hawthorne Lord opened his mouth and drank.

Some of the liquid escaped down his chin and darkened the blankets as Avantor coaxed the contents of the mug into his patient. But enough went into Lord Calithilon that the healer seemed satisfied. Finally, when over half the mug was gone, he let the Hawthorne Lord slowly sink back against the pillows.

Bran watched, half expecting some miraculous transition—but none was forthcoming. His father's hand lay quiet in his grasp.

"It will take a little time," Avantor said, giving Bran an intent look. "But I promise you that your father will recover."

At this, Lady Tinnueth gave a little snort of annoyance. "Don't make vows you can't keep, Avantor."

Expression calm, the healer turned to her. "I assure you, my lady, I do not. Even now, the shadows are withdrawing from your husband."

Disbelief plain in her expression, Lady Tinnueth took her seat once more. "We will see if you're right," she said. "Bran, have the kitchen send up some food. I'm weary and in need of nourishment."

Curbing his impulse to tell her to summon it herself, Bran rose. For Avantor's sake, he would make sure a lavish meal arrived, with more than enough food for two.

"Come back after moonset," the healer said. "I will have good news for you."

"Thank you." Bran laid one hand on Avantor's shoulder.

Then, without a glance at Lady Tinnueth, he left the room. Mara waited before the hearth, and he wondered how much of his mother's vitriol she'd overheard. As he swung the bedroom door half shut behind him, Sindor hurried into the room.

"My lord," he said in a hushed voice, glancing from Bran to the bedroom, and back, “your presence is urgently needed in the throne room.”

“Why?” Bran asked, as Mara came to stand beside him.

The soldier swallowed. “The Oracles have just arrived.”

“The Oracles?” Bran stiffened. “But they never leave their sanctuary.”

It was unheard of. His people went to the Oracles. Not the other way around.

“And yet they are here, demanding an audience.”

“Well then.” Mara slipped her arm through Bran’s. “I suppose we’d better go see what they want.”

CHAPTER 40

Despite the need for haste, Bran insisted they stop back at their rooms. Mara didn't argue. She was curious about the Oracles, but she was also more than ready to wash her face and don new clothing. Especially as, judging by Bran's reaction, meeting the Oracles was tremendously significant.

At least it would be easy to keep the promise she'd made to him, that she'd speak to the Oracles before deciding to leave Elfhame forever. Which, of course, wasn't a question any longer.

She was staying.

Despite the brightmoon's wan light, the Dark Elves' prejudice against mortals, and the small fact that someone there wanted her dead.

"Do I get to ask the Oracles a question?" she asked, as she opened her side of the armoire.

Her elvish gowns hung within, an array of silks without buttons or buckles, and she smiled briefly as she ran her hand over the smooth fabrics.

"You can try." Bran, too, was laying out a fresh change of clothing. "Whether they answer..."

He lifted his shoulder.

One question, that may or may not receive a reply. Too bad she had a half-dozen at the ready. What should she ask?

As she sifted through her clothing, a small roll of parchment fell to the floor. She bent to pick it up, but Bran was quicker.

"Take care," he said, scooping up the paper. "You avoided one poisoning attempt in these rooms already. This time I'm here to protect you."

"If it's poisoned, then aren't you in danger?" She frowned at him.

"I know several runes of purification," he said, then flicked his fingers at the parchment and spoke a quiet word.

Blue light danced briefly over it, then faded.

"Is it safe?" she asked.

He nodded, then carefully unrolled the paper. It appeared to be a note, and Mara moved to his side so that they could read it together.

Mara,

You do not belong in Elfhame, but if you are reading this, then you have returned with Prince Brannonilon. If that is the case, and he is still content to be married to you (for whatever unfathomable reason) then I suppose I cannot rail against fate any longer.

At any rate, I have come to an understanding with Prince Deldarinnon, and will be imminently departing Hawthorne with him, to take up life in Cereus as a princess of that court.

I feel it is my duty to let you know that Lady Tinnueth hired an assassin to pursue and kill you. It is only for my dear Brannonilon's sake that I tell you this, to spare him any sorrow, since I am no longer there to offer him solace.

As this is valuable information, I have no doubt an adequate payment can be made. Although Prince Deldarinnon is a noble of Cereus, the life of a high-ranking princess carries certain costs.

If, by some chance, you are considering visiting Cereus, I urge you not to do so. Although I have very magnanimously forgiven you for stealing my betrothed from me, and will expect some tokens of your gratitude for this warning, I would not welcome your presence.

. . .

Lady Mireleth Andion

Princess of the Cereus Court

Bran held the note steady as they read, but Mara found herself shaking. There was one question answered.

"Steady," Bran said, catching Mara's elbow and guiding her to the low couch.

"I can't believe it," she whispered.

"I can." Bran's voice was grim as he rerolled the note and tucked it into his pocket, then settled beside her.

She turned to him, grateful for the warmth of his arms around her. "What will we do?"

"Confront Tinnueth."

"Is Mireleth's note enough evidence?"

"If it's not, I'll summon Mireleth from Cereus to give testimony."

"Oh, Bran." Mara's heart twisted. "Your own mother."

He was silent a moment, then exhaled; a low, weary sigh. "Tinnueth never cared for her children. I'd thought she held some affection for my father, no matter how remote that emotion might be—but now I think she is only concerned for herself."

"I'm sorry." She leaned against him, seeking comfort, giving it in return.

"As am I." He brushed her hair back from her cheek. "But dealing with my mother will have to wait until after we meet with the Oracles."

Mara gave him a tight nod. She dreaded seeing Lady Tinnueth again, but she would trust that Bran would keep her safe.

It did not take long for them to dress and make their way to the Hawthorne Palace's throne room. Instead of entering via the main arched doorway, however, Bran led her to a small side corridor, then pushed at the intricate paneling. It slid aside, revealing another entrance.

"The rulers come and go this way," he said. "It opens just behind the thrones."

Mara nodded and followed him into the room. A quick glance reassured her that Tinnueth wasn't in attendance—at least, not yet. The room was filled with courtiers and urgent, low-voiced conversations. In the center, before the thrones, the Oracles stood—three figures veiled in white from head to toe.

The courtiers had given them a wide berth, and the air around the visitors seemed strangely still.

"Stand with me," Bran said softly, taking Mara's hand.

Together, they stepped onto the polished white stone of the dais. Ignoring the two thrones positioned in the center, he strode to the front and stood there, surveying the court. Mara let go of his hand, but remained at his side.

A renewed buzz of whispers hummed in the air, but Bran held up his hand, and slowly the courtiers quieted.

He inclined his head to the figures in white. "Oracles of Elfhame—on behalf of the Hawthorne Court, I bid you welcome. To what do we owe this surprising visit?"

The middle Oracle took a step forward. Through the gauze of her veil, Mara could just make out the delicate features of a Dark Elf woman, her expression serene.

"Prince Brannonilon Luthinor," she said. "We come to tell you the terms of your prophecy."

Bran blinked. "Didn't defeating the Void fulfill the destiny you foretold at my birth?"

"Do you recall the words?" The Oracle tilted her head and began to recite. Her resonant voice filled the room.

"Evil lurks and soon will fall,
A door long closed must open wide,
Elfhame's greatest need will call
A mortal woman as the bride
The Hawthorne Prince must surely wed,
Else all our kind shall perish, dead."

"I haven't forgotten my own prophecy." A touch of annoyance crossed Bran's face. "But we defeated the Void."

The Oracle pivoted, sweeping the room with her veiled glance. "And yet our kind is still fated to perish. Without children, what will become of the Dark Elves?"

A low murmur greeted her words.

"What are you trying to say?" Mara's patience frayed. "Either Bran saved his people by marrying me, or he didn't. Which is it?"

With a soft exhalation that pushed out the delicate fabric concealing her face, the Oracle turned back to the dais. "So impatient, you mortals. The balance is much more delicate than that."

"You mentioned terms," Bran said. "Explain."

The Oracle lifted her delicate hands. "It is not that simple. Your understanding is flawed—but I will try."

She glanced at her companions on either side, who each gave her a slow, silent nod. Mara leaned to brush her shoulder against Bran's. Whatever the woman was about to say, they would face it together. And overcome it.

"The answer to the Dark Elves' future lies beyond the gate," the Oracle said. "You returned with it from the human world."

"I am weary of your riddles," Bran said.

"Wait." Mara pressed her lips together. The answer teased at her mind... "The flowers. The ones blooming around the doorway, with the golden petals."

"Yes." The Oracle nodded. "It is the cure for the Hawthorne Lord's ailment—a weakness that will, sadly, remain with the ruling line of all the courts."

"That only solves our immediate need," Bran said.

The Oracle regarded him for a long moment. "It is also the cure for our people's infertility. But it comes with a price."

The taut silence gripping the court broke into gasps of gladness, a clamor of questions.

"Quiet," Bran called, raising his hands. When the crowd quieted again, he frowned at the Oracle. "What price?"

"One easily paid, at least for this generation." Her voice carried the hint of a smile. "The gateway will open once every thirteen double-moons—three years' passage in the human world—so that your people may go forth and harvest the blossom, which will only grow on the mortal side of the gate. Its distillation will keep the rulers' sickness, and the Dark Elves' inability to bear children, at bay."

"On what condition?" Bran's voice was hard.

"A noble of Elfhame must wed a mortal, or a mortal ruler must marry a Dark Elf. As long as an alliance holds, and a mortal dwells in our land, or a royal of our blood in the human world, the gateway will open and the flower will bloom."

"That's convenient," Mara said under her breath.

"What of future generations?" Bran asked.

"They must uphold the bargain, or perish."

This caused another spike of conversation, and Bran glanced at Mara. "Good thing my people are now accepted in Raine, or this would be a difficult undertaking, indeed."

She managed to smile at him. "And good thing that Anneth stayed, just to be doubly sure. But it's wonderful news—the Dark Elves are saved!"

"For now." His brows drew together. "I worry for the future."

The Oracle glided forward to the edge of the dais. "Do not fear for what is to come," she said. "Tend to the present."

She lifted her head, gazing behind Bran and Mara.

They turned, to see Lady Tinnueth step through the doorway. Mara's breath caught in a mixture of fear and dislike.

"Holding an audience without the Hawthorne Lady?" Tinnueth's voice was cold, her eyes flat with anger as she stared at her son. "You could be banished for less."

Bran took a step forward as his mother paced past the thrones, and pulled the roll of parchment from his pocket.

"Lady Tinnueth Luthinor," he said loudly, holding up Mireleth's note. "I have here testimony that you plotted against my wife by hiring assassins to murder her. How do you answer?"

Tinnueth's eyes narrowed as she glanced from her son to Mara. "I was doing you a kindness, Brannon. The Hawthorne Court is better off without the taint of a mortal in residence."

Her words were caught by the nearest courtiers, some of whom hissed in reaction.

"You would doom us all," one of them called. "Step down! Let Prince Brannonilon rule."

This idea was met with approval, and Tinnueth jerked her head back, blinking at the shift in the court's favor.

"You cannot rule if you're imprisoned for life." Bran's voice, low and menacing, was pitched for their ears alone.

Tinnueth gave him a scornful look. "I have committed no crime."

"Call off your assassins," Bran continued. "Or I'll ensure you'll never see the light of the moons again."

His mother made a dismissive gesture. "That incompetent guild is no longer my concern. I've no interest in employing assassins whose target slips from their grasp."

"I want your assurance you will not attempt to harm my wife ever again." He could barely get the words out past the rage tightening his throat.

Tinnueth merely looked at her son, unspeaking.

Claws fully extended, Bran took a step toward her.

"Wait." Mara caught his arm. "Much as I'd like to see your mother taken down, maybe the middle of the throne room isn't the place."

"Indeed." Without asking permission, the Oracle mounted the dais and, quickly but firmly, took Tinnueth's arm in her grasp. "Lady Tinnueth will be coming with us."

"I'll do no such thing." Bran's mother attempted to jerk away.

Despite the Oracle's seeming fragility, her grip was apparently made of steel, as Tinnueth was unable to free herself.

"Tinnueth Luthinor," the Oracle said, her voice suddenly deep and booming. "You are the next chosen of our order. Your temporal titles are hereby stripped from you. You will be escorted to the sanctuary, and all your power turned to the service of the moons."

"But I am the Hawthorne Lady! You cannot simply—"

"The Oracles have spoken." The veiled woman nodded to her companions.

They came to the dais and flanked Tinnueth, taking her arms.

"Show our newest acolyte out," the Oracle said calmly, then looked at Bran. "This is your chance to say farewell, before she no longer knows your face."

"Mother." Bran faced Tinnueth. "I want you to know that, even though you didn't ask after Anneth, she is well and happy. And remained in the mortal world, to marry their king."

Tinnueth's lip curled. "Then I raised two fools, instead of just one."

"You did not raise us at all." Bran turned away and glanced at the Oracle. "I wish you good luck with her."

"She is the one in need of such wishes." The Oracle's voice held a touch of menace that made Mara shiver.

It seemed that Lady Tinnueth was not going to escape punishment after all.

CHAPTER 41

Bran dismissed the courtiers, and he and Mara accompanied the lead Oracle to the gates of the palace. His mother was already ensconced in the rounded coach they'd arrived in, a strange vehicle the likes of which he'd never seen before, pulled by four horses.

"Wait," Mara said, as the Oracle stepped away. "What about my vision?"

"What vision?" Bran glanced at his wife.

A shred of guilt crossed her face as she looked at him. "Before I left Hawthorne, I had a vision in the Pool of Reflection. We were in the Darkwood, fleeing, and you..." She swallowed. "You were lethally shot with a black arrow."

"Why didn't you tell me?"

"I was afraid." She caught his hand. "Afraid that speaking the words would make it come true. But it didn't." She turned to the Oracle. "Or is there still a danger it will?"

"No." The veiled woman shook her head. "Cross-world visions are not always accurate. Your actions—or rather, Anneth's—changed the timeline of what might be."

"So her alliance with Prince Owen..." Mara trailed off.

"It was the soldiers of Raine, in the vision," Bran guessed. "Pursuing us. Or the Athraig."

"It matters not." The Oracle flicked her fingers. "Your sister's ability to trust, to love, turned the tide of time. That possible future now lies in the past."

"Can we visit her?" Mara asked. "When the doorway opens, can we see our family in the mortal world again?"

The yearning in her voice made Bran want to pull her to him in a strong, reassuring embrace. He settled for squeezing her hand.

"The gate will open at dawn on the appointed day," the Oracle said. "And close at midnight. Whatever your business in the human realm, it is best concluded within that time frame. I advise you to spend the bulk of it in harvesting the flowers."

"What are they called?" Mara asked.

The Oracle studied her a moment. "*Nirwen* will do," she said at last. "Now, I must be gone. Rule well, and long. I will not see you again."

She turned, despite Mara's outstretched hand, and gracefully entered the coach. At some unseen signal, the horses started forward, and the vehicle glided away.

When it was gone from sight, Mara glanced at him.

"What does it mean, *nirwen*?"

"Maiden's tears." He slipped his arm around her shoulders. "Your grief is the salvation of my people."

She leaned against him. "I hope that my happiness will be equally beneficial."

"It will." He smiled at her. "To both of us."

She laughed, and his own joy blossomed, as bright and golden as the mysterious flowers. And just as potent.

THE NEXT SEVERAL moons were a flurry of activity. Lord Calithilon slowly recovered, and did not seem overly concerned about his wife's departure. Or perhaps he was still too weak to fully comprehend what had happened. Bran resolved to have a long chat with the Hawthorne Lord, once his father regained his strength.

Hestil arrived with the rest of the Dark Elves who'd camped by the gateway, including Ondo. The four of them—Bran, Mara, Hestil, and Ondo—met in Bran's rooms soon after their return. Seated around the low table, Bran and Mara told the others everything that had transpired since their return. The scout was greatly relieved to hear that no assassin was threatening Mara's life, and satisfied that Lady Tinnueth was now the Oracle's problem.

"Are you certain she's no longer a danger?" Hestil asked, a crease between her brows.

"Yes." Bran met his second's gaze. "She cannot harm us—in fact, she may no longer even know who we are. Or care."

He'd gathered that the Oracles would change his mother's memories, and he trusted them implicitly. They would tend to their own business. Just as he'd tended to his, taking up temporary rule until Lord Calithilon was ready to reassume his position as Hawthorne Lord.

"Ondo." Bran turned to the scout. "Now that the gateway between worlds will be opening regularly, Mara and I think there should be a Dark Elf presence in the Darkwood. A guardian, if you will, to watch over the forest and the doorway. We were hoping you might take up the mantle of *Galadhir* on behalf of Elfhame."

The scout's eyes widened, and he glanced from Bran to Mara. "It is a great honor. But I do not think I'm qualified for such responsibility."

"Of course you are." Mara leaned forward and lightly touched his forearm. "There's none better. Other than us, and Anneth, you know Raine best of anyone."

"And you don't mind the solitude of the forest," Bran added dryly. "We're not asking you to act as a diplomat to Castle Raine—only to tend to the gateway and keep humans out of trouble in the Darkwood."

"And be there for Anneth," Mara added.

"Well then." The apprehension faded from Ondo's eyes. "As long as I'm not required to dwell at the castle, I think I could accept such a duty."

"We'll come through the doorway every three years," Mara said, smiling. "We'll visit everyone then."

"It will only be thirteen doublemoons here," Bran reminded her.

"Yes." She sobered. "It will be hard to watch our families age, while we don't."

He dropped a kiss on her head. "Don't carry that sorrow until you must, beloved."

"What of your magic?" Hestil looked across the table at Mara. "Ondo tells me you're finally able to control it at will."

"Mostly." Mara gave her wry look. "As long as there's a similar concept in my language, or if the Dark Elf word is simple enough."

"We've created new runes, as well," Bran said. "Though not everyone will have the power to cast such magics."

"And the *nirwen* essence?" Hestil asked. "Is there enough for all the courts?"

Bran shook his head. "I wish there was more elixir—but for now we have been able to treat Hawthorne, and give the rest to Nightshade. I will ask all the courts to send help for the harvest, when the gateway next opens."

He was certain of Nightshade, and perhaps Rowan. Nehta, their commander, had returned to the lords there, and was a strong ally. If the Rowan rulers listened to her, they would at least send a few of their people.

"Once the courts see babes being born in Hawthorne, they'll come," Mara said confidently.

"I suspect you're right."

A knock sounded at the door, and Bran went to answer. It was Avantor, his expression weary.

"My father?" Bran asked, apprehension flaring.

"He's well enough," the healer said. "But he's asking for you—quite insistently."

It seemed the Hawthorne Lord had recovered—at least enough to be making demands.

"I must attend Lord Calithilon," Bran told the gathering, shaking his head as Mara made to rise. "Stay, love. I'll return soon."

With a worried expression, she sat back, her gaze following him until he closed the door.

Bran and Avantor silently strode the hallways. There was no use in speculating about what Lord Calithilon wanted—they'd be there soon enough.

As they entered the Hawthorne Lord's suite, Bran was relieved to see his father sitting in a chair before the hearth. Though his eyes were weary, the usual imperious expression had settled back on his face.

"Brannon." Lord Calithilon nodded to the chair across from him. "I must speak with you."

Keeping a wary gaze upon his father, Bran sat.

"I've come to a decision," Lord Calithilon said, nodding to himself. "In the best interests of our land, I am stepping down as Hawthorne Lord."

Bran sat back, blinking. He hadn't expected those words.

And yet... perhaps he had, in some small corner of his mind. The balance had shifted, between the worlds and even here, in the Hawthorne Court.

"I understand you are handling the current issues competently enough," Lord Calithilon continued. "I want you to assume the rulership."

"Are you certain?" Bran lifted his chin, ready to take the mantle of Hawthorne Lord—provided his father was honest about relinquishing it.

In the past few moons, he'd begun to find his own style of leadership within the court, drawing from his experience as commander of Elfhame's forces, and tempered by his wife's empathy.

"Of course." His father's tone was brusque. "Who else? But I will remain as your chief advisor."

Ah, there it was—the thorn inside the rose. Bran held his father's gaze.

"I would welcome your advice," Bran said, putting iron in his voice. "But I will not always follow it."

Lord Calithilon's eyes narrowed, but he was the first to look away. "Very well. It's not as though I'm feeble, you understand."

"Indeed not." Bran kept his opinion of his father's reduced strength to himself.

In former days, Lord Calithilon would have met him standing in the royal study, not wrapped in a robe before the bedroom hearth.

"It's simply time." His father glanced at the flickering foxfire in the hearth, shedding light but no heat. "And it's better for Hawthorne to have both a lord and a lady. Even if one of them is human."

"Thank you." It was the closest his father would come to approving of Mara.

It was enough.

"I'm tired." Lord Calithilon waved his hand. "Avantor, help me back to bed. Bran, you may inform the court of my decision."

"You don't want to do so yourself?"

A wave of utter weariness crossed his father's face. "No," he said shortly. "But call me when you convene your first council meeting."

"I will." Bran stood and made his father a low, formal bow—that of a prince to his liege.

It would be the last time, and they both knew it. Then, spirits rising, the new Hawthorne Lord went to inform his wife.

He paused at the threshold of their rooms, the door half-open. Mara sat on one of the low couches, a pensive look on her face.

They had both made hard choices, but despite the challenges that might lie ahead, he was no longer worried that his wife would find him lacking. His gaze lingered on her, moving from her earth-colored hair to her sweetly rounded cheeks, her serious eyes and square chin.

So many twists and turns had brought them there, so much difficulty and sorrow. But he could finally believe that the worst was behind them. The Void was defeated, his people saved.

And Mara had chosen Elfhame.

She glanced up and, seeing him, smiled—a look of such tenderness and honesty that it made him weak-kneed.

"Come here," she said softly, rising.

He strode forward and enfolded her in his arms, inhaling her scent: mint, salt, and the memory of golden flowers.

A new era was beginning at the Hawthorne Court, full of brightness and hope, and the laughter of children. He had no doubt his own would be among them.

At long last, his prophecy was fulfilled.

~ END ~

Acknowledgments

Thank you to my long-time friend and fellow author Chassily - couldn't have done this one without you! Big thanks is also due to another friend and writer, Laurie, for excellent editorial advice. Your passion and grace help make me a better storyteller.

Another big round of thanks to my mom, Ginger, for catching a lot of little things in the MS during your nightly read-throughs, and to Will, for listening (and making a catch or two himself!) - hugs to you both.

I also want to thank everyone in basically the world for doing the right thing and sheltering in place during the early days of the COVID-19 pandemic. I was behind on this book by a month, due to life upheavals caused by the virus - but the fact that it didn't sweep like an out-of-control wildfire through my country enabled me to dial back the panic and immerse myself in the fantasy world of the Darkwood Chronicles to get this book done. Humans are amazing, and resilient, and we will get through this...

Another big tip of the hat to Arran for the fine work and quick turn-around, not to mention cleaning up my comma abuse.

Finally, I'd like to acknowledge the work of Leonard and the wonderful folks who compiled Parf Edhellen, a free online dictionary of Tolkien's languages. The Dark Elf language is deeply inspired by Sindarin, with many thanks to this excellent resource.

https://www.elfdict.com/about.page

ALSO BY ANTHEA SHARP

~ THE DARKWOOD CHRONICLES~

The hidden world of the Dark Elves is discovered by a mortal girl... romance and adventure ensue~

ELFHAME – Book 1

HAWTHORNE – Book 2

RAINE – Book 3

HEART OF THE FOREST (A novella)

~THE DARKWOOD TRILOGY ~

WHITE AS FROST

BLACK AS NIGHT

RED AS FLAME

Have your read the *USA Today* bestselling FEYLAND series yet? Fae magic, high-tech gaming, and a touch of romance await~

Feyland is the most immersive high-tech game ever designed, and Jennet Carter is the first to play the prototype. But she doesn't suspect the virtual world is close enough to touch — or that she'll be battling for her life against the Dark Queen of the faeries...

~ THE FEYLAND SERIES ~

THE FIRST ADVENTURE

THE DARK REALM

THE BRIGHT COURT

THE TWILIGHT KINGDOM

FAERIE SWAP

SPARK

BREA'S TALE

ROYAL

MARNY

~ VICTORIA ETERNAL ~

Victorian Spacepunk! Steampunk meets Space Opera

STAR COMPASS

STARS & STEAM

COMETS & CORSETS

~ STORY COLLECTIONS ~

TALES OF FEYLAND & FAERIE

TALES OF MUSIC & MAGIC

THE FAERIE GIRL & OTHER TALES

THE PERFECT PERFUME & OTHER TALES

MERMAID SONG

Visit www.antheasharp.com for a complete book listing!

ABOUT THE AUTHOR

~*USA Today* bestselling, award-winning fantasy author ~

Growing up on fairy tales and computer games, Anthea Sharp has melded the two in her award-winning, bestselling Feyland series, which has sold over 200k copies worldwide.

In addition to the fae fantasy/cyberpunk mashup of Feyland, she also writes Victorian Spacepunk, and fantasy romance set in the magical forest of the Darkwood. Her books have won awards and topped bestseller lists, and garnered over a million reads at Wattpad. Her short fiction has appeared in Fiction River, DAW anthologies, The Future Chronicles, and Beyond The Stars: At Galaxy's Edge, as well as many other publications.

Anthea splits her year between sunny Southern California and the enchanted forests of the Pacific Northwest. When not writing, she hangs out in virtual worlds, plays the fiddle with her Celtic band Fiddlehead, and spends time with her small-but-good family. Contact her at antheasharp@hotmail.com or visit her website – www.antheasharp.com

Anthea also writes historical romance under the pen name Anthea Lawson. Find out about her acclaimed Victorian romantic adventure novels at www.anthealawson.com.

Be the first to hear about new releases and reader perks by subscribing to Anthea's newsletter, Sharp Tales.

www.antheasharp.com